To Jody
Be Blessed
Be Bona-Fide
Enjoy
BJ
8-26-17
BJ Historical

BONA-FIDE

Bona-Fide

BJ Tassin

ISBN: 1532855915
ISBN-13:978-1532855917

DEDICATION

To Scott, my husband and best friend. I wrote this book especially for you because I know how much you enjoy reading. I hope this story is as much a pleasure for you to read as it was for me to write.

CONTENTS

ACKNOWLEDGMENTS

I'd first like to thank God that I'm this far on getting this story out of my head and on to the pages of this book. Just as always, He was faithful to answer my prayers in sending me the perfect editor and assistant to do all the formalities of getting this book published. After eight and a half years of sitting on a finished manuscript, I had no idea it would turn out to be my husband Scott. Now a published author himself, who better for this position than he? I'm so very blessed to have his love, support, encouragement and know-how to "get er done!" Thank you My Love!

Scott and my sister Margie, both seasoned readers, were the first to hear me read out loud a couple of pages and hear my idea to write this novel because I trusted them to be honest and with me as my best critics, before I'd write any further. They liked what they heard and wanted more.

Each week I'd turn out a new chapter in time for our "Friday at Four Coffee Time". I'd have Margie read it out loud to me so that I could hear for myself if the story flowed. As word got out as to what we were doing, Margie found that she was supplying coffee by the pots full to a growing fan club of the characters in this book. Thank you Margie, I appreciate you and all the "Third Street Coffee Drinkers" of those days.

To my Uncle Johnny Miller; thank you for believing in me and sending me that check for $25 twelve years ago to start my publishing account, when I told you and Aunt Renee that I had started writing a novel. I appreciate your love and support…and that check! You will be one of the very first to receive a copy of this book. No charge!

It was my sick and dying Daddy, John Justice, who was after me to finish the last few chapters so he could find out how the story ends. I finished about 3 monthes before he died but by then he was too sick to read anymore or even listen to anyone read it to him. I appreciate my Daddy for pushing me to finish what I started.

To my Mom, Dott Justice, who came up to the hills to stay with me for a month to pre-edit my work but instead got so lost in the story and the dialog that she forgot all the grammer rules. Thank you Mama for doing that and for staying after me to get this story published! I'm glad this pushed you into getting your own book published! I want to thank you and Daddy for providing me with 10 siblings to grow up with and giving me plenty of material to write about!

Thank you Lavonda Hulbert, for being a dear friend and allowing me to read this whole manuscript to you at work, as if this was part of your job. You were so kind to listen, consult and encourage me to finish that last chapter and get it out there. You were the first to hear the whole story!

To my Mother-in law, Gladys McKamie, who has been a great encouragement to me and has faith that I can do anything I set my mind to do. Thank you MamaG!

To my daughter Monica, "The Grammar Hammer". Thank you for your love and encouragement, trusting me to pronounce the dialog phonetically "any ole how" and being able to read between the lines.

To my son Nick who has only heard the first 17 chapters of this book and said time and time again, *"Mom, I can't wait to read the rest of your story, when are you going to get it published?"* Thank you for waiting Nick; if you are reading this, then it is published!

To my son Stevie, who years ago said to me, "*Mama, you dream big but you never finish what you start!*" Well son, if you are holding this novel in your hands, this dream came true for me. I made it to the finish line. Wow! What a long race!

To all my brothers, sisters, nieces, nephews, aunts, uncles, cousins and friends who cheered me on along the way. I appreciate you all!

BONA-FIDE

1
THE PLACE CALLED HOME

The needle had rounded the circle and pointed to the one hundred degree mark, making it the highest number I had ever remembered seeing it get to in my lifetime.

Had it ever been any hotter prior to this, they failed to tell me about it, as I didn't recall having felt this particular kind of agony before then.

"This is just awful!" I heard myself saying *"I'm feared the end is commin soon fer us."* However, it didn't seem to faze the curly orange haired lady, who was enjoying her cool refreshing Coca-Cola, on the face of the rusty, faded thermometer.

She'd been hanging up there on the trunk of that sweetgum tree, drinking on that soda pop for as long as I could remember. Well, long enough for the tree bark to grow over the rim and frame the edges.

It had been discarded as junk when Daddy brought that old thing home for Mama, one day shortly after they moved here to Chinquapin Holler. It was new to her and that's all that mattered.

Apparently, it still worked because you know what they say; "The numbers don't lie" and I'm here to tell you the number 100, on any thermometer, is some kind of hot!

My eyes and mind were fixed in amazement on this newly discovered record. Unaware this was only making matters worse, my mouth grew dry as my whole body began to feel parched.

I wanted to break open the glass, snatch that cold drink right out of that woman's hand and guzzle it down! Apparently she wasn't thirsty and was content just to sit up there tempting me with it! It wasn't fair that she could find something to smile about when I felt the way I did. How could she tease me like that when I was already so miserable?

I had always admired her before, but at that moment I could only feel contempt! More than the Coke, I wanted to get inside there and move that needle back to a cooler sixty eight degrees; like it was when things felt better. In my ten year old mind I believed that thermometer really controlled the weather.

I remember watching Mama pace before it and beckon for the temperature to read higher so that she could get her seeds in the ground. I've seen Daddy throw Sweetgum balls at it in a fit of rage when a late frost would sneak in and destroy our measly young crops.

Late one winter night I woke to the sound of my Daddy's voice. As I peered from one of the many windows in our home, I could see him just beyond the flickering light of the night fire. He was kneeling in a foot of snow under that sweetgum tree, praying for God to please make that thermometer read above freezing real soon before we all froze to death.

Oooow, snow! I thought as I closed my eyes to imagine having such a break from the heat. Snow would be real nice about now…we could make some ice-cream and it would cool us down.

Overtaken by reality, I bent down and picked up a few gumballs, though their prickly points made them hard to grasp. I hurled the whole handful at the thermometer, but to no avail, the needle didn't move… it was still hot! The woman didn't so much as even blink! Not a curl was out of place as she held her grinning pose.

My baby sister Learline was standing at my side and tried to mimic this act but the sharp burrs were too much for her tender little hands. As she started to cry, I kissed her chubby little fingers and gave her a hug to comfort her pain. I began to feel a little ashamed as I realized I had only achieved a bad example with my behavior.

I turned back to the thermometer and nothing had really changed; the orange haired lady was still smiling. However, a closer look into her eyes told me that I perhaps could have misread her. It was then that I noticed a hint of compassion and understanding in her polite gesture. I concluded that with the drink, she was merely offering an idea to relieve my discomfort by suggesting that I…. *"Drink Coca Cola!"*

I could smell the smoldering cinders from the cook pit as I turned to see my big sister, Earldean, putting out the fire in our homemade stove. She had recruited our six year old brother, Ed Earl, to help with the task, as I had been too distracted to do much of anything that morning. I couldn't even eat the oatmeal she had cooked for our breakfast. Even if I would have had much of an appetite it would have been hard to swallow Earldean's oatmeal because it was much stiffer than the creamy kind Mama made.

Although she was only a year or so older than me, she was used to the extra responsibility our parents had given her and had often taken advantage of the privileges that followed. I reckon everything has a price though, because without Mama tending her own chores, most of them fell on Earldean and she grew to be a bit sour minded about not having any time left over to play.

Often times she'd take it out on the rest of us as if we had something to do with it, even though Mama had already warned her about … *"gettin too big fer her own britches"*.

Well, to tell ya the truth, I was just about fed up with her *"stinkin-thinkin"* and thought she needed *"a good woopin"*!

I took Learline by the hand and guided her toward the others just as Ed Earl was slinging the last coffee can of dirt over the fire. Earldean caught me staring wide-eyed down at Ed Earl's bare feet. They were buried in at least an inch of dry powdery dirt, his toes digging down to the cooler soil that had not yet faced the sun that day and dust was clinging to him like flour on a buttermilk biscuit.

"Will you quit makin yo eyes so big Sassy…They gonna git stuck atta way!" Earldean said in a mothering voice. *"…What cha starin at anyhow?"*

"He'z gonna need some shoes" I said, still staring at his feet as they stepped out of the prints he had made.

"Go git yo shoes on" Earldean scolded just after she splashed her face with the water in the wash pan from the night before. *"…and 'fore ya do, best getcha cleaned up boy…how come ya git so dogone filthy already?"*

My little brother then turned and darted towards the woods in an attempt to escape such a dreadful torture. She started to run after him but she knew she would be in for a long game of chase and was in no mood to play games. Instead, she stiffened up and screamed at him as he disappeared out of sight.

"Get back over here …Ed Earl…ED EARL!

"They don't fit!" I said back to her.

"What cha talking bout? Ed Earl…DON'T MAKE ME COME AFTER YOU!" she continued, not waiting for me to explain.

"His shoes…They don't fit him no more."

"Well, he ain't gonna be able ta walk that far without um! …He'll be whinin with stone burses ana wantin me ta tote him outa ezz here hills!" she snarled back at me, as if I had been responsible for his out growing his shoes.

"Well, he'll have blisters the size of muscidines before we ever git past Cove Creek!"

"HE"S GOTTA PUT ON HIS SHOES, SASSY, HE"S TOO HEAVY TO CARRY!"

"THEY-DON"T- FIT- I DONE TOLD YA!" I yelled back with my hands on my hips.

"I-DON"T-CARE!" she snapped back with her head bouncing from side to side now imitating my stance and trying to get in the last say…again!

Neither of us backed down when our exaggerated steps had drawn us almost nose to nose. We both slowly drew in long breaths of air through tightly gritted teeth. All puffed up and ready to go at it; we each had that rebellious stare in our eyes that dared the other to make the first move.

Usually about this time Mama would step in and break up the bickering before it tore into hair pulling rolls on the ground, but this time she didn't come.

We were almost dizzy for a number of reasons but mostly from holding our breath so long while we waited…but still…she didn't come. With our hands still stuck to our hips, we both stood frozen…chilled to the bone on the hottest day of the year.

The quietness was almost deafening as it rung in our ears. We were waiting for her voice to call out our names…but it didn't. The glare in our eyes softened to mist as we read each other's mind….she wasn't coming.

Earldean finally broke the silence to ask, *"Why ya wonna sass me like that?"*

"CAUSE YOU AIN'T MY MAMA!" I screamed at her, wanting an excuse to beat some of that meanness out of her and rid myself of the anger that welled up inside of me too.

Instead, it all got stuck inside my throat, backed up into my sinuses and come pouring out in the form of tears from my eyes.

"Oh, here we go again" she said *"...you're gonna start cryin on me too!"* She looked down at Learline who was sitting in the dirt pouring hands full of the sandy stuff on her stretched out legs. Her bottom lip stuck out between the words. *"Mama...Sick?"*

"No-No! Earldean fussed, grabbing her up and dusting her off. *"ED EARL!"* she started yelling again. *"ED EARL, GET BACK HERE NOW!"*

"Oh leave um alone Earldean, cant'cha see they's tore up inside? Ain't cha got no mercy?" I said as I stomped about pouting.

I grabbed a cloth that was hanging from a nail that we used for a hook. It was stuck in the side of a rickety table that Daddy made from an old sign advertising Lincoln Apples...Ozarks Juicy Reds. Sliding the wash pan of stale water off of the table, I then carried it over and poured it on top of the smoldering coals.

As they hissed and steamed, I could see Earldean dusting the seat of Learlines' britches. She paid no attention to my antics when I stomped about so I turned and headed to the creek for fresh water to bathe Ed Earl with.

In late summer Cove Creek seemed so much further away as opposed to the spring. Then the water was so high at times we would have to move our gear back to keep the flood waters from carrying off our things downstream. But, this particular summer, we were in the midst of a heat wave with no rains to cool things off and the creek bed was down to a trickle in some places.

For the most part we had four definite seasons here in the Ozarks with pleasant days and cool nights. Spring would always be full of the sights and sounds of new life. Aromatic buds, dotting the branches of the various trees, clung close together, waiting their day of debut. Fresh blossoms would paint the purple hazed canyon with splashes of pastels.

As the weeks grew warmer, the bright greens of the forest would grow richer and deeper, lending a canopy of protection to the ferns and tender moss on its floor. Fragrant blooms of clover would spill over the hillsides on the long days of summer.

For all our hard work and Mama's special attention, the garden would be blessed with enough homegrown vegetables for good eating. Some years better than others but at least enough to get by.

The sun would rise early, filling us with anticipation of exciting adventures. There was plenty of time after chores for exploring, fishing or a splash in our favorite swimming hole. After supper, there would sometimes be enough daylight left for a game of Kick the Can or Freeze Tag or we'd take a blanket and climb up on the rock bluff to watch the sunset.

We would stay up there and count the stars as they came out. When we could no longer count as high as the many stars there were, we would find our way back home with the flashlight.

Autumn had always been my favorite time of year. The wide variety of maples, oaks, and pines would turn and fill the hills with splendid color that would take your breath away.

Palettes of warm colors spread across the mountains that looked like crazy quilts. Crisp cool air that was so easy to breathe after summers end. Adventures of hiking, exploring caves, discovering new things with our parents would be the best schooling a child could ever have.

Every day was a lesson in creative ways of getting things done in order to survive this life we lived. The only kind of life us kids ever knew of back then was to prepare for the harder times to come. So, as we gathered wood, food, and other provisions, we found pride in our achievements of sufficient accumulation.

Fall would be the better time of year to market our homemade goods from the back of Daddy's truck. Parked just off the highway, our business picked up as travelers out and about, coming and going to trade fairs and festivals would stop out of curiosity.

They would "ooo" and "aaa" over the baskets and wreaths Mama made of raw materials she had found in the woods. Daddy would have whittled a few things or cleaned up some junk he found that the men would be interested in.

We kids might display and peddle a few of our crafts that our parents might have helped us with. I was proud of the things I made and liked to look at the people while they shopped.

Other times we might just sell jars of berries in season but in the fall it would be different kinds of nuts we had gathered and put in containers Daddy had recycled from the trash bins behind a store in town. Later, Daddy would take what little money we made to the store and buy food that we couldn't get from the land.

The woods were stocked with active wildlife that were, to me, more entertaining to watch than hunt. Hunting was more for survival than for game; however, coming home with anything to eat was considered a trophy. My kind of game was to hunt for and gather black walnuts or hickory nuts. Counting our find, we'd see who could collect the most then Mama would reward the winner somehow. If we were lucky it would be an extra nut roll or shortbread she baked for a treat.

Nonetheless, we all were winners if she had enough staples to make them. When she did, it would be enough to last several days…with rations.

Pumpkin soup was something I always looked forward to in the fall. I can still taste that smooth buttery flavor that warmed my palate with a hint of sweetness. Mama would save her best cooking for Thanksgiving which came at the final end of harvest and lasted over a week.

Daddy would cook a big piece of venison on a stick that hung over an open pit. Our neighbor kept us stocked with his homemade barbeque sauce; his secret recipe that had won several ribbons at the county fairs. Daddy would mop the sauce on the meat then turn the stick several times throughout the roasting. In doing so, he licked his fingers so much you would think he should be able to figure out the secret.

With colder temperatures came shorter days. I think God made it that way so we would get under the covers and do some Bible reading and rest a while from all the work and play. On the stone fire pit Mama kept a big pot of soup going for days at a time. Well, it might have started out as a pot roast, but after we ate, she might add some water to the pot, cut up some potatoes and carrots to make stew out of it.

After a few meals of that, she might add more water, some tomatoes, peas and corn. If needed, she threw a rabbit or squirrel in and as you might guess…soup was on! We might eat from that kettle for eight to ten days without it ever leaving the heat.

The snowy winters seemed longer than they really were as the pure white powder preserved the life beneath it. Though we struggled at times, we managed to stay warm and fed on those bitter cold days.

However, we were limited to the small confines of our sleeping quarters, which was an old school bus. It had once served as Daddy and Mamas' traveling home and portable playpen for Earldean when she was just a baby. After settling in the hills, they set up housekeeping in it and felt they couldn't have found a more perfect spot to raise a family.

Daddy salvaged a little potbelly stove and rigged it up inside for means of heating. He ran the vent pipe out of one of the windows, then with a piece of scrap tin cut to fit the opened space, he plugged the hole to keep out the bitter cold.

In the midst of hardships my parents would find a little joy in the memories they had made with one another.

I remember sitting around that stove at night listening to them talk about all the places that they had been in "Ole Yeller", the name Daddy had given the old bus after his favorite story book. He loved reliving the memory of how he had come about getting that old thing.

He had worked for two years after school with his uncle Leonard, who was the head mechanic at the Bus Barn.

"Ever thang I ever lernt bout fixin thangs, I learnt frum my Unka Leonard." Daddy would say as he'd start his story. He told us how he had moved up from Murphysboro to Winslow to live with his Aunt Verdie May and Uncle Leonard when he was sixteen. He and Mama shared with us how they came about meeting and falling in love with each other in their high school years. They rode the bus to school together in the mornings and on the afternoons that Daddy didn't have to work after school. The rides on those long country roads were the biggest part of their courtship as they sat on the backseat together, holding hands and dreaming of making a house out of a bus. They fantasized of traveling all over the country seeing things they might not ever see if they stayed in Winslow.

Daddy would talk about how they could take the seats out for more room but leave a few for a sitting area. Mama imagined having checkered curtains and doilies sitting on milk crates turned upside down for tables; an affordable home for the two dreamers.

They had talked of marriage but Aunt Verdie May said they were too young to think about that and should focus on their school work and make something of themselves. When Daddy found out that they were selling one of the busses out at the county auction, he and Mama made plans to attend.

We would draw in closer as Daddy primed his voice to tell the tale again. *"They said it had too many miles on it to tote little children back and forth to school but with some fixin up I could get her runnin fine and dandy."*

Daddy would start out as if it was the first time he had ever told us the story. And…we would listen as if it were.

"So…ya mama and me plan to run off and git hitched and have a bunch of youngins. I took all the money I had saved up from workin out there at the Bus Barn…mowin yards and such…showed up with two hundred and seventy seven dollars and sixty two cents. A might purdy penny in those days, and ya mama with her thirty one dollars she had saved up from babysittin and takin in ironin. We had it planed we'z ta run off that day iffin we'z to git the bus…Had me a mess of tools that Unka Leonard give me through the years that I'd worked wit him…they'z all in a lit'lo tool chest I had bought with my first paycheck. I toted it wit me…'case I needed to use um to git the bus on the road…Atta way we figured we could fix er up along the way."

"And…" Mama would add, *"I had stopped off along the way and hid some clothes and a box with pictures and what-nots under the foot of the bridge on Filpot road…We'd go back for them on our way out of town."*

Mama would smile and stare into the fire and say something like, *"Oh I'z as nervous as a long tail cat on a porch full'a rockers!"*

Daddy would pull her closer to him as he'd continue with his story. *"There was a preacher man from the First Baptist Church of Rolling Hills there to bid on the bus…Said he wuzza needin it fer pickin up folks and brangin um to church on Sunday mornings. I told him bout me a workin out there at the bus barn and knowed a thang or two bout all em busses out there…made out like this here pa'ticlur bus wuttin fittin fer nuttin, said it needed a great deal a work done on it. But the preacher man didn't act like it seem to matter to him…wanted to bid anyhow."*

About this time Mama would add her part to the tale saying how scared she got when that preacher man grew curious enough to ask Daddy if he planned to bid on the bus too. When Daddy told him yes, he wanted to know what such a young fellow like him would do with a bus like that if he had it.

Mama was afraid the secret of their plans to run away together would be revealed and she would be in a lot of trouble if the preacher told on them.

She would shake her head and say, *"Well…I stepped away not wantin him to know we'z there together…incase I had to make a run for it…watched to see how he'd answer…Seen ya Daddy put his hands in his back pockets, arched his back and rocked proudly from heel to toe and told him…as a matter a factly like…"*

"What cha tell him Daddy…What cha tell um?" we'd ask him, as if we didn't know yet.

"Well, I told him I'z thinking bout startin my own church with that bus…Goin round to places a tellin folks about the Lord Jesus, inviting um in ta pray and sing…Yep a church bus…Church on wheels…Thinkin bout callin it the Second Baptist church of Rollin Hills…Or maybe…The First Baptist Church on Rollin Wheels!"

Well, needless to say the preacher didn't out do my daddy's bid of two hundred dollars.

He was able to get the bus started and with the money they had left they would be able to get out of town. When he started up the bus that day to leave, he reached for the handle to close the door. Just as he did a man's hand reached in and grabbed the door, pulling it open.

At this part of the story we would all gasp for air like it was scary or something. It could have been the way Daddy was telling it. With his eyes open so big we could see the reflection of the flickering flames in them.

In a soft low voice he'd say, *"There…standing in the doorway…was that preacher man! Ya mama was a sittin there on the seat behind me a figurin he'z there ta tell me how I'z gonna burn in Hell fer lying bout the bus and usin the name of the Lord Jesus for my ill gotten gain!*

It was a serious look on that preacher's face…just knowed he done figgerd us out…We looked and seen he had some sort a lynch mob with him…figgerd was there to string me from a high tree for lying to a preacher like I done…I'z about ta mess my britches for fear of what might do to us before we got away…Long bout that time he stepped in, then reached and handed me two books bound in black leather like covers with gold letters on um.

I looked and seen a'z Holy Bibles…He says I'd be a needin um for my church...One for me…and…one for the sinner to follow along. He prayed a quick blessin over us and them bibles then…just like 'at…he smiled and walked away…long wit them other fellers what wuz wit him…guess a'z some kinda deacons er sumpin other frum down at the church house!"

After a moment of silence, Daddy would take off his cap and rest it over his chest, then looking toward the sky he'd softly say, *"Lord, forgive me."* Placing his cap back on his head he continued. *"But I'm sho glad he gave us em Bibles cause they come in handy!"*

Mama would agree with him then tell us how scared she was that day when they left Winslow and never looked back.

I loved hearing their stories over and over though I never understood much why they didn't want to return and see their families. They never talked much about things back home either. Anyway…at my age it had never occurred to me that they might have been children themselves at one time; they had always been grown-ups to us. It was though life for them began when they met.

They went on to tell us how they headed west and saw the Grand Canyon, a painted desert and a forest that had petrified. It all sounded so pretty.

They met all sorts of people, even some real live cowboys and Indians like in the western books. They told us of hitch hikers they had picked up along the way and how they were glad to have the company. Some folks even paid them to take them to where they were going. They didn't at all mind, on the account of them not having any particular place they were heading, they were just glad to go along.

Mama told how she tried to get Daddy to study his bible and become a preacher man. She felt that his fibbing would be readily forgiven and justified if he at least would give it a go. She believed it was by the grace of God they were not caught and that the notion to have come up with such an idea must have already been stirred up and put there inside his head by God Himself. It would only be like the devil to leave it as lie!

Daddy would argue that he couldn't pronounce half the words and names in the "Good Book", nor could he make sense of it all and would never be able to pull it off.

"Who'd believe me? he'd ask. *"…B'sides…I got too much dog-on madness left inside me…too much foolishness left to spend!…naw…don't think I'd make much' a preacher."*

They said thay got as far as the California coast when Mama discovered she was pregnant with Earldean and sometimes the bus ride would make her sick at her belly. There they stayed with some strange folks that went by the name of "Beat-Nicks".

Daddy said at first he thought they were just one big family because they'd all go around calling each other brother, sister… or baby. At the time, my parents thought they sort of fit right in with these people because they too appeared as though they couldn't afford haircuts. One had long blond hair almost to her knees and went by the name "Sunshine". She took up with my mama and they became friends.

Having two children of her own, Sunshine knew a thing or two about having babies and was glad to share her knowledge. She taught Mama how to string beads and make pottery that they sold at the coffee shops in town. Sunshine had a fellow who lived with her who she introduced to Daddy as her *old man.*

Daddy thought it was strange being that this man was only two years older than him but five years younger than Sunshine. They told us that when Sunshine's old man saw that Mama was pregnant he coupled her belly and with a slow wiggle of shoulders he said *"Ooooow...Little Mama!"*

Then he turned to Daddy and his slapped him on the shoulder calling him *"Cool Daddy".* He referred to them as *"Little Mama"* and *"Cool Daddy"* for the longest time until Daddy told him he had a name...it was Earl and wished he would please call him that.

He laughed and said his name was Dean but Mama was still was a *"Little Mama."* He called the bus a "pad" but after a while they learned that was another name for a place where people lived, like a house or apartment.

Daddy said that though Dean talked funny, he chose to overlook that and all his other strangeness. According to them, all the Beat Nicks acted that way. In turn, the other couple took up for our parents when they were teased about their backwoods ways. It wasn't long before they all became good friends.

Dean would help Daddy find parts for the bus to keep it running. Together they pulled out some of the seats to make room for a dinning and sitting area. Being handy with wood, Dean helped Daddy build a table for a booth, bolting seats on either side. Two more seats were pushed together against the wall and bolted to the floor for bench seating. Across from it, on the other wall, was another seat for visitors.

The back area was reserved for storage and sleeping quarters where they placed a mattress that had been discarded. Beside it, they placed a shelf they had made for books and the few what-nots Mama had.

Dean surprised them with a little cradle for when the baby came. He had made it out of scrap lumber but sanded it smoothly so that it would not splinter. It could be locked down during travel, or removed to use outdoors.

Sunshine took Mama down to the Salvation Army to shop for maternity clothes and a coat. While they were there she got a few more baby pieces to go with the ones Sunshine had already given her. At a thrift store, they bought old sheets, some of which they cut up and hand stitched curtains for all the windows for privacy.

Dean and Sunshine had taken Mama and Daddy to the Charity Hospital when Mama started labor. While they waited, Sunshine checked in on Mama when she could sneak past the maternity ward nurses and the fellows paced the floors. Daddy told Dean if it was a boy that they would name it after him for all the kindness he had shown them. But Dean thought a father should name his first born after himself, Earl. Daddy settled for liking the idea of both names then declared it so.

The men were a little disappointed when the baby turned out to be a girl, but they came around when Mama said she liked the name *"Earldean"*.

We didn't know Mama's name at that point and never thought to ask. "Little Mama" became "Mama" that day and Daddy just called her by that name from then on.

They said that along with the baby came new challenges and struggles that they weren't prepared for. For one reason or another they didn't stay much longer in California. So, they said farewell to their friends, promising to keep in touch, though I don't think they ever did.

They had made their way back to Arkansas in 1957 after almost two years on the road. They said they had seen enough of the world and didn't care to take in any more. When "Ole Yeller" came to her final resting place here in these hills, she was not too far from where she started. They figured this was as good a place as any to make a home and raise a family…sheltered from any wickedness of the world.

For years Daddy would tinker under the hood of that old bus trying to get her started. She would just spit and sputter and on occasion blow a backfire that would scare us half to death. After several years, he finally gave up and sold off most of the parts. He used the hood to make an awning out over the door so that we could step out on rainy days to relieve ourselves without having to get soaked.

Mama found some paint to spell out the words SECOND BAPTIST CHURCH on the sides in attempt to keep daddy out of the pits of hell. She believed their misfortunes and the breakdowns were God's way of punishing them for Daddy's fib telling about the bus needing some work. She didn't even want to think about what was in store for them if they didn't make a church out of the thing.

To make it more authentic, she'd see to it that we said our prayers in it and every night before we went to sleep and they would take turns reading those Bibles out loud by candle light. Mama would have us singing songs like…Jesus Loves Me this I know for the Bible tells me so…and other things we'd later learn about like rocks of ages and old rugged crosses.

Sometimes, when she would be down at the creek washing out clothes or bathing, Mama would often sing this one song we called "Gather at the River". It was as though I could almost hear her singing it off in the distance that very day as I headed down the path to the creek for fresh wash water.

2
ALL WE KNEW TO DO

I stood at the creek bank with the wash pan and rag, entranced by the sun reflected in the sparkling water. The air was very still and it was too hot, for even the birds were in no mood to sing. Behind me, over my left shoulder, I could hear the dry brush and sticks cracking so I turned, but didn't see anything. A squirrel, I thought, as I squatted down and dipped the pan beneath the surface of the gentle stream.

The water was crystal clear and felt very cool to my hands as I took the rag and sank it beside the pan. Swirling it around, I watched the water cloud from the grime that was released from the soiled cloth. After swishing and twisting several times, I then took and stretched it out over my face.

My forehead and cheeks felt so hot against the coolness of the wet cloth, I wondered if I had a fever like Mama. I was weak, with a knot in the pit of my gut but not in any way I had ever felt sick before.

With my eyes covered, absorbing the refreshing moisture, my ears were more sensitive to the familiar sounds around me. I could hear the calm trickle of the droplets as they fell from the wet cloth and hit the top of the water. I could hear the babbling of the creek traveling over rocks in its path and a hawk screeching in its descent.

Off in the distance I could hear Earldean still fussing, though I wasn't sure what about; it didn't matter at that moment. About ten feet away I could clearly hear the rustling of leaves; probably a rabbit.

After a few moments I removed the cloth that had drawn the heat from my face and dunked it again. After ringing out the excess water, I held it firmly to my face and enjoyed another brief moment of the soothing coolness.

Again, I heard movement in the weeds behind me, closer, now over my right shoulder. Startled, I turned to see a flash of something that left the sumac swaying from the disturbance so I knew it was not my imagination. It was bigger than a rabbit, I thought, but every bit as fast. Wild boars with long tusks had been known to charge for no particular reason and though I had only seen a few, I didn't want to get caught off guard.

Pretending not to be afraid I slowly pulled the rag around my neck. I kept an eye out as I turned back to pull the pan from the creek. It was so full the water was spilling as it splashed from side to side. Coming up with it I turned to catch a glimpse of my little brother dodging behind a big maple tree. I pretended not to see him as I climbed the creek bank, heading back toward the path.

With caution, I walked slowly, spilling water along the way. Ed Earl was not a stranger to playing Hide and Seek and was likely to try to jump out from behind the tree any minute, so I would play along.

I passed the Maple but he did not jump out and say "Boo" as I expected. Instead, I heard Ed Earl sniffling and I turned to see him curled up on his side with muddy tears rolling down his cheek.

"What's a matter?" I asked stepping toward his hiding place.

"Leave me lone!" he cried. *"Don't want you to give me bath…just Mama!"*

I set the wash pan down and sat beside him resting my back against the trunk of the tree.

"Mama cain't do it now Ed Earl" I said in an easy way. I didn't want to upset him any more than he already was. He was lonesome for her, as he had not been able to go inside the bus to see her for two days now. He had gotten mad at her for getting sick in the first place and he didn't understand why he couldn't be with her.

He rubbed his face with his fists, getting dirt in his eyes. He grabbed at them kicking and screaming.

"Don't do that! You'll make it worse!" I yelled as he resisted me. I held him to me with one arm while I reached and grabbed the rag from my neck with the other. Stretching, I dipped it into the pan of water saying, *"Here…Let me help you!"* I held the cool cloth over his eyes while the tears did the rest of the work. When he calmed down, I repositioned him in front of me and said, *"There now, let me git a look at that."* I wiped his face, asking him, *"Ya ok now?"* Still sniffling, he slowly shook his head yes.

I rinsed the rag out and reached for his hand saying, *"Here, let's git that dirt off so'z ya won't do that again."* He sniffed as I washed his dirty palms while he managed to compose himself enough to ask, *"What we gone do, Sassy?"*

"We're gonna go find Daddy…He'll know what to do." I said, taking advantage of his distraction so that I could wipe him down.

"Where'z he at?" he inquired.

"Mama said he's working in a town somewhere…heard him tell her one time bout gettin some work over to a place called Tulsa…whereever the heck that is…Recon it's in a town some place…but I don't know whichin it is. We been ta three differn't towns ba-fore ya know…Aint quite sure where ta find him… but we gonna walk till we git to one and look fer him…If he aint there… well…we'll just keep a walkin…When we see his truck…we'll know we done found him." I said.

Ed Earl was oblivious to my bathing him when he asked, *"Why come Daddy cain't jes come git us in his truck?"*

I rinsed the rag between questions and tried to answer as best I could. *"Daddy don't knowed we'z a needin him or he'd a done been here Ed Earl…then it wuttin be no need ta go fetch him, ya see?"*

"Mama gonna walk wit us ta find Daddy?" he asked, leaning in for a hopeful answer. I quickly turned away so that he wouldn't see me about to cry as I was trying so hard to be a big girl.

I was so afraid to go without Mama because we had never gotten too far away from her before. I took the rag and wiped my own face that felt so hot and flushed.

Keeping it hidden, I answered him in a soft cracking voice. *"Naw Ed Earl…Mama cain't git up…we have to go alone."*

"But Mama done told us we'z best not ever go off or we gonna git …" he was saying before he was interrupted by Earldine's beckoning call.

"*SAAAA-SYEE…EEEED-EARRL!*" Her voice sang through the cove, sounding a whole lot like Mama's call. *"YA'LL COME ON!"*

I got up dumping the water out and held out my hand to Ed Earl. He took the offered assistance but didn't let go as we walked back.

On the way, we heard Earldean shouting out instructions that we needed to follow to prepare for our trip to town. However, they went in one ear and out the other with only bits and pieces sticking in between. Something about drinking water…Ed Earl's shoes…extra britches…Learline's' accidents…peanut butter...doin ever thang round here!...bla…bla…bla!

We prepared for the twenty two mile hike to town as best as four young children could prepare. Of course we had no idea how far twenty two miles was on the hottest day in August. In fact, we had no idea how far twenty two miles was on any given day of the year.

We had only gone to town once or twice a year and then it was riding in the back of Daddy's old pickup truck.

In our urgency to find our father and get him home we knew walking was the only way. Earldean and I gathered some things we thought we might need for overnight in case we didn't make it back before dark. We had a change of clothes for Ed Earl and Learline, because they were both susceptible to messing up one end or the other.

Though they were all worn out, we took a hair brush and our toothbrushes…Mama would insist. We had seldom seen a tube of toothpaste so we weren't accustom to using any; it was just as well, we didn't want to tote more up that hill than we had to.

We laid these things in the middle of a tattered sheet we had spread out on the ground and then folded the sides to meet the center. After rolling it up, we tied it off with a cloth belt from one of Mama's old dresses that had been worn out and didn't fit her any more. I was sure it never really fit in the first place but she kept it in case she needed it later.

Out of habit, I bit the buttons off and put them in the baby food jar; the one that Mama had there for buttons. She saved and sorted all parts that could be used again. I wadded the rest up and tossed it into a box of rags under the bus.

Many times we had helped Mama pack a bedroll for Daddy when he set out for road trips looking for work. Ours was not as neat as hers but it would do fine for us.

While we were doing this, Learline sat playing with her baby doll on our bed covers that were still laid out on the ground from the night before. We had been sleeping outside because Mama said it was too hot for us to sleep on the bus. She also thought it was best if she slept inside away from us that first night that she got real sick. I guess she didn't want us kids to catch whatever it was she had.

We had taken over her chores as well as taking turns going in and wiping her down with a cool rag when she started running a fever. With honest effort, Earldean took over the cooking when we saw that Mama was too weak to get up. We had never seen our mother like this as she usually stopped at nothing and was not one to just lie around.

At first I thought it was just the poor taste of the food but she had gotten to where she would barely eat or drink, and what little she did, she couldn't seem to keep down. I had to spoon feed her like a baby up until that night before when I seen she was too weak to even drink a spoon of water.

Her raspy voice cracked as if she were struggling to get the words out, *"You…go on honey…eat ya supper…babies might git scared ifin theys' ta see me like this…tell um Mama's restin."*

She suddenly gripped herself as if she were riddled with pain and her face cringed tightly as she slowly curled to her side for some sort of relief.

"Mama? Does it hurt…like when ya belly aint had no food? Ya aint eat nuttin in a great long while…Ya ain't got ta be hungry ya know…we have food now! Won't cha please try ta eat sumthin-nother…please Mama…I don't want ya ta hurt like iss."

We had known the pangs and weakness of hunger before but never so bad that we didn't have the energy to eat when we finally got it. She didn't say she was hungry, but her foul breath indicated she was nearing starvation.

"Please…jest one little ole bite…might make ya feel better!" I begged. She didn't say no but tightened her lips and refused as though it would taste bad.

"Maybe Earldean can make ya somethin else ya like better…What'cha want Mama? I'll try to git it fer ya." I asked and waited a bit for her to answer. She tried but couldn't get her words out.

"When's Daddy commin home…Maybe he can go fetch some kind of tonic to git ya well?...Earldean said he might not be a commin fer a few more weeks…Is that right…can you wait that long Mama?…Mama? Still, she couldn't answer. It was as though it took too much energy for her to talk so I didn't try to force her any more.

"Here just sip this spoon of water…it aint got no taste." I suggested, putting the spoon to her mouth. *"Open up…come on Mama."* I coached her trying to hold up her heavy head. When her lips barely parted I hurried to pour in the water but most of it fell across her cheek. I tried again lifting her face up off the pillow but still no luck; it just ran across her lips then onto the pillow. Then I put down the spoon and leaned in to dab her face with my shirttail.

Leaning back, propped on my arms, I sighed at my defeat trying to think of what else to do. All I could do was just sit there and stare at her as she dared not move for fear of pain. I watched her body gradually start to relax as the pain seemed to subside, yet she stayed on her side while drifting off to sleep again.

As I got up and started out, she reached out her hand and slowly waved it around as though she were trying to find her way in the dark even though it was still plenty light outside. It was strange in that her eyes were wide open, but strained as if she couldn't see. I felt afraid for her when she reached but couldn't find me. She looked right through me as though I weren't there. I reached out and took her hand instead and quietly sat back down holding it for a moment before I rubbed it against my face.

Her lips were cracked and dried, sticking together as she started to say something. With my other hand I dipped my fingers in the cup of water that was sitting on the crate beside her mattress. I wet her lips and let the water drip in her mouth. I dipped again and waited for her to suck the droplets off but she only licked them and barely smacked.

"Remember Mama…?" I asked. *"Remember when Nanny Goat was too little ta eat? We taught her to suck our fingers and get the milk off…remember?...It felt so funny! Huh? Mama?...Remember?"* I was trying to get her to laugh. Oh, how I wanted to hear her laugh again. She barely turned up one side of her mouth, but she slightly squeezed my hand to let me know she heard me.

I leaned over and kissed her forehead still hot with fever. She started to move and softly groan. Finally she found enough energy to respond. Straining to get the words out, she whispered, *"ssss…Sassss…You and sssSister…doin good ta help me like this…gettin ta be a big girl now."* She drifted between mumbling her broken sentences. *"I'm sorry…I'm so sick…but ya Daddy…come…home…know what ta do…. Tell the babies good night…I love um…sss Say…prayers and…sssSassy?* She drifted.

"Yea Mama." I answered.

"I love ya…so much." she said with a dry mouth and her lips getting stuck together. But she managed to work up a crooked smile, before she closed her eyes again.

That night, after the others had gone to sleep, I took the flashlight and climbed into the bus to check on Mama. She was still on her side; just as I had left her, only she was shaking hard like she was cold. I couldn't understand that with it being so hot and stuffy in there. I pulled the sheet over her and up to her shoulder, tucking it around her as she had done for me many times.

I knelt down beside her and kissed her head. Her chestnut brown hair had drawn up in tight ringlets around her pale face. The rest of her hair was in knotted curls that sprung out all over her pillow.

When she feels better, I'll brush it for her, I thought. She likes to look pretty when Daddy comes home.

She had a smell about her that didn't smell like Mama usually did. It made me think of honey and sour milk mixed together.

I reached across and picked up her Bible from the shelf where she kept books and what-nots. Sitting on the floor next to her I held the flashlight over the opened book. With my finger sliding across the pages, I searched to find some words that I knew so that I could read to her.

"Father uh…Holy…in you shall make…uh…naw, let's see…" I flipped the thin pages; I liked hearing the sound it made when my parents did that. It sounded so…important.

"Oh, here's some I can read" I quietly announced then cleared my throat. *"I-cried-out-to-God-with-my…vvv-voice and he…gave-me…ear. In-the- day-of-my…ttt…trrr…trob…Table! Wait naw…its trouble…yea trouble. I sssssssss…sought-the-Lord. My hand was ss…st..strrrrrrr…eeech..da …stretched… out in the night wit…withooo…with out… without…ce-sssss…uh…oh! Cleanin…no wait…uh cesin..uh…dogon it! What is that word?"* I pondered out loud.

"Ceasin." I heard my Mama say in a weak voice. *"That means without stopping."*

"Hey Mama!" I said softly then asked, *"ya feeling better?"*

She repeated the whole verse by memory while I followed along with my finger. *"I cried out to God with my voice and…he gave ear ta me…In the day of my trouble…I sought the Lord…my hand stretched out in the night without ceasin...My soul refused to be comforted."* She said finishing with a sleepy smile and though it was for that brief moment, she was more coherent than she had been in days.

"…That's Psalm seventy seven…verses one and two...I..I think."

Mama had taught Earldean and me how to read using the Bible as one of her teaching tools. She knew a bunch of verses by heart. There was plenty of reading time out there in the woods.

One of my goals in life at that time was to learn to read out loud, real smooth like Mama did. She and Daddy made it sound like the books themselves were doing the talking.

"Mama?" I asked softly. *"Is ya pain gone now?"*

Except for the involuntary quivering, she had barely moved when she spoke. Still lying on her side she had not tried to reposition herself. I knelt down beside her and drew in closer, waiting for her to answer me. *"Soon, real sss…"* then she drifted off again; unable to keep her eyes open.

She was shaking so hard I didn't know how she kept from waking herself up. I folded my hands and whispered my prayers asking God to please help her stop hurting then lifted the sheet and crawled in beside her, nestling my back in the curve of her body.

I reached and pulled her arm over my side, cradling her hand in mine as if she had the strength to scoop me up there herself. I could tell by her occasional groaning, she was not resting well and her body was very hot, causing me to sweat all over but I didn't want to leave her. Eventually, her shaking rocked me to sleep.

The next morning I woke up still spooned up to Mama. She had finally stopped shaking and was sleeping so sound that her arm felt as heavy as a bale of hay. Trying not to wake her, I quietly slid out of my spot so that she could get some sound sleep.

Learline and Ed Earl were climbing up the steps of the bus when I stopped them. *"Sssssssssssh....Mama"s sleeping"* I signaled with my finger over my mouth.

"I want Mama!" Ed Earl insisted.

"Mama" Learline followed.

"Ok." I said. "*…but be very quiet.*"

Learline kept her finger over her mouth as I had shown her. We tiptoed over and kissed her softly on the head, then back out again, me hushing them all the way. That seemed to be enough for them at that moment to hold them off for a while.

It was later that morning that Earldean had decided to go get Daddy and bring him back. She had gone in to take Mama her breakfast and was only in there a minute before she came back out crying.

She told me that Mama didn't wake up and it didn't look like she was breathing. I was hoping she was wrong but deep inside I was afraid she was right.

"Why?" I asked. *"do you think she's…"* I just couldn't say it. The word would not come out of my mouth.

"I don't know Sassy, what cha think?" she asked, wiping her tears. She looked up and saw Ed Earl and Learline playing in their oatmeal. They were not disturbed yet by Earldean's discovery. If they were to see us upset, it was sure to set off an uproar of frustration. She grabbed my hand and pulled me to the other side of the bus to finish the conversation.

We had seen our fair share of death in animals, but knowing only a hand full of other people, we had never known a human that had died. We had heard our parents talk very little about people they knew who had "passed on", or as they might say, "the Good Lord took um". But this was our first experience.

What are they passing? Did Mama die like the animals? Could she wake up and live again? Is God going to come and take her away from us to live with Him in Heaven? Will He let us go too? Are we going to die too? What are we going to do? We will be all alone! What was going to happen to us? The questions flooded out with the tears.

We had to tell Daddy as soon as we could. Maybe he could fix her back up. He would know some answers.

It didn't set well with Ed Earl when Mama had gotten sick in the first place. How on earth could he handle this? Learline was not quite three years old and didn't understand all of our words anyway. So, we agreed not to tell them until we knew more about it ourselves.

We were just coming to that conclusion when Ed Earl poked his head from around the front of the bus.

"BOO!" he said. *"I found you!"* Learline followed up behind him. *"Boo…Boo…Boo…"* she said with a giggle. We quickly wiped our tears and tried to compose ourselves but they had caught us. Of course, the questions followed. We stuck with our plan and told them we were just worried about Mama being sick. There were plenty of things to do to try to keep our minds off our worry.

Our parents had taught us a whole lot about surviving in the Ozark forest and living off the land. Daddy said that one of the most important things a person needed to know about living was not to worry about anything but to do something about it instead. Earldean had decided that we would set out to find the one who always knew what to do when the rest of us couldn't figure it out.

Mama had spent the biggest part of her days teaching us things not only in books but also about our surroundings. She taught us how to milk the goat and take care of the chickens and other varmints that may one day be our supper. We followed her around learning how to cook, sew and tend the garden. We learned how to draw drinking water from the springs, wash clothes, gather kindling and build a safe fire.

Although Daddy did most of the wood chopping, Mama showed us how to use a saw to take limbs off trees that had fallen to the ground to make firewood. We had lived among bugs, spiders, snakes and animals long enough to know which ones were friendly and which ones to stay away from.

Going into town had always been a big deal to us so we knew there were things we had to do to prepare. We remembered that before previous trips to town and other outings, we had to hoist the baskets of food up by ropes on an A frame, to keep the wild varmints out of our supplies. By the time we finished feeding the animals, putting out the fires, and tying things down, it was just after noon. The sun was getting higher in the sky and hotter by the minute.

Earldean heaved the bedroll over her back and secured it with wide strips of fabric from the rag box. She turned and motioned for Learline to come take her hand. She did, but not before she ran back for her baby doll.

With the exception of his bare feet, Ed Earl was standing ready to go. He was carrying a brown paper sack with a red pig face on the side. Earldean had told him it was for a pick-nick we would have along the way.

She had packed up some peanut butter, a jar of Mamas homemade jelly, saltine crackers for lunch and some small tomatoes from the bumper crop of Mama's wilted garden. She thought we might eat those for supper if we weren't back before dark. I suggested we bring a flashlight in that case and dug through one of the supply trunks for some spare batteries to take along. After tucking them into the sack we were set to go and started toward the path.

After only a few steps I said, *"Wait here!"* then turned and ran back to the bus. As I climbed aboard, I looked toward my mother and saw that it looked as though she were just asleep. What if my sister was wrong about this I wondered.

Maybe Mama was just sleeping real sound. I thought about taking a closer look and double checking. I watched for a moment but she didn't move…at all. I turned away looking out the windshield of the bus, I could see the others waiting impatiently for me. The heat had strengthened the smell of Mama's sickness making it hard to breath.

Digging through a box of shoes that was stored under the steering wheel, I found a pair of ladies sneakers. They were bright pink with striped shoe strings. Brand new, never used shoes that Daddy brought home to Mama but they were too small for her. She wouldn't mind me taking them this time.

I turned and darted toward the back to get the Bible. She would want us to have our lessons. As I proceeded, I couldn't help but see her there. Her face was the color of goat's milk and her eyes were closed in deep dark circles. She didn't look like herself at all.

Again, I thought what if we were wrong? We don't really know what a dead person was supposed to look like; what if she started breathing again after we left? I wanted so bad to believe she would take a big breath right then but she didn't move. Nothing moved but the flies that swarmed around her so I shooed them away and pulled the sheet over her head to cover her face. I could hear Earldean calling for me but I didn't want to get in trouble for going off without permission so I thought I would ask, even if it weren't granted by either parent, at least I had done my part.

"Mama? Me and Earldean wanna go lookin fer Daddy…so'z he can help take care of ya…We both gotta go…ya told us don't ever go off by ourselves, I know…a-a-and it aint like we don't wannna mind ya Mama…We know better than ta do that…but we gotta go and we takin the lit'ones 'long wit us…on account they won't have nobody here ta look after um after we gone…well…you caint git up an all…I-I-I sho hope we are doin the right thang…Ya hear me Mama? Mama?" I waited, wanting her to answer me.

"SASSY…COME ON!" I could hear Earldean yelling impatiently, echoed by Learline.

I stood up over mama's body and said, *"Well…gotta go now Mama… I just wanna be able ta say I talked wit ya bout all this…I caint help it if you aint able to give me a answer. I tried Mama…I really tried, ya hear me? …Mama?*

A tear rolled down my face when I told my Mama I loved her then said goodbye.

In leaving, I grabbed the Bible and shoes then ran out without looking back. I went up to Ed Earl and handed him the bright pink sneakers and said, *"Here, Mama said ta wear these…They'z a little big but they better-n-nuttun."*

"But…" Earldean started to say something to me about fibbing but I widened my eyes and glared back trying to indicate that I needed to and for her to let me handle this situation. She complied by turning away.

Ed Earl was thrilled at his new possessions and slipped them on not even having to untie the striped laces. *"These purdy!"* he said, not knowing back then that boys weren't suppose to wear pink.

"Thank ye Mama!" he yelled back at the bus, not knowing she couldn't hear him. At that point it was best he didn't know.

There were a lot of things we didn't know that day as we headed up the path to the dirt road.

We didn't know how to tell time or what the rest of the world did with their share of it. We had no idea where they lived, how they lived nor about the things they thought were essential in order to survive in society; things like planes that fly like birds, flags that fly on poles and sprays that kill flies.

We didn't know that Johnson and Johnson were more than two people, neither of which had a daddy named John. Nor did we know that Lyndon Johnson was the president or even what a president was.

We didn't know where to find our Daddy or where to begin to start looking for him. We didn't know where he worked or for sure what kind of work he did. We didn't know which way he went when he last left for work because we couldn't remember or we just didn't pay attention; different jobs took him different ways. It never mattered before as we always stayed behind…how could we have known?

We couldn't have known that hot August day in 1968 that our fate was at hand when we reached the end of the path that led to the dirt road; we didn't *know* which way to go…left or right.

We picked right.

3
LOVE THY NEIGHBOR

Our youth was in our favor for the climb up the steep path carved into the hillside.

Daddy had been working on it for years by removing rocks and trees so that he could make a driveway from the upper graveled road down to our home.

The tire tracks were still there in the soil from when he had left eight days earlier. Ed Earl had the idea that we could find Daddy if we followed the tracks to his truck. We decided that might work, at least until we got to the main highway.

Creek Bed Road would have been the shorter distance for walking but that old forgotten road over time had grown to be nothing more than a wide trail after the storms and rains had taken its toll on that old rotten bridge. Daddy had said that dilapidated antique would have collapsed long before it did had "Ole Yeller" ever crossed it. He claimed it was by the grace of God that the bus broke down when it did just before it reached that point. Otherwise, he might have risked crossing it in his younger, more daring years.

It was under that old bridge that they first met the most unforgettable person in our lives. That morning, after the bus broke down, Mama and Daddy took out walking carrying ten month old Earldean. They were in search of food and supplies with the little money they had on them. It certainly wasn't enough to buy any parts for the motor, so they had planed to just camp out there just off the side of Creek Bed Road where the bus had stalled out. At least until they could come up with a better idea.

They had walked about a mile or so when they came upon that shaky old bridge. Mama said she was afraid it was going to collapse before they reached the other side and shuddered at the thought of having to cross it in that heavy bus when they continued their journey.

Though Daddy tried to assure her that if he got a good running start he could speed across it before it fell in, Mama insisted that she would walk back the way they came in before she'd ever let her baby ride with him across that bridge on the bus.

She had already tried to tell him that they were going the wrong way in the first place; way back when they turned off the highway and on to the first side road but Daddy would never admit that they were lost. Even when they wound up in the back woods on yet another dirt road, he claimed that he was just taking a short cut; though Mama could find no such thing on a map.

They were in the midst of bantering about this as they nervously crept across the bridge watching the waters stir beneath them. It was about that time that they heard a man's voice yell, *"Howdy!"* Paddling his fishing boat out from underneath, he introduced himself as Mr. James Denby from across the lake.

When Daddy told him that they had broken down, the man offered to give them a ride to town for help. Daddy explained that with him being a mechanic he could fix it himself if he only had the parts but the money they had save to come home on had about all dwindled out.

Having been traveling for weeks with a baby, they all looked a bit scraggly, tattered and worn out but the man didn't think they looked too out of place for this neck of the woods. It was so far out from civilization that there wasn't much call to bathe, shave or get dressed up. There was no one out there to impress but the wildlife and in some folks opinion, a body was better left un-kept rather than to try to draw attention from the beasts who populated the area.

Seeing that they were down on their luck the man decided to do the neighborly thing and help out as best he could. He first took them by boat to his house where he fed them a good hot meal and came up with an old sheet to make diapers out of so that they could keep their baby changed and dried. He dug through a back closet and found a few worn pieces of clothing that had once belonged to his late wife.

"Don't rightly know iffin these ta fit cha little mama but you'z welcome ta try um on fer size…Keep um iffin ya like…I aint got no use fer um. They usta belong to my wife Virginia when she wuz a livin…she'z been passed on a great long while now or she'da give um to ya herself…I almost forgot they'z back here…you'z the first gal besides my sister ta come along…sis said she didn't need um…so they'z yourz iffin ya like."

Mama said that she could tell that they might be a little big for her but didn't want to refuse his kind and thoughtful generosity. Sometime later she would alter them with a needle and thread.

Though they had just met Mr. Denby, the trip to and from town allowed them to get better acquainted and he offered this little family a place to stay for the night. Mama and Daddy were also used to meeting strangers themselves. Some were pleasant and trustworthy, others not quite so. They would sort this particular man in the former ranks; so there wasn't a problem with his offer. They simply knew that their stay could end up being longer than his offer and neither wanted to wear out their welcome.

After explaining that the bus offered more than their just their transportation and that it had actually been their "mobile home" for two years, the man didn't feel so bad about taking them back to the other side and just dropping them off. However, he would save them some steps by taking them further up stream, closer to where the bus was located.

Mama had always claimed that this man was an angel sent straight from God that day as their meeting had turned out to be a real blessing. Without any money or a way of getting any, my parents had no clue as to how they were ever going to be on their way without just abandoning the bus where it sat.

This idea was no good as it left them on foot and they couldn't possibly carry the entire collection of things necessary for a baby. Even when their new friend offered to take them by car to where ever it was that they were going, it was of no use as they really had no place left to go.

They didn't provide him with any information as to why they couldn't return home, nor did he ask them about it. In fact, he never questioned their past at all, making his only business being that of helping them feel comfortable during their stay there in the hollow.

After his assisting them with getting their supplies back up to the bus, Mama offered to give the man a tour of their living space while Daddy wanted to show him what was under the hood. He obliged them both then complemented them on their clever contraption that seemed to accommodate all of their needs.

He left them feeling proud of themselves in what they had accomplished for such a young couple and grateful for him not having ridiculed their weird ideas of a dream come true. Early the next morning he returned with some fresh baked biscuits and ham along with a little applesauce for baby Earldean.

Realizing that this young man must have been a pretty good mechanic to have kept that old bus on the road for that long, Mr. Denby offered Daddy a way to make a little money by helping him work on his tractor.

He kept a few old vehicles around his place and told Daddy he could have that old 47 Ford pickup in exchange for helping him out with odd jobs he needed done. The truck wasn't all that old but when Mr. Denby couldn't figure out how to fix it he just parked it out there with all the rest. It didn't take long for Daddy to get it running using parts from the other junkers around there. New belts, hoses and a carburetor were the only things he had to spend any money on besides oil and gasoline. He then had a way to go look for a job.

Mr. Denby seemed delighted and entertained that Daddy was capable of accomplishing so much in so little time. With him not being as spry as he once was, the older gentleman was very appreciative of the help of a younger fellow and paid him accordingly.

Daddy was as grateful for the chance to get out of the bind he was in so the feelings were mutual. Both of my parents admired his wisdom about things they weren't sure of. And even some things that they just thought they were sure of until he was able to politely show them a different point of view.

I believe this must have been the pivoting point of Mama's faith. She often testified that many of her prayers were answered when God sent this angel of mercy to help keep and guard over them.

He would laugh at her every time she suggested that he might really be one, saying, *"Awe now…just git a good look at me Lit' Mama…Do I look like an angel? Where's my wangs…and my shiny halo? Why, I'm jest an ole man a tryin ta do what's right is all."*

No, this fellow didn't look at all like what most folks would figure an angel to look like. This widower was a tall, thin man in his late sixties. His face had sharp features with tanned weathered skin and his head was bald on top where his hair had fallen out so he wore a ballcap to keep the sun from burning it. The hair that he did have stuck out like straw on a scarecrow and was white as snow.

He was a good cook and often tried out his new concoctions on us. However, he wasn't much for keeping house. Mama wouldn't take any money from him when she would sweep out the house and tidy up a bit for him. She told him she was just returning the favor for all the kindness he had shown. Besides it would give her something to do while the men folk worked on projects around his place.

After he got the truck going Daddy found a few odd jobs in the area working the fields and on farm equipment. He came back late one afternoon announcing to Mama that he had finally made enough money to buy the parts for the bus engine.

Instead of being excited about it, like Daddy thought she'd be, he found her acting a little disappointed because they would have to be leaving this beautiful place and their new friend. He said that he too wasn't as eager to get back on the road as he had been at first.

Daddy admitted that the thought had crossed his mind to just homestead right there where they broke down. Mama approved of the idea but didn't think staying parked there on the side of the road for the rest of their life was the safest place for a baby who was about to start walking at any time. Other people would be driving through their front yard and throwing dust.

Daddy reminded her that only two other cars had passed them the whole time they had been out there, neither of which had stopped and questioned their being there. He figured that those people passing through must have assumed that theirs was just another campsite like others scattered around the lake.

Mama loved the area but she still didn't see how they could get by without having to move the bus someplace back off the road. But, if they had to spend the money on the parts to start it up again, they might as well move on along.

Though Daddy thought she was silly when she suggested it, Mama told him that they ought to pray about what to do. When he asked her how were they suppose to know what God's answer would be, she didn't really know how to respond. All she knew to tell him was that whenever she quietly talked to God in times of despair that somehow things would straighten out much faster than they did if she didn't.

She told him that there had been times in her life where she would be in impossibly bad situations but not long after praying, things would miraculously change for the better. She said that she was beginning to believe in all that stuff she'd been reading in those Bibles because the same sort of things happened to those other people too; some in much bigger ways. She confessed that it only happens for her when she prays but she still couldn't tell him how it works.

So when she went into the bus to lay the baby down she brought the Bibles back out with her for them to search for an answer to that question. Though they really didn't have a clue as to where to start, they fumbled through the pages searching for some sort of answer. One of them stumbled across the story of how God sent Moses a burning bush as a sign. Then the other read where they shouldn't ask God for signs; that they should just have faith so they still weren't sure how they would know.

When they went to bed that night they prayed together for the first time; they figured it wouldn't hurt to ask even if they never actually heard the voice of the Almighty. They didn't have anything to lose by doing so.

Not long after they went to sleep that night a powerful storm moved in with forceful winds that almost blew the bus over. They had weathered many a tempest in that bus before but none that had ever matched the force of this one. It shook them up so much that when it finally blew over they had a hard time getting back to sleep.

The next morning when they woke up, they found out just how bad it really was. Huge trees had snapped into, like toothpicks, while others had been pulled from their roots and crashed to the ground, clearing a large area just outside the bus.

Mangled tree tops lay across the roadway and were piled so high that you couldn't see over them. They were held in place with their enormous twisted trunks all blocking the path going either way, leaving no means of access for anyone to get in…or out. Denby was just making his way on foot through the rubble carrying an ax and a chainsaw figuring that he would have to carve his way in to rescue my parents and sister.

Instead he found them safe and sound without a scratch on them or the bus. He told them that the radio news reported several tornadoes in the area the night before and that there was no doubt to him that one of them had touched down right there in that spot.

He said that his house got only a little damage but his shed was floating somewhere out there in the lake. He advised them that if they ever tried to get back out of there that they would have to turn the bus around and go back the other way for that old bridge, which was on its last leg anyway, didn't have even so much as its feet left.

Daddy turned to Mama and said, *"Looks like we got an answer!"*

When they told Denby about their prayer, out of respect, he removed his cap and responded in amazement, *"The Good Lord works in mysterious ways…don't cha thank?"*

With that he placed his hat back on his head, smiled, then yanked the pull cord on the chainsaw saying, *"Let's get your yard cleaned up so'z we can go a fishin afterwhile!"*

In no time at all the two men had become really good friends and enjoyed hunting and fishing together. Mama would cook up their catch of the day and with Denby around there always seemed to be plenty.

When I was a baby learning to talk, I called him *"Denby"*. Wasn't long before they all started calling him that. Over time it became a common name around our place.

Mama said Denby was there the day I was born in Chinquapin Hollow. She didn't know much about insurance and there wasn't enough money to go to a doctor. She was about five months pregnant when Denby took notice and told her about the free clinic in one of the nearest towns.

She claimed that the only sickness she had was morning sickness and didn't see the need to bother a doctor with natural causes. Denby said it wouldn't be a bad idea to go in for a checkup or two just to make sure everything was alright. She agreed and had planned to do so but somehow she lost track of time and her labor came by surprise.

There wasn't time to make it to a hospital when she went into labor. It was fortunate the men came in from hunting when they did. Denby had delivered a baby once before when he worked for the volunteer fire department.

He said the woman does most the work anyway. He probably told her and Daddy that just to ease their minds so they wouldn't panic.

Daddy would tease him about being so calm during the delivery but when it was all over he went off into the woods and cried like a baby. Mama said it was much more natural than what they put you through at the hospital and that the rest of her babies would be born right there as well. And…they were.

When Denby came to visit, he took time out with us kids to play tic-tac-toe, checkers and I spy. He was the one who taught me to bait my own hook when Mama thought I was too little.

Mama would send Denby home with a jar of pickles or some of her homemade preserves. Sometimes she would pick a mess of butterbeans or peas and have them shelled before the men would get back from their fishing trip. She would cook half for supper and send the other half home with Denby to cook another day. He never came or went empty handed.

He would bring us watermelons or peaches and on occasion an ice chest full of sodas. Ice was a rarity for us in the summer months so this would be such a thrilling event. I loved holding a cube in my hand and watch it melt like magic. It felt so nice and cold.

I would stand beneath that thermometer and pretend I was the Orange Haired Lady drinking my cool refreshing Coca Cola and looking so pretty! A good burp contest was bound to follow an ice chest full of drinks. Daddy was a sure winner with Denby a close second. There was guaranteed to be laughter in the camp with Denby around. He was so entertaining and always a welcome sight.

We called him our neighbor but he was more like a grandfather or uncle…like family. It was in the winter of 1964 that Denby slipped on the ice and broke his leg. He might have frozen to death out there if Daddy didn't happen to show up for his weekly visit across the lake. Daddy drove him to the hospital where they set his leg and nursed his pneumonia for two weeks. After he came home, Mama would cook him up some soup and send it over by boat with Daddy.

Ed Earl was still too little but Earldean and I would go over to help Daddy do Denby's chores and visit with him. He never quite made it back to his old self. Early that next spring his sister and brother-in-law came and took him off to live with them in Sikeston, Missouri.

They sold off his car and most of his things. When we went to see him off, he sent us home with several boxes and things to remember him by including his old fishing boat. He shared it for so long with Daddy he thought he ought to just have it. He wouldn't let them sell his home. He said he'd be back as soon as he got well…but he never came back.

"Reckon how Denby is doin? Think he'll be back soon?" I asked Earldean as we walked.

"Don't know if he's well enough." she replied.

"I wish Denby still lived cross the lake…I sho miss um." Ed Earl chimed in, though he was hardly old enough to remember him except in the course of our accounts.

"He'd of taken Mama to the hospital iffin he were still our neighbor." Earldean added.

"He'z still our neighbor ya'll. He'z gonna come back when he gits well ya know!" I informed them.

"He might not ever come back Sassy! Some people don't ever git well…and some people just die!" Earldean cried.

"Earldean!" I shouted.

"Is Mama gonna die?" Ed Earl inquired.

Nobody answered him. Earldean ran ahead and Learline followed her, crying for Mama.

The next closest neighbors were the Riley's who lived about four miles down the road. Lester Riley was a small man who made me think of a boy in a grown up body. He was half the size of his wife Myrtle. He was quiet and seldom spoke other than a nod for hello and good-bye. He would busy himself whenever we would occasionally visit them unless Daddy happened to come along. Then the two men would find enough to talk about as they walked around the property looking at first one thing then another.

Myrtle Riley on the other hand was just the opposite as she was a talkative, large, slow moving woman who didn't care too much for "youngins" and she let us know this in no uncertain terms. She would be kind to us in an artificial way whenever Daddy would visit with us. Then she would act all prim and proper. I believe it was because when she first met our folks she asked where we were from and Daddy answered her by saying, *"We have the Rolling Hills Baptist Church…just down the road."*

She assumed there was a church there and he was the preacher. Truth was she seldom got off the front porch to find out any different. She excused herself from attending services on account of her feet hurting all the time and couldn't wear shoes. I believe she just got too big to wear them anymore.

She had often made remarks about the way us kids ought to be able to behave better, with our daddy being a preacher and all. It didn't make much made sense to me then but now, I get it. Daddy didn't pay her too much attention on the rare occasions he visited them. However, from time to time we would walk with Mama over there to help Myrtle put up vegetables or jars of jelly on halvsies.

Their house had a big porch with rockers where they would sometimes sit and shell purple hull peas or snap beans. Myrtle Riley would do most of her snappin at us. *"You youngins git on out in the yard and play. Leave us be so'z we grownups can do sum visitin!...and don't be hangin frum my trees either!"* She would sound so mean like. Mama said it was because the Riley's never had any children of their own and we made them nervous.

The closest thing to a family they had was a pack of hound dogs Mr. Riley used for retrieving his kill on his hunting trips. He referred to them as his babies and each one had a name, though they all looked the same to me. When we visited their home, he would have to tie them up to the bumper of his tractor.

He claimed he did this to keep the dogs from jumping on us and knocking us down but looking back I think they may have served as security guards for his prized possession. With our curiosity about the tractor, it's safe to say that the dogs did their part to lower the odds of any injury to ourselves or the tractor.

On a few occasions we got to go inside their house to use the indoor toilet with flushing water. This was a real thrill for Ed Earl who got yelled at a time or two for flushing more than necessary.

They had electric fans that hummed like a song and moved from side to side and made a breeze on hot summer days. In the largest room, they had a soft chair that stretched out like a bed when the old man sat in it. He would fall asleep in the middle of the day and snore with his mouth stretched wide open.

Myrtle Riley kept pretty what-nots sitting around on furniture that was so smooth and shinny it looked to be as still as the lake on a calm, moonlit night. Her house had a smell. Not a bad smell; not a good one…just a smell.

She might not have been friendly to us kids but she was nice enough to Mama. We had gone over there the day before Mama got sick. It was hot that day too when we took the long walk up the road for a visit. Mama took along some empty mason jars that she had been saving to use next time they did some canning.

That day, while Mama was talking to Myrtle Riley, I was looking over some of her what-nots when I knocked over a vase of flowers and they fell to the floor. Broken glass shattered across the floor, flowers bent and twisted as water splashed against the wall, then began to run down on to the rug. I threw my hand against the wall in an attempt to try to stop the water from dripping. Then, I turned in a hurry to get the glass picked up before she saw it but it was too late.

When Myrtle Riley started yelling from the kitchen, I got so scared that I peed my pants!

"YOU AINT GOT NO BUSINESS IN THERE…WHAT WUZ THAT NOISE ANY HOW?"

The whole house shook as she stormed across the floor and into the room. *"LOOK AT THE MESS YOU MADE…YOU A BAD LITTLE GIRL!"*

I was so scared that I started trembling and felt like I was about to throw up. She was still yelling at me as she stomped toward the mess but I can't recall what she said. All I can remember was hearing the tinkling sound of glass and ceramic figurines as they bounced across the table tops. I could feel the boards on the floor moving and heard them crack. I was hoping she'd fall through so I could break and run free.

Mama acted panicky as she rushed in and squeezed passed the large woman in order to pick up the broken glass. Squatting down, she busted out the seat of her snug fitting shorts leaving no doubt as to what had just happened. We all heard the *rip*!

The moment was frozen in time for me, Lester and Myrtle but without missing a beat Mama picked up the tiny fragments with one hand and piled them into the other being careful not to cut herself. We all just stared at her in surprise; me, standing with my wet bottom in a puddle of pee, Myrtle Riley towering over the scene in disbelief, her husband stretched out in his reclined chair, eyebrows raised, mouth hung open, just taking it all in.

"You git on outta ere Sassy. I'll clean it up Myrtle…I'm so sorry bout this!" Mama said nervously without looking up. I broke and ran out through the screen door forgetting to ease it shut.

"STOP IT!…WHY COME YOU YOUNGINS GOTTA SLAM THAT DOOR?" I could hear Myrtle Riley yelling from inside the house. *"I AINT GONNA TELL YA NO MORE! YA'LL HEAR ME?"* I could still hear her yelling in my escape.

Of course, Earldean and Ed Earl came running to see what had happened inside the house. I just knew Earldean was going to give me a hard time about wetting myself, but she didn't say a word about it. You can bet your sweet taters I wasn't going to tell her! I believe they all assumed it was just the water from the flower vase.

Awhile later, Mama came out in a change of clothes. She was wearing an oversized sleeveless dress, faded brown with dingy white polka dots. It was cut full and looked much cooler as it hung loosely around her making her appear larger than she did in her other clothes. However, standing next to her hostess, she was still the smaller woman.

As she stepped off of the porch, Myrtle Riley handed her several other pieces that she had out grown herself and couldn't wear anymore. I was sure they were going to swallow my Mama, probably would wrapped around her twice with room to spare. Never the less Mama was no slave to fashion and was grateful for the woman's generosity.

Mama had mentioned that her own clothes had been getting tighter so she was grateful for something more comfortable to wear, especially in this kind of heat. I kept my distance as they said goodbyes, being careful not to do anything wrong before we got away from there. Standing as still as I could, hoping not to be noticed, I focused on the large armholes of Mama's new hand-me-down that revealed the sides of her swollen bare breast.

"That was nice of her to give you them there clothes, Mama." I said to her on the walk back, preparing for the price I had to pay for the trouble I had caused. *"If she was still mad at me, she didn't take it out on you."* I said, in hopes that would be the end of it.

Mama had plenty of time on the way home to scold us about meddling with other peoples stuff and slamming doors. She knew we had not been around that many doors before to have enough practice in opening and closing them. She didn't punish me for it. I guess she figured I'd learned my lesson when I saw how angry it made Myrtle Riley. Truth was I think it scared Mama too. She had never seen the woman move that fast before.

Here we were a week later on that same road, chancing another encounter with this ornery, ole woman just by passing her house.

The afternoon sun was burning bright in the sky and the heat was beginning to get unbearable. My sweat could have been blamed on more than that as I grew nervous when we rounded the bend just before the Riley's place. I thought about the broken vase with the mess I'd made and wondered what Myrtle Riley would do if she got her hands on me. My belly started to ache at the thought of not having Mama there to bail me out again.

"It's so hot and we need something to drink...why don't we stop at the Riley's? Earldean suggested.

"Naw!" I responded immediately. *"We cain't do that...That lady is mean and she don't like us much."*

"Yea, she's mean!" Ed Earl agreed.

"Mean. Mean. Mean." Learlean said, just wanting in on the conversation.

We laughed at her cuteness then told Earldean she was out voted.

"Ole Meany Myrtle" Earldean called her, *"...She's a mean woman alright but that Mr. Riley ain't so bad and he might give us a ride to town. I'm tired of walkin!"*

"NAW!" I protested *"...We gotta pass her to git to him...and I'm tired of talkin!"*

"Walkin...Talkin...Walkin...Talkin...Walkin..." Learline rhymed and repeated as Ed Earl giggled at her and then joined in.

As we reached the corner of the Riley's pasture, we could see the roof of their house that sat back off the road under a grove of shade trees. We heard a few thuds and bumping around as their hound dogs scrambled to get out from under the porch and commenced to barking. Those howling hounds weren't about to come all the way out to the road to get us so we weren't in any danger of getting attacked. They should have known who we were by then but I guess they didn't recognize us without Mama alongside us.

"All that barkin is sure git ole Meany Myrtles attention." Earldean said.

We agreed to keep going and spare ourselves the heartache of being barked at by her too. We didn't see Mr. Riley's truck so a ride from him was out of the question.

We had just reached the driveway and the constant barking of the dogs when Myrtle Riley came through the screen door yelling, *"WHATA YALL YOUNGINS DOIN OUT YOUNDER? YA'LL DON'T NEED TA BE MESSIN ROUND HERE ...NOW GIT...GO ON...GIT!"*

Then we heard her tell the dogs, *"Sickum!"*

Well, the hounds gave chase and were well on their way before we realized what happened. Earldean grabbed up Learline and broke into a run with Ed Earl and me hot on her tail, kicking up dust with our long strides. Ed Earl ran right out of his pink sneakers, never looking back.

I turned to go back for the cherished shoes; we just couldn't leave them behind. As I bent over to pick them up, I looked down the driveway, tunneled with rows of corn down either side. The hounds had made it halfway to the road, barreling and barking all the way. They were all legs, tails and teeth so I grabbed up the shoes, turned on my heels and ran as hard and as fast as I could. The barking got louder as they closed in on me. I could feel their breath bouncing off of my backside. I was tempted to hurl the hot pink sneakers at the dogs in attempt to scare them off. I opted to try to out run them instead.

They snapped at my heels as I ran blindly into the dust my sisters and brother left behind in their escape. The hounds gave up as they reached the property line. They just stood there barking as if there were a glass wall to keep them from going any farther.

When we saw that the chase was over we slowed down from our hard sprint into a panting trot. The harmless hounds had been misjudged for sure as I felt like those dogs could have eaten us alive if they really wanted to. They continued to bark and howl until we topped the next hill and went over out of their sight.

When we got far enough away we stopped to catch our breath. If we weren't thirsty enough before, we were now. We were hardly able to make saliva as we tried to spit out the dust. Our mouths were so parched and dry; my lips were sticking to the sandy grit on my teeth.

I looked down at the paper bag that Ed Earl had been carrying. It was crumpled and damp as it had absorbed the sweat from his hand.

"Hey...Got…any…thang to drank…in there?" I asked, panting and pointing toward the bag.

Ed Earl started to open it when Earldean answered, panting too. *"Naw…I forgot!"*

"What?" I gasped. *"We...ain't got no water?"* I shook my head and bent down from exhaustion, resting my hands on my knees trying to get my breathing under control.

Thinking better that I should save what air I caught, I decided not to waste my breath fussing at her for not packing any drinking water. I should have seen to it myself but like her, it just didn't come to me. We weren't thirsty when we left.

After we rested a little and got our heart rate down, we straightened up then got on our way. Our faces were beet red and the sun was hotter than ever, hammering down on us as we pressed on. Around every bend, over each hill and every few minutes, somebody would ask, *"Are we almost there yet?"*, but the answer would always be the same. *"Don't see it."*

"How'z anybody spect us ta eat peanut butter and crackers without water?" I mumbled after Ed Earl and Learline started complaining of being hungry and thirsty. It was getting late in the afternoon and we had not yet eaten lunch. I looked around for the creek to get a dip of water to quench our thirst but didn't see it anymore. We ate the tomatoes so we could at least get the juice from them to quench our desperate thirst. However, after we finished we realized that only made it worse. We walked on and looked for a water source along the way. In this part of the country, underground springs and waterfalls were plentiful but were harder to find during a summer drought.

Ed Earl was fussing about his legs and feet hurting. We could tell by Learlines' whining that she wouldn't hold out much longer as the day grew hotter by the minute.

4
GETTING ALONG WITH A FRESH CLEAN START

Up ahead in the distance, heat waves from the dehydrated hills met with rain clouds. Competing for space, they forced a merge and created an almost forgotten fragrance that indicated a summer storm. It promised of a possible change in the temperature that guaranteed relief from the heat; a much needed change that would be welcomed with opened arms…and we did just that.

When the first bit of breeze came in on a short gust, it passed through us and took with it some of the gloom that weighed us down. The second one that reached us was slightly cooler and that gave cue for the four of us to throw open our arms and begin to twirl around as if this act had been rehearsed.

Dancing in the fresh air, we cheered with gratitude and fanned our clothes out away from our bodies so that the sweat beads eventually evaporated. Our hair, which had been plastered to our heads with perspiration for hours, began to move about. As the winds gained strength, it brought with it dark heavy clouds that now totally shaded us from the blistering sun.

Puffs of dust rose up like smoke signals as large rain drops pelted the path before us. They disappeared into little powdery craters they had made on impact leaving holes the size of dew berries. In the process it made a pattern along the dirt road that looked to me like polka dots; much like the polka dots on Mama's hand-me down dress.

"Mama was wearing that Pokee-dot dress the last time we walked down this road." I found myself mumbling out loud as I stared at the image in my mind, wondering if it had been too much for her to walk that far in the hot sun in the shape she was in.

"She would'a put some drinkin water in a mason jar and toted it with us along the way." I muttered. My mouth was parched just thinking about it.

"Come on Sassy! Don't just stand there! Lets git a movin!" Earldean yelled from six paces away; breaking my concentration from the polka dots and my Mama. Though it had only been hours I was already lonesome for her. I tightened my face muscles to hold back any tears that might leak out in front of the others.

Earldean was constantly after me about being a 'cry baby'…as if she never cried about anything and I was in no mood for one of her lectures. Besides, the two younger kids might start up with their whining and that would only magnify the racket.

I caught up with them and filed back to my place in line. Trying not to let them see my face, I shot a side glance at my younger siblings now skipping around trying to let as many raindrops wet them as possible. They were so cute and oblivious to the seriousness of our situation that it caused me to momentarily step out of my depression which released the tension that had built up.

I chuckled at their innocent freedom as they began to dance around without a care in the world. When Learline started giggling uncontrollably even Earldean couldn't help but break a smile. Sweet sounds of contagious laughter echoed through the canyons which amplified the sound making it seem as though we weren't alone.

Ed Earl stopped, tilted his head back and opened his mouth to catch raindrops to quench his thirst. *"Goo idea."* said Learline in her tender squeaky little voice. Then we all joined in the quest.

The sprinkle turned into a downpour, pushing the dust back to where it belonged. With rain slapping against our faces, we found it hard to see as the shower we so longed for, and needed, cleaned our bodies, clothes and hair. We had often taken advantage of the free falling water in warm weather to bathe. We didn't have our bar soap with us but we rubbed our legs and arms as if we did.

I leaned forward with my head down to rinse the back of my neck and scalp just as Mama taught me. It was so cool and refreshing as I felt the heat leave my body. I never fought her when it came to bath time like Ed Earl did, but Daddy would always take up for him when he'd raise a ruckus.

Bathing had never been a priority with Daddy as he felt he didn't need to impress anybody and didn't care much if it offended them either. He would say, *"Aint nobody out ere but us…sides, it helps keep the wild animals back…they have a way a knowin iss ere's our neck of a woods!"*

Mama disagreed with him on that and insisted we tried to keep clean. She felt it helped to keep down illness and sores. *"Well there ain't nuttin better fer washin troubles away than a good soakin in the creek."* she'd argue. *"…and the skeeders an' fly's ain't such a bother while'st ya tryin ta git a good night sleep either!"*

Sometimes she'd get after Daddy for going too long without bathing and finish off the discussion by saying to him in her flirty voice, *"You might be a bit more tolerable iffin you'z ta fall off into the water on your next fishin trip!"*

He'd wink at her and say something like… *"Well that might jest happen iffin you'z ta come along with a rag to wash my back!"* He would go over behind her and softly kiss her on the neck saying, *"Why I'z kindly hankerin fer sum fish fer supper. How'z bout you?"* She'd grin and give him a nudge with her elbow.

After Mama would get us started on our daily chores she would watch for Daddy to pick up his fishing pole and head down the path to the lake. Often times such as these, he didn't bother to take the cricket box Ed Earl kept stocked for him.

Mama would place Earldean in charge of holding down the fort. She'd grab a towel and wash cloth off the line she had strung up for drying clothes and such, and then she trotted down the path after him. When she caught up with him, he'd reach behind and grab her in the rear end, the *"hinny"* we called it.

I don't know how we knew, but somehow we figured out, with this indication, that we were not to follow them. Earldean would explain to us would be this meant they were *"Gittin 'long jest fine".*

They didn't fight much; at least not in front of us kids. Mama wouldn't have it that way. After spending all day refereeing our bickering, she didn't want to set a bad example. If a disagreement grew into a full blown argument, she would drag him off into the woods to settle it or he would send us off to fetch something we didn't really need.

When we did hear them fussing, it would scare us half to death and we would all cry about it. Mama would try to explain it away by saying that they just weren't getting along right then. She'd ask us to give them a little time alone promising everything would be alright. And, sure enough, after a while, we could hear them off in the distance just laughing, giggling and sounding real silly trying to make some kind of animal noises.

This would get Learline's attention and cause her to stop her playing and head their way; wanting to get in on the fun. I would have to go get her and carry her back saying, *"Now you stay right here and play cause Mama and Daddy is out younder gittin 'long...ok?*

I was just getting old enough to realize it was good for parents to get off away from their "youngins" from time to time; just to be alone with one another. Understandably so, grown-ups can get irritable when they have too many worries on their minds.

Sometimes it's ok to go fishing without bait, and a change of pace or a step off the beaten path can be just the antidote. At ten years old, I had no idea what they possibly had to say that they couldn't say in front of us kids. I couldn't imagine what kind of game they could come up with that we hadn't already thought of. However, they managed somehow to have fun out there and it didn't matter because whatever it was, they always seem to "get along" better after they returned.

Oh, they were never further away than ear-shot from us; both, one or the other was always close by. That was up until now. We were never this far away from them and it was a bit scary for us. This unfamiliar feeling of loneliness manifested in my throat as the rain wet and cooled my entire body.

Just as we had gotten good and soaked from the downpour, a loud clap of thunder warned us it was time to seek shelter. We ran up ahead to a thicket of trees just to the side of the road.

The winds began to blow harder, bending the brush far to its side. *"We need to find a better place than this!"* Earldean shouted over the storm.

About sixty feet ahead was a bluff near where the road started to curve. She figured at least that would block the wind off some. *"There."* she said pointing in that direction. *"Let's get over there by those big rocks!"*

She grabbed up Learline and threw her on her hip. I snatched Ed Earl by the hand and drug him along with him bent down trying to keep the rain out of his face.

I remembered passing this landmark. It had been one of my favorite spots to look for on our trips to town. About twenty feet off the road stood a massive bluff of gray limestone that towered over us about forty feet tall. Years of erosion had carved out the foot of the colossal wall, leaving an indention large enough to provide a little shelter from the storm.

We stood with our backs against the wall as the rain poured steadily for the longest time. Above us, from the edge of the overhang, the runoff was spilling down in a sheet of water that pelted the stone floor below it. The splashing from this was so hard, we had to take turns holding Learline to keep her from getting wetter than she already was.

Bolts of lightning hit all around us followed by loud crashes of thunder so we huddled in close together. We held tight and cringed with each earsplitting boom. Learline buried her head in my shoulder as I wrapped my arms around her and held her securely to me. Her back was getting soaked but her body shielded mine and helped to keep me from getting so drenched. I didn't complain about holding her when it was my turn.

Ed Earl held the brown paper bag in front of his face giving the allusion he had a pig head. Earldean pointed this out and we laughed as the rains started to slow down.

As we stood there with our feet underwater watching the storm move off, Ed Earl handed the bag off to Earldean and stepped toward the drip line at the edge of the bluff. He cupped his hands together to make a bowl and caught himself a drink of water. We all took turns doing the same but when Learline wasn't satisfied with her catch she held out her shirt tail and filled it till it bulged. We got tickled at her as she tried to bring it to her mouth to drink.

When the water splashed to the ground she just stood there and sucked on her wet shirt till she got her fill. I was tired and wanted to sit down but there was no place there that wasn't under at least an inch of water. I decided I was already wet so it wouldn't matter if I sat down and made myself comfortable there next to the wall.

Earldean handed the guarded sack off to me then she untied the bed roll from her back and held it up as she found a spot next to me. She slid it behind her neck and used it for a head rest. I rested the soggy bag on my head in effort to keep its contents dry, then we watched the two younger ones splash and play with a new energy that came from relief from the heat.

Across the road from the bluff was a narrow shoulder, then a drop off that allowed us to look out over a canyon. Beyond that we could see other hills and mountain tops. This panoramic view made the world seem so big, beautiful and uncharted. New lights and colors began to form as the sky started to clear and the rain dwindled to a fine mist.

We were getting hungry and decided to go look for higher ground to eat our crackers. As we stood up, squeezing the excess water from our clothes, we could hear the sound of a motor off in the distance.

"Daddy's commin!...Daddy's Commin!" Ed Earl shouted as he ran out into the road.

"Get back here Ed Earl!...That might not be Daddy!" Earldean yelled.

" Whoever it is, izza commin fast and can run you over when they round that there bend! I 'member at time daddy hit dat deer a standin in the road round a curve atta way! Lets git back ere 'ginst iss rock till we see fer sure who it is. It might be a stranger we don't even know!" I said.

We all stood pressed to the side of the stone wall as we listened to the sound draw closer.

" Dat's Daddy?" Learline asked.

"Don't know yet baby…shsh…listen." I said to her.

"I think it's Daddy…What if it's Daddy and he don't see us?" Ed Earl asked.

"Well if it's Daddy we'll jump out when we know fer sure." Earldean told him.

We waited hopefully as we heard the sound of tires against gravel and splashing in the puddles just around the bend. We watched a truck go past us, never slowing down except to make the curve. It wasn't Daddy's old truck and we didn't recognize the driver.

"They must nota seen us…Probably lookin at that purdy sky out there." I said.

We had been on that road for hours and had not seen a vehicle all that time. There weren't many turn offs from that point so it had to be someone that had business back that way unless they were just cutting through the back roads. Folks would do that every once in a while.

After they were out of sight we walked down a bit and found some boulders to sit on and dry out a bit. There we spread peanut butter and jelly on our crackers and ate them. I still didn't have much of an appetite and by the way Earldean was nibbling at hers she didn't feel much like eating either.

When Ed Earl and Learline seemed to be getting full, Earldean suggested we save the rest for later so we gathered our things and got back on the road. The fresh rain had seemed to have stirred up the wildlife in the woods along the roadside. Squirrels barked and chattered back and forth as they scurried about. Birds chirped and sang as they splashed and bathed themselves in the fresh puddles. It hardly seemed fair that life was going on without our mother.

As we walked on, not much was said about anything but we were all thinking about Mama. The lump that had been in my throat all day would get painful at times as I struggled not to cry when memories of her would flood my thoughts. It was tough but I tried to occupy my mind with everything...anything but her.

It helped being surrounded by new scenery. We had an up close opportunity to examine things by walking as opposed to seeing them through a cloud of dust from the back of a pick-up.

I found myself quizzing the others on the various kinds of trees and plants like Daddy would do when we would go for walks. He taught us about all the different trees that grew in this region. He had learned most of it through an Audubon book that he picked up at the agriculture fair one year.

He took pride in what he had learned and wanted to pass that information on to us. One he had taught us about was the Ozark Chinquapin. This is the only tree species with a natural range limited to the Ozark region, for which it was named. And, we lived in the heart of that region where the most of them grew. This was one we knew well. Denby said that must be where Chinquapin Hollow got its name from.

Earldean wasn't much into playing along that day as she was tired and worried about it getting dark before we made it to town. She talked about what we needed to do to find Daddy when we got to town. I was nervous about talking to strangers so I was hoping to just look for where his truck might be parked then just sit and wait on him to come back to it.

We hid in the edge of the woods when a car, then a truck, came by. That last one we were sure was Mr. Riley heading toward his house but he didn't realize we were out there.

When Earldean and Ed Earl jumped out to try to flag him down; he just kept going. He didn't even slow down. I'm sure he wasn't expecting anyone to be out there in the middle of nowhere so he probably didn't bother to look in his rear view mirror.

They were disappointed that he didn't stop but I wasn't. I didn't trust him enough to ask for help. He might say no and I don't think we could have handled the rejection just then.

We stood there in the middle of the road a minute just looking at one another wondering what to do next. Should we go back to the Riley's for help…or keep going? We really didn't want to face those dogs again, but we were so tired. We weren't *sure* Mr. Riley would help us…and by this time and the distance we had already traveled…we knew it was a long way back to his house!

What if town is even farther away than the Riley's, we wondered. Or, what if it is just around that next bend?

The sun looked like a big red ball as it started to sink on the horizon splashing purples, pinks and oranges across the sky.

We had not gone far enough but we had gone too far to go back. We were running out of daylight and would have to make another decision soon.

5
CAT GOT YOUR TONGUE

Deciding to pursue our mission to get to town before dark, convinced it couldn't be much further, we continued to make our way down this rocky road. Our baby sister whined for her Mama and was in need of a nap as she cried to go home. We were all tired but we walked on and on…and on, passing tree shaded rock bluffs on one side then the other. We trudged past places where the road had no shoulder as it hugged the mountain side dropping off into steep crevices and deep ravines.

We would catch an occasional lake view as the road winded up and down hairpin curves, rounding each one in hopes of seeing signs of a town where we would find our Daddy.

Frustrated and confused, there wasn't much to say at this point and if it were, we were too tired to say it. We would save our energy for the long stressful hike out of there. We weren't accustomed to wearing shoes in the summer, or for long periods of time in any season. Having our feet constricted all day, plus all that walking, compounded the suffering we already had on us.

We had passed a few forks in the road that probably led to the lake. It was quiet with no traffic, except for a truck that came out of the last fork. The pickup was pulling a boat trailer behind it with two young men inside the cab that we recognized having seen on the lake before.

They had fished there often so I had just assumed they lived somewhere around the lake. When they passed by, they slowed down enough to make me real nervous. I couldn't see the driver very well but they both had on ball caps, like the kind Denby wore and I wondered if they were going to be as nice as he was.

I lost that glimmer of hope when nether of them spoke a word as they slowed to a stop and stared curiously at us. When we caught up with them the driver veered closer to us forcing us to walk on the narrow shoulder.

Keeping with our pace, they rolled along slowly, intimidating us with their gawking. The exhaust fumes from the tail pipe were suffocating and causing my eyes to water.

Unlike like these fellows, Denby would have greeted us, smiling whole heartedly with a "Howdy" and comments about the weather.

The one on the passenger's side had a beard like Daddy's but was younger looking. His beady eyes were squinted as the bright sun peeped from the passing clouds. With his head resting on his folded arms, he hung out of the open window. They just rode alongside us without saying anything for a little while before the bearded one, who was staring at Earldean, spoke up.

"Hey…What's new pussy cat?"

Earldean stopped momentarily and started to say something but thinking better of it, she turned to catch up with the rest of us. Her name was not pussy cat and she wanted to let him know it but she didn't want to get in trouble for talking to strangers again.

Having seen and greeted them out on the lake fishing before would not make them friendly acquaintances according to Daddy and he had said he didn't want her talking to them anymore. The way they acted made us feel strange and uncomfortable.

"Hey boy, where ya git them girly shoes?" he sneered as he pointed towards Ed Earl's feet then forced a ridiculing laugh.

It wasn't what he said but how he said it that scared me so bad. His tone was haughty and his laughter sounded devilish. I could hear the driver ask, *"Where you punks goin?"*

"Does ya paw n'maw know ya'll way out here?" the passenger mockingly asked.

They kept gawking and laughing so we walked faster. The driver sped up to catch up with us asking, *"Hey...did you hear me?"*

The passenger, still hanging out the window with a sheepish grin, followed that query with, *"…or did the cat gitcha tongue?"*

We didn't answer them as we struggled with our steps; walking close together and staring timidly back at them.

"Yea…bet the cat got their tongue…or maybe they just dumb…don't know how to talk!"

After a long silent glare, Learline hid her face in my side when he stuck out his tongue at her. They laughed as they spun their tires, slinging mud and rocks everywhere! This caught us off guard and we screamed, covering our eyes as the debris flew in our direction.

They drove off down the road, honking and hollering, *"DUMB HILLBILLIES!"*

Getting us all dirty again, we brushed off the mud and were relieved that with the exception of our pride, no one was really hurt. Now, with our adrenaline pumping, we had energy enough to make the next big incline without too much complaining; except for Learline, we had to take turns carrying her when she would get too tired.

We had something new to talk about as we agreed those two weren't interested in helping us and probably weren't even going into town anyway. We didn't feel bad about not asking them for help as we were sure they weren't the neighborly kind. However, our curiosity was aroused and we wished we had been brave enough to inquire about this sadistic *"cat"* they mentioned.

The procedure of this peculiar *"tongue getting creature"* was enough to keep us engrossed in conversation for a good thirty minutes, which made the time go by. We kept a close watch over our shoulder for such a ruthless critter that might be on the prowl.

We had passed a few abandoned camp houses that were falling down and another road that may have led to a home. We weren't sure how far it went so we didn't take a chance going down it looking for help.

Learlines' bottom was wet from one way or another and all that walking made things worse as she was getting badly chapped. We found it made it easier for her to squat and pee-pee after we just left her shorts and panties off. We'd try to put them back on after they aired out a bit but when we did she would just fuss and say, *"Me don't like it my shorts…Me don't like it my panties…Me jest like it my hiney!"*

So we just let her go butt naked…who cared? We were just too tired to argue with her. Far off in the distance we could hear the sound of an outboard motor revving up. It was soon followed by a muffled sound that led me to believe it was too close to the bank and may have hit mud.

The lake was real low in some places and you might drag bottom if you didn't know where those shallow spots were. Usually, this late in the summer, there weren't as many fishermen out on the water. It was just too hot to fish unless you had to have food.

Mama used to warn us about sunburn and heat strokes when it was like this and wouldn't let us go out on the lake in the boat. Daddy didn't let us go out on our own and even if Mama was with us, we didn't get out too far.

After Earldean and I proved to be good swimmers, he'd sometimes take us out on the lake in the fishing boat. We'd go to deep enough water so that we could swim and dive off the cliffs. Ed Earl got to go for the first time that summer and he just couldn't get enough of it. Especially jumping off the cliffs…the higher the better! He got upset with Daddy when we had to leave only because some other people showed up.

One time we were out there having just a grand ole time by ourselves when a few other boatloads of folks showed up to go diving there too.

"Look at them scrawny little ole kids going off them rocks like that!" one passenger said to the others in their motor boat.

"Check out that little one…he's jumpin off of there like a bull frog! Watch him!" said another. Though Ed Earl liked showing off for them, Daddy insisted it was time to go. I remember thinking that he was overprotective and somewhat cautious of strangers. I guess some human behavior is learned by how we see others react, because much of how we reacted was like one or both of our parents.

Then, there are other parts of our behavior that must come from within. Something we were born with that pushes to get out and causes us to disagree with what we're taught. Bits and pieces mix together, stir around in our hearts and heads, and then meet in the middle of our mouth to form the words we say…or *don't* say.

I myself could be pretty timid at times where as Earldean was a bit more daring, at least when it came to people. I was so curious about them and wanted to know more but was afraid they might not like me if I asked too many questions. Instead, I would just watch people, when I had a chance, and try to figure them out in my head. Not Earldean. She would take a chance of getting scolded for being nosey. A few times when we were in the lake swimming, a fishing boat would troll by and she would be the first to swim out and ask them what they were doing… as if she didn't already know.

"They're fishin Earldean! Shhh." I'd softly say. *"Why you gotta all time ask folks the same ole question? You know what they a doin…can't cha see them fishin poles?"*

Acting like she didn't hear me she would ask them again and again until they heard and answered her. *"Hey, whatchaw dowin? Hey…hey ya'll…Whachaw doin I said?"*

And if they took the time to talk with her, it went something like this... *"How many fish ya done caught?" "What kina bait cha usin?" "Where ya git dat fishin rig ya got tere?"*

I felt like she was wasting her breath asking about fishing. Everybody knows about that kind of stuff. No...not me, if I would have had the nerve back then, I'd have asked such questions like... *"What's your name?" "What's it like where you live?" "What do you like to do for fun?"* or... *"What are you and the other people in the world like?"*

Being that she was friendly and liked to talk, I wish she would have asked better questions. It appeared she was just interested in hearing her own voice as she would do most of the chatting. She would talk on and on, trying to tell about everything she knew to tell, to anybody who would listen. Back then, she had a lot of one sided conversations.

If somebody happened by our place, they were probably lost but Earldean didn't mind giving them misguided directions in exchange for idle words. Daddy would call her motor mouth when she chattered at length about the same events.

He had warned her not to bother folks while they were fishing and to come get him if anybody comes around there asking questions or as he put it... *"nosinround"*.

Whenever he would have to leave for work or town, he would give us the same list of instructions and he always finished with *"...and don't talk ta strangers."* We knew he meant that mostly for Earldean.

Truth was I was the one who would have been accused of being nosey if I weren't so afraid to open my mouth. However, I was able to exercise that bottled up curiosity by exploring the hills we called our home. Ed Earl was always up to it too. Mama used to say we were two peas in a pod in that we were both involved in some kind of expedition that could hardly wait till after chores.

There were times we'd spend an entire day clearing paths to places we wanted to find again. We cut undergrowth, moved limbs and sticks, rolled away rocks and swept away debris until we were down to a thin layer of dust over a stone path. We would cross streams with hanging vines or fallen trees that bridged the gaps in the trail.

We examined every creature we encountered with caution and inquisitiveness. There were times we would detour our paths in an effort not to disturbed their nests or beds. This didn't always sit well with our big sister as she saw it as extra work.

Ed Earl and I would insist because we had seen them get aggressive otherwise. We didn't blame them!

Ed Earl didn't mind playing subordinate in whatever adventure we were on no matter who thought of it. By the same turn I was willing to assist him in his trailblazing fun. Whereas Earldean wanted to be the leader, no matter whose idea it was and when we didn't give in to her way, she would quit and go play with baby sister.

That's probably why Learline took a shine to her because she took up time with her. Earldean was good with babies. She had helped Mama with the babysitting as soon as she was big enough to carry me. Learline still liked to be carried even as heavy as she was getting to be. She liked the undivided attention she got with all her cuteness and we poured it on, especially Earldean. The trouble was she treated me and Ed Earl like we were still babies and now I was almost as tall as her!

I don't know if it was me or her that had started the disagreements between us. It would make me mad and sad at the same time but most of all, sorry. But, we were beginning to bicker over the littlest things. Maybe it was our ages, the competition for special privileges and attention from our parents or perhaps it was those small differences in our personalities that caused the friction between us.

Ed Earl had learned to take advantage of us during those quarreling times as he would play favorites to get what he wanted. Learline was still too young to wander out much back then. She and Earldean spent a good deal of time playing baby dolls around Mama's feet as she sat and hand stitched doll clothes out of rags.

Sometimes Mama would play dolls with them or explore with us. Other times we would pack a picnic basket and go for a hike on the trails we made. Sometimes we would venture off on some of the paths cut through by the deer and other wild animals. We were sure to find wild berries and there was plenty there for snacking and cobbler making. It was nothing for Mama to tear off a piece of her shirt tail and tie a place to mark the spot so that we could find it again. She was very creative in that she would find something to make out of things nature provided.

When we would search and gather things to fill our handmade baskets, Mama called it "scouting". When we got back home we would sit and examine the contents and show off our finds.

Mama would say, *"City folk do the same thang, only they scout for thangs in stores and markets where somebody put it there for them to find. They call it shoppin."*

On very rare occasions, we got to go into town to a big place called the grocery store. There we saw lots of people gather in their cars in a big lot out in front of it. Most of them went inside and came out with brown bags filled with things they got from inside. Mama said they had been, *"Grocer shoppin"*.

We always had to wait out in the truck and watch the babies. But *once*...on my fourth birthday, I distinctly remember getting to go inside this magnificent fortress of food that was lit up with florescent lighting.

To my amazement, in the midst of cold weather, there were large racks of fresh fruits and vegetables. They had already been grown, gathered and stacked against the walls at the entrance and wrapped clear around the corner. Much of it was already canned and labeled with pictures of its contents, all lined up in neat rows, just waiting on shelves for folks to come get. Towers of paper goods were there for the taking and I was amazed at how little of all this my parents took.

Some folks who passed us in the isles had little room to spare in their metal baskets with the squeaky wheels. As I peered into the cart my Mama was pushing, I wondered why we only had a few items; things I never would have picked out.

It was there I got my first lesson in how money worked. After begging for almost every new thing I thought would be good to eat, the only response I ever got was, *"Put that back Sassy!" "We aint got the money for it!" "Do I look like I'm made of money?"*

Earldean and I had already gotten in trouble by a fellow in the produce department for eating some grapes. But you'd have thought we committed the unforgivable sin when we bit open a pack of wieners and ate one.

"You really should cook those first!" said the man behind the meat counter, startling us as well as getting our parents attention.

"What the...Earldean!...Sassy!...Git over her...NOW!" Daddy yelled.

"What wuz ya thankin...you caint jest open up stuff and commence eatin...ya have ta buy it and we ain't got the money fer that!" Mama fussed at us.

"But we'z hungry, Mama!" I cried.

"It don't matter...ya can't take thangs that don't belong to ya!" Daddy snapped. *"We have to buy this food! We caint jest open it up and eat it on account of beein hungry!"*

"We're sorry...aint we Sassy?" Earldean said trying to get me to apologize too, though I wasn't sorry at that moment. I was hungry and it was worth getting fussed at about. That was until we were promised a whoopin.

"Now see what ya gone'n done?" Daddy said, taking the open package from me. *"We'll have to put sumptin back!"*

He looked up to see that the man behind the meat counter was watching. *"I'm gonna have ta skin yo hide fer this...now gone' git in the truck!"* Daddy said with his teeth gritted. *"...and don't git out. Jest wait till we done here!"*

"Oh Daddy!" we cried as we turned to walk toward the door.

"And don't be a talking ta strangers...ya her' me?"

"But Daddy!"

"Go on. GIT!" he huffed while pointing his finger toward the door, rerouting our protest.

"Oh Earl, this is spost' ta be Sassy's birthday outin, reccon they didn't know no better!" we heard Mama say in our defense as we sadly walked off.

I turned to see the man step out from behind the meat counter wiping his hands on his bloody apron. He said something in a low voice to them before Daddy handed him the weenies. Needless to say, we cried for the rest of the wait just thinking about what we had coming to us.

When they emerged from the grocery store they were both in a better mood. Mama explained that the butcher had kids of his own and understood we didn't know any better. He said he didn't think a kid ought to go hungry. He had rewrapped the wieners in white freezer paper to keep the juice from spilling on everything and paid for them out of his own pocket.

Daddy handed me a tiny brown paper sack and said the man told him, to tell me "Happy birthday."

"For me?" I asked, unaccustomed to receiving gifts. My first store bought present, I thought, treasuring the moment while Earldean rushed me to look inside.

I opened the sack to find two candy bars...one for me and one to share with my sister. We didn't get to go inside the grocery after that though. What few times we went for the ride we were made to wait in the truck. Most of the time Daddy would pick things up on his way home from work. At least, he'd bring home what he could afford.

The rest of our provisions we grew ourselves or picked from the wild. There was enough to survive on if you knew where to look and Mama was a natural for scouting food sources. Denby used to say she could spot a berry from a mile away and when it was "slim pickins" he would always show up with something to make a pie out of.

When he'd hand her a peck of apples, she would smile and say, *"Are you tryin ta jest keep me busy?"* But, she was always glad he did it in a way that didn't hurt her pride.

She sometimes allowed us stir up the batter for a blackberry cobbler. We loved to sit and watch it bubble up and bake through the opening of the stone oven Daddy made for her. The smell would fill the woods and lure in some of the more curious varmints.

Playing with the animals was an entertaining pastime for us as we made games out chasing the few chickens we had back in the pen when it was time for them to roost. We would laugh when Ed Earl would try to ride the goats like horses though they didn't think it was so funny.

Once Daddy came home with a small pig that he said he was keeping out there for a feller. We fell in love with that thing when it followed us around everywhere. We taught it some tricks, like how to sit and how to fetch a stick. Over time it had grown big enough to slaughter and it broke our hearts when it had to go but Daddy said the feller would be sharing with us some pork for raising it. It was some good meat too but I didn't know at the time that it was from the pig that we had grown to love.

Fondness for animals came natural for me as we were surrounded by all kinds of critters. There were times we would put out crumbs for the wild animals trying to make friends with them. When we would try to bring them home with us, Daddy would get upset and tell us it's just another mouth to feed.

He would say such things as, *"If we let one wild animal in theyz all wanna come in and we fight hard enough to keep um out! Let um find theyz own food!"*

Personally, I felt like they were more at home in the woods than we were. According to Mama, they were there first. When he saw that we were getting too attached to one of our animals he would say things like, *"They ain't for pettin, aze fer eatin and ya ain't sposta play witcha food!"*

Mama told us it's wasn't that he didn't like animals; he didn't want us to get attached because he was afraid we might get hurt.

I remember the time I had made friends with a little yearling who lost its mama in a hunt. First, I put out some dried corn cobs, then the next day, a few carrots. I would talk real soft it each time I saw him. It wasn't long before he would walk right up and eat out of my hands. Mama knew I was doing it but she didn't tell Daddy about it. She figured it didn't hurt as long as it didn't follow me home.

One day Daddy came dragging a yearling out of the woods with a broken arrow in its side. I knew this was my friend but couldn't say anything for fear he would find out I had disobeyed him. He was proud of his kill for we needed the meat but was disappointed that he had worked so hard to whittle that arrow only to be used one time, and on a little thing like that. One thing for sure, he knew the meat would be tender.

Now that Denby had moved away, we didn't have a deep freeze to keep extra meat from a big deer anyway. Daddy thought this one was about the right size without too much waste and what we didn't cook that day, we'd hang the rest in the cold box down on the creek.

He had asked me to help him clean and dress it but when I started throwing up he decided I might contaminate the meat and had better go lie down. He recruited Earldean to help him promising her top choice of meat from the kill.

I buried my face in my blanket to keep them from seeing me crying. That night at supper when I couldn't eat any of it, they figured I might be coming down with something. When Mama saw that I had no fever, she kind of figured it out and covered for me till the meat from that deer was all eaten up.

Now don't get me wrong, I liked to eat just as much as the next girl, but for some reason that little yearling didn't seem to be like all the rest of the deer in the woods. He was my best friend! When I looked into his dark eyes I could see somebody looking back at me. Maybe it was my own reflection, I don't know, but he was more like a "somebody" instead of a "something."

These hills are full of deer, why did it have to be that one?

Death was painful in that it hurt to think that I wouldn't ever see my friend again. It hurt to think I would never see my Mama again....alive...what will we do with her if she is dead...we can't eat her...the scavengers would...I got sick at the thought and put my hand over my mouth to keep from puking.

We can't just leave her there to rot...we have to find Daddy, my mind raced. What if we were wrong...what do we know about humans dying...we're not like the animals...they don't live like us.

I was tired and didn't want to think about it anymore. In fact, I didn't want to think at all! All of my daydreaming was halted by a horrified scream. I was instantly yanked back to reality. Something was wrong with Earldean!

When she could no longer take Learlines' whining, she had slowed down her pace and fell to her knees, pulled at her hair and began to scream to the top of her lungs! Having been taken by surprise all I could do at first was just stand and stare at her. It scared Learline out of her wits so bad that she panicked and started screaming along with her!

Ed Earl was in defense mode looking for some wild animal that she might have seen! All he could see was a flock of birds that took off and a few squirrels scampering away from that horrible noise Earldean was making!

"What! What is it? Whatcha see?" Ed Earl asked her as he circled her still looking over his shoulder. *"Is it that cat? Where is he?...Did he getcha tongue?"*

"Why?" she kept screaming out, over and over. *"Why?"*

Tears rolled down my cheeks as I watched her do what I had wanted to do all day. I wanted to scream too but the lump that was stuck there in my throat would not let any sound out at all.

The other two looked at me to do something... like I could make her stop. So I sat down the sack and walked over and squatted down beside her. She turned toward me and we embraced. I knew why she was crying but all I could say was, *"Shhhh"*... *"Shhhhh"* while I rocked her side to side, patting her back...just like Mama would have done had she been there.

After a bit I helped her get up and out of the middle of the road and walked over to sit under a canopy of trees. Learline followed along crying from exhaustion, dragging her dirty wet baby doll along side. Ed Earl grabbed the sack and met us over there. We had sat on a bed of moss that felt soft and cool to our skin and though still a little moist, was dry enough. We were so tired we could hardly talk…we just gathered our emotions as best we could and settled down to sniffles.

Learline lay down next to me cuddling her bewildered looking dolly. Resting her head in my lap she soon fell asleep. The edge of woods would get darker as the sun set so we decided to make use of what little light that was left and set up camp. It was still a little damp from the earlier rain but Earldean opened the bed roll and spread the sheet out on the moss. She lifted our baby sister from my lap and laid her across the pallet. She stripped her sleeping body from the damp clothes and hung them over a low limb to dry.

Not wanting to wake her, she took the change of clothes we carried for her and laid them across her tiny worn out body. I snapped off a sapling from its skinny trunk and used it for a broom to sweep away the area where we would build our fire for the night. Ed Earl scouted for dry kindling and I searched nearby for enough dry wood to hold us over.

Being the only one allowed to handle the matches, Earldean dug through the little box in hopes to find one dry enough to strike. She had to blow on the side of the box to dry it out enough to get any of them to work. It was almost pitch dark before we saw the first spark.

We all worked together without talking much. We just knew what had to be done without being told. In a way, it was an adventure to have a change of pace and getting to sleep in a different place…just us kids. However, it was lonely around the campfire without at least one of our parents.

We snacked on our tomatoes and peanut butter crackers till we got full enough. Not having water, we got out of brushing our teeth but we all promised not to tell on one another, as if it mattered that night.

We kept the flashlight close by as the fire died down. As we settled down on our pallet, we missed our usual bedding but as tired as we were, the thick velvety moss felt nice.

Longing for Mama and something normal about our strange new environment, we said our prayers like we usually did when we went to bed. The familiar song of the night bugs kept harmony with a whippoorwill that perched close by and helped us to relax a little. However, we were so tired, it didn't take long to drift off to sleep.

6
A CRY IN THE NIGHT

It was a warm sunny day but the vigorous breeze made the heat tolerable. The wind was whipping through the trees popping the clothes that were hanging on the clothes line. Mama's polka dotted dress would fill with air giving the appearance she was inside of it. I watched as it would fill, deflate, and then fill again. It had a smock shape and the belly would swell bigger and bigger each time it filled with air.

Mama approached the line with a basket resting on her hip. She reached and unclipped a pair of jeans and let them fall into the basket. Next to the jeans hung one of Learlines' little shirts and a pair of her shorts, both of which were still damp so she left them to dry.

A sock with a hole, an old worn out brazier and a clean, but blood stained towel all dropped into the basket. She bent over to set down the basket in order to use both hands to take down the sheet that was dancing in the wind. As she came up the sheet blew over her face to where she couldn't see. She got tangled up trying to get out of it but the wind kept it twisted it around her so that she couldn't get free. My little brother and I got tickled as we watched her wrestle her way out. You should have seen the look on her face…it was so funny….and her hair…it was all over the place!

She looked over when she heard us giggling and smiled a big smile with a wink. Picking up her basket, she gathered a few more pieces before she reached to release the pins that held her dress. A sudden wind gust snatched the dress off the line and hurled it toward the woods. Mama dropped the basket and ran after her polka dotted treasure. Each time she would reach to pick it up, the wind would take it farther away. Soon she disappeared as she went into the woods after it.

Seconds later I heard a horrible blood curdling scream…It was Mama! She screamed again…a scream that sounded like she was in pain. I ran into the woods to help but I couldn't find her. It sounded like the screams were getting farther away. I could hear Ed Earl calling for her too, not realizing he had followed me. We both saw her squatting down behind a big maple tree but as we drew closer I thought I saw her get up then fall to the ground. *"Over there!"* I said to Ed Earl, pointing in that direction.

Dodging through briars and stickers I shouted, *"WE"RE COMMIN MAMA!"*

She called out to me, *"Sassy?"*

"YEA, MAMA…ARE YA HURT? HOLD ON…I'M COMING!" I was struggling to answer while I stopped to help Ed Earl through some thorny bushes. But, in haste I let him go so that I could get to Mama who I could still hear screaming for help.

"Sassy…Sassy!" He beckoned for my attention not wanting me to abandon him in his struggle. Torn by both demands for my attention, my own feet got tangled up in the hearty ivy vines that grabbed at my ankles and I tumbled, getting my wrist caught too. Once I managed to break free, I chose to untangle my brother who was closer so that he could go with me to help Mama. When we turned back we couldn't see her any more.

"Where ya at Mama? I can't find you? I said, heading in the direction of the maple tree, near where I had seen her fall down. I could see the tall weeds rustling as something made its way, rolling down the steep hillside into the ravine. At first I thought it was Mama but I couldn't tell. It was more like a big hunk of rock that had broken free from the bluff but Mama's screams let me know that she was in that direction.

I could hear her screaming as it tumbled all the way to the bottom and it sounded like she was hurt really bad. My heart was beating so loud it was pounding in my ears as we ran through the woods trying to find her but couldn't see her. We knew we were getting closer for the screams were louder and close by.

"Mama…Mama! Where are you?" I was trying to yell but was so terrified about not finding her that I could hardly force the sound out of my mouth.

"Mama…Answer me!" I tried again as I felt an uncontrollable shaking take over my body.

"Mama…Please! Mama…"

"Sassy…Sassy! Wake Up! Earldean was saying in a hushed but desperate voice. Though she was right in my face I could barely make out that she wasn't Mama as she shook me in an effort to bring me to my senses. *"Come on Sassy…wake up Please!"*

A ringing sound rushed in my ears as I felt hot and cold at the same time. I could barely make out her face in the dim light of the flashlight. I came up on my elbows up realizing the dampness of my clothes from the perspiration. I could feel the chill bumps growing on my body.

"Maaaw…Maa." Ed Earl was mumbling as he tossed around.

We must have been having the same bad dream. I sat up further and tried to shake him too. *"Listen!"* Earldean whispered.

Ed Earl was waking up, still calling for Mama when we heard another scream.

"Mama!" he yelled as Earldean grabbed him putting her hand over his mouth to keep him quiet. His eyes bulged and he began to kick as she hushed him then slowly let her hand free so he could breathe.

"*Shhhhhh…hear that?*" she asked softly.

"Wuz at Mama?" Ed Earl inquired quietly.

Off in the distance we heard another scream in response. It was a sad, lonesome sound.

"Panther!" she whispered.

"Panther…Whatzat?" he asked still feeling groggy.

"Quiet! they will hear us!" she said with a desperate grind in her voice.

"It's a big black cat!" I answered him.

"Cat!…the kind that gits tongues?" he asked imaginatively.

I crawled toward the burning embers of the dying fire and felt around for a stick to stoke it with. Earldean reached over and pulled Learline onto her lap; drew Ed Earl up next to her and gathered the bedding around them. After I managed to get the fire to flickering again, I crawled in with them. We huddled close and listened to the cat calls crying back and forth across the canyon blindly in the blackness.

Now, I don't know if you've ever heard the sound of a panthers cry but if you haven't, or if you ever do, it is a sound that you will never forget. It is a sound that will make the hair on your neck stand straight out. I later learned to compare it to the hurting cry of a woman who is in grief stricken pain. The kind of pain she might be feeling as if her heart was being ripped out of her body and torn in two. It is such a sad, lonesome cry. It's a cry that comes from deep within, with volume and purging.

We had heard the panthers before over the years but it had been a while. They had not been accustomed to coming around our place.

Daddy said that they were too timid to invade human territory unless they were provoked.

Black panthers are big cats that could hurt you if you messed with their babies or tried to take their supper away but they aren't interested in fighting you for yours. Whatever you do, don't ever sneak up on one. They like to find you first.

When they cry out like that in the night, they are on the prowl in search for a mate. He would say, *"It's bess ta stay out the way of um and let um find each other instead of you."*

The cries in the night pierced the darkness and seemed to be coming from about fifty yards away. Each blood curdling scream seemed closer than the one before. I took the flashlight and from where I was sitting panned the ground for firewood. Spotting some small twigs close by, I scurried over and gathered them, tossed them on the flickering flames, then quickly returned to my post for safety. We pulled the sheet up over our faces only peeping out when the light from the fire lit the edge of the woods.

We could see nothing but the shadows dancing around, bringing life to the night. The local crickets raked their legs in rhythm and harmony with the frogs and beetle bugs. The crackling of the fire sent orange squiggly ashes floating up through the tree tops.

With Learline still asleep in Earldean's lap we sat looking like a six eyed bundle of dirty laundry all huddled up in that sheet. The cries from the closest cat had stopped. Her mate still cried for her in the distance but she didn't respond.

As the flames died down, so did the song of the insects, tapering off again to silence and deep darkness. We were barely breathing trying to keep quiet. When we thought we heard something in the edge of the woods I aimed the flashlight in that direction. It was so dark that it was of little use. I thought about changing the batteries but the bag was too far away and I was too scared to get up again.

Learline moaned and stretched then squirmed to get out of Earldean's lap.

"I bess git eez here clothes on her, case we ta have ta break n run." Earldean whispered. She rustled under the covers to dress baby sister in spite of not being able to see what she was doing. Needles to say, the sleepy two-year-old was not cooperative in assisting in this procedure.

"Ouch!" Ed Earl yelped after a stab in the side with an elbow.

"shhhh!"

"That hurt!"
"shhhhhh!"
"Sorry!"
"Ya'll hush up!"
"Shhhhhh!"
"DON'T shhhh me…YOU shhhh"
"SHHHHHHHHHHHHHHH!" we finally all agreed as we settled back down.

We must have sat there another thirty minutes without a sound except for a sniff or two from one or the other of us. With the fire light almost gone and the batteries played out on the flashlight we couldn't see our hand in front of our face. It was up to our ears to be on guard and they were fine tuned to every little sound around us.

I knew I wasn't just hearing things when Earldean grabbed my arm and drew me in closer to whisper, *"Did–you–hear–that?"* The snap of a small stick just a few feet away followed by a soft grunt affirmed we were not alone.

"Wha-sat!" Ed Earl whispered. Earldean squeezed his hand. We were listening so intently that when a partially burnt log shifted in the ashes, we liked to have jumped out of our skin as we gasped for a breath. The embers cracked and whistled under the rearrangement sending a whirl of lit squiggles through a cloud of smoke.

Our focused turned back to the edge of the woods. We peered into the darkness as we drew tighter into our bundle. We still weren't able to see anything but we kept our eyes peeled in that direction anyway. From our peripheral vision we could see a small flame struggling to gain height as it licked the side of the fallen log. With a soft puff of air it succeeded and gave instant light. We could see two tiny sparks glowing. It was the reflection of the camp fire growing brighter in a pair of eyes that were staring back at us. I got a quick glimpse of Daddy's face with the flames reflecting in his eyes; a comforting but fleeting sight as they faded again. Leaning forward, I strained to focus and find the familiarity of protection I so desperately needed. When the light source returned in fullness, I realized instead, it was the silhouette of the biggest black cat I'd ever seen, standing about fifteen feet away from us. We stared at it in amazement as it stared back at us in the same way. Though my heartbeat was racing, the panther was too close for us to make a run for it. We all had to be thinking the same way, wondering if we were going to be eaten alive. Oh Lord no! Please help us! I prayed silently.

What should we do?

Right then, at that very tense moment, when any of us least expected it, we heard… *"AT-CHOO!"*

It was as if God Almighty Himself answered our plea instantly and stirred up the most powerful sneeze that could possibly come out of a tiny six year old boy such as Ed Earl!

The startled panther turned on a dime and darted into the woods. I was astonished at how something that size could move so fast as we listened to it pounce across the forest floor in its escape. Thank God it was headed in the opposite direction of us!

We hesitated to breathe our sigh of relief until we were sure that kitty was far enough away. When we did, it was followed by a roar of belly bouncing laughter!

I crawled out for the batteries to replace in the flashlight so we wouldn't be caught in the dark again.

We relived the experience over and over, wide eyed and giggling, entertaining one another but mainly to reassure our bravery. When the panthers cry started up again it was far enough away that we were sure she would find her mate soon and we fell back to sleep in each other's arms.

The next morning came too soon as did the end of Learline's sleep. She was up and hungry for breakfast and thought that anyone left sleeping in the forest ought to know this.

"Haaaaaaeeey…time a wake up…itzz not dark no more…Wake up! Wake up!" she wailed in her waking little voice. *"Everybody…I'm hungry now! Wake up!"*

She didn't seem to mind peanut butter and jelly crackers again but made a big demand for a drink of water this time. The need for quenching our thirst would set us out on a new quest first thing. Along the way we would look for a stream and maybe some discarded containers to collect drinking water in.

7
THE BULLY

A typical Ozark summer morning would be cool and crisp with the sun being its greatest source of warmth, but with the heat wave going on it was already starting to get hot. By the time we were back on the road to town it was about eighty-five degrees in the shade.

Rains from the previous afternoon caused the woods to be a bit steamy; however, the runoff had filled the creeks and replenished small waterfalls throughout the hills. Plenty of water filtering through canyon walls provided cool refreshment, ready to drink and we helped ourselves to the bounty often over the course of the morning.

By late morning, walking was easier for us as the hills started to flatten out a little. We were now out of the woods and passing pastures. Shade trees by the road were fewer and far between as they had been replaced with posts and barbed wire fences.

The smell of cow manure lay heavy with the heat but tiny whiffs of fresh cut grass could be captured and welcomed as a break from the stench. The sputtering of a tractor starting up could be heard off in the distance. At a nearby farm, a dog's barking was interrupted occasionally by the lowing of cattle. A rooster could be heard giving a late wakeup call and it made me think about our chickens back home.

Who was going to feed them today? What about the goats and the other animals? What about Mama? Mama…I just tried not to think about her, it was just too sad.

We got over to the side of the road when a truck came up behind us. The driver slowed but didn't stop when he passed. It was Lester Riley but I guess he didn't recognize us being so far from home and without either of our parents.

We didn't try to stop him this time. I guess for some weird reason, as kids, we thought he would scold us for being out so far from home by ourselves.

Still trying to keep our secret of Mama's outcome from the two little ones, we would have to reveal our suspicion or tell a lie to protect them. We could only guess what Mr. Riley might have to say about leaving our sick or dead mother to fend for herself…one of us should have stayed behind…but which one?

He might have wanted to take us all the way back home and wait there for Daddy to come back there…that could be days!

Or worse…What if he made us wait at *their* house until Daddy came back? Then we'd be stuck there for days…with " *Meany Myrtle and them hateful ole hound dogs!"*

The fact that we were in need of help didn't override our fear of the Riley's dislike for children. We felt it was in our best interest to stay out of their way and not bother them with our problem. The deciding factor was that we had come such a long way from home and we should be getting close to town by now…there we would find Daddy and everything would be alright…we had gone too far to go back now!

After a brief discussion about it, the vote was unanimous that we pursue our task of reaching town on foot. At first we thought our grand scheme was in ruins when we saw the brake lights come on and the truck come to a stop. But, instead of Mr. Riley coming back for us, he turned his truck right and picked up speed.

It soon disappeared behind a farm house then with the same momentum appeared again on the other side. It was then that we realized he had reached the highway to town, "*The blacktop road!*"

We watched him drive faster as he followed the bend of the asphalt road back around the other side of the pasture we ourselves were passing, then disappear into the distance.

"That's a road ta town! That's where he'za goin'!" Earldean shouted.

"Yea!" we all cheered.

"Let's cut across this here pasture on over to the blacktop!" I suggested.

The pasture had slopes but seemed shorter than walking on down the road then all the way around again. I was tired of walking and wanted to save some steps.

"Yea…Let's make a short cut!" Ed Earl shouted in agreement.

Without hesitating, Earldean grabbed up the baby and jumped the ditch yelling with enthusiasm, *"Comeon, ya'll…lets go!*

We held the barbed wire for each other to pass through while Ed Earl, who had gone through first, had a new found energy that set him running ahead of the rest of us.

Of course, he kept coming out of those pink shoes so he'd have to turn around, come back then stop and put them on again. At that pace it didn't take long for us to catch up with him.

The cattle snorted at us as we crossed the pasture while a few more aggressive cows mooed and moved toward us. With us being that close to them, we became aware of just how big they really were. When Learline looked up and took notice of this, she froze and let out a scream that sent them backing off and bumping into one another.

It was difficult for me to pretend that this was no big deal when apparently they associated us with food and I was not familiar with what cows eat. I was really hoping that small children weren't on their diet. Maybe they thought we were there with feed for them, I don't know. We were more used to a few little goats that could get a bit rowdy when they were hungry but we had never dealt with cows before.

We were about half way across when we heard a man's voice yell, *"Hey! What are ya'll doin out yonder? Yall better git on outa here!"*

I turned to see a man standing up on his tractor just atop a small hill there in the pasture. He must have been on the other side when we passed that way. We didn't hesitate after his command.

"Run!" I shouted as I grabbed up Learline and threw her on my hip, bouncing her in stride as I trotted down the slope. Earldean reached the barbed wire fence first and hurried the rest of us to come on.

I saw a bull across the way moving in our direction, so I picked up speed passing Ed Earl as Earldean pulled the wire and crawled through.

In the rush, I lost my balance and stumbled downhill, losing Learline from my hip. I got my footing before I picked her up again noticing the bull was now trotting straight towards us. Ed Earl was still behind trying to stay in his shoes.

"Hurry Ed Earl!" I shouted, keeping an eye on the bull as I turned to run again.

When I approached the fence I reached up, passed our screaming baby sister over to Earldean, and then stretched the wire to crawl through myself as fast as I possibly could! Once on the other side, I held the wire apart for Ed Earl, hurrying him all the while. When he reached the fence, he tossed over the sack he had been carrying. Freeing one hand, I held the bottom wire with my foot then reached to help him through but instead, he ran back to go get the shoes he had stepped out of…again!

"No…come back! You don't have time!" I warned him *"…ED EARL…NO!"*

"MY SHOES!" I heard him say as he ran off.

"Ed Earl! Come on!" Earldean shouted over Learline, who was still crying about the big cows that scared her, the tumble that she and I took and now…all the commotion of our distressed concern!

I was horrified at the thought of what was about to happen if he didn't get out of there!

"Forget um, Ed Earl! Come on, hurry...THE BULL!" I yelled with my arm still reaching out, waiting to help him through.

Over his shoulder, I could see this huge bull making his way down the slope never taking his eye off of my little brother who was very small by comparison. I could feel the ground rumble beneath me as the gigantic animal charged toward his tiny target with his legs about to buckle under its great size.

Ed Earl slid into a stop, grabbed up the shoes and headed back at full speed to his exit. The bull had picked up speed as he made his way down the incline and I was sure the barbed fencing wasn't going to be able to hold him back.

All our screaming seemed only to antagonize him as it appeared he was gaining on Ed Earl. *"HURRY!...RUN…THE BULL IZ BOUT"A GIT YA! COME ON…RUN FASTER!"*

By the time he made it the opening of the fence, I was in such a panic about getting him out of there that I pulled at him when he bent down to crawl out. With all my efforts to assist him I had only made matters worse! He had not yet cleared the opening when his leg snagged one of the sharp barbs on the fence tearing the flesh on his shin.

The pink tennis shoes were clutched tightly in his hands throughout his escape. Terrified the bull would come right through those wires after us; we took off running as hard and fast as we could. Conjured up from deep within us, came enough force to run for our lives with energy left over to deliver the sound effects for anyone within half of a mile to hear!

Over our squealing, I thought I heard the voice of the man from the tractor yell out something then whistle. Closer to us were the sounds of reverberating bumps and thuds mixed with an awful clamor.

I was sure I heard the screech of metal wire stretching, popping then recoiling. I couldn't tell you what was going on behind us because I was so focused on out running our aggressor that I wasn't about to turn around to find out. It wasn't until we felt safe enough to slow down that Ed Earl started suffering with the injury on his leg. It was a pretty nasty cut that was bleeding quite a bit.

Unaware of how far we had run, we looked to find we had covered a good stretch down the blacktop road and out of sight of the pasture. Relieved to be out of harms way, we searched for an out of the way place to stop and catch our breath.

Just off the roadside, a natural row of Black Oaks lined up and hung over the wide ditch providing a cool shady spot to retreat and examine the injuries of our small troop.

As we reached the back bank of the ditch we all fell out in exhaustion, stretching our bodies to absorb the cooler air tucked in the shadows, hidden from the bright sun.

After several long sighs of relief, Earldean sat up and tugged at her shirt to stir a breeze to her overheated body. She then looked over the baby for bumps and bruises from the tumble she took when I fell with her.

Other than a little skinned elbow and grass stained knees, nothing hurt but her feelings. But, by this time, Learline had found it was useless to continue crying as her voice had grown hoarse and she was just too tired to do it anymore.

My scrapes and scratches were minor compared to the gaping hole in Ed Earl's shin. We wrapped and bound it with his extra shirt to stop the bleeding. There we'd sit and try to rest while we gave the blood a chance to clot before we moved on again.

I reached over in the paper sack to find something to eat and saw there were two small tomatoes left. I took a bite out of one and tossed the other to Earldean to share with Learline. After a few bites, I handed the rest of mine to Ed Earl.

We nibbled on crackers, peanut butter and jelly and discussed the fact that we were running out of food. I forgot we had Mama's Bible and decided this would be as good a time as any to get some reading in and it might be a calming distraction after all that excitement.

A few vehicles passed by while we waited but we didn't recognize the drivers. We so wanted Daddy to come driving up and find us.

We were exhausted, frightened and homesick which put us in a desperate need of being rescued. We had to find him soon.

When Ed Earl felt like he was going to be alright we continued on our journey. We paid close attention to the newly poured surface of the road we were walking on. We had only seen it from the back of Daddy's truck before and then we were going too fast to notice it had tiny rocks in it. I don't know what I thought it had been made of; black dirt or melted rubber I guess, I'm not sure, but I had never remembered smelling tar before that day.

As the scorching sun bore down on us, it softened the asphalt beneath our feet and little bubbles rose up and would pop with each step. Ed Earl chose to walk alongside the road because now the sticky steps were causing his feet to slip out of his oversized shoes.

When he started to limp, we thought it was because of the cut on his leg but when Earldean asked him about it, he said in a hesitant voice, *"Blisters."*

She suggested he take off his shoes and go barefoot, however, he soon found out that the sizzling hot black top would only aggravate his tired feet causing them to sting more than the blisters.

"We need to hitch a ride with the next car that comes along." Earldean suggested.

"No, I aint ridin' wit no stranger! You know we ain't spose ta be even talkin ta strange folks, Earldean, much less ridin in cars wit um!" I protested.

"This is aint the same thang Sassy! We gotta find some help." she replied.

It was getting miserably hot and Learline was getting whiny again. We had come across a few houses along the way but had not seen anybody stirring around out of doors. They must have all been up in their houses getting ready to eat because I could smell the appetizing aroma of chicken frying as we passed one house.

Passing another, a window was open with a screen over it. Seeping through was the all too familiar smell of speckled butterbeans just about done. Along with it came the sound of a woman's voice singing off key with a song on the radio.

"I' Hungry!" Learline whined.

"Me too!" I said, finally getting my appetite back.

"Well we have some jelly and a few broken crackers left." Earldean said.

"Ain't hardly a nuff ta taste there…I'm a needin sumpin fittin ta eat! …like fish?" Ed Earl exclaimed.

"Fish!" Learline agreed.

Walking on discussing other things that would be good to eat if we had a choice we came across one house that had some children playing around it. We could hear their laughter as we got closer and was distracted by the sound of their voices. They stopped playing and stared at us as we passed. We stared back of course, watching them draw close together while we did the same. Other than ourselves, we had not seen many other children before that time, except maybe a few when we went to town, but none that we'd ever talked to.

Mama had gotten on to us before for staring at people. We couldn't help it! The temptation was too much as our opportunities to look at other people were few and far between.

It was strange to see people with different kinds of colored hair, eyes and skin tones. Some were round in places like Myrtle Riley but not as tall and some were skinny like Mr. Riley, but not as short. A few of the men we had looked at were a little like Denby or a little like Daddy.

A few women would have hair like Mama or cut shorter. Some had different textures and styles of curls circled around their heads. Most of them wore pretty bright colors with pictures on their clothes.

It was strange…some folks were funny looking and some were just pretty to look at. But to me, it was the other kids who were the most interesting to watch. I guess some folks felt the same way about us because everywhere we had ever gone, people stared back at us.

I had wondered if any of these children we saw there playing were the ones we had seen in town before. I had a pretty vivid recollection of what they looked like and if I could have just gotten a closer look at their faces, I could have told you.

One of the little girls waved as we kept our pace down the road. She seemed friendly enough so I waved back.

Learline pointed and said *"Look!"* as one of them stood up his bicycle and rode it over toward us. Nervously I grabbed Learlines' pointed finger and pulled her along.

The boy sped up and rode up alongside us asking, *"Ya'll new round here?"*

We looked at each other wondering if we should answer him.

"Whatcha name?" he asked, looking at our little brother.

Earldean answered for him. *"His name is Ed Earl, I'm Earldean, and eez here are my sisters Learline and Sassy. We live in Chinquapin Holler."*

"Up there by the lake? What ya'll doin way off down in ezz parts?" he inquired.

"Mama took sick and aint doin so well so'z we're on our way to town to find Daddy and let him know 'bout it" she answered.

"Town! At's a fer piece from here. Y'all walk all this way?" he responded.

We all nodded our heads yes.

"That a take all day! Cain't ya'll get a ride?" he continued.

"Aint got nobody ta ask." Earldine said.

"My name is Huey….I live just down the road here…let's go ask my maw. Maybe she might can help." he said as he circled around us scooting the bike with one foot.

We didn't know what to say to that so we just kept walking and looking at one another. This boy, Huey, pushed at the peddles on his bicycle making one more, larger loop around us then said, *"Well… alright then…Let's go see what she has ta say bout it!"*

"SEE YA'LL LATER!" he yelled as he waved bye to the other kids in the yard before racing past us again with instructions.

"Ya'll come on and meet me down at that white house there on the left."

He pulled up on the handle bars of his bike and rode off on one wheel for a ways before it dropped back down. Then he came up off the seat and pushed the peddles furiously, picking up speed as the bike rocked fast from side to side beneath his lanky body.

"Wow! Did ya'll see that trick he done?" Ed Earl said as he watched in amazement.

We had seen folks in town on bikes but we had never seen anything like that!

"He seemed like a nice feller. Maybe we should go over there. What do ya'll thank?" Earldean asked with a bit of hope in her voice.

"I duno bout that…We should probably keep goin…We don't know them." I said.

"We don't know anybody Sassy! Look around!" Earldean was saying when she stopped and spun around with a pointed finger. *"There's people living everywhere round here! Sure, we don't know um. That's cause we ain't met um yet! You heard 'at boy...We are still a long way from town!"* she rattled on, throwing her arms around in the air. *"It's too blasted hot to be out here, Sassy!…Let's just go over there!"*

"My leg hurts and my blisters sting…I'm tard a walkin!" Ed Earl complained.

I too was tired and hungry and now Learline wanted to be carried again. *"I guess we can stop by there."* I consented.

We stopped a few yards away from their property line which was clearly marked by freshly cut grass. The place looked well kept except for a couple of yard toys and bicycle parts scattered about under a single, large shade tree.

Still not sure if we would be welcomed, we watched from a far distance as the boy rode his bike up the muddy driveway toward the large house with aged white paint.

We could see movement on the porch but in contrast with the bright sun, it was hard to make out what it was.

To keep from getting hit by a passing car we stepped off of the road and stood in the bottom of a big ditch. Ed Earl sat down and adjusted the makeshift bandage we had tied around his leg then wrapped his hands around it and moaned.

"Do it hurt?" Learline asked sympathetically as she sat down beside him.

I was tired and needed to rest but I felt too nervous to be still. We were about to talk to people we didn't know. Being shy, I didn't want to have to do any of the talking when it was obvious that Earldean was much better at it than I was. I wouldn't know what to say to them except that I was about to wet my pants! That's all I could think of I was so nervous. I had the urge to go behind a tree but now these people were all looking at us.

Huey yelled and motioned for us to come on up to the house. As we approached, we could see him straddling his bike with the front wheel propped up on the first two steps leading to the front porch.

He was talking to these two women who were perched on a glider sipping iced tea. We could hear their voices but couldn't make out what they were saying.

We were cautious in our steps as we slowly made our way, stopping short of reaching the big tree. The two little ones ran ahead to inspect a few toys they spotted beneath it, then plopped down in the shade and began to play.

Huey motioned for us to come closer. Earldean nudged me and I liked to have lost it. I spun around and nudged her back. She stumbled forward and reluctantly walked toward the porch. Ed Earl and Learline got up and followed her. And me…well, I lagged behind them straining to hold my bladder.

Ohh! I wish Mama or Daddy were here! They would know what to say to these people. But, if they were here, we wouldn't need to be here asking for help. Mama and Daddy didn't ask for much aid so we weren't sure how to go about it.

As it turned out, we didn't have to ask them for anything. Huey had explained what he knew about our situation and we just had to answer their questions. Well, at least as best we could.

"This is my Maw and my Granny." Huey said. *"A'z wantin ta talk to ya'll."*

The younger of the two women stood up and walked toward the railing of the porch. She was tall and thin with high cheek bones and sharp features. Her brown hair was a little darker than Mama's and it was pinned up on top of her head. Some of the hairs had fallen loose and stuck out around her neck and face so that they flew about when she fanned herself with a paper fan.

My dry tongue got stuck when I tried to lick my parched lips as I watched her taste her tea then swallow while she waited for us to reach speaking distance.

"Huey here, says ya'll from round Chinquapin Holler. Ya'll walk all a way down here?"

"Yes um" Earldean answered.

"Well, that's a good eight or nine miles back up in them hills. Where's ya'lls folks? Do they know ya'll off down here by ya self?" she asked.

"Our Mama got sick so we're on our way to find our Daddy and let him know." Ed Earl said. I looked over at Earldean who swallowed real hard about that time. He still didn't know yet.

"Where is your Daddy, hun?" the woman asked as two young little boys ran out of the screen door and onto porch, working their way around her legs to see who was there.

Peeping through the railing we could hear them whisper to Huey *"Who's that? What they want?"*

"He's workin a job in town.... Aint due back fer several days so he wouldn't know about Mama gitin sick n' all." Earldean explained.

"Did ya Mama send ya'll to fetch him?" she went on asking.

"Uhh...I...Uhh." Earldean, lost for words, cut her eyes at me when she was interrupted by the older woman. *"Good Lord, son, what happened to your leg?"* she said, sliding off the glider then stepping up for a closer look at Ed Earl.

When I looked down at his leg, the shirt we wrapped around it was saturated with blood.

"Oh Ed Earl, it's a bleadin really bad now!" I exclaimed. We should have wrapped it better or something, maybe gave it a little more time before we made him walk on it.

"Cut it on a fence…It don't hurt bad as ez blisters on my feet do." he responded.

"We better see to it. Come on in here." she said as she stepped toward him with her hand stretched out. *"How long has it been a bleedin atta way?"* Huey's mother asked.

"He done it a ways back down the road. We thought it was alright but we tied it up case it commence ta bleedin 'gin! Some that blood wuz from when it first happened. We held it on there quite a spell!" Earldean said as she helped our brother up the steps.

"I gotta pee pee!" Learline blurted out.

"I'll take her out there…I gotta go too." I whispered to the back of Earldean's head.

"Ya'll come on in. Let's get that leg cleaned up. Ya'll can use the bathroom and get a drink a water here." Huey's mother said as she opened the screen door inviting us in.

I grabbed Learlines' hand and turned to take her out behind a tree.

"Where ya'll goin?" Huey asked, still holding the door and waiting on us.

"Gotta pee." I said softly, more embarrassed about talking than revealing a personal matter to a boy I had just met.

"Well you can use our bathroom, come on." He said with a big grin on his face.

"I wuttin a lookin to take a bath…mind ya…I guess I could wash up a bit…. I really need ta pee first" I mumbled.

"I said you could use our bathroom…we got a toilet in there." he repeated with a chuckle. It was then that I realized that they must have had indoor plumbing like at Myrtle Riley's house.

We followed him in to the house where we found Ed Earl center of attention as the two women fussed over his injury. They had him sitting on the edge of the table with an audience of Earldean and the two little boys eagerly waiting for the unveiling.

Huey pointed to a door across a short hallway then hurried to see the drama taking place across the room.

I was relieved to get my turn on the toilet for, like her brother, Learline was fascinated with the flushing and took her time. She also wanted to turn every water faucet and play with the light switches which made me nervous and I was ready to get out of there.

As we were rejoining the others, we saw the Granny lady was coming across the room with some bandages and tape.

"Oooowee! That hurts!" Ed Earl shrieked as tears were running down his cheeks. His red face showed signs of anguish as the tears flowed enough to wet the front of his dirty tee shirt.

Daddy had always told him big boys don't cry and he did all he could to keep from it too. He worked hard to gain Daddy's favor by appearing to be as big as a boy could be. He must be hurting pretty bad to let tears leak out like that, I thought.

Looking over Earldean's shoulder, I could see a wash pan of bloody water and rags under his leg that was propped up on the back of a chair. His filthy pink shoes lay in the floor, one spotted with blood and both with black tar stuck to the bottom and sides.

The blisters on his feet had made bubbles and the biggest ones had ruptured. Dust had stuck to his feet and the only spot clean about him was the sore leg that had just been washed.

Huey's mother was dabbing the cut with a dry towel but the blood kept oozing.

"Looks like it could take several stitches to close it up." she said. *"Guess we could run him down to the clinic before Doc leaves for the day."*

"Stitches? You mean like sewin stitches?" Earldean asked.

"Yes, we better get him down there purty quick…They close early today." she suggested.

Huey and the other boys were right up next to Ed Earl pushing to get in closer to see some blood and guts. This had to be making him worried in addition to the pain.

Over their chattering, I heard Earldean ask, *"What's a clinic?"*

Huey looked back at her with a puckered brow, surprised she had to ask. He replied, *"What? You ain't never been to the Clinic? Where you go when ya git sick?"*

"We don't git sick much…when we do, we lay down till we feel better…we don't go anywhere!" she answered.

Across the way, into another area, I noticed the two ladies were at the kitchen sink talking low and looking back at us. When Huey's mother caught me staring back at them, she reached and got two tin cups from the counter and walked toward me and Learline.

"You gals want a cool drink of water?"

Neither of us was shy at all at that moment when we took and drank the water down, hardly stopping for air. It was so refreshing and thirst quenching…I just couldn't get enough. That's why I was glad when the baby finished hers because between hard breathing she held out the cup saying, *"More!"*

We followed the woman back to the sink and watched as she refilled our cups from the faucet where the clear water flowed freely with a simple twist of a knob.

While I was downing my second cup full, she put her hand on my shoulder then asked, *"What did you say your name was?"*

I hadn't told her my name yet but I answered her anyway because she was so kind to me. *"Sassy."* I said in a voice that was barely more than a whisper.

"And…your last name is…?" she had a questioned look about her as though she were waiting on an answer from me. I stared back thinking maybe she was trying to tell me that she didn't hear the *last* thing I said.

"Sassy…My name's Sassy." I repeated, slightly louder than before.

She turned to Earldean, who had already been through introductions of sorts, and said, *"Well...I guess that'll wait…we'd better tend to the boy…My mother is going to take your brother down to the clinic and let Doc Murphy take a look at him. Huey tells me ya'll need a ride to town anyhow. She lives over that way and says it won't be much trouble."*

She walked over and began to wrap Ed Earl's leg with heavy bandages.

"Your Mother?" Earldean asked, looking around the room.

Huey could tell she didn't understand what his maw was trying to tell her.

"My Granny, Earldean…She says she can get you to town…the clinic is in town!"

We didn't know at the time that mothers could have mothers of their own. Our mother never had one…that she spoke of. Neither had daddy but at any rate, I was relieved to hear we had a ride to town. Now that we'd talked with them a bit they didn't seem so much like strangers so hopefully we wouldn't be in trouble about it.

I was really tired and didn't think Ed Earl was in any shape to walk with those blisters and a bleeding leg. Learline wouldn't hold out much longer either. I was still a little scared but these people seemed nice…like Denby.

"After we get Ed Earl's leg fixed up we could go look for Daddy." I said softly.

All this talk about stitches reminded me of the time Daddy cut his knee on a sharp rock in the creek. It made such a hole that Mama took a needle and thread and sewed it up. It must have hurt pretty bad because Daddy stuffed a rag in his mouth to bite down on to keep from crying out. At least that's why Mama said he was doing it.

It made *my* knee hurt watching her pull the thread tight through the holes in his skin. I was just glad I didn't have to be the one to do it. As far as that goes, I didn't want to think about anybody doing that to my little brother because I could imagine the pain it would cause. However the older woman explained why it was better to sew it up than to leave it open and I didn't want my brother to lose all his blood.

I watched Huey's maw tenderly tend to my little brother as she finished by putting a piece of tape on to hold the bandage. She took a clean rag and wiped the tears and dust from his face, then cleaned his hands. For some reason he didn't resist the help she tenderly gave him.

She made me think a whole lot about my Mama, that's the kind of stuff she would do if she were there. It made tears well up in my eyes as I missed her so much it hurt.

Ed Earl was still crying, though not like a baby but like a boy who was tired and hurt. *"Sniff…My Mama could sew it up…sniff…when we git back home!"* he told her, afraid of what was in store for him at this clinic place.

"Do ya think he might git sick and die?" Earldean asked Huey's maw with concerns about bleeding to death after her explanation.

"No hun…not if yall go on and let Doc Murphy tend to him down at his Clinic!"

She carried him to the car and put him over into the back seat. Reassuring us that everything was going to be alright, we all crawled inside the car with him.

Just before she shut the back car door, she caught me staring at her again. Embarrassed, I quickly turned away and caught myself waiting to hear my mother's voice scold me again. Peeking back, I saw her smile softly in a way that let me know she didn't really mind. She took time to single me out to say, *"Bye now Sassy. You take care now, ya hear?"*

As Granny backed her car around, Huey stood there with Maw and what I was sure were his little brothers. When they waved goodbye, I felt a warm sense of fondness for our new friends, such as they were. Suddenly, an urge to respond to their kindness overwhelmed me.

"Bye Huey! Bye Maw! Thank ya for the water…I'll take care! Aw ite?" I yelled out of the open window. I surprised Earldean by speaking up. Heck, I surprised myself! It started a series of waves from the rest of the gang as we pulled out of the driveway with the boys running alongside the car. The cautious driver grinned and waved with one hand, keeping the other on the wheel and both eyes in front of her moving vehicle.

The fourteen mile ride to town gave us plenty of time to check out the inside of Granny's car. The cloth seats were protected with clear plastic coverings with bubbles on them that Ed Earl and I couldn't resist punching down with our finger tips. We did not see the harm in mashing the tiny bumps that had kept us so preoccupied.

Looking back I feel bad and can't believe we did that to that lady's car seat. She was so nice to help us out and all. After I was satisfied with all the bubbles I could smash, I sat and stared at the woman's head from the back seat. I was amused by her short silver curls that were so perfectly placed about her head. They barely moved while our hair was blowing around making massive tangles.

I noticed often her eyes would catch mine looking in the rearview mirror; they were a familiar color green. I wanted to touch her wrinkled skin and see if it felt like Denby's.

I couldn't help but stare at her as she put on a pair of sun shades. I wondered how she was able to see through that dark glass.

Earldean and the Granny lady did most of the talking on the trip into town. I couldn't hear much of the conversation over the wind noise coming through the car windows so I decided to sit back and enjoyed the scenery that this opportunity had given me. I had seldom seen outside the hollow so this was a treat to be inside a moving car.

I held Learline tightly in my lap for fear that she would blow out of the window when she tried to hang out of it like her brother. She fought me for a while about it before Earldean pulled her over into the front seat with her screaming like she was in pain.

Before too long she was asleep, dozing only between Ed Earl's shouting for us to look at something he'd seen out the window.

Being our first ride in a car and feeling a little uneasy with a stranger could have attributed to the ride seeming to take longer than what it had in the back of daddy's truck.

I remember thinking how much things had changed from the last trip to town and wondered had we ever gone this way before. We had taken the hills and curves, passing farms and such that were new to me as nothing looked familiar. It was as though were seeing this all for the first time.

After a while, we topped a big hill to where we could see clusters of houses and other buildings that nestled down the slopes overlooking a big lake.

Ed Earl was the first to notice something real big far off in the distance.

"What'zat? Lookie over yonder!" He said, pointing and hanging his head out the window.

Before any of the rest of us could see what it was, the view was obstructed by large trees and the landscape next to the highway. He was trying the best that he could to describe what it was he saw when we rounded a curve in road. *"Yonder it is again!"* he screeched, pointing in the direction of an enormous structure that towered over everything including the trees.

It appeared to be a gigantic ball resting on huge tall post with a skinny ladder rising up one side.

"That's the water tower." Granny answered. *"That's where they keep the town's water supply."*

"Way up at the top of that thang? That's a fer piece ta go fer some folks to fetch water, don't cha thank?" Earldean asked.

It was much bigger than the rain barrels we kept and I wondered how the water got in there without a hole in the top.

"Why come um to keep it up so high like that? Ta keep the critters out n' all?"

The Granny lady laughed a little as she tried to explain as best she could the modern methods of plumbing, though it still didn't make much sense to us. At any rate she went on answering our questions as we kept an eye out for this curious landmark around each bend as we drew closer to town.

"Almost there!" Granny said as we approach a big road sign that Earldean attempted to read out loud.

"Waa-his-pear-rrrride-ga! Pop-u-lat-I-on…Eight-six-five! Recon wha 'zat means?"

"Whisper Ridge…that's the name of our town…" Granny explained.

"A name?…Like a person?…I didn't know town was called anythang but town!"

"Sure…and the population is eight hundred and sixty five."

"What ta heck iza Pop-u-lation anyhow?" Ed Earl asked her, now hanging over the back seat pressing in on the conversation.

"Population? Well, that's how many people live here in town."

"Man…atza lotta people!" Earldean exclaimed. *"…Why…that's more than the stars up in the night sky!"*

Granny laughed and said, *"Well…not quite that many!"*

8
THE CLINIC
(*WHO WANTS PIE*)

It was mid afternoon, when the sun was its brightest, that I caught a glimpse of our pathetic looking group in the reflection of the glass entrance at the Whisper Ridge Health Clinic.

Granny stepped in front of us and pushed hard at the heavy door. As it opened, a cool, brisk, breeze rushed through that felt truly refreshing and wonderfully delightful!

It was as though we were walking into the midst of another season, any season but summer. Inside the air remained cool and judging from the funny sounds Granny made with her mouth, I think she appreciated it too.

"Afternoon Mrs. Pane. What brings you in today?" I heard a woman's voice asking.

I looked around to see who she was talking to. Was granny in pain? I wondered. I just thought she was enjoying the break from the heat.

"Hey Alma. We're lookin ta see Doc Murphy. He here?" Granny responded, bending down to talk through a hole that was cut in the big glass window on the wall near the door.

"He'z gone out to check on Ralph McMillen's mare. She was havin trouble passin her colt and he called for Doc to see iffin he could oblige her. He probly won't be back today. Sumpin I can do fer ya?"

"We were needin the Doc to sew this boy up!"

The lady, sitting in a chair behind the glass, pushed herself away from the desk and slowly rose to her feet. Although she did not get much higher than she was sitting down, I could see now who it was that was talking to Granny. Her face was quite large and round with several chins that rolled into the neck of her blouse. Her dark brown hair was cut short and rounded her face like she had a mixing bowl turned upside down on her head. Just beneath her bangs were slits were her eyes were suppose to be and they widened as she leaned forward to peer over the ledge to investigate.

"Reccon how bad is it?" she asked.

"Not too, but it's deep enough to call for a stitch or two…maybe eight to ten!"

Granny said, lifting Ed Earl up onto the counter, his shoes dangling from his feet.

Chuckling, the woman amused herself by saying, *"Well, cain't be too deep on a boy that skinny. He ain't got no meat on his bones! Whatca do little feller…Trip over them fancy shoes ya got there?"* Ed Earl didn't answer but struggled not to let the shoes fall off.

The lady looked over at us, then back at Granny and asked, *"These some yo kinfolk?"*

"Naw. They's from up around Chikipin Holler. They come a long way to fetch their Paw. Said their Maw wuz sick and needed him a come home. They wandered up to my daughters place out there. We figured we'd better get um fixed up first." Granny told her.

"Well, let's take a look at it before we call Doc back to the office."

As she stepped around from behind the dividing wall I couldn't help but stare at her.

"Bring him on back. The rest a ya'll have a seat there in the waitin room." she said pointing to a small area filled with metal chairs. They took Ed Earl to a back room and shut the door behind them.

When we sat down on the chairs, they felt as cold as ice to the back of our bare legs, so I pulled at my shorts to shield my skin from the seat. Earldean wiggled around a bit before she stood and removed the bed roll from her back. She had been wearing that thing for so long I almost forgot what she looked like without it. She put it on the chair and sat on top of it. *"It's cold in here, huh?"* she said with a shiver. *"She feels warm though."* referring to Learline as she pulled her into her lap to cuddle.

"Did you see the size of that woman! I ain't never seen nuttin like at before!" I said.

"Yea, and I saw you starrin at her too. She wuz a biggin alright but Mama says we shouldn't stare. Itta git us in trouble cause folks don't like it nun!" Earldean scolded.

"Lardy! She was as big as that there bull at got after us!" I went on, still amazed.

"Oh, she wuttin at big Sassy, you a stretchin a truth a might aren't cha? Basides you arta be glad she's lookin after our little brother. She prolly cain't hep it!" Earldean said.

I sat and thought about what she said. I didn't mean it in a bad way, she was just so big and back then, Myrtle Riley was the only one I could come close to comparing her size to. Not that I had ever seen that many people…but still!

Myrtle carried it in her height where this woman carried it *everywhere.* I wondered if she was as mean too. I pondered the many times Mama and Daddy would be after us to eat all of the food on our plate so that we would get big and strong. She must have minded her folks real good, I thought. Bet they had some big plates too. I would just have to keep my thoughts to myself. I didn't want to make her feel bad about it. I had heard a few folks before make comments about all of us being so skinny and it made me feel terrible for a long time. Maybe she just liked to eat more, that's all.

While we waited we heard Ed Earl in the back room let out a scream followed by crying. We were all afraid, worried and wondering what was happening to him. We could hear the ladies trying to calm him down. I stood and paced the floor until the sound of a little bell rang. I didn't remember hearing it when walked in but it hung over the glass door and moved when the door opened. In walked a tall man with a cowboy hat.

He looked at us real hard as he stood in front of the glass wall where the big lady sat. From the back room she yelled, *"BE WITH YA IN A MINUTE!"*

He stood there with his hands on his hips like something was bothering him. I wondered if he was sick or needed stitches or something. I didn't see any blood anywhere and he seemed to walk just fine in his pointed toed boots.

He glared at us as he walked across the waiting room and bent over a metal box that was stuck to the wall. After a few seconds, he stood straight, then bent again staying a little longer. I wondered if he might be looking for something in that box and was curious as to what he might find in there.

When he stood up straight again he turned and taking a piece of white cloth from his pocket, he wiped his mouth. About that time the large lady opened the door and poked her head out to see who was there. The tall cowboy man took a large step in her direction and in a grouchy voice, said to her, *"Where is she?…My wife!...She here?"*

"Why…yes Mr. Pane, she's in the back here. Should I get for ya?" she answered him politely in spite of his ill temper.

Just then Granny came to the door. *"Ben, Whatcha doin here? How did ya know that I…"* she was saying when he interrupted.

"Woman! Where you been? I called out there a lookin fer ya when ya didn't come right straight home. Jane told me what you'z up to…said you wuz here a tindin to somebody else's bid'ness! You need to git on to the house woman!" he said in a loud mean voice.

"Ben, these little youngins needed some help! Didn't Jane tell you that?" she asked.

"I don't care what THEY need. What bout my supper? You give any thought ta that? HUH?" he shouted pointing his finger in her face. *"Now I'ma sick n tard all iss!"*

Granny glanced over at us only to see our frightened demeanor before she tried to defend her actions. *"B-b-but Ben! I…just…"*

"Don't but Ben me! What I tell you? You all the time pickin up strays and puttin out time and money on um…messin round wit thangs ain't none ya bid'ness…I aint gone be the one ta pay fer this! Well, I'll tell ya one thang …YOU BETTER start thinking bout me…Ya hear?...NOW COME ON!"

The large lady put her hand on Granny's shoulder and said, *"You go on Mrs. Pane. I'll handle it from here."*

"You sure now?" Granny asked her, as if she knew it was really best that she leave.

She nodded yes and patted her back. Granny turned and walked over to us, squatted down and softly said, *"Ms. Alma here is gonna help you now. She'll get your brother fixed up and maybe help ya find ya daddy, so ya'll can git on back out there and tend to ya mama. Ya hear?"*

She stood and walked toward the door where her husband was impatiently waiting.

When she passed by the back room door she waved bye to Ed Earl and started to speak when her husband snapped at her again. *"Come ON, woman!"*

I felt bad that he yelled at her and partly responsible for her getting in trouble. If we would have just kept on walking out there on the highway she wouldn't have been there helping us. Though, it was a nice thing she was doing, she really didn't know who we were and I'm sure like Daddy, he had probably already given her plenty of warnings before. *"See what happens when you talk to strangers?"* I whispered to Earldean as the fussy old man aggressively assisted his wife out the door.

Ms. Alma, the large lady, turned to us and said, *"Don't think we gonna need the Doctor. I can put in those few stitches myself and have ya'll on ya way in no time. I'll need one of ya'll to come help hold him down though."* She turned to go back in the room when I stood up to follow. I really didn't want to watch but I just couldn't leave my little brother in his time of need. *"I'll do it Sassy. I know how you are, you'll be cryin too and you aint even the one hurt."* Earldean said. *"You stay here wit Learline."*

I was fine with that because I didn't want to see him in any more pain. I was, however, interested in discovering what was in that metal box on the wall.

After the door to the back room shut I looked around at the empty room. Learline followed me over to see what we could find. I stepped up on a wooden box that sat on the floor beneath this thing. Looking over, I saw that the top of it had a knob of some sort that sat on the corner of a shallow silver basin. Wondering what the man might have been looking for, I stretched to look down through some tiny holes that were in the center of it but couldn't see past the darkness. After closer inspection I could tell that this was some sort of strainer stuck in a bigger hole. I tried to pry it out with my thumb nail but it wouldn't turn loose. So, I squinted my eyes and tried to see past it but still couldn't see anything.

Coming up, I examined the entire top again and found only a blurred reflection of myself and a few water drops. I'd wondered if that man had turned this knob when he was here. I hadn't seen any lights come on that weren't already burning when he had arrived.

This didn't look like the electric fans like at the Riley's', or the ice box at Denby's, nor even his deep freeze. However, it did have a quiet hum like all of these things but no way to open it to find out. I contemplated several possibilities.

I looked down at my baby sister who as eager to find out what it was as I had been, and wondered...should I turn the knob or should I hold Learline up here and let her do it? Yea! She liked to turn knobs, I thought. That way if it was wrong to do it...I could blame it on the baby!

With my fingers gently caressing it, I pondered several ideas before working up the guts to turn the darn thing myself.

With a gentle twist...out squirted a long stream of water! I jumped back a bit in surprise and said, *"Water, Learline! Water!"*

I knew it was safe to drink because I had seen Granny's husband do it...yes, I'm sure he did. That's why he was so cranky in the first place! He was hot and thirsty like me! I twisted and held the knob and watched as a perfectly arched stream of water flowed then trickled down through the tiny holes. I held my mouth as close to the base of the flow to catch all that I possibly could. I remember thinking how easy this was to obtain as it quenched my desperate thirst.

It was so good and cool…I just couldn't get enough! I drank until I had to come up for air with my sister pulling at my shorts for a turn.

"Let me! Let me!" she exclaimed.

"Lookie here Learline…It's like this here water iz magic…It comes out of nowhere and shoots out this little ole hole somehow er nuther when ya turn this thang here! Now don't tat jest beat all you ever did see?"

We took turns drinking until we got our fill. Then we just watched in fascination, turning the knob, running the water and watching it trickle down the drain. I imagined it was recycling back and coming out again, though I couldn't figure out how it worked.

"This must be pluming stuff like that Granny woman told us about." I told Learline.

I thought about drinking after Granny's mean old husband and wondered if some of his spit might have gotten in that water and come back out when we drank it. Mama had warned us about drinking after other folks when they don't feel good…they could be sick or coming down with a fever. We might catch whatever illness they had.

Oh no! I thought I remember him claiming he was sick! Or, was he just sick and tired. I thought back to a time I heard Mama explain herself when she said those same words… *"its jest a figger a speech…whatcha say when ya don't wanna put up with the way thangs iza goin…don't mean a body's really ailing!"* I remembered her saying.

Never the less, the man was not happy. He acted more like he was hungry and needing some food to eat. Hunger can make a person feel angry and tired like that. If you go too long without anything, you can start to feel weak and sickly. Mama says a body can starve to death from not eating. I knew all too well how that felt and tried not to judge him by the way he was acting; at least we had eaten a little bit…that was better than nothing! If I would have thought about it I would have given him those last few broken crackers and he could have scraped out at least a spoon of jelly that was left.

I looked around for the paper sack with the pig face but didn't see it. *"It must be yonder in the back wit Ed Earl and Earldean."* I mumbled to myself.

I had started to get chilled from drinking the cold water and being in the cool air. I could feel heat coming off of Learline's body when she sat next to me. I felt her forehead for fever hoping she had not caught germs from the old man just in case he really was sick. She was really hot but not pale like she was sick. Instead, she was a dark shade of pink. I could see redness under my dark tanned skin as well. Sunburn, I thought. We had been in the sun too long and now we were blistered. It stung when I touched it or bumped next to things.

We played around the chairs and on the rug looking at pictures in the books that were stacked on the short table. It was quite entertaining to say the least, with about twenty trips to the water fountain, and at least that many magazines to look at until they were finished.

With a lollypop in his mouth, Ed Earl came out of the back room limping and his leg neatly bandaged up.

In his fist were two more suckers that we assumed were for us by way he had his arm stretched toward us as far as possible. Earldean's cheek was puffed out with one stuck in her mouth too, so we were pretty sure to get one of our own.

"It's a prize for bein a big boy and not cryin…so much." Ed Earl said. "… *and I got eight stitches!...and some Band-Aids wit…uuhh…Who?"* he asked turning back toward Miss Alma.

"Casper." she said smiling back at him.

"He's a friendly ghost…for my blisters!" he went on to say.

"You mean Holy Ghost?" I asked, reaching with shared excitement for my treat.

"No! Sassy…Casper! See?" he said as he showed off his boo-boos.

Learline struggled with the wrapper of her candy while I went to show them the water fountain. After they had several turns Ms. Alma called us over to where she sat behind the glass wall.

It was hard for me to listen to what she was saying, for I was distracted by all the things on her desk. She answered our many questions about this and that as she pulled out a writing tablet and a fancy pencil and prepared to write.

"Ok, I need to get some information about cha…What's your last name Ed Earl?" she asked turning to him with a big happy smile.

"My last name…whatzat?" he said wondering why she would ask such a question.

"You know…last name…like Ed might be your first? Or is it Edward? Then your middle name is…" she started to explain before he blurted out what he thought was the right answer.

"…oooh…it's Earl" he declared as he studied his red lollypop before the next lick.

She was waiting to write down his answer when she turned to him and repeated what she thought he was claiming. *"Earl?...Ed Earl Earl?"*

We all laughed at how funny that sounded then she looked at Earldean and asked her. *"Tell me your last name?"*

"Why Mizz Alma…It's Dean of course!" she said matter of factly.

Alma slowly said the whole thing as she wrote down the name. *"Ed-Earl-Dean."*

We broke into a giggle and took turns repeating it under our breath before she caught us.

"So…Your name is Earldean Dean?…Wait…is that right?" we laughed again.

"Sure, septin it is only its one time Dean not two!" she chuckled.

"Dean Dean? Ha-ha...Dean-Dean." Ed Earl duplicatingly rattled off with the two-year-old following with her own version of what she heard. This had us giggling with giddiness, almost beyond control.

"Oh. Ya'll bein silly! Now what's all yall's last name?" she insisted as she showed only a hint of impatience.

Not wanting her to get irritated, I spoke up over their laughter and told her, pointing them out one by one.

"That's Ed-EARL, that's Earl-DEAN, that's Lear-LINE, and Mine is Sas-SEEE!"

"Goodness Gracious, don't you know your last name? Ok, how about your mother, what is her whole name?" she asked as she turned to write again.

"Mama!" we all said in unison.

"And I guess your father's name is Daddy, right?" she asked, getting a little frustrated.

"No." Earldean answered. *"God is our father and our Daddy's real name is Earl but just we call him Daddy, but other folks call him Earl!"*

"Ok." Alma said with a smile. *"Seriously, I need to know your last name for the record."*

"It's my turn…Let me play dis time!" Ed Earl requested, thinking it was a game.

Alma set the pencil down and turned, putting her hands on her lap…such as it was. Her smile softened to a concerned look that she kept fixed on Learline for several seconds before she spoke again. *"My word sugar pie…look at you… poor little thang… you're cooked!"*

Now with that being the first time I'd heard that phrase, you can imagine the scene rolling in my head…Cooked Sugar Pie?…Learline laying in a great big skillet…head and toes sticking out of the pie crust…baking in the cook stove…hot fire going...

"You aint gonna eat her are ye?" I shrieked.

Alma busted out laughing; she shook so hard her chair squeaked as her whole body jiggled uncontrollably! *"No!"* she said with the first breath she caught, then started laughing again. When she was finally able to get a hold of herself she showed signs of near exhaustion. *"WHEEEEEW! That was a good un!"* she affirmed, still fighting it back. *"That was the best doggone laugh I had in a long time!"* she was saying when she noticed I was still concerned.

"Oh…Hun…why would you think I'd wanna eat ya lit'lo sister?"

"Well…you'z a lookin at her like youz a study'n ta eat her up…like you thought she'z some kinna cooked up pie!"

Well that answer set her off to laughing again and still unsure why, I pulled Learlean further back away from this big gal.

"No…no hun. I just mean she stayed out in the sun too long and now she's blistered…cooked by the sun…Sunburned? ...Look atcha, ya all are!"

Turning her attention to our sunburns, raising our shirt sleeves and comparing the difference, she started with questions about how long we had been out there and how it led up to us being there.

Granny had filled her in on what she knew and Earldean said she kept asking Ed Earl questions to keep his mind occupied with other things while she stitched him up. She was rubbing some cold cream on our sunburns to cool it down; when Learline said she was hungry. I looked around for the sack with the pig head to give her some cracker crumbs. It was then that we realized we hadn't seen it for a long time, not since we were walking down the road.

Miss Alma told us not to worry, she would see about getting us something to eat and help us find our daddy. I wasn't worried about the sack; I was worried about what was in it; Mama's Bible.

"The Clinic closes at three thirty on Friday so I have about ten minutes left to get some thangs done 'round here before I go. I've got enough money on me to git ya'll a burger or hot dog from over yonder at Trudy's Eat-a bite. Maybe

somebody over there knows where to look fer ya daddy…alright? Well, ya'll play in yonder in the waitin room till I finish up here." Miss Alma told us while she shuffled some papers on her desk.

There was a race to the water fountain with Ed Earl in the rear cause of his handicap. We discovered they too had an indoor toilet and we all took several turns there as well. I had noticed that I had gotten taller when I caught a glimpse of my reflection in the long mirror hanging on the back of the restroom door. It reflected a much larger and clearer image than the aged and weathered side rearview mirrors Daddy had salvaged from the bus to use for his shaving.

Myrtle Riley's mirrors hung too high for me to see myself in. Other than store front glass on those occasional trips to town, my reflection before that time might have only been found in the deep spots in the creek or lake. Those places provided for me small glimpses of the progress in growth and changes in my appearance over my first ten years of life.

As I stood staring at the skinny girl in the mirror and though I resembled my siblings, it was as if I was looking at somebody else I had never seen before. I had seldom wondered what other people saw when they looked at me. It was at that point that I became self-conscious and aware that I even had an appearance. No wonder folks would stare back, if they saw what I was seeing in my own reflection. Before me stood the image of a skinny, snagged toothed, red faced, shaggy haired, skinned up girl in bad need of a bath.

Earldean came and stood next to me and I couldn't get over how much we looked alike, only she was slightly taller and was proud of the fact that the mirror proved it.

We admired the haircuts we had given each other only days before, when Mama first got sick. She had been lying down all day and we got bored having to stay close to home watching the little ones. By the time she found out, she felt too bad to yell at us.

She had done her best to keep it neat and the ends trimmed with a dull pair of scissors. Part of her daily routine was to tie it back or braid it for us. She had started teaching us how to braid our own but we thought short hair would be easier to keep. Daddy took pride in our long hair but now that it was shorter it had more curls and less tangles so that it didn't hurt as bad to brush and was a lot cooler to wear.

Learline and Ed Earl stepped up in front us for a quick look at themselves and the cuts we had given them too. We were so pitiful looking…just a mess! At the time we were too ignorant to know the difference or perhaps too tired to care as we made fun of ourselves and each other. We stood for a while making exaggerated faces back at the mirror and doing what comes natural to people when they are momentarily "care free" and see something funny…we laughed!

Alma didn't seem to mind at all when the younger ones started up with their repeated flushing but Earldean took advantage of her rank in age and size and insisted they stop.

I was starting to shiver from the coldness and wished I had something to cover my skin. I didn't know a person could get goose bumps in the summertime but I sure had them that day. We were not accustomed to the cool inside air and our fingers and toes were growing colder by the minute. We didn't want to complain as it was better than the heat outside.

Instead, we all found a warmer spot on the floor by the front windows where the warmer afternoon sun filtered through some sheer white fabric.

While we made ourselves comfortable there, we looked through the brightly colored magazines. About that same time we heard a loud noise that scared us into each others arms bumping and scratching our now sensitive, burned skin. It sounded much like a spoon hitting a pot lid repeatedly and real fast. It stopped for a second than rang out again when we heard Alma say, *"Hello?"*

We ran to see that she was holding a phone receiver to her ear. *"Hay Doc, Glad you called…That colt come yet? Good…good, listen…there's some kids over here…one of um a patient…they've got a situation…well… I'm not quite sure what to do with um yet…"* She went on talking while we went back to playing.

We had seen pay phones when we went to town and had asked Mama about them. She let us hold the receiver to one once and told us how they were used. First you have to have a nickel to put in the slot and then you have to know the phone number to the person you are calling.

She attempted to explain how they worked but it was too hard to comprehend. It still is! We had heard one ringing once outside the Five and Dime store when we were there waiting on our parents to come out but forgot how it sounded until then.

We had gone to town with Daddy before and waited in the truck when he had to make a call. I think he had to call somebody about a job or something. When she finished with her call, Alma asked us to pick up the magazines and stack them back on the short legged table she referred to as a "coffee table". Of course, we had to ask why it was called it that. And, though they didn't serve coffee there that's what it was supposed to be used for.

She turned off a switch on the wall that stopped the cool air from moving around and it got real quiet. She walked past doors and turned off light switches and with each one it got even quieter. Even the hum of the magic water box, hanging on the wall, had automatically shut itself off as we followed her to the glass door where she flipped the last two light switches.

We stood there for a moment in total silence realizing we had not been aware of the noise we had walked in to. Alma reached and turned the open sign around to the other side to where it read the word "closed".

The little bell over the doorway jingled as the door was pulled past it.

As we stepped out of the clinic the heat from the afternoon tried to take our breath away, bringing us back to reality and reminding us it was still summer.

With the hot sun stinging our blistered skin, we watched closely as Alma fumbled with some keys that locked the glass door then checked it with a push. Yet another "first time" thing to see that day.

9
GETTING A BITE TO EAT

I shooed away the fly that kept after my face as we crawled into the booth at the café, located just across the street from the corner of the Whisper Ridge Health Clinic. We had hardly settled in our seats before a young, enthusiastic, blond teenager approached us carrying a tray of glasses filled with ice water. Her presentation was entertaining to say the least as she spun the round tray of glasses from above her shoulder, bringing it to rest on the edge of the table. With a sweet tone in her voice, both highs and lows, she greeted us with words that sounded as though they could have been mistaken for a song.

"Welcome to the Eat-a-Bite! My name is Debbie and I'll be your waitress!"

She was about the happiest person we had come across all day with a big smile and the whitest teeth I'd ever seen. I just couldn't keep my eyes off of her as she went about her business of setting the water glasses down without spilling a drop. Then, in an orderly fashion, she placed one in front of each of us and followed suite in the distribution of gifts that were wrapped in soft white papers; all maneuvers that indicated this girl had a plan of action.

We wiggled around with delight because we hadn't seen ice cubes in the summertime since Denby left and were excited about getting that treat. We tore the paper from the wrapped gifts only to find eating utensils, but we were none the less happy about the idea of a "present" to celebrate our very first restaurant dining experience.

"Will ya'll be needin menus or...are you here fer afternoon ice-cream?" she asked.

Alma leaned in toward her like she didn't want anybody else to hear her, and said in a soft voice, *"Don't worry with the menus, Deb, I know that thang by heart."*

Then sitting up real straight, she cleared her throat and spoke a bit louder, *"These kids are hungry...so, bring us four grill cheese sandwiches and...four orders of French fried tatters will do just fine, thank ya!"*

The charming young waitress' hair was pulled up in a pony tail and fastened with a pretty clip that sparkled as she moved about conscientiously achieving her tasks.

"Okie-doke, Mizz Alma...let me git this down fer ya..."

She held the tray under her armpit while she reached into her apron pocket to pull out a small pad of paper that she flipped open. Patting her pockets, she searched for her pencil before finding it stuck behind her ear.

"*...That was five GC's and five fries, right?*" she asked as she wrote on her pad then stopped to count the number of people in our booth.

"*Naww...well...yea...better make it five of each...incase I get caught up with these kids...don't wanna miss my supper...And, it looks like we'll need more napkins...they have torn these to shreds!*"

"*Okie-doke. I'll git this order in right away for ya Mizz Alma!*" she said with a big smile as she tore the top sheet from the pad then turned to leave.

I remember thinking how charming she was to look at. I watched her as she walked away with her pony tail swaying from side to side, keeping time with each lively step.

Alma, in the meantime, was explaining to us about how you aren't supposed to play at the table with knives, forks or spoons. She repeatedly had to ask us to set them back down in place when we would tap them on the table.

In a matter of seconds, Ed Earl had figured out the trick of flipping his fork in mid air by slamming his fist down on the pronged end of it. It took several ties but I showed him how I could do a double flip by doing the same thing to my spoon.

Learline made use of her knife when she attempted to stab holes in the plastic tablecloth but Ed Earl showed her how she could achieve her goal faster by simply sawing along the table ledge with the serrated end of it.

It wasn't until baby sister had almost poked her brother's eye out trying to get her knife back from him that Alma decided she'd have us turn in our weapons. Earldean, who had already tucked her set into the bed roll for safe keeping, was saddened to find out these gifts were not for keeps.

The two younger ones grew restless in the excruciating long wait it took to grill cheese. How quickly they diminished all options of things to do in the marginally small space they shared with Alma on their side of the booth.

Ed Earl was catching the water droplets from the moisture that had accumulated on the sides of the water glass, while Learline had pulled up to the top of the table trying to lick the side of hers. She was just about to knock it over when Alma caught it, saying to her, *"No-no hun…be careful!"*

Then, pulling her back down to her seat, she assisted her with a drink. *"Deb forgot to give us some straws."* she said. *"That's Trudy's niece. She's tryin to teach her the business so's she can pass it on to her one day…on account Trudy ain't got no youngins of her own…she never settled…works all time! Well, bless her heart, I know Debbie's still in training but if she's trying so hard to get a big tip…she needs to remember to offer a straw!"*

"What we gonna do wit straw?" Ed Earl asked with a puzzled look.

"A straw? Well, that way we aint gotta drink straight out the glass that other people's had theys mouth on. I've learnt a whole bunch about germs workin in a doctor's office and sometimes… they might not get them glasses clean enough. A straw, I think, is safer!" she informed him.

I don't know if he got the answer he was looking for but I pictured in my mind some kind of pine straw or dried grasses that had a medicinal purpose. I just assumed we'd have to chew on it to keep from getting sick like animals do sometimes.

I looked up to see a tall, thin lady walking toward us. I'm not sure if she looked tall because she was so thin or if she was thin looking because she was so tall. Either way, she was as high up there as any *man* I had ever seen. One of the things that may have given her some of her height was the way she wore her orange colored hair piled high on top of her head. I just knew she was the Coca-Cola lady come to life! She had to be the woman that posed for the picture on our thermometer back home, only she looked somewhat older now and her hair had a little deeper tint to it.

She had on a white shift dress with a red apron just like the waitress, Debbie. She too was all smiles as she headed our way. I saw that she was still chewing her food and assumed that she must not have been through eating her meal.

"You eatin a little late today aren't cha Alma?" she asked as made her way toward us.

She turned and waved bye to a fellow who was on his way out, pushed his chair back close to the table then approached our booth placing a small stack of white paper napkins in front of Alma.

"Debbie said you requested these…Who'z these little folks ya have wit cha?... Hey Hunny!" she continued still chewing and smiling as she bent over a little to make eye contact with Learline.

"Hey Trudy! Ya'll this is Trudy…my best friend in the whole wide world! She owns this outfit and is a very successful business person here in Whisper Ridge." Alma stated proudly with her opened hand stretched out toward this woman in awarding her such high honors.

"Oh Alma! It's good customers like you that make this place what it is!" she said as she leaned over and put her arm around Alma's shoulder.

Well, that explains it, I thought…Miss Alma is so big because she wants to help her friend out by buying all this food from her. It must be nice to have a real friend like that!

She introduced us by name to Trudy and told her what little she knew about our situation including the part about Granny Pane having to leave and tend to her grumpy old man's supper.

Trudy stood there with her hands on her hips half cocked, still chewing and listening intently. Her head was shaking back and forth in disbelief, as if to show off her sparkly earbobs that were catching and reflecting the lowering sun through the window. Her lips looked as though they were perfectly painted on her face in a very healthy red that matched her apron. Curiously, I watched her stretch them around to one side then the other causing her chin to move in small circles. Trying hard to get a look at what she was eating, I wondered if she could be gnawing on some of that straw that Alma talked about.

Earldean squeezed my knee under the table in order to distract me from my staring at this fascinating lady. I jumped back, startled and asked her what she did that for. She shot me one of her glaring looks then stretched her eyes open to let me know she had caught me gawking again.

I huffed, and then sat back in the seat with my arms folded to pout. I didn't like her bossing me around and wanted her to know it. I sat there thinking of all kinds of things to say to set her straight, but not wanting to attract attention to myself, I decided not to make an ordeal out of it.

I shooed away a couple of flies from around my eyes. It triggered the memory of me shooing the flies away from my mother, then pulling the sheet over her face, just before we left. I closed my eyes and shook my head, trying to shake free the image from my thoughts. I didn't want to start crying again.

"Poor little thangs and just look at them sunburns…well if that ain't just a rotten cherry on top of a scoop a bad luck! And, for old man Pane to come up in

there, spitin anna sputterin like he done…he ortta been shot! He'za ole crazy nut! Probably skered these youngins half ta death!" Trudy responded when Alma finished filling her in.

"Well Alma…what cha'll gonna do?" she asked with concern in her eyes.

"Well, I told Doc these kids had to be fed as part of their tendin to…they ain't had much to eat in about a week with their Mama bein sick n' all. He was ok with me sewing up the boy under the circumstances but he wanted to take a look at my needle work and see how I done. He would like to see me go through nursin school but…I don't know who he would get to help out at the clinic whiles't I 'z gone." Alma told her.

"Well, He would have to pay ya a heepin more money to go all out like that. I'd sure miss ya while you'z off schoolin. I'd be afrade you would get a better payin job in one them big hospital buildins in the city and never wanna come back ta Whisper Ridge…a lotta young folks do that ya know?" Trudy assumed.

"OH Trudy! For one thing…I hardly think thirty one is young, besides, I have roots here! I can't possibly leave this place. I'd be lost in the city. Naw…I aint gowin nowhere. We're just yalkin bout it, that's all. And, ya know what? I'm not just gonna go off and leave my best friend. I'd never find another'n like ya…you know that!"

Trudy bent down cheek to cheek and squeezed Alma's shoulders with another big hug to show her adoration in return. Alma patted the back of her friend's hand sealing her promise she'd just made. Trudy squeezed her eyes shut to restrain her sentimental tears.

"I truly want what's best for you, Alma…I'd just miss ya is all!"

I must have been mesmerized by those earbobs again, unaware that my mouth was hanging wide open. About that time, a fly flew in there and landed before I realized what had happened.

I huffed and spit several times before he came out. When he did, he spun around and tried to get back in. I swatted and swung at it, knocking my glass over. In spite of my attempt, there was very little I could do to stop it when the contents spilled everywhere! Thank goodness I didn't have much water left, however, for a split second my greatest concern was that I just blew my one and only chance to eat ice cubes in almost four years!

But then, I realized that was the least of my worries for I became aware of the mess I had just made. I instantly recalled the consequences of such actions that I had suffered before at the likes of one Myrtle Riley.

Embarrassed and scared, not knowing how these women would react, I grabbed my crotch in attempt to keep from losing the contents of my full bladder and further humiliating myself. I could feel my heart beating fast and loud as I squeezed tight and prepared myself for what I had coming to me.

Earldean, Alma and Trudy flew in to catch the spinning crystals from falling to the floor. It all happened so fast but things were in slow motion for me as I couldn't think of what to do next.

Trudy quickly grabbed up the stack of napkins and dabbed them across the water that was running toward the edge.

Alma set the unbroken glass back upright and with Earldean's assistance, proceeded to drop the cubes back into it. I scrambled around to help but the ice kept slipping out of my hands, sliding further away, causing me to be even more fidgety!

Noticing my nervousness, Trudy wiped her hands on her apron then patted my shoulder. Her fingers were cold and it stung a little, I think she forgot about my sunburn, but she meant well, as she said, *"Now honey, don't you worry yourself none! It was an accident…those pesky flies will drive you crazy. Let's get you something else to drink. How bout it… y'all wanna coke?*

"Coke...you mean like Coca-Cola?" Earldean asked excitedly.

"That't right!" she answered.

I was convinced then, by her offering that particular drink, she was indeed the orange haired lady on that thermometer back in Chinquapin Hollow!

"I don't know if I have enough money for drinks too, Trudy…unless you let me put it on my tab." Alma told her.

"Oh Alma…your money's no good here today, let me git this…I wanna help… it's the least I can do. I'll get those drinks and check on your order." Trudy said stuffing the wet napkins in the glass before she carried it off to the kitchen.

"...And more napkins please!" Alma requested loudly as Trudy walked away.

"Napkins…you got it!" she replied

When Debbie returned with our drinks, Alma got some straws from her and showed us how to use them. Surprisingly enough, with little mishap, we found it fun to drink that way even though the bubbles burned the inside of our noses.

Learline had to have lots of help to keep from tipping hers over so Alma spent most of her time tending her. We got tickled watching her eyes water after every sip.

Before we knew it Debbie was coming toward our booth with our food and wearing a big, stiff smile. She had not yet learned to manage five plates so Trudy had followed behind her with the overload. The aroma of freshly prepared food raced before them and I found myself trying to compare it to the familiar scents of Mama's cooking. Indeed this smelled appetizing and I couldn't wait to try it! But, for the life of me, I couldn't imagine how they would grill the cheese without it melting away into the hot fire. At any rate, I was looking forward to seeing the miraculous results.

Having been deprived of such pleasures before, it was that very day, at that moment, that I would learn to appreciate the art of fine dining.

During the brief interlude, I was spellbound by the presentation as I watched this delightfully orchestrated performance take place. Each and every plate of evenly proportioned food was set before us in the exact same way, keeping a level pace, even space and smooth grace. Atop of each plate sat a sandwich made of warm, brown laced bread that had been cut diagonally so that it exposed the melted cheese slightly oozing from its covering. It hinged open from the top corners so that it cradled a pile of golden fried potatoes that were cut in a peculiar way.

My first instinct was to applaud to show my appreciation for the entertainment but when I started clapping with such giddiness, I think it was mistaken for gratitude of the food itself….of which I was…but it was so much more than that!

"You youngins really are hungry aren't you…poor little thangs. How long has it been since you've had a good hot meal?"

Well the answer was obvious when they saw we were too busy to reply. In fact, Mama would have been ashamed of us for being so rude. We just dug right in without even saying a prayer of thanks over this food!

Learline couldn't reach the table very well, so she kept coming up on her knees before Trudy rescued her with a cute little chair called a booster seat.

We had a wonderful first time experience of eating grilled cheese sandwiches for they were a big hit with our taste buds as well as our hunger pangs. We had never seen fried potatoes in crinkle cuts like that before and we watched Alma dip each one of hers in fancy ketchup before she ate them. Ed Earl was the first to ask if he could try it. She found it hard to believe we had never had ketchup before, which led into a series of questions about a number of things.

After we told her how old we were, she wanted to know how girls our age didn't know our last name and how we got by with that in school. She was surprised to hear that we had our schooling at home and had never been visited by a Truancy Officer from the county. We weren't sure what she was talking about but told her we didn't have many visitors out there where we lived.

She was asking about our mother, wanting to know some of the symptoms she had so that she could tell the doctor.

Having heard us mention the subject, Learline started whining for her Mama. Alma turned her attention to the two year old, putting her arm around her in an effort to comfort her. Instead, she must have rubbed against her sunburn because Learline let out a blood curdling scream that alarmed the whole place.

This sent Debbie and Trudy rushing over to see what the commotion was all about.

"I must have hurt her sunburn!" Alma explained.

"I'm so sorry sweetie…Alma didn't mean to hurt cha!" she told her as she worked herself out of the tight fitting booth to give room for the help to get in.

Trudy reached in and pulled the baby from the booster seat, scraping her burnt legs on the table edge, which turned the crying into total hysteria!

By this time several of the other customers came over to see if there was anything they could do. You could hardly hear what anyone was saying, over the earsplitting racket she was making as several of them did their best to calm her down.

She was crying so hard that she lost her breath, turning her red face into an odd shade of purple. The chatter from the people crowded around her tapered off when the screaming went silent, leaving them all waiting to see if she was going to come back at all. Trudy was bouncing her around, yelling, *"Somebody do somthin! She ain't breathin!"* when Alma reached over and grabbed Learlines' face and pulled it close to hers. She blew a quick puff of air from her mouth into Learlines' face…but nothing…she still had not taken a breath.

I climbed to my feet, standing on the bench of the booth to be able to see over the crowd what might be happening to her. I could see Learline's discolored face, taut with fear and panic struggling to take in air. Her hands were clutched over the top of Alma's hands, trying to pull them away, not realizing that Alma was there to help her. She cut her eyes in my direction and caught a glimpse of me, peering over Debbie's shoulder, when Alma blew another hard, quick gust of air into her face. Caught off guard, she bucked back as the sound of air struggled to get in the collapsed airways.

Finally, after what seemed like forever, she caught enough air to let out a little cry…then a cough…then another…then broken sobs that ended with a wail. "*MAMAAAA!*"

Everyone was so glad to see her breathe that they broke into applause. We had never heard that many people clap at the same time and were amused at the sound of it. Learline benefited from it the most, as the applause had distracted her from her crying…but only for the moment. When she realized that all eyes were on her, she scanned the crowd to look for the familiar face she had spotted seconds earlier…mine.

"SASSEEE-HE-HE!" she whined, as her arms stretched out for me to rescue her. My heart went out to her as did my arms, when Debbie stepped aside to let me through to her.

"Aweee…she wants her sister!" Trudy said as she passed Learline off to me, noticing her apron was damp and a puddle was on the floor at her feet. It was at that point that we realized she was also in need of dry britches.

Earldean took the bed roll where she kept the extra set of clothes and followed us, as Debbie led the way to a restroom. Learline cried with exhaustion from lack of sleep as well as suffering through the disrobing of her dirty clothes. The ammonia from the urine stung her raw blistered skin as her wet shorts were drawn over it.

The clothes from the day before were all we had to put on her, in spite of the fact that they were soured and slightly damp. Debbie wet some paper towels and tried to lay them across Learlines' sore legs but she wouldn't have it. After a several attempts, Debbie excused herself as she had to get back to her tables.

I tried everything I could to sooth Learlines' pain but it was to no avail. She was one miserable child and didn't care if the whole world knew it. After a long spell of sympathy I gave up and left Earldean sitting alone with her on the cool tile floor.

When I returned to our booth Ed Earl was alone, up on his knees, dipping his fingers in a blob of ketchup and then licking them. He had finished off Learlines' fries and didn't have anything left to dip but fingers.

The table had been cleared and wiped with the exception of Learline's empty plate and a half a glass of coke on ice. The puddle on the floor was gone. There were two men sitting on stools at the counter, still drinking coffee. Trudy was ringing up an elderly lady at the register and the rest of the customers had finished up and cleared out.

I turned to find Alma sitting at another table with a man whose back was to me so that I couldn't see his face. It wasn't until she nodded and waved at me that he turned around to see me standing there.

He must have come in while I was in the restroom with Learline because I didn't remember seeing him in there before. I turned away so as not to stare and climbed into the booth in time to hear Ed Earl slurping around on the bottom of the glass, indicating he had finished off the rest of the Coke.

I sat, enjoying the uneventful moment of peace and quiet, as I looked about, taking in the different sounds and smells of the Eat-A-Bite. I let my eyes absorb the bright cheerful colors scattered about the café. The red checkered window toppers matched the red checkered, vinyl table cloths that were stapled to the tops of all the tables. On top of each, was a green vase that held a single white plastic daisy.

The bench seats in the booths were covered in solid red plastic that was worn out in choice places. There were eight chrome framed tables that had matching chairs with padded seats of shiny, red marbled vinyl.

On the walls without windows hung posters advertising soda pops; like Chocolate Soldier, 7up, Orange and Grape Nehi…and of course, Coke-Cola. Plate glass windows covered the top half of the wall across the front of the café, letting in plenty of indirect light. They reminded me of the many windows on the bus only these were much bigger. I thought about how Mama liked to tie up the homemade curtains to let in the light and how she might would like how these windows were dressed.

The café was located on Main Street in the heart of town. Out the window, from the booth I was in, I could see down Laurel Street, where a big three dimensional sign with a face of a smiling pig was raised high in front of The Piggly Wiggly Grocery…it was the same smiling pig face printed on the side of the sack we had lost along the way that contained our mother's Bible.

I closed my eyes and prayed for God to help us find it so Mama wouldn't be disappointed in us…if she was able to be disappointed.

Seeing the familiar icon made me realize that in order for us to have had a paper sack from this place, Daddy must have shopped there before.

Looking out on to the street at the different buildings, I wondered if Daddy might be working inside one of them. I didn't remember town looking like this but I had never seen it from the view of the Café. To me, everything I looked at was different as I was not accustomed to being on the inside looking out.

By late in the afternoon there seemed to be more vehicles weaving their way around the buildings making their way down Main Street.

I found myself searching among them for Daddy's old red truck but all I could see were strangers that I had never seen before. I had no idea the world had this many people in it as I counted close to fifty cars. I wondered where they could all be going in such a hurry.

At any rate, I was glad to be out of that traffic and in the cool air of the café where I was beginning to feel a little safe with these friendly ladies. From a distance I could see Trudy chatting with a customer who was working her way toward the door. I couldn't make out what they were saying but their laughter carried across the room. I watched as Debbie picked up some change from a table she was cleaning and dropped it in her apron pocket. She had a cheerful smile on her face as she finished that task.

Two men at the counter were having coffee and carried on with the cook who conversed with them through a big opening on the other side. He must have told a funny joke or something, because at one point, they busted out into knee slapping laughter.

After the lady left, Trudy walked over and picked up the coffee pot and gave refills to the coffee drinkers. She carried the pot over to the table where Alma and the gentleman were sitting and sipping a cup.

I was wondering if we should get on with our search for Daddy when about that time Alma leaned out and motioned for me to come over to where she was. I took Ed Earl by his sticky hand, getting ketchup all over me too. Letting go, I wiped it off on my shirt while he licked the rest off of his fingers. As we approached their table, the man turned out toward us, resting his arm on the back of his chair. His salt and pepper colored hair was thin and was combed over the top of his head from one ear to the other. His eyes were a nice shade of blue and were magnified behind his wire rimmed glasses that rested on his fleshy nose. The hair on his face grew only over the top of his eyes in one straight, thick line. The rest of his face was smooth. His teeth were perfectly arranged behind his thin lips, giving him a pleasant smile.

"Hello, you must be Ed Earl" he said as he held out his hand for a shake. *"How do you do? My name is Hank Murphy."*

Ed Earl stepped back and put his hands behind his back.

"DOCTOR Hank Murphy…Ed Earl, this is Doc, I told you about him remember? It's ok…he wants to shake your hand!" Alma assured him.

Ed Earl looked at me and asked, *"Like Denby?"*

"Who's Denby?" Alma asked.

"He's our friend." I said. *"Denby says if a feller offers a handshake, that theyz offerin friendship and you should shake on it...It's alright...go'on, Ed Earl…Shake his hand."*

When he stuck out his hand again, Ed Earl obliged him with a firm six year old handshake followed by a snagged tooth grin. Doc smiled back and didn't seem to mind Ed Earl's sticky fingers. He then turned and offered me a handshake with a smile asking if my name was Earldean.

"Naw, I'm Sassy!" I corrected him. *"Earldean is my bigger sister but I'm pert 'near big as her!*

"Pardon me Sassy, you're such a tall young lady I thought you might be the oldest." Doc said apologetically.

Ed Earl thought it was funny that Doc thought I was a lady but I was flattered.

I was standing close enough to him to notice he had recently had a bath with soap. It was nice that he smelled like Ivory soap with a back note of fresh coffee.

He pushed out a chair from the table with his foot and offered it to Ed Earl asking him if he could take a peek at his stitches but he seemed more concerned with our sunburns.

Trudy offered some ointment she had for burns she kept in the kitchen for the cooks, but Doc said we needed to clean the skin before we sealed the burns with ointment so that the bacteria wouldn't set in and make us sick.

I thought about Mama getting sick and wondered if it was from sunburn. Her skin was hot to touch but she looked pale, not red like us.

I wondered if we were going to get sick and die too. Maybe we should have given Mama a sponge bath, I thought, so nothing would set in.

"They could defiantly use a bath and some clean clothes!" Alma said

"Do ya'll have any clean clothes witcha?" Trudy asked us.

"We still have a clean pair of drawers and a pair a shorts fer Ed Earl, but Learline done dirtied up hers…they stank purdy bad too! We didn't thank we'd be gone this long, so didn't brang none fer me n' Earldean." I told them.

"How long did it take you to git here?" Trudy asked.

"We left yesterdee n' walked a long ways till we got to Huey's house…his Granny gave us a ride to the Clinic." I said.

"…An I got blisters and Alma toll me I ought not wear my new shoes fer a while." Ed Earl added. *"They're pank! Mama gave um to me… fer walkin!"*

"Alma tells me your mother is sick. Was she too sick to drive to the Clinic?" Doc asked.

"Mama got sick…she caint git up! She don't drive none no how…Just Daddy." Ed Earl informed him.

"Does your mother know you came here to look for your Daddy?" Alma asked.

"I already toll ya Alma…at's how come her ta give me em pank shoes!" Ed Earl snapped at Alma. I knew he was tired and uncomfortable but I couldn't believe he talked to her in that tone of voice after all she had done for us.

"Ed Earl! Shame on ya! You aint got ta be so sassy! You ought not ta be talking atta way ta Ms. Alma. She's our new friend!"

Ed Earl turned away in shame when Alma forgivingly said, *"That's ok, sometimes friends git tard, ya know?"*

"Well maybe we need to find your father so he can get you back home and get you cleaned up. Your mother is going to be worried sick if you are out after dark.

I've got to get ready for the supper rush." Trudy said as she turned to walk away.

"Did you stay the night at Huey's house last night" Doc asked as he leaned in with half of his brow raised.

"Naw, we slept off the roadside when it got dark." I answered him.

Alma gasped and put her hand over her mouth. Trudy stopped in her steps and turned back around and stood there for a second before anyone said anything.

"Ya mean ya'll slept up there in them woods…all by ya'self?"

I was afraid to answer her because by the way they were reacting, it gave me the notion we might be in trouble.

After a bit of silence, Alma sent us off to find our sisters. I think they wanted to talk grown up talk. On our way to the restroom I thought about us being in trouble for making Mama worry. I didn't know a body could get sick from worrying. She worried about us a whole lot. I wondered if that was what made her sick in the first place and if it was contagious.

I *had* been feeling sick at my belly for two days and my throat was sore from that knot that wouldn't go away. If I *had* caught it from taking care of Mama, I wondered if I might have carried it over to all the people we had met.

At this point, they too were starting to look a little worried and could be getting sick from it. This could be a really bad epidemic! I didn't want to get sick like Mama, but if we died, we could be with her and Jesus in Heaven. But then, I thought, we would miss Daddy and when he got off work, he wouldn't know where we were. Then…he would be sick with worry and there wouldn't be anybody left to take care of him till he died! Oh…this was making me feel weak and light headed.

Maybe…I thought…Learline was already sick from it and that's why she couldn't stop crying. Earldine was sure to get it because she sat as close to Mama as I did.

My thoughts were spinning in my head as I pushed on the heavy restroom door.

That loud squeaky noise it made as it opened scared Ed Earl so he hid behind me.

I peeked in to see Earldean sitting on the floor, leaning against the wall with her eyes closed and her arms hung loosely out beside her. Laid out across her legs was our baby sister's limp body. At first I thought they were asleep but they didn't even flinch when the door made that shrill racket.

They were so still that I could clearly see from where I was that they weren't breathing…it was too late!

I gasped and covered my eyes for I didn't want to look at them and I didn't want my little brother to see them like that. So, I quickly turned and blocked his view, backing him out the door.

"Don't go in there Ed Earl…They're Dead!" I screamed. Fretfully I shook his shoulders and announced the dreaded truth of the matter *'We all are gonna die!"*

I started feeling dizzy and could barely make out Ed Earls fading face through my blurring eyesight.

Now…something inside me let me know it was my turn…I'd be the next to go.

What started out as a slight ringing in my ears grew into a loud rush of white noise. Deep in the center of it all, I could hear the sound of my mother's voice calling me home. As my knees began to buckle underneath me, I could feel myself falling to the floor but was too weak to fight it any more. I closed my eyes and gave in to it so that I could die peacefully and be with Mama.

On my way to Heaven I could hear Ed Earl trying to call me back. *"SAAASEEeeeeee!"*

Then…It was over…I too was dead.

10
LIFE AFTER DEATH

It was as white as new fallen snow as far as I could see in any direction. It seemed to go on and on forever! Up, down or side to side it didn't matter how hard I strained my eyes, I just couldn't see an end to it. There were no extraordinary, brilliant colors like I expected, just white…plain ole white.

I had started to feel a little disappointed and forgot where I was going and why I had to go there until I heard singing across the way. I looked all around but I still couldn't see anything. I listened closely to the sweet notes of the prettiest voice I had ever heard as it carried me through the air.

I recognized it as the voice of Jesus Christ himself, even though I had never heard it before. I'm pretty sure it was Him…yes, I know it was him! He was singing my favorite song…"Oh, how I Love Jesus" and that's my favorite part of the song too! But…why was He singing a song about Himself…to Himself?

When he finished I could hear Learline saying "Sing it again!" So, He did but this time, after he sang the first verse and started in on the chorus, it started to sound more like Mama's voice. It was still nice, but not as pretty as Jesus singing by Himself.

I could not see them but I was sure they were singing it to Learline. That had been the song Mama would sing to put all of her babies to sleep by. So if Learline made it to heaven, then that meant Earldean must be here too, I thought. I tried to call out to them but I couldn't make the words come out of my mouth. I remember Mama reading in the Bible about how when we get to heaven we would have new bodies. I thought something must have been wrong with the one I got because it didn't work.

I couldn't see or talk…but I could hear!

Maybe I hadn't made it all the way into Heaven yet but I was close enough to hear Mama call out to me…her and Jesus!

They were calling my name over and over. I tried to answer but I couldn't speak! I started to see tiny fragments of muted colors through the thick cloud of whiteness.

I could hear Earldean's voice off in the distance. I turned in every direction but could not see her at all. I had guessed that she must have already passed through those Pearly Gates of Heaven and had been given her new body because her mouth was working.

However…the only words she could say were, *"Sassy! Come on!"* I was trying hard to get there but my legs wouldn't work so I tried to pull myself closer with my arms. My body was heavy and I felt so weak. I didn't know getting to Heaven was going to be this hard. As I struggled, I could see blurs of color fading in and out. I could hear Earldean's voice closer now, calling my name, telling me to come on as more of her words came. *"Sassy! Can you hear me?"*

Yes…I wanted to say…I can hear you…but I just can't get the words to come out of my mouth to let you know!

I strained my eyes to see her but couldn't bring her into focus. I strained my voice again to say *YES*, but still…nothing came out.

Far off to my right, I could see something small and brown coming toward me. It made its way through a thick patch of clouds fading in and out until I recognized what it was. I was happy to see again my little yearling friend from the woods back home. I struggled to hold out my hand to signal for him to come to me. When I managed to do so, he licked my hand and I worked up a smile to let him know how happy it had made me to see him! I had missed him so much and was glad he made it to Heaven. Though his earthly body had been killed and eaten, it was apparent he was given this new one. He stepped toward me and wet my face all over with kisses. It tickled at first but then it started to feel nice, so I just let him lick me again and again. I reached to hug him but he turned and sprinted off back into the clouds. I smiled as I kept an eye on his little white tail as it bound out of sight…just like I used to do when he frolicked back into the woods.

I noticed the singing had started up again as well as the sounds of other voices close by. Before I knew it, I could hardly hear the song over the all the voices that were caught up in different conversations. Some were voices of strangers while others were almost recognizable as I strained to listen to what they were saying to one another.

I heard Earldean telling someone that she had told me to put some water in a mason jar but that I had put the water in Mama's pink sneakers instead. I wondered if it was God she was talking to. I wanted to defend myself so I tried to stretch my mouth open to tell her to stop but I couldn't speak. I wanted to tell her that He knows all things…You can't lie to God, Earldean…He knows the truth!

My heart was saying it but I couldn't get the words pushed out!

I could hear two men loudly discussing the topic of their boat sinking in the lake when one of them forgot to put the plug in. It sounded like Daddy and Denby at first but how could they be in Heaven? They weren't dead yet and besides, those two would never argue.

One was blaming the other about whose fault it was and who caught the most fish. I started to think that it might be Peter and one of those other apostles in the Bible, when they talked about throwing out their nets and catching so many fish saying that's why the boat sank. It sounded like one of them said something about *"Sweet Jesus!"*

Could it be…they were blaming it on Jesus now?

It was hard to tell because I couldn't see who was there but it was a whole bunch of fish because I could smell them!

I wanted to tell them "Make no mistake…That was not a mishap…it was a miracle!"

But still I could not speak!

"Sassy." I could hear Mama saying. *"You are gettin to be a big girl now. You're are a tall young lady…pray without ceasing…and Sassy?...Sassy… where are you?"*

I managed to push out in a whisper, *"I'm here Mama! I caint see ya though…here take my hand so I can feel you Mama."* I reached my hand out into the whiteness to feel for her. I thought I saw her hand and stretched to grab hold of it but it moved away quickly.

"Sassy?" I heard my Mama's voice close to my ear.

"Yes Mama?" I strained to respond to her.

"I love you." Then she came closer to kiss my cheek and when she did, she licked it like my yearling had done. Startled, I turned to see her face but all I saw was the little deer leaping away again, only this time he looked like one of the wet paper towels that Debbie tried to lay across Learlines' sunburn.

As I watched it turn and come right back at me, I flinched when it landed across my face. I reached and pulled it off and I could clearly see Earldean starring me square in the eye!

She was saying to me, *"Sassy…Can you hear me? Sassy…Come on! Sassy, say something!…Please!"*

I stared at her a moment before I said, *"You ought not tell lies, Earldean...God knows!"*

With that I sat up to find myself on the floor of Trudy's Eat-A-Bite, in downtown Whisper Ridge. I was surrounded by people like Earldean, who was wiping my face with a wet paper towel from the restroom, Doc who was sticking something under my nose, Alma and Trudy holding and kissing my hands.

Standing behind them was the cook, two coffee drinkers and Ed Earl.

On a chair at the closest table sat the waitress Debbie holding little Learline. She was swaying and singing to her that song of "Oh How I Love Jesus" and was finishing up with… *"Be-cause-He-first-loved-me."*

11
HAND IN THE COOKIE JAR

Whisper Ridge was living up to its name as the hush of a placid breeze played a symphony on this timbered crest. It chose for its instruments a collection of brick buildings with alleyways and lighted street signs, accompanied by vast variety of thirsty vegetation.

Along with restrained percussions from the various slow moving automobiles, who were abiding by the rules of paved streets, this small hidden town orchestrated subtle sounds of a juicy secret being told.

The cool air off the lake and the sinking sun took the edge off the heat, bringing the mercury down at least twenty degrees.

The town folk were making their way around, celebrating the week's end. Local courtships, young and old, a special occasion of birthday or anniversary participants all took their favorite seats in the Eat-A Bite for the Friday Night Special.

A younger crowd migrated down at the Burger Doodle Drive-In and hung out on picnic tables sipping malts or drinking cherry Cokes.

As the sun hovered low in the western sky, it unfolded a mantle of orange and crimson that highlighted the silhouette of the geometric shaped buildings.

It tinted the sidewalk a ginger hue, casting shadows of our bodies like we've never seen before. They made our legs look as though we were walking on tall stilts as we made our way back over to the clinic.

Alma had a hard time getting us to hurry up and cross the street, as we were still amused by our long legged shadows on the perfectly flat surface.

Horns honked and drivers waved and some just drove by slowly, staring ever so seriously, as we climbed into the back seat of Alma's rusty old Buick, which she proudly kept somewhat clean.

Alma dug around in her handbag for her keys and politely said, *"Now, if ya don't mind, let's not put our feet on the car seat, ok ya'll? I've got to go back inside the office and get some cream for your sunburns. Ya'll wait here and I'll be right back."*

With a slight limp, Ed Earl followed her anyway but she didn't seem to mind. We were settling in the back seat when they promptly returned. With a slight expectation Ed Earl asked, *"I like your car Alma, want me ta sit up front witcha?"*

"Sure, thata be jes fine Ed Earl...I might wantcha ta do that...but don't climb over the seat, go round to the other door...ok? ...alrighty then!" Alma said, glad for the company.

There is a certain kinship you feel toward someone who nurses your wounds. That bond is sealed by sincere appreciation and gratitude.

Now, Ed Earl felt indebted to Alma, for going over and beyond the call of duty of a secretary at a medical clinic. He now wanted to oblige her with his close presence and constant companionship. He, having rapport with her already, felt comfortable enough to do most of the inquiring on our way to Alma's place.

We rode around the back part of town, where we saw large metal buildings with motor boats sitting on trailers lined up in rows. The whole area around it was incased in a tall fence made of cleverly twisted wire.

I wondered why anyone would worry about penning up such things. It wasn't like they were going to take off and run like chickens or goats. This led Ed Earl to his first question. *"What kinna tall wire zat round at their place?"*

"That's called cyclone fencing," Alma said. *"I figgure they got it up there ta keep folks from a totein them boats off down to the lake."*

Ed Earl followed with, *"Well, Alma, at's where boats sposta go! Aint they'z?"*

Alma laughed at his smarts as she answered him, *"Yea, but I reckon ya have ta pay fer it first fore ya pull it down there!"*

"My Daddy might like ta have one em big un's over younder. At there red un's a might purddy...aint it ya'll? Yep, he'd probly like it just fine!" Ed Earl said as he stretched himself looking out the window of the car door.

Then we turned onto a road that winded up the hillside. At its foot we saw white framed houses all lined up in rows on streets. We "oohed" and "aahed" as we had never seen so many houses. There must have been forty to fifty houses stuck close together in a group that Alma called a neighborhood.

That would have been nice if our neighbor Denby had lived that near to us. We could have kept a closer eye on him and maybe he would not of have to gone to live with his sister.

As we traveled up the steep undulating road we saw more homes scattered about the hillside. The higher up we climbed the better we could see in between and over the trees until we came to a clearing overlooking the heart of town. Alma considerately slowed down for Ed Earl's sake. Sitting half turned on the edge of the seat, his arm stretched out the window and his finger pointed in that direction, he said with excitement, *"Hey. Ya'll looky down younder! I see the top of town! See it?"*

"That's right Ed Earl...but you better sit back in that seat, ba-fore you go clear out that door...best scootch over here by me so'z ya won't fall out!" Alma warned him.

"Yea...then I'd have walk the rest the way... huh?" he said responding to her warning.

Alma got tickled and assured him that if he *could* still walk after falling out of the moving car, she would come back after him. However, she would probably get another sewing lesson in with more than just a few stitches.

The light of day hung on for a while after the sun slowly set but it had been dusk long enough to catch the electric lights, twinkling like stars that had fallen from the sky and sprinkled on top of the town.

It was a fascinating experience that was expressed with more mouth opened *"WOW!"s.*

"We're almost there!" Alma said, although it seemed we just got started: it wouldn't be much of a ride. Just a bit further up the road on the left, we came to a wooden sign that hung from two tall posts. Alma turned and drove under the sign that read: Shady Grove Trailer Park.

Up a long driveway, nestled under a small grove of walnut trees, along with nine others just like it, was the home of our new friend.

"Look at all them purdy silver busses!" Ed Earl shouted!

"Naw, hunny, them aint busses, them are mobile homes! Guess which one is mine... go on...ya'll guess!" Alma played.

We all took our guesses, as the excitement of getting to explore a new place, built up inside us. We counted each one until Alma turned in and parked next to the seventh one. She turned off the engine and turned and said, *"Welcome to my humble home...ya'll come on in and sit a spell."*

I thought it was a beautiful home on wheels, with two plastic pink flamingos next to the three steps leading up to the door.

"We got steps at our place, cept theyz on the inside not the outside." Ed Earl said making conversation.

"Is that right?" Alma carried along trying to get in the door and turn on the lights.

"And you got one door. We got two doors that go together." he said as he crossed the threshold.

I think it was at that moment that Alma got the impression that we lived in an elaborate, two story lake home, with a winding staircase just beyond these huge drawing doors at its entrance.

She had started wishing she had gone with Doc instead of offering to bring us kids home with her. She would have loved to tour such a home like that but didn't personally know anybody who lived in one. Well, except Doc, and his home wasn't as big as some of those others she had seen while out on the lake.

But that would have to be another time. Doc thought it best that us kids be bathed and treated for our sunburn pain. Back at Trudy's, they had agreed we had been through too much for children our age and were in need of attention. It sounded to them like our mother was not in any condition to take care of us anyway, so Doc agreed to ride out and check on her and pick up some clean clothes for us. If she was as bad off as it sounded then it might be days before she would be able to resume her chores of motherhood and housekeeping.

He had asked if one of them were willing to keep us for the night or until they could locate our father.

Trudy had the Friday night rush about to come in and was already running behind in getting prepared. Even though she had only one bedroom, Alma volunteered.

When Doc asked Earldean for directions he didn't tell her what he needed them for or she might have told him that it was too late for Mama now.

It wasn't until he had already gone that Trudy and Alma told us of their plans. We didn't know what to say that would make it right so that he wouldn't go all the way out there for no reason. We had not had a chance to say anything to any of the grownups with Ed Earl or Learline around all day.

Deep down inside I hoped that we might have been wrong about Mama. Given the circumstances of the afternoon, she could just be unconscious or maybe she was just sleeping real sound. Deep down inside I had hoped that Doc could make her come around to feeling better; like he did for me.

In the back seat, on the ride to Alma's, Earldean and I had exchanged secrets about what we knew and what we were going to do. Alma had been nice to us but didn't we know her enough to stay overnight with her without permission from our parents. We had never had to ask permission to stay anywhere else before. We were still none the wiser after all the whispering.

Looking back, I wonder what Alma must have thought of us standing there in amazement, in the middle of her living room, looking all around at how well everything was lit up at night. I didn't understand a whole lot about electricity but I knew it was brighter than batteries or candles. Denby had electricity and so did the Riley's but we were never anywhere at night to appreciate how bright a light bulb could be after sunset.

The most amazing thing to me was when Alma went over and turned the knob on a big contraption that stuck through the kitchen window. The whole place started vibrating with a low drone as air moved about the room. Within forty five minutes the entire six hundred square feet was chilled to a nice cool seventy five degrees.

During that time Alma had drawn two rounds of tepid bathwater. Earldean had taken Learline into the tub with her, so that she could assist her with a shampooing. Ed Earl went next, convencing Alma he was big enough to bathe himself. She had to ask him several times to stop splashing around before he soaked the floor. She was not surprised to see mud running down from behind his ears and his hair plastered to his head and still smelling like a wet dog when came out of the bathroom.

He did at least step out with a towel wrapped around him this time, he usually just liked to drip dry.

Earldean and Learline were spinning and dancing around the living room to a song on the radio, wearing oversized shirts that Alma said she had out grown.

"I wanna play! I want one em dance shirts…can I have one too, Alma?" Ed Earl asked.

"Got one for you right here sweetie and one for you too Sassy." she said, handing us each a clean garment. *"I'll get your bath ready for you in a minute, let me just get a wash cloth after your brothers ears first."* Alma said to me.

"That's ok Alma. I watched how you did it before so I can get it by myself." I told her.

"Ed Earl forgot to shampoo his hair…you won't forget now will you?"

I shook my head no as she reached and got me a dry towel and mopped up the floor with the towels my sisters had used. I plugged the tub and filled it with water from both the hot and cold faucets. I turned the cold off first leaving the hot to scald my sunburn. Alma rushed to the door when I screamed out in pain, asking if I was ok. She helped me adjust the water and I settled in the tub for a soak and shampoo. It was so refreshing and enjoyable that I didn't want to get out. When I finally did, I dried off, put on my big shirt and joined the others in the living room.

Alma was dressing Ed Earl's stitches worried that they were starting to pull. He might have been a little rough splashing around in the tub.

Learline was walking around looking at things in Alma's living room and asking questions about everything she saw. She didn't have the what-nots Myrtle Riley kept but it was just enough to make it cozy. Alma mostly had pictures of people hanging on the wall and sitting about the room.

Earldean was washing out our dirty clothes in the kitchen sink and when Alma finished with Ed Earl, she went to help out with the clothes ringing. We hung them by wire hangers over the tub to drip dry.

Alma then painted us up with the cream for our sunburns and it gave us some relief.

We pulled up to her snack bar and visited with her while she made us fried baloney with scrambled eggs on top of a piece of toast made with white bread from the store. Store bread was a real treat for us as the only time we got to eat it was when we went to town or Daddy would bring back an occasional loaf, when he had the money for it.

Alma made remarks about us being funny little kids and how we were wearing her out. She said she was from a big family and was used to being around a lot of children but seeing as she had never married she didn't have any of her own.

She told us that she was the oldest of seven children, three brothers and three sisters, and that they all had grown up right there in Whisper Ridge. Most of them were still there, married with families of their own except her youngest two brothers, one of which was in the service and the other who had drowned in a boating accident when he was sixteen.

Her being the oldest, she had helped her mother take care of her younger siblings. She later went back to help her father take care of her mother after she had a stroke. Alma told us her mother never got over her brother's death and suffered with heartache for such a long time that she was eat up with grief and worry.

"A body cain't take that kinda stress for too long before it will cause ya ta have a stroke, then ya cain't do nothing but just lay there." Alma was saying as she gazed at the floor in deep thought.

"Did Sassy have a stroke, Alma? Is that why she just laid there and wouldn't move?" Earldean asked her.

"No hun…she fainted. Doc said it was probably from too much sun and goin too long without water and food…then takin it in so much too fast like she done. She's gonna be alright now. Every one of ya'll could use a good nights sleep. You'll feel much better in the morning."

She spread out some blankets on the floor for us to sleep on, and tried to settle us down for a good nights sleep.

Learline started crying for Mama which set off a chain reaction in us all. Alma sat on the couch and carefully pulled baby sister up into her lap trying not to scratch her sunburn.

"What does your Mama do to get her to sleep?" she asked.

"First she reads from the Bible, then we say our prayers, then she sings us a song." I said. *"But we lost Mama's Bible."*

Alma opened a drawer in the table next to the couch and reached in and pulled out a red book and said, *"I have one right here."* It looked different from the ones Mama and Daddy had but she assured us that it read the same.

It wasn't that unusual for us not to understand all of what was being read to us but the familiar thee's and thou's were comforting enough to help us relax.

Alma, like Mama, would do her best to explain the hard parts in her own words. It was interesting to me that, though she just opened it up at random, she came to this particular reading that was about life after death. After all I had been through in dealing with the idea of Mama being dead and, more recent, what had happened to me that very afternoon, it was comforting to know there was hope.

According to what she read to us that night, we are promised to have a life beyond this one here on earth that is far greater, or worse. She clarified that the choice is up to us as to which one we picked. Personally, I could not comprehend why anyone would want to choose the latter but according to Alma, some folks do. She said it was because they just get tired and give up. Then they don't care anymore what happens to them or anybody else for that matter. It almost sounded like a kind of selfish thing. How does somebody just quit caring?

We listened as she continued with the passage in hopes of finding some answers to the many questions we had for her.

Learline was asleep after five or six verses. As Alma read on, I drifted off with thoughts about what had happened to me earlier that afternoon. I wondered if I had really seen a little bit of heaven and thought if my sisters weren't really dead, that maybe Mama was still alive too. Maybe she had fainted like me and will wake up. Maybe she had a stroke like Alma's mama and was just laying there because she couldn't move.

Alma was still reading when I interrupted, *"Is your mama still jest a layin there?"*

Alma stopped reading aloud but still kept her eyes on the word. She took a deep breath and said, *"No Hun, we lost our Mama summer before last."*

"I can help ya find her when we look fer our sack wit Mama's Bible tomorrow!" Ed Earl said sympathetically as he volunteered our services. When Alma smiled at him with appreciation for his concern, her eyes squinted, pushing a tear out. It rolled down her round cheek and ran into the corner of her mouth. She closed her Bible and laid the baby across the couch. She turned to him and softly patted his shoulder and said, *"It's not like that Hun… My Mama died."*

"She did! I didn't know Mama's could die!" he said.

"Yea hun we all have to die sometime…even mama's…"

"Do they die cause thez git sick?" he asked.

Earldean and I sat up a little waiting for her answer, hoping she would tell something that would make a difference in our suspicions.

"My Mama's heart played out on her ya'll. She was sick for a long time…not like your Mama. Doc is out there with her right now, don't worry, she probably has a bad virus or something."

Ed Earl sat up Indian style and held his head down while he poked at the blanket. *"I wanna go see Mama wit Doc."* he mumbled.

I could feel the lump in my throat forming when I heard Earldean sniffle then turned to see her bury her face in the blankets. Alma could see the worry in our eyes and wanted to comfort us each one.

She scooted herself out of the sunken spot she had worn and sat on the edge. She pulled a small throw from the back of the couch and spread it out over Learline. She gently tucked it around the sound-sleeping child who remained undisturbed by the deed then indicated accomplishment of the task with a long sigh of relief.

She sat for another moment with her lips pursed and tapping her fingers on her knees. *"How about a bedtime snack?"* she offered, wanting to make us all feel better.

It was plain to see that Alma knew about comfort food and kept some handy snacks available for emergency comforting. We followed her to the counter where she kept a big, pale green ceramic jar. It was round like a ball and rested on tiny little nubs to keep it from rolling to the floor. On its side, were three faded, hand painted flowers; orange, red and a white one that with age had turned to a pale yellow.

She told us how she had been eating cookies from that cookie jar all of her life and that her mama, and her mama before her, had also. She told us that hundreds of hands had reached past that opening and pulled out thousands of cookies over the years.

She didn't know how old it really was but it belonged to her great-great grandmother who had for the most part kept vanilla wafers in it but on occasion would surprise it's takers with butter cookies that had holes in the middle so you can dress up your fingers. This old green cookie jar had been with her family for a long, long time and it was an inheritance that was valuable only to the memories of the heart. Alma removed the lid then held it down for us to reach in and get a hand full of vanilla wafers. She poured us a glass of cow milk that came from the dairy and showed us how to dunk our cookies in the milk.

After cookies and idol chat, she dressed for bed and had us wash our teeth with toothpaste on a rag. She said we might be more at ease in a strange place if she slept on the couch to be near us if we needed her. She laid Learline on the pallet then fluffed a big sheet over the top of us, just like Mama would do. She turned out the lights except one she left burning over the gas stove that we could see from where we were laying.

I stared into it thinking about Mama and Daddy and how much I was missing them. I thought about the overwhelming day we had with the bull and Ed Earls stitches.

In one day, we had discovered so many new things like water fountains, the ring of a telephone, the taste of grilled cheese sandwiches and crinkled fries with ketchup, fried bologna and homogenized milk.

We had made new friends and knew their names. I counted them on my fingers as I laid there listening to the hum and felt the vibration of the air condition window unit.

"Let's see…" I whispered to myself. *"Huey and his little brothers, Maw, Granny, Alma, Debbie, Trudy and Doc."* Now, I knew twice as many people as I did yesterday and had ridden in two of their cars! We had bathed in a bathtub and now…we were spending the night with a person who I never knew existed seven or eight hours earlier.

I fainted for the first time in my life…all because of such a day. It all seemed so unfamiliar, that still I was not sure that I had not died and gone to heaven…but without my parents…I was homesick…sunburned….but too tired to think about it anymore. At some point, I had fallen into a deep sleep giving my mind, body and emotions a much needed rest.

I felt my body jerk hard as the ring of the phone shot through the air breaking the sound of silence. It pulled me out so fast that I jolted straight up wondering where I was. I could hear Alma scrambling around trying to get up and felt the floor thump as she took her heavy steps toward the snack bar where the phone sat. She was trying to keep from waking us so she answered softly. I could barely hear her talking over the hum. *"Hello…Yes?"*

After a long pause, I watched her turn and face the wall wrapping the cord around her. Though she spoke softly with a sleepy, raspy voice, I could make out some of her words.

"They will be worried sick…what are we spost ta do?" She mumbled a few more things into the receiver cupping her hand over her mouth to funnel her voice.

I wondered who she was talking to on the other end and why they were calling so late. Sleep was trying to take me over again as I kept drifting in and out fighting it to hear what was being said.

The last thing I heard her say was, *"Well, you're right…let's wait till the morning."*

With that she made her way back across the room to the couch and settled in. It was safe to go back to sleep because whatever it was…it would wait until morning.

12
OUT OF THE ORDINARY

It must have been that sound first, and then the smell, that woke me that Saturday morning. Rolling over, I stretched, then realized that I wasn't dreaming anymore. I took in my surroundings trying to figure out just where the heck I was.

Absent were the usual sounds of the woods that I had awakened to every day of my life for those first ten years. That in itself was so unfamiliar that at first it was a bit disconcerting.

I rubbed my eyes then pulled the bed clothes a little more securely around my chin. When my ears recaptured the gurgling sound, I curiously sat up for further investigation.

Diffused dawning light peeked from around the sides of the pulled shades that covered the windows. Encircled by large dark unfamiliar shapes, it was evident that I wasn't among the trees and plants. And, I was pretty dog gone sure that bizarre sound I was hearing was *not* the morning call of the neighboring birds but possibly, the purr of a big cat or more likely…the strain of somebody trying to start an old worn out motor.

Through my squinted eye lids I could see the light burning on the stovetop and recognized the antique cookie jar on the counter that Alma had introduced us to the night before.

Alma, standing on the kitchen side of the snack bar, was leaned in on her elbows and resting on its top. She was talking to Trudy, who I hardly recognized out of uniform.

They were engaged in a weighty conversation and had not noticed that I was waking up. Though she talked softly, I could hear Alma telling Trudy something about how some of the wealthy people who own those big lake houses just use those places for vacation homes in the summer.

She was saying that Lucille somebody's sister worked as a housekeeper for one of them and had told her those people had more money than they knew what to do with. Her guess was that *we* were from one of those families and that's why they hadn't seen us around before. From what she could gather we had a two story home because Ed Earl talked about the staircase and the big double

French doors at the entrance. Also, that our parents had to be wealthy enough to afford to have a full time tutor come in and teach us at home. It sounded like she was trying to convince Trudy that we were probably from out of town, visiting for the summer.

Trudy's voice carried a little better than Alma's and it was obvious she had her doubts. *"Oh Alma, you don't think these kids are from one of those kinda houses…do ya?…dressed like they are in mixed matched rags and the boy wearin them ladies pink tennis shoes?…Really now…come on…I hardly…"*

Alma looked over to see me up on my elbows, still sleepy eyed and bleary. She patted Trudy's arm to get her attention stopping her in mid sentence.

"Shhhhhh! One of um's awake." she whispered, just loud enough for me to hear her.

"Hun, it's ok, you go on back to sleep. It's still early you need more rest." she softly said trying not to wake the others.

Surely, I thought, they must hear that noise too but they didn't seem to be bothered by it. I had to know what it was that sounded so weird, so I made mention of it in a groggy but quiet voice.

"I…I heared some sorta racket…I'z wonderin what it wuz…listen…yonder it go'z agin!

"Oh that?…well that's just my new electric percolator." she responded. *We're makin us some coffee…it's alright…just go back ta sleep now ya hear?"*

Lying back down, I curled to my side rubbing my eyes again before closing them to get those last few winks in until the rest of my senses were aroused.

Snoozing in and out while the aroma of fresh brewing coffee filled the small living quarters made me feel at home. It had always been the first chore of the day for Mama to brew a pot each morning. That was one of the rations she seldom ran out of and when she did, it didn't set well with her. Daddy saw to it she stayed stocked by buying large quantities at a time. She would rather do without most anything but her coffee, and there were times she did.

Coffee must be more significant to some people than it is to others and it apparently tastes better if the pot is shared with good company.

Personally, I had learned to appreciate a good cup at a very early age, when on rare occasions, Mama would invite me to sit and drink coffee with her. Though she said it was because she didn't want it to go to waste, I often suspected she just wanted to pretend that I was a visitor come to call.

She would pour me a half cup of coffee and the other half of it being goat's milk as to not burn my mouth. We'd sit sipping while chatting about how good the coffee tasted or she might talk of a recipe she would like to try if she could get all the ingredients. Or, she might have a creative idea she just had to share about putting together something useful or pretty.

On rare occasions she would tell melancholy stories of a little girl that lived once upon a time, a long time ago. I suspect now, they may have been pieced together by vague memories of her own childhood, though she never told me that.

Then there were those times she just wanted to sit there, with her eyes fixed on something and drink coffee.

Earldean didn't care for the taste and refused to drink it saying it left a film in her mouth. Quite truthfully, I had acquired a taste for its flavor for the sole purpose of getting quality time with Mama.

Trudy reached and pulled two cups from the cup hooks and passed them across the counter to Alma.

I had figured that coffee time was important to these particular two women for them to get up that early and meet to drink some together.

I watched Alma pour two cups then pass one to Trudy. One stirred in a little cream and the other a little sugar, tapping the spoon on the side of their cups before laying them across their saucers. They picked up their steaming cups, blowing over the rim, before they took their first long and cautious sip. It was as though this was a routine they had rehearsed a million times and they had synchronized this performance to perfection.

Drinking coffee indeed was an important aspect of this friendship. I couldn't help but overhear parts of their conversation. Apparently, the two had different views on what kind of background we might have come from, but somehow the coffee was the glue that held them together, no matter their difference of opinion.

Alma's theory was that our Daddy must have been off in some oil field making millions while Trudy's was that he must be a truck driver, who was on the road and gone for weeks at a time.

At any rate, they both agreed that our parents were probably worried sick about us being gone for two nights now and by this time had probably reported us missing.

"We aught ta check with the Sheriff and see if anybody has called about um. They could be out there looking everywhere!" Trudy quietly suggested.

Alma agreed and added, *"We have got to get to their mother and let her know that they are safe and sound right here."*

I must have dozed off again because when I opened my eyes, the sun was up, making the room was much brighter and they were pouring more coffee in their cups.

It was about that time that Learline started coming out of her sleep, stretching and kicking the covers off when she whacked Ed Earl right on his sore leg. He woke up crying, which woke up Earldean and distracted the women from their coffee.

Learline sat staring at him for a moment, still half asleep with that "What's the matter with you?" look, before she too started whining about not knowing where she was.

The two women darted across the room as fast as they could to rescue the wounded. After they saw that Ed Earl was ok, Trudy began trying to calm Learline by picking her up and carrying her to the kitchen. She was attempting to remind her of where she was when she offered her breakfast.

"How bout we cook you kids up a nice breakfast…ya hungry?"

This got Earldean to her feet, stretching and calling out orders.

She reached down and pulled the sheet off of me and my brother saying, *"Ya'll come on! Git up! I gotta git these covers folded up 'fore breakfast!"*

Folding up our bed covers before breakfast, without being told, had always won favor with Mama. She would have us shake them out and fold them to keep leaves and other debris off so they would be more comfortable to sleep in.

In winter it would be necessary to fold them, turning our sleeping quarters into a living room. On those real cold days, she didn't mind us leaving them layered over the hides that lined the floor to keep out the draft.

Alma didn't have much floor space, so picking up the covers wasn't such a bad idea. However, I think Earldean was just so excited about not having to do the cooking that she didn't mind doing a few other chores to help out.

As far as I was concerned, I was glad we weren't going to have to eat her cooking again because she still didn't have it down yet and though Mama said that would come with practice, her experimentations were challenging to eat.

Trudy had picked up a few groceries to bring not knowing if Alma had enough food in the house for her unexpected guests. She and Alma bumped around each other in the tiny kitchen making such a fuss over scrambled eggs, bacon and toast served up with juice from an orange that had been frozen in a can.

We were accustomed to eggs, but once again, we were treated to what we called back home, "Special Occasion Food".

I pulled Ed Earl's arm back when he reached for his toast. Trudy saw that we hadn't started eating yet and said, *"Well ya'll go on before ya eggs git cold!"*

"We have ta say the blessin first" I told her.

She looked at Alma who was handing her a plate and hesitantly replied, *"Alright, that's a good idea, who's gonna say it?"*

Earldean volunteered. *"Dear Lord, we thank ya for this here food and thank ya for our new friends that cooked it for us…and God please forgive us for forgitin bout sayin our prayers fore we went ta sleep last nite…And Lord please help us find our Daddy real soon! Amen."*

"Amen." we said in unison, then dug in and enjoyed.

While we ate, Alma took our clothes that were still a little damp outdoors to hang in the morning sunshine while Trudy got on the phone to make a few calls.

The first was to the Eat-A-Bite to make sure everybody showed up for work on the breakfast shift.

Second, she called the Sheriff's office to see if any children had been reported missing and to let him know where to find them if they did. She went on to let him know about the situation when Alma returned from outside. We all listened to her tell the Sheriff the story and the part we hadn't heard about yet; the late night phone call from Doc.

She told him that Doc had gone out to check on our mother but could not find the place. He had followed the directions Earldean had given and had even drove around in the dark on those back roads until late in the night before he gave up and came back to wait on daylight.

The sheriff told her she should bring us to his office so he could question us and try to find our Daddy as soon as possible. He had a hard time believing that our mother would send her young children for help instead of calling the Doctor herself.

Trudy explained that it was a little more complicated than that and asked if he would come to us because the only clothes we had to put on were still drying in the sun.

Agreeing to send out a deputy, the sheriff said they would do what they could to help. Then Alma tried to call Doc but his wife Estelle answered and said that he was already on his way over and that he had been trying to call but kept getting a busy signal.

Apparently, she was not too happy with the idea of Doc spending the whole day doing good deeds after he was out all night on a wild goose chase, because it wasn't until she hung up that we heard Alma say anything but, *"uh-hum…uh-hum…uh-hum."* and so on.

Then, she had been animated in telling Trudy what all Estelle had to say. She finished up by saying, *"Well…I don't know why she snapped at me…Doc is the one who volunteered to go out there and he's the one who told me to call him back this mornin…so, I don't know…I don't want the woman mad at me!"*

Earldean and I looked at each other knowing that if we had told them about Mama by now, maybe Doc's wife wouldn't be mad at him and Alma. We felt bad about that and agreed we would have to pull one of them aside to tell them as soon as we could.

If Mama had in fact died, we were still going to have to break it to the two youngest. Feeling sad about that again, I asked Alma if she minded me using her bathroom.

"Why sure honey, you don't ask that while you are here. You just go anytime you want to, that's fine wit me…ok? Alright then."

Of course it was a race for Ed Earl and Learline to beat me there and I really just wanted a place to hide and cry without having Earldean fuss at me for doing so.

I was hoping that she would take advantage of the time alone with Trudy and Alma to tell them about Mama. It wasn't long at all before Doc showed up at the door. Being the gentleman, he waited for Alma and Trudy to refill their coffee cups before they stepped outside to talk with him.

It was the proper thing for them to do, as not to give any of the neighbors a chance to take advantage of an opportunity to start any gossip about a married man up in a trailer house with a single woman and a divorcée.

We all ended up following them out there within minutes. The grownups were standing around talking as I sat down on the steps within ear shot of their conversation.

I pulled the oversized shirt over my sunburned legs to keep the sun off as well as to conceal the fact that my panties were still drying in the sunshine a few feet away. Learline was following Ed Earl around when he started up a game of hide and seek with her. Although Ed Earl favored his sore leg it didn't stop his play being the toughskin he strived to be.

Learline's sunburn didn't look as bad as it did the night before but it was still evident that she was a bit uncomfortable when Ed Earl would jump out from his hiding place and grab her shoulder or arm. She rustled with the oversized tee shirt stepping on the hem pulling it off her shoulder and rubbing the skin.

Earldean had gone over and felt of the clothes to see if they were dry. She turned and shook her head letting me know they weren't. *"Almost."* she said as she took a seat next to me on the steps, pulling her shirt over her legs too.

Doc was telling the women how far out he drove and that he couldn't believe how far we walked before we stopped for help. He wondered why we didn't check at one of the other houses that were closer to home. Apparently, he was ready to go out there again and this time he was sure to find it with our help.

Stepping over by the steps, he asked again, *"You said that ya'll don't have a phone right? Is there a neighbor we can call?"*

"We got some neighbors by a name of Mr. Riley and Myrtle Riley, but theyz aint got no phone either." Earldean told them.

Trudy felt it necessary to point this out to Alma, that rich people have phones. Doc let her know that he was not looking at taking sides in their guessing game, however, that there were a great deal of places out by the lake where the phone lines didn't run yet so it wouldn't be unusual not to have one. He was more interested in facts and getting the show on the road as time was wasting.

He asked if we felt up to riding out there to show him the way so he could get us back home to our mother and check on her too.

"Doc we're waitin on their clothes to dry. They caint go like that!" Alma informed him.

Trudy stepped over and squeezed Earldean's shirt and shook her head saying, *"Nope, it's still a little damp, besides, the Sheriff said he was sending a deputy out to help. He's going to wanna talk to them if he's gonna be able to find their daddy."*

Doc seemed a little frustrated as he stood there with his hands in his pockets, dragging the toe of his shoe in a semicircle across the gravel in the driveway.

He took a deep breath to gather his patience with the two women, and then thought he would make good use of the wait and check on Ed Earl's stitches.

Doc called him from his hiding but Ed Earl didn't answer, getting Doc involved in his game. When he found him, Doc played along for a bit before he lifted him up on the hood of the car telling him he wanted to take a look at his boo-boo.

Learline struggled to climb up on the car to sit beside him, wanting some of that attention, as it was her strongest craving in those days.

Doc, not wanting to get dirt in the wound, was careful as he pulled back the bandage. No longer than he was out there, Ed Earl had already found a way to get dirty, giving him an excuse to take another bath in Alma's tub. The wound looked red and puffy, and concerned the doctor.

"Did you take a bath in Ms. Alma's tub last night, Ed Earl?" he asked.

"Yea, her let me go swimming. I wanna go again. It was fun!"

"I wanna go too! Let me too!" Learline shrieked at the thrilling idea.

Doc told Alma that it wasn't a good idea to put the boy in the tub with a fresh wound like that because infection could set in. Alma told him she forgot that you weren't suppose to submerge stitches in water that soon but that he was so dirty and she thought the cool water would help his sunburn.

"Gee, I feel so bad! I just wasn't thinking Doc…There was just so much goin on...How could I be so stupid?"

Alma slapped her hands on the side of her face; it was clear that she felt bad about it. Trudy went over putting her arm around her shoulder saying, *"Oh now Alma, you had a lot on your plate with havin ta take care of all them sun sick…homesick…heartsick, tard and sleepy little orphans! You didn't mean no harm! It's all right!"*

I was starting to get confused with all the sickness Trudy was talking about until she referred to us as being the orphans.

We had a goat back home whose mother died, leaving her tiny baby to die too, if we had not taken care of her. Mama used that word *orphan*, referring to our little Nanny Goat who had to be trained to drink a bottle by first sucking our fingers. She struggled with the loss of her mother; nudging all around looking for her. Mama said that she wouldn't have made it if we hadn't *adopted* her.

Wondering why she would call us orphans made me think Trudy may have already suspected that our mother died. Not ever finding Daddy would leave us without anybody to take care of us.

Sadness grew inside me as I sat rocking back and forth; pulling tighter on the shirt I was wearing while watching my knees as they bulged through it.

I tried to picture life absent our parents and how we would be lost without them. What were we to eat if Daddy said that we weren't to shoot guns without him around?

Who would hunt for food for us if we weren't allowed? How would we ever be able to grow a garden of vegetables like Mama? We had not yet learned enough about seeding as she had only started showing us that part so what were we to plant?.

Who would referee our differences about who was the boss of whom and was Earldean going to be the mother now? Would I have to mind her even though I was almost as big as she was? I didn't want her to stop being my sister because that's when I loved her most. She could try to comfort us when we needed it but who would comfort her?

She couldn't do things like my Mama or Daddy because she wasn't them, she was Earldean. I just wanted to go home and have things the way they were. Now I know why the little Nanny Goat kept nudging around and crying for her mother was because she needed to know she was there.

Pining for the two most significant people in my life made me feel lost for I was overwhelmed with the urge to find them and touch their physical presence just to know they were there. Was I really… an orphan?

That lump in my throat was back and was pushing with vengeance to break free from its confinement. When I could no longer suppress it, a steady stream of tears leaked from my eyes running beneath my chin, down my neck and into the opening of the stretched out shirt. I could feel my tears rolling along my belly and felt their warmth on my skin.

Straining to keep from making any sound so as not to attract attention, I buried my face in the shirt to hide my shame.

Earldean never looked over at me as she got up to see the stitches when Doc, referring to the wound, said that it needed to be cleaned up. He suggested that instead of putting another bandage over it that it could dry out better if uncovered. Alma reached and picked up Learline from the hood of the car to keep her from sliding off when Trudy volunteered to go get a wash cloth for him and turned to go up the steps.

When she did, she caught me in the midst of my sorrow and was taken back that she hadn't noticed before.

"Oh Sweetie! What s' a matter?" She sat down on the step beside me, pulling me into her side then kissing my head. *"Are you worried about Ed Ear? Huh? Cause if ya worried bout Ed Earl…Oh Honey! He's gonna be alright! Ok?*

Doc lifted Ed Earl off the hood of the car, swinging him down to his feet, telling him that he needed to take it easy and that maybe he should stay indoors for the day being still so that he wouldn't pull his stitches out.

He walked over and squatted down beside the steps. Looking at me with compassion he asked, *"Are you worried about your brother Sassy? Or is it something else?"*

Well, that just made me cry more and this time it came with little sobs and sniffs. Sure I was worried about my brother but it was not just those stitches that concerned me but more over what was to become of him.

Without a daddy, who was going to teach him the things that boys need to know. What's Learline going to do for a mother to rock her and sing songs?

Earldean and I couldn't sing a lick! Earldean wasn't big enough to be a mother and was a terrible cook…we'll starve to death, I thought as I sat drowning in my grief. Ed Earl stepped up on the first step putting his hands on his hips and stooping over to tell me, *"It don't hurt Sassy! See…it aint bleedin no more! Don't cry!"* losing his balance as he lifted his leg. It was a good thing Alma was standing behind him to catch his fall.

The whole performance made the group laugh and I myself mixed a slight chuckle in with the tears before I wiped my face on the sleeve of the shirt. But now, I was weeping harder as I thought they were laughing at me.

"What's wrong now, Sassy…come on, you can tell Trudy!"

Earldean moved in to answer for me. *"She just cries for the heck of it sometimes…don't even got to be nuttin wrong! Aint that right Sassy? See… look at her…Sassy!…Come on stop cryin! You just sittin there cryin for no good reason aint cha?"*

Trudy decided it was time to rescue me when she pulled me back to her side with a hug saying, *"Ok now that's enough…Poor little thang! Sometimes a girl just has to cry for no reason just so she can stay in practice for when theyz a call for it!"* She rocked with me back and forth to sooth my hurt.

"Whatsa matter wit Sassy?" Learline was asking.

Alma suggested to my sisters that they go inside with her to wipe the dirt off of Ed Earl's leg, leaving Trudy and Doc figure out my problem.

It was a minute or so after they were inside, with the door shut, that my crying began to ease off and Trudy asked again, *"Sassy, you can talk to us…tell us what's wrong…we want to help."*

I sniffed and wiped my face on my shirt again, then cleared my throat and wailed out, *"I don't wanna be an orphaaaan!"*

"What?" she asked with surprise in her voice.

"An Orphan Trudy…She heard you tell Alma that while ago." Doc explained to her.

"Oh Honey, I didn't mean that literally! I just meant it like you were missin ya Mama and ya Daddy, that's all! Oh Trudy didn't mean ta hurt ya feelins hun!"

I tried to gather myself together to tell them what my sister and I had not been able to all along, but I was afraid that they would be mad at us for not telling them right up front.

"Trudy, if we don't find my Daddy soon we really will be orphans!" I told her trying to find a way to lead into it.

"We are gonna find him hun." she reassured me. *"We just had to take care of you kids first…you know…get your brother sewed up, get some food in ya bellies, take care of those sunburns…well by the time we got all that done, it was dark and ya needed a good night's sleep!"*

Doc leaned down to tell me, *"We also tried to go out and check on your mother too, Sassy. If she is so sick that she had to send you for help we should get to her soon…she might need some medical attention…I'm a doctor. Even if we knew where your father was, and told him about your mother, by the time he got to her, there is a good chance he would just have to load her up and bring her back to see me!"*

This was the perfect opportunity to tell them why it may not be necessary to go out there before finding Daddy. I had wanted him to be with us in any case but now, we couldn't just leave Mama lying there, dead or alive.

I could still feel a glimmer of hope inside my gut that there was a chance for her.

Willing to risk them being upset with me and Earldean, I had to tell them now or give up hope that Doc could save Mama and make her well. Feeling that I had nothing to lose I began to explain.

"Doc…Trudy…w-w-we walked a long way to find Daddy…c-ca-cause he would know what to do but then Ed Earl cut his leg and Huey's Granny said we had to go to the clinic and…"

Before I could finish telling them, a horn honked as a big black and white car pulled up and stopped. It had two big red cylinders on top, with writing on the doors.

As Doc and Trudy stood up to see who it was, a tall brawny man got out and smoothed his hair back with his hand before he placed his big hat on his head, which shaded his face, making it hard to make out who he was as he walked toward us. I could see that he was wearing a star shaped badge on his shirt and had a gun in a holster that hooked on his belt.

He looked a little like the ranger who had come around our place a long time ago.

"Doc." he said as he nodded then tipped his hat and said, *"Miss Trudy"*

"Hey Nolan! Sheriff said he was sendin a deputy over. He didn't say he was sendin the good lookin one! How you doin?" she asked in a flirty way.

"Purdy good…and you?" he answered as he got closer.

Doc stepped over and stuck out his hand, wanting to make friends with him no doubt.

"Doc you know Deputy Nolan Reed don't cha?"

"Sure, how's ya Daddy doing? He feelin better these days?" Doc asked him.

The deputy laughed and said, *"Mean as ever!"*

Doc chuckled a little saying, *"Good! Good! That means he's gonna be alrite!"*

"Yep, he might be feelin too good!"

Well, I guessed that they were already friends and a handshake just reseals the deal.

Trudy pointed at me and said *"…And that's Sassy."*

The deputy looked down at me and said in a deep voice, *"How do young lady? I hear tell you're lost?"*

Nervously I answered him, *"Naw...I aint lost! I'm right here!"*

He smiled and looked up at Trudy and said, *"Sheriff said y'all had some kids wander up here or somthin. Wanna tell me bout it?*

As Trudy started talking the deputy reached into his pocket and pulled out a pen, then began writing on the pad he had been carrying. He stopped writing long enough to look at his watch before he resumed, then asked a few questions.

Trudy began telling the story from the part when Alma had come into the Eat-A-Bite with us. Shortly after, Alma and the others came to the door so I got up from the steps to let them through. My siblings took seats on the steps and Ed Earl made room for me when I tried to sit back down.

He was still hyped up about this whole adventure, with all the discoveries it unveiled and could hardly sit still as he studied the officer and the paraphernalia attached to his uniform. He leaned in toward me and softly said, *"Hey, he's gotta gun!"*

"Shhh." I said, trying to listen to what was being said.

We listened as Alma told how she came about meeting us, followed by Doc, who told the parts that involved him.

Ed Earl, who lost interest in the conversation, was more fascinated by the squad car and went over for a closer investigation while Learline was in her own little world.

Petting and talking to Alma's pink plastic flamingos there by the steps she couldn't care less about what was being said.

When Doc finished Alma and Trudy felt sincerely that it might help if they each shared their ideas and theories too.

When they got caught up in another mild difference of opinion, the officer took the opportunity to break from them and squatted down by the steps to talk to us.

"I'll need to get your full names and ages for my report, let's see… which of you is the oldest?"

I of course, was flattered that he would have to ask but Earldean was quick to point out that she indeed, was the oldest, while I, not wanting to waste time on formalities, was anxious to ask him if he was going to help us find our daddy.

He said that we would get to that but he needed this information to start with. We went through the whole last name routine again with him and he too had a hard time believing we didn't know our last name. We spent a great deal of time on that subject.

"You mean in your whole life your parents never told you what your last name was?"

Earldean answered, *"We didn't know a body was sposta have one...what cha need it fer anyhow?"*

Puzzled he asked, *"They didn't teach you that for school?"*

"Mama did our schoolin, she learnt us how ta write our name, spell words and put um together ta read." Earldean told him.

Mama was a good teacher and I wanted him to know there were more important things besides last names to learn about in schoolin, so I added, *"... and she learnd us bout addin and takin away numbers and such...she teaches us bout most anythang ya wanna know!"*

Getting a little impatient with the whole idea, he said, *"Anything but your last name!"* He took a deep breath then stood up shaking his head. It was quiet for a moment until Doc called Ed Earl back over to the group. *"Ed Earl! Why don't you come back this way so ya won't get hurt playin round that car!"* He was reluctant but he obeyed and Alma took him by the hand and pulled him in for a hug saying, *"You better stay by me so'z I can keep an eye on ya!...You don't want to bust up them stitches now do ya?"*

Deputy Reed tried one more time for a last name asking Earldean, *"Have you ever heard your parents call themselves by another name?"*

"Naw, just Earl, but Daddy has a friend in California that goes by a name a Dean and that's where they got my name, Earldean!"

"Do you know of any relatives we can call, such as grandparents, uncles, aunts or cousins?"

"Daddy's gotta Unka Leonard and a Aint Verdi May." I said.

"Ok...do you know their last name or how to get in touch with them?" he asked hopefully, but was soon disappointed when we shook our heads no.

"Alright...Alma here says you know your Daddy works in town but do you know where in town or what kind of work he does?"

Ed Earl, getting back in on the conversation, now volunteered information. *"My Daddy goes to work in his truck!"* he said with confidence.

The deputy looked at him and asked, *"Is your daddy a truck driver?"*

"I knew it…I just knew it!" Trudy exclaimed, nudging Alma and causing her to almost lose her balance. *"I told ya Alma! He'z a truck driver!"*

"What kind of truck does he drive, do you know?" Deputy Reed continued.

"Orange." Ed Earl answered. *"Brown and orange."*

"Oh! I bet he works for that Jones Truckin outfit down there in Springdale! Their trucks are red and black! You mean red and black don't cha Ed Earl, not orange and brown?"

Ed Earl looked at her as a matter of factly and said, *"Naw, brown…orange and brown."*

Doc asked him if our daddy's truck had a name on it and he confidently answered, *"Yep, it's gotta name on it but I caint read big words yet"*

"Did it say Jones Truckin Company on it ya'll?" Trudy asked us.

I thought for a minute then said, *"I remember!…It said Ford and the color is sposta be red but it's faded and rusted some since he had it."*

Alma folded her arms and threw her head back, then looking down her nose said to Trudy, *"Truck driver huh?"*

Trudy pretended not to hear her when she said that it was getting late and that she had to get on to the café and relieve Yvonne and the rest of the morning shift; plus she still had to go by the house and pick up Debbie.

Doc agreed that time was wasting and felt his services could be best spent going out and checking on our mother. He felt it would be better if Alma could keep the two younger ones, wanting Ed Earl to be still and knowing that the little one would soon need a nap, while Earldean and I went out with him to check on Mama.

Deputy Reed said there wasn't a whole lot he could do about finding our daddy with no more knowledge than he had gained from us.

He thought he might be able to get more information out of our mother then go from there if it was still necessary to find him.

He was very interested in asking our mother a whole lot of questions about her child rearing anyway.

Trudy said her good-byes, not knowing if we would still be around after she got off of work but told us that when Mama got well, she wanted us to bring her and Daddy to the café so she could meet them.

She gave us all hugs before she climbed into her car, then we watched and waved as she drove off down the drive.

Earldean might have used a little too much soap in washing our clothes out the night before but by the time we came up with our plan, they had dried enough to get dressed, though they were a bit scratchy against our blistered skin.

Alma and Ed Earl were disappointed in that they weren't included in the part of the plan that had them going out to Chinquapin Hollow. Alma was looking forward to a tour of our fine lake home and Ed Earl really wanted a ride in that squad car with Deputy Reed.

Learline was getting whiny and would probably go down for her nap as soon as she ate her lunch.

Alma bit the bullet and agreed to stay behind, convincing Ed Earl that tarrying there with her would be worth his while because she was going to teach him how to go fishing with playing cards. With that she promised that when they got hungry, she could cook up something good to eat…something he could dip in ketchup.

Learline wasn't buying it though. As soon as we stepped out the door, she went into a screaming rage of panic for Earldean.

As it ended up, she stayed. Deputy Reed offered to give us a ride in his squad car out to Chinquapin Hollow, but Doc said he would take his car just in case he had to stay longer to tend to our mother.

I reluctantly climbed into Doc's car to ride out with him with Deputy Reed following.

I was a bit nervous about riding with somebody I didn't know that well but I felt that if Alma and Trudy trusted him then it was ok for me too; besides we shook hands. He did offer friendship.

There was not a whole lot said on the first part of the ride back out there so I took advantage of the quiet time to talk to God about our situation.

I bowed my head, folded my hands and uttered my prayer under my breath. It was just as hard to talk to Him as it was to talk to the grownups in that I wasn't sure if he would be mad at me for withholding the truth. Mama had told us that could be as bad as an outright lie if it did the same kind of damage.

So I started out with small talk like thanking The Lord for the pretty flowers, birds, and trees, you know, the usual, giving an extra special thanks for Him finding us somebody to give us a ride into town, saving us more steps than we cared to count, even if it took my brother tearing his leg open like he had done, before we had an offer.

Being ever so grateful for our new friends that we had met along the way, I took time to praise him for being so creative in His making of such kind people. Pondering hard, not to leave out a single bit of praise and thanksgiving before moving on to the petition part of my praying, I struggled to recall all that had happened over the previous three days.

Once I finished praying about all the good things, I slowly moved into the hard part. The part I really wanted to talk with Him about.

"Oh God, this is the hard part, but in your words you said that we should bring our burdens to You and you will tend our needs. So God…We need to find our Daddy soon! I hope you won't be mad at me and Earldean for not telling what we know about Mama. If you really do see all, then you already know that we didn't mean it like a lie, we were just not wantin our little brother and sister to be sad…that's all! Only you know for sure how she is right now and we will be so sad if she's dead so please don't take her to heaven yet! Please let her be alive Lord cause we need her more than you do! I should have stayed with her to make sure…I hope I didn't let her die! I didn't know…I didn't mean it if I did mess up! Oh Lord! Forgive me!

I turned my face as far as I could to avoid letting Doc see my tears. He reached into his pocket and pulled out a white piece of cloth, the kind I remembered Granny Pane's husband having. Offering it to me, he said, *"It's clean."*

I reached and took it from his hand and examined it carefully. Woven into the soft fabric was tiny little stripes that outlined the edges. In one of the corners, were the letters **H.M.** sewn on with dark blue thread in perfectly even stitches.

"It's ok, it's my hankie. You can use it. It's clean…go on…you can use it to dry those tears."

I took the hankie and wiped my tears then folded it back, laying it on the seat between us. I ran my fingers back and forth across the letters, thinking what a nice person this man was to give me a ride. He wasn't as talkative as Denby but he was every bit as polite.

Denby would do nice things for us too and it made me feel good and want to do nice things back. I wanted to find a way to show Doc how much I appreciated what he was doing.

After shyly thanking him for letting me use his hankie, I asked if he wanted me to sew a letter between that H and M when I got home making a word that would make sense.

He smiled real big showing his pretty teeth and asked, *"What letter would you put?"*

"Well, I could put an A." I told him.

"And what sensible word would that make?"

"H-A-M…ham! That's a word." I just knew he liked the idea because he smiled really big and told me so when I offered it back.

"Or, I could put an 'I' on it and spell the word him."

"That's an idea." he said.

We drove on making small talk about things my Mama taught me to sew. Making things and hobbies, somehow led the conversation to talking about horses.

Doc told me about him having raised horses and that he loved riding them. I remembered seeing horses in the magazines that were at the clinic and enjoyed looking at how pretty they were.

We looked for horses in pastures along the way and he pointed out the different kinds. Before I knew it we were to a familiar area on the route.

Looking out the window, I recognized Huey's house and pointed it out to Doc. I looked for Huey and his brothers out in their yard but didn't see them.

I asked Doc to slow down because I thought we would be coming up to the turn off pretty soon. We must have drove two miles before we came to the pasture where the bull was.

"That's it! The dirt road is just past this farm!"

My heart was beating fast and I was lost for words because of mixed feelings. I was excited about getting to go home and be in the comfort of familiar surroundings but was nervous about having to face Mama, as bad as I missed her.

As we turned onto the road I looked behind to see Deputy Reed still following but he was soon lost in the cloud of dust. *"I don't see him anymore!"* I said. Doc slowed down as not to stir up the dust too much and so that he wouldn't miss any turn off's.

"You'll have to tell me where to go…I found out yesterday evening that there are several forks and turn offs on this road." Doc said.

I hadn't recalled that many but I had paid attention to landmarks on our walk out of there, so it helped in the navigating.

When we would come to a fork in the road, he was patient to wait for me to recall which way to go.

Doc commented on how pretty this wooded area was as he pointed out rocky bluffs, small waterfalls and lots of caves that could be seen high on the cliff sides.

"I love this place!" Doc said with passion. *"Did you know that the Ozarks are the oldest living formations on the earth? There are caves all over these hills; stalagmites, stalactites and there are some being formed right now!"*

"My friend Denby told me bout um…you'd like him…he likes ta shake hands like you…Iffin he wuz here…that's what he would do iffin he'z ta meet ya."

"Denby?" Doc asked. *"Does he live around here?"*

"Useta be he lived cross the lake from us…but not no more…He had to move to Sikeston, Missouri wit his sister soz she could tend to him... He fell' n broke his hip and got a bad ole cold in his chest…He's commin back tho…when he gits well from it."

"You don't say." Doc said as he drove slowly past my favorite landmark that was in the curve of the road. This was the place that provided a little shelter from the storm we had encountered that first afternoon.

He looked off down in the valley keeping one eye on the road. In spite of the drought, the observation was a gorgeous terrain, a living forest in luscious shades of green that climbed into the heights of the hills and mountains beyond.

His stopping the car in the curve of the road to sigh as he gazed upon it, made it obvious that he thought it was a breathtaking sight as well.

"Denby use to say that it wasn't that these Ozark Mountains were so high, it was that the valleys were just so darn deep!"

"That is so true…You know Sassy, from up here you can see things better than when you are down there in the forest floor. When my life seems like I'm stuck in a rut or at a very low point in my life, I can come up here to places like this and it seems good, like I can rise above it all."

"That's because you are closer to Heaven…Closer to God." I told him.

He rubbed his chin still staring out the window and said, *"You think?"*

I climbed up on my knees looking over his shoulder at the view then answered, *"At least I always thought about heaven being up…and that other place…where the devil lives…well, it's down yonder!"*

"Oh? I don't know about that Sassy…look how pretty that is…Do you think God would let the devil live in that beautiful place like that for an eternity?"

"Well I jest know that ever time Ed Earl gits too close to the edge of one these cliffs, Daddy goes to hollerin…a telling him to git back or he'll have hell to pay! I jest figured that meant he would be payin a visit to the devil! Hell…that's where the devil lives ya know…sepptin it aint nice to say that word…H E double L…lessin ya talkin bout where the devil lives and Mama says we ought not even let that nasty word come out of our mouth!"

Doc chuckled as he checked his mirror when we heard the Deputy honk his horn and yell out his window, *"Ever thang Alright?"*

Doc kept his big smile as he waved and rolled on down the road. Pointing the way in the right direction when the road would fork, I noticed that it would narrow with the ones less taken.

The closer to home I got, the more relaxed I felt about talking to him. Maybe it was because I was on my own turf, but I felt I was shedding some of my shyness.

"Doc, have you ever read a book called the Bible?"

"Well, I've read most of it, but not all at one time…but over the years. Why?"

"Cause, There's this here story in there that tells bout how the angels would praise God with real purdy angel music. Then…one day…one of them named Lucifer thought he could play better than the others and grew proud. He thought it was better than anything. He thought a whole lot of himself too and became selfcentered. Mama says that's when a body gits all tangled up inside themselves and caint get out and consider anybody else. Well…soon nuff he started liking himself more than anythang else…even more than God! Well…God wuttin to crazy bout all that. He even tried to take Gods place, by telling lies…lies that would try to fool others into thinking he was the greatest thang ever wuz…but that's a lie…cause God is!

God tried not to pay him any mind but he just kept on…wuttin long bafore that bad angel got jealous of the other angels that God was paying attention to! God warned him ta quit it but he jest wouldn't let up! He kept on with his foolishness till he got some em others ta follow him and they became fools too…like him!

Well…God had jest bout 'nough of that and throwed him clear out of Heaven! And, the Bible says that when he fell, he fell far down in the pits, as far as the deep goes. Yep…God said he wuttin nuttin but an ole devil and he would burn in the pits of hell along with all the other fools who decided to follow him!

There have been many times that I have seen smoke a commin up from down there and where there is smoke there is fire! So…Ya see Doc…Heaven is up…and Hell is down!"

"Ok." Doc said. *"I see. I didn't remember all of that; where is that at in the Bible?"*

"It's in there…several places...Isaiah, fourteenth chapter…Psalms fifty five Revelations…buncha places. Yortta read it again! Mama says he'z still a tryin to pull fools down there ta join him! Now God…well, He has a throne in heaven…Bible always says that Heaven is up"

"How is it that you know so much about the Bible…but don't know your last name?"

"I don't know. I guess we aint had no call to use another name but the ones we got, cause what would we do with it? We all know who we are. None of them people in the Bible had but one name and nobody thought anythang of it!"

"Where did you learn so much about the Bible? Do ya'll have a church up here?"

"That's right Doc, how did you know? I don't remember telling ya bout that!"

"Oh, just a wild guess." he said with both hands on the wheel and his eye on the narrowed road.

"Yep. The Second Baptist Church of Rollin Hills. That's our church alright."

I recognized the pasture of our closest neighbor and got excited about seeing our own animals that had to be pretty hungry by now.

We were about six miles from home when I thought to myself, it wouldn't be long now. I pointed out the Riley's house as we passed by and when the dogs came barreling down the driveway to chase the cars, I felt compelled to tell him the story about those dogs chasing us down the road. When he asked why we didn't stop for help there, I told him how she didn't take kindly to children and how mean I thought she was to sic those dogs on us. *"It's just a little ways from here."* I said as we passed their place and the dogs quit chasing us.

Doc commented on the heat and distance as he drove for the rest of the way in disbelief that we walked all that way. He said that we were lucky we didn't get hit by a car or pass out from heat exhaustion. Not to mention any meanness that could have come upon us kids being out there all alone.

Finally, we were coming up to the paths that lead to our place so I asked Doc to slow down so he could turn in.

When I spotted the opening that was mostly hidden by underbrush I shrieked, *"There it is! There's where we live!"*

Doc stopped the car and looked around then said, *"Where?"*

"Turn here...just past that tree!"

"Sassy I don't see anything...where is your house...Heck! Where is your driveway?"

"Daddy aint done makin it yet but he parks his truck just down there then walks the rest of the way." I said pointing in that direction.

Looking around he said, *"My car won't make it down there, I'll bottom out, I'd better park here."* He pulled off the edge of the road, stopped then turned the car off.

Deputy Reed pulled up and parked behind us. We all got out and stretched, giving the deputy an opportunity to tell Doc that he was pretty sure that he was about eight or nine miles into the next county, and if so, he was out of his jurisdiction. However, since he had come this far, he might as well follow up.

Though they couldn't clearly see any signs of a house through the thicket of trees and brush, they could barely make out signs of life and the subtle sounds of our animals moving about.

"This way, come on!" I said to them, leading the way and so glad to be home.

On my way down the steep path I realized that I might not be able to tell Mama about all the adventures we had on our trip to town. I wanted her to meet all of our new friends.

I slowed my pace when I got to the driveway and waited on them to catch up with me.

Doc almost lost his footing before he caught hold of a small tree close by.

Animals, both wild and tame, scurried about the edge of the woods and in their pens as we stepped into the clearing.

The clothes that were hanging from the line were barely moving in the gentle breeze and gave the appearance that they had just been hung there.

Hanging from the A frame was but one of the bags that we had tied up. The other lay on the ground partially opened just beneath the rope that still dangled above it.

The chickens that had flown the coop shuffled toward us in search of feed as they had always done upon our return.

The goats neighed and pushed around in their small confinement as we made our way further into the camp.

I noticed the stone cook stove sat cold with nothing cooking, but the fire pit barely smoldered under a heavy layer of ashes.

Opened was the lid to the supply trunk where I had retrieved the extra batteries for the flashlight. That puzzled me as I remembered securing it before we left.

The men stopped in their approach. Looking around, they saw the remains of an old rusted out school bus that was being held captive by a tangled mass of vines. Its tires were missing, as well as most of its engine, with the hood removed and placed securely on tall logs over the door for obvious shelter.

Hand painted in black letters along the sides, just beneath the curtained windows, read the faded words, *Second Baptist Church of Rolling Hills.*

Deputy Reed asked if this is really where we lived and if so, where was our house?

I didn't remember one question past that as I found myself standing under the hooded porch Daddy had made for Mama, staring through the doorway.

Doc suddenly realized that I was standing at the foot of our stairs, just outside the double doors, of our home by the lake…and asked me, *"Sassy, is your mother in there?"*

I stood paralyzed with fear of the disappointment I might find inside, as Doc rushed passed me and climbed aboard. He called me to come there as the deputy lifted me up to the first step then followed.

I stood astounded at what I saw.

The bookshelf that Dean had made for her had been knocked over and all of her treasured little curiosities were thrown to the floor.

Scattered about and covering the floor were little pieces of paper that had landed everywhere!

Next to the wall was the black leather binding to a Bible…its pages missing.

There on the mattress, where I left Mama three days ago was nothing…not even the bed clothes!

13
LAW & ORDER

The ticking of a clock, measuring time by minutes within the hours of a day, days into weeks, and weeks into years then into decades and so on, is but one example of man's pursuit for order.

Every aspect of creation thrives on routine and organization for its survival on this earth.

All matter of mineral is organized in its buildup and breakdown. Plant life routinely depends on the arrangement of the passing seasons for balance of nature. Every living creature, from the time of conception until death do it part from this earth, clings to life itself through its daily regimen and habitual lifestyle.

It was woven into mans congenital composition by his Creator to have order. Given time to ponder it, sooner or later you will end up where you started. From ashes to ashes…dust to dust.

One of my earliest lessons in organization was seeing a flock of geese in chevron flight and asking my Daddy how they knew how to fly that way. He told me that they kept an eye out on one another working together like a tag team and when the leader got tired he fell back, then the next in line took a turn at leadership. However, in order for them to be good leaders they must first learn to follow. So they earn respect and status in time spent with the flock.

I recognized it again in the straight and even stitches on the seams of my clothes that made them form to fit my body for comfort. They kept their form and stayed fastened if the whole row of buttons lined up to meet with the button holes.

It was good, I had learned, that pages of the Bible were cut evenly on the edges, so that it stacked neatly and stayed in numerical order in its binding.

I found that organized ideas can work, like the windows on the bus. They were able to open and close if they stayed on the tracks that were made to keep them in line. If one of them got off track, it didn't work right any more then became a hassle to use. It was out of order…and…order made things work better.

Whisper Ridge was a good example of this and would leave a lasting first impression of the result of order and pattern. I could see the visual effect of the neatness in the rows of tables in the café, the rows of boats outlined by straight lines of fences as well as houses that lined up neatly on the streets.

Upon our arrival to this quaint little town my younger brother had asked what those silver boxes on posts were and why they all were lined up on the same side of the road.

At the time I couldn't answer, not knowing they were mail boxes but later would learn that they were yet another example…a result of cooperation and order. It was apparent that rules and regulations were followed by the towns' people, who enjoyed sharing close spaces and found the give and take was worth the effort. Much like the exchange of respect we had back home for each other in our daily routine, only on a much larger scale.

I had heard it said that we are all creatures of habit. We adapt and become comfortable in a situation if we stay in it long enough. A way of life will become a habit and habits, once they are formed, good or bad, are hard to break.

Our habits and routines become part of our lives, and over time become not our first, but our *second* nature.

It's part of what makes up our character that becomes who we are when we think nobody is looking.

If a person doesn't enlist a set of rules and regulations to follow they will simply live by their own rules. They may make up their own…but if it's not set in good standards, they can haphazardly destroy their chance for a full life.

During the late sixties and early seventies a popular phrase circulated that said… *"Do your own thing".*

Some folks used that statement to encourage talents and ambition whereas others abused it by taking it to mean, "do what you want to do and don't worry about anybody else or the consequences that were sure to follow".

Trouble is when so many people try just doing "their own thing" and only what *they* want to do, it creates chaos and disorder, wreaking havoc in every area it is played out.

The same malfunction can be found in those scriptural readings where Satan made fools of many by telling them, *"Do as thy will"* as opposed to God's will being done.

I would guess that our parents had already started to see that sort of behavior in those days, prior to coming to Chinquapin Hollow.

That may have been the reason for their hiding from such a world that had gone mad and, in their opinion, heading straight to the pits of hell.

Could it have been that they adopted this philosophy to fit their own needs and were in fact doing their own thing?

Pondering such thoughts to form rhyme and reason is where I would spend most of my time in those days that followed our finding Mama gone from her sick bed where I had left her.

Our problems had gone from bad to worse as now we were in search of both our parents.

The odor of perspiration and stale ashtrays occupied the little available air in the cramped working quarters of the Sheriff's office. Two desks sat side by side piled high with papers, clip boards, pens and pencils, along with empty pop bottles and potato chip bags. Each one had phones that were ringing simultaneously with only one young deputy left to man them.

On top of a small table sat a big metal box with knobs and tiny lights that blinked. Occasionally, I could hear a voice and some static come out of it and the deputy would pick up this thing and talk into it. When he caught me staring at it, the deputy explained that it was a police band radio that they used to talk to the officers in the patrol cars.

File cabinets topped with extra loads, lined the walls except for a gap that was left for three chairs, leaving very little floor space where the tiles were loose and worn from concentrated traffic. In this case, the Sheriff gathered a crowd of men in the parking lot along with some other police to form a search party.

Some of them were in and out of the office making calls while others were asking me questions to get a description of Daddy and Mama.

The Sheriff came in, then sat on the edge of one of the desks knocking a drink over and sending a stack of papers to the floor. Another man who was wearing a different uniform followed him in picking up the mess before stepping over the Sheriff's big boots that stuck out in the pathway.

This man sat in one of the chairs next to me and pulled out his pen to write on some paper that was clipped to a thin board.

They asked if I could remember and describe what Mama and Daddy were wearing when I last saw them. They asked me what kind of truck they have and were there any other vehicles they could have been using. Then, once again, I was humiliated by not knowing Mama's first or last name.

"Are you sure?" one asked.

"Think girl…think!" the other persisted.

The one who was doing the writing seemed angry with me when he didn't get the answers he wanted. He jumped up from his chair with frustrated huffing and pivoted in the small space with little room to pace the floor.

"What kinda people don't teach their kids their last name? Are you retarded or something that you don't know a thing like that?" he asked in a loud voice.

I sat staring at his red face without making a sound. Because I hadn't known the answers to those questions he'd asked, I thought it best not to answer at all rather than giving him a wrong one and frustrating him more.

"Look at her Sheriff! She don't know nuttin! I think she's a retard and that's why they kept her hid up in them woods!"

"Now Virgil." Sheriff said, *"There's no call for that…Sassy why won't you tell us what ya folks names are…Did they threaten to beat cha or somthin if ya told the police?*

Beat me? What did he mean *beat cha…* like…in a race? I wondered.

The other officer sat back down and asked me, *"Zat it? They tell you not to talk to the police?"* They both leaned in eager to hear my response.

"Girl…you understand I'm the law, don't cha? And, by order of the law you have to answer me!"

"Now Virgil…back off…ain't no law been broken here!" The Sheriff told him.

Still confused and staring at the first man, I hesitated to answer, not knowing what they wanted to hear.

"Come on girl! What kind of game are you playin?"

Game? I wondered. What was it that they wanted to know…what kind of game would my parents…*beat* me in?

I studied his face to try and figure out if he was asking me to play a game. Maybe, I thought, he might want to play some kind of name game but I wasn't sure how to play.

I watched his face grow a deeper shade of red with the ticking of the clock. I was concerned about it and was about to tell him that he looked a little sunburned when he snapped.

"GIRL, WHAT YOU LOOKIN AT!"

Jumping back in my chair, I hadn't realized I had done something wrong. The man stood up, throwing his clip board across the desk and shouting... *"I DON'T KNOW WHY WE'RE WAISTIN A GOOD SATURDAY EVENIN ON A BUNCH OF HILLBILLIES THAT DON'T NOBODY GIVE A HOOT ABOUT NO HOW!"*

"Alright Virgil...settle down."

"I HATE THIS JOB! THEY DON'T PAY ME ENOUGH TO SPEND MY TIME LOOKIN FOR A COUPLE OF STUPID INBREEDS THAT AINT GOT BETTER SENSE THAN TO GIVE BIRTH TO A BUNCH OF STINKIN RETARD YOUNGINS!"

"Virgil!"

"...THEN, THEY WON'T STAY OUT THERE AND TAKE CARE OF UM!"

"VIRGIL! I said that was enough!"

The Sheriff stood up and grabbed him by the arm and lead him to the door while bumping their big bodies on the file cabinets. On their way out I could hear him say..."*Is that any kinda way ta act! I don't know how ya'll do it over in Clifton but that aint how we get answers here! We aint interrogatin no criminal here!"*

Shaking in my skin I sat scared but too afraid to cry for fear of upsetting anyone else.

The deputy sitting behind the desk had hung up the phone during the yelling, shaking his head as they walked out, he said, *"Don't pay him no mind...them fellers over in Clifton think if aint a shootin involved it aint any fun for um! If they caint be a bully, then they'd rather sit around on a Saturday night drinkin beer and watchin Perry Mason reruns on the television set!"*

I wasn't sure of anything he was talking about but it sounded like he was taking up for me.

Sheriff came back in with another man that asked questions, who didn't get upset if I didn't know the answer.

When any of them would think of another question, they would come back in to ask, then tell me to wait there…as if I had any place else to go.

Emotionally drained, I sat waiting in mayhem for what to do next. The only order I could find was the ticking in a big clock that hung on the nicotine stained wall. Its rhythmic pattern kept time with the skinny red arm that traced the circle and could only be heard between the ringing phones, the ten-fours on the radio or the voices that got louder each time the door was opened.

The only clock that I was familiar with was the one in the cab of Daddy's truck and I had never known it to work. We never really needed a clock out there in the woods, we just used the light of day to let us know when it was time to do what.

However, Denby had a watch that he tried to teach me how to read time on and though I had not yet mastered "time telling", he would make a game of it by letting me count the tics.

He would hold it up to my ear so that I could hear. I could still see his green eyes light up and his bushy brows rise when I would count past sixty and he would cheer, *"That's a whole minute! Yea!"*

It was good to see a familiar face when Doc came through the door with a gentle smile. He sat beside me and softly asked, *"Are you ok?"*

I shook my head and forced a smile as not to worry him any more than I already had.

"Maybe we ought not tell Ed Earl you got to ride in the Sheriff's car. He might be jealous…You think?"

I whispered, *"I was really scared…I didn't know him…we didn't even shake hands."*

"Well he had a whole lot on his mind trying to find your mother and all…The Sheriff is not a bad man. He's here to help you. I heard that other officer from Clifton yelled at ya. That aint right…he ought not done that."

"Well…that Sheriff feller…he talked to that man on that radio most of the way back from out younder…when it wuttin makin all that static noise and such…still…I'z scared."

"Alma is on her way to pick you up. I have to take care of a few things first then I'll meet you over at Trudy's Eat-A-Bite. Bet you're hungry, we haven't eaten since breakfast!"

"I'd like ta eat a little sumpin other."

With that he gently patted my hand then got up and left.

I occupied my time counting file drawers then ceiling tiles while I waited for Alma. Getting restless and tired of sitting, I watched through the dusty blinds for her car to pull up in the parking lot that had emptied from a line of police cars and pickup trucks.

I felt so all alone in the world for the first time and I now understood what it meant to be lonely.

The seemingly eternal wait took almost twenty minutes.

Reuniting with my siblings was somewhat emotional with that being the longest time of separation, as well as distance.

It felt like I had waited forever before Alma had pulled into the parking lot of the Sheriff's office to pick me up.

Running out the door to meet them without waiting for her to park, I felt tears well up in my eyes. However, these, unlike all the others I had cried earlier, were tears of joy in seeing the faces of my brother and sisters.

They hung out the windows of the car, waiving and yelling my name. I had missed them so much and realized that they were all I had to my name…whatever that was. They were the only things I could be sure of that day.

Alma slammed on her breaks, screaming, *"WAIT!"* when the car doors flew open before she could come to a complete stop.

Earldean, Ed Earl and Learline met me halfway with open arms where we then locked up in a group hug.

To Alma, we must have looked pitiful there weeping and hugging like we had not seen each other for years though it had only been six and a half or seven hours.

"SASSY!"

"What Happened? How did it go?

"Oh, Earldean…"

"Did Doc give Mama some medicine soz she can git well?

"Well…when we…"

"Why did the police bring ya back? Did ya'll find Daddy?" Where's Doc?

"He'z commin but…"

"Did you git ta ride in a squad car?"

"Mama come too…Were Mama?"

"Oh baby sis…"

"Sassy…Did ya'll find Daddy or something?
"Naw, It's just…"
"Did ya. Huh, Sassy…Did ya git ta ride?"
"Ed Earl, I'm trin ta…"
"Sassy! Answer me…what happened?"
"I want Mama…where is she?"
"Wait!"
"Well what happened?"
"Sassy…Did he turn on them lights?"
"Wait…I'm tryin ta…"
"MAMA!"
"WAIT…PLEASE..Wait!"

There were so many questions to answer and so many things I needed to tell them, although I rehearsed it in my head over and over it wasn't coming out like I planned.

Alma got out of the car and attempted to corral us back in when she came to my rescue. *"Now…Now…Let's back up and give your sister some room…Hey Hun…you ok?* she asked as she worked her way in for a hug. I was glad to see her too and returned the embrace, feeling her spongy flesh press against me as I stretched my arms to reach around her.

She took my face into her hands and asked again, *"You ok Hun?"*

"Yes'um, I'm alright."

"You have been through a hard day, I know…Ya hungry?"

"Sortta."

"Ya'll come on." she said turning and scooping us around back towards the car.

"She can tell us all about it in the car, ok? She aint eat chet so let's get ya sister over ta Trudy's place fer a bite ta eat."

"We goin to the Eat-a-Bite…for a bite ta eat?" Ed Earl asked with a little sarcasm as we headed back to the car.

"That's right! Eat-A-Bite for a bite ta eat!"

Learline made up a cute little tune to go with the catchy words and as she climbed into the car she sang; *"Eat a bite…bite ta eat…eat a bite…bite ta eat…"* She was so adorable and entertaining at that age. We laughed and sang along with her. Well, everyone except Ed Earl, who was placing his food order as he climbed in and shut the door.

"I 'ont summa em fried taters…and sum ketchup fer dippin…ok Alma?"

In the car, on the way over to the Eat-A-Bite, I made a challenging attempt to tell them about us getting all the way out to Chinquapin Hollow and finding Mama gone.

Earldean stared at me in disbelief with her mouth hung wide open saying, "*What?*"

I told them how shocked I was to see her empty bed as we could only guess where she might be.

I was glad to see that she was up and about and had gone out of the bus looking for us.

When we didn't see her right there around the camp I called for her. The men, not knowing her name just called out, *'Ma'am!...are ya out here?* "

I told them I'd looked for her down by the creek thinking she might be washing the sickness off of her body and out of her bed clothes as she was known to do such a thing to prevent spreading any plagues. They held back up the trail just a bit in case she was undressed because they didn't want to catch her off guard or embarrass her.

Through the woods I could hear that the recent rains had provided sufficiently to replenish the creek so that the water babbled, as it rolled over the rocks downstream. I could hardly keep my eyes on the path before me for trying to peep through the trees for a preview of my reunion with Mama.

When I reached the edge and didn't see her I started calling for her again.

Doc and Deputy Reed came running down the path, thinking I had found her asking if she was ok.

We followed the creek on down to the lake, looking her for down around there but still nothing.

Thinking maybe she might be out on the lake, we looked for the boat but it was still securely tied up under the bushes where we kept it.

Doc wondered if she might have gotten to feeling better and in her deliriousness might have gone out looking for us, not remembering that we had gone to town for help.

She was just nowhere in sight so we started looking throughout the woods in all of our favorite play places.

Deputy Reed had a notion that she might have gone to a neighbors' house for help and he left us still searching the area while he went down to the Riley's and a few of the other houses down by the lake.

Doc had his doubts about her having enough strength to walk that far if she had been in bed for three to six days.

I had kept fears to myself in that if Mama had gone looking for us that she wouldn't be upset about us going off to town by ourselves. I had hoped that she wouldn't be angry with me about letting Ed Earl wear her pink shoes; they were too little for her anyway.

I told them about us looking all around out there for her before Deputy Reed called Sheriff McCoy to come out and help us to find her.

As it turns out, our place was just over the county line so he had called for the police over in Clifton, the next county, to assist in the search.

Only two of them showed up to help saying that it was so close to the line and that if we were to find her on this side of the line they would still have to bring them in on it.

Agreeing to work together, they decided to meet and form a search party before it got too dark.

Doc was going by to gather some of the volunteers so I rode back with the sheriff to give them what information I knew.

By the time we reached the café I had given them the highlights of the event as best I could, which would be enough to hold them off until after I ate.

From the moment I had said that Mama wasn't in the bed, Earldean had folded her arms and kept them locked without uttering a word. As we walked in Trudy was putting out a chalkboard that listed the "Saturday Night Special" of fried chicken, pinto beans, turnip greens, mashed potatoes and cornbread. For desert there were two choices, peach cobbler or banana pudding.

"Well, if it aint my new favorite customers! Ya'll come on in here and get a seat before all the good ones are taken." Trudy said with a big welcoming smile.

I looked around at the near empty café with only one lady sitting at a booth and Debbie and two other ladies rolling silverware into napkins at a corner table. We exchanged waves with Debbie as we took our place in Alma's favorite spot, the same booth where we sat the day before.

Trudy soon followed with a tray of water glasses that she served up with a smile and howdy do's.

I couldn't help but notice that she was wearing a different pair of earrings that were even prettier than the ones she was wearing the day before. They complimented her uniform with clusters of red sequins fastened with tiny silver beads and fashioned on little balls that dangled from her earlobes.

I kept my eyes on them as she bent down to serve my glass of water and asked, *"So did Doc git ya Mama fixed up?"*

"She aint eat since breakfast. We'd better feed her purdy soon!" Alma told her with a signal to hold off on the questions.

"Oh Sweetie! Let's get you some vittles then! Wha cha hungry for?" Trudy sympathetically said. *"Cody's gettin the grease hot n ready ta start fryin up some chicken back there…shouldn't take too terribly long ta git ready. Howz at sound to ya?"*

"I like chickens…I like how the skillet sounds when it frys just fine…kinda like fish."

"Like the sizzle do ya? Well how bout the rest of ya? Ya'll like chicken?"

We all responded with a positive nod and Ed Earl asked if it would be alright if he could dip his in ketchup.

"He really likes ketchup." Alma smiled and told Trudy who took advantage of an opportunity to snag Alma aside from us for information by saying, *"Well maybe we aught ta go fetch an extra bottle for this table, ya think Alma?"*

Promising to bring him back a whole bottle of it, Alma asked us to stay there while she took her water and walked to the kitchen with Trudy.

While Alma was giving Trudy the scoop, Earldean pulled me over to discuss what we had found back home.

Ed Earl and Learline entertained themselves by rearranging the condiments on our table while we talked under our breath.

"Sassy, what do you mean Mama wuttin there? Are you sure…it wuttin like she could just get up and walk away…You saw her! She was…"

"Naw she wuttin Earldean! She was just fainted or stroked or something, we just thought she wuz dead! She musta woke up and got well cause she wuttin in the bed!"

"Sassy! Where wuz she then?" she persisted.

"Well, I don't know! That's why all them people are goin out there to look for her…They gonna find her…Maybe she went to go pick some berries or somthin!"

"Berries?…Sassy, the drought done got all the berries, you know that! You know what this means don't ya? If she's alive she is gonna kill us for takin off by ourselves…we'll be the dead ones then!"

"EARLDEAN!"

"Shhhhhhhh! Quiet, Sassy!"

"I can't believe you said that! You'd rather Mama be dead than ta take a wippin?"

"Naw…It's just…this is nuts! Sassy what are we gonna tell Daddy?"

"Hey, maybe Daddy went home and fount her and theyz a out lookin fer us right now!" I suggested optimistically.

"Or…maybe he went home and seen she's so sick so he took her to see the doctor!"

"No Earldean, that aint happened…Doc wuz wit me all day!"

We were so engrossed in our conversation that we hadn't noticed that the little ones had climbed out of the booth and gone looking for Alma. They found her at the end of the counter talking to Trudy and holding a bottle of ketchup.

They made their way over for a visit with Debbie who had stopped rolling the utensils long enough to chat. She took them each by a hand and led them back to our booth.

"Hey ya'll! Sassy, are ya feelin better today? Debbie asked *"…You sure gave us a scare yesterday. Does your sunburn still hurt?"*

"It's a little achy…but I aint fainted no more."

"Aunt Trudy's says ya'll had ta stay the night with Alma last night… I bet ya'll was bored ta tears. She aint got nuttin to do out there at her house but listen to the radio and there aint no cute boys over there in that Shady Acres trailer park…nuttin but old people. Where'd ya'll sleep at in that tiny place?"

"We slept just fine on the floor." I told her and noticed she wasn't wearing her big smile. She was still real pretty to look at, though I could tell she wasn't fishing for a tip like she had done the day before.

Alma was coming back with the ketchup just as Debbie was asking if we were going to stay again tonight. Alma answered for us as she worked herself into the booth to sit next to Learline. *"They are welcome to stay as long as they need to…Ya'll know that don't ya?…I mean if they don't find ya Mama or ya Daddy."*

Earldean cleared her throat but still sounded a bit fretful when she said, *"Maybe we could look around for him Alma…That's what we come to town for."*

"Heck, Earldean, I know that, but unless we can come up with a place to start, well, we'll be just goin round in circles! Can ya think of any names of places ya heard ya folks talk about him workin we could go there and see? Anything Hun, can ya think of anything at all that might help?

"I heard Daddy say one time about him findin work in a town called Tulsa." she said.

Trying to recall when that was and what was said about it, I closed my eyes to picture my parents. I had a hard time seeing their faces in my mind but I managed to remember that conversation. *"Yea, I heard that too...but that was a long time ago...Earlden, he come home after that!"*

"Tulsa! That's still a ways from here and you were gonna try to walk there?" Alma asked.

"Who's walkin ta Tulsa?" Trudy asked as she walked up and pulled a chair from the adjacent table to the end of the booth then sat down.

"The kids here say they think their daddy may be in Tulsa or may have worked there at one time."

"Maybe we aught to tell Sheriff McCoy so they can call the police over there and have them look for him, while they're tryin ta find the Mama."

"They still don't have a name to run a check on or a clue ta know where ta start." Alma reminded her.

Trudy turned to me and said, *"Sassy, Alma told me what happened out there when ya got home and couldn't find ya Mama. What did the sheriff say he was gonna do?"*

"The Sheriff said he sus-pected a bird of some kind ...maybe the chickens came up in the bus and played around and tore thangs up!"

"The chickens?"

"Yep, probably a couple of big one ta cause all the mess...why, he took one look at it and said it looked like fowl play to him. Then, that's when he got on his radio and called them other fellers"

"What is this about Fowl Play?" Trudy asked as she and Alma both leaned in waiting for me to answer.

"You know...chickens like the kind we gonna eat fer supper? Septin he called um fowl. Same thing...Anyway he must a thought theyz the ones who got up in the bus and tore up the place like they done but I told him aint none ever got up in there ba fore and made a mess like that!"

"Bus...What bus?" Alma said with a totally confused look on her face.

*"What did the chickens have ta do with...OH-MY-GOSH! Alma...**Foul play!**"*

14
IN THE WAITING
(*MAKING A HABIT OF IT*)

Noticing the traffic flow was different on this day than it was the day before I still caught myself watching out the windows of the Eat-A-Bite for my Daddy's truck to pass by. I don't know what I might have done if I had seen it; run out after him I guess.

Doc had come in with a woman and was talking with Trudy and Alma at another table when our food was ready.

There was more on our plates than we could possibly eat at one sitting as Cody, the cook, brought it to our table himself. I guess in his own way, he thought we had to make up for any lost meals we might have missed.

He stood and watched us as we asked God to bless it before we dug in. He listened to the pleasurable moans we made over the crispy fried chicken. He helped Ed Earl pour some of the stubborn ketchup on to his plate for dipping. Learline, not wanting to miss out, had to have some too.

"I'll get that for her, Cody we don't want to take ya away from your work." Alma said walking back to our table with Doc and the other woman.

"Oh I don't mind... I had better get back to the kitchen though...I have a feelin we in for a busy night." Cody said as he trotted off toward the back.

Doc stepped over next to the table and took the woman by the arm pulling her closer to him. *"This is my wife... Estelle. She has agreed to help take care of ya'll until we find your parents."*

Strangely enough she didn't look at all like what I had imagined. When I first heard that Doc had a wife, I sort of expected her to look like Mama. I don't know any other reason why I would think that, except Mama was the only *wife* I knew of besides the ones in the Bible and I just assumed that all wives looked like her.

"Well, I only agreed to help Alma and Trudy. I'm not going to take on the fulltime position... I've raised my children and I'm not crazy about babysitting."

I could just sense by the look on her face and the tone in her voice that she was not too thrilled with the idea of hosting us misfits as she went on to say, *"Alma…you're going to stay here with um tonight, right? I have to wash and roll my hair for church in the morning. Hopefully, the Sheriff and them will find their parents and we won't have to fool with rearranging our schedules."*

"Sure…" Alma said… *"I didn't have anything more important to do tonight than help out with these kids…I want to do my part to help!"*

"Well, so do we…isn't that right Estelle?" Doc said putting his arm around her and giving her a gentle shaking kind of hug.

"Well I think you have done enough Hank! You spent all afternoon out at the McMillan's helping Fred deliver that colt then the rest of the evening and on up into the night trying to find these people! Then, you were up early again to deal with these children…gone all day! When's it going to be my turn? Am I going to have to get lost for you to spend time on me?" Estelle said with grievance.

"Shhh…Estelle, not here...Let's get something to eat and we'll both feel better." Doc said as he turned her body by guiding her shoulders.

Alma watched them walk over to a table across the way before she turned and fixed herself back into the booth.

"Ya'll have to excuse Estelle. She aint all bad, it's just she's a goin through the change of life and ya might not know from one minute to the next how's she gonna be. Why just a few minutes ago she couldn't wait to have ya'll out to their place, talkin about bakin some cookies and ridin horses and such…she'll be alright after while."

In most cases the folks of Whisper Ridge would be done with their supper time by eight o'clock at the latest on Saturday night. However, this particular Saturday night, Trudy and the crew were still serving till almost nine, even though she had run out of the special by seven thirty.

Word had got out about the search party that was formed to find the missing people and rumors spread like wild fire as to what might have happened to them.

The Eat-A-Bite was like Grand Central Station with the comers and goers of folks who wanted to help and then there were those who were just looking for something new to talk about.

Some of them were the regulars who found out when they got there and were a little perturbed if they found somebody else sitting in their favorite spot.

Others would pass by our table and stare at us and maybe make a comment or two.

Alma explained that some people get set in their ways and don't take kindly to changes or strangers in town. *"But that's just some people for ya....Those same kind of folks like to sit in familiar places and eat the same familiar foods with the same familiar people so they will know what to expect. It becomes a habit and a way of life and they don't like anybody messin with their lifestyle."*

Doc and Estelle said their good nights as they made way for more folks that had come in. Before they left, he told Alma that he was only a phone call away and the Sheriff had his number too if there was a need out there but unless it was a real emergency, he could use a good night's sleep.

Trudy did what she could to accommodate the overflow as they kept coming in with the same question... *"Have they found them yet?"*

I guess it's just in our human nature to be curious as even the owner of the Burger Doodle took a break long enough to come looking for his regular customers as well as a chance to sneak a peek at the little orphaned hillbillies.

He walked up to us with an introduction and invited us to come down to his place for a burger if we got hungry. He told us not to worry if we didn't have any money and that our parents could pay for the food we ate when they showed back up.

I thought that was awful nice of him to want to help out with feeding us knowing that we probably didn't have any cash. It hadn't occurred to us that we might need any money when we set out for town. We had little knowledge about currency, probably because we never had much of it.

We never thought about buying food that somebody prepared for us but it looked like a chore some folks would give up money for.

At any rate, I thought he was trying to give us one less thing to worry about by his offering. That was until Trudy set us straight.

She was busy turning in an order at the window when the man had come in. Being surprised to see him there in the first place, then talking to us, had her curiosity aroused.

Between turning in an order and serving another she made it over to us to ask what we wanted. When we told her what he said she responded with a bit of disgust. *"Well that sorry no good son of a gun..."* She came back and said after he left. "*... aint interested in nuttin but* *wantin ya'll at his place to draw folks in down there! He's just out ta make money 's all! He aint lookin out for nobody but himself... Ya'll don't got ta worry none bout what cha goin' eat! Aint nobody down here gonna let you go hungry... And... Don't worry none bout money either! Ya'll gotta 'nuff troublin ya mind without thinkin bout that!"*

She huffed off back to work shaking her head and chewing on a bite of something I had figured was some of her supper.

We volunteered to give up our booth as we had long since finished eating and were just visiting with some of the wives who were waiting on their husbands to meet them there after they found Mama and Daddy.

Trudy had to call in some extra employees to help with the supper rush and had even recruited Alma to fill and serve water glasses to the customers until their orders could be taken.

Earldean and I had volunteered to help clean tables with the bus boy who didn't care to do much talking. We couldn't get over how much food was going to waste.

Alma had told us that we shouldn't eat the food that people had left on those plates after I passed off a half eaten chicken leg to Ed Earl so he could mop up a big blob of ketchup somebody left on their plate. When her explanations to our "why not's?" were not sufficient to us she grew flustered.

Trudy overheard the dilemma and stepped in for a quick fix by saying, *"As a rule... it is not polite to do that in a restaurant, Ok ya'll?... If you're still hungry I can fix you somthin other ta eat sides other peoples leftovers... understand?"*

"Yes 'um." we all agreed with her, looking at one another as if it all made sense.

Alma, after all her talking watched Trudy walk away with having only to explain in those few simple words.

Shaking her head she said, *"How does she do it? For somebody who aint got no kids, she's sho gotta way with um!"*

What Alma didn't know was that Trudy gave us a word in her explanation that we understood the meaning of... that word was *Rule.* We understood about rules. Our parents had told us that we didn't have to always know the why of a rule; we just had to follow them for our own good.

When the hustle and bustle started to slow down and everybody got fed, Trudy and the other waitresses took a break. Most of the people that were still there were mostly just hanging out waiting on the searchers to get back with Mama and Daddy.

Trudy had sat down at the table with Alma and two other women who were waiting there for their husbands who were out on the search. One of them had her children with her; two little girls that were older than Learline but younger than Ed Earl.

They played with some crayons and coloring books that their mother brought along for them to keep them entertained.

When Earldean and I finished cleaning the tables with the busboy I took a break with Trudy and the others while Earldean went to look for Debbie.

Trudy made a little room for me to sit by her at the booth so I sat, half in and out of paying attention to the conversation, but mostly intrigued by the assortment of looks of the different people there.

One of the ladies that was sitting at the table with us had the others spellbound in a captivating story she was telling. Her bleached blond hair was most impressively light and fluffy. Her eyelids were colored with a shiny powder blue that almost matched the color of her eyes.

At one point the colorful blond began talking about some new stuff they had come out with that you paint on your lips to make them look wet and shiny.

The mother of the girls interrupted her to ask, *"Why on earth would ya want ta make um look like that?...I've always blotted my lip stick to keep um from lookin wet...and keep from gittin it all over my teeth."*

"It was one of Marilyn Monroe's beauty secret's called lip gloss, darlin..." the blond said secretively, "*... All the movie stars are wearin it now...Ann Margaret...Raquel Welch...ya know...all those...s-e-x symbols.*"

"Well that's the last thing I need...two kids is enough for me thank ya...I've got my hands full as it is...I certainly don't want my husband any more stirred up..." she stopped and caught herself when she noticed me sitting there. *"...well...you know...he don't need me to look more...s-e-x-y"* she whispered.

"Oh, sweetheart...I don't think it'll hurt ya nun ta put a little spark in your marriage..."

"Hut-Hum! Excuse me..." Alma broke in, tugging at her ears and almost singing a tune, *"...little ears listen in...we need ta change the subject."*

"Alma's right..." Trudy said. *"...anyway back to the lip gloss...when can I git some? You know, you're always lookin for a new representative to recruit...have ya give any thought ta askin Yvonne over there?*

"Yvonne?...Alma...how could you do that to me? I don't want to go losin my head waitress!"

"It's only a part time job Trudy...besides...she could use the extra money."

"Well...it don't matter anyway'z...we live in the same territory...she'd have ta work across town."

"Well...she might iffin ya's ta ask her to...maybe she might"

"Yea, right Alma...You know Cody would be all over that one."

"Whatta ya mean?"

"Well just think about it...Yvonne the Avon Lady?"

They all laughed and joked a little but I really wasn't sure what it was about then. It was just refreshing to hear a little laughter in the place. It didn't last long though, they went on talking about something else I didn't understand either. But...they were fun to watch; especially the Avon Lady.

Trudy wore color on her eyes and lips too but it was her orange hair that stood out most on her. I liked her pretty earbobs as well. They were different than the ones she had worn when we first met her. These were small red balls about the size of cherries, which dangled from tiny chains and were fastened somehow to her lobes with some sort of buttons. They bounced about her jaw line with every little move she made.

Staring at Trudy's face, watching her chin go round in a rocking sort of swing, her jaw bone moving under her cheeks each time her lips pursed then drew back again and again, gave me the impression that she stayed too busy to sit and finish her food.

I figured this accounted to her being so thin but when it went on for so long I couldn't help but wonder why she didn't swallow whatever she had been chewing or spit it out for lack of its ability to be pulverized.

I've had that happen to me on some tough pieces of meat that might have had too much gristle in it or sometimes a bite of undercooked turnip would do me that way.

Watching her chew like that set me to thinking about chewing on a piece of sugarcane and how we would sit on the back of Daddies truck, parked on the side of the road, waiting on buyers for our goods.

The stuff didn't readily grow in these parts but when traders would come through, Daddy at times might barter one of Mama's baskets for a few canes that would last quite a while. He and Mama used to cook it down for the sugar before they had realized it was more trouble than it was worth and Daddy decided to add a big bag of white sugar to the rations list.

On occasion he still liked to get some purely for entertainment pleasure. He would take a saw and cut the cane in small pieces, then with his pocket knife would peal the bark revealing the long, stranded pulp. Handing us each a piece to chew on, we would wallow that thing around in our mouth for the longest time, trying to release the sweet flavor.

We had been known to take some along on fishing trips as it seemed to help the time pass while we were waiting on our cork to bob.

Thinking maybe it might even be a chew of sugarcane Trudy was chewing on I looked around for some stalks that might be leaning against a wall or something. Not finding any in sight, I ended up fixing my eyes where I had them before…on Trudy's mouth.

"Would you like a piece of gum Hun…is that what you're a want'n… some gum?" Trudy asked me. I looked up at her eyes and found them looking back at me.

I smiled back at her with a big smile revealing my missing teeth and I guess she took that as a yes because she reached into her apron pocket and pulled out a small flat yellow package. She grasped the end and slid out a wrapped piece, handing it across the table to me and said, *"Juicy Fruit?"*

Taking it out of the paper I held it between my thumb and pointer trying to figure out what it was and what she wanted me to do with it.

"What's a matter Sassy, you don't like Juicy Fruit? It's the only kind I got on me right now."

It didn't look like much of anything in the way of fruit and it certainly couldn't contain very much juice, it was dry as a bone and about the same color.

"What's it for?" I asked still holding it and bringing it to my nose to smell.

Daddy had said it's always a good idea to smell of something when your eyes can't figure out what their seeing, especially before your put it in your mouth.

I recalled him saying many times when we were learning to check for spoils in our food supply, *"If ya smell it and it stanks…then it could be that its rank…but if ya smell it and its sweet…then most likely it's a treat!"*

Trudy stared back at me in disbelief. *"You don't know what it's for?"* she asked. *"Ain't ya ever had no chewin gum before child?"*

"Naw ma'am, I aint never had none!"

"Well go'on try it…it's good!"

Slowly sniffing it again just to be sure, I could smell the sweetness...like that of sugarcane. I licked the end to get acquainted with the taste on the tip of my tongue and liked what I tasted. I bit off a little piece and chewed for a moment until it became soft then I swallowed it before taking another bite.

"You didn't swallow it did you? Naw Sassy, its chewin gum! Ya sopose ta chew it!"

"What for?"

"Cause… well…its sortta fun… It's delicious…Gives ya mouth somthin ta do while your waitin your turn to talk…I guess…just try it!"

Putting the rest into my mouth, I worked it around getting the wonderfully sweet juicy flavor each time I chomped down on it. The more I chewed the juicier it got!

I could feel my expression change as I watched Trudy mirror the image on my face. We were both lit up with wide eyes and great big smiles.

"It's so…so…tasty!" I said as I fell in love with the flavor.

Trudy seemed to be as thrilled as I was at this new experience for me. *"I tried ta tell ya! I knew you'd like it!…Good huh?*

It was about an hour after dark when some of the men started showing back up from the search. Several had walked in with dismal looks on their faces saying that they hadn't found them yet.

Trudy got up to put on a pot of coffee when the Sheriff came in with some of the other officers. He said that they were giving up the search for the night as it was too dark to see anything out there. He announced to the crowd that gathered there that the search would resume in the morning at daylight and anyone interested in helping could meet at the police station by six.

As the crowed thinned out Sheriff McCoy came to Alma and told her that we might be able to be of some use to them out there in the investigation. He commented that the Clifton County police had not been a lot help with their Sheriff being on vacation.

They gave up the search after about two hours saying they were going to look around their town to see what they could find, although there were already two other of their deputies on that job.

Sheriff McCoy had his doubts about those guys; excusing them for being young and inexperienced.

Alma said she would work something out to get us out there with the help of some of the other volunteers who showed up to help.

We went home with her for a good nights sleep, as if there was such a thing under the circumstances. I felt such emptiness within me as now my hope was back on the downside of the rollercoaster, plummeting down fast.

Ed Earl had asked Alma what was going to happen to us if we couldn't find our parents and she assured him that she would see to it that we were taken care of. Her instructions were for us not to give up hope in finding them; for that it was in hope that we would find the strength to keep looking for them.

It was late that night before we spread the pallet out on the floor and took our place on it. She gave us all hugs before she spread the sheet over our tired and weary bodies.

Setting on the edge of the sofa she reached and took her Bible from the drawer in the table where she kept it. Flipping through the pages she came to Luke and found the story where the boy Jesus was separated from his parents when he was about twelve years old. It told how his parents searched for three days to find Him and how frustrated and worried they had been.

She closed the book and said, *"Ya see, they didn't give up till they found Him and when they did He had been takin care of important business! Don't give up on finding ya Mama and Daddy…They'll turn up soon."*

With that, we said our prayers and turned out the lights. There in the darkness, I strained to recall the sound of my Mother calling me. It had now been over three days since I had last heard her voice and its tender sound was fading from my memory but the words she last spoke, still played strong in my heart.

"I cried out to God with my voice and He gave ear to me. In the day of my trouble, I sought the Lord, my hand stretched out in the night without ceasing. My soul refused to be comforted…Soon, real ssss…"

15
THE SEARCH PARTY

Numbness is a word that would best describe how I felt that Sunday, in early August of 1968, when my whole world had been toppled over and went spinning in another direction.

It was playing in my head, like a bad dream, seeing and hearing everything that was going on around me but it was like it was happening to somebody else. In which case you might say, I was not myself.

Alma had to cut the gum out of my hair that had fallen out of my mouth in my sleep. She fussed a little about Trudy not warning me to get rid of it before bedtime. My cheeks were a little sore from overworking those muscles. I didn't know I was supposed to spit it out when it lost its flavor.

This was an unexpected chore for Alma and she was rushed to get the job done. Otherwise, she might have used peanut butter to loosen the gum from my hair but that would require a head washing after it was worked in. That…she said, she didn't have time for.

At any rate, she had every one of us up, fed and dressed before day break, then took us down to the police station where we waited on the crew of searchers to gather.

We were sitting on the edge of the sidewalk out front by the parking lot as folks drove in to meet with the Sheriff who was to show them the way out to our residence.

Trudy had showed up with Debbie and a thermos of coffee and volunteered to take us out there because she thought it best Alma not have to miss church services. Trudy claimed she wouldn't be missed on account she wasn't much of a regular attendee at either one of the two churches there in Whisper Ridge.

I could tell she apparently had felt unwelcome and that she had been shunned by the Christian community when she turned to me and Earldean who were sitting next to her and confided in us, *"Folks at the church house commence treatin me different ever since my husband Otis run off with that ole tangled eyed woman who tended bar down at them, dat, blastit VFW hall dances!*

When I decided to attend that other church…well, they was the same way toward me when they seen I didn't wear my weddin rang, knowin I'd been a married woman. Them church goers don't believe in di-vorces and made me feel plum shame about attemptin ta show up in the presence of the Lord under my circumstances.

Some of um down there thought Otis was a real stud…I reckon they thought I should sit round waitin on him, ta wear out that ole mare and a come trottin back ta my back door! Lordy No! That wuttin his first rodeo and probly wuttin his last the way he gallivanted out a here…Nope, he was back in the saddle again and I wuttin putting up with it."

Trudy picked up her cup and took a long sip of coffee swallowing hard enough to make a gulping sound then turned her head away.

We were a little confused about what she was talking about at the time but sat listening anyway because she said it with such emotion that we figured it was pretty important. I had taken her words literally when she had said that her husband was a gallivanting stud…and that he trotted at the back door…and something about the rodeo and a saddle.

I tried to picture in my head Trudy being married to a horse and how she might have lived with an animal of that size in her house.

Alma overheard her talking and came over to comfort her by saying, "*Now Trudy…Everybody aint like that down there! Just a few of them high floutin do gooders who thank they're holy'er than Thou. Thay aint got a clue what you went through with that cowboy you'z married to! Come on now…it's been nine…almost ten years since he took off and left ya like he done. That's too much time and foolishness to let that stand in the way of you and God Almighty!*"

Trudy took one more hard sip of her coffee before she said, "*Well I sure hate it for um 'cause when they started that mess…they got rid of the best pie baker of the Sunday socials!*"

"*Sure did!*" Alma responded "*…But God and the rest of us down there love ya anyway…wish ya'd come on back.*"

I might have been a little mixed up about the horse talk but I was smart enough to know what *foolishness* was. It had the word *fool* in it and couldn't nothing good come from it. I recognized it as the devils play and felt it necessary to warn her that he was just trying to play a trick on her mind.

I turned and rested my hand on her arm saying, "*Trudy, don't let the devil try ta make a fool out of ya…you can come to our church we got back in*

Cheek-pin Holler...we don't care none about you not havin a husband or a horse...and we like pies!"

After a short pause, she turned and hugged me with tears in her eyes saying, *"Oh Hunny! That's so sweet of you to say!"*

Alma leaned in to her and said, *"Out of the mouths of babes."*

Alma had already decided to skip the morning service and go along with us. She thought maybe we could pick up the clean change of clothes that Doc had forgotten in all the chaos the day before.

With that she suggested maybe we would get back in time for Sunday night prayer meeting. She was sure we would find our parents soon and we would all be able to go to church together.

Sheriff McCoy announced that if any one needed to gas up for the trip out that Collis would open his gas station to oblige and that they needed to go right then before it got any later. He also suggested that we use the restrooms and to fill water coolers if we had them before we take off.

Offering to take her station wagon because it would carry more people and she had a full tank already, Trudy rearranged the boxes of dried goods she had picked up for the café on Saturday and had not yet unloaded.

Granny Pane came with a basket of sandwiches she had made and some red Kool-Aid she had in a gallon jar that had been used for pickles. She said she wanted to go along but her husband had given her a hard time about it and she had better not rock the boat. She did say however, her daughter Jane and her husband Inky had volunteered for the search and that Huey wanted to help too. From what she understood they were to meet us out there along the way.

We had guessed that Estelle had a change of heart and/or mood, when Doc showed up with a batch of homemade cookies that he said she had stayed up late making for us, after she got word that our folks hadn't been found yet.

He said she was a little more agreeable this morning when she woke up and hadn't given him a hard time about going out on the search in the event there was a need for medical attention. In which case, he would need Alma's assistance so he was glad she was going along.

We climbed in Trudy's car for the long ride out to Chinquapin Hollow.

Sheriff McCoy led the way in his squad car with about twelve vehicles behind him. His lights were flashing and his siren would sound through the blinking traffic signals in town, as I'm sure it was a thrill for Ed Earl who was in the squad car with him and Fred McMillan.

We kept an eye on the long line of cars and trucks as we wound up and down the hills along the way. Trudy described this as looking like a funeral procession and I wondered what she was talking about.

Passersby would pull over to the side of the road until we proceeded as they gazed at us in wonder.

When we got out as far as Huey's house, he, along with his Maw and Paw, were waiting in their car at the end of the driveway. I came up on my knees and turned, looking out the back window to see them as they pulled out, then fell in line behind the last car who was Deputy Reed.

Up and down the dusty road, we wound through the mountains, as the morning looked promising for good weather for the search.

The barking hounds had brought Myrtle Riley and her husband out on their front porch to see what all the commotion was about. They stood with their hands on their hips and looked as though they wondered what was going on as we passed by their place.

Upon arriving home Learline, who was sitting in Debbie's lap, started jumping up and down getting excited about seeing Mama. She didn't understand about her being gone and was calling out her name. Debbie tried to calm her by telling her that we were there to find her Mama but she was out of her lap trying to crawl over us to get out the car door.

"Maybe we ought notta brung her out for this." I commented, but Trudy said it was too late to take her back. Debbie said she would look after her while we did what we had to do and would see what she could do to help her through this.

Huey and his Maw had parked and made their way over to see us. *"Hey ya'll...member me...Huey?"*

Ed Earl had already climbed out of the squad car and was on his way back to give his report on the experience of his ride. When he finished his tale, Huey asked to see his stitches saying his Granny told him all about him having to get sewed up.

Ed Earl was proud to show it off and sat right down in the middle of the dusty road and proceeded to work at the bandage Alma had put over it to keep it protected from the dirt and further injury.

When Alma saw what he was trying to do she went after him to stop and was backed up by Doc who told him the glue would not work again on the tape if he pulled it loose.

Sheriff McCoy had gathered the people at the entrance of the path where they waited for instructions.

He first sent Deputy Reed and another man down to check out the place, hoping our parents might have come back in the night. When they returned not having found any sign of them, Sheriff went on to explain the procedure of an organized search.

He asked for Trudy and Alma to take us children on down the path and wait there at the home sight while he divided the rest of the crowd into two groups.

Huey and Debbie came with us and helped carry the food and drink that was sent along to feed the helpers.

Alma had a hard time with the inclined path but did better once she reached the clearing.

We had told her and Trudy the night before about us living in a school bus but the look on their faces when they actually saw it told me that it had not sunk in. They stood at the opening for a minute before proceeding in to set down the snacks they had carried from the car.

Huey put one of the coolers of drinking water on top of a make shift shelf that was wedged between two maple trees. He pushed the button and held his mouth open under the spigot for a drink. Wiping his mouth with the back of his hand he made a quick evaluation of the place then headed over to get a closer look at the goats.

Thinking they might be hungry, I decided to go feed the animals.

The barrel of corn feed was almost empty when I reached in to scoop out a bucket full. Spilling a few kernels on the ground, I made way for the loose chickens and a goose that shuffled over to eat them.

When I got to the penned up goats, I could hardly get through the gate for their nudging me trying to get to the bucket. The chicken feeders were empty and needed to be restocked so I scooped up as much as I could from the bottom of the barrel before heading to the coop. I grabbed a hand full and scattered it out and about the ground to get them out from under foot.

Huey asked me if I needed some help, so I swung the bucket over to him so he could pour its contents in the feeding trough.

"Granny said ya'll aint got no house out here…said ya'll stay out here in that ole bus, zat right?" he asked, throwing his head a little and pointing with his nose as he poured the feed with both hands.

Still a bit shy but glad to be entertaining company, I softly answered him, *"We don't stay up in there all time…most time we just stay out round here."*

He worked his way around the crowd at his feet saying *"I thank ad be sortta fun…like campin out all time, huh?"*

I looked back over my shoulder to see the old bus resting in a nest of small trees and vines. It was surrounded by various storage containers of diverse shapes and sizes, made of anything from pasted board boxes or weathered wood to an assortment of tarnished metals.

Scattered about the grounds were a variety of home spun contraptions used to make life simpler for us. Our things were not stacked neatly about in tidy cupboards or folded to fit in cabinets with drawers but it was all kept sorted by arrangement so something could be found if there was a need for it.

It wasn't near as nice as Alma's trailer or Huey's house or any other homes we had seen and at that moment, for only a slight second, I felt a little embarrassed that I couldn't offer a nice place for our guests to sit for a visit.

The rest of the gang was looking around as Ed Earl and Earldean led them on a general tour. The women took a closer look and admired the homemade cook pit. Trudy asked if our parents had built it and commented on how neatly it was laid out. I could hear them making small talk and asking questions to Earldean about how we made out in winters out there.

They were about to take a tour of the bus when Sheriff McCoy stepped into the clearing and said, *"Hold it! Yall don't go in there just yet!"*

Stepping in closer he continued with an explanation, *"It's best ya'll not tamper with anything in there till we know more about whats goin on round here. We got some suspicions about this disappearance of the mother and if we're right … well…"* He hesitated to say anything else when he looked down at me and Earldean who were hanging on his every word in search of an explanation.

"Yea, what's that all about?" Alma asked.

Then Trudy added before he could answer, *"We heard somthin bout some foul play…wha cha thank happened here Sheriff?"*

"I shouldn't say anything about it just yet…We just got our suspicions so it's best everyone stay out here and wait until we find these people or till they show back up." he responded. Taking a deep breath, he went on to say, *"Doc seems to think that she would be too weak to go too far if she had been sick in bed for days before sending her children for help.*

We checked all the hospitals within fifty miles to see if any of them had a Jane Doe show up or anyone fitting her description…but…nothin. We've checked with most of the homes in the holler, to see if she showed up at any of them but she hadn't. Nobody had seen her…It would help if we had a name or a picture or something to show um.

Nolan will be making a second round today to recheck and to get the ones who weren't home when he went by. All we can do at this point is to search these woods or wait for her to come home. If we haven't found her within twenty four hours from the time we discovered her gone, we'll have to file a missing persons report with the state police."

"What will they be able to do to help?" Trudy asked.

"Well, they will try to find a picture or have a composite drawing made then post it around towns, announce it on the TV, radio news and get other communities involved."

Concerned about us, Alma asked, *"What will happen to these kids in the mean time?"*

Sheriff shot a glance at us then shook his head saying, *"Ya know Alma; they will turnthem over to Children's Services…You don't have to worry about them."*

"OH! Sheriff! They're gonna stay wit me till we find their Mama and Daddy! They aint gotta involve Child Services!" Alma insisted. *"I've already told these kids we'd all look after um till then!"*

"It's not up to me Alma, even if we do find them I have a feeling Child Services is gonna check into their living conditions…take a look around here…you think their gonna let um stay here?"

Alma reached back, putting her arms around me and Earldean and pulled us in to her sides with a reassuring double hug. She said with confidence, *"Well, we may not know what their names are or what they look like but these kids do have parents and they are bound to show up sooner or later. Their Daddy is off workin and is not expected back till sometime today or tomorrow…Why don't we just give him some time and wait till he shows up then at least one of their parents will be here to give you the information you need to find the Mama?"*

Sheriff put his hands in his pockets and shook his head *"…As I said before Alma, it's not up to me."*

Tugging at the Sheriff's pants leg Learline asked him, *"You gonna get Mama fa me?"*

Ed Earl, who had paid more attention to the conversation than I thought, stepped over in front of him and said, *"If Mama is out in them woods I can help find her…I know all the hidin places…she likes ta play hide an seek wit me…sometimes she lets me find her."*

"Me too" I said. *"…We have trails all over these woods…I can show ya!"*

Trudy bent down and picked up the baby, who straddled her hip after an adjusting bounce then with her fingers, she brushed the hair from Learline's face as she asked the Sheriff, *"Do ya really think she'd still be out there looking for um…Surely she'd come back by now to see if her kids came home or something! She might be asleep up in that bus right now! Why cain't we go up in there and see?"*

"Nolan already looked for that…everything is just like we found it yesterday when we came out…Nobody's been out here since we were here last night…That woman either walked out of there or somebody took her out…We have reason to believe that if she is alive…she's in bad need of medical attention."

"Why do ya think that? Maybe it was a bad virus or something…those things could last for three days at a time and take a lot out of ya but once they run their course ya git back to ya old self." Alma supposed.

"Ladies, I don't know how much you've been told but there are some things here that don't add up and we won't know the answers until we find one or the other of these people." Sheriff paused a moment before going on, *"…That old mattress where this girl supposedly left her Mama layin sick, was empty. When I got out here yesterday, I looked around for clues as to what might have happened to her. The mattress was pretty old and somewhat soiled but I noticed a spot of what looked like blood. When I touched it, it felt moist so it had to be fresh. After further investigation, I discovered that the mattress must have been flipped because the other side was saturated with blood."*

"Blood!" we all gasped.

I had not been in the bus when that discovery was made and they had not said anything to me before that point about their find. I would guess that it must have been after that that they decided to contact the Clifton police and form a search party.

The day before, Doc and I were returning from our second search in the woods and we had heard voices back around the bus and thought maybe Mama or Daddy had returned while we were out. It wasn't them of course but instead a group of various uniformed police, one of which was Sheriff McCoy. There were no formal introductions, as Doc had told me later, that there were more important things on their minds. They set me down and asked all sorts of questions including the ones I had been through with everybody else.

Sheriff and Doc together quizzed me about Mama's illness and wanted to know if she had fallen down before she got sick or maybe cut herself on something. When I couldn't recall anything like that, the Sheriff asked if Mama and Daddy ever fought or if I had ever seen Daddy hit her.

I told him that Mama didn't take much off us kids when it come to quarreling and didn't put up with the bickering between us.

She was easier going than Daddy was and had always sidestepped him to keep from butting heads when his feathers were ruffled. If he had any qualms with her, she went out of her way to smooth things out so that they would get along.

I told them that whenever a disagreement started up between the two, they took it to the woods. They didn't bring it out in front of us kids to see.

He asked me how soon after Daddy left, had Mama started to get sick. I told him that Daddy had left before daylight that morning and that when I woke up, I could hear Mama just beyond the edge of the woods throwing up.

She didn't go to bed with her sickness right away but it was after several days of not being herself, that she started taking spells of lying down and resting between chores.

When her fever started up she was too weak to get up, except to relieve herself. I had told them about her not having much of an appetite and Earldean and me taking over her chores and such but we hadn't done as good a job as she could.

I still didn't get a chance to tell them that Earldean and I thought she might have passed away when we didn't see her breathing. It never came up about that being the real reason for us taking out on foot to look for Daddy.

At first we had skirted the issue around the younger ones but just like all the times before, when we had tried to tell somebody that we thought Mama might have died, there would be some sort of interruption that would change the subject.

Not getting to tell that part in any of our conversations with the adults had seemed to work in our favor. It was Doc's thinking she was sick that got me back out here to see that it wasn't true anyway with her being out of bed and all. By that point I had decided that if we had told them she was dead there wouldn't be a need to drive back out there until we found Daddy. Mama might not ever think to look for us in town which would explain why I thought she would still be looking for us out in the woods. However, with a chance she was alive and well; she would soon grow tired of looking for us and she would have to come home and find us waiting for her.

It had not occurred to me that someone could have carried her out, except to take her to a hospital. When that idea was checked out and she had not turned up anywhere for medical attention, I put all my hope in the theory that she had gotten well and went out looking for us in the woods.

But now, all that talk of blood had my stomach in knots thinking some wild animal might have gotten in after her. That would account for the mess that was left behind. This was too big of a job for chickens and why would an animal want to flip a mattress?

The guilt of leaving her unattended was breaking my heart as I sank into a morass of silence and remorse.

There was nothing left to say about anything to anybody. I needed to be left alone but there were too many people around for that. There were more people than had ever been there before, more than I had ever seen in one place. There was no place to hide.

Debbie took up with Learline and kept her entertained, as well as Ed Earl who seemed to have had a crush on her. He had started following her around every step she made. It was a load off our minds for me and Earldean not to have to keep up with those two for a little while.

Alma and Trudy had done a whole lot to help but now were a bit nervous to be out there with potentially wild animals or whatever it was that got after Mama. They kept looking over their shoulders as they tried to find a place to make themselves comfortable for the waiting.

Huey, talking with me and Earldean, made mention of a boy he went to school with who Child Services had placed in some kind of foster home.

"They done 'at on account a him not havin no Mama and Daddy to look after him. Before that, he lived in one em places with a bunch a youngins called an orphanage." he warned us.

The word "orphanage" sounded a whole lot like the word orphan and caused me to crawl deeper into quietness, figuring there was a lot of truth to Trudy calling us that the day before, although she said she didn't mean it literally.

It was about ten o'clock when the Clifton deputies showed up with a couple of forest rangers, who had more of the same questions we had been through before with the others.

I recognized the one officer called Virgil among the group and was hoping he would not want to talk to me again. He made me feel nervous and shot mean looks at me when he thought nobody was looking.

Alma too had notice those two deputies from Clifton acted like they were put out to be there as I had overheard her mention this under her breath to Trudy.

At that point the volunteers came in for a drink of water and to re-divide into smaller groups with an officer leading each one.

The rangers told Sheriff McCoy that they had plenty of rescue gear incase it was needed and encouraged the group to stay within eyesight of each other so that nobody else would get lost.

They used hand radios to stay in touch throughout the woods. As we sat on blankets from our bedding we could hear the voices calling back and forth as they faded deeper into the forest.

The morning drug on for the longest with us waiting for the results of the search, hoping and praying for anything to be found that would change the uncertainty.

Making things more difficult for everyone was the fact that no one was exactly sure what they were supposed to be looking for.

Sheriff had the volunteers combing the grounds and woods looking not only for a woman who's name they did not know, with only a hint of what she might look like, but also, for anything that may possibly be a clue to what might have happened to her.

Eager were those who wanted to play detective and would question every foreign object they came across.

Not realizing that our family made our home and lived among these hundreds of acres for thirteen years, they were surprised to find scraps of paper, discarded containers or perhaps, an old piece of clothing or two that the strong winds had taken from our dwelling and strode about the woods.

There were those who were amazed and would later comment on the well worn paths they had found that lead to some of the most beautiful displays of nature out there.

They found our favorite places that were decorated with our homemade play things that were fashioned from whatever we could find to make them out of.

In a small cove by the creek, they found our cane poles. There were those that we used for fishing and the shorter ones, with the knotted and frayed fabric tied to one end that we liked to pretended were stick horses.

Up the path toward the bluff, just off the side, was a small area that nature had encircled with rock walls. Its notched ledges and jagged edges provided shelves for keepsakes such as carved pieces of wood that took on the shapes of toy boats or buses without wheels.

Clay that had been rolled into small balls served as marbles and kept in a pouch that was made of ash bark. Also made of clay, were miniature primitive figurines that had been shaped then baked in the sun until hardened.

Emerging from the well worn ground in this inlet, were the tops of boulders that provided seating for the weary to rest on or, a flat surface to roll out clay. Under a thicket of chinquapin trees, where the underbrush had been pushed back, they discovered our handmade, tied grass, twig dolls dressed in rags stitched for clothes, lying in hollowed logs that served as their cradles.

Down another path, they found the place that Ed Earl and I named "Crying Rocks" because water fell like tear drops from an underground spring, and for the most part provided a wading pool or at least, a fun mud puddle to play in.

It was here they found some old tin cans that were rock hammered into shape for a variety of play dishes. They were setting about in a miniature version of the cook area our mother used, with a petite homemade table and little stone cook pit that looked just like the one she used.

As the volunteers trickled in from the woods with their discoveries, some seemed impressed and showed enthusiasm, saying that we were creative and showed artistic ability when it came to amusing ourselves out there. Whereas others showed their pity on us for being too poor to afford real toys. Then there were those who showed off with smart-alecky comments about us being dumb for playing with garbage and too stupid to know the difference, adding that they thought we were nothing more than no-count, stinking hillbillies.

They all *showed* something…but…none of them *showed* up with Mama!

16
AROUND TOWN

Why do little kids think that if they whisper, nobody could hear? You could tell by our body language that something had disturbed us. But we just wanted to be sure first before we made an issue over this.

It was Ed Earls finding, that we were so secretive about, that we drew first Huey then Debbie over into our hushed conversation. The commotion of this discovery had shed a new, but distorted light on the mystery of the missing parents. It didn't take long before the rest of the folks that were out there searching for them to add this clue to the puzzle.

We were sure that Learline had left her baby doll somewhere along the roadside on the way to town, because the last any one of us remembered seeing it was when we stopped to make camp that first night out.

Earldean and I were convinced that someone had been there and brought it back, though I'm not sure why they would bring it all the way back out there only to leave it down by the creek and chance it being washed back downstream.

We pondered over several scenarios of how the doll made it back home before we did. It couldn't have come by waterway because the creek runs down stream and empties into the lake. We lived up stream about a hundred yards from the mouth of it.

Whoever found it must have known that it belonged to one of us and brought it back. We could only guess that Mama came looking for us, found where we had made camp and discovered that Learline left her baby doll.

I started crying again when Huey said, *"What if she got eat up by them panthers? That's probably why cain't nobody find her!"*

This time Ed Earl lost it with the thought of his mother being eaten alive by wild animals. He was so upset that even Doc had a hard time trying to convince him that that was unlikely to have happened.

Alma had to promise him some fish sticks, dipped in ketchup to calm him down. It worked too, as he was distracted by the thought of trees that grew sticks that tasted like fish.

It helped when other more positive possibilities were mentioned.

We considered the idea of Daddy coming home and finding Mama feeling better, then the both of them setting out to look for us and only finding the doll. When it got too dark for them to see any more, we assumed they might have come home to wait for daylight before setting back out on their search for us the next day. One of the two of them must have left it down by the stream by accident. Maybe Mama wanted to wash the dirt off so the doll would be pretty and clean when Learline came home.

Our best guess was that we must have showed up after they left that next morning and we had just missed one another, coming and going. So, we decided on our own that we were never going to find each other if one of us didn't sit still and wait. Against these odds, none of the adults would agree to let us stay there and wait for our parents to come home.

The heat was almost unbearable as the day went on, so we figured that most of the town folks were eager to get back to their electric fans and air conditioners.

Sheriff McCoy thought it best if we went on back to town and let the police do their business. He said that he and Deputy Reed would check the houses around there again to see if anyone had seen anything yet. He promised that before they left they would leave a note as to where our parents could find us when, and if, they came back.

Doc and Fred McMillion said they would look around town and see if Mama and Daddy might be there looking for us. Earldean and I were reluctant to leave again. However, we had learned to respect authority and do as we were told, for our own good.

Ed Earl and Learline whined for Mama as expected but came around on the way to the car. Getting to ride in a vehicle was still a new enough adventure that would distract them from their heart aches.

With that we left; hungry, tired and hot, and ended up at Trudy's house just in time to eat a cool tuna fish sandwich before Cinderella came on the TV set. We had a hard time getting Learline to sit down so the rest of us could see. She was spellbound with the moving pictures and the talking that came out of such a contraption.

Of course we too, were impressed with the images that played across the screen, agreeing we had never seen such a beautiful girl/

lady as Lesley Ann Warren, who portrayed the mistreated stepchild that could sing like a bird.

Trudy and Alma couldn't enjoy the program for all the questions we were asking about what was going on. After they attempted to explain what a stepmother was, I found it hard to follow the story for fear of what might happen to us if our parents didn't show up soon. It was scary to think that women draped in such elaborate fabrics and fancy hats could be so hateful as the wicked stepmother and her daughters.

The edge was taken off when I was taken aback by the thought of the Fairy Godmother, who came out of nowhere! With the tap of her wand she could clean a girl up, twist up her hair and fasten it with shiny jewels and dress her in the prettiest store bought dress money could buy.

I didn't think she looked all that bad to start with, but after that, she was truly a sight for my sore eyes.

It was no wonder that handsome Prince Charming took a shine to her.

Me and Earldean oohed and aahed over the kind of dancing they did. Unlike the step stomping, jerky kind of dancing we had always been taught, these two were very smooth as he took her in his arms. Never looking at their feet, he swept her across the ballroom floor with her dress flowing like the patterned wake of waves a motorboat makes on water.

They kept time with their steps and made their own music as they sang their words instead of regular talking. The prettiest song we had ever heard came out of their mouths while they floated into the courtyard and ended it with the longest kiss in the world.

I admit, I remember being sort of concerned about her dancing around and running in those glass shoes. I just knew she was going to cut her foot half into if she stomped down too hard, and then thinking she'd have to get stitches like Ed Earl did.

Yet, before that could happen, when she had seen she had missed her ride home, she stepped clean out of one of those slippers, then ran off into the night. Unlike Ed Earl and his pink sneakers, she didn't go back after it.

It was probably a good thing too because that prince liked to have run himself ragged trying to find the mate to it before he ended up at her house and rescued her from those mean people she was living with.

That was the first movie I had ever seen on TV and the details of that experience are still vivid in my mind to this day.

When it was over, I wanted so desperately for a Fairy God Mother to appear out of thin air and wave her magic wand over me.

I wasn't looking to get a new dress or shoes or even a ride in a carriage pulled by six white horses. I only wanted my Daddy, who was my Prince Charming, to drive up in his old, rusty Ford pickup and rescue me along with my siblings and take us home where we belonged.

Alma tried to talk Trudy into going with her and taking us to Sunday Night prayer meeting so we could get the congregation to pray our parents home but Trudy didn't go for it. She said we didn't have clothes fitting to wear to church and Ed Earl couldn't possibly wear those lady's pink sneakers down the aisle without causing a big distraction.

I suspected that she was the one who was a bit self-conscious about being the distraction after what she had said that morning about divorcees not being welcome down there.

After she passed off every excuse she could think of as to why she thought we ought not go, Alma quit pressing the invitation.

She did however, agree to turn off the TV and circle up for a prayer right there in her own house. Admitting that 'The Good Lord' was welcome to her home anytime, she claimed to believe that where two or more were gathered in His name that He was bound to show up. These were familiar words as we had heard Mama say the same thing before.

After the prayer Trudy insisted that we stay there with her as she had an extra bedroom besides the one Debbie was sleeping in. She also had extra food in the house so the extra mouths to feed wouldn't put Alma in a bind before payday.

Alma appeared to be sad that we didn't go home with her but Trudy told her she could see that she was tired and needed a good night's sleep. She had made arrangements with her before she left to get us over to the Clinic after breakfast the next morning.

It was a bit less crowded at Trudy's house with the extra floor space. She had a big piece of cozy furniture to sit on. It was a brilliant shade of turquoise and would have been almost a perfect match to the color of some beads Mama kept; ones that Sunshine had strung up for her years ago.

Trudy kept these big pieces pushed up together, wrapping around the corner of the room, making it nice to sit close for talking or watching the television set that sat in the opposite corner. She told us it was called a sectional sofa.

On either end of it were tables that held nice lamps with plastic covers to keep the dust off the shades.

In front of the curve of the sofa was another short table like the coffee table at the Clinic, only this one had an odd, crooked shape to it. Instead of magazines on its top, it was dressed with a centerpiece made of glass balls that were wired into a large cluster to a thick wooden stem. Debbie said they were supposed to resemble grapes only I had no idea that grapes could be that big or the color of turquoise but they did, however, match the sectional sofa.

The walls in that same room were covered with a printed pattern of big flowers. Some type that I had not yet learned to identify but they were various shades of pinks, yellows and purples. The stems and leaves leaned closer to a green that would fade and give shadows of the pale turquoise, keeping with the color scheme that Trudy had going on in that room.

When I was in her house, it made me feel like I was in one of those pretty pictures in one of the magazines of the waiting room at the Clinic.

Every room in Trudy's house was an adventure but I worked hard to keep from meddling.

I had learned my lesson at Myrtle Riley's house. Trudy seemed to like kids and I didn't want to mess up that relationship by taking a chance on breaking one of her pretties.

After our supper Trudy insisted that we take another bath even though we had just had one two nights before. We were surprised to find the tub filled with white foam that gave off an aroma, like a field of sweet clover and wild jasmine mixed together.

Debbie couldn't believe we had never taken a bubble bath before.

When bedtime came, Learline and Ed Earl squabbled over who was going to get to sleep by Debbie. To settle the difference she let them both crawl up in the bed with her along with the baby doll, which had been cleaned up like the rest of us.

Trudy turned back the covers to the bed in her guest room and left a lamp burning on the nightstand. The room of pastels looked femininely soft and had a clean fresh smell.

That was the first time I ever remembered feeling cool and dry at the same time…it was so comfortable and relaxing.

Earldean and I knelt down on the soft rug to say our bedtime prayers. I ran my fingers across its fibers feeling the texture that reminded me of the goats back home. Once again I had to choke back the homesickness which I was learning to overcome.

We crawled onto the bed that was layered with soft pink sheets and a light blue blanket. My skin had never felt so soft as I stretched my legs beneath the cool bed clothes.

Earldean fumbled with the lamp for a while before she managed to figure out how to turn it off. We settled in the dark with a street light shining through the high window, casting shadows on the walls. We could hear Debbie in the next room telling the little kids a bedtime story.

Being my first time to ever get to sleep in one, the bed felt like nothing I had ever laid on before. Unlike the solid ground or the firm floor of the bus, the springs beneath the mattress gave way to our bodies and squeaked as we moved about. I felt like we were so high off the ground that it was easy for me to imagine that I was floating on a cloud.

Earldean reminded me of the time we found that deflated water raft that had washed up on the shore of the lake. After Daddy blew air into it, we took turns floating around on it. *"That's what layin on this fluffy bed makes me think of."* she said.

"What ever happen to that thing?" I asked her.

"When we pulled it out of the water so it wouldn't float away, it was all soggy and limp…Daddy said it was too tore up ta fool with fixin but he might could put some tape on it that might hold it for a while…but it wuttin no count."

"Daddy is good bout fixin thangs, aint he?"

"Yep, most time."

"Do you think Daddy can fix this mess we in now…I mean…you think he would know where to find Mama?"

"Daddy always knows what to do…He'll find her. He's the smartest man in the world!"

"You think he'll be mad at us fer leavin without Mama?"

"Why you keep brangin that up Sassy? You know at the time we didn't have no choice in the matter…we thought Mama was dead! How was we to know she was just sleepin off a hot fever?"

"Why do I feel so bad inside…why didn't I just stay there and wait on Daddy?"

"Sassy, you gotta stop this…aint no sense in makin blame…we did what we knowed ta do, that's all there is to it…we cain't go back and change things!"

"What if they don't find us and give us up for gone…forget all about us?"

"That ain't gonna happen…Mama's and Daddy's don't just forget about their kids!"

"Well, they forgot about their Mama's and Daddy's!"

"That aint the same! They wuz just kids like us back then and they didn't forget theyz Mama and Daddy…They aint around that's all!"

"That's what I mean…They run off and left um!"

"Naw…That aint right…Daddy said after his Paw died and his Maw couldn't take care of him, he moved off to live with his Uncle Leonard and Aunt Verdie Mae."

"What about Mama? Ever time I axed her bout her folks, she told me to forget about that or she would change the subject or somthin."

"Well she told me one time that she didn't have no parents."

"What happened to um…did they die?"

"She didn't say nuttin bout that…claimed she aint never had none."

"I guess some folks have um and some folks don't."

"I guess…she didn't really need um…she had us kids and Daddy."

"Well, what about Daddy? Why would his Mama not wanna take care of him?"

"Sassy, I don't think he said she didn't want to take care of him. He said she couldn't!"

"Was she sick like Mama?"

"Didn't say…I guess so...Mama couldn't take care of us…that's why we had to go look for Daddy…get some help."

"Is that why we're staying here…So Trudy and Debbie can take care of us?"

"Yea…I could take care of us by myself…but I was missin Mama and Daddy's help."

"Wonder why they never told us about our last name?"

"Don't know…reckon they never thought we would need one."

"Do you think we have one…They would have taught us how to spell it if we did."

"Yea…guess so…now hush and go to sleep" Earldean yawned.

"Don't ya wanna know what ya whole name is Earldean?"
"Yea, but I wanna sleep right now so hush".
Though the bed was the best thing I had ever had the opportunity to sleep on, I had a hard time falling asleep with all the quietness in the house. I missed the sound of the night bugs that normally would sing me to sleep.
I lay awake and wondered if Earldean also was having a hard time getting to sleep. *"Sister?"* I asked in a hushed voice, not wanting to wake her if by chance she was asleep.
"What?"
"Do ya still miss um?"
"I miss um real bad Sassy."
"Me too." I said with a sniffle, then rolled on my side to cry myself to sleep. I could hear her sniffle too, before she rolled over and kissed me goodnight then spooned me up like Mama would do if she were there. It made her feel good to mother me so I let her.
I was in need of mothering.

Over the next three days, the town of Whisper Ridge would do their best to go about its business, working with the four of us underfoot and altering their schedules.
On Monday, the Detectives came by with their sketch artist who drew a vague likeness of our parents based on the description we gave them. Earldean thought the pictures looked exactly like them but Ed Earl and me?...well, we couldn't see it.
Ed Earl made that clear enough when he said to him, *"You a purdy good picture drawer...who ya makin a picture of?"*
The artist pretended not to hear him, while the detectives were distracted. I guess he had spent enough time with us and was ready to move on.
Learline hardly gave them a second glance when he finished. I figured she didn't recognized Daddy or Mama in the sketches or we would all know about it.

We didn't want to make him feel bad about it after all his hard work. He did the best he could do with us trying to describe our parents who we thought were the most beautiful people in the world.

Estelle picked us up from the Clinic and took us out to their place for the day. She was in a fussy mood again but she wasn't complaining about us, she was complaining *to* us...about every little thing from the pesky flies to the hot flashes she couldn't control.

Staying out of her way was no problem with all the open grounds out at their place that were neatly groomed.

Most of the grass had been cut to the same level as it rolled over little hills and into the pasture. I could see from their back door all the way down to the lake.

We were a little intimidated by their dog at first until Estelle assured us he wouldn't bite. She said Doc named the old dog Festus after the character on his favorite T.V. show Gun Smoke.

She gave him a big bone to chew on to keep him busy so that he wouldn't bother us. I spent the biggest part of the day hanging on the fence post watching the horses. Doc had three of them in the pasture that were absolutely gorgeous!

One was a tall, lean, solid black stallion, who was so jet black that he looked navy blue. As he galloped in the sunshine, I could see his muscles move under his shiny coat and his long black mane flowing in the breeze. He ran as though he had some place particular he was going but turned short of the fence and kept in stride, heading for his imaginary destination.

Another horse in the pasture was a white quarter horse. A mare, with the youthful spirit but a graceful trot. Her mane was long also as it flowed down her neck.

I thought she might have been one of the six white horses that pulled that carriage in that Cinderella movie because she was so quiet and timid, she could have been a mouse at one time.

I spun around as if I might find a Fairy Godmother. The movie seemed so real to me I thought it could really happen. But, I guess she was just a regular horse. She occasionally peered at me between her long bangs with those black shiny eyes. I would catch her staring at me but when I looked into her eyes...she would turn away.

She kept her distance but something inside her wanted to come closer. Something inside me wanted her to.

The third one was a paint horse. That's what Doc called that kind. This one was a pretty one too, with splashes of brown and black on mostly white. She was friendly toward me and liked to be petted on her forehead and would turn her head to guide my hand when she wanted to be rubbed on her neck and under her chin.

I stooped down and broke off some tall grass that was on my side of the fence and held it to her face. She sniffed it first before she ate it, just like you're supposed to do before you eat anything, to make sure it's fitting ta eat. Therefore, I knew she was a smart animal, unlike some of those goats and other scavenging varmints I had watched back home. I had seen some that pounced and bit into something only to find out they didn't like it.

She showed me her big teeth to let me know she could hurt me if she wanted to, so I rearranged the grass and held it with my fingertips incase I needed to pull away real fast.

She was careful not to harm me as she used her big lips to pull the grass into her mouth. Her lips felt soft and wet as they brushed across my fingertips.

Giving her another handful took me back to thinking about my best friend, the little deer in the woods, who took much longer to warm up to me. This new friend wasn't shy at all and was growing bored with the grass. I wished I had one of those vanilla wafers from Alma's cookie jar to feed her. Bet she'd like that.

She didn't like being in the sun too long, so after she had been petted enough she would strut over and stand in the shade for a while. There, she would swat the flies with her tail and keep the air stirred.

Every time I would try to walk away, she would neigh and walk back towards me. It was apparent to me that horses did their talking with their eyes and their bodies. If I didn't know better, I would have thought she was saying to me, *"Come…stand in the shade with me Sassy and tell me what's troublin ya."*

I thought back to what Trudy had told us about her husband that left her and wondered if I had really just misunderstood her about being married to a horse. I was beginning to see that Trudy had a way of saying things that just sounded silly. How could a person be married to a horse anyway? It just wasn't right.

She said people called him a stud but maybe they meant he was big like a horse or was a man that galloped like a horse…or was the word gallivanted.

Well, she did say she had been to the rodeo before…and rodeos have horses…that's right, he was a cowboy! She probably met him there…oh…how could I be so stupid?

Estelle had already told us not to play in the pasture and after that encounter with the bull, I wasn't going to take any chances with large animals until I understood them a little better.

Ed Earl had kicked off his oversize pink shoes to freely run barefooted in the wide open yard of plush green grass that was free of rocks and debris. His sore leg didn't seem to slow him down much and though he had a slight limp, he didn't complain.

He was out of breath every time he came by to look at the horses with me. He came in a little closer to the fence each time he stopped by.

I think he was still intimidated by their size after being charged by that huge bull. Who could blame him?

Learline was riding on Earldean's shoulders when they came over to look at the horses. They had been out picking Black Eyed Suzy's that managed to survive the late summer's drought and Learline had a bouquet of them in each hand.

Racing by, the Stallion seemed to be showing off when he turned, making a figure eight before he slowed down to a pace that didn't kick up so much dust.

The white mare stepped closer turning her body sideways, and stood staring at us through her long pretty bangs.

Then the friendly paint came out from under the shade trees to meet my sisters. She quickly made a bee line, coming right to us. Earldean took a half step back, wobbling, almost losing baby sister off of her shoulders. Learline managed not to drop a single flower as she wrapped her arms around Earldean's face and held on for dear life.

By the time Earldean was able to see again the horse was right there in front of her. Her eyes widened as she softly said, *"Look at the size a that thang!"*

"Go on…pet her…she won't hurt ya." I said.

The horse slightly flared her nostrils and sniffed at them like she wanted them to pet her.

"Her wants a smell da flowers." Learline told us.

"Hold um out there…let her have a smell!" I said. *"She thanks they purdy!"*

Ed Earl came running up and asked, *"What cha'll doin?"*

"Lookin at these horses." Earldean said. *"They big aint they?"*

"Sassy wuz pettin um a little ago…said they don't bite or nuttin." Ed Earl commented.

"Didge ye pet um Ed Earl?" Learline asked.

With his hands on his hips, he confidently said, *"Not chet…but…I'ma gonna do it in a minute…I jest gotta catch my breath from all this runnin I been doin round here."*

I reached up and patted the horse on her neck then ran my hand down to her shoulder.

When Learline got the courage to let the horse smell the flowers, she bravely, but cautiously, stretched out the bouquet with her full arms length.

Earldean wasn't standing close enough, so I urged her forward with my hand around her back.

Learline chuckled with a nervous laugh as she talked to the large animal asking her if she wanted to smell the pretty flowers.

Eagerly, the horse stretched forward and sniffed the flowers like she knew what she was talking about.

"You wike my purdy flowers…don't cha Horsy?"

Our laughter rang out when she sniffed again then rocked her head in agreement.

"She wikes um…her says yes!"

Still laughing, she held them out again with expectation. *"Do it again…Do it again!"* she said, looking toward us for encouragement with her arm still stretched out.

Before she could turn around good the horse sniffed then pulled the flowers off with her big lips. Letting go of the stems, Learline jerked her arm back and shrieked before she allowed her fear turn into laughter along with the rest of us.

Earldean squatted down to let Learline off of her shoulders then pulled the straggling flower stems from her hair. *"Daddy said he got to ride a horse one time…said it's fun!"*

Daddy read to us out loud from his paperback western collection, so we knew a few things about horses and had seen pictures of men riding them on the covers of his books.

He did have five books in his collection before Mama had to use the pages from two of them to start fires in the cook pit. When dry leaves and kindling were hard to find during the rainy season sometimes that's all she had.

Daddy was a bit put out with her at first for tearing up his books but she claimed the stories inside weren't fit to read. With the mischief some of them bad guys got in to, she didn't want to plant any ideas from bad seeds in the minds of young readers that were still learning.

She kept the pictures from the covers with the good looking cowboys riding their horses. She didn't find a thing wrong with that part of the book.

In the stories, some of the cowboys gave their horses names like "Lady", "Black Jack", "Lucky" or "Lightning". Whatever name that was fitting to the horse and meant something to the rider.

I was beginning to see how a name could be important to identify an individual from the rest of the crowd.

"Reckon Doc gave um names?" I wondered out loud as I stepped up on the first rail of the wood post fence and hung my arms over the top one.

"Don't know." Ed Earl said as he pulled up beside me. *"...but when I grow up I'm gonna get me three horses just like these...I'm gonna name um 'Whitey', Blackie'...and Wild Flower!"*

By supper time we were back at the Eat-A-Bite with Alma. It was a slow night except for a few folks who stopped by to see if we had found our parents.

I still wasn't saying much as gloom set in by that night with the hope of finding them, slowly fading away.

Nights were the hardest to handle, for we would grow lonesome for our parents as the sinking sun would fall behind the ridge.

That night we stayed with Alma again so she could practice her healing exercises on our depression. Her sweet talking voice was calming and when she thought we needed more comforting she took us to the kitchen, which she referred to as her operating room.

Her protocol for a bedtime snack, she believed, would help absorb the excess acid that would produce in the stomach after a day of worry or sadness. Feeling this treatment was more effective if the food was fun and/or distracting, she selected something that she felt should do the trick.

Now, Alma described "Fun Food" as things like cotton candy that melted in your mouth; or Jaw breakers that didn't; pretzels that you could lick the salt off of or a slice of watermelon so juicy that it dripped from your elbow.

Fun food, by her standards, could be anything that your tongue had fun tasting.

"Distracting food" she claimed, would be things that you eat that make noise while you chew it…chips, popped corn, crispy fried foods…stuff like that. It could be any food that distracted you from your worries by keeping you busy while you eat it, for instance, food you might dip in sauces or gravy…chips and dip…donuts dunked in coffee and so on. She said that this keeps your hands and your mouth busy so you have to think about that instead of whatever it is that had been bothering you.

Her claim was that if the food tastes good, the flavor will entertain your tongue, while the sustenance will absorb the excess acid in the belly.

Back then, when she tried to explain all this, most of it went right over our heads. We had never heard of many of the foods she talked about but were eager to learn.

We had already finished off all the vanilla wafers that were in the old green cookie jar and Alma had put it on her grocery list to get more for a refill.

So this particular night, she introduced us to the crunchy fish sticks she had promised Ed Earl the day before; dipped in ketchup of course.

Just before daylight Tuesday morning, I was awakened by the puttering sound of a vehicle not too far off in the distance. With all the strange noises that a town makes, I was still having trouble sleeping soundly.

I found it was going to take some "getting used to" sleeping indoors no matter where I stayed but Alma's little trailer was the closest thing to a bus we were going to find there.

At first I would easily be pulled from a deep slumber by the racket of the compressors on either the refrigerator or window unit shutting on and off.

A flushing toilet would have the same effect on me as maybe a bomb going off. Then, I'd be restless trying to get back to sleep, being afraid of the unfamiliar noises such as a squeaky door hinge or the roof settling from the hot day.

I would lie awake disturbed by distant traffic with an occasional backfiring of an old engine trying to make its way up a hill.

I'd try to focus and listen for more familiar things, like frogs and crickets, to help me get some rest but instead I'd be distracted by the constant barking of a neighborhood dog.

I remember trying to settle my mind by thinking that it could have been Doc's dog, Festus, I was hearing; not knowing then that they lived eight miles in the other direction.

Before I knew it I'd be wide awake with fine tuned ears and my thoughts running in every direction. It would seem hopeless to get back to sleep with all the noise I detected by then. I would just have to lie restless and listen to every little tic of the clock and wait till time to get up.

However, that morning I sat straight up when I heard the gears change on the vehicle that seemed to be getting closer. It sounded a whole lot like Daddy's truck would sound when we'd hear him coming home up the old dirt road. The closer it got the more I was sure it was Daddy's truck I'd heard out there.

I got up from my pallet and tiptoed across the floor to the kitchen window to peep out. Quietly, I slid one of the chairs over to climb on so that I could see out and over the kitchen sink.

I didn't see anything at first but it sounded like the truck was sitting idle before it started moving again. This happened several times before I saw headlights round the curve then turn into the driveway of the Shady Grove Trailer Park.

My heart skipped a beat to recognize the familiar rumbling of the motor and the bright headlights on Daddy's truck. I rubbed my eyes to be sure I wasn't dreaming.

When the truck stopped at the first of the silver trailers I was convinced it was him, though it was still too dark to see yet. I'd know that sound anywhere.

He must have found out from the police where we were staying but wasn't sure which of these trailers belonged to Alma; they did all look alike.

Judging from the headlights, the truck was stopping every so often making its way toward lot number seven. I thought I'd better go let him know that we were at this one, before he wakes up everyone in the park trying to find us.

I jumped down from the chair and ran to the door. The racket I made getting there had woke Alma up and startled Earldean enough for her to ask what was going on.

"Daddy's here…he's out there looking for us! I exclaimed as I fumbled with the locked knob on the door.

"How ya know…did ya see him out there?" she asked in a sleepy voice.

"Yea…I heard his truck a commin…I looked out younder an seen its him!"

Ed Earl rolled out from the covers and mumbled, *"Whazamatter?"*

"It's Daddy Ed Earl…He'z comma lookin fer us…just like I knowed he would!"

In no time at all I was out the door and down the steps yelling, *"Daddy! Daddy!…we're over here!"* Having been used to being barefoot, my callused feet didn't feel much pain from the sharp gravel as I ran across the driveway to get his attention.

"Here we are…Oh Daddy…you found us…over here!"

"Sassy?" I heard my name called out over the barking dogs and the rumbling of the idling truck engine.

"Over here, Daddy!"

I could barely make him out in the shadows but I saw him running back to his truck from the corner of lot numbers five and six. At first I was afraid he couldn't see me so I ran toward the headlights as he slowly pulled forward.

"Here Daddy…here I am!" I yelled. *"Stop!"*

"Sassy!…Look out!"

The truck was just about to run over me when I dodged out of the way and dove over into the grass on the side. He drove past me a little then came to a halt at the end of Alma's parking space.

"Sassy! Are you alright?…you almost got run over!…What are you doin out here?"

I was a little wobbly from hitting the ground so hard. I must have bumped my head or something because everything seemed to be spinning around me for a moment or two.

"Sassy…say something…are you ok?"

"Daddy?"

"Oh…Thank the Lord!" I heard Alma say. *"…Oh Sassy, you scared me half to death!" What on earth were you thinkin child?"* she asked as she and Earldean hovered over me on the ground.

"Mornin Miss Nettles. You up awful early this mornin aintchee…plantin some flowers this late in the year?" a man's voice said coming from behind her carrying something that made a tinkling sound.

"…Aw…uh…uh…pardon me ma'am…uh…uh…uh…but…well…is…a su…su… summpin a matter there?"

"Oh my goodness…Charlie Wayne…I…I…don't know what ta say!"

Straining my eyes to see through the darkness, I pushed myself up past Earldean then stumbled over the top of Alma. Struggling to steady myself, I managed to come to my feet only to be surprised and gravely disappointed. *"You ain't my Daddy!"* I exclaimed.

"No hun…I don't believe so…Iffin I wuz…sombody fergot ta tell me anythang 'bout it."

Alma was struggling to get up off the ground when the man set down what he was carrying and went over to help her.

"Need a hand there, Miss Nettles?"

"Oh…Thanks, Charlie Wayne…if ya don't mind." she said, expressing her gratitude.

Though she was embarrassed to be caught out in her nightgown she figured that it was dark enough that the man couldn't see much. She reached up and grabbed hold of his extended hand in order to take him up on his offered assistance.

"Did I miss somthin here?" the man asked Alma as he struggled to pull her up.

"Whewwww…You barely did miss somethin…Sassy here…was…out in the street…and almost got hit…by your truck there!" Alma panted.

Still trembling from the excitement, she wrapped her arms around herself while she worked on catching her breath.

"I DID?? OH MY GOODNESS!…are you ok punkin?…why… I never even saw ya till just now…I'm so sorry…ya didn't git hit did ya?"

"Naw sir…I'll be alright." I tried to assure the upset man.

"Well, I'll just be dog gone…It's sa dark out there… It's hard ta see everything till ya pert near on it…a little ole gal your size is hard ta see anywayz…even in the light of day…that ain't no place fer a youngin ta be playin…ya have ta watch out fer these big ole cars and trucks…"

"Didn't ya hear her yellin and screamin at cha?" Earldean asked.

" I cain't hear nuttin when that truck is a runin…its sa loud. I never heard a thang till I got out and came over and saw ya'll here. What wuz you a doin out yonder so early in the mornin anyhow?"

Alma was still shaking as she tried to conceal herself so that this Charlie Wayne person couldn't see through her thin cotton gown. *"That's… what…I wanna know too!"* she said still slightly out of breath.

"I thought you'z my daddy drivin that there truck."

"Ya Daddy?…Oh…He a milk man too, darlin?"

"Milk Man?…wha'sat?"

"Ya know…a feller like me that delivers fresh milk to folks round town." he said as he bent down to pick up the milk crate. He then held it up for me to see in the dawns light.

"Naw…my daddy ain't no milk man. We git our milk from a goat when we need it."

"Ya don't say…goats milk huh?" he was saying as he walked over and set two big glass bottles of milk on the steps. *"Well… I don't carry that none…all I got is cow milk…ya like that don't cha? Got eggs too on the truck iffin ya need um".*

Alma made her way past him, then up the steps and into the trailer. She hid her body shamefully behind the edge of the doorway.

"I'm so sorry ya had ta see me without my clothes Charlie Wayne. I'd just got up out of bed when I heard the commotion. When I looked out here and saw her a standin in them headlights…well I didn't think about my robe… I just ran out her after the girl. I'm so embarrassed. Please don't tell nobody ya seen me like this…alright?

Even though it was starting to get light enough to see a little by then, he said to her, "*What?…Oh naw, Ma'am…I ain't seen nuttin…It's too dark out here ta seen ya…uh…I ain't a been a lookin no how…so don't you worry bout that none…now ya hear?*

Earldean and I both were wearing Alma's big tee shirts with no pants on and wondered if we should be embarrassed too. I didn't feel ashamed except for the fact that I had made such a dumb mistake.

"I'd heard 'bout these kids a bein over here…I'd didn't plan to run into um while I'z on my delivery route so early in the morning but…" he stepped back and laughed a little, then after clearing his throat he continued. *"…I didn't mean ta make a joke…that just kinda slipped out there…git it…run into…he-he"*

Alma didn't laugh though.

"…uh… well…anyhow I'z brangin ya an extra half gallon of milk. Ya know for the youngins n all…no extree charge er nuttin…I mean I'm a givin it to ya fer free."

"Why, thank ya Charlie Wayne…That's right nice of ya!"

"Ya welcome, ere Miss Nettles…It's good of ya ta take in these orphans like ya done…I'm gonna run back to the truck and git ya some eggs too…alright?"

"That's real nice of ya too."

One of the other neighbors came out of his trailer to see what was going on outside. He met the Milk Man at the truck and I guess he explained what had happened.

Alma went on back to her room to get her robe and I waited at the door for the eggs.

When he returned, I told him thanks and let him know we weren't really orphans and that we had parents but we just couldn't find um yet.

Ashamed of what I'd done I was talking so softly that he couldn't hear me and I had to repeat myself several times. He took the blame for that though and claimed that driving that loud milk truck for so long had been hard on his hearing.

By the time he was climbing back on his truck, there was a slight contrast between the tree line and the sky. It was just enough light to see that I had clearly made a huge mistake in thinking this could have been my Daddy.

This truck was twice as big as his and was boxed in, sort of like a bus but shorter. Daddy's truck was a rusty red and this one was a dirty white with a big cow painted on the side. And, last but not least, this milk man named Charlie Wayne looked nothing at all like my daddy.

By the time that was all over, everybody in Shady Grove Trailer was awake and fabricating stories about a case of hit and run and another about our daddy being the Milk Man!

After breakfast Alma got dressed for work and went out to tell her neighbors what had really happened and to apologize for the commotion.

We still had not mastered the habit of getting dressed first thing and going places. So, Alma had to keep sending us back to finish getting our clothes on, then our shoes and then to brush our hair. Needless to say she was late for work.

Doc was already at the Clinic with his first patient and another one waiting when we arrived. He didn't fuss at Alma like she thought he would but instead he understood; especially after she told him about the episode with Charlie Wayne.

Alma found some writing paper and pencils and had us draw some pictures while we waited for some answers from the police search. We thought surely they would come looking for us soon.

However, by ten o'clock, when we still hadn't heard from either of our parents, Estelle declared it to be a day of shopping.

"There's nothing like a day of shopping to take your blues away!" she declared. Her goal was to get Ed Earl a pair of good fitting shoes…boy shoes! So, our first stop was at Albert's Shoe Shop, two doors down from the Clinic.

Most of Albert's business consisted of shoe repair and sizing but he kept a small stock of shoes there on consignment from one of the bigger stores out of Fort Smith.

He was only open Monday through Thursday because he was semi-retired and spent the other three days of the week on the lake fishing, when the weather permitted.

Estelle said, "*When shopping with Albert…You gotta git while the gittins good!*"

Not only did our brother get a new pair of shoes, but with the end of summer clearance sale, 'Buy one pair-get one free' she said it would be a sin to pass up such a sale.

I studied that claim for a while, trying to figure out where missing out on a shoe sale would fit in the Ten Commandments. But, with her being a regular church going Christian and all, and a grown up, she had to know what she was talking about.

Anyway, she felt it necessary to buy us each a new pair of shoes. We were so excited about getting them too.

With the two pair in her younger years, Earldean was the only one of us who ever was blessed with a brand new pair of shoes before.

All of the shoes we had prior to that had been hand-me-downs or came from a second-hand store.

We were always grateful just to have shoes and we hadn't really been bothered by not ever having new ones as we had never known the difference.

These were so nice and clean we couldn't keep our eyes off of them as we walked. Mine and Earldean's were penny loafers. Estelle gave us each a penny and showed us how to put it in the slot provided for it and told us they would bring us good luck. I already felt lucky just to have them!

Ed Earl got a pair of navy blue tennis shoes with fresh white laces. The other shoes he had out grown never had laces, even when Daddy brought them home.

Estelle was impressed to see how fast he learned to tie the laces, although he really already knew how from playing around with ropes and strings back home.

She told him these would stay on better than those pink ones and Mr. Albert told him they would help him run faster. He took every opportunity to try them out and we had a hard time trying to keep up with him as he kept running ahead of us. If it were not for his sore leg slowing him down we might not have ever caught up with him.

Learline picked out a pair of white patent leather shoes that were so shiny that Mr. Albert guaranteed that they would never need polishing.

Estelle mentioned to him that she wouldn't get to wear them much longer with Labor Day coming up soon…

"…and you know you're never are supposed to wear white after Labor Day!"

But he gave her such a good deal on them that she couldn't pass them up! She later told Alma she got them for a song but…I never heard her sing.

We walked down the sidewalk to the Dry Cleaners that was located on the same side of the street. There, Estelle picked up Doc's white lab coats and pants, along with one of her dresses. She gave somewhat of an explanation of how they got the clothes clean without washing them in water. We were amazed at how stiff the fabric was and how clean they had gotten them without any water.

We held the ends of the plastic bags off the sidewalk, while Estelle carried the clean laundry on our way back to the Clinic.

When we got there, she hung Doc's uniforms in a closet behind the door and gave a sigh of relief that we had all made it back there safely without losing Ed Earl in his new racing shoes.

Alma shared our enthusiasm over the purchase of our new shoes and grinned from ear to ear over Ed Earl's darting across the waiting room to show her how fast he could run.

Estelle had to lecture him about why we don't run indoors and why it's important to stay on the sidewalks and off the streets in town.

Learline watched her feet as she tapped around on the tile floor, making a clicking noise that was a new sound to our ears. She danced about with excitement and pride.

Estelle sat on one of the metal chairs in the cool waiting room, fanning another hot flash and wondering out loud if she was going to be able handle another day with us.

She came around when the hot flash was over and was ready for the next round of shopping!

We rode in the car down Loral St., past the Piggly Wiggly and on to Flechers Filla-Sack, the local general store.

Stepping on the rubber mat at the entrance made the door open all by its self, sending a cool blast of air through it, that was filled with an exciting aroma that I'll never forget.

I didn't know how to describe the scent back then but I would learn, the factors of its contents could only be found in the conglomerate of items that abided together at the Filla-Sack.

It was a buttery, salty, perfumery, leathery and new plastic smell mixed with a lemony fresh, sweet, Juicy-Fruity scent that most general department stores had in those days.

There, we were greeted by Mr. and Mrs. Fletcher who we had learned were good friends with Estelle and Doc, as well as sister and brother-in-law to Alma.

Helping Estelle push the shopping cart up and down the aisles was a blast! We had no idea that wheels could roll so smooth on a flat surface. It didn't take long for us to discover how fast the cart could go to as we made our way down the aisles of neatly stacked merchandise.

Ed Earl climbed inside an abandoned 'buggy' as he called it and Earldean and I took turns racing down the opposite aisle from Estelle.

Other shoppers dodged out of the way so as not to get hit by the speeding, wobbling, wheeled contraption that eventually knocked over a tower of sunglasses that Earldean had been spinning around just as Estelle rounded the corner.

Fortunately, most of them hung on for dear life with just a few pair being slightly damaged. With Estelle being good friends with the owners they didn't make her pay for our badness. She insisted that we help the stock boy pick them up after she scolded us for running inside, then made us put back the extra cart.

She then told us we had to stay close to her cart with Learline riding in the toddler seat. Barely able to push the cart for us hanging on the sides of it for a ride, Estelle filled it with a variety of plastic household gadgets that we examined and quizzed her on.

She did her level best to explain what each item was and what it was used for but that would only prompt more questions. She made each one of them sound absolutely necessary and couldn't imagine how she would function without these vital essentials.

Let's see…I remember a few things she got…a new ironing board cover pad for one thing. That was the day I first learned that wrinkles could be pressed out of clothes like at the cleaners.

She also picked up a package of rubber caps that snapped on the tops of soda bottles, in case you couldn't drink it all.

She got a dish to display her guest soaps in, a jar of Oil of Olay cold cream, and a red, leather handbag. She didn't explain why she got those pretty dish rags with strawberries painted on them but she said out loud, *"Oh, I just have to have these! Aren't they pretty?"*

I hated to tell her they were just going to get ruined when she used them!

But to me, the strangest thing she bought was a new dust pan, of all things, to sweep up dirt in! First of all I couldn't believe she had an *old* one she wanted to replace…why didn't she just sweep it out the door and save her money for something else?

She picked up a couple of pairs of socks for each of us…real pairs that matched! The few socks we had before seldom mated with another but Mama kept them darned as best she could when we wore holes in them.

We stood still as she held clothes up to our backs to see if they might fit. She ended up buying us each a new pair of shorts and a tank top, again, all on a sinful summer close-out sale.

In the back corner, across from the last aisle was the soda counter where customers could buy refreshments and rest while they shopped.

One lady shopper was resting on one of the stools while her little girl stood at her knees licking a big colorful circle on a stick. We all stood there staring at her wondering what it was she had. Ed Earl asked her, *"What cha got there girl?"*

"Lolly Pop." she said in a squeaky voice then returned to her licking.

It didn't look like the ones that Alma gave us after Ed Earl's stitches. This was almost the size of a saucer.

Not seeing any harm, he asked, *"Can I have a lick?"*

After a strange look from her mother, she jumped off the stool, snatched her child by the arm and pulled her away.

When they were out of sight Estelle informed us it was not polite to stare and told Ed Earl that it was downright rude to ask a total stranger such a thing!

We had always been taught to share and were told that Jesus said we were suppose to!

I was surprised that Estelle didn't learn that at her Sunday school.

Fresh popcorn bounced in the big glass box with bright lights as we stood amazed watching the batch grow. The smell was so inviting to my taste buds that it made my mouth water when Mr. Fletcher offered us a complimentary serving.

Alma was right I thought, it *was* fun and distracting as we all stood around with our very own little red striped box, shoveling the buttery flavored kernels into our mouths and enjoying the satisfaction of the crunch.

It was a challenge to hold on to it with our fingers without dropping any before we put it to our mouth.

Ed Earl and I were eating most of ours off the floor before Estelle told us not to do that because the floor was dirty. I thought she was crazy! It shined brighter than any floor I had ever seen, so when she turned away Ed Earl put his in his mouth and ate it anyway.

I told my brother that when I got to know this woman a little better I would explain to her that all food had come from or lived on the ground at one time or other before we ate it…so a little dirt never hurt anything. Apparently town folk didn't like to fool with dirt.

I tried to be obedient but I couldn't find a trash can. Alma had told us not to throw things on the floor or ground because if everybody done that the world would be a big mess. I surely didn't want that to happen. So, I examined each kernel that I picked up, even a few pieces that other folks had littered the floor with. I didn't see any dirt at all but I wiped each kernel off on my shirt just in case, before I put them into my mouth.

When Estelle said it was time to go pay for everything, we headed to the front of the store passing friendly folks that Estelle knew by name. Once there she found some more that she greeted and spoke with as we stood in a line with our carts and waited our turn.

There were racks on both sides of the narrow checkout line that were just loaded with last minute purchase opportunities. The temptation not to touch anything there was almost unbearable for a child to resist with its brightly colored packages and sweet sugary aroma.

All kinds of candies and gums were sorted and stocked in little bins that were tilted so that anyone at least two foot tall would be able to view the entire selection. They were stocked so full that just about anything you looked at long enough would almost jump out of the bin and into your hand.

Estelle was engaged in idle chit-chat with the Mayor's wife, who was in line behind her, and kept having to excuse herself so that she could get on to us about playing with the packages.

It took Learline getting fussed at for pulling down a whole stack of boxes of jaw breakers to get everybody's attention.

"She aint da one done it!" Ed Earl shouted, jumping to her defense for fear she would get in trouble. *"...it jest popped off a there all by it's self...I'z just standin ere a lookin and next thang I knowed...that all just came a dumplin down on my head...but I don't know how come it ta fall all by itself...ain't nobody even touched them one's...I'z lookin at these ones here next to um!"*

Mr. and Mrs. Fletcher heard the racket it had made; they rushed over from the tall manager's cage to make sure everyone was alright. By that time most everybody around there had helped to get them all picked up.

Estelle apologized for the mess and offered to pay for any damage we might have caused.

'No harm done here, Estelle." Mr. Fletcher said. *"Why don't we send these children off with a little snack...my treat."*

She told us that we could each pick out one thing that we would like to have for a treat after our lunch. I can still remember what each of us picked out because we all shared out treats with one another…later…when Estelle wasn't looking. We didn't want to get in trouble about that again.

Earldean picked out a 'Clark' candy bar; Ed Earl picked out some 'Boston Beans' and Learline had picked out some 'Red Hots'. Estelle warned her that they would be too hot for her to hold in her mouth but she insisted.

I myself had a hard time selecting with so many options to choose from. Finally, I spotted on the top row something familiar that I knew would be a tasty treat. I picked up the package and held it to my nose and sniffed then said, *"Ahh…Juicy Fruit!"*

After the checker finished pecking on the cash register and explaining his actions to Earldean, he carefully filled the sacks with all the things Estelle paid for.

"Hey! I git it…" she told him. *"Iss ere's why ya'll call it the Fillasack…cause at's what you do here…fill eze ere sacks with store bought thangs…huh?"*

She might have stayed and gabbed all day with the man had Estelle not hurried her along.

By this time we were getting a little hungry so from there we went to the 'Burger Doodle Drive In' where Estelle suggested we eat out on the pick-nick tables so we wouldn't make a mess in her car.

She ordered chilli dogs for us which was something very similar to what Mama would make only she would cut the weenie in half and wrap it up in a homemade biscuit with mustard. We never had chilli on it but were accustomed to eating chilli beans by themselves.

We were delighted to get both at the same time and were eager to find out if Alma knew about this sort of food combination.

They were good but very messy to eat as Estelle had to ask for extra napkins to get us all cleaned up afterwards.

She was in the process of wiping down Learline, with Ed Earl in line to be next, when four big guys sat down on top of the table next to us.

Estelle had already told us not to get on top of the tables and I figured her to get on to them guys too.

However, she hardly looked at them when they came over there but just kept wiping Learline down.

Maybe it was because she thought they were adults, for two of them were as big as or bigger than her. You could tell they weren't all the way grown up because they still had boyish looks with maybe a little peach fuzz where their whiskers were supposed to be.

Except the one that had a full beard, he looked a little older. They were all wearing blue jeans that looked two sizes too small with white tee shirts and ball caps.

"Hey boy…where's them girl shoes at you been wearin…huh?" the bearded one said.

I recognized his voice but couldn't place him. I tried to think about where I had seen him before, as I stood staring too long before I realize I had offended him.

"Wha cha lookin at hillbilly girl?" he sarcastically snapped at me.

I quickly turned away and felt embarrassed that I had gotten caught again. Why can't I learn my lesson about that? I thought to myself. I just wanted to study his face and so I could remember who he was. I don't mean to make folks angry I thought to myself.

Trying to focus on something else I kept my eye on Learline as Estelle finished wiping her hands then went on to Ed Earl.

I didn't realize Learline was staring too until I saw her tongue poke out of her mouth and toward the other table. I glanced up to see the same one that had snapped at me was now sticking his tongue out back out at her. The other fellows laughed with one saying, *"Look at that ugly tongue on that little squirt!"*

It was then that I recognized two of them as the fellows in the pick up on the dirt road we had seen on our way to town. The same ones we had seen out on the lake before.

I turned and scanned the parking slots and found that same truck, only now, it didn't have the boat trailer behind it.

I don't know what it was about this feller but he made me feel a little sick and nervous inside. Debbie said that when you're around someone and you keep getting that same feeling that means *"they are giving you the creeps"*.

Her explanation helped me to understand how such a person can have an effect on others. I remember feeling grateful that it is an illness that don't last long and usually passed when the contaminated person goes away and you are no longer exposed to it.

"He gave me the creeps", this guy; with his beady eyes and his ugly tongue sticking out like that.

Estelle finished cleaning the chilli off of Ed Earl's face and hands, gathered us up and headed for the car.

After we were in the car and the doors were shut, Estelle said, *"I tell you…this place has gone to the hoodlums, them boys just hang out here and are up to no good…They'll have this place destroyed in no time with no more respect for other people's property than they have!"*

With it being mid-afternoon before we finished up the shopping having gone to the Piggly Wiggly after leaving the Burger Doodle, Learline was getting tired and needed a nap.

Estelle said that by the time she got out to their place and put the groceries away, it would be time to turn around and bring us back to meet Alma.

"Maybe she could take a nap at the Clinic…in Doc's office or something." she suggested.

When we got back to the Clinic, Jane, Huey and his little brothers had stopped by there and left a pair of brown shoes that Huey had out grown. Normally, they would have been passed down to one of his little brothers but it would be a while before they could fit into them and Jane felt like Ed Earl needed them more. Especially after Huey suggested it in the first place. She was proud her son was willing to be charitable to Ed Earl.

Now he had two pair of boy shoes and still didn't want to let go of the pink ones he thought his Mama gave him.

Doc was busy with other people but I was hoping he would want to talk to me about his horses. I didn't want to be the one to strike up the conversation but I was willing to listen if he had something to say about them.

Going from room to room, he only found enough time to smile and ask about how my sunburn was and if Ed Earl had anymore problems with his stitches. My sunburn had faded and was starting to itch but it didn't hurt any more. Ed Earl had no complaints so that was all I had to say in answer to his questions. However, he walked away before I could ask him if his horses had names.

After the last patient left Alma got ready to close up the Clinic for the day. She had washed us down with a rag and combed our hair and made us look presentable before we headed to the café for supper.

Trudy and the rest of the employees shared in the excitement when walked into the café that evening all dressed up in our new clothes with shoes and matching socks.

I had never felt so pretty before, thinking that this must be what it felt like for Cinderella when she got to the ball in her new dress.

We slept better that night at Trudy's. Learline didn't even mention Mama's name and with all the attention she was getting from Debbie and Trudy it was no wonder.

By Wednesday there was still no sign of Mama and Daddy except for the 'Missing' posters that hung all over town. The story was in the morning paper and had made it on the five o'clock TV news at Estelle's. We heard it all again on the radio's Late Report at Alma's that night.

We were originally going to stay that night with Trudy but the plans changed so that we could go to the Wednesday night prayer meeting with Alma.

The congregation made a big deal about the "Little Orphans", and they had us come sit down on the front row so that folks could see us better, then they'd know who it was they were going to be praying for.

It was a bit uncomfortable being the center of the attention, especially with that many people. There must have been close to forty in attendance on that most holy night for us.

Chills ran up my spine at the thought of being in God's own house and though I couldn't really see Him, I just knew He was there. Alma reminded me that He was there in the Holy Ghost form and that was why I had that feeling.

That was our first time to be in a church house and we were quite impressed. Though it was originally just a little country church, it had been modified with stained glass windows and carpet. At some point the back wall had been expanded out to incorporate a baptismal, with classrooms included in a side addition.

Nothing fancy now, but all that I had to compare with it was our church bus; so to us, this place was absolutely beautiful.

We were overwhelmed and had never seen so many people in one place in all our lives…and praying people at that!

The songs they sang sounded like angels as there were so many people singing together. Our mouths fell open as we looked all around watching the people reading the music and the words from books called hymnals.

After church service it was still light enough to see outside so the grownups stood around talking while the children ran around and played chase.

At first we stood close, holding on to Alma's dress tail until some boys asked Ed Earl if he wanted to play. He never answered them with words but broke loose and ran in circles like a crazy chicken showing off his new shoes. Later he showed them his stitches and told them the story about the bull getting after us.

Earldean and I saw some other girls there our age but were too shy to say anything so we just stood there and stared.

They were all wearing pretty dresses and I didn't feel like I belonged there even though my clothes were new.

It was sad listening to all the grown-ups talk about the disappearance of our parents and the comments about us being nameless. They weren't trying to be mean or anything; they just didn't realize how bad it hurt.

That night as we lay down to sleep, we were so tired from our busy day with all the attention we got from all the publicity about our missing parents. All of Whisper Ridge would know about our problems.

It was shortly after nine p.m., just as we were about to fall asleep, when there was a phone call from the Pastor of the church saying that one of the church members had found our parents and asked Alma if she would bring us to meet them. We weren't sleepy any more as we were overwhelmed with excitement that God had answered our prayers. Alma didn't waste time dressing us but we grabbed our new shoes and socks to put on in the car.

We chattered all the way as we rode down Hillside Road and were crying tears of joy while asking Alma loads of questions about where had they found them and where had they been?

I couldn't wait to see them. The first question I'd planned to ask was, what's our last name? And…why did they call me Sassy? Finally I would know!

17
THE LOST AND FOUND

Pulling into the church parking lot, on the corner of Loral and Hickman, we could see by the street light there were at least three cars waiting there for us but no sign of Daddy's truck.

We were greeted by the Pastor and his wife, who had already changed from their church clothes into blue jeans and overalls like regular people wear.

Behind them we could see a small group of folks, some of whom I had recognized from the services earlier that evening.

Ed Earl bounced on the edge of the seat, with his hands gripping the dashboard while we girls were wiggling in the back seat giddy with delight.

Learline stood, hanging over the back of the driver's seat, bracing herself with one arm; in the other, her baby doll hung limp from the choke hold she had on it. Peering through the windshield, she expected to see her Mama in the headlights that were shining on the folks that had gathered.

Earldean and I came to the edge of the seat too, trying to seek out our parents among the small group.

When the car came to a stop the Pastor walked over and waited for Alma to open her car door then leaned in to reintroduced himself.

"Hey Alma, Hello children…Remember me? Brother Hemphill?…And ya'll remember my wife here, don't ya?…Sister Hemphill?" he said with his arm stretched out toward her.

The woman stepped in closer with her arms folded, as if she were cold, then leaned down next to him looking into the car.

"Suurrrre…they remember me." she said in the sweetest kind of talking I had ever heard! It sounded like she was trying to sing a song or something.

"…Hope we didn't get ya'll outta bed…but…me and Brother Hemphill, knew ya'lled wanna know!"

At the time, I wasn't sure if this woman was his sister, his wife or both. Maybe it was just their names. In any case, they both seemed to be related to a lot of people at that church because that night at the preaching, he kept talking to everybody saying, "Now, brothers and sisters this" and "brothers and sisters that."

Anyway, I was glad they didn't wait till morning to tell us about finding our parents. I certainly didn't mind getting up for that!

"That's right Sister." he agreed. *"We believe we mighta found ya folks…Sam Hully's wife Clarice, says Sam knows right where they're at. They've probably been lookin for ya'll all this time!"*

It was dark and I could hardly make out his face but I recognized his voice from his preaching earlier that evening.

"Look…Sister Alma, thanks for bringing them down. I uh…know they are anxious to see their parents, but could I have a word with you first?"

Alma worked her way out of the car asking us to wait there and that she would be right back.

Brother Hemphill shut the car door behind her and the cargo light went off. We could hardly sit still as we waited for the arrangements to be made to see our parents. They stepped away from the car to talk. Eventually the group that was standing in the headlights, moved to the shadows with them. When they didn't come back right away, Earldean asked, *"What they sayin?"*

"Theyz probly talking bout Jesus or sumpin…ya'll hurry up n-come on now…lets go!" little brother replied in assumption, never missing a beat.

I hushed them and strained my ears trying to listen though I couldn't hear a thing for the squeaky springs in the seat from Ed Earls' bouncing.

Learline too, was now jumping up and down and laughing with Ed Earl, both chanting in between the giggles, *"Mama! Mama! Mama!... Daddy! Daddy! Daddy!"*

"HUSH!" Earldean shouted. *"We cain't hear nuttin fer all that racket ya makin!"*

They were quiet for less than ten seconds before Ed Earl, just teasing her, started a little bounce again and softly chanted, *"mama. mama. mama…"* Learline started her giggling again.

"Ed Earl!" she snapped. *"LEEESTEN…PLEASE!"*

I figured the two little ones could feel the tension building and settled back in silence. We could only hear muffled parts of the conversation but not enough to understand what was being said.

It was so quiet in the car, that when it made a settling sound, Ed Earl whispered, *"What'sat!"* scaring Learline, causing her to jump into Earldeans lap.

"Don't know…why come we caint just go? I said getting impatient.

"Roll down the window…it's gettin hot in here…" Earldean said *"…maybe we can hear better what they sayin."*

I grabbed the handle and cranked the wrong way in frustration causing the irritation inside of me to grow. I don't know what come over me, except that I was anxious and couldn't understand why they had to talk about anything.

"Why can't they just take us to them?" I said. We had been missing our parents long enough and couldn't understand why these people couldn't see that?

"DAT BLAST-IT THANG WON'T GO DOWN!" I shouted.

Immediately, I started shaking inside after I screamed out like that. Ed Earl flew into the back seat to show me how to do it. He had become the expert, being that was the first thing he did, every time we climbed inside a car now.

"You wuz goin the wrong way with it!" he explained.

The adults were finishing up their ten minute conversation, which at the time, seemed like hours.

The only thing we got out of what we could hear being said was something about the *"…responsible thing to do…"* followed by Brother Hemphill's voice saying, *"Well it's the Christian thing to do…Amen?"* The group answered and dispersed with a big, *"Amen!"*

They walked back over to the car with Alma saying, *"I'm going too…I know I can help verify the truth. They've been with me most of the time and have told me so much about their Mama and Daddy, I feel like I know um, already! I ain't about to quit on them youngins at an important time like this!"*

With that, she opened the car door and reached in pulling the keys from the ignition. She turned off the headlights then grabbed her purse. *"Come on ya'll…we takin ya to your folks..Brother and Sister Hemphill are gonna drive us down there!"*

We crawled out of that car and were getting into the Pastor's car when one of the men there suggested that we could fit more people in the church van and could save taking so many vehicles to the same place.

The Pastor's car was sort of small with bucket seats in the front. I think he was worried about fitting Alma in there with the rest of us in the back seat with her.

I worried about it hurting Alma's feelings with them thinking she was too fat to fit, especially when two of the men had to help push her up inside the van.

By the time we all loaded up, she was too out of breath to worry about what they thought. If she was embarrassed about it, she showed too much concern about us to let on about it.

The man who offered to take the van in the first place was the regular driver for the Sunday school pick up service. He waited until everybody was in before he slid the door shut then went around to the driver's seat.

Alma told us on the way out of the parking lot that the church held several fundraisers to get the money to buy this "near new" 1967 Volkswagen van,

"...We got it so Brother Jessie here, could go around picking up old folks who don't drive, and little kids whose parents are too lazy to get up on Sunday morning and get their children to church...the way they aught to. In all...it's come in handy!"

Talking in her singing sort of way, Sister Hemphill began to tell her version of why the church got the van. She made the whole explanation sound like she was singing it out of one those hymnals stored on the back of the pews. *"Now Sister Alma...we pick up those children because they need to be comin ta church! Their parents may be as the lost sheep, who have fled the flock...or... might not have come to know the Lord Jesus as their personal Savior yet...We feel...that until these lost souls, have dedicate themselves to serve their Master...The Creator of the Universe...that it is our Christian duty...and...Love of God, to see that the lambs of the flock are fed and nourished by His Word."*

Her explanation made their Brother Jessie's job sound like more of a privilege instead of a chore.

The thought came that maybe Brother Hemphill might be the same preacher man that gave my Daddy the two Bibles that day at the County auction. Daddy had told us that story many times and I knew it by heart. He said that preacher was looking for a bus to go around and pick up folks to bring them to church. Daddy had out bid him that day so I would guess they ended up with this van.

Earldean and I must have been thinking about that same thing about that time.

I had almost overcome my shyness enough to ask Brother Hemphill about it, but before I could, Earldean said, *"That's what My Daddy did one time…He bought a bus to go around picking up people too…seppin he just had church right there in the bus."*

"Your Daddy drives a church bus…for what church?" Sister Hemphill asked.

"Second Baptist Church a Rollin' Hills." Earldean answered then asked, *"Ya'll any kin?"*

"Whatta ya mean honey…Like the same denomination?"

Earldean looked at Alma with a questioned look and asked, *"Zat mean the same as name…the-name-a-nation?"*

The women got tickled. *"Denomination."* Alma corrected. *"That means the kind of church…like Baptist, Methodist, Pentecost… Assembly of God like ours."*

"Naw." Earldean said. *"I a talkin bout family name'z…like Hemp hill…Rollin hill…like a last name…aint ya'lls last name Hill?"*

Alma slapped her hand down on her leg and said, *"That's right! I remember seeing that on the side of ya'lls bus out there…Is that ya'll's last name, Hill…or is it Rollinghills ?"*

"Don't know…could be…I believe that's a name Daddy give it…the bus that is…when he turned it from a school bus into a church on wheels." Earldean informed them.

"He used ta call it Ole Yeller before most all the yeller paint wore off it…ain't a much a yeller color left to it…most all brown now…wit a little bit orange color mixed in".

Alma tilted her head toward Sister Hemphill and confirmed under her breath, *"Yea, she's right…it looks purdy weathered and rusted with age."*

The pastor, who was sitting in the front seat, had heard parts of the conversation and turned to ask, *"Were your parents missionaries at one time, maybe?"*

Earldean shrugged her shoulders saying, *"Aint sure…Whatsa missionaries?"*

Sister Hemphill did her best to give a brief definition of what one was, saying, *"A missionary is a person who goes out into the mission field and works for the Lord".*

Earldean rattled on with a quick answer to what she thought they wanted to know. *"I heard Daddy tell Mama one time he got a job a werkin the fields over near Siloam Springs but other than that he and Mama just had a little garden round there…theyz able to grow what we needed, I guess…Mama said them hills up where we stay, don't have enough dirt to plow…just rocks is all…trees an rocks…so naw…ain't got no fields…they just werk round yonder…but I don't know how they would go about werkin fer the Lord when he's way up younder in Heaven…"*

Something she said seemed to get them tickled as they turned to find each other chuckling.

"*…How'z a body ta go bout doin such a thang?"* she asked.

"Oh darlin…" the woman explained with a grin, "*…When you help others out in their times of need…or tell them about Jesus…You know?" Well…theyz just tell us bout the Lord a bein everwer!…ya ain't gotta be out in no field er pasture."*

The pastor, still facing back to hear the conversation, looked over at his wife who was smiling and nodding her head in agreement with Earldean. He cleared his throat as if to send some sort of signal then turned back around. Perhaps, he was simply indicating that he was satisfied with an answer to his question.

In the dim light from the dashboard, I could see the two women communicating with gestures. Sister Hemphill smiled and winked at Alma then said, *"Honey, what I think he wanted to know was if your parents traveled about preaching the gospel…that's working for the Lord."*

Ed Earl felt it was time that he set everybody straight on what they needed to know. With his six years of wisdom and insight, he felt he could give them the information they were fishing for. With confidence, he said loud enough for everybody to hear from the very back seat, *"My Daddy don't work for the Lord…he works for money! And, he don't drive the bus no more cause it broke down before I was ever even born! He just drives his truck to work and we sleep in the bus when it rains…or it gits cold! And now we gonna go home with him and Mama cause its bedtime and somebody name Sam, found um!"*

Learline had forgotten all about being sleepy. She had been sitting with her back arched and looking out the windows for her parents since we got into the van. She broke from her vigil watch to put in her two cents worth *"…An I gone sleep wit my Mama and my Daddy a night…me and my bae'doll!…Mama gonna tell Bible story, den her a sing me song bout I wove Jegus!"*

"AUUWEEEEE." the adults sang out like it was a well rehearsed hymn all sung in tune, followed by Alma saying, *"Aint that the sweetest thang you ever heard?"*

"Sooo precious!" Sister Hemphill confirmed.

She was cute to say things like that. Big thoughts would come out in baby words and had a way of making your heart feel soft.

Everything fell to a hush for a short time after that was said, except the hum of the tires on the road and the wind noise the van was making, as it drove on in the night air.

That sound seemed to fill my ears while the van slightly swayed and rocked its way to the place where we would meet our parents. Although I was tired, I was so happy and looking forward to the reunion of our family.

Alma reached and pulled Learline and her dolly close to her and gave her a kiss on top of her head just like Mama would do at times like that.

I would miss Alma after we went home, I thought; so would my brother and sisters. She had been so good to us. Trudy and Debbie had been good to us too. I wish we could have told them all goodbye. I wish we could have said goodbye to Doc and Estelle. I tried to remember if I said thank you to Estelle for buying us the clothes and shoes.

I think we were all too excited to remember that important thing. Mama had done well to teach us manners just in case we ever needed them.

The memory of Mama's words she had repeated time and time again, would surface in my mind too late to do anything about it. *"Always say your pleases and thank ye's; for it's such a small effort for the blessings we receive."* her voice echoed in my thoughts.

Her and Daddy both taught us to answer them with *ma'ams* and *sirs.* We had never had much call to say it to anybody before we came to Whisper Ridge, except Denby and the Rileys. Never the less, Mama said if we practiced good manners at home, they would come natural for us when we were at other places.

I'm not sure who it was that taught her all those things like that but she had lots of little sayings that came from somewhere in her past life.

Mama had told us of a fine elderly woman she called Mammy-maw Davis, who she had taken up time with on a porch, somewhere far away.

This woman apparently had lots of "sayins" too, such as, *"Wear your velvet at home"*. A saying, Mama told us, that meant the same thing as being on your best behavior at all times. That way it would eventually become part of "who" you are and you wouldn't have to try so hard to be good…it would just come natural.

Now this one took some explaining for Mama, especially with us having no idea what velvet was, having never seen it before. She described it as best she could and told us that rich people had clothes made out of it…important people like the kings and queens of the Bible. I could only imagine what velvet was when she said that our royal robes we'd be given when we got to heaven might be made of such a fine fabric.

I bet velvet feels like some of those soft sheets at Trudy's house I thought to myself as I reminisced…or her soft fuzzy footstool she kept by her chair.

I reached down at the pocket of my new shorts I was wearing. I could feel that the package of Juicy Fruit gum was still there with two sticks left. I had meant to give her another piece because I knew how well she liked it. I had seen how it made her eyes light up when I offered her a stick before. That look on her face made my heart feel so warm and soft.

Taking the package out of my pocket; I held it to my nose drawing in a long sniff. I could smell the sweet flavor through the waxy paper. The memories of Trudy's smile froze in my imagination as I felt that same sort of expression come across my own face.

I must have drifted off on the night ride without realizing it, because when my eyes opened I heard the Pastor's voice. It sounded like he was talking from under a pile of blankets or as if his words were muffled far away and I couldn't make out what he was saying. I thought he might have ended it by asking something like, *"Did the man ever get the bus fixed? Is he still picking up converts for their church?"*

"That ole thang won't pick up nuttin but flies now." I heard Alma's voice a little closer and clearer. She turned to Sister Hemphill and said, *"It's stalled out there…That's what they been livin out of all this time."*

"I see…Poooor little youngins…stuck out there for sooo long." Sister Hemphill said with pity, sounding as if she was singing a pitiful sweet tune.

The Juicy Fruit package was hanging loose in my hand and I clutched on to it before it fell to the floor of the van. I stuck it safely back in my pocket for another time.

As I listened to the two women talk on about first one thing then another, I began to drift off to sleep again.

Suddenly, the whining of the van's wheels dropped to lower tones as did the humming of its engine when we slowed down the fast pace we had kept against the wind. I sat up on the edge of my seat and peered out the window at the darkness wondering where we were and was curious as to why we seemed to be stopping out in the middle of nowhere.

Sister Hemphill leaned forward, peering through the windshield into the night, lit only by the headlights and asked, "*Is this the right place?*"

"Must be…Sister Hulley is in the car up ahead with the others and she said this is where Sam claimed they were when he saw them." Brother Jessie said.

We turned onto a dirt road near a big sign that read something about The Ozarks Cider Creek. I was trying to read what it said while the headlights were shining on it but we were turning too fast and the words spun off into the darkness.

We watched as the headlights wound around, up and down a road that was wide enough for two cars but we stayed near the middle and drove slow.

The tall trees of the dense forest lined both sides and for a little while I thought we were back home in Chinquapin Hollow, but I wasn't sure because I had never seen it at night lit up by headlights.

The car in front of us that was leading the way had slowed down when its red brake lights flashed before they held steady, then came to a stop. We could see up ahead a deer stood in the road and stared back at them. It was good to see a familiar animal and I thought of how her stance looked sort of like Doc's white mare standing there.

"Ooooh it's a deeeer! Look children!" Sister Hemphill sang out.

"…ats a doe…prolly bout three er four years old." Ed Earl said. *"Daddy would let her go…she's good for makin babies but the meats not as fittin ta eat…too tough…she hardly got nuff ta chew! She's lucky she aint got shot yet…Daddy says some folks these days just kill one her size fer a trophy."*

"My goooodness! You sure know a lot about deer for a boy your age!" Sister Hemphill said. *"You can tell all that about a deer from just lookin at it?"*

The doe darted on across the road into the woods like it had seen a ghost or something as we slowly proceeded.

"He'z smart as a whip…I'm telling ya!" Alma proudly complimented.

"Ya Daddy a hunter, Ed Earl?" Brother Hemphill asked.

"Ye sir…He takes me wit him most time, after he seen I got big nuff ta walk a long wayz off and could keep up wit him!"

"Yep, that's where we get most all our meat from." Earldean added. *"Daddy's huntin or him and Mama a settin a trap fer rabbits and squirrels."*

"Is that the only kind of meat ya'll eat out there? Do ya'll ever have beef, pork or chicken? Brother Jessie asked from the driver's seat.

"We eat all kinds of birds…we eat chickens some…but mostly we got them fer egg layin." Earldean answered.

"Lotta time we eat fish…when the bitin's good." I said, not realizing I hadn't done much talking the whole time we were in the van.

Sister Hemphill leaned forward and look over in my direction saying, *"Weeell I'll Beee! Miss Sassy, I was beginning to think you couldn't talk…I thought the cat got your tongue!"*

"Sassy is sortta on the shy side." Alma informed her, patting me softly on my leg as if she were trying let me know she liked me anyway; ignoring the part of what she said about the cat. *"…but, she aint no trouble at all! She's really gonna be glad to see her Mama, aint cha hun?"*

I smiled nervously, then leaned my head back pressing it against the seat. When they weren't looking I reached and pulled at my tongue to see just how hard it would be to come out. I couldn't imagine why a big cat would only want that part of a little girl without eating up the rest of her.

"Them ole mean fellers told us bout that tung gittin wild cat out there…we aint never seen it yet …but if I had my Daddy's gun… I'd shoot it…atta way it cain't git my tongue outa my mouth!" Ed Earl bravely announced.

"Tongue Eating Cat? What mean ole fellers you talking about Ed Earl?" Alma asked, again, ignoring the part about the cat.

"Them mean ole fellers that scered us out younder when we'za walkin ta town that day!"

"Oh…He talking bout them hoodlums…at there's what Estelle called um…hoodlums!" Earldean told her. *"…We seen um again when we went fer a chilli dog over at the Burger Doodle with her…Alma you ever tried one em*

chilli dogs…az real tasty…you'd like it…ya oughtta go over there an gitchee one ta eat one day."

"Hoodlums? She didn't tell me anything about that. Did they give ya'll any trouble?"

"Naw…they just called us a bunch of hillbillies…talked to Ed Earl bout his shoes…stuff like that…"

"…And when they stuck out they'z ole ugly tongue...Learline stuck hers out too…showed um that she still had hers…aint no cat gonna git it…huh baby sister?" Ed Earl finished with reassurance and protection for his younger sibling.

"As long as they didn't try to hurt ya…I guess no harm done…huh? Still…there was no call to pick on you bout them shoes…or that ya'll live in the hills…cain't help it!" Alma declared, though she still didn't have any comment about the absurdness of that strange cat's behavior.

The road twisted and turned until we came to a clearing with a few trees scattered about.

I knew we were close to the lake because I could see it a little ways off down the hill, lit up by the moonlight.

Scattered about were small camp fires and lanterns hanging about here and there. Lines were strung up with towels and a few clothes hanging from them. To me it appeared that people like us were living there by the lake. There were even a couple of trailers that resembled small buses there in the dark.

"Where we at?" Earldean asked.

"Cider Creek Camp Grounds." Brother Jessie said. *"Don't look like as many campers out here during the week, huh?"*

"Too hot this time of year to enjoy it." Pastor Hemphill answered.

"This is the place they found ya folks at!" Alma informed us. *"Least we hope they still here."*

"Sister Clarice said her husband Sam had headed back down here to keep them from leaving until we could get here with the children." Brother Hemphill said. *"He was commin to let them know we were bringing their children to them and not to worry…We are gonna do what we can to get this family together and keep them together."*

Apparently, this sister of theirs, Clarice, told her husband about us being at church that night as soon as she got home. They, like everybody else in Whisper Ridge, had heard bits and pieces of the story before it was told from the pulpit.

Sam, her husband, who was the camp ground attendant, had come in from work and seen it on the local TV news, while his wife was at church.

He thought he recognized the sketches as being two campers who had shown up just about the time these two people were reported last being seen.

Sam and Clarice had wondered why they had not gone to the police if they were looking for their children, and thought there might be something more to that. Sam said he thought they acted kind of suspicious to him.

"Maybe it was because they looked like a couple of them beatnik dope-heads." he had told his wife. *"...They sortta look like they might be the type to run off and leave their youngins for somebody else to tend to."*

Clarice, who was not as judgmental as her husband, thought that maybe they were just too poor to take care of their children and that the only way to see that they were fed was to give them away.

But Sam wondered if we were run-a-ways that had lied about what happened to our parents, to keep them out of trouble with the law. He also suggested to his wife that if he was right, it might be that they had abandoned us out there to fend for ourselves while they were off having a good time...smoking dope and doing drugs and Lord knows what all!

With us being so skinny, he implied that our parents could have been starving us and with our brother having to have stitches, we could possibly have been victims of abuse.

Clarice told her husband that he sounded like he had been indulging in a little gossip with some of the locals who were just bored with their own lives and looking for some dramatic entertainment in thinking the worst of people.

Her first instinct was to get this family the help they needed and to her, the best help would be from the church family.

Sam argued otherwise. He thought that the police should handle this kind of situation. Up ahead we could see red flashing lights like the ones on the patrol cars. The lights made the darkness look like a storm was going on without all the noise or wetness and instead of white bolts of lightning flashing against the trees, these flashed red ones.

Sister Hemphill pushed herself forward on the seat and softly said, *"Uuuh- Ooooo. Looks like Sam went to the Sheriff after all!"* Alma said with disappointment.

There was a small crowd standing back away from the patrol car. Other campers, I guess, had come to see what all the commotion was about.

We were out of our seats ready to jump out of the van before it came to a complete stop.

When the door was slid open we were crawling over Alma and Sister Hemphill who we thought weren't moving fast enough. We could hardly wait to lay eyes on our parents!

As we broke through the crowd we looked for them thinking they might have been standing among all the people.

"Wait for me!" we could hear Alma's voice cry out, over the mumbling crowd. However, she was still trying to get out of the van so I left it up to the others to wait for her; I just couldn't. I had waited long enough to see my Mama and Daddy!

I ran past Brother Hemphill, through the folks that were standing there, then up to where the Sheriff was standing talking to a Park Ranger.

"Where they at?...Where's my Mama and Daddy?" I cried looking all around.

"Now hold on a minute, little missy!" Sheriff McCoy responded to my cry.

"My name is Sassy not Missy...Where's my Daddy and Mama?" I pleaded with him unaware I had overcome any shyness I might have shown before.

"Your name uh...Hold on!" he said, holding his big hands on my boney shoulders.

"Did Miss Alma come with ya'll?" he asked, while I tried to see past him.

"Yes Sir. She'z a commin...Where they at?"

The rest of them followed up behind me asking the same thing I wanted to know.

The Sheriff stepped aside to greet Alma saying, *"Hope we didn't get ya'll out this time a night for nuttin."*

"Ain't it them...Please Sheriff...fer these kids sake...tell us it's them!"

"Don't know. Unless these folks are toatin a fake ID, they from Monroe, Louisiana! At least he is...she didn't have a driver's license or nuttin... Said

they's just up here on a vacation. The ironic thang is…His name is Earl…Earl Posey…You youngins know anybody by that name?" the sheriff asked us.

"My Daddy's name'z Earl too…Daddy and Earl…thems his names!" Ed Earl answered.

"I don't know…could be!" Earldean said. *"Where's he at?"*

"We have um sittin over here waitin for yall to positively identify them before we turn um loose." He gathered us up close to him with the group from the church standing behind us now. He squatted down to get at eye level then took off his hat so that we could see his eyes with the headlights that were still on.

"Now, ya'll understand that if these people are your folks…well, ya caint go home with um tonight."

We all started to cry out, *"Why?"*

"Listen!" he said softly. *"…Your folks have got some explaining ta do before ya'll can get back together. They might have to get some help!"*

"We always help them when they need us to!" I said, crying bittersweet tears.

"It's not like the kind of help you kids can give um." Sheriff replied. *"They need the law and a head doctor to help sort this kind of problem out."*

"If they'z both sick…they gonna need us to take care of um…We know how!" Earldean told him, stepping from one foot to the other like she was nervous or needed to pee.

"We won't go off and leave Mama no more!" I assured him.

"I want my Mama!" Learline cried.

"Meeeeeeee Tooooo!" whined Ed Earl *"…and my Daaady!"*

Sheriff McCoy stood up and straightened out his pants legs then slid his hat back on. *"OK, I'm going to let you see ya folks…make sure they're the ones that belong to you...and if they are, well, you all can ride to the station with us…get in a little visit for the night…but…then ya'll have to go back with Miss Alma till we have this all sorted out."* Then looking at Alma he asked, *"That alright with you?"*

"Sure." she said stepping in closer and putting her hands on my shoulder. *"They welcome to stay as long as they need to!"*

"We'll help her out, Sheriff." Brother Hemphill said with the church folks all following it with, *"Amen!"* making it sound like a closing to a prayer.

Sheriff McCoy took a deep breath then hissed a sigh of relief. It must have been pretty hard to be in his shoes that night. To have to tell us grieving, homesick children who had already been separated from our parents long enough, that we couldn't go home with or without them. At least not that night; there would definitely have to be some changes made first and it appeared as if it was going to take a long time.

He reached for Learline's hand. She tucked her baby doll safely under her right arm, and with her other, reached out and took the large man's hand. He led her to the squad car with the rest of us following close behind them.

Steady streams of tears were rolling down my cheek as the Sheriff opened the back door of the squad car. We looked in…our parents weren't in there!

18
RESPECT

Episodes of tears and nightmares took their toll on Alma by day break. She had been up with one or another of us all through the night, blowing noses, drying eyes and rocking on the edge of a straight back chair.

She even took a turn with me and Earldean, as big as we were, acting like big ole babies! We couldn't seem to control the overwhelming sadness that had replaced the joy we had in thinking we had found our parents. Where could they be?

Turns out, the people who were in the back of the squad car that night, were who they said they were, Earl Posey from Louisiana and his wife Patricia, of four years. They didn't look anything like our parents, although they did resemble the composite drawings enough that I could see how Sam Hully and the Sheriff could have made such a mistake.

I didn't see it as a mistake right away though. That night, we were so let down in not finding our parents where we had been told they were, it felt like a dirty rotten trick had been played on us. Just a cruel mean joke!

Ed Earl cried so hard that he wore himself out, curled up on his side and fell asleep still shaking. I had never seen him get that way. We all took it pretty hard but he took it the hardest all. I guess those last few years, before his sixth birthday, of having to be a big boy and trying not to cry, had been building up all that time. It took something like this big dose of disappointment to pull it out of him. He was in bad shape, for even long after he was asleep, he moaned and whimpered.

Poor Alma! She had no idea what she was in for when she turned down the help some of the church ladies offered that night. Several of them volunteered each to take one of us home with them but Alma didn't think we should be separated at a time like that. She was probably right. It was hard enough as it was, to be missing the main two people of our family without us missing one another. "Each other" was all we had that night holding us together…Each other and Alma, bless her heart!

The ringing phone woke me up the next morning. It was Doc, looking to see if Alma was alright. When she didn't show up for work he got worried and called to check on her. It was not like Alma to miss a day of work and not call in. She was never even late, so this had the Doc worried and concerned. When she gave a brief and sleepy sounding explanation of what had happened the night before, he told her not to worry about trying to come in that he could handle the few appointments he had that day. He said he would send Estelle over to get us kids so that she could rest but she wouldn't have it.

Learline and Ed Earl were still sleeping and she didn't want to wake them. In fact, we all went back to sleep and stayed there until almost noon.

When we woke up Alma had Ed Earl up on the couch with a cool wash cloth over his eyes and a small throw spread across his little body.

"He'za runnin a fever…Hotter than a firecracker!" Alma said.

"Reckon he cried too hard?" I asked. *"He aint use to cryin sa much as us girls."*

Earldean stretch then got up to take a look at our little brother. Feeling his cheek with the back of her hand she said, *"Hope he aint commin down wit that mess Mama had…It put her out fer quite a spell."*

Alma repositioned the wash cloth across his forehead saying, *"I ought to take him in and let Doc take a look at him…need to cool him down some first though."*

Ed Earl was barely strong enough to open his eyes because he was so weak. The swelling in his eyes we figured had come from all the crying he had done.

"Look at his arm!" I exclaimed. *"His skin's a commin off!"*

He was pale and splotchy, with small loose sheets of skin cracked and pealing from the one arm that was hanging out of the covers.

"That's where his sunburn is a fadin and peelin off." Alma informed us.

"Why come it to do that?" Earldean asked.

"That's what it usually does after ya git blistered by the sun like that…bad as ya'll got it, I'm surprised it didn't make sores all over ya!" Alma said.

Examining my own arms and legs for sores or peeling, I found that a few small flakes floated off when I rubbed my skin.

Earldean made mention that she thought she remembered that happening to her once before, after she had stayed in the swimming hole too long on a bright sunny day and got sunburned from it.

"Seemed like I remember it ichin and I ended up scratchin all my skin off!" she said, as she scratched around on her own arm.

"...Just thinking bout it makes me itch!"

"Well truth is..." Alma told us, *"...all that is dead skin that is comin off you have new skin underneath all that mess."*

I was glad too. It scared me there to think what we might look like without any skin on our bones. I had seen skeletons of people in a picture on the wall in the back room of the Clinic. It was pretty scary! I knew about the skeletons of dead animals out in the woods as me and Ed Earl would always be poking at them with a stick. On occasion we would make things from the bones of animals that we had eaten the meat off of.

But something about the bones of a human made me quiver inside. I guess, like the animals, a body would have to be dead to see all their bones. I had never seen a dead human before to look at any bones but I knew we all had them.

"Are we all gonna git fever from that skin peelin?" I asked.

"No Hun, you don't run a fever from that...Your brother must be comin down with that same bug that got your Mama had when she was sick."

"You think it was a poison bug that bit um...caused um to get sick like this?" Earldean asked, while I scanned the floor for a spider or some other little critter that we might have carried in with us on our new shoes.

"Not that kind of bug." Alma said. *"Sometimes we refer to bacteria as bugs...that's what they look like under a microscope...crawly little bugs!"*

"Is a mike-a-poke some kinda leaf or log them kinda bugs hide under?" I asked.

Alma smiled and said, *"No, a microscope has a special kind of glass that lets you see things you caint see with the necked eye. Germs and bacteria are so tiny you don't evenknow they're there just by lookin...certain ones can cause you to get sick with a belly ache or fever when they get in your blood stream."*

Alma knew a whole lot about stuff like that, getting sick from germs and all, I'd guessed from working at the Clinic there with Doc and helping the sick folks that would come in.

"I hope they don't git the rest of us sick like that!" Earldean said.

Me too! I thought.

With all the talking we were doing we managed to wake up Learline, who was lying on the pallet on the floor. She sat up, looking around in a daze with her hair going in every direction. *"I hungry."* she said with a scratchy little voice, her crying all night must have made her a little raspy and congested.

"Good mornin sleepy head...Or I should say, almost noon!" Alma said.

"I can fix her somethin ta eat...I know how." Earldean told Alma.

Alma scooted off the edge of the couch and stuck a throw pillow under Ed Earl's head to rest on. *"You lay right hear sweet boy...I'm gonna get you some aspirin for that fever and fix you and your sisters a bite to eat."*

Ed Earl hardly responded to her comment about cooking something to eat. He had been requesting something dipped in ketchup every time anybody mentioned food. But this time, he just curled to his side and pulled the covers over his shoulder.

Alma found the bottle of aspirins, then took a knife and spoon out of the drawer of utensils. She cut the aspirin in half then crushed one side of it into the spoon. In the refrigerator she found a bottle of syrup and poured some over the top of the aspirin then gently stirred it around in the spoon with her finger until the tablet half dissolved.

"What cha makin Alma?" I asked her as she carefully mixed the concoction.

"Aspirin for your brother...this will make him feel better and hopefully break the fever. He aint big enough to take a whole aspirin... and this syrup will make it easier to swallow than tryin to chew up a bitter pill by itself."

She held her hand under the spoon as she walked across the floor to the couch where he was laying. We were following behind her every step like little puppy dogs anxious to see if it would be something we would like to taste.

"Ed Earl" she said, *"...wanna sit up and take this? It'll make ya feel better".*

"I aint hungry." he said in a weak shaky voice.

"Come on hun...its just a little ole spoon full...make ya feel better!" she coached.

Ed Earl slowly shook his head no then closed his eyes tight.

Earldean sat on edge of the couch next to him and lifted him up from under his shoulder saying, *"Come on Ed Earl, mind Miss Alma...you know better...she's a grown up!"*

Ed Earl moaned like it hurt to move him, sort of the way Mama did just before she passed out. *"Don't hurt him Earldean!"* I scolded *"...He might faint!"*

"We need to try to get the medicine down him to settle the pain and break his fever." Alma said. *"Taste sweet, like honey... you'll like it!"*

Learline had worked her way in front of Alma and under the spoon saying to her, *"I like it…can I hab sum?"*

"Naw, sweetheart…this is for Ed Earl…he's sick." Alma replied.

"Come on brother…sit up and eat this so you will get well!" I pleaded.

With a groan, he struggled to be obedient when Earldean barely managed to help him sit up enough so that Alma could spoon in the potential antidote. He hardly got a little taste in his mouth before he spit it back out.

"Now look at cha! You have to swallow it…taste sweet…its not bad!" Alma said.

"Just swaller fast!" She scooped the spill off his chin and tried again. *"Come on…you wanna feel better don't ya? Be a big boy now…open wide."*

With that he took the rest then shrugged his shoulders.

The show was over when Alma said on the way back to the kitchen, *"I should have thought to mix it with ketchup…He wouldn't have given us any problem with that, I bet."*

She fed us then spent a great deal of time on the phone with Trudy, filling her in on the latest, as well as the many callers from the church who were concerned.

She had shown us girls how to play her record player without scratching her records and allowed us to go through her album collection. That kept us busy while she drug the long corded phone out to the steps so that she could hear.

We were entertained by great artists we had never heard of. She had the likes of Gary Pucket and the Union Gap singing "Woman-Woman", "Lady Willpower" and his latest hit…"Young Girl."

She had some with Otis Redding, Neal Diamond and another with Aaron Neville singing "Tell It Like It Is". But, Alma's newest ones were my favorite. They were those with Bobby Vinton's pictures on them. I would just sit and stare at how pretty he was for a man. He sang pretty too. My favorites were "Mr. Lonely" and "I Love How You Love Me".

Alma had said her favorite newest hit song was one of the ones she had on little records called "forty fives". We got tickled at her when she played it for us and sang along with Aretha Franklyn and did a funny dance that looked like she was a bouncing ball. The whole trailer shook as she put on a show for us.

"R-E-S-P-E-C-T, that-is-what-it-means to me! AAAAAAAWW!"

She didn't seem to mind us laughing at her. We couldn't help it! She was so funny! She was glad to see us laughing instead of crying.

When two o'clock came and Ed Earl still hadn't eaten anything and his fever was about the same, Alma put in a call to Doc.

He came there to check on Ed Earl instead of making Alma get out with him. Estelle was with him when he came to see if she could be of any help.

Doc looked Ed Earl over, mashing around on his throat and belly and listening to his heartbeat with a thing he call a "stethoscope".

Doc had asked us when was the last time Ed Earl had seen a Doctor for a shot of any kind. We told him that we had never known him to get sick enough to need to go.

He told Alma that he checked before he came and didn't find a chart on the boy. Before she could remind him of why she had not finished it yet he asked her if she had given him a Tetanus shot when she put the stitches in.

Alma gasped and put her hand over her mouth. She never answered him yes or no but the look on her face told him what he needed to know.

"We need to get him to a hospital right away!"

19
THE VISIT
(*LOCKED UP INDEFINITELY*)

They're all the same. No matter where you go, no matter what state of the nation you're in or state of mind for that matter, they're still… all the same.

You could put a blindfold on me, not give me a single clue as to where you're going take me, spin me around and put me through the door and I can identify this particular place by the distinctive smell it will have.

It would be a mixture of pine oil and other cleaning fluids, alcohol, camphor and medicine, with a back note of wiped up puke. It's the same smell that all hospitals have. They say that your nose is a secret passageway to your past. Often times it will pick up a scent that will trigger a memory of a certain time or place. A reminder, you could say, to let you know that you haven't forgotten that part of your past. It's there, tucked away on a shelf in your brain somewhere, waiting to resurface from your subconscious to your conscious mind.

Every time I walk into a hospital, it's the smell that brings back to my mind that first time I had ever been inside one. It was on that miserable summer Sunday back in 1968 when Trudy took us to visit our little brother who was very sick.

Unlike it is today where some folks think they ought to take a pill for every little ache or pain; back then we just rubbed the sore spot until it eased up or we'd soak in the creek.

Eventually we'd feel better. But it's not like that anymore. Nowdays people take handfuls of pills every single morning, noon and night, to keep from dying. They're convinced they've got an illness that will surely kill them and short change them on their numbered days.

Nowdays, with some people, all it takes is so much as sneeze, then they think they should seek emergency medical treatment immediately so that they can start pumping drugs into their body faster…so they can live longer…pain free.

We sort of had the understanding that a person must be near death, in order for it to be necessary just to go to the doctor and if *he* says you need to go to a hospital, well…we thought that meant that you might as well give up the ghost.

It scared us to tears when we overheard the adults saying that Ed Earl might die.

Walking down the halls, that seemed wide enough to drive a car through, our steps echoed off the highly polished floors and the shiny ceramic tiles that neatly lined the walls.

Out of nowhere, dings of a bell would sound just before a lady's voice would make an announcement to get the attention of a particular doctor or nurse.

"Ding, ding…Attention please…Dr. White…please report to E.R…Dr. White, to E.R."

Most everyone there wore white clothes. The whitest white you ever saw. They walked real fast, like they were in a hurry to get to where they were going, carrying clip boards or trays filled with pills or tubes of blood. Some pushed carts filled with strange objects, some pushed chairs on wheels that carried people.

Stainless steel pipes hung horizontally along the walls and served as hand rails for those patients who needed something to hold on to in order to keep them stable.

The air was cool in spite of the heat outside but the light inside was as bright as a warm sunny day, magnified by the pale aqua colors in the background.

Other than the moans and groans, an occasional beeping machine or visitors that talked in whispers, the place was quiet compared to the other noises the city made outside.

As we made our way down, what I thought at the time was the longest hallway in the world, I wondered if the police had checked this hospital to see if Mama and Daddy had been there.

Rounding the corner, we came upon an area where a few people, two ladies and a young man, were just standing quietly. When Trudy stopped to talk to them we did the same but instead, we all just stood there waiting for somebody to say something.

One woman looked as though she was about to speak when a rumbling noise came from the other side of the wall and we all turned to see what it was. Learline let out a frightened squeal but the sound of it was muffled when she buried her face in Trudy's dress tail. Sister and I looked at each other not knowing what to expect.

About that time a bell rang then the wall opened up and an old man with a cane stepped out of a tiny room. After he stepped out, Trudy and the other folks who were standing there stepped through the opening and into the small space.

I looked through the opening to see if Ed Earl was in there thinking that might be his room but the space was too small for a bed.

"Well…come on girls!" Trudy said. *"…Hurry up!"* We stepped forward and were about to enter when the wall started to close up again. *"Yikes!"* Earldean shrieked and we all jumped back while the young man reached and grabbed at the opening. He pressed hard against it, asking, *"Ya'll commin er not?"*

Reluctantly, we walked through and joined them just in time before the wall closed back up and locked us in! There was a jolt that made the whole place feel like we might have been caught up in the middle of a cyclone and with a squeal, Learline grabbed hold to Trudy's leg causing her to almost fall.

"Goodness Graicious!" Trudy said with a chuckle as she caught the pale nauseous look on mine and Earldean's faces. *"…I forgot…I bet this is your first elevator ride!"*

The same woman that started to say something before we got on, decided to warn us, *"You know…children are not allowed past the first floor, don't you?"*

Trudy hesitated only a second or two before she came up with a clever response that disturbed the woman as well as the other two passengers.

"Oh…These girls are checking in as patients…they have a highly contagious disease."

The woman looked surprised then pulled the collar of her dress over her mouth, not saying another word. Turning her face to the wall, we heard the other woman say, *"Contagious! Oh no...That's all I need!"*

The young man frantically pushed at the buttons on the wall causing the whining hum of the elevator to lower its tone before we felt another slight jolt. The thing opened up and they all rushed off.

When the door closed Trudy busted out laughing saying, *"Smarty Pants…Teach her right to be a snooty know it all!"*

"Are we sick too, Trudy?" I asked.

Wiping the sides of her lips with her thumb and finger, without messing up her lipstick, she pressed her smile back down as if she had been guilty of being out of line.

"No Sweetie…You as healthy as Jack Lalane…I was just foolin with them people…te-he-he…I just couldn't resist!"

We didn't understand the joke she had played and stood silently staring at her straight faced. Probably feeling a little guilty she tried to make it worthwhile for somebody besides herself. Looking down at Learline she asked, *"Did you see the look on her face?"*

The toddler, who was still unsure about the safety of her elevator ride, mistook the laughter as a sign of security and responded with a forced giggle.

As a rule, in those days, kids weren't allowed up on the floors with the patients but Doc had made arrangements with the resident Doctor and the nurses, who had been treating Ed Earl, to let us come up there to see him.

He had been diagnosed with Tetanus; Lock Jaw they called it, and was in the painful stages of its rapid progression.

He had not been responding well to the treatment, partly due to his emotional state of mind. Without his parents to be with him through this trauma, they felt that a visit from his sisters would be encouraging to him.

We girls had been staying with Trudy at night and during the day with Estelle, except for a few times when her hormones were flaring up and she couldn't handle the stress. On those particular days, Trudy kept us with her at the café and we did our best to help or stay out of the way.

Alma was turned inside out over Ed Earl's condition and seemed to be taking full responsibility over him getting sick. She claimed that if she would have thought about giving him a tetanus shot after his getting cut on the barbed wire and needing stitches, he wouldn't be going through all this pain and suffering. She regretted not calling in the Doc to do the job of putting in the stitches. Although she had done it before with his guidance and assistance, she wished she would have waited and let him do it this time.

Trudy, being the friend she was, did everything she could to keep Alma from blaming herself for fear she might give up her dream of becoming a real nurse. She reminded her of all that was going on that day we first showed up at the Clinic and how we didn't even know our names much less whether or not we had been vaccinated against such things as Tetanus. It was something anyone might have done in her situation.

Doc too, did his best not to let the blame fall on Alma, who without the proper training or such records of immunization, couldn't have known for sure. Doc himself felt like it was his responsibility and that he should have followed up with Alma by asking to make sure Ed Earl had a tetanus shot if he needed it. He too was distracted when he called the office that day and found out about our dilemma.

They both spent a lot of time at the hospital. With Alma not wanting to leave his bedside, she did her best to make Ed Earl feel as comfortable as possible but it wasn't enough.

When the doctors didn't think he would live through the week, they consented to let his sisters come in to see him. We were shocked to see him in such poor condition. He had not complained about his stitches hurting nor had he even acted sick for days after Alma sewed him up. Doc said that was not unusual as it takes four to ten days for the incubation period and for the bacteria to get into the blood stream well enough before symptoms start to occur. By then it had been seven days before he started running fever and his neck started to get sore. When he first complained about it, Alma thought he might just have a crick in his neck like you get from sleeping with your neck bent or holding your head down too long. We all just thought it was because he had been crying so hard from the letdown of the night before.

We would have never thought of "Lock Jaw" if we were still back at home in the hollow. We would really be in trouble without Doc and Alma.

If we had been vaccinated against such things when we were babies, it could have prevented this from happening. Mama must not have known about this or she would have seen to it that we were shot with the medicine we needed. She wouldn't want us to get sick and die! Maybe she did know and took care of it when we were babies but I couldn't remember. You would think I would remember a thing like that.

Now, more than ever, we needed to find our parents. With the situation Ed Earl was in, Doc told Alma there was a good chance that the rest of us may be behind on our vaccinations as well. If that were the case, we were due for shots and unless we knew where our parents would keep such records at home indicating otherwise it would need to be soon.

Alma suggested they could check with state health department but without a last name they were at a dead end. Until we found them, all the hospital could put on his chart for a name was…"Little John Doe/Ed Earl".

This name hung on a sign outside a big door that squeaked when we pushed it open. Alma rose to her feet with stiffness from the straight back chair where she had fallen asleep next to the bed. She looked worn out and tired but smiled when she saw us come through the door.

She slowly stepped forward to greet us with a hug and tears fell from her eyes. She said she was happy to see us but the tears were a bit confusing.

My little brother looked so tiny lying in that big hospital bed with the silver rails pulled up on each side. He laid sound asleep while silver boxes with tiny flashing lights blinked and flickered at the head of the bed. There were tubes and wires connecting Ed Earl to these contraptions. It scared me to think that he might get electrocuted by them.

"He aint dead, iz'e?" Earldean asked as she cautiously tiptoed towards the bed.

"It's ok…sniff…he'z just sleepin." Alma tried to assure her with a whimper as she wiped the tears from her swollen face before she turned to follow.

"Are ya sure?…he ain't a movin 'round er nuttin." she requested assurance with whining concern.

"Shhhh…they give him sumpinuther ta ease the pains…sniff…poor little feller…sniff…been so sick." she answered sympathetically, putting her arm around Earldean.

"How in the world can he be a sleepin through all 'at beepin racket?"

Of course there were questions as to what for and why each one was there. Alma did her best to explain through the tears.

When Trudy saw how upset Alma was getting she dropped her purse next to the wall then put her arm around her friend and coaxed her to sit in a big chair in the corner.

"Oh Hun…When was the last time you had any sleep?" Trudy asked her when she squatted down next to her.

"Well…sniff, sniff…I've been sleepin off and on since I got here." Alma replied.

"That was four days ago, Alma! Sleepin in a chair don't count! You've got ta go home and get some rest…you aint gonna be fit for nuthin without some real sleep!"

"I just cain't leave him like this…sniff…he's got to have somebody here at his side, bless his lit'lo heart!"

"Alma, you take the kids back to my house…they can stay with Debbie…I'll stay here with him till ya git caught up on ya sleep."

"But you need to be at the café in the mornin don't cha?"

"Well…I'll make a call and git Yvonne to schedule some of the others to come in…we'll work it out…don't you worry bout that now!"

"The girls just got here…let them see their brother first!"

"I don't mean right now…I mean when they have to leave…Why don't you find a place to take a nap…maybe in one of those big chairs in the waiting room at the end of the hall. You need to sleep a little before that long trip back home." Trudy insisted.

Ed Earl barely moved, then moaned, which distracted them from their conversation. His muscles had stiffened up so tight that he could hardly move voluntarily but Alma was afraid that he might be about to start having muscle spasms again.

She pushed herself back out of the big chair and rushed over to his bedside. *"I've got to rub him down…when he starts that shaking it throws him into a fit of pain and his little body gets stiffer after each time!"*

"What does rubbin do for him?" Trudy questioned as she watched Alma gently massage Ed Earls arms and chest and work her way down to his feet.

"I want ta try ta keep his muscles loose…when they tighten up like that they get locked up in cramps…It pains him so much he tries to scream out but his jaw is locked up so tight he caint make the noise he'd like to."

Ed Earl threw his head back and arched his back pulling out the tube that was taped to his mouth. Alma scrambled to put it back in before his teeth clenched together.

"Why's he makin that funny noise?" I asked.

"I thank he'za tryin ta say sumptin-er other!" Earldean said.

"He cain't open his mouth too good…that's why they call it Lock Jaw!" Alma answered, still wrestling with the tube. *"He has to be fed through this tube… if it comes out he won't be able to eat or drink…He gets most of his nutrition from that IV."* she said nudging her head up toward a bottle

turned upside down on a pole, *"...but they want to keep his plumbing working."*

Trudy had a fretful look on her face then asked Alma, *"How often does he do this?"*

"They have been giving him something to help him to relax and of course the serum treatment for tetanus...Doc said he believes they get it from horses."

"Horses?" Earldean and I sang out.

"Horses...Whatever it takes...I hope it takes soon!" Trudy said as Ed Earl started to settle back down. I peered through the bars at his bony little body that Alma kept massaging. Trudy went around the other side of the bed to assist Alma from that end.

"Me wanna see himz." Learline insisted. Trudy pulled a chair up to the bedside then lifted her up to stand on the chair so that she could see.

"Why he sleepin in dis big bed...its daytime?" she asked.

"He don't feel good hun...he's sick!" Trudy explained.

Learline leaned over the bedrail and softly said, *"Wake up Bubba...me don't like it when you be sick!"* Ed Earl could hardly move but attempted to smile so I know he heard her.

I reached through the railing and held on to his hand. I felt so sorry for the poor little fellow just laid out there, all locked up like a prisoner inside his own body that was being tortured.

He looked so pale and weak lying there as Alma pulled the covers up and tucked them around him.

"Ed Earl...your sisters are here to see you...Miss Trudy brought them all the way to the city just to visit you...can you open your eyes and look at um?" she tenderly said.

He fluttered his eyes that were hidden under dark circles as he struggled to wake up. I gently squeezed his hand and said, *"Ed Earl...it's me Sassy...can you hear me?"* He still didn't open his eyes but sort of squeezed my hand back in response.

Earldean reached over and placed her hand on his forehead. *"Ed Earl...We been missin you runnin round in your new shoes...When you git well we gonna go back to that church and you can play wit them other boys that go over there...They asked bout ya this morning after church and Brother Hemphill had everbody pray fer ya...all them people was prayin just fer you...our little brother! Wit that many folks prayin fer ya...surely God couldn't help but hear um!"*

Alma gasped as she stared up at Trudy with a questioned look on her face. Trudy turned away and bent down picking up her purse.

Alma turned, following her with her eyes then started to ask, *"Did you…"*

"Yea! Yea!...We went to church this morning! They talked me and Debbie into getting up and takin um down there." Trudy mumbled as she dug through her purse like she was digging for something important.

"Oh! Trudy…Praise the Lord! I'm so proud of you!"

"Now don't go ta makin a fuss about it…I did for them youngins, that's all…I aint lookin to join the choir or the the sewin circle so don't git your panties in a wad!"

"Trudy…bless your heart! I know that wasn't an easy thang for ya ta do…Ya make me proud ta be your friend!"

Trudy dug around in her purse a little more before she pulled out an opened pack of gum. Holding it out to Alma she said, *"Juicy Fruit?"*

Alma just smiled and turned her attention back to Ed Earl.

I turned loose of his hand long enough to take a piece of gum from Trudy when she passed out some to the rest of us.

"Chew on it now…don't swaller it." she told Learline after she opened a piece for her.

"Want sum Ed Earl?" Learline said looking at her brother, waiting on an answer.

"He's too sick baby…we'll save some for him for when he feels better." Trudy said.

Earldean asked Alma, *"When do ya think that might be?"*

"Doc says he should have started pulling out of it by now…We were hopin that with him seein you girls, he would fight this thing off and wanna go home."

"Home?" I asked. *"You mean back to Chinquapin Holler?"*

I might have guessed that was never going to happen by the way Alma looked at Trudy. It was one of those looks that adults would give one another that would send a message without a word ever being said. Earldean and I had learned to communicate like that when we wanted to keep things from the little kids. The women didn't realize we understood the language or they might have been a little more discreet.

When she saw their reaction to my question, Earldean pulled herself stiff and with a clenched jaw she said, *"Oh…Sassy! Can't you see we're never going to get to go back home until we find Mama and Daddy! Aint nobody gonna let us do that!*

Her face turned red before tears started leaking from her eyes. She turned and went to the window. Looking out over the city she finished with a quivering voice, "*…We caint take Ed Earl home…after we let him get sick like we done…we ain't got no mama er Diddy ta look after um!*"

"*Oh Darlin it's not your falt!*" Trudy proclaimed as she and Alma made their way over to her. "*No…you had nothin ta do with your brother gettin sick, Hunny!*"

I felt bad for Earldean but she was right, they weren't going to let us go back by ourselves and it didn't look like we were going to find our parents.

If anybody was to blame for Ed Earl being there, it was me. I'm the one who hurried him through the rusty barbed wire fence by pulling on him before he could get himself over. However, I was afraid the charging bull would kill him! Either way Ed Earl was to suffer for it all!

I stood staring at him and how he just looked so helpless. I couldn't help but think about Mama and how she looked when I last saw her. She was in the same kind of shape only worse and she was able to pull out of it. She got well enough to get up and leave her sick bed so surely Ed Earl getting the medical treatment ought to do at least that well.

But we had no home to take him to. "*Lord.*" I found myself praying out loud. "*Please help us out of this mess…Don't let him die…Don't take our brother from us...Lazarus wuz plum dead when ya give him back to his sisters! Ed Earl is just sick…you made all them other people git well …please…In the name of Jesus, make him well!*"

"*AAA-man!*" Learline said just before she started clapping, sending us all into a round of laughter at how she sounded like the church ladies.

"*Well now…*" Alma said, "*…you sound like a regular church go'er, don't cha think so, Miss Trudy?*"

"*She aint been two Sunday's in a row yet.*"

"*Not yet…but she learn't that after two services!*"

"*Now Alma, you know them kids been prayin since the first time we seen um…caint nobody take credit for that but their own folks who brung um up that a way!*"

"*I'm just sayin…*" Alma tried to finish before Ed Earl stirred from all the commotion going on in the room and opened his eyes.

He tried to focus on my face then managed to mumble something with his locked jaw. His limitations were obvious as he strained in an effort to talk.

"Sazzz-zyeee." he managed to get out before he turned and worked up a shallow smile for Learline.

"He'z waked up!" she said when he looked at her. *"Reddy go home now?"*

All of us gathered at his bedside to ask him how he felt. He was still too weak to talk but listened and smiled with his eyes as we filled him in on all he missed while he had been there in the hospital.

We must have been too loud because a nurse came in and tried to run us out of there saying children weren't allowed to be up there unless they were a patient in the ward.

Alma and Trudy tried to explain that we had been given special permission to be there. Apparently, she was not the same nurse that had made the arrangements.

"Rules are rules!" she snapped shrewdly before she held the door open for us to exit immediately. Trudy refrained from saying anything back to her but I could tell she instinctively wanted to resist the womans forceful attitude. However for Ed Earl's sake she complied and asked us to wait downstairs in the lobby while she and Alma arranged some accommodations. We reluctantly said our goodbyes to our brother and followed the nurse who assisted us to the stairwell.

"Quietly follow the stairs down to the first floor… go through the door on your left…down the hallway…the lobby will be on your right…and don't stop until you get there."

Well, we found our way to the main lobby and were grateful we didn't have to ride in that scary elevator to get there.

Trudy stayed that night with Ed Earl so that Alma could get some rest.

Over the next few days he would get better as several volunteers took turns relieving Alma of her duty as temporary guardian of the "Little John Doe".

As the days passed, Trudy reported that Ed Earl was showing signs of improvement but still had a ways to go before he was well enough to leave the hospital. They had moved him out of the special care unit and into children's ward which they said was a good sign.

She informed Alma and Doc about a woman from the Welfare Department coming by the hospital to check up on Ed Earl on Monday. She had told Trudy that someone from the hospital had reported the nameless child to them and she needed to ask some routine questions.

Trudy said that she seemed like a real nice lady at first until she started asking questions about the Clinic over in Whisper Ridge. She asked Trudy if she knew if the physician or any of the medical staff who ran it, were licensed. Trudy, in their defense, set the woman straight giving her friends what she believed was good creditability.

"I wuttin quite sure what she wuz insinuatin but I let her know right quick like, ya'll was a bona-fide establishment and had gone over and beyond the call of duty in takin care of that child!" Trudy said.

Alma looked at Doc and asked, *"Oh Doc…Can they close us down on account a me not givein Ed Earl that shot?"*

"Hardly!" he answered. *"As matter of fact, you weren't authorized to administer it...don't you worry about that…I'm sure the lady was just doing her job."*

It was on Tuesday afternoon when the same woman contacted Doc with questions about Ed Earl. Alma answered the phone at the Clinic, not realizing who it was or she would have offered her the information she knew about him.

Doc didn't say much about it when Alma quizzed him after the phone call. This made her nervous and she worried the rest of the day thinking they might try to close the Clinic down for her practicing medicine without a license. Though, all she did was put those stitches in for Ed Earl. It seemed like everyone was making a big deal out of it.

Personally, I don't know what we would have done without her but nobody asked what I thought about it. In my opinion, if all these folks were as concerned about our welfare as they claimed they were, then they should have been helping us look for our parents instead of studying Alma's qualifications to sew up a bleeding wound. She and Trudy had done more for us than anybody.

20
ANNOUNCING THE BIG EVENT
(WITH BISCUITS & GROOVY)

By Wednesday it had been fourteen days since we had set out looking for Daddy and now, Mama too was missing. I constantly wondered where they could possibly be. It was beginning to feel like we never would find each other and be a family again.

Though it seemed to always be on our minds, the town's talk of it had started to taper off and had been replaced by the buzz of the upcoming event.

The 32nd Annual Labor Day Celebration had been the event used to mark the transition of seasons for the townspeople of Whisper Ridge. It was the Grand Finally of Summer and the Grand Opening of Autumn.

The whole weekend would run on an excitingly organized schedule. This event was originally put together by the Town Council of 1936, who saw a need to pull the township together and boost morale during the midst of the Great Depression.

Its structure of festivities had only slightly altered over the years with the changing of the times. The original idea was to take advantage of a day that had already been set aside to celebrate and do just that…and a celebration it would be!

Announcements were made of a big picnic with checkers for the men, a recipe contest for the ladies, games and races for the children and music for the whole family. They were posted everywhere for miles and the news of the event was passed by word of mouth for all to come.

In 1936 it was a justifiable excuse to take a break from the hardships of that day and age. Time was set aside for a relaxing day of entertaining fun as well as an opportunity to prepare and fill orders of supplies for the long winters.

Folks would come down from out of the hills and from miles around to bring to the table what food they could, for what was then called "The Crop Swap".

Some would bring in their goods and wares to show off their trade for a weekend of bartering in the "Barter Barn".

Local politicians would find their way to the public gathering to do their campaigning. They would come with promises and hope of the possibility of new government jobs; it was low paying wages, but never the less employment that would bring new roads and better highways. They promised new schools that would educate their children for a better tomorrow and a thriving generation.

By 1968, the concept of the celebration was the same but the bartering had been measurably modified to fit the exchange of legal tender.

Local merchants would start the weekend with Summer Clearance Sales to liquidate the stock that had been pulled from the shelves to make room for the fall and winter merchandise. It was put out on tables and racks along the sidewalks out in front of the stores.

On Saturday, the camp grounds would fill up with campers and tents for those who were there to be spectators or contestants in the boat races; sponsored, of course, by Woody's Boat Sales and Service of Whisper Ridge.

The sack races of the earlier years had long since been replaced with the boat races, after Woody took on his oldest boy, Jimbo, for a business partner. Jimbo had broken his right leg once and his left leg twice in the sack races of his boyhood years. Feeling that the game was too dangerous, he had convinced the 1955 committee to omit them from the schedule. Being a well liked fellow, it wasn't hard for him to pursway them, though most of the committee secretly agreed that Jimbo had brittle bones and he had passed this curse on to his next generation. Throughout all those years, his had been the only bones ever broken in the sack races…that was, up until that last year thcy had them.

In the spirit of competition, Jimbo's daughter Rebecca, twisted her ankle and fell and broke her arm when she tangled up with her twin brother Robert at the finish line. Robert was declared the "winner by a nose"…a broke nose that is.

In 1956, when the committee wanted to fill the void of the sack races with another event to take its place, it was Jimbo who suggested adding the boat races. The idea became a big hit; especially with the men folk who still harbored their boyhood inside them. They like things that go fast and make loud noises so the boat races were ideal to the males of all ages. Over the next thirteen years this particular event proved to draw in larger crowds who were attracted to the water sports.

Needless to say that in those same years following the amendment, Woody's became a thriving business, making Jimbo "top dog" over there.

By this time, in order to hype it up, he had a huge sign made that read;

32ND ANNUAL LABOR DAY CELABRATION
SEPETEMBER 6TH
SIGN UP HERE FOR THE BOAT RACES.

He and some other fellows were out hanging it on the outside of the cyclone fence that surrounded the boatyard. Traffic in town had increased as Crafters made their way to the Bargain Barn to set up their booths.

The large vacant lot on the south end of Laurel St. had been mowed and set up to accommodate for extra parking.

The Farmers Market would replace the Crop Swap of the earlier years, as most of the farmers had gone commercial.

The Recipe Contest had grown to become the Grand Labor Day Cook Off sponsored by the local Piggly Wiggly who gave away fifty dollars in free groceries to the winner.

The ballpark would be used for the games that had become somewhat competitive now that there was an entry fee being charged to cover the trophys and cash prizes.

The musical entertainment would basically sound the same with the second and third generation of musicians, still "pickin and grinnin" the same songs with pride of tradition. An occasional young, up and rising local would make their singing debut with their grandpaw announcing their plans of stardom in the music industry.

Families would cheer on their loved ones, who were in the spotlight with faith that they would make a name for themselves in Nashville, reminding them to never forget their humble beginnings in Whisper Ridge.

Labor Day weekend was certainly something to look forward to and the more folks talked about it, the more excited everybody got.

When Trudy asked if we had ever come to town for the celebration before, we couldn't say for sure. From their description of it I think we would have recalled such a gala event had we ever been to one.

More than likely that would be one of the times of year when we would sell vegetables or Mama's crafts from the back of the truck on the side of the road. As we had told them before we didn't get to town much unless we needed something. Daddy wouldn't have seen any need in skipping chores just to celebrate the labor of them.

I thought again about all the catching up on the chores we would have to do when we got back home. That is if we were going to ever get to go back. I was beginning to think we never would if we didn't find our parents soon.

Alma suggested how it would be perfect to find our parents before that weekend, then that way, the whole town could celebrate the reunion of our family and Labor Day at the same time, making this a year to remember.

Debbie was getting ready to go back home before school started. Trudy had grown close to her niece with her spending the summers there in Whisper Ridge and was a bit melancholy about her leaving. Her parents both worked all the time and had been sending Debbie to stay with her aunt for the summers since she was a little girl. Although Debbie was old enough to stay alone without a sitter now, her parents felt that working with her Aunt Trudy would be good experience for her as well as keeping the teen out of trouble.

While Trudy dressed for work that morning, Debbie had talked her Aunt into promising to take us to church again that Wednesday night. Some of her summer friends would be there as well as some cute boys she wanted to get to know better before she left. Her parents were to come for her on Labor Day weekend and she was running out of time.

After breakfast, Debbie tried to come up with an outfit to wear to the Wednesday night prayer meeting. She went through some of her nice dresses that she thought might fit me and Earldean. She took one of her wrap skirts and was able to wrap it around me almost twice before she decided that a couple of safety pins would hold it just fine.

Although it still was a bit loose, I noticed that the one she selected for Earldean fit a slight better as Debbie commented on how my sister was maturing in certain areas.

While we were changing, I caught a glimpse of Debbie's under clothes. Being that she was sixteen, I knew she wasn't a little kid but she almost looked like a grown woman standing there. I hadn't noticed before that morning that my big sister had started filling out a little as well.

When Debbie brought this to our attention, she suggested that Earldean might need a brazier soon and insisted that she try one of hers on for size. Of course it was too big and she didn't have enough yet to fill the small cups so Debbie recommended she start with a training bra. After explaining what that was, Earldean just stood there in front of the tall looking glass saying she couldn't imagine growing a pair of breasts like a grown woman.

Debbie thought she'd help her get an idea of what that might be like. She reached into the drawer and pulled out a pair of socks then rolled them into small balls for Earldean to fill the bra cups with.

Earldean was giddy at the thought of having breasts like a lady and even though they weren't real she snatched up a pillow from off the bed and hid herself behind it. At first she curled up and wouldn't let us see but once she got use to the idea she seemed to like it and stuck them out for all to see.

Debbie searched her hand bag for the tiny white tubes of lipstick samples that the Avon lady had given her when she delivered her Aunt Trudy's last order.

She then opened each of them and offered to let us try the color of our choice. I, of course refused for fear it wouldn't come off but Earldean couldn't resist the temptation; she just had to try that "Hot Pink" shade.

Debbie selected the "Ruby Red" and commenced to show her how to go about putting it on. When Earldean failed after several attempts she gave up and let Debbie apply it for her while she stood very still.

When she finished they turned back and peered toward the looking glass. Shocked at how it changed her appearance, Earldean slapped her hand over her mouth smudging the fresh application. She could hardly stop giggling long enough so that Debbie could fix it for her.

It was so funny looking to see her like that and we laughed at the poses she made but in reality I could see that my sister was growing up too.

It made me a little sad to think I'd be left behind as one of the little kids. Debbie had seemed much older than us when we first met her but not as mature as Mama. Though her slim figure appeared to be every bit a woman, she and Earldean giggled at the silly faces they made in the dressing mirror still acting like little girls do.

I looked down at my skinny body then slid into my clothes as fast as I could before they saw me naked. By comparison, I did not fit in with the "big girls" and did not want give them a chance to point that out. I had not worried too much about modesty before that but now the words "Skinny Little Hillbillies" echoed in my memory and made me feel self-conscious.

In anticipation of the dress up occasion, we laid out our clothes with our shoes so that getting dressed for church would be easier. Debbie wanted to make sure we got there early enough to do some socializing before service started.

When Learline woke up from her afternoon nap, we walked the eight blocks with Debbie to the Eat-A-Bite so that she could work her four hour shift. Along the way, we were greeted by some kids playing ball then some girls who were skipping a rope. A few boys swiftly passed us on bikes but were in too big of a hurry to stop and talk; one did ring his bell for us to get out of the way though.

We also met up with the pretty blond Avon lady who was walking her door to door route. She identified by name the stains on Debbie and Earldean's lips, even though they had tried to wash them off. Taking a moment, she mentioned a few other products for the young ladies Debby's age.

We all got a kick out of Learline repeating over and over again, the commercial slogan she had learned. *"Ding-dong…Avon calling! Ding-dong…Avon calling!"*

She reached into her shoulder bag and pulled out a small tube of hand cream for Debbie to try in hopes of her being a potential customer now that she was earning her own money. She also gave her some perfume samples for her to pass out to the other waitresses at the café.

We rounded the corner and headed down the sidewalk of Main Street noticing flyers that had been printed up on orange construction paper, were hanging in the windows of the various businesses.

When got to the doors of the Eat-A-Bite, we stopped to watch Trudy who was taping one in the window of the café. She was chatting with a woman who was standing there with a stack of the orange papers in one hand and a roll of tape in the other.

The woman was introduced to us as Martha Barnett, the Event Coordinator from over at the town's chamber of commerce and who was out promoting the Labor Day Celebration.

Debbie got excited when the woman began to go over the list of events and the highlights of what all this year's celebration would entail. I was too distracted to take in all she was saying for as myself, I was entertained enough just trying to figure out how that tape was sticking to the glass like it did.

Shortly after we arrived, Learline sat at the corner table and colored in some color books that Trudy had bought to keep there for her so she would be occupied while she worked. Earldean sat with Debbie, folding silverware into napkins and stacking them in a container. I had been helping Cody, the cook, put away some supplies that Trudy had picked up when she made a trip to Fayetteville to see Ed Earl at the City Hospital.

I noticed in the back room that there was a chest type deep freeze like the one we had back home. Daddy had drug it up from the dump and brought it home where he found a use for it.

He thought it was just the right height to place behind the bus just under the emergency exit, to serve as a stoop. Even though the motor had burned out in it and was useless without electricity, he thought it would serve well for dry storage, or keeping valuables in, especially after he found the key to it stuck under the hinge with a magnet.

Daddy had a key ring with two keys on it, one for the truck and one for the deep freeze. They were the only two things out there that had locks on them. He took the two keys and had copies made of both of them for spares in the event he lost his set. He gave Mama the extras and she strung them on an old shoe string and hung them around her neck where they stayed tucked inside her clothes most of the time.

The old deep freeze kept the bulk of our dry goods in there like flour, sugar, coffee, gun shells and such. For the most part, you were likely to find one or the other shotguns stored in there for safe keeping but seldom would they both be locked up. Daddy liked to keep one handy when he was home and insisted Mama keep one loaded and under the mattress for safety reasons while he was away. As soon as he was gone she would unload it and tuck the shells in her pillow case. Even then, she only kept the gun out at night. During the day she locked it up in the deep freeze, especially after Ed Earl took a masculine interest in hunting and guns.

She had always been more afraid of one of her babies finding the loaded gun before she would find the need to have to use it.

Sometimes they kept valuable things in the freezer, like the money for our supplies. I knew that's where they kept it because sometimes when he came home from working a job, I would see Daddy put money in a big jar and place it in the bottom of the freezer under an old flour sack among some dry goods then take the key and lock it up.

They had managed to save a little back each time after buying the supplies incase Daddy hit another spell of not finding work. However, in spite of the war going on, he had had a good year and was building a good little nest egg in the bottom of the freezer. Well, to a ten year old it seemed like a lot of money but I never got a real good look at it.

I wondered about the contents of our makeshift safe back home. I knew that before we left from out there, the supplies were getting low and we were due for a "ration run" as Daddy called it. My main concern was about the shotgun and the money.

I heard Daddy tell Mama the reason we needed to keep it locked up was to keep anybody from stealing it. We never had to worry too much about that, as we were hidden back up in those hills so far it was seldom anybody came around. However, with all those people who had been out there for the search, somebody was sure to find it. What if they took it? I pondered the idea and knew Daddy would be upset if it came up missing.

Then I thought better of it, given the situation, nobody had a key to it except Mama and Daddy. Besides, the people who were out there were there to help, not steal. They were our new friends; they would not want any spoil to come to us; all except that Virgil feller.

The thought of him left a bitter taste in my mouth.

Cody walked in and saw me standing there just starring at the freezer.

"Daydreamin again, are ya Sassy?" he asked.

Startled, I spun around and busied myself by moving some jars around on a shelf.

"What wuz ya lookin at girl? Ya look like ya seen a ghost!"

Cody, a tall gangly man, about in his mid thirty's, stood there in the doorway a second or two before bringing in a stack of small boxes. After setting them down in the floor against the wall, he stood back up and rested his hands on his hips and scanned the floor around the freezer.

"See a spider or sumpin?" he asked stepping toward the freezer. *"I know how you lit'lo girls are skierd a bugs an all…well…I guess you aint tho, huh?"* he continued saying before he froze in his next step with caution. *"Wuttin no snake wuz it?"*

It tickled me how such a grown human being like him could be afraid of a little critter like that.

"Naught aint no snake…Iz just thinking bout that freezer…We got one em back home."

"How'd ya'll git ta werk…Off a generator er sumpin?" he asked. *"Trudy said ya'll aint got no electricity runnin to ya'lls place out there."*

Cody took a short break sitting on some boxes while I explained what we used it for and asked him if he thought anybody might steal anything from it while we were gone.

"Ain't nobody gonna mess with it iffin it's locked up like ya say…If ya worried bout it we could git ole Nolan to check it out whilst they out there next time."

"Nolan?"

"You know him don't cha…Deputy Reed?"

"Oh…Yea he's alright…I'll git Earldean ta tell him bout it."

"I can let him know fer ya iffin ya want…I'd better git back ta werk fer that blazin red headed hussy tries to run me off for loaffin round here!"

"Who ya talking bout?"

"Miss Trudy…She'z a mean un don't cha thank?" he said as he stood to his feet and stretched his arms almost touching the ceiling, then turning to leave the room.

"Trudy ain't no such cha thang…Why, I thank she's a real nice lady!" I informed him as I followed him out.

"Oh…you just don't know her like I do…" he was saying as he crossed the threshold, *"…You aint seen her with her feathers ruffled like I have…she's a real pistol!"*

"Who's a Pistol?" Trudy asked catching his last part of his comment from the doorway to the dining area.

"YOU ARE!" he yelled across the kitchen with a glaring grin.

He ducked and laughed when she threw a cold biscuit at him through the pickup window behind the counter.

"…a real Smith and Wesson ya are!" he said just before he dodged another flying biscuit.

"Yep…A REAL SON OF A GUN!" he yelled loud enough to be sure she heard it as he stood at the grill scraping it with a spatula. A few moments later, another biscuit appeared flying over his shoulder, hitting the wall and breaking apart all over his clean grill.

He never flinched. He just kept on scraping and egging it on. Never looking back he yelled, *"AINT NO SHARP SHOOTER THAT'S FER SURE!"* Then looking at me, he winked and said, *"She's out of ammunition… or a customer is out there and she cain't misbehave…I told ya she'z mean…Ya see how she does me?"* He shook his head and hung it for a minute pretending to have self-pity.

Just about the time he had raised his head back up; ssssSSS-SWACK!

Another biscuit came flying through and hit him smack dab on the back of his head. He dropped his spatula and grabbed his head and yelled, *"HEY…WHAT YA DO THAT FOR?"*

I thought at first he was hurt until I seen he was laughing with his back turned to her.

Cody had been the cook there at the Café long before his cousin sold out and it became Trudy's Eat-A-Bite. I had heard Trudy tease him about being like one of the old fixtures that came with the place. Being that Cody had been working there since he was a teen and trained on the grill at age eighteen, this was the only paying job he had ever had.

Even when he was in the service he was assigned to KP duty and was made a cook; giving him even more experience. So, when the Café came up for sale, Trudy was obliged to keep Cody and a few of the other old waitresses on. This way she would have some experienced employees and in turn, they wouldn't have to be without a job.

Trudy herself had been the head waitress at one time when the previous owner had the place.

When it first opened, with its fast food service, it was the Burger Doodle that became the new "hot spot" in town. However, after four years of struggling, finding the competition more than he could stand, Cody's cousin closed his café, put the building up for sale, then left town.

The Café had been a landmark there in Whisper Ridge for a long time and some folks felt sad to see the vacant building just sitting there empty for several months.

Cody didn't have the money, nor was he interested in the business aspect of running a restaurant, so he put in his application to work at the Burger Doodle.

Alma said that when Trudy found out about that she lit into him like a crow on road kill with a lecture about being a traitor and tried to make him feel bad about it. But after he explained that cooking was all he knew and that he had to have a job, Trudy seen fit to try to buy the café herself and open it back up. She really had always dreamed of owning one of her own. She managed to get a business loan from the local bank based on her reputation for being loyal to her job.

Well…that's what Alma, her best friend believed. Cody has his own version of how she got the loan. He claimed that Trudy got the deal because of him putting in a good word to the lender on Trudy's behalf.

He had stopped Mr. Barnett, the banker, out there on the sidewalk one day and commenced to have a discussion about how sad it was to see one of town's oldest sources of commerce fading away. They talked about how dreadful it would be if just any ole "out-of-towner" bought the place. They might have tried to turn it into some other kind of business and sent the profits off to somewhere else to be spent.

Though he was grateful to have the burger business generating cash flow in his town, Mr. Barnett was one of the few faithful customers who had kept his routine of eating his lunch and entertaining potential clients at the old café. Day after day he would show up, if for nothing else but to drink a cup of coffee with some of the other old timers. He was one of the last customers rung up on the cash register on closing day.

Cody knew how Mr. Barnett had a strict regimen and how he had been frustrated with the change in his routine. He knew the old man had sentimental ties to the place and used this for his playing card to get in a good word for Trudy.

Apparently, the man had been coming over every day and sitting on the sidewalk bench out front, meeting up with some of his buddies, where they would eat cold sandwiches his wife Martha would bring over. She couldn't stand seeing her husband and his friends so melancholy so she did what she could to cheer them up.

Every day the topic of discussion was the same. They talked of how they would miss the old place and all the good fishing stories that were told there. And…everyday, for old times' sake, they would tell a few tales just to get them through the transition.

So, when Cody suggested that with a coat of fresh paint, some new fixtures and replacing the old griddle with a new grill, it would make a nice money making business for somebody. He recommended somebody like Trudy could be the one to really do something with the old place and bring it back to life. Mr. Barnett was thrilled with the idea. After all, Trudy had been his favorite waitress and he had always sat in her section.

But without a lot of money down and a little extra for the fix-ups, Trudy's chances of getting the loan looked grim so the banker would have to come up with some creative financing to work it out.

When all was said and done, Mr. Barnett said it was a good business decision when he and the other old timers invested a little of their own money to get the place up and running again.

With some help and support from their friends at the town council meetings, Martha promoted the Grand Reopening of the old café. She had them run a full page story in the "Town Talk" circular, which included the new name and Trudy's new menu.

In the meantime, with all the reconstruction and painting going on, Mr. Barnett and the other old timers wouldn't stay out on the sidewalk where they belonged. Their excitement and eagerness for the job to be done kept getting in the way of progress.

They were so excited about getting their "old stomping grounds" back that all they could do was stand around talking and distracting the workers who were getting paid by the hour.

Trudy saw this as an added expense and had to find something for them to do to keep them out of the way yet make them feel a part of it all.

She and Martha had them migrate over to the benches in the town square where they would be out of the way and could make better use of their lunch hour.

Martha had printed up a stack of flyers with the new menu that also included a coupon for a free cup of coffee or soda pop. She and Trudy kept them supplied with sandwiches and a big thermos of coffee every day while they passed out the flyers to all the folks that passed by. These unlikely fellows turned out to be her best source of advertisement.

It was a real big deal when they closed off part of the street for the new sign to be raised. The faithful crowd that gathered there waited for Mayor Scott to give his speech before the ribbon cutting ceremony.

It was a big day for everybody involved; especially Trudy who could hardly wait till dark to see her name lit up in big florescent lights.

Though the bank still held the mortgage on the building, in no time at all she was able to buy back those small shares of stock, with interest, and became the sole proprietor.

Mr. Barnett and his buddies personally made a little pocket change but to them, the best part of the deal was that they were glad and able to be back on their scheduled lunch appointments. His wife, Martha, was grateful too as the "sandwich making" had been interrupting her social life.

Cody took credit for the whole idea and would occasionally remind Trudy that without him, she'd be off somewhere broke and chasing after "that no count ex-husband of hers."

Alma said that Cody teases her about that all the time, especially whenever he feels threatened by her.

At first I didn't know how to take their relationship. I'd never seen anybody play acting before. I'd feel sorry for one or the other of them until Alma had seen how it worried me so; not knowing that it was all sort of a game. She told me that they didn't act that way unless they had an audience to perform in front of. It took some explaining to translate what she meant but before too long I comprehended that they were both just showing off.

Still, they were so good at it that sometimes it was hard for me to sort the difference but when I finally could, I'd find it entertaining…like the flying biscuits for example.

A few days before that, we had gone to work with Trudy. According to others, she had been so preoccupied with our problems that she was not acting herself.

That day, after Yvonne had pointed this out to Cody, he saw fit to fix this problem with ways of his own.

We had all been walking around in gloom and despair with Ed Earl sick and not finding our parents yet. Cody was doing his best to get everybody in better spirits by cracking jokes and making goofy faces at everybody, especially Trudy. He didn't give up when she tried to ignore him until finally she jumped back poking fun at him.

"Alright now…If you don't behave I'm gonna trade you in on a newer model….one that's good lookin like Elvis!"

"The customers would starve to death too!" he snapped back with a half cocked grin.

"Just the men folk…us girls would be so in love, we wouldn't eeeven think about food!"

"OH EEEELLLLVIS!" he said, mimicking the girls of the times in a high pitched falsetto, *"…you're just sooooo haaaaandsome!"*

"Oh…you can only wish you was half as good lookin as he is…ya…ya ole buzzard you!" she came back at him laughing. *"…and he has more talent in his little pinkie fanger than you ever thought about have'n!"*

Pulling a frying pan from the rack, he pretended it was a guitar as he held it low then strummed it, breaking into his perceived rendition of Elvis singing Heartbreak Hotel.

"SINCE MY BABY LEFT ME, da-dum…I FOUND A NEW PLACE TO DWELL…da-dum…DOWN THE END OF LONELY STREET…AT…HEARTBREAK HOTEL…dum-dum-dum-dum…"

He spun around the kitchen with long dance steps and a serious look on his face as the rest of the staff drew in for the show. He gyrated with his hips the way Elvis might have done, while he sang in a deep exaggerated voice, *"I FEEL SO LONELY BABY…"*

He was jerking his whole body and bobbing his head so hard keeping strong time with the rhythm, that his slick comb over fell completely back the other way, until the long greasy strands bounced around on one side of his head looking hideously funny!

He made his way over to Trudy and acted like he was serenading her. She tried to keep a straight face while she nudged him away saying, *"Well it aint a wonder why ya so lonely...look at how ya actin!"*

"I FEEL SO LONELY I COULD DIE-IE-IE-IE-IE," he'd drag out the drama as she would walk away.

"Well then get a clue Dick Tracy…just look at ya…goin round actin a fool…ya aint never gonna find a woman to put up with the likes of you!"

Everyone was laughing by the time he'd finish singing. So, when he took a bow we all started clapping and cheering. Yvonne pretended to be one of those screaming Elvis fans.

"Ooooooooo Eeeelvissss! You're soooooo h-h-h-handsome!"

Trudy shook her head at him and made out like she was disgusted with his behavior, though her suppressed grin nearly gave it away.

"Ya'll….don't fan his flame…he's gonna get the big head and get all puffed up!"

Cody just stood there with a silly grin, his hair all a mess and soaking up the attention.

When Trudy grabbed the frying pan from him and acted as if she was going to hit him with it, he broke and ran off hollering with his arms in the air. He hid behind Yvonne, using her for a shield of protection, knowing Trudy wouldn't hurt her.

"Save me Miss Yvonne…she's gonna git me!"

She was laughing and didn't seem to mind when he grabbed her shoulders and twisted her in the direction of Trudy's attempts to swat him with the pan.

"…you a mess...ya know it?" Trudy said as she swung and missed several times around either side Yvonne. Her aim was off as she got tickled watching Cody duck and dodge.

"Don't you have anything better to do than to pester me?…like…an ole…fly?"

"Flies like stinky stuff!" he cantered back from behind his hiding place then jolted over and hid behind Debbie, thinking Trudy wouldn't hurt her own flesh and blood.

"She'za gittin a ripe stanky attitude don'tcha thank? That's why I like her so much." he said softly over her shoulder before Trudy went in for another swing. Laughing at them both but not wanting to get caught up in the middle, Debbie spun around leaving him defenseless. He threw his long arms over his face and head and cowed down to a squat. *"I'z like ya…I like ya! Please don't beat me Miss Trudy…please!"*

Out of breath from laughing, she gave up and staggered away. *"Well…get back to the kitchen and do some work!"* she said before turning and chunking the pan down on the counter. *"…and tie up that hair of yours before I get them scissors after you!"*

From the kitchen we could hear his call for sympathy, *"Ya'll see how she treats me?"*

Everybody was laughing at their silliness. And, once I figured out they were just playing, I laughed along with the rest.

It was a good place to be to keep a girl's mind off her worries. For helping, Trudy would give us a little pocket change to save or spend at the store on "a pretty" we might want.

I would buy a pack of Juicy Fruit and put the rest in a little jar. Cody put a slit in the lid of it with butcher knife so that I could just slide the money in without opening the top every time.

Debbie showed me how to take the wrappers of the Juicy Fruit and by folding them a certain way, and locking them together, I could make a chain out of them. She had a green one made of the wrappers from the Double Mint flavored gum fashioned into a bracelet and another white one made from the spearmint kind.

She was working on another chain made from all three Wrigley's flavors that she said she thought would make a "groovy" necklace.

"Groovy?" I asked, with that being the first time I heard it.

"Yea…Ya know…Groovy!"

"What zat mean...sortta like gravy?"

"No! she laughed "…you Silly Billy…Gosh! You have been out of circulation…I guess you might not have ever heard it said livin way out there in the sticks Huh?"

She wasn't trying to hurt my feelings but it still made me feel a little stupid like Virgil said I was. Never the less, when she called me Silly Billy, it didn't sound as mean as being called Dumb Hillbilly.

"Well…What does it mean?" Earldean asked.

"It means something that's in the groove with what's popular…The in thing!" she said.

Still wondering what the heck she was talking about, I said, *"Whaaaat?"*

"Something that's hip…ya know…uh…" she was still looking for a way to define the word; she stopped, rolled her eyes up and kept them fixed that way, while she took in a long drawn in breath then blew out a blast of air.

Following her eyes, I too looked up as if the answer would be written up there on the ceiling of the Eat-A-Bite.

The busboy, Willie Jay, took his summer job seriously and didn't have much patience for the likes of city girls like Debbie, who worked when they felt like it and didn't appreciate a hard working young man like himself. He had worked his way up from sidewalk sweeper and trash boy to stock boy and errand runner and this summer he was promoted to busboy.

He had a chip on his shoulder and didn't think it was fair that Debbie waltzes in and lands a waitress job making fifty cents an hour plus tips, just because she's the boss's niece. He usually went about cleaning tables and not saying much but something about her prissy ways got on his nerves.

"*Nice,*" he said as he walked by the table, looking at us and ignoring Debbie, "*…it means nice…that's what regler folks say…Nice! Hippies say groovy…normal hard workin people just call it what it is…Nice! If you see something you like say nice…not groovy!*"

"*Whatta you know about nice? Country boy!*" she retorted.

"*I know it's a real word…you can find it in a regler dictionary.*" he claimed.

"*OH…and I guess…regler…is a word huh? Is that in a regular dictionary?*" she poked.

Trudy was behind the register and could hear the two of them starting to get riled up, so she stepped in to break it up before it got worse.

"*Hey you two…BE NICE!*" she said.

"*Yes ma'am.*" Willy Jay said as he walked on. When he was out of hearing distance, Trudy pointed her finger at Debbie and said, "*…And you young lady you…be groovy.*" then she winked at me and went back to the register.

21
A BONA-FIDE PERSON
(*TO BE OR NOT TO BE*)

On Tuesday, the twentieth of August, the heat wave held steady all day until it burned itself out sometime during the night. This made way for a severe thunderstorm that came in with a vengeance just before dawn on Wednesday, waking everybody in the house. It was so loud that it had Festus scratching at the door to get in. Estelle barely had it opened when the dog managed to force his way through to safety, soaking the floor and walls as he shook off. She quickly pulled off her houserobe and threw it over him to keep him from making a bigger mess than he already had. She then led him into the washroom where she told him to stay and surprisingly enough, he obeyed.

We gathered and huddled close at the foot of the stairs until the worst of it blew over. By then, it was light enough to see that the fierce winds had taken their toll on a few large branches and all that was not tied down. Though the sky was still gloomy, and rain was still dripping from the trees, Doc put on his mud boots then headed out the door with Festus to check on the horses. Meanwhile, Estelle sent us girls to get dressed while she started breakfast.

By nine thirty we were out the door, in the car, and on our way just before one last rain shower hit that moved out as fast as it came in. It left behind dense clouds of steam that rose from the canyon floors, so heavy that they could hardly get any higher than the crest of the lower hills. It was a weird and wonderful sight to see as we had never been above the clouds before, though the humidity was so thick that it made it a little difficult to breathe.

Fog on the mountain roads made it a little difficult to see as Doc and Estelle drove us down to pick up our brother who was being released from the City Hospital.

He had made such an improvement in those days after our visit that the doctor there saw fit to let him go, if he went home with Doc and Estelle who could keep a close eye on him.

They had to meet first with the woman from the welfare office to sign some papers saying that they would be responsible for our wellbeing until which time we found one or the other of our parents.

This woman, Miss Patterson, had told them that she would be out to check on us after the boy got to feeling better. At that time she would be interviewing all four of us for an evaluation of some sort.

Alma seemed to take it personal that she wasn't appointed our temporary guardian, since she had pretty much been taking care of us from the beginning, especially after Sheriff McCoy had already verbally given her that job.

I heard her talking to Trudy, telling her that she didn't think it was fair that Estelle ended up with us after all of the complaining she had done. She was under the impression that we got on Estelle's nerves too bad for her to handle us full time and that she had a good mind to talk with the Sheriff about it.

Trudy suggested to Alma that she might be putting her job on the line if she stirred things up with Estelle and got her mad. Alma was already feeling a little insecure after neglecting to ask about the tetanus shot. Estelle was Doc's wife and was in a position to influence him into having his assistant replaced, if she let her jealousy get in the way of the well being of his patient.

Trudy smoothed things over by telling her to take a break and rest up because knowing Estelle, she would be asking for help before the weekend was over.

It felt sort of nice to have them all making such a fuss over us the way they were doing. It gave me a sense of value.

I gave Alma several hugs that day, as she just seemed like she could use some extra ones. She appeared to appreciate the affection and it helped me too.

I wondered what Mama was going to think about Ed Earl getting sick enough to have to go to the hospital. She would have been there if she had known about it so I could only wonder why she and Daddy had not come looking for us in Whisper Ridge yet.

By then everybody in town knew just who we were, should they come looking there. Folks questioned every stranger that came around, wondering if they were there to find the "Nameless Hillbilly Kids"; the general reference we'd been given.

It was not like them to run off and leave us like some of the people had accused them of doing. I would later learn of horrible rumors passed behind our backs to protect our innocence. These were just mere speculations with nothing else to go on but somebody's guesses. It was a good thing the excitement of the Labor Day Celebration was there to distract them from such evil thoughts.

As the days turned into weeks, the sheriff had stopped coming by daily to report on the search. When I asked Trudy about it she said that they had looked everywhere and were doing everything they could to find them. However, it appeared to me that everybody had all but given up on the idea of ever finding them.

Most folks had learned not to ask about it when they saw us, as to not upset us anymore than we already were.

Still, there was that group of mean ole boys that acted like they were born to live their lives just to tease us. They seemed to thrive on calling us names like stinking hillbillies, stupid heads, and other names and words that the adults said we shouldn't repeat. Alma said they were words so dirty that it would take a bar of soap to wash them out.

In their meanness they would make up lies about why our parents weren't ever coming for us, planting seeds of doubt that would sprout into fearful nightmares.

They made fun of the bug bites that speckled our legs and arms. Some we had scratched so much that they had turned to sores and over time, many had left scars. These fellows made out like we had some sort of disease.

When one of them said I looked like a leper, I thought he was saying I looked like a leopard, which wasn't so bad in my opinion. On one of the walls in Doc's study hung a huge beautiful picture of a leopard and I thought the big spotted cat was sort of pretty.

One night, while reading a Bible story to us, Estelle explained what leprosy was. It wasn't until then that I realized what he had called me. In a delayed reaction, I burst into tears with my hurt feelings. I cried more about being *ignorant* to what he had said than I did about him saying it in the first place.

They were right, I was stupid! Estelle had a hard time trying to convince me otherwise, as she attempted to comfort me while I cried myself to sleep.

We did our best to stay out of their way but these hateful fellows ran in pairs and sometimes we didn't recognize them until it was too late.

Unlike like most folks around town who thought these immature boys were just bored troublemakers, I personally was afraid of them.

Estelle and Alma called them "hoodlums" while Trudy called them by their whole name, having known most of them since they were babies.

She would shame whichever one she happened to catch misbehaving and embarrass them with clever come-backs that would put them in their places. Doing this in front of the other boys would cause them to laugh at each other instead of me or any other victims of their rebelliousness.

Trudy seemed to know their language and have a way with them that Alma and Estelle didn't. You could tell she wasn't afraid of them and they seemed to respect that in her.

"They're just little ole boys inside…insecure and scared of the world…all that tomfoolery is their way of trying to make themselves feel better. They have it in their head that makin folks scared of um gives um some sort of special power. Like it's gonna make them bigger than they really are…but it don't. I ought ta know…I'z married to one just like um!" she'd tell us.

Doc stayed close to home with Ed Earl there, checking his temperature and carefully administering his medication.

By Saturday morning he was feeling well enough to come downstairs for breakfast and to watch some cartoons on the television. Casper the friendly Ghost and Bugs Bunny made him laugh, which seemed to be the best medicine of all for little brother.

Estelle was on the phone with her dear friend and hair dresser, Melba Jean Hogan, making appointments for us girls to get haircuts. Doc pulled on his boots, reached for his straw cowboy hat and was headed out the door. He turned to see me watching him with my curious expression and then swung his head to the side, motioning for me to come go with him.

When he heard the door open, Festus staggered from around the side of the house and came up to Doc for his daily petting.

"Even though he's gittin too old to do much a nothing in the way of tricks…" Doc said, stopping to rub his friend behind the ears, *"…the old boy makes good company…still good to have around to talk to."*

Doc squatted down and brushed his hands across the dog's back knocking the dust off of his coat where Festus had been laying in a hollowed out place on the ground. *"Yea…you're a real good listener…huh old boy?"* he said to him as he finished up with a scratch under the animals chin, holding him face to face to look into his eyes.

Festus seemed to agree, and with a wagging tail, he adorned his master with kisses. Doc chuckled and almost lost his balance as the dog tried to lick him on the lips.

I enjoyed watching the two of them interact with one another and wanted to be a part of that type of affection. I hadn't been around that many dogs, with the exception of the ones out at the Riley's place, but this one sure seemed friendly with people.

"I aint never knowed a dawg wita name…other'n just dawg…I call pigs, pig…chickens, chicken...deers, deer." I said as I watched Doc pull a tick off of Festus then smash it.

"Sure…gotta have a name of their own…so they'll know who they are when you call them to you. Otherwise, you just yell dog…and all the dogs in hearing distance might come running up…Yea…Festus here is my sidekick…he's real loyal like that deputy is to Marshal Dillon…huh boy…yea…that's right…good boy."

"Reckon itta be alright iffin I'z ta pet um?" I asked with hesitation, getting the owner's permission as well as assume my own safety from the animal.

"Sure…He'd like that...it's ok…go on…he won't bite…he's all bark but you'd never know that if you're a stranger commin up in the yard…He can make some racket, now I'll tell ya!"

While Doc was still petting him I let my hand follow along behind his. Festus turned first to lick my ankle then my hand when I drew it back.

"See…he like's ya!" Doc assured me.

I held my hand out, palm down, for more of this acceptance before I tried petting the dog again. It made me lonesome for my little deer friend that was killed. I wanted to discuss it with Doc but I didn't want to get sad and start crying about back home stuff.

Instead, I chose to just talk about his dog. *"What sortta dog is this un?"*

"Oh…he's just an ole mut...part Collie and part Retrever…I believe." Doc answered as he turned to walk on. Festus stood only for a little more petting before he turned to follow his master, with me behind him running to catch up. As we strolled across the yard with the dog between us I found the courage to ask Doc more questions about Festus.

"Where didgee gitum…had him very long?"

"He was old when he wandered up here all tattered and hungry…skinny as a bone. He took a shine to me and decided to stay...so I let him…he follows me around makin sure I get all my chores done…keeping me company…" Doc was telling me as he watched his four legged companion pursue his predicted behavior. *"…aint that right ole boy?"*

Festus looked up at him and wagged his tail with a few brisk waves. Somehow the dog knew the difference between when Doc was talking to me and when he talking to him.

"You right Doc…he is good at listenin…aint he?"

Doc just looked at me and smiled then bent down and rubbed the dog's head while we walked along. He let me and Festus follow him around the barn and the pasture tending to the horses and such.

Doc, like me, wasn't much of a talker but when we were out there with the horses we were both like different people. He explained what things were, what he was doing as he did it, and why it was done that way, before I'd ever ask. It was as if he could read my mind.

He made me feel good about myself for wanting to know more about my surroundings. He never made me feel dumb for asking when I did have a question to request further information. He was real nice, like Denby, and I knew he was a good person from the first time we met that day at the café. He had complemented me and shook my hand, offering friendship and making me feel important.

What little we had visited before, he didn't talk down to me, as if I didn't know anything. Yet, he didn't assume I was suppose to already know everything either. He treated me like I was a *bona-fide* person, not as if I were just some poor, pitiful, hillbilly kid that had wandered in to town and was too dumb to know anything.

Doc was like Denby in that when you were around him all your troubles seemed to fade away. He never made light of my worries but had a way of helping me look at the brighter side of things then keep moving on.

When he had seen that I was getting more comfortable with the horses, he told me I was a real natural and asked if I would like to ride with him around the pasture. He didn't assume I had never ridden before, nor did he ask me if I had. He just had a way of knowing that a short ride around the pasture, along with him, would be sufficient for me to get familiar with this particular horse and for her to get familiar with me.

I paid close attention as he put the reins on the paint horse and guided her toward the barn where I stood in the doorway.

As they approached Doc said, *"Patches, this is Sassy...Sassy meet Patches."* Then he stopped to let me pet her.

"We've already met...but I didn't know if she had a name"

I gently patted her neck and she sniffed at my shoulder. *"Hello Patches...that's a pretty name for a horse."* I said. Then, running my hand down her neck, I asked her, *"Howgee git a name like that...bein' a horse and all?"*

Doc also was stroking her neck and answered for her in babyish voice, saying, *"Amy Sue named me that because I was born with patches of several colors!"*

"Who is Amy Sue? Her momma?"

"Amy Sue is my little girl." Doc answered in his own voice again.

"Ya have a little girl, do ya...how come I aint never seen her?"

"Well...She's not so little anymore. She grown up and gone off to collage out west in California...We have pictures of her in the house. Haven't you seen them?"

"I saw some pictures sittin round in there. I didn't ask who they were. Mama's got some pictures too but they aint the big ones like that. Her and Daddy's got friends in Californey too. Maybe they know your little girl!"

"Oh, I don't know...she's only been there a little over two years and California is an awful big place."

"Why come her to run off like she done?"

"Well she claimed she wanted to live her own life...Not that she didn't love us but she wanted to venture out into the world...do her own thing she called it."

Doc looked kind of sad when he pulled at the reins and made a clicking sound for the horse to follow him into the barn. After a moment or two of silence, I looked up at Doc and saw his eyes had glistened over with tears, then I asked, *"Do ya miss her?"*

"Sure do. Amy Sue will always be my little girl...no matter how big she gets."

"I know how ya feel...I miss Mama and Daddy too."

"I know you do, Sassy. I wish there was more that I could do to help."

We stopped at the stall where the saddle was resting on a padded rail. Doc pulled it off and hoisted it over Patches' back. She staggered a little at first before he wooed her with a calm voice then patted her neck.

"Doc?"

"Yea Sassy?"

"Do you think Daddy and Mama might have ventured off out in the world…to do their thang like Amy Sue done?"

"Don't know your folks well enough to say. What do you think?"

I thought seriously about the question, it being the first time anyone had asked me what I might have thought happened to them.

I closed my eyes and tried to think back about my parents. I tried to capture their faces in my memory. I tried to remember anything they might have said or done that would indicate them wanting to leave our home and go back to California and live. Sometimes Mama seemed lonely out there when Daddy was gone but she stayed so busy doing chores that she didn't have time to complain.

Her and Daddy *did* seem happier when Denby was living across the lake. They both cried when he moved away. Mama seemed sad for a long time after that but she got a little better when she started canning with Myrtle Riley. I don't know if she liked the woman as much as she pretended to but I think she liked the company.

I thought living out there was just how it was. I never knew anything different to compare it to before. That was our life. We were a family and that *was* "our own thing".

"I don't reckon they had no call to run off and live some place witout takin us wit um…but with Amy Sue leavin you the way she done, shows me, folks don't live wit theyz Mama and Daddy forever…guess Mama and Daddy thought we wuz big enough to take care of ourselves…That's what all the animals in the woods do." I said.

"People aren't like animals." Doc replied. *"There is a difference between living and surviving out on your own. Human children need more time with their parents than the animals do. We live a lot longer and have different needs. Humans are delicate to the environment but are intelligent enough to build complex shelter to protect themselves from most all of the elements.*

Humans have to look after their young much longer than other animals. We mature much slower than they do. Take ole Festus there…he was born about the same time you were…but in dog years, he's older than me.

"My goodness! That's purdy old huh? How did he do that?"

"Well now..." Doc responded with a big grin *"...it don't seem that old to me and Festus but he ages about seven times faster than we do so it didn't take long for him to catch up with me. Yea he and patches here are full grown. They've gotten about as big as they can...learned and done just about all they're going to by now...but me and you...we'll still learn something new every day...and you have a lot more growing to do to catch up with me."*

"You mean I'll keepa growin till I get as big as you?"

"Well...maybe not quite as big as me," Doc said with a soft laugh *"...but one day you too will be a grown up. Until then you need an adult to look after you...tend your needs."*

"But it's not like I'z a lit'lo baby...I can look after myself"

"That's true...you're no baby...and probably are smarter in some areas than most kids your age...but still, a ten year old girl shouldn't have to worry about where her next meal will come from or whether she'll have a safe place to sleep at night...stuff like that."

"Mama was learnin me to do some cookin just fore she took sick...said I'z gittin big enough ta learn how."

"Tell me again...how long did you say she had been sick?" Doc quizzed, still fishing for answers for her mysterious disappearance. I didn't hesitate to tell him again still leaving out the part about me and Earldean thinking she was dead. I didn't want Doc to think I didn't know the difference between being dead or just unconscious; especially after he had just told me how smart he thought I was.

"Don't rightly know fer sure...long bout a week, I reckon...least ways that's when she slowed down some...she didn't take to stayin in bed 'til ' long bout three or four days before we left from out younder...ta come find Daddy and all. But she must have gotten better and got up and around lookin fer us fer her not ta still be out there...she must be awful worried by now."

"She knew you were coming for help...right? I mean...unless help showed up before we returned, it could only mean, someone took her for help...or like you said...she got better and has gone out looking for you."

"She has to be a lookin for us...you said she wuttin at the hospital...where else could she be?" I answered with a question, avoiding the fact that we didn't really have her consent to leave in the first place. I just knew we would be in trouble enough with our parents when we reunited without having being scolded by every adult we had met along the way.

Earldean and I had already agreed to avoid that subject at all costs. I had to stay true to her. I liked this man and didn't want him to think I was some disobedient little kid.

"I don't know. Sheriff and his deputies are checking again with the neighboring houses to see if anyone might have taken her in…with her being sick. Someone might be looking after her not knowing she had been reported missing."

"Don't rightly know of anybody round them parts that would do that…aint that many folks livin up there!" I felt grief and despair taking me over again as I talked on about it. *"Where could she've gone off to…and why come we cain't find our Daddy nowhere?"*

"We'll find them…they'll have to show up sooner or later…don't you think?"

"I still don't know why come we can't go back and just wait fer em up there."

"Oh Sassy…I know you're homesick but we've told you, you can't stay out there alone…and all the rest of us have our own homes to stay in…you are welcome to stay here as long as it takes to find them. Sheriff is doing all he can…ok?"

I swallowed hard then reluctantly responded with a nod, choking back the tears.

"In the mean time…I could sure use some help lookin after ole Patches and the other horses here…you seem to be a natural with them."

"What kinda help?" I asked, gladly changing the subject.

"Well…helping me keep the water trough filled with fresh water…maybe puttin out a bucket of feed for um…you know…they really like to be brushed, maybe I can show you how to do that…whatcha say?"

Still feeling a bit melancholy I asked, *"How ya know they like it…Animals can't talk to tell ya what they thinkin…how ya know what they want?"*

"Well ya have to pay close attention to their body language…how they behave".

"Yea…sometimes you can almost hear what they thinking huh?"

"You're catchin on…animals use different sounds and behavior to get their point across…People use words to communicate…and in many languages."

"Many words." I added.

He smiled and said, *"Yes…many words…and sometimes with no words at all."*

"Like the animals!" I compared.

"Like the animals." he concluded with a smile then pulled tight on the strap under Patches belly.

"Want to ride with me? Or all by yourself?" he asked.

"I don't know how to do it." I admitted.

"I'll hold on to the reins and guide her this time…you crawl up and hold on to this saddle horn, that way you can get use to each other first." he said, then hoisted me up so that I straddled the seat that seemed much wider as I sat in it.

"Reddy? Hold on tight now."

Petting Patches on her neck, he talked more baby talk to her before he made the clicking sound with his mouth again causing her to step forward and turn toward the barn door.

This animal seemed a whole lot bigger from up there, for even with the saddle between us, I could feel her gait beneath me. Every muscle in my body was tight as I resisted the movement and held on for dear life.

I was terrified and thrilled at the same time as I locked my feet tight and grabbed hold of her long mane for security. I felt her shoulders come back as she threw her head upward then stopped and dropped it almost out of my sight.

I shrieked as I felt my butt come off the saddle and my body just about turn upside down with the pull of gravity. Just before I completely fell forward, she brought her head back up slapping my face with her mane and bumping the tip of my nose with the back of her head.

She let out a loud sound of disapproval and jerked her head to the side causing me to slide off , hanging by my leg, to one side and both hands gripped tightly to the mane.

"WOOO Patches…It's alright girl!" Doc said as he pulled tight on the reins and patted her neck again, saying, *"Grab that horn on your saddle!"*

When she was calmer he reached back and pushed my near petrified body back up in the saddle.

"Try to relax a little Sassy…she can feel you resisting her…let her take you for a ride…try to go with the flow of her body and hold tight to the horn not her."

My legs weren't long enough to fit in the stirrups so he repositioned them down the sides of the straps. *"You could use a smaller saddle…but this will have to do…Now don't dig in her side with your feet, she won't like that. Try to keep them here. I won't let her go...ok?"*

I took a deep breath then said, *"OK…I want to do this but…please go slow!"*

Smiling again he said, *"We'll take it easy"*.

With a double click sound Doc made with his mouth, Patches stepped forward and moved slowly walking next to him. I started to relax and so did she. I began to enjoy the adventure and didn't want to stop.

I had often imagined riding through the woods on the back of my little yearling and what it would be like to go as fast as he could. Although we were only trotting, the fact that this big animal was carrying me, without resistance was thrill enough for me at the moment.

Doc coached me and Patches as we circled the corral three times before Estelle called me in to get ready to go to town. I asked Doc if I could stay there with him instead but he said I'd better go with the other females to the beauty shop because Estelle had planned a day of "girly things" and he'd better not spoil it for her.

"We'll ride again another time." he assured me. Doc seemed pleased that he had someone around again that appreciated the horses.

I felt as beautiful as Cinderella when I walked up the steps leading into the church house the next Sunday morning.

Estelle had taken us girls shopping for our first real church dresses and new underwear, including panties, more socks, and a slip for each of us as well as a training bra for Earldean.

"Bra," that's a nickname for brazier, which was a new fangled undergarment that all the town ladies wore including Debbie who wasn't even a woman yet…and now my own sister was wearing one.

Trudy and Debbie were sitting next to Alma on the pew for the Sunday services. They stood and greeted us and were excited about our "real" haircuts we had gotten from a Bona-fide beautician.

"Ya'll just look beautiful!" Alma exclaimed, reaching out to us for a hug and looking as rested as she did the day we first met.

"Fancy Smancy!" Trudy complimented as she picked up Learline. *"Don't ya'll just look darling!"*

"I got a braw like you Debbie!" Earldean bragged.

"Shhhhhhh! Somebody might hear you!" she responded.

"Estelle got it for trainin Earldean to get use to wearin one…ya know…incase she wants to move to town and all when she grows up to be a lady." I informed them in a soft voice.

"Ed Earl still not up to getting out yet?" Alma asked.

"He's doin much better but Doc said he'd better keep him in a few more days." Estelle said as she fussed with the bow on the back of my dress.

"Look how precious you are!" Debbie said to Learline as she took her from Trudy's embrace. *"Ya'll gonna sit by us?"* she asked as she sat back down with her in her lap.

"Well, this is not my usual pew..." Estelle said as she turned, longing to keep her routine seating.

"Now Estelle, surely there's no church rule that says you have to sit in a certain place every Sunday, now is it?" Trudy asked.

"No, but..." Estelle went on, looking around then back across to the empty spot that had automatically been saved for her by the regular church goers.

"Reckon why they to do that?" Alma asked, turning to sit back down then looking around at the congregation as she continued; *"Folks do have a tendency to sit in the same place every service. What...are we afraid that God won't recognize us if we sit someplace else?"* then, amusing herself, finished with a chuckle.

"Or Maybe..." Trudy leaned in whispering, *"The preacher can tell who's here and who aint...so he can keep tabs and tell Jesus on um later!"*

"That's not so Trudy!" Estelle denied. *"People are just creatures of habit...no different than over at the Café and folks wantin to sit in the same place all the time!"*

"That's probably it..." Alma added, nodding her head in agreement. *"...We get comfortable in a routine...It helps to know what to expect."*

"Well, it aint good when we become so complacent, a havin thangs our own way, that we won't make minor accommodations when the need arises...especially if it hurts feelins!"

"What are you tryin ta say, Trudy?" Estelle asked, trying to read between the lines.

"Well for example...over at that other church, I seen a whole family get up and leave before the services ever started when Old Lady...well...a lady, whose name we won't mention...got after them for sitting in her family's favorite spot...like she owned that place herself!" Trudy said, then sat back crossing her arms and pursing her lips.

"Shame on her...Who was it? Old Lady Kitchell?" Alma responded. *"I bet it was her, she can be a real horses..."*

"Alma Fey Nettles! Listen to you!" Estelle fussed. *"You know better than to spread gossip like that! Trudy was just giving an example...She left the woman's name out for a reason."*

That was the first time I remember hearing Alma's whole name being said and I had to ask, *"Is all them names yours?"*

"Shhh…service is fixin ta start." was Alma's response.

We all took a place on that same pew except Estelle who was still standing in the aisle. She looked around and smiled at a few people sitting close by who were watching her and who might have over heard the conversation.

"Well I guess we can sit here." she said as we all made room for her.

Trudy leaned in and said, *"Maybe you will see things from a different point of view."*

Looking back now on what she said, I believe she meant several things by that. I think she wanted Estelle to see how hurt Alma was about not being asked to take temporary custody of us kids; especially after she had invested so much time in tending to us and putting her 'heart and soul' in every minute of it. She had already bonded with us so it was hard for her to just let go.

Poor Alma, she didn't have anybody at home to love. Estelle and Doc had each other and their grown children who would be coming back for occasional visits. Plus, they had Festus and the horses to take care of.

Alma didn't have a husband like Estelle did, which is precisely why the Welfare Department didn't ask her to be responsible for us. They told her that children should be placed with couples, not single people.

When Doc and Estelle heard that they were planning to place us with other families in another county until the matter with our own parents could be settled, they offered their assistance.

They weren't trying to take the job away from Alma. On the contrary, they were just trying to keep us together and closer to home. Given what little they knew about our situation, they felt we would be more contented around the folks that we had become familiar with; like Alma. This way we would at least be together in the same town with her.

She had a job she had to go to and if we ended up with her, she would have to find a sitter for us to stay with. Doc and Estelle didn't think it was a good idea to have us kids waiting there all day while Alma was trying to get her office work done.

Estelle had a more flexible schedule and they felt that they could better afford the added expense of caring for children as well as offering medical care for Ed Earl while he was recovering.

After a little further investigation of Doc's clinic, seeing that it was on the up and up with him being a bona-fide medical doctor, the Murphy's were awarded our temporary foster care at their request.

It was agreed by the authorities that in the best interest of the boy, that he stay there with them along with all three of his sisters.

After church Estelle had seen how much we had missed Alma and how sad it was for her to go home alone. So she asked both the women and Debbie to come to Sunday dinner, saying there was plenty there to feed an army.

She had cooked up a big batch of spaghetti and it was waiting on the stove at home. Trudy was reluctant at first, feeling she had already spent the first half of her day off at church appeasing Alma but she finally agreed to it if she could go home first and change out of her high heels.

Alma agreed, as she too wanted to change out of her church clothes feeling that the girdle she was wearing would be too constricting when she sat down to her plate of spaghetti.

There was a wonderful aroma that greeted us as we walked through the kitchen door. Doc stood there with an apron on and was stirring the sauce that he'd kept hot on the stove while the pasta was cooking. Fresh bread rolls that had been rising overnight were now baking in the oven. This only stimulated our hunger pains and we were excited about trying out this spaghetti stuff that we had never had before.

Ed Earl was so excited to see Alma that threw his arms around her neck and held on tight.

"Wow! Boy…you sure are getting your strength back…that is unless you have lock arms now instead of lock jaw!"

As Doc asked the blessing over the food he also asked for peace in our hearts over our longsuffering and new beginnings, which later I translated as, *"Hurry up and help us find our Mama and Daddy, cause we just caint take it no more!"*

The dinner conversation was mostly lighthearted chit chat, about the rain in the forecast, what Brother Hemphill had to say in his sermon at church that morning and of course the Labor Day Celebration.

We managed to avoid such subjects like, missing our parents, Ed Earl being sick or them mean ole boys in town; just nice pleasant conversation.

It was wonderful to sit at the big table, all together with our new friends who meant so much to us now. I could only wish our parents were there too. I wondered if, after we found them, would we still be able to gather together like this.

Doc would make a good friend for Daddy like Denby had been. They could fish together in the lake out back and could ride horses together.

Mama would enjoy drinking her coffee with these women and they would fuss so over the crafts she makes. She could show them how to weave baskets and string beads and put up preserves. Then they could swap recipes. I know she would want the one for this spaghetti that Ed Earl had decided was his new favorite dish because the sauce tasted like warm ketchup.

After dinner we all sang songs as we cleared the table and washed dishes.

After the sun settled more in the western sky it shaded the back yard and Doc thought it would be alright if Ed Earl got a little fresh air.

He sat in a lawn chair by the adults while Debbie showed us girls how to make a necklace out of wild clover by slitting the stems and sliding the next flower through.

Although there was a gentle breeze blowing, Estelle would loosen her blouse and fan her hot flashes as she sipped iced tea. When she saw Trudy and Alma both fanning she decided it was too hot for Ed Earl to be out and suggested the women take him back in the air conditioning.

"Doc, why don't you take the girls down to the pasture and show them the horses, I'll scoop us up some ice cream in about a half an hour. That will give us ladies time to cool off!" she said.

Doc agreed it was a good idea, thinking after they got Ed Earl settled watching TV; being women, they would just want to talk about menopause and prognosticating their menstrual cycles.

He figured, if they got that far, they would probably go ahead and cover the topic of feminine protection and other such subjects he wanted to steer clear of, so he was glad to oblige.

He wanted to be sure they got it all out of their system, so he allowed enough time to pass by letting us each take a turn riding Patches. Earldean was surprised to see that I already knew the painted mares name but not disappointed that I didn't know the other horse's names.

"The white mare over yonder, she's a little shy but she's a good breeder. She is the mother of Patches here." Doc explained as he began to saddle up Patches.

"Why…she's as big as her mama, huh?...What's her name?" Debbie asked.

"Butter Cup." Doc replied. *"…but I call her Ole Gal most of the time… She'll respond to either, if you call her in with a piece of watermelon or a sugar cube…as long as it's a treat…she likes to be invited."*

"Is the black one her Daddy?" Earldean asked.

"Dats da Daddy one?" Learline followed with assumption and pointed at the black stallion still grazing in the pasture. Doc smiled as he pulled tight on the straps beneath the belly of the horse.

"No Darlin…That's not patch's Daddy…more like a cousin."

"Ma-lik-a-sin?" Learline attempted to repeat.

"His name is Acouzin?" I asked.

"Nu uh," Doc chuckled, *"…his name is Feather Foot."*

"Fetafoot?" Learline tried to pronounce.

Debbie got tickled at how she had said it so serious like.

"That's right!" Doc said, still grinning when he squatted down to be at her level. *"You're a real baby doll…you know it?"*

Only long enough to get her point across, did she look away from the black stallion in the pasture in order to make eye contact with Doc. Shaking her head in disagreement, she meant business by saying, *"I not Baby Doll…Hers inna house, sweepin…I Learline!"*

Debbie, who was easily amused by Learline's baby talk, cracked up laughing while Doc played ignorant saying, *"Is that right? Learline? How did I ever get that mixed up?"*

Picking her up high in his arms, he said, *"I hope you forgive me…you're both just so cute…I get you two mixed up!"*

Everybody had been entertaining her by playing along and pretending with her that her Baby Doll was a real live person. Learline appreciated the respect of her imagination.

"Your Baby Doll is sweepin the floors?" Debbie asked her.

"No Dabby…Her too wittle…her don't know how!" she replied.

"Ya mean she takin a nap?" Earldine quizzed.

"Yea…her sweepin." Learline said in a tone of voice that let us know she was glad she made her point.

Doc set her back down and asked us to take her over by the gate and wait for him while he untied Patches.

I, being the experienced one, got to go first to show them how it was done while Doc led the horse in a big circle. Though I was a tad bit nervous, I was able to overcome it as long as I could hear Doc's voice. I found things to ask him just so that he would have to answer and keep talking.

"How did your black horse get the name Feather Foot?"

"We named him that because the day after he was born, we could tell he was going to be light on his feet. Sure enough, he turned out to be a graceful swift runner. He's the reason I had to buy that piece of land back over there…to expand the pasture and give him more distance."

"I reckon horses like plenty of runnin room…they don't know how to play other games do they?"

"Sometimes when I watch him race across the pasture, he goes so fast, it's like he's floating…his feet never seem to touch the ground!" Doc said like a song with passion as he gazed out at his beautiful horse.

"He really belongs to my boy Hank Jr. who is over in Vietnam…in the war. I told him I'd take care of Feather Foot till he got back."

"We saw that war on TV. Estelle turned it off cause she said she don't like him being over there."

"She worries about him."

"Estelle showed us pictures of him on a horse. Is that the same one?"

"Probably."

"Do you ever ride that one?"

"Sometimes…when my back's not giving me problems. I'm getting to old to be riding fast horses. Even though he's a smooth ride when you bend in and go with him…it's the bending in that stumps me…Arthritis."

"What's that?"

"Old age." he said. *"Yep…Foots still gets a good workout when Fred McMillan's boys come around."*

"Foots?"

"Feather Foot…Foots is a nickname."

"Trudy says Hun is a nickname…so is Sugar…Sweetie Pie…says they play names ya give somebody so ya don't wear out they real one."

"Could be…is Sassy your nickname or your real one?"

"It's the only one I ever knowed of…till I come to Whisper Ridge…Now its Honey, Hun, Darlin, Little Lady, Sugar, Sweetie Pie, Stupid Hillbilly."

Doc hesitated for a moment in his steps, then turning back, he looked at me he asked in a disturbed tone, *"Who calls you stupid?"*

"Them mean boys in town…and that Virgil feller that works for the po-lice."

"You're not talking about Nolan…Deputy Reed?"

"Naw, not him…he's a nice un…I'm talkin bout that feller Sheriff calls Vergil."

"Was that the same officer that yelled at ya'll out there that day…the day of the search?"

"Yes sir…that's the one…he don't care much fer me…told me I was stankin…I couldn't smell nuttin…he might a been foolin but it sounded loud and mean."

"Well, don't you pay him no mind. He's got social problems. I'm pretty sure that's why he's not in the service. I'm not sure how he got that job working with the police."

"He's a mean un alright."

"Well, you let me know if he gives you any more problems…we'll talk to the Sheriff."

We were both quiet the rest of the way back around the circle. I didn't want to spoil my ride by talking about bad stuff.

Doc helped me down then helped Debbie get her foot in the stirrup for her turn.

She had ridden a pony at the fair before but never a big horse like this.

Earldean was so excited she laughed a nervous giggle all the way around the circle never stopping. We all got tickled at her and laughed along.

Then, I got to go again with Learline because she was too little. Doc put her up behind me and she held on around my waist for a short ride before she got too scared and wanted off. When we took her in for her nap she couldn't wait to tell her brother what she was allowed to do.

Ed Earl was jealous when he found out but Doc promised when he got better he would let him have a turn.

It turned out to be a beautiful, memorable day with our new friends that felt like family now. They had shown us the compassionate side of the cruel, mean world our folks had warned us of and went out of their way to see to our needs.

As we waved good-bye to Alma, Trudy, and Debbie, we noticed that dark clouds were moving in fast from the southwestern skies. When Doc said he'd better corral the horses, I followed him to help in whatever way I could. I just wanted to see them one more time. We had finished up and were on our way across the yard when the bottom fell out of the rain clouds. The smell was so refreshing we took our time, letting the drops soak us.

Estelle came to the back door and yelled for us to get in out of the rain. She greeted us with big fluffy towels that smelled like spring flowers.

During the night the storms got worse before they got better as the bolts of lightning and peals of thunder would wake me from time to time but I would pray myself back to sleep, thanking God for the soft, dry bed to sleep in.

By Tuesday of that week, Ed Earl was looking much healthier. Although he was still a little weak, he had started to pick up a pound or two and his scar from his stitches was was healing just fine. Even his bug bites were all cleared up.

Doc had told Alma that it was no surprise that we had so many bites on us with us living in the woods. He had recommended using calamine lotion on them to help them heal. When we were at Trudy's, she would paint us up good after we got out of the tub. We'd have so much on, we would have to stand in the bathroom until it dried, before we put our clothes on. However, it paid off because for the first time in my life that I could ever remember, I didn't have some kind of sore on me.

Doc said Ed Earl's probably healed faster because all the medicine he was taking was helping him to heal all over.

Personally, I believed it was all them prayers that done it. I had prayed one night after one particular Bible story, for Jesus to come heal Ed Earl like he had done for that leper in the story. It wasn't too long after that that we all began to notice a vast improvement.

It had been raining all morning so we couldn't go out to play. It was different to be this dry on a rainy day and I wanted to play in it like we did back home but after Estelle warned us of the dangers of lightning we lost interest in the idea.

We were in the kitchen with Estelle who had taken a little time before lunch to plan some menus for the rest of the week.

She reached and took the calendar from the wall next to the back door. After checking the number of days we had left in August, she scratched around in a drawer for something to write with then sat down at the table with a pen saying, *"I've been so busy lately I forgot all about some of these things I had planned to do. I can't believe I missed Clarice's Tupperware party. And look at this…Hank and I had planned to have Jessie and Sharon over for a cook-out last Saturday night. I completely forgot to call Sharon back to confirm all that; she must think I'm terrible! Well, she didn't say anything about it on Sunday morning…I'll have to call her later and explain…Clarice too…they'll understand with all that's been going on around here."*

She made a few notes on the remaining squares then turned the page over to the month of September and after a contented sigh she went on with her comments. *"Look it's a whole new month…a fresh start. I just love a clean slate to write on. Lets see…Sunday is September 1st…so…we need to fill in all the Labor Day events we want to attend. Wonder what day school starts? Now that my kids are grown I haven't had to keep up with those sort of things."*

"Debbie says she starts school the Wednesday after Labor Day." Earldean informed her as we all stepped over to watch what she was doing.

Mama kept a calendar too but it was the kind that comes on a flour sack that showed the whole year. She didn't write on it but used it to count the days and teach us how to find our birthdays, Christmas and Easter. We didn't know about other holidays like Labor Day.

She used the cardboard from the occasional boxes of cereal we'd get, cutting it open and turning it over to the blank side to write on. She'd take a pencil and write down a list of the days in the weeks of that month. Putting a date then a dash with something written out beside it she would have us find that day on the big flour sack calendar, making a learning game out of it.

Learline had not learned how to play that yet but the rest of us knew where her birthday was on the calendar.

"There's Learline's birthday…right there!" I said pointing to September fourteenth.

"You know when her birthday is?" Estelle asked, with a surprised look on her face.

"Sure do!" I proudly replied.

"And mine too!" Earldean cheered. *"Mine is the very first day in October. That'll be October first, then I'm gonna be twelve years old. Right now I'm still lebum but won't be long now cause October comes right after September, ya know!"*

"I know." Estelle said still looking puzzled.

"…And Learline's gonna be three!"

"I TWO!" Learline insisted, holding up two fingers.

"Yea, but ya gonna be three on ya birthday Learline…this many!" Earldean said, showing her the correct amount.

Ed Earl proceeded to help fix his baby sisters hand teaching her to hold up three fingers instead of just the two she had already learned.

"Do you know when your birthday is Sassy…and Ed Earls?" Estelle asked me, sliding the calendar toward me in case I needed assistance to find it for her.

"I know it by heart…It's April ninth…go to April and count nine days…and when that day comes it's gonna be my birthday. I turned ten last time so I'm gonna be…" I stopped to count on my fingers until I ran out and looked around for what to do next. Earldean came from the other side of Estelle and stopped beside me holding up one of her fingers for me saying, *"Lebum!"*

"I'll be lebum years old then. I calculated.

"Eleven, huh?"

"That's right eee-lebum…that's how old I am right now." Earldean reminded us.

"I'm gonna be…uh…When'z my day…Maybember two-many six?" Ed Earl inquired. We laughed, then together, Earldean and I sang out to correct him, *"May twenty-sixth!"*

"May two-eney six…That when I was six but now is it ganna be May two-eney seben?" Ed Earl said.

"No…that aint right…" Earldean corrected him. *"Ya birthday is still gonna be on May twentysix…but you gonna be sebum this time!"*

Estelle then asked, *"Why didn't you tell us that you knew when your birthday's were?"*

"Ain't nobody axed us iffin we knowed it." I said.

Earldean added, *"All anybody wanted ta know wuz our last name…we coulda told um if they wanted ta know when we's born and when we have birthdays…"*

"…And Christmas and Easters…don't fer git them!" I inserted in the explanation.

"Do you know when your parents' birthdays are?" Estelle asked.

"Daddy's Birthday is a next day after Ed Earls' cause Mama always said she give him that boy fer his birthday present so's he could have a son to carry his name." Earldean told her.

"And…what name would that be?" Estelle asked, trying to see if our last name would surface in the answer.

"Well, that's why come he ta be called that. The Earl part come frum Daddy, just like mine done…Earl…Dean, Earldean, ya see?"

"What about the Ed part, where did that come from?" Estelle asked her.

"Daddy said he give him that part from his own Daddy who go'ed by the name of Ed."

Estelle sat up straight in her chair and asked, *"Your Grandfather's name is Ed?"*

"Huh? We don't know nobody called Grandfather…but Ed's a name what come from he name of my daddy's daddy."

"That's right…and his name is Ed?"

"Daddy said we'd probly be callin him Papaw Ed."

"So, Ed is your Papaw. Where does Papaw Ed live?"

"He don't. Daddy said he died down there in Murphysboro long time ago when Daddy was still just a youngin. Then his Mama brung him up alone fer a little while afore she took sick with sadness and wouldn't git outta bed."

"Murphysboro…your folks are from Murphysboro, Arkansas?"

"Just Murphysboro's all'z I knowed of." Earldean said.

"Naw…he lives in Heaven!" I corrected her. Then, looking at Estelle, I said, *"That's where ya go when ya die incase ya wanna know."*

"That's iffin ya take Jesus in ya heart Sassy…ta live in there!…Daddy said his paw didn't have nuttin but hardness in his heart…probly why come him not ta have no room fer Jesus…said all he cared bout wus whisky and bein mad at folks cheetin him outta money!…But still…Daddy said he'z a the only daddy he ever had, so he seen fit ta name his boy after him…guess ta carry on his name an all."

"Jesus is in my heart!" Ed Earl exclaimed, stepping to the edge of the table with his hand over his heart.

"Awee…is that right darling?" Estelle said scooping him to her side.

"Yes um." he replied with sincerity, still pledging his love in its location. *"When I'z in that hospital…that doctor was listenin to the inside of my heart…with this thang ya put up in ya ears…an he let me have a listen…and I heard Jesus in there!"*

"You did?" Estelle asked with delighted enthusiasm.

"What did he say?" I questioned him.

"Reckon how ya knowed it was Him?" Earldean followed with her inquiry.

"Couldn't hear what he was sayin cause he was whisperin like this…sshwit-sshwit-sshwit. But I knowed it was him in there…cause I heared a bumpin round inside there a tryin to git out…who else could it be?"

"Jegus is in there Ed Earl?" Learline asked pointing to his chest.

"Yep…right here." he answered patting the place over where he heard it.

"Opin ya mouth and let him git outa dare, bubba!"

Ed Earl dropped his hands to his hips, tilted his head and asked, *"Now, Learline…if he gits out…hows I posta git ta heaven?"*

Estelle laughed then lifted Learline up into her lap and assured her Jesus would be alright and for her not to worry; that she would one day understand.

"Yea…maybe when ya three you can know bout it…this many." he told the baby as he went back to teaching her to hold up three fingers.

"Back to Papaw Ed…does he...er a da…did he have a wife?…Grandmaw maybe?"

"Don't know…but my Daddy said his Maw took sick after he'z Daddy died."

"Do you know if she still lives there?"

"Don't know nuttin bout that neither…We ain't ever seen her…could be…"

"Estelle?" I interrupted. *"Reckon our folks are down there a visitin Daddy's Maw?"*

"I couldn't say…did they talk about goin down there to see her?"

"Mama was talkin to Daddy bout it long time ago…sayin sumptin bout payin respects."

"Hummm…Sounds like she might have passed away." Estelle said.

"Duno…they didn't say nuttin bout that but…I thought Mama died one time…like she passed away…but I guess she just fainted wuz all…like I done that time." I told her.

It was like I could see the wheels turning in Estelle's brain. She didn't know what to do with all this new information we had given her. Should she call somebody and tell them or keep probing in hopes of solving this puzzle?

Learline still had her pinned in the chair but now she and her brother were almost in her face as she dodged flying arms from their play that was sliding into bickering.

Ed Earl was persistent in teaching Learline how to hold up the right amount of fingers, as if she were going to run out of time before her birthday and not be allowed to turn three years old.

She pushed his hands away yelling for him to stop. *"No! Leave meeeeee lone Bubba!"*

Still trying to get his lesson across, he grabbed her hand again before she yanked it back. *"Me don't wanna be dat many I wanna be dis many!"* she cried waving her two fingers like a flag before she broke into a sleepy cry.

Estelle knew she still had to fix lunch before Learline's nap. She needed more information and was on a roll, now that she knew what kind of questions to ask. She wanted to call her husband or somebody and tell them what she found out. Yet if she waited, she might find out more.

She couldn't think clearly over the sleepy, whining cries of the two year old who was defying this lesson her brother was insisting on teaching her about turning three.

All at once Estelle slid Learline down out of her lap then pushed herself from the chair bouncing around in circles and fanning herself with both hands.

Ed Earl watched her with wide eyes before he yelled out, *"Hot Flash! Run for your life!"* then darted out of the kitchen scaring Learline half to death, causing her to scream.

"Ed Earl! Quit runnin…you'll git sick again!" Earldean yelled into the other room.

Learline ran out after him screeching, *"STOP IT BUBBA!"*

Estelle's face was turning red as she ran her fingers across her head messing up her big hair do. She picked up the phone and dialed the number to the Clinic but hung up when she got a busy signal. She paced the length of the kitchen floor twice then tried again.

"Still busy!" she sternly said. *"Who could they be talking to for so long?"*

About that time Festus started barking outside indicating somebody was pulling down the driveway. *"Somebody's here…who could that be…I hope it's not the Watkins man! I'm in no mood to fool with him too right now!"* Estelle exclaimed in panic.

We children all ran to look out the living room window to see who it was. Standing on the sofa, pulling back the drapes, Ed Earl yelled, *"IT'S THE PO-LICE!"* Then, he jumped down from his look-out and ran across the room in a big circle doing his impression of driving a squad car and sounding his siren.

Estelle pulled at her hair and yelled, *"CALM DOWN!"* just before she broke into tears.

"Ed Earl! Look what ya done did…jumpin on the furniture, makin Estelle cry and all…after she done told ya bout that! Shame on ya! That was her purdy sofa too!"

Earldean scolded him as she wiped the seat of the sofa where his feet might have been.

I reached and picked up Learline who was still crying and tried to calm her down. When the two little ones realized that this grown woman was sobbing real tears they stopped their racket and looked concerned.

"Are you alright Estelle?" I asked, being a little concerned for her myself.

Trying to pull herself together, she wiped her face with her hand and said, *"I'm so sorry about your Grandpaw Ed…and…and…your Mama and Daddy! It's just a shame…It's not supposed to be this way! They should have found them by now…It's just not fair!"*

Then she collapsed on the big chair behind her and sobbed some more.

I put Learline back down and walked over to her. Resting my hand on her shoulder I told her it would be alright and asked if she needed a hug. Learline darted to her and hugged her knee not waiting to find out if she needed it or not.

"I give ya hug, itta be are-ite." she said.

"I'm ok hun." she sniffed. *"I don't know what come over me…I better get myself together before I answer the door."* she said, standing to her feet and wiping her face again.

She reached and got a tissue from the box next to Doc's recliner then blew her nose.

Fluffing her clothes and combing her hair with her hands she asked, *"Do I look ok?"*

"You look just fine!" Earldean said, though we all knew she was lying because she didn't want to hurt her feelings. Estelle's face was blotchy red and her hair was a mess compared to her usual neatness.

She smiled and asked Earldean if she would answer the door and ask the Sheriff to come on in while she went and freshened up. *"Tell him I'll be right there!"* she said as she headed down the hallway to the bathroom.

Ed Earl didn't wait for the officer to knock or ring the bell, he just opened the door and rang it himself. Again and again he rang it until Earldean grabbed him back away from it.

"It's Deputy Reed!" he shouted back toward the hallway to let Estelle know who it was.

"She knows that!" Earldean told him trying to restrain him from ringing the bell again. *"...uh...hey there...Estelle says come on in...she'll be right out."*

After dodging the heavy rain drops on his way from the squad car, Deputy Reed stepped in through the doorway, taking his hat off, then turned back to shake the water off of it. We took notice of his consideration as he wiped his feet on the mat at the entrance then shut the door behind him.

"Ya'll doin alright today?"

"Yes sir." Earldean and I answered in unison.

"Estelle said she's gonna be alright now...she was cryin!" Ed Earl told him. *"She's back er inna batchroom!"*

"Her gotta pe-pe inna potty." Learline said, giving him more information than he cared to hear. He pinched back a smile ignoring her response then quickly changed the subject by asking Ed Earl if he felt better now that he was out of the hospital.

"Yeaser...mighty fine...mighty fine." he answered, mimicking how Doc might have done.

"Better than he should..." Estelle said as she walked back into the room, *"...he's got more energy than he knows what to do with...just won't sit still!"*

She walked over and stuck out her hand saying, *"Hello Nolan...what brings you out today?"*

"Hey Estelle...I hate to bother you like iss but Sheriff McCoy sent me out here on official police business."

"What is it?" she asked.

He reached in his shirt pocket and pulled out a piece of paper of some kind saying, *"They found a truck that fits the description these kids gave us…might be their Daddy's."*

"Did ya find my Daddy?"

"Really? Wuz they alright?"

"Please tell us you aint foolin this time!"

"Oh Nolan…where?"

We all bombarded him with questions at the same time as we moved in closer to each hear their own answered first.

"Hold on." he said, gently putting out his hand to halt the questions. *"We don't know for sure but we got a call early this morning saying they found a truck fitting that description, abandoned on the side of Highway 72 over near Gravette. Said they figured somebody was just broke down out there…maybe caught a ride into town for parts and would be back to fix it…or send a wrecker back for it…said it was there over a week before they hauled it in."*

"A week...I thought the law was trying to help find these people for us. How'd they miss it on the side of a major highway?" Estelle asked.

"That's just it…they had a wrecker haul it off the highway on the thirtieth of July and impounded…waitin on somebody ta come along and claim it…said it had been sitting there at least a week by that time, meannin it must have been abandoned out there on or about the twentyfourth."

"The twentyfourth…of July…that was around the same time the kids said he left for work." Estelle noted.

"Exactly…but the APB didn't go out until late on the evening of the third…that was back on that first day Doc and I rode out there to check on their sick mother. But, when we found nobody was there, we called for a search and put out the APB."

"The APB…what's that?" Earldean asked.

"That's an All Points Bulletin...lettin all the police in the area and the region know what to be on the lookout for." he explained.

"I don't understand…today is the twentyseventh of August…If the police had hauled it off on the last day of July…why are they just now telling ya'll about it?" Estelle asked.

"Well from what I can understand of it…when the truck was picked up by the wrecker, it was sometime late in the evening and they had already closed the books for that month. They hauled it out there to one of their wreckin yards and everybody just sort of forgot about the old clunker, until the wrecker service sent out this month's bills. By the time the processing department received the statement for the wrecker service, the officer who had it towed in was just getting

back from vacation. He had not been aware of the APB and it had been over looked somehow…anyway…We don't even know for sure if this is it. That's why we need one these kids to take a look at this Polaroid and see if it might be their Daddy's truck."

Deputy Reed turned the picture over that he'd taken from his pocket and laid it across the palm of his big hand.

We all rushed over to see it with Ed Earl getting to it first. After only a second he shouted, *"THAT'S IT!...That's my Daddy's truck!"*

We all looked at and agreed.

"Are you sure?" he asked. *"We need to be really certain about this."*

I looked closely and was reminded of how it used to sit when it was parked by our home in the hollow. I recognized every scratch and dent, as well as areas where the paint had cracked and peeled. I wanted to see my parents seated inside the cab of the thing but the truck was empty; like the empty feeling inside me at that moment. I turned and looked back up at Deputy Reed and said, *"That's my Daddy's truck alright."*

22
ALL DRESSED UP & NO PLACE TO GO
(*ROOM TO LIVE*)

Sheriff McCoy had said that the case was out of his jurisdiction and that it had been turned over to the state police. However, as long as we kids were in his town, he would see to it that as soon as he had anything to tell us, he would make it a priority.

There were so many holes in the case that it was hard for anybody to know where to start. For the first three weeks after the police got involved, all they had to go on were the words of four small children, claiming their parents were missing.

They had circumstantial evidence that somebody had in fact, existed for quite some time out there in the hollow, in the spot we called home. However, with no more shelter than an abandoned old school bus and nothing there to claim who we really were, this left their imaginations running wild with concern and suspicion.

The only name they had to go on was Earl but that just wasn't enough as we discovered how common the name was.

There was no legitimate address for where we lived, so the name couldn't be found on a mailbox. They had started a search for court records on the track of land out there, thinking this Earl person's last name would show up as property owner.

There was no real proof that a crime had been committed, except for maybe trespassing if it turned out we were not authorized to subsist on the land.

By this time, talk of desertion played a strong role in the case with our parents not coming forward yet to claim their children. The officials said that unless something tragic had happened to them, more than likely neglect and abandonment would be the criminal issue here.

If that were the case, it was only a matter of time before a decision would have to be made by the state on placing us in permanent foster care.

Everything else had just been suspicion of misconduct and speculation on the part of the investigators. They found nothing at our home site that could help them make a case for anything illegal such as drugs, stolen merchandise or wrongful death as they first suspected. Therefore, the traffic out to our home in Chinquapin Hollow had slowed down quite a bit.

There was not a lot anyone could do with the file that was slowly but surely getting lost under a stack of other official business; like traffic tickets and potato chip wrappers.

When Nolan came into the café Cody remembered to ask him about checking out the deep freeze for me like he had promised.

Nolan, thinking if we had used the thing for storage, figured that maybe some sort of records identifying the parents might be kept there. He said that he would pass the information on to the State Police who were working the case and that maybe they might find our birth certificates and shot records next time they were out there.

Finding Daddy's truck seemed to put the wheels back in motion again for the search. Once the Detective got the vehicle identification number he tried to trace it back to a name. The Arkansas license plates had long expired and were last registered to James Denby, who they thought at first might have been our father.

When they followed up on the address, they found the place had been abandon and suspected Daddy might have stolen the truck.

I could have saved them the trouble if they would have just asked me but they contacted Denby first, through a long forgotten forwarding address in Sikeston, Missouri.

He assured them that the truck was not stolen and was a payoff to a close friend of his by the name of Earl Johnson, who had done some work for him.

Denby was terribly disturbed about what was going on. He told them he was the next best thing to kin and in our case, probably better. The detective wasn't sure how to take that comment because with that, Denby hung up the phone saying something about making a way to come home and help us out in our time of need.

The welfare worker, Mrs. Patterson, was scheduled to come out early that afternoon on Thursday, the twentyninth of August, for an interview with us. Estelle felt she needed to clean the whole house in case the woman wanted to do something she called a white glove inspection. When she started acting a little nervous about the whole thing, we jumped in to help before she exploded into a full blown panic attack.

Alma and Doc closed the Clinic early in order to be there when she came and were on their way out. When Alma told Trudy about it, she was unclear as to exactly what kind of meeting it was going be, so she made arrangements with Yvonne to cover for her at the café. She was afraid that this woman was ready to put us in an orphanage somewhere and forget about us. She had to go out there to make sure that wasn't going to happen.

When Debbie had asked to go along Trudy refused saying, *"No Hun…you don't want to be there…this could get ugly…If this woman tries to take them kids away from us…it'll be like stealin cubs from the bear's cave …them others might be intimidated by her but she aint met the likes of Ms. Trudy Pearl Tefertiller…I aint a goin down wit outta fight…I'll tell ya that right now!"*

"Hey! It ain't rainin no more!" Ed Earl had yelled from the stoop just outside the front door, sticking his leg out in the path of the droplets that were falling from the roof.

"Can we go outside now?"

"Ya already are outside, Ed Earl!" sister yelled back as she went after him. *"Now git back in ere…Estelle's gonna tan your hide, boy!"*

He resisted her tugging at the neck of his shirt but she was able to get a hold of his arm and swing him back toward the door. He finally gave in but not before he reached and rang the door bell a few times and yelled, *"Avon Calling!"*

"Look at cha gittin the floor all wet after she done mopped!" she fussed, as she shut the door behind him. Estelle came running from the kitchen with a dish towel and used it to dry his feet and wipe the floor.

"I wanna go outside! Can we huh…can we?" Ed Earl pleaded to a higher authority.

"No sir…it is too wet out there and you need to settle down and rest a bit…you could get sick again!" Estelle said as she finished wiping up the puddle.

"But Festus aint got nobody to play wiff out yonder!" he appealed with an excuse.

"Festus will be just fine…Now, why don't you go get your shoes and socks on so you will look nice when Mrs. Patterson gets here." she suggested.

"Is she gonna take us to town or someplace?" he asked.

"No, Sweetheart, What makes you say that?" Estelle asked, wondering if he was concerned about being taken off to live in an orphanage.

"Well, if we ain't goin no place…why we gotta put our shoes on!" he asked.

Relieved that's all it was, she combed his hair with her fingers and said, *"Oh no, Darlin, I just want you to look nice is all…see how nice your sisters look in their pretty dresses and shoes? So…why don't you go put on your pretty shoes so Mrs. Patterson will think you're a handsome young gentleman…ok?"* she coached, turning him toward the staircase. *"…Sassy…why don't you help him find um."*

"Yes um." I said and complied by guiding his shoulders from behind.

"…and not the pink ones…his new ones I bought for him." she yelled back up as we climbed the stairs.

Doc and Alma had made it there about ten minutes before Mrs. Paterson pulled into the drive. They were greeted and adorned with excited hugs before they made it all the way inside the house.

The two of them commented on how "spiffy" we looked and after we fished for more compliments, they bragged about what a good job we had done on helping clean the house.

Estelle explained to us on how we needed to sit and be on our best behavior while the Welfare Woman was there. She had instructed us to keep our answers simple and not to say any more than we had to.

Doc told her she had been watching too much Perry Mason and not to worry, that this wasn't a court of law.

When the lady arrived, we all stood, pretty as a picture, while Doc and Estelle went to meet her at the door. When the bell rang we had to convince the two little ones that it wasn't the Avon Lady.

"Hello Doctor Murphy…Mrs. Murphy." We heard in a pleasant voice before the petite woman appeared through the doorway.

"Who's Murphy?" Ed Earl asked when he heard the greeting.

Alma explained to us who she was referring to as they welcomed her in, offering to take her rain coat and umbrella. While Estelle put them away, Doc did the introductions.

She seemed to be pleased when we all, including Alma, extended our hands to greet her.

She had met Ed Earl at the hospital but he had been too groggy to remember her coming by. When she said that she was glad to finally meet us, at the time, I remembered feeling honored to shake the hand of someone who was looking forward to being *my* new friend.

When Doc introduced Alma by her first and last name, Mrs. Patterson told her that she was glad to meet her as well and that she had heard a lot about her. She kindly thanked Alma for all she had done in taking care of the emergency with the boy as well as looking after us children until something official could be done with us.

We all took a seat in the "living room" as they called it. It was a very well kept room that Estelle kept reserved just for special company. There wasn't much living going on in there so I wasn't sure why she called it that. Most of the time they kept the drawing doors shut to that part of the house with Estelle warning us that she didn't want to see a single *living* soul in there. She seldom went in herself except to dust all those pretty things she was saving like new so that just didn't make sense to me. I just couldn't figure out why anyone would want to hide such a lovely place. Whatever the reason, this day was different and I felt privileged to be part of such an extraordinary occasion.

Estelle offered her a cup of coffee and a slice of pound cake from the service set on the short table in front of the sofa.

There was a bit of ice breaking chit chat as she began to fill and pass each shallow cup that rested on a matching saucer. However, I was so entertained by the tinkling sounds of the fine china during the performance of Estelle hosting, that I paid no attention to what was being said during the interlude.

After a wave of compliments over the cake there was an awkward moment of silence. Mrs. Patterson sat down her coffee cup then pulled a tablet of paper and a pen from her briefcase.

She asked Doc about Ed Earl's recovery first, then if there was any more news about our parents. Estelle told her about them finding Daddy's truck broke down on the side of the road and that the police were searching the area over closer to the state line.

The woman was not as awed by the news as we were so I figured she must have already known about it.

She asked the adults questions about themselves, how long they had lived there, their work and how much money they made. They gave her their background experience on being around children as she made notes on her tablet of paper.

Though Earldean and I found the conversation between the adults to be intriguing, the two little ones were easily bored and were crawling all over the formal furniture.

This caused Estelle to get a little antsy as she tried to calmly handle the situation. Ed Earl was jabbering ninety to nothing over the adults as he hopped around needing to go to the bathroom. Before we knew it he had opened the front door and was relieving himself in front of God and everybody!

Estelle and Alma made out like that was the first time that ever happened, though all but Mrs. Patterson knew better. Doc pardoned himself then calmly took care of the matter by escorting Ed Earl to the bathroom where I'm sure he must have explained why gentlemen don't do that in front of the ladies.

Estelle, in trying to make light of his misconduct, drew attention instead to how well the youngster was getting. She nervously snickered a little while commenting on his energy level.

Alma backed that up with a comment to all of his chatter saying, *"It's hard to believe he had Lock Jaw just a few weeks ago...His jaws ain't locked any more…that's fer sure."*

We laughed because we could hear Ed Earl talking ninety to nothing all the way to the bathroom, hardly stopping for a breath.

"He's makin up for lost time now…all those days when he couldn't talk…I guess." Estelle said as if she needed to cover that too.

When they returned, Mrs. Patterson asked to speak to us alone so the other adults went to the kitchen table with their coffee. It was about that time Trudy arrived and Ed Earl ran out the front door to greet her, splashing through the puddles of water on the front lawn.

It was an ordeal just to get him back in and dried off so that the woman could do what she came for.

When she started with the questions, she like everybody else, wanted to know our full names so that she could write them on her tablet.

At first she asked us a lot of the same questions we had been asked by all the others, which caused me to wonder why we had to give her a special audience.

Earldean answered most of them before the rest of us could say anything. I gave up trying, whereas Learline and Ed Earl would cause us to laugh at some of their attempted answers. Even Mrs. Paterson got a kick out of Learline's cuteness.

She was glad to see that Ed Earl was doing better physically, but was concerned with his manic behavior. He hadn't been sleeping well, getting up all hours of the night wanting somebody to wake up and play with him. He couldn't sit still for a minute without fidgeting, bouncing his bare feet on the seat of the big chair and playing with a loose button on his shirt while the lady was trying to ask him questions.

"Pay attention, Ed Earl!" Earldean scolded. *"Mrs. Patterson is a talkin to ya...tell her how ya cut cha leg on that there bob wier fencing…go on tell er!"*

"What really happened to you son?" she asked like she didn't believe the story.

Earldean scooted forward on the edge of the sofa saying, *"There was this bull ya see…"*

"Let him answer, please." she said nicely to her. *"I want to hear what he has to say."*

He told basically the same story Earldean had repeated so many times; only in his own words.

She scratched some more words on her pad then turned to me and asked, *"What have you got to say about it, Sassy?"*

Unsure what she meant I pondered the question a moment then answered her with, *"Well…what she said."* pointing my thumb to Earldean who was sitting next to me.

"Did your sister tell you to say that?" she asked me.

I looked at Earldean, wondering why she would ask such a question, then back at the woman and answered, *"Naw Ma'am."*

"Do your Parents ever hit you?" she asked, still looking at me.

"Ya mean like woopins?" I asked.

"Yea, whenever we git in trouble about sumpin we git a woopin…" Earldean started.

"Earldean got a woopin one time fer sassin Mama…I don't sas Mama…" Ed Earl broke in to tattle.

"Yea ya do to done it! One time he …"

"I WANT MAMA!" Learline began to cry letting everybody in the house know it.

Estelle and Alma ran into the room to rescue her and put her down for her afternoon nap that she was late for.

Earldean began to chatter on about how cranky the baby gets when she hasn't had her nap. I had to remind her of what Estelle told us about not saying any more than we had to. When I did, Mrs.

Patterson got a funny look on her face and asked why Mrs. Murphy would say such a thing.

"I don't know why come her ta tell us that...." Earldean answered first.

"She talks a lot!" I told the woman, stopping my sister from rambling on again.

"She watches Perry Mason…that's what Doc said." Ed Earl added.

"Who…Earldean?" the woman asked.

"Least I know how to talk!" Earldean huffed with her arms folded, and rolling her eyes.

"Hey…make your eyes do like Debbie's again! Ed Earl shouted with a giggle, *"…come on…do it a-gin…its funny!"*

Earldean didn't think it was all that funny. The fact is, she got mad about it.

"Ok children…let's get back to the matter at hand." the woman insisted.

She went on with her inquisition; efforts to find out our level of education and why our parents had not sent us to school. She seemed somewhat impressed that our mother had taught us as much as she had outside the formality of a classroom.

After a series of questions about our parents, our home, what kind of food we ate and whether or not there was enough to go around, she jotted down a few more notes then looked at her watch. Closing her tablet she then began to gather her things saying, *"I have to go now…but I will be meeting with you again soon."*

The adults seemed a bit disappointed that she didn't have much to say to them on her way out after she told them she would be getting back with them after she met with her supervisor.

Trudy felt it necessary to let her know that she believed that our parents would show back up soon and it probably wouldn't be necessary for her to come back.

She told her that there were enough people in town that could help our folks get back on their feet and she couldn't see any reason to split up a family.

Mrs. Patterson said that it was not their goal over at Children's Services to stock the orphanages with unwanted children and that her job was to see to our well being. She agreed that the children needed to be with their families, providing they were in a fit environment and it was not a decision to be taken lightly.

"Good day Ms. Tefertiller." she said. And with that, she was on her way, leaving Trudy's face almost as red as her hair.

23
DON'T LOSE YOUR HEAD

"Look at the traffic...I ain't never seen it like this!" Estelle claimed, as we drove at a snail's pace down Main Street. *"It's all the folks commin ta town for the holiday, I guess...Look at all the campers and boats! The lake is going to be packed this weekend. I hate that! All that oil and gasoline smell gets in the water...messes things up!"*

Estelle went on fussing for anyone who might have been listening. I didn't mind, I thought her crabbiness was better than when she restrained from talking at all. It was when she kept quiet for long periods of time, that was scariest for me. Doc had once compared her to the pressure cooker that blew up the pot of beans she was cooking out there one day.

"Made the biggest mess you ever saw!" he told me. *"Butter beans all over the counter...on the floor...slidin down the wall...some stuck clear up on the ceiling...so, be careful..."* he had continued with a warning. *"When she gets quiet like that...it's best to stay a safe distance because I guarantee ya...she's gonna blow! It's been my experience that it's better to listen to a whistling tea kettle, blowing off a little steam, than to clean up the mess of an exploding pressure cooker!"*

Doc then went on to explain the comparison of his wife with the cooking techniques he had used, assuring me that her body would not literally explode. Though I understood the account of how heated liquid would create forceful steam, it was the image of Estelle's detonated body parts, all over the kitchen that had already displayed itself clearly in my imagination. It was enough to make me nervously nauseated during as little as a moment of her contemplating her next sentence.

"I like em there fast boats...I wish my Daddy would git us one em kind." Ed Earl said as he gazed out the car window. *"I miss my Daddy...wish more...he'd come git me."*

"Looks like the sun's commin out...at least we might have good weather for the

celebration." Estelle commented, trying to change the subject before her mood plummeted from just being a little irritable to being profoundly hopeless and full of sympathy. *"Anybody hungry?"*

Getting her attention, Learline stood up with her doll on the back seat to look out of the window for an eating place. *"My baby doll's hungry…Her wants nanner puddin...huh baby doll?"* she said, then held the dolly to her ear pretending to wait for it to secretly confirm. "*Her says yea…her want some."*

"I could use a little sumpin ta eat." I said, not really hungry but willing to help boost Ed Earl's moral.

Finding him in the rearview mirror, Estelle asked, "*Something with ketchup sounds good…don't cha think Ed Earl?"* She forced a smile hoping he would do the same.

The traffic came to a complete stop seeming to make time stand still. There was a long, agonizing moment of silence where we all waited for his response.

When he didn't answer her, she called his name to get his attention. *"Ed Earl?"*

"I ain't much hungry…" the grieving lad mumbled, as he sat back in the seat, just staring out the window. *"I'm just ready ta go home now."*

"Are ya fillin sick again?" Earldean asked him, placing her hand on his forehead. *"Aint got no feaver or nuttin…Why come you wanna go back? We aint got out no place yet!"*

"Naw…not back ta Estelles house…I wanna go home and wait over younder fer Mama and Daddy to come back!" he sadly clarified.

In the immobility of the car, distant traffic noises broke through the tender silence as we tried to maintain a hopeful attitude after his request.

"*My baby doll's sick …like bubba…her wants Mama too."* Learline muttered, as she held the doll face to face, sticking out her lip with pity.

I was riding in the front seat with Estelle and couldn't help but notice her bottom lip was now stuck out too and quivering. Her eyes welled up with tears just before she reached and bumped the horn sounding three short honks.

"Come on people! What's the hold up?" she fussed.

"I don't thank they heard ya...you want me to git out and go ax um fer ya?" Earldean asked reaching and pulling at the door handle.

"No, no...stay in the car...it's not time to get out yet!" she frustratingly cried out. *"...j-just...just stay in the car!"*

About that time, the car in front of us honked their horn in response, then another, then another, starting a chain reaction.

Estelle held tight to the steering wheel until her knuckles turned white. With her lip still quivering, tears rolled down her cheeks and dripped on to her blouse, while she kept a blank stare at the car in front of her.

As I watched the pressure build behind her facial expression, I drew my legs up underneath me preparing to jump out of the window at any given moment. I found myself squinting my eyes tightly, not wanting to see the possibilities that were before me. Every muscle in my body grew tense in anticipation of what was about to happen to her.

Without warning, she turned loose of the wheel and pressed both hands firmly on the horn, blowing out a long, hard blast of continuous noise, scaring us half to death!

Once again, the other drivers joined in the song and dance of horn honking, as if this would help the congested streets.

Her body still tense, she sat stiff armed, braced against the horn forcing her back into the seat.

When she could no longer take the noise herself, she threw her arms over the steering wheel and rested her head on them. I could hardly hear her over the racket but I knew by her bouncing shoulders that she was crying again.

The traffic started to move a little, clearing about three car lengths ahead of us but Estelle was so emotional, with her face buried in her arms, she had not noticed.

"Estelle...we can go now." I softly said, still afraid to interrupt her episode of tears. I wasn't sure if she just didn't hear me or if she really didn't care but I wasn't going to bother her again.

The traffic behind us sent waves of blaring horns to let her know the road was clearing but I guess she thought they were just mimicking her frustration. When she still did not rise up to see for herself, Earldean scooted forward on the seat and asked, *"You alright?"*

The car behind us raced his engine before he pulled into the other lane, squealing his tires to go around her then dodged an oncoming car to get back in front of her.

The next car that came up behind us did the same but shouted obscene words as he shook his fist out the window at us.

Mr. Albert must have been observing out the window of his shoe shop and noticed Estelle was slumped over in the car and was not moving. He came running out of the doorway jumping over a stack of shoe boxes on the sidewalk and leaping to the car window.

"Mrs. Murphy!...Mrs. Murphy...Are you alright?" he yelled through the glass before he reached and opened the door.

Estelle gradually raised her head as she came back to reality letting her foot accidentally slide off the brake. The car began to slowly roll downhill past Mr. Albert who then yelled, *"LOOK OUT!"*

A few folks along the sidewalk stopped to see what was happening as horns began honking again.

Estelle screamed in panic while Mr. Albert yelled for her to hit the brake. In the confusion Estelle must have put her foot on the accelerator and floored it. Mr. Albert ran after us yelling, "*HIT THE BRAKE!...HIT THE BRAKE!*" But, before she realized what she had done, we crashed into the car in front of us throwing me, Learline and the baby doll to the floor.

After we got over the initial shock, Mr. Albert was there, opening the doors and asking if anyone was hurt.

Thank goodness the other two cars had filled in the gap between the third or otherwise we might have picked up a lot more speed, causing more damage than it was.

I had banged my head on the dash and bruised an arm and a leg but no blood. Learline had wet her panties and busted her lip when she hit the back of the front seat. Never the less, next to the bumpers, it was Baby Doll who suffered the most severe injury.

When Learline fell against her dolly, the headlock she had held tightly around its neck caused the head to be pulled apart from the body!

Learline let out a blood curdling scream, letting us all know the degree of pain and shock she was suffering when she discovered her beheaded loved one, there, in the floorboard. Still clutched tightly in her arms was Baby Doll's head. The headless body had landed on its feet, standing there in a pose that suggested she was searching at her feet for her lost head.

To add insult to misery, when Mr. Albert yanked the door open to rescue the screaming child with the bloody lip, he jumped back at the shocking sight of what he thought was the headless body of a "real" baby. In doing so he lost his balance and fell back into the crowd of onlookers who were now exposed to the same sight.

Some of those hoodlums who found their way through the crowd made out like it was the funniest looking thing they ever saw. It was sort of funny looking but to Learlean it was horrifying. Poor baby, she was hysterical.

Deputy Reed had just arrived down the street to direct traffic and came running when he got word about our wreck. When he had seen that we were all OK he ran the hoodlums off then radioed for back up help with the traffic so that he could work the accident report.

A lady from one of the offices close by came with some wet paper towels for Learline's lips just before Trudy got wind of what happened and came running down the sidewalk. She took us kids back to the Eat-a-Bite to get us out of the way, where she summoned Doc to go see about Estelle.

Learline was still hysterical when Debbie took her to the restroom and cleaned her up.

"She's so upset about her dolly!" I told Trudy.

"She thanks itsa real baby…but it aint even alive!" Ed Earl pointed out.

"Maybe we shouldn't-na played along like at…makin her thank it was a person." I reasoned with the complicated matter.

"Don't blame ya selves for this, now ya'll…ya baby sister a'll be alright…she is just goin through the same hard time ya all are…lovin on that baby dolly was a way to help her feel secure…maybe we can sew its head back on…fix it fer her." Trudy said.

"Alma can put some stitches on it!" Ed Earl suggested. *"She's the one who sewed me up wit some stitches."*

Remembering the previous miserable weeks I added, *"Don't forget the tetanus shot or she'll have to go to the hospital like…"*

"Like me, huh Trudy?" Ed Earl asked for verification.

"Oh! We wouldn't want no more of that, for sure!" she said as matter of fact.

It was about forty five minutes later when Estelle showed up at the café with Doc. She appeared bewildered and distressed when she asked if we were alright, apologizing for losing control and causing the wreck.

"I just don't know what come over me…I cry at the drop of a hat, these days." she said as Doc pulled a chair out at the table for her.

Trudy poured them both up a cup of coffee then took their order as we rallied around Estelle in support, wanting whatever was making her so emotional to go away so she can be happy again.

"Maybe you need a stronger prescription of hormones. I'll have to check into that for you, right away." Doc suggested.

"Hank, did you ever think that I might be crying for a reason?" she exclaimed.

"But, you said…" Doc attempted to defend his offer.

"It don't have anything to do with hormones…I got plenty of reasons to cry...Here's four of um right here!"

"Estelle, I…" Doc tried to explain before she interrupted.

"How are you suppose to know why I keep crying when you ain't never around to listen to a word I say?" she protested.

"I just thought you…" he tried again.

"That's the problem…You don't think, Hank! If you did, you'd be cryin all the time, just like me!" she went on. *"Have you thought at all what these kids are going through? What they must be thinking about their parents not coming home! Huh? And…what on earth are they thinking…leavin their kids to tend to themselves! I just can't take no more of…sniff, sniff…you're not with um all day to see how sad they are!"*

"Shhh…Sweetheart…calm down. It's OK." Doc said, putting his arm around her.

"It's not OK…just so sad, Hank!" Estelle started crying again. *"Their hearts are breaking right before my very eyes. It just hurts, ya know?"*

"I know it hurts, Darling, Shhh…"

"It's not fair..." she protested, then blew her nose.

"No…It's not." he consoled her, patting her hand then holding it.

Alma had walked over to the café on her lunch break and happened in on the midst of Estelle's frustrating remarks. We had not noticed her standing behind us until she spoke.

"I know it hurts, Estelle…I feel for um too!" she said with tears in her eyes.

"*ALMA!*" we kids screamed, as we rushed her for a hug.

"You came!" Ed Earl said with excitement. *"We had a wreck and Sassy bumped her head and the po-lice come and…and dolly's head come off so Learline was bleadin and them boys wuz laffin then Learline was cryin real loud like cause she was bleadin and so I told um you can you stitch it like ya done my leg!"*

"Learline needs stitches? Are you OK baby?" she asked, bending down to examine Learlines swollen busted lip.

"Baby Doll broke her head." Learline sadly reported.

Alma stooped down to comfort the tiny child, took her hands into her own and compassionately said, *"Doc told me... poor little Baby Doll...I was so sorry to hear about that and..."*

"Me cried-n-cried an cried." Learline told her.

"It made me sad too, to see her hurt like that...so when Doc...." Alma was saying with empathy when Learlean interrupted her saying, *"Me and Dabbie told Jejus a prayer for ta git Baby Doll's head back on and help me don't cryin bout it no more!"*

"A prayer?" Alma softly asked then looked up to see Debbie standing beside her, *"...you said a prayer for her doll?"* she asked her.

"I ahh...I didn't think it would hurt anything!" she responded.

"Come...let me show ya something!" Alma said, getting up then taking Learline's hand, guiding her to the booth closest to the door. She helped her climb onto the bench where she stood to be able to peep inside a box on top of the table.

There, cradled in a small towel on the bottom, was Baby Doll whose head was securely fastened with bandage tape. Across one knee was band aid with pictures of Casper the friendly ghost on it.

"Baby Doll...You all better!" Learline exclaimed.

"Well what do ya know?" Debbie mumbled.

"I know prayers are answered in one way or another." Alma proclaimed. *"Ask and you shall receive."* she said pulling the doll out the box and placing it in Learline's arms.

With the exception of Ed Earl's Hospital stay, that night was the first time we had voluntarily split up to spend the night at different homes as not to over burden any particular one of our care takers.

Earldean and Learline stayed with Trudy at Debbie's request.

Ed Earl wanted to go to Alma's and I went back with Doc and Estelle.

It was one long, lonely evening without my siblings there to share the bed. I had never slept alone before and had a hard time falling asleep but once I did, I slept so sound that it was without nightmares. I didn't even remember dreaming.

24
LABOR DAY WEEKEND
(*IN NEED OF SOME THERAPY*)

I often found myself scanning the faces of the crowd in hopes that I would find one or both of my parents that Saturday morning as we gathered in front of the Eat-a-Bite. I didn't see any sign of them but I picked out some of the faces from down at the church, some of the neighborhood kids, and a few of the regulars from the café.

I hardly recognized Charlie Wayne out of uniform when he stopped in passing to say hello to our group we had standing there on the sidewalk. He had been there a few minutes talking to Doc and it wasn't until Alma said his name that I realized who he was.

He was bragging about the fact that he was finally getting a new milk truck and was looking forward to a quieter ride. Alma said that the whole town had been spoiled to not having to set their alarms for years because every morning when they heard that old milk truck coming down the road they knew that meant it was soon time to get up.

Granny Pane and her husband came walking up greeting the adults with handshakes. They told us they were meeting their daughter Jane and her husband Inky there in front of the café. She informed us kids that they would be bringing their grandsons along too, saying that Huey had been wondering about whatever happened to us. She thought that he might be glad to see us again.

Granny Pane's husband acted like he was mad about something but Trudy had said he was that way all the time and told us that we shouldn't pay him no mind.

I didn't know his real name but Trudy referred to him as Old Man Pane so that's what I called him when I greeted him and Granny. He didn't extend his hand to shake mine when I offered but instead tucked them both under his arm pits and ignored me.

Granny, on the other hand, ducked and turned away from him before tucking her lips under her gums. She put her hand over her mouth to hide her growing grin as she bent into a stoop reaching one arm out to hug me.

Alma leaned and whispered in my ear, *"I think you hurt his feelings when you called him Old Man Pane."*

"Well aint that his name?" I asked her.

"Naw hun…" she couldn't finish because she and Granny started snickering too hard.

"Oh…I didn't know…I figured that was his nick name!" I softly said.

"Its OK…he **is** *old."* Granny whispered back.

Estelle had left us waiting out there with Alma, Cody and Doc while she, Trudy and Debbie ran off to hit the sidewalk sales. I heard Alma ask Doc, *"Does it bother ya that she goes shoppin so much…what can she possibly need?"*

"Therapy." he answered quickly, with his arms folded, casually inspecting the crowd.

"You think she's gone crazy?" she asked him with concern.

"All women are crazy if ya ask me." Cody inserted. *"Most of um have more shoes and junk like at than ever necessary!"*

"I used to think that." Doc answered. *"I thought my wife was crazy for spendin a lot of time goin out shoppin for things she didn't really need…until one day she explained why. She says it's not because she needs what she was goin after…but to fulfill the need to go after it. She went on to compare it to my goin out huntin for wild game when we had a freezer full…more than plenty meat ta eat. I thought about it…then realized it wasn't the prize trophy but playin the game that compels us to want to do such things. Hunters want to return from their hunt with the game limit or the biggest kill. The best trophy in the woods. Shoppers want to return from the shop with the nicest thing their money can buy or as many good deals as they can find…whether they need it or not…they'll find somebody to give it to if they have to but they've got to bag somethin to bring home!"*

"Their trophy…right?" Alma figured out.

"Right!" Doc expounded, *"It's somethin therapeutic about the game of it all…huntin gives me pleasure…a sense of accomplishment if I bring home the trophy."*

"Shoppin does seem to calm Estelle down…Trudy too for that matter." Alma said.

"…Like therapy!" Doc concluded.

Imitating a person in deep thought into Doc's analogy, Cody scratched his head then said, *"Ya know…I read up in some books on cavemen one time…I seem to recall sumptin bout the men being hunters brangin in meat and all…the women a bein gathers…would gather up vegetation and such….thangs they need round the place."*

"Sounds good to me...Men are hunters and women are gatherers." Doc agreed.

"I recon it's been goin on for a long time then…huh?" Alma asked.

Old man Pane stood close enough to get in on the conversation. *"My wife spends all my money…ain't never none left to buy shell and huntin gear cause she's out gettin and gatherin."* he complained.

"Just gittin groceries is all!" Granny said in her defense.

"Yep…a great long while." Alma answered herself, cutting her eyes at Doc to let him know she was really referring to the Panes' relationship.

Cody, trying to make light of the twist in the conversation said, *"Now Miz Pane…Ya ortta turn loose the grocery funds…give the ole man some his money back fer some shells…a man's gotta git a little huntin in, ya know…git a little thur-rpy!"*

"I don't care if he goes huntin! He's got bullets in a drawer at the house!" she said.

"Them ain't bullets, woman!" he rudely said, *"…them's shells an a'z aint the kind I need…thems fer duck huntin…don't you know nuttin?"*

"Well…caint you go duck huntin?" she asked him.

"Woman…We ain't even talkin bout that…We're talking bout cavemen!" Old Man Pane said loudly trying to get out of admitting that he just wanted to fuss.

"At's right…" Cody teased them both, *"…real cavemen didn't mess wit lit'lo birds…theyz went out a huntin big meat like dinosaurs…then theyz drug um back fer the women ta clean and dress wilst they rested up and tole lies bout the ones they missed! Then, the women went up in the cave and cooked it fer their old man…they wuttin off runnin the trails a draggin up stuff to clutter up the cave walls with!"*

"Cody that ain't right!" Alma protested. *"They didn't cook inside them caves…they cooked out on an open fire!"*

"At's only ist thez a havin a Bar-b-Q…ait that right Doc?…Then the men do the cookin while'st the women folk stayed up in the cave with the youngins and shelled nuts…cut up them fruits 'n grass…at kinna stuff…fer salads!" Cody teased.

"Well…you a cook…zat make you a woman?" Alma picked back.

"Naw…what happen wuz…em cave men had to git in there an cook az own supper cause az cavewomen done gone of on a shoppin spree…turn'z out az better cooks!…at's what happen to my great-great-great-great-cavepaw!

They all started laughing at Cody's joking then changed the subject.

As the previous conversation was in progress, I had thought about how my Daddy had been teaching Ed Earl how to hunt. They were excited when they brought in their kill but most of the time we had to hunt for food. It was more than a game.

Mama had encouraged us girls to learn to gather wild berries and nuts. She taught us to look for and gather things that might have some fundamental use. She had called it scouting and had compared it to shopping.

"Cody…am I a caveman?" I asked.

"Naw girl…you a hillbilly just like me!" he exclaimed.

"I'm a hillbilly too…like you Cody!" Ed Earl said proudly as he stood next to Cody.

"Yea ya are boy!" he said as he laughed and rubbed the youngster's hair, messing up his part. A few days before, this simple male approval might have sent Ed Earl off into space with more energy than he could contain. But, after Doc took him off the medication he was on, he went back to being a normal six year old boy. A simple discovery Doc noticed when Estelle forgot to give it to him.

Instead of getting rowdy and running out into the street or something, Ed Earl just laughed along with the rest of us when he saw his reflection in the glass door of the café.

"Looka me…my harr's a goin ever whicha way!" he said.

"Do me…Do me…I a billy too!" Learline told Cody.

"Naw I caint go a doin that!" Cody teased. *"You a billy al'ite…but, I go ta messin up them pig tales a yours, at Estelle will tear me up! She a tryin ta turn ya into a city girl…ya thank?"* he said as he picked her up. Then he pointed through the swarm of people, down the sidewalk and asked her, *"A lookie there…who'z at a commin yunder?"*

"Dabby!" she said with her arms reaching out for Debbie who had walked back from shopping.

The women weren't gone long before they too came back with big bags of "good deals". They seemed thrilled with their trophies as they pulled new clothes from the bags showing Alma and Doc the price tags with their slashed prices.

Although we kids were each wearing new 'hand-me-down' clothes, donated by some of the church members, they found reasons to buy us some more new outfits to wear over the next several days.

"They're coming…they're coming!" Huey loudly announced as he came trotting alongside his family to meet up with his grandparents.

I leaned over to look around Debbie and down the street to see a patrol car coming. We all responded when we heard the sirens with Sheriff McCoy waving as he passed us by. His deputies walked beside the squad car asking folks to move back onto the sidewalks.

The Labor Day Weekend festivities began with a parade of farm tractors that made their way down the length of Main Street, turned right on Ridgecrest Rd. then left on Lakeview Drive, leading the way to the Farmers Market. Some of the rigs slowly pulled behind them trailer loads of harvested fruits and vegetables.

Walking alongside them were farm boys who would occasionally pass off a 'prize pickin sample' to a pretty young spectator, inviting her to visit his stand at the Crop Swap.

There were a few strange looking characters, tagging along, being friendly and shaking hands with some of the kids. I had learned by then it wasn't nice to stare and did my best not to do so. Worse than that, the crowd laughed at them and pointed their fingers. Folks poked fun at these fellers far worse than they had ever done us hillbillies.

I felt sorry for them. One of them acted like it didn't bother him at all, he just kept grinning from ear to ear while another looked like he was torn up about it. He had the saddest face I'd ever seen.

I was startled at first at the grotesque features of their pale faces and bizarre hairdos of various bright colors that clashed with the misfit patterns in their clothing.

Being disturbed by the thought of their feelings getting hurt, I consulted Alma about it. She laughed, saying they were dressed that way on purpose because they were clowns…they were supposed to look funny and make people laugh! However, they scared Learline half to death and made her cry!

The adults could hardly enjoy the parade for having to answer and explain all our questions about every little thing that rolled by. Cody said he had never in all his life heard the one word question, "Why?" asked so many times within one short period of time. He had fun with it though; it got to the point that if one of us wasn't asking "why?" about this, that or the other, he would...just to spite Alma and Trudy.

They explained the "what-for's" and "what-ever's" of the things they called floats that were made of truck beds and anything that could be pulled.

Woody paraded three of his top of the line boats that included one for fishing, one for going fast and pulling folks on things called ski's and the last one was a great big one they said was just for cruising and floating in the water. It looked to be bigger than a bus and Doc told us that some folks even use them for a house and live in them on the water.

Collis's Wrecker towed an old rusted out car that looked a lot like it could have been one of the ones Denby had kept around his place. This old wreck, they said, was to be used for a "Big-Bash" fundraiser for crippled people.

For a donation of a quarter a whack, a person could take their frustrations out on it with a sledge hammer. Then when it was smashed to smithereens, the rest would be sold off to the scrap iron yard with the proceeds going to the cause.

A couple of show-offs walked alongside, promoting the idea and demonstrating the procedure. Cody purchased two swings on the spot...one whack for Alma and another for Trudy.

The town's small marching band played their same unpracticed tunes that they had played every year according to Cody. I had never seen anything like it and some of the instruments they had were unusual, so I was easily impressed to say the least.

A few folks laughed when Cody ducked and covered his ears saying that I must be tone-deaf because this "happy little haphazard band" played some of the worse racket he'd ever heard!

Mayor Scott, along with a few others from the town's council, sat in lawn chairs riding in the bed of a red Chevy pick-up truck that was driven by the mayor's brother-in-law, Sam Hully. They waved and carried signs reminding folks to be sure and vote in the upcoming presidential election.

The Mayor's voice was amplified as he spoke through a horn like instrument that Doc said was called a megaphone.

"WELCOME TO WHISPER RIDGE...WE'RE GLAD TO SEE ALL YOU FINE FOLKS WHO CAME OUT TO CELEBRATE WITH US TODAY. ...BE SURE TO VISIT ALL OF THE

CAMPAINE BOOTHS NEXT TO THE BANDSTAND IN THE PARK…WE HOPE TO SEE YOU AT THE VOTING BOOTHS NEXT MONTH….”

As they passed, folks would clap and cheer. Some of them yelled out, *"Go Goldwater"* while others chanted out, *"Nixon, Nixon he's our man…If he can't do it no one can!"*

About a half block or so later, the mayor and his group would repeat the same thing for the folks waiting down the street.

They were followed by "The Whisper Ridge Twirlers" of Miss Beverly's Baton School. The entire student body was made up of girls whose ages ranged from six to sixteen and they all got to participate in the performing march regardless of their level of expertise or degree of talent.

This could have explained why the crowd was wise enough to move back when they attempted to do that "Double Toss, Spin and Catch" maneuver. Though most of them missed it and had to retrieve their batons from here, there and yonder; Miss Beverly and her well seasoned students on the front row did it perfectly.

Their teacher marched on and proudly led the way for all twelve students to follow. One of Beverly's brothers followed alongside with a portable eight track player so that the girls would have music for their routine. Her other brother ran from side to side passing out enrolment forms for the fall classes to the eligible young ladies. Earldean and I were tickled pink to qualify and Debbie said she'd like to do it just to get to wear those groovy costumes with the short, tasseled skirts and white boots.

Of course she would have to be leaving to go back home soon but she thought it would be fun for us to try it.

Another truck drove slowly behind the girls carrying four of the retired soldiers from down at the VFW hall. In the midst of them were various flags with an American flag raised higher than the rest. On the tailgate two more vets sat holding up a banner that read the words **Support Our Troops**.

Marching behind them were a small group of men, some of which wore their different uniforms representing their branch of the service. One was being pushed in a wheelchair and another was missing an arm.

They all were waving little American flags at the crowd who applauded them as they passed by. A few men in the crowd solemnly saluted the war heroes through their procession.

Cheers from the onlookers swept down both sides of the street when the final tractor rounded the bend pulling a flat bed trailer, skirted with the legs the young 4-H club members.

It was pulling a trailer of mixed fruits and vegetables adorning the foot of a throne made especially for the 1968 Crop Queen; Miss Brenda Jo Higginbotham. Her name was proudly displayed in big bold letters on a banner across the back of the trailer.

The bright sun caught its reflection in the sparkling tiara she wore atop her head and it was plain to see that this crown was filled with jewels that I was sure at the time were real diamonds. She wore it proudly as she smiled and waved her stiff hand at all the folks who were standing across the street then turned and waved toward us. At one point she looked right at me then smiled even bigger…I felt so honored.

The excitement of being such a part of an extravagant event felt unreal to me. If I hadn't have been so sore from the wreck the day before, I would have pinched myself to see if I was awake. I thought I was in the presence of a real live queen.

The crowed fell in behind the old fire truck that brought up the rear with its volunteer firefighters hanging from the sides. Occasionally it would backfire sending screams through the unsuspecting crowd of followers.

Unforgettable were the impressive memories that this celebrated long weekend provided for us. As each eventful day of it passed, it brought forth new discoveries of what the world outside Chinquapin Hollow had to offer.

It divulged a host of first time experiences that included the likes of candied apples, kettle corn and some fried pig skins called cracklins. I was ultimately dumbfounded at what happened to the cotton candy when I put it in my mouth. After eating all of mine, I finished off Learline's.

I was puzzled when Doc blamed my belly ache on too much cotton candy being that the stuff disappeared before I could chew and swallow.

Learline had fallen asleep on a quilt Alma spread out on the grass beneath the shade of a huge Hickory. It was close to the bandstand so we kicked off our shoes and rested for a spell before the show.

Debbie ran off with a few other teenage girls her age, who had been her summer friends for several years. They said they were going to just walk around the grounds there but Trudy accused them of scouting for boys when they didn't want me and Earldean tagging along.

Earldean sat pouting about it but I didn't care; I wasn't interested in flirting with any ugly ole boys, especially any of them mean ones.

The adults visited with Alma's sister and brother in-law, the Fletchers, who were there with two more of her sisters and all of their children.

Melba Jean and Clifford Hogan were there with their new grandbaby and had stopped to show off their beautiful offspring a bit before moving on.

While Fred McMillen walked over to chat with Doc about his new colt and his other horses, Huey and a few of his friends ran past us, waving on their way back from the snow cone stand.

Yvonne, from the café, had just spread another quilt next to ours when her son and daughter-in law came up with an ice chest full of drinks. Following them were their two little girls that Learline had played with a few times before.

There was so much going on all at once that I found it hard at times to concentrate on any one particular thing. I had no idea that this many people existed in the world, for there had to be over a thousand there in Whisper Ridge alone. With all those shapes and sizes of bodies moving in all directions, it would be effortless for one to get lost in the masses and easily overlooked in a search.

Mama and Daddy both could have been there looking for us and we would have never known it unless they just missed the mayor making his announcement about us at the end of his welcome speech.

With anticipation we waited for them to come forward through the crowd and claim us while the other folks who gathered there anxiously waited on the hog calling contest and amateur talent show to start.

Without any further "a-do", baby sister had managed to get in a few winks before the first, *"Sooooo-WEEE!"*

I was impressed to see individuals standing before a crowd that size who didn't seem to be bothered by the fact that everybody was staring at them. I certainly wouldn't have had enough nerve to do that; I would have been too embarrassed.

Instead of being shy, the contestants were showing off their talents. Some performed better than others and there were a few that might have just been making fools of themselves thinking they were good. However, I found it all to be entertaining because of their fearless attempts to compete in the first place.

While the judges made their final decision, Mayor Scott got back on the microphone and called all the contestants back to the stage for a round of applause for their participation.

After several rounds and poor attempts of trying to carry a tune himself, the mayor announced the winners.

The one who got first place walked away with a blue ribbon, a nice badminton set donated by Fletchers Fill-A-Sack, and a voucher for free voice lessons from Sister Turner.

The prize for the best hog-caller also got a blue ribbon as well as a gift certificate for a free oil change and tire rotation down at Collis's Car Care.

After a long anticipated wait, cheers poured out at the introduction of the well practiced "Ozark Brew Boys". This group had unpolished looks and a variety of well played, crude instruments that lined the stage as they tuned up.

Estelle said that in spite of their appearance and backwoods behavior, they were pretty good musicians. So Alma suggested she close her eyes and pretend they were angles sent there to delight our spirits. I on the other hand, couldn't keep my eyes off the live performance.

I just thought I had heard real music before…on a clear night, bleeding through the static on that old radio in daddy's truck… and on those scratchy old records of Alma's…or that canned sound coming over on Cody's transistor…or maybe even through the noise of the crowd on that portable 8-track player…but I hadn't…not really.

Not even in the "imitation" of real music played by the marching band nor as much as I enjoyed Sister Clarice's organ playing when Sister Turner sang along…nothing had come close in comparison to what I was hearing that day.

Most people are brought up being exposed to such things as this but as for me…at ten years old, seeing and hearing anything like this for the first time would have been next to impossible for me describe what was going on right then; I didn't know enough words to define it back in those days. I'm still not real sure if I can now…but I'll try.

Of all I'd ever seen in my whole life before this; nothing had impressed me more. I was mesmerized by how this group of seven rugged looking men, together could take these instruments and make their different sounds come to life.

Two of them would fashion their fingers in different manners, thrust and rake their bows across their fiddles along with others, who even with their eyes closed, could bend and pluck strings as naturally as most folks breathe.

One kept rhythm for the rest to follow with the beat of different drums while yet another played no manmade instrument at all except one he was born with…his mouth.

No, he didn't sing but instead he whistled the most beautiful sounds I'd ever heard. This human being could whistle as good as any bird I had ever heard and do it with the power of the winds in that he didn't seem to tire too easily; yet, its tones were as pleasant as a gentle breeze.

An awesome vibrato carried its weight as he held his mouth close to the microphone to be heard ever so slightly over the rest.

Occasionally, during the culmination of the performance, some of the others would join him in harmony by humming or wailing "O" sounds that mixed for the perfect blend.

To spite their raw looks, this group of hillbillies was able to create the most articulately refined composition that showed their audience another side of who they really were.

Sweet and beautiful sounds flowed through the air and seemed to have some sort of magnetic force that would draw me in and captivate my total attention. It was as if I could feel the tempo in my veins and it sent chills up my spine.

My thoughts danced with the musician's blend of harmonizing notes that played a delightful melody in my ears. Without effort, it ran down my right leg and into my bare foot, causing my heel to roll back, lifting then dropping the ball and toes.

Again and again, with the exciting flow of rhythm, my toes instinctively tapped and kept time with beat of the music.

In its own language, the notes played as words spoken to tell a story to the listeners. Although I couldn't comprehend how such implicit sounds were produced, I felt that understood what they were trying to communicate.

At the end of each amplified feat, I would turn to see the spellbound audience had grown larger, drawing folks in from across the way.

Perpetual smiles accompanied the roaring applause and several shrill whistles would ring out in approval of the latest performance.

Familiar tunes would follow shouts of request while an enthusiastic volunteer would stir up the crowd to clap in time and sometimes sing along.

An old timer took the opportunity to show off some fancy foot work and hand jive. He would occasionally invite a partner to partake in his dance by locking the arms of different ladies who were walking past him, swinging them around in circles. Some played along, while others got embarrassed and bashfully pulled away.

Working his way over to where we were he saw that his style was familiar to Learline and Ed Earl who had a show of their own going on. Baby Sister was delighted to take hold of the man's hands and spin around and around with him, in his quest for fun. Even I twirled around a few times before I got embarrassed and sat back down.

He moved on leaving Ed Earl to partner up with Learline. Giggling and laughing encouraged all of us to join in the spirit of the dance. Cody rolled around then jumped up off the grass circling around them clapping and stomping as if he was imitating the old man. We all laughed as he did a pretty good job of doing so and we all broke into encouraging cheers when he began to tug at Alma to get up and join him.

She resisted at first but Cody kept persisting by pulling at her arms in order to get her up off the blanket. Once Earldean and I got on either side of her pushing and prodding for her to comply with his request, it wasn't long before she started working with us and began to help herself up.

Everyone around us shouted with approval and they began to clap their hands in time with the music while these two momentarily stole the show. The odd couple that they were, somehow managed to synchronize their comical moves in a way that they didn't knock each other down in the process of Alma twirling under Cody's arm while still holding on to his fingers.

Earldean and I were laughing so hard when they reached out and pulled us in with them that our sides were sore. Our laughter and excitement seemed to be their driving force for the brief time they played along. It was so much fun as we spun around with each other until we were dizzy.

When Alma had just about enough she slipped out of the commotion and took her place back on the blanket to be part of the audience. Still laughing Trudy put her arm around her, patted her shoulder and fanned her exhausted friend with a campaign brochure.

Out of breath, Cody fell sprawled out on the ground as if he couldn't go any more. No matter how much we begged him to get back up he just closed his eyes and pretended that he couldn't move.

It frightened us kids to think that he might be really hurt when Learline fell across his chest and he didn't flinch. We turned to see the adults were still laughing at him so we figured he must have been joking as he knew all too well how to do.

Ed Earl, who wasn't sure, thought to test him again to find out, he too fell across Cody's body saying, *"Now try to git up Cody…I bet cha caint do it."*

Learline decided she'd throw out a challenge for him. *"Cody…cain't git up!"*

Just for fun Cody laid there for a few seconds before he suddenly jumped and grabbed them both then began to tickle them.

They shrieked for help between hard giggles, with arms and legs going in every direction during this playful torture. When Earldean and I both went to rescue our siblings we were pulled down into the pile up and tickled too.

When Trudy thought we were getting too rough she sent Debbie running over to pull the baby from the bundle of bodies. Cody didn't have enough arms and legs to hold us all so it wasn't so hard to do. Debbie stood Learline safely back off and out of the way but when she turned to walk away, Cody reached out of the mound and grabbed her ankle.

He was obviously going for a bigger target as she hopped around on the other foot trying to break free from his grip.

She laughed and screamed, *"Help me Ed Earl…he's gonna git me!"*

Ed Earl crawled over and started trying to pry Cody's fingers from around Debbie's ankle.

Before it was all over, with Debbie's help, we were able to get Cody to cry uncle before we turned him loose and let him get up.

"Toodie…you seen um pickin on me like that…why come you let um do me that'a way?" he said, as he pulled his comb from his back pocket to slick his hair back down.

"Maybe ya aught ta be pickin on somebody ya own size, big boy." Trudy told him.

"Alright…" he said, pretending to scan the group for a worthy opponent.

"…Come on Alma…lets me and you go roll around over yonder on the grass and tickle one another…ya 'ont to?"

"Cody…I hardly think we're the same size…now do you?" Alma asked him rhetorically.

She flinched when he stepped over onto the blanket and sat next to her. In a lower tone, he leaned in and responded, *"Well now…I don't know Miss Alma Fey…"*

"What?" she asked, leaning away, grinning at him as if she weren't sure what he might be up to.

Then even more quietly than he had spoken before and thinking no one was paying them any mind I overheard him tell her, *"I think you're the perfect size for me."*

Deputy Reed, who was working crowd control, came over to see what all the commotion was. *"Everything alright over here…from a distance it looked like a fight broke out?"*

"Wa-uh…hey Dep…Naw…aint no trouble here." Cody reassured him.

"Just Cody is all…ya know Trouble is his middle name." Trudy told him.

"Naw real trouble, Deputy Reed." Earldean said knocking the grass off of her clothes.

"Didn't really think so…just wanted to come over and see if everyone was having a good time."

Yvonne had seen Nolan walking over their way looking hot and thirsty so she passed an Orange Nehi from her ice chest over to Estelle.

"Well that's mighty nice of you to check on us." Estelle said as she removed the bottle top with a pop opener. *"I think everybody is having a wonderful time, don't you Hank?"*

"I think so." Doc replied. *"Ya hear from anybody yet, Nolan?"*

The Deputy just made a disappointed expression and slowly shook his head no.

Estelle had passed the bottle of cold drink over to Trudy who knew that this was Nolan's favorite drink…being that he was one of her most favorite customers, she would know that sort of thing about him.

"We havin lots a fun…" Ed Earl said with a laugh. *"We made Cody say uncle!"*

"Doin all right, Nolan? Thirsty?" Trudy asked as she stood and handed him the drink.

"Orange…my favorite…why thank you Miss Trudy…don't mind if I do."

He turned the pop up and drank it down. In one long pose he emptied the whole bottle.

"Thank ya…that was mighty thoughtful of ya." he said as he wiped his mouth with the back of his hand then handed her the empty bottle with a wink.

Trudy who had sat back down just waiting and watching said, *"Ya welcome Darlin!"*

She tilted her head to play with one of her red curls around her neck. *"…ya wanna sit down here with us…we'll make room…get up Cody… let this tired officer rest."*

"No, no that's quite alright Miss Trudy. I'm on duty."

"Toodie dootie." Learline said again and again as she crawled over Trudy's lap then around behind her and back again. *"Tootie dutie…"*

Ed Earl liked the attention his little sister got from it so he started chanting it with her and circling around Trudy as well. Though this was getting on her nerves, Trudy tried to keep her composure while talking with the officer who was competing for her attention.

The Deputy rescued Trudy from her distress by picking up Learline and tossing her up in the air. *"That's right baby girl…tell Miss Trudy I'm on duty…"* he said before he rested her on his shoulders for a short ride. *"But maybe I can meet up with ya'll after I get off. Where will you be around four o'clock?"*

Trudy stood up again and followed Deputy Reed so that she could talk with him while he gave Learline her ride on his shoulder.

"Uncle huh?" Cody said to Ed Earl in efforts to get the boy's attention when he started to follow them. He was successful in doing so as the tickling started back up.

When Alma attempted to protect Ed Earl from any sort of relapse, she asked that he settle down some as not to get over heated. Cody took this as a cue to include Alma in on the tickling attack. It was so funny to have them play with us. And though she hollered for him to stop, I think she really was having a good time too.

It was a blessing to be momentarily carefree of worries that had held us captive in the idle efforts of unifying our family once more.

Our caretakers were elated to see how easily we were amused by the simple pleasures of life that would give us temporary separation from our anxiety.

Alma turned to Cody and made a rhetorical statement by saying something to the effect of, *"This was just what the doctor ordered."* Doc smiled and said to them, *"For this group…this was the best therapy of all."*

After the Labor Day picnic, we had to say goodbye to Debbie and wondered if we would ever see her again. We parted with the faith that the circumstances that had brought us together in the first place, would be far better when we reunited again.

School would be starting up in a few days and with no sign of our parents we would be faced with the dilemma of the next step with the social workers.

On Tuesday, the third of September, the day after Labor Day, Sheriff McCoy came with an update on the search. He said a salesman from Mason's Used cars over near Jay, Oklahoma had reported a man fitting the description of our Daddy. He was said to have been on the car lot looking around and claiming that he was looking to trade in his old truck in on a newer model that was in better shape. He had identified the trade in as being the same truck from the picture we had; the one found on the side of the road.

When he couldn't find anything in his price range he sent him over to see his cousin that had a fixer upper he might would sell to him real cheap.

Further investigation had found that the cousin had indeed sold a truck for cash on the 2nd of August. He had signed the title over to a man by the name to Earl Johnson with an address in Winslow, Arkansas. The cousin said that there was no trade-in mentioned and that this Earl Johnson had hitch-hiked over to his place carrying a backpack of some sort.

Neither of the two men knew anything else about him and had never remember seeing him before. They both said that he seemed preoccupied and in a hurry to get back on the road.

He had asked me for more information about the contents of this supposed deep freeze I had told Cody about. He said he would see that the investigators got the information.

He was about to leave when he remembered something else. Stopping to pull a piece of paper from his pocket, he opened it then asked us if we new anyone by the name of James Denby.

When we told him that he was our friend that moved away, he informed us that Denby had contacted the Sheriff's office sending a message for us.

"Says here that he'll be arivin on Friday with his niece and will be a stayin with some kinfolks over near Bugtussel. Says he'll look ya'll up as soon as he gets settled in and can get one of um ta bring him in ta town." Sheriff said as he read off the note.

"Denby's commin back?" I asked.

"What it says here." he answered.

"Does he know bout us not finding Mama an Daddy and all?" Earldean inquired.

"I'm purdy sure he does" he said, *"...bein he contacted the police to get a message to ya. We wanted to make sure he was on the up and up before we told him where ya'll was a stayin. We'll get back with ya on that when he gits here... alrite?"*

"Thanks Sheriff." she said.

After he left we were giddy with joy about getting to see Denby again. It had been so long and we had really missed him. Daddy and Mama wouldn't want to miss seeing him either.

Me and Earldean agreed that we had to do everything we could to try to find them before Denby came for his visit. We'd have tried to find them ourselves if we could...if only we knew where else to look.

25
ONE STEP FORWARD…TWO STEPS BACK

It was Doc's persistence that urged the police to go back out and search more for any records that would let him know more about our vaccinations.

The State's Social workers were doing everything they could to research any records, now that they had a last name to go by. Yet, with school starting up there was an urgency to find out for sure. In the efforts for the state's health department to help control contagious diseases, it was necessary for all students to have their immunization shots.

They couldn't take the risk of revaccinating within a certain time frame without putting our health in danger.

At first, from their point of view, the police and just about everyone else was sure that with the way that the inside of bus had been found, it was apparent the place had been vandalized. With everything in there overturned and torn up it appeared as though there might have been a struggle. With all the blood they found on the scene, somebody was bound to be hurt but if so, where were they? If someone was murdered there, the killer made a poor attempt to cover it up. However, without any body, or bodies, to prove otherwise, most just gave up on anything more than abandonment.

Doc had not told me at the time but from the beginning, he had a gut feeling that there was something more to this case than the presumption of abandonment. Especially after he had spent so much time with us and had gotten to know us better, he couldn't help but feel that these parents of ours wouldn't just walk away.

When the detectives were tied up with all the paperwork, they weren't seen around as much, so, most people thought they had done all they could do and just moved on to more important cases. Without any new information to broadcast it seemed to have lost interest in the public view.

They soon had replaced the story on the TV and radio with accounts of other more important news; mostly about the war,

President Johnson's last days in office and the new presidential candidates.

None of that stuff made any sense to me at the time but I watched closely just in case my parents showed up on the screen. I was especially interested after Doc explained how, with modern technology, they could film something way out in California and other faraway places and have it on the five o'clock news that very same day.

Estelle must have thought it was a waste of my time because she was always after me to turn off the set and go play. She was particularly sensitive to some of the violent battle scenes they would often show, probably because of her son still being over there in Vietnam. These were more than any of us could bare, especially her.

Newspapers no longer carried the story about our search; they too were just a repeat of the television news. However, the Town Talk circular did still have that tiny article in the exact same spot on the second to the last page every week but most folks just skipped over it; you can only read it so many times before you know it by heart.

Some of the "missing persons'" posters had been pulled down and replaced with promotional signs for the Labor Day Celebrations, then those were replaced with political campaigning. There were a few posters about our missing parents that were still left hanging about in remote spots, faded by the sun and wilted from the rain beyond legibility.

According to some, the Clifton police had passed it off, assuming this was another example of worthless, irresponsible people that were too lazy to work and would rather starve to death than pay taxes. They weren't worried about having to deal with us and were glad that we took a wrong turn at the top of the path and went the other way.

Of course, this just made us look even dumber but how were we to know Clifton was the closer town? Personally, I'm glad we went the wrong way…turning right instead of left was in our favor when we ended up where we did…so right was right! The State police originally had their suspicions that this couple must have been hiding out, maybe dealing with drugs or some other form of illegal activity. With other more important cases on their work load, it seemed that they too had let this case grow cold when they found no evidence to support their suspicions.

Since there was no signs of abuse, the overburdened welfare department was not in a hurry to remove us from danger or place us in an orphanage, especially since we had a safe place to stay for the time being.

Most of the townspeople had started getting used to seeing us around and had other things to worry about besides the fact that we were still there waiting for our parents to come find us.

We did however, have a small support group there in Whisper Ridge who stood behind us and didn't turn us away. From the beginning they showed compassion and concern about our predicament. They had shown us that they cared about what was going to happen to us. They accommodated and fed us, making us a priority in their lives.

Although they had no answers for us, they were patient, kind and consoling. Most importantly, they had shown no signs of giving up on us.

The Wednesday afternoon showers had left a trail of assorted cloud formations for the sun to paint, as it settled in the western sky. Estelle and Doc were commenting about the spectacular beauty of this sunset on our way to the church early that evening.

We were at the end of the road and about to pull out on the highway when we saw the police in two different squad cars signal to turn.

They were coming from the opposite direction of town and the first of these got Doc's attention when he turned on his flashing lights.

When he recognized it was Sheriff McCoy, Doc rolled down his window and waited to see what he wanted.

"Howdy Sheriff!" Ed Earl shouted from over the back seat, waving his hand through the opening.

"Hey son." Sheriff responded in a serene voice lifting only his fingers in a subtle wave.

"Doc…" he said, bringing his car up beside us, *"…sumppin's come up…we gonna need to see ya'll bout it…can we meet back at your place?"*

"Sure...that'll be fine…meet ya there." Doc responded without hesitation.

As the sheriff pulled on down the road, we could see that a state trooper was driving the other car. He was carrying a passenger but we couldn't tell who it was.

"Wonder what all that's about?" Estelle mumbled.

"Don't know, but I guess we'll find out." Doc said as he turned the car around in the road to head back.

"Why didn't you ask him?" Estelle asked, turning her head to assist him in maneuvering the big car on the narrow turn around. *"...I hope it doesn't take long, we don't want to be late for prayer meeting!"*

"It must be important if the state police came along." he calmly responded. *"If it was just a tad bit of news, I don't think he would have asked us to turn around and go back...he could obviously see we were on our way out."*

"Ya thank maybe they'z found Mama and Daddy?" Earldean asked.

"Bet he found um in theyz new truck...I thank at man told my Daddy he wuz a gonna git him a new truck!" Ed Earl said hopefully.

"I saw somebody up in that other police car...recon it wuz Daddy?" I asked.

"Don't know who that was...couldn't tell...didn't get a good look." Doc said.

"It looked like a man in there...to me it did." Earldean added.

"Hey, Maybe it's that neighbor friend of yall'z...what's his name...Denby?" Doc guessed, eager the meeting would be a happy one like that.

"He's not suppose to be here until Friday." Estelle informed him.

"He might a come early...ya recon?" I supposed, although, I still preferred it be Daddy as eager as I was see Denby. If it was in fact our father, we could cut through the chase and get back out to the hollow where our mother would be waiting for our happy return.

We would need to remind Daddy that we were low on supplies so he could buy some while we're in town, before we go back. Mama would want some sugar so she could cook up a cobbler with company coming. There might still be plenty of black berries if they haven't dried out on the vine or the birds eaten them all. I'd hoped whoever was taking care of our animals remembered to milk the goats so that they'd still be giving plenty.

We could tell Mama about all our adventures while we shelled a mess of peas and Daddy and Ed Earl skinned a few rabbits. Over supper, they could tell us about all the places where they had gone looking for us. We'd laugh about how we waited for them to find us in town, where we had been there all along.

After supper Earldean could help Mama clean up and spruce up the place a little before Friday when Denby was coming for sure. Ed Earl and I would help Daddy dig worms for bait so we could all go fishin.

"We'll need lots a worms!"

"Worms?...Fer what...What cha needs worms fer Sassy?" Ed Earl asked me, waking me from my daydreaming.

"What cha mummblin bout over there?" Earldean asked me.

"Nuttin...Iz just thankin out loud." I said not wanting to get our hopes up again.

"I show ya were ta find sum worms...under them flower pots by the back door...I seen sum big uns out younder when..."

Ed Earl was volunteering this knowledge when Estelle interrupted with a thought that she'd better warn him not to get his good church clothes dirty.

"This might not take that long so ya'll don't run off diggin in the mud!"

We held our breath when Doc turned the car into the driveway, never taking our eyes off the passenger in the troopers' patrol car.

"Should I wait in the car with the kids, while you find out what's goin on?" Estelle asked.

Doc didn't answer as the car came to a stop and he put it in park...he too kept an eye aimed at the passenger as he got out of the car.

"Aww Heck! That aint my Daddy...it aint Denby neither!" Ed Earl affirmed with disappointment, falling back on the seat and folding his arms.

Earldean physically showed obvious signs of discontent herself when she blew out a strong sigh, shaking her head saying, *"I should a known...they aint never gonna find um!"*

Sadly enough, it wasn't either one. Just another man that didn't look anything like Daddy or Denby.

At that moment I was angry with myself for getting my hopes up, only to be let down, yet was hungry for answers and couldn't help but wonder what information, if any, that Sheriff McCoy had to offer.

Doc killed the engine when he saw that the men were waiting by the Sheriffs car for us to get out.

"...*Well?"* Estelle questioned, still waiting for an answer.

"Yea, ahh…wait here." Doc said looking at his watch before he got out.

Through the windshield we watched as the men greeted him with a handshake before Sheriff took off his hat and fanned his perspiring face with it. He was only there for a minute before he returned to the car with instructions for his wife.

"Best take the kids on into the house…and put on some coffee…" Doc said looking at his watch. *"I have a feelin we might not make it in time for services…Sounds said this might take a while."*

"What is it Hank?" she asked, reading something more in his voice than he was trying to let on.

"Ya'll go on inside now ya hear? I'll be along a minute." Doc instructed in a protective manner.

Estelle didn't hesitate after that. Getting out of the car she proceeded to corral us up into the house saying, *"OK…Lets let see bout getting these men folk some refreshments, make um feel welcome."*

Turning back I found my little brother shaking hands with the officers, standing eye level the trooper's holstered gun. He was asking him if it was the same kind of six shooter the Cartwright Boys have on the TV show Bonanza.

"…come on Ed Earl...you too!" she coached him to follow. With dejection he trailed behind dragging his feet.

Once inside, Estelle went to the kitchen to make coffee while we kids watched the exchange from the window.

Their conversation was muffled by the distance and glass but I could tell by their body language, that it was an intense one. Doc had his back to us so I couldn't see his face but I watched, as he shook his head just before he stepped into a pace with no more than four steps either way.

I saw Sheriff McCoy put his hand on Doc's shoulder as if to get him to stand still and listen to what he was trying to tell him. Doc resisted and it looked to me like it wasn't something he wanted to hear.

All kinds of bad scenarios raced through my mind. Could it be that Denby called to say he wasn't coming, because maybe he fell again and can't get up? Were they telling Doc that they were tired of dealing with us and were officially giving up the search? Was he irritated that we were still infringing on his life and was angry because they couldn't find our parents?

My biggest fear was that they were there to take us away to live in an orphanage with other misfits.

Estelle called us away from the window and into the kitchen, pretending to need help. She tried to busy us with simple tasks that she could have easily done faster. Things like counting out enough napkins for everyone and wiping off the already clean table. She had Earldean fill the creamer while she filled up the sugar bowl.

"Reckon I'z ta git ta eat another slab a that chocolate cake, Estelle?" Ed Earl asked her.

"Maybe…lets wait and offer our guests some first OK?...maybe after you change into your PJ's." she bribed.

About that time Doc came through the door with Sheriff McCoy, the state trooper and the other man who I recognized as having seen somewhere before.

After Estelle was introduced, she offered them a seat at the table where she would serve them their coffee. She noticed that the men seemed to be somewhat anxious, almost reluctant to sit, indicating this was not a social visit.

Sending us off to get out of our church clothes and into our new pajamas gave her a chance to find out what was going on. Ed Earl raced ahead to finish so he could get back for the cake.

By the time I had changed and made it back downstairs, Estelle had sliced the cake but nobody was eating any of it, except my little brother.

She appeared to be on the verge of another change in disposition about the time I reached the kitchen. At first I would have guessed that she was insulted that her guests were refusing her offer of refreshments, so I asked for a piece for my sake as well as hers.

Her hand was shaking as she laid a slice across a small plate then excused herself to make some phone calls from her bedroom.

Learline thought it was a good idea for her baby doll to have her own piece of cake so Earldean cut two tiny pieces to appease them both.

I turned to find a place at the table when Doc got up and offered his seat then found some more chairs to accommodate everyone.

The State Trooper, still persistent in standing, found it more comfortable to lean next to the counter, holding his hat in his hands.

There was tension in the air and even Doc had a certain manner about him that was a bit out of character for his nature.

Sheriff McCoy cleared his throat, then looking at the other man said, *"While we're waiting for Mrs. Murphy, Detective Glenn has some questions I think he wants to ask ya'll…"*

"Yes…We should do that first…" the man said in a deep gentle voice. Something about his voice sounded vaguely familiar to me.

I slowly savored the rich chocolate flavor of the homemade frosting in my mouth and watched as he reached for a small pad and a pen he carried his shirt pocket. Trying to place where I'd seen him before, I studied his face as he began to speak.

"I understand you told the sheriff here all about why you came here looking for your father. I want to go over everything to make sure we didn't leave anything out." he said, flipping over a few pages then wetting the tip of his pen on his tongue.

"You the one who made my piture…aintcha?" I asked him, remembering then where I knew him from.

"I believe so…yes."

"I still got it…I showed it to some folks…but I'm gonna keep it forever!"

"I talked with your parent's friend James…" he said *"…and he told me that your parents have been living out there for some time. How long have you known this…James Denby?"*

"We knowed him all our life…he's just all time been there cross the lake…till he took too sick from his fall." Earldean told him. *"Then his sister come an took him off ta stay wit her over'n Sikeston. He said he's a commin back…hear tell he'll be ere Fridee!"*

"We thought you'z him when we seen't cha in that car out younder on the road." Ed Earl said with a mouth full of cake.

Earldean, mothering him, fussed saying, *"Ed Earl you gonna choke! ...Swaller Ya food fore ya speak, like Estelle done toll ya already, boy!"*

When Ed Earl made a face at her, the man smiled before he continued with his questions. *"…this Mr. Denby told us on the phone that your last name is Johnson…is that correct?…Are you the Johnson's?"*

"Naw…don't know no John…I'm Earls son…My name's Ed Earl but sometimes he calls me son…Doc calls me son too…but Mama sometimes calls me boy cause sometimes she sayz…how'z my boy doin taday…er where'z my boy at…stuff like that…Earldean sayz boy too…but Daddy and Doc call me son…And Sheriff McCoy…that's what he calls me most timez." When he finished rattling off all that, he quickly stuffed a big bite of cake in his mouth that had been waiting on the fork only inches away. It was as

though he had to get it all said between bites so Earldean wouldn't fuss at him again.

Doc smiled as straightened up in his chair, then under his breath he said to the Sheriff, *"Oh boy…this could take a while…getting answers is not a problem…but getting the right ones…well…"*

Sheriff McCoy rephrased the question, *"Ok son…Johnson is a last name…Did ya'll ever hear ya Daddy or ya Mama call that name?"*

"Johnson ya say?" Earldean answered. *"Naw…we don't know any Johnson."*

"Yea we do…well…sorta like that." I said, reminding Earldean of where we had heard the name before. *"You know…Johnson, Johnson, Johnson…that shakin box Daddy brought home fer Learline when she wuz a lot'ole baby? She kept that empty box long time even after Ed Earl shook all the white stuff out."*

"That's right!" Earldean recalled. *"I plum fergot bout that…Mama wus glad to get it for the baby but she liked ta use it too…Said it made her soft…smelled good too."*

"Yea…it did smell right nice didn't it?" I agreed. *"She gave Daddy a big ole hug and told him 'Thanks fer the Johnson, Johnson, Johnson; but that's the only Johnson we knowed about."*

"Three Johnson's?" the state trooper asked. *"I thought it was just two…you are talking about Johnson and Johnson baby powder aren't you?"*

"Yea that's it!" Earldean yelled in agreement as she spun around in her chair toward the officer. *"Baby powder…But it's called Johnson Johnson Johnson…least way'z that's what Mama all time calls it."*

"Really?" he said scratching his head, *"…'Cause…we've got a new born… and I was pretty sure…"* his voice tapered off as he slipped back into thought.

The men sat quietly puzzled for a few seconds before Detective Glenn turned and asked the other men.

"Do you think that… maybe she was just trying to be witty in thanking her husband for the baby gift?"

"What do you mean?" Sheriff McCoy asked.

"Well think about it…John's son…Johnson…Mr. Johnson…"

"OOH…I get it!" the trooper replied. *"Thanks for the Johnson-n-Johnson, then his last name must have been Johnson….Hey, you're pretty good at this detective work."*

"Yea." Doc countered with a smile. *"We could use you around here full time just to get through some dinner conversation…not just with these kids…*

but… maybe you can help me figure out what my wife is talking about half the time these days."

Sheriff shrugged his shoulders and added, *"Yea, mine too…I know what ya mean Doc."*

"Just doin my job is all." the detective said as he jotted something down in his notes then continued with the questions for us.

"Can you tell me about the last time you saw your father…The day before he left for work…how was he acting? Tell me everything you can remember…" he asked looking at Earldean first. *"…one at a time, please."* he said when Ed Earl had attempted to answer at the same time.

We each told our own account of what happened in and around our last weeks out there. For the most part, it was the same as we had told them before except this time, Earldean told them about Mama passing out and her and me thinking she was dead.

We could tell by everyone's reaction that this was new news to them. Even Estelle, who had slipped back into the room from the phone calling, was flabbergasted and drilled us over why we would leave out such an important bit of information. *"You knew this all along…why didn't you tell me?"*

After we explained that we were protecting the little kids, not wanting them to cry, I reminded her that I had mentioned it to her before. She barely recalled me telling her about Mama fainting and thinking she had died. When she did, she said she didn't realize that I was talking about the last time we saw her.

It appeared to be a simple mix up to us but the adults managed to make a big deal out of her fainting. We told them we didn't think it was anything serious after I had passed out that first day in town.

"I didn't die…ya see?" I said. *"…at first I thought I did…but I'm OK!"* I informed them.

Earldean told them that she and I assumed that when we had found her bed empty that day, that Mama too must have fainted, "come to" (regained consciousness), then went out looking for us.

We only assumed that she and Daddy were together because he was due to come home soon and they were both missing.

"The last time you saw her she was in bed…right?" Detective Glenn asked.

"Right! We left her sleepin…in the bus." Earldean said.

"She might of been fainted…that's why come we ta go lookin for Daddy…to make sure."

"Was your mother bleeding when you left?" he asked.

"Bleedin?" I repeated.

"We didn't see no blood...naw she wuttin cut or nuttin...just sick s'all" Earldean assured him, nudging me for confirmation, *"huh...aint that right Sassy?"*

"I didn't see no blood." I said backing her up.

"Which of you were the last to see her?" he asked.

"Sassy wuz...when she went in fer them pank shoes." Earldean answered.

"Mama give em to me...Didn't she Sassy...told her ta give um to me so I'z whouldn't git sore feet...but I still got blisters!" Ed Earl said.

"That wus when we left for town, walkin."

"Did she say anything else that day to ya, Sassy...other than about the shoes?" the detective asked leaning in for an answer.

I shook my head no and looked away, I didn't want to fib. Mama didn't really say he could have the shoes. In fact, she didn't say anything at all, so that part wasn't a lie but I really didn't want to hurt Ed Earl's feelings.

"So she knew you were going to town on foot...and that was OK with her? he asked.

"We had to go find Daddy!" Earldean exclaimed.

"But did she give you permission ...did she say it was alright for you to go all the way to town? This is a long ways from home...a long ways to walk."

"Naw sir..." she mumbled as she squirmed in her chair, *"...but she was too sick to do any talkin...we had to go look fer my Daddy...to tell um bout Mama n'all!*

"Did he know your Mama was sick when he left?"

"She wuz a little bit...but...she got ta feelin too sick ta git up any more...that's why come us to go fetch him from town!"

"Why did you think you could find him here?"

"Well...This is town aint it? Mama said he worked in town." I answered for her when she hesitated, feeling we were on the verge of getting in trouble.

"But he wasn't here...Do you think she might have meant another town?"

"We didn't know there was more than one town then...town wuz all we knowed bout."

"Well...we've checked all the other ones around here..." he said as he rubbed his forehead like his head might have hurt. *"Girls...do you think your Daddy might be hiding out somewhere..."*

"Hidin! Why would he do that?" I asked *"This aint no game or nuttin..."*

"I know to play hide-n-seek..." Ed Earl chimed in. *"...wanna play?"*

Learline slid quickly off her chair and tugged at her brothers pajama sleeve. *"Me too!"* she begged, *"…I play too bubba?"*

"Well…iffin I can eat the rest yo cake." he bargained with her as he reached for her last few bites.

"We don't really know where they at, for sure but I don't thank he'd be hidin for this long a time…do you?" Earldean told the detective. *"We just hope they are both together…out lookin for us…Maybe we aught ta go back out there to stay…wait on um to come home…don't you thank so too Sassy?"*

"They probly out younder right now…maybe when theyz couldn't find us, the'z gave up and went back home." I said, suddenly feeling real homesick again.

"Bet cha at's were az at…I wanna go find um." Ed Earl mumbled, helping Baby Doll finish off her cake too.

"Me too…" Learline added. *"…Me want Mama play hide too!"*

Estelle pulled Learline into her lap, tenderly kissed her on her forehead, and then cuddled her up close to her.

Nobody said anything for a minute. When they just gave one another dismal glances, I thought they might be toying with the idea of letting us go. That was until the Sheriff dropped his head and stared at the table. *"I'm sorry…"* he muttered. *"This is hard…"*

"No, we just came from out there…your parents aren't waiting for you." the detective told us. *"We're sorry."*

"Maybe they wuz down at the creek fishin…did ja look down younder?" Ed Earl quizzed while their heads shook with disappointment.

Doc took hold of Estelle's hand and sighed. Leaning toward her, he quietly asked her, *"Did you get a hold of Alma on the phone?"*

"She's at church…I called Trudy…she's on her way…she may go by the church first." she answered softly. I felt by the way they talked that something was wrong.

"They'za coming over after church?" I asked trying to figure out what was going on.

"Doc…" Sheriff McCoy said getting his attention, *"…it's gettin close to bedtime…huh?…maybe we should finish this tomorrow."*

"Just a few more questions…" Detective Glenn said, *"…tomorrow may be too late, we need to clear up some answers before..."*

"I don't know…" Estelle said. Then with a puff of air, she blew Learline's hair from her eyes while the baby examined the woman's concerned face. *"…think about these kids!"*

"Just one more question tonight." Detective Glenn requested. *"The last time you saw your mother…are you sure she was on the bus?"*

"Yea…she wuz still there when we set out for town!" I answered quickly, wondering why he had asked several times by then. Did he not understand? *"…why?"*

Sheriff McCoy got up to pour himself another cup of coffee, stacking the dessert plates and forks, taking them to the sink.

Detective Glenn closed up his little pad, clicked his pen and tucked them back in his pocket. Pushing himself away from the table he said, *"That's all I have for tonight...thank you for answering my questions…I'm sorry we had to put you through this again."*

Ed Earl was climbing down from his chair when Doc asked him to come to sit by him. He pulled him close to him and said he had something he needed to tell us.

"There is no easy way to say this…" he hesitated while Estelle shifted the baby in her lap. *"We don't know where your Daddy is…but…"* he cleared his throat. *"We know your Mama won't be coming for you…I'm so sorry…but…she's gone."* he said in a gentle voice, his eyes misted over.

Streams of tears now rolled down Estelle's cheek as she held tight to Learline with one arm and with the other she reached out to hold my hand.

"Where did she go?" Ed Earl asked.

"Well son…She's gone to meet her Maker." Doc tried to explain.

"Dead?" Earldean asked. *"…are you sure?"*

Doc, staring into her eyes, pulled his lips taut then slowly shook his head yes.

"NOoooooo!"

26
HOMECOMING

It was as if a nightmare had come to life when suddenly, all that was around me felt distant and unreal, as though it might be happening to somebody else.

My ears took in noise that sounded like rushing wind while the rest of my whole body went numb except for the pain of my breaking heart.

Time stood still as the notion of life without Mama forced its way to my mind. Momentarily, I felt constricted and couldn't move. It was just as well as there was no place to run and hide from the hurt that held me bound.

As hard as I tried to resist what was happening to me, the certainty of my mothers' death was the very thing that made me aware that I was in fact alive…and awake.

I could now feel my small hand being held and squeezed by Estelle's larger one as she pulled me in next to her. I felt the pain deep within me purge its way out in a loud cry breaking the barrier of the initial shock.

Realism had barely set in yet when Alma and Trudy came through the door with their ruddy faces. Having already heard the news, they had mourned for us all the way out to Doc and Estelle's house where they cried along with the rest of us. Alma, Trudy, Estelle and Doc huddled close for the worse part and held us through the sobs and tears.

Learline wasn't quite sure what to make of the news so she mostly cried out of fear of what was happening to the rest of us.

Ed Earl was not prepared to accept the fact that we were never going to see Mama again, whereas me and Earldean had held the secret of her death; hidden behind denial and the false hope of our youthful innocence.

As word got out, the house filled with neighbors and church folks who came after the prayer meeting had been interrupted with the news of Mama's death. Some showed up out of curiosity but most showed up for support and to help grieve our loss. People that had never met our mother cried along with us as if it had been their own.

We didn't think our sadness could get worse until this. It was hard to understand why such a thing could happen. It hurt so bad I just wanted to die too. The pain in my chest was almost unbearable as I cried uncontrollably for the longest time.

Detective Glenn and the state trooper had left shortly after some of news reporters from the papers, T.V. and the local radio station arrived. Sheriff McCoy stayed behind for a while trying to explain what they had found when they went back out to Chinquapin Hollow.

The rain storms we had recently had washed away some of the dirt from Mama's shallow grave.

"We must have missed her somehow when we were out there searching around the first time…" Sheriff McCoy told the reporters, trying to answer their flood of questions. *"It…the body…was hidden deep in the crevice of a ravine…Ya cain't dig more than an inch or two before hittin a rock bed in them parts...guess a bottom of a wash out's bout the only place ta find nuff dirt to cover a body. She was mostly buried under a pile of small stones and gravel…the only thing left holdin her down after the recent rains…The swarm of flies and the stench is what give it away…The coroner figured she'd been there for about a month or so. We're not sure how she got buried there…the cause a death aint been determined yet…No we're not rulin out murder yet…We're sendin the body to Little Rock for an autopsy…We'll know more when the test results get back…NO! Ya cain't take a statement from the children! What kind a question is that? Them youngins don't know any more than the rest of ya!…We don't know where their father is…NO the children aren't suspects! That's all we have right now…No more questions…Please! Let's move out and give the Murphy's some time to help sort this out with them kids in there…Thank you."* he said as he tried to help clear the house and yard by sorting the real help from the curiosity seekers.

It was almost ten thirty when Alma and Trudy left, saying they would be back in the morning to help Estelle.

My head hurt from all the crying that would come and go in waves throughout my sleepless night. Doc and Estelle got up several times in the night, more with me and Earldean than with the two younger ones, to console us.

"Doc…what's gonna happen to us if we don't find Daddy?" I asked, needing to know the truth. *"Are they gonna send us to the*

orphanage…Huey says he heard it's a bad place to live…Kids that ain't got nobody to take care of um there!"

"Oh sweetheart, that's not true!" he responded passionately, drawing me close to his chest. *"They have people there who take care of the orphans…good folks that love little children. They work and live there so that they can look after them full time. They see to it that the children have warm dry beds and good food to eat. They see to it that the children go to school and have lots of other kids to play with."*

"But theyz ain't got no mamas and daddies to love um!"

"Some don't but they find others to love…love finds them."

"If we don't find Daddy can we stay here with you…and Estelle…we can be your youngins…ya'lls is all gone, ain't they…don't cha want some more?"

"Sassy…you would be a wonderful little girl to have for a daughter and so would your sisters…and Ed Earl is a good son…Your Daddy's son…Don't forget about him…his family might would have some say so in all this!"

"Family?" I asked. *"Mama and Daddy wus my family…now it's just us kids…that ain't much a nuttin wit out nobody to look out fer us. I'm scared Doc!"*

"You have every right to be afraid…that's perfectly natural…I know you can't see clear to what is going to happen at this point and neither can I tonight, however, God knows!"

"I wish He'd tell me then!"

"I guess this is one of them times your just gonna have to trust Him, huh? Faith, Sassy…Faith and trust."

"Who's gonna wanna fool wit us orphan hillbillies if Daddy don't come back for us?"

"Don't you worry no more about that…You are loving children…I believe the Good Lord is looking out for you, I have a feeling everything will turn out all right."

I wanted to go to sleep on those reassuring words, *"…every thing will turn out all right."*

The next few days were long but filled with folks stopping by to offer prayers and comfort food, while the adults made arrangements for some kind of memorial services for Mama. Brother Hemphill said we could wait for the body and have a funeral then but they weren't sure how long that was going to take. Then too, there was a cost involved with the funeral home, so someone volunteered to look into what could be done under this kind of circumstance.

When the flow of good deeds tapered down to a handfull of close friends and an occasional phone call, Estelle would find us counting the hours until Friday, when Denby would make it into town.

We were ecstatic when she got the call announcing his arrival. Our enthusiasm had us begging her to let us wait for him by the end of the driveway. Much to her disapproval she consented only if we promised to stay out of the road. With that we were out the door before she changed her mind when Alma volunteered to go with us to keep us out of the way of cars turning in. Figuring it might be a while before he got there, Alma grabbed a folding lawn chair from the carport to sit under a shade tree in the front yard. Festus, being the self-proclaimed guard dog he was, scurried from his wallowed out watch post to follow us.

It seemed to take forever as we took turns stretching our necks in competition of the first peek of Denby turning down the road. Alma did her best to keep us preoccupied with guessing games and silly songs as time drug on.

We bounced around with giddiness when we saw him coming, chasing the car all the way down the drive. Alma was trying to keep up the whole way, yelling, *"Ya'll wait…Be careful!…Stay back!…Let them park the car before you git run over!*

Denby was grinning from ear to ear as he pulled himself out of the car and walked toward us with the help of a cane. He was much thinner than I remembered and had aged a little but his light green eyes sparkled still the same.

"Denby!" we all yelled over and over, *"Ya come back!"*

He was bound in the doorway of the car by hugs that almost made him lose his balance. Each of us were pushing our way to him, including Festus, who's constant barking rolled into howls amongst all the commotion.

"My, my, my…How you have all grown!" he exclaimed. *"Earldean…Look at you!...and…Ed Earl…is that you?…what a big boy! Why you were just knee high to a grasshopper when I saw you last!"*

I kept one hand on his waist, afraid to let go, making sure it wasn't just another dream. *"You're really here!"* I said.

"There's my girl…Sassy just look at you! Yes…I'm really here."

"I missed you Denby…I knew you'd come back…like ya promised." I proclaimed.

"I've missed ya'll too!" he said with sincerity. *"…and who is this little whipper snapper?"*

"That's Learline!" I said *"…My baby sister!"*

"Baby?" he responded, as he bent down and gently patted her on top of her head. *"Why she's much bigger than a lit'lo bitty baby. Why just look at her…She'z walkin around and talkin…"*

"She aint gonna be no baby no more, she turns three purdy soon!" Ed Earl claimed.

"Three…My Goodness…has it been that long?"

"I TWO BUBBA!" she loudly insisted, holding up her two fingers to prove it.

Alma stepped forward and picked her up when Ed Earl again tried to change her mind.

"How ya doin?" she said, extending her hand to introduce herself. *"My name's Alma Nettles…I've heard a whole lot about you Mr. Denby!"*

"All good, I hope…" he said taking her hand in his. *"Glad to meet cha."*

"Oh it's my pleasure…these kids are crazy about cha." she said.

"She's our good friend that helps take care of us." I told him.

"Well then…you can call me Denby too!"

"Yea, she's our new friend! She give me stitches when I cut open my leg…wanna see my scar?" Ed Earl said, sticking his leg out to show him.

"Let's back up and let him get out of the car good…bet he would like a cup of coffee." Alma said.

Denby introduced everyone to his cousin, Harold, who had given him a ride over there. He then reached into the car and pulled out a brown paper sack that was rolled shut at the top. Assuming he was planning to stay and that the sack contained his change of clothes, I offered to carry it for him as we made our way into the house.

Estelle and the other folks who were there met us at the car. A person would have thought some famous movie star had arrived with the red carpet treatment Denby was given as he walked through the door. Truth of the matter was this man was the only known person outside of us four kids, to have had any ties with our parents and could possibly solve some of the mystery behind the dead woman and her missing husband.

Once settled in Denby marveled once more over our growth and told us how much we looked like both our parents; Earldean and Ed Earl more like Daddy, and me and Learline more like Mama.

He had been gone for over three years and I didn't remember him being so thin. His clothes were clean and neatly pressed and his shoes were polished. His whiskers were shaven and his hair was cut neatly to his hat-less head.

When I asked about where his cap was he said that in the weakness of his recovery, his sister did away with it saying it had a smell to it.

"Yea, she done her best make me citified." he said. *"She seen fit ta clean me up…make me fittin to socialize and tolerable to be around…like I was fore my wife Virginia passed on, God rest her soul."*

Estelle told Denby and his cousin Harold to make themselves at home while she and about six or seven women scrambled about the kitchen simply to fix two plates of food from the bounty of provisions that had made its way to Estelle's kitchen. We gathered around the table while they ate, not wanting to leave his side. The rest of the folks talked in hushes around the kitchen, pretending to have business in there in hopes that they might be able to hear some of the conversation. Denby had always been a good listener and never minded us kids rattling on about first one thing then another and this visit was no different. With his pale jade eyes fixed on our facial expressions and his ears fine tuned to make out our chattering, he would soon be absorbed in the tales of adventure in our coming to Whisper Ridge.

Though Learline had never met him, she had heard of us talk of Denby like other kids might have talked about Santa Clause. She followed our lead of affection and interest in this old man and took up with him right away. He had hardly finished eating before she had crawled up into his lap where I used to sit. He made over her so and said he remembered when I was her age, how he use to call me his little shadow because I followed him around everywhere.

Not wanting to miss meeting Denby when he arrived into town, Trudy made arrangements to come out and meet our beloved friend we had told her so much about. She arrived just about the same time Doc made it home, after finishing his early day at the clinic. Several other interested parties were there to meet this possible missing link.

Estelle offered coffee as we all made our way to the living room where Denby told his awaiting audience of his accounts in Chinquapin Hollow.

27
FOR OLD TIMES SAKE

Still not quite sure why everyone was so receptive to his arrival and making such a fuss over him being there, Denby appeared to be a little shaky with a room full of people waiting to hear what he had to say.

Letting the adults take the proper seating, we kids found a place and sat on the floor at his feet in front of the oversized chair. He scanned the room over the rim of his hot coffee cup as he drew a long cautious sip. *"I don't know if I can be of any help to anybody seein's how I aint got no idea where to start lookin fer Earl."* he said resting his cup on his knee then making eye contact with Earldean. *"I wuz sure sorry to hear bout ya mama."* he whispered with his raspy voice, choking back his sorrow.

Estelle came from across the room with a tissue for the tear that escaped the well in his eye then ran down his leathered cheek.

Turning back to Doc he explained his emotions. *"Earl and Little Mama have been like family to me..she wuz jest so young...it's a cryin shame, I tell ya."*

After a brief lapse of silence that was broken by the sound of him taking another long sip of coffee, Denby went on to tell of how he met our parents and the history of their relationship.

He shared a few interesting details of how they all looked after one another and got along so well that they grew to be more than just friends and neighbors. *"They's wuttin nuttin but yungins themselves when I met um…Didn't have much except a broken down old school bus and a little ole baby…playin house out there in the woods. They never talked about movin on…like they wuz stuck out there with no place else to go…I figured they wuz tryin to hide out from their folks being so young and with a baby and all…and from what I understood, they never really had no legal marriage. Well it wuttin too long before I realized there wuz another baby on the way…You Sassy…I wuz there when you'z born…Right out yonder in the woods!"*

"The woods…really? Trudy asked.

"Yep, didn't have time to get to the hospital, she wuz pert near born when I got there. I cut the cord and was the very first one to hold this lit'lo peanut!" he said with a grin as he patted my head. *"It was just as well…"* he continued,

"Earl didn't have much fer hospitals and doctors no how…uuh…No offense Doc…"

"None taken." Doc replied as he rearranged himself in his chair.

"Naw, ole Earl had some bad encounters or some sorrta dealins wit um…he'd git mad just talking bout it. So, I done my best to steer clear of the subject as to not get his feathers ruffeled…Specially seein how a birthin ought ta be a happy time!

He'z glad he didn't have to take his gal off way down there just to have a baby. Oh, he seen to it she wuz made as comfortable as he could and though I thought she'd be better off with a woman's help…she come through just fine…sayin she would do it again iffin she had to...and…she did! Bout four years later…Ed Earl there come along!"

Ed Earl perked up with his big toothless grin when he heard his name and asked, *"Me?...Ya talkin 'bout me?"*

"Aaat's right lit'feller, you!" Denby proudly told him when he stopped for a moment to pat little brother on the head.

"Little Mama just knowed it was a gonna be a boy all whilst she wuz a carryin…kept rubbin her belly a sayin 'It's a little Earl'…said she knowed he was his Daddy's boy cause he kept a polkin at her ribs tryin to git her to laugh though she didn't thank it wuz so funny!

Well, I missed that birthin…Earl brought that un in own his own…but they give the boy baby my middle name…Ed…Short for Edward…Stuck it on the front so's it would sound a little different when me or them gals would call um fer sumpthin….Earl and Ed Earl. I felt a might honored to have a name sake…Believe Earl also took it from his own Daddy…name's Edward too…said they called him Ed…If I remember right."

"Now Earl…well he does what he can ta keep um fed and warm in the winter. He might have to go off from time to time to make enough money to take um through till some local work would come along. Back when I'z a livin out yonder, I checked in on um almost daily whilst he was away.

Marline was a good little ole gal…worked all time makin a home…tendin chores and such…doin what had ta be done and makin so over them youngins. I never heard her complain…they's both good ta me."

"That's it!" Earldean exclaimed. *"Marline…that's my Mama's real name, I couldn't ra-member! We all just called her Mama for so long…I just plum forgot it."*

"Well I wuttin much help…" Denby replied, *"…I called her Little Mama for so long, I almost forgot myself."*

He went on to tell how he had not seen any of us since he moved and how he missed his life back home.

"I heard from them a time or two but the letters had no return address and I didn't think to ask before I left if they had a post office box where they got mail so'z we could drop a line er two…I recon Marline got the address from my sister sometime b'fore we took off up yonder to Sikeston."

"My sister made out like I was goin home wit her to live up there…wanted me to shut the house down fer good and wuz after me to sell it. I figured I'd be a commin back in a few months when I got ta feelin better…Never had any idée I'd be away fer so long."

"I took awful sick for spell…like ta never got my strength back I aint fer from feelin better right today but I mustered up enough to come look after these youngins till we git holt of Earl."

With a bit of difficulty he set his coffee cup on the side table then reached down to get the brown paper bag that rested beside his chair. Opening it he reached inside and drew out a small stack of letters that were bound together with rubber bands. He clasped them with both hands as if to protect their content saying, *"I recognized the papers these letters is written on…For Christmas one year, I give Marline a writin set …a tablet that come with flowerdy lookin envelopes and a ink pen in a nice lit'lo box..She made over it so…said it was too purdy to write on and was afraid she would mess it up! Looks like she got over it…I saved all the letters to read over again…she kept it up I guess till she ran out of paper. They kept me up on the news there in the holler…such as it was…the weather…the ole home place…the kids and the news about little Learline being born out yonder. I kept up wit where Earl wuz workin by lookin at the postmark."*

"I figured he'd mail um when he went off to work…Looks like he might have had to drive off a fer piece for a job at times." Walking his fingers through the stack he strained his eyes to read the faded names of the towns' postmarks. *"Lincoln, Tulsa, Fayetteville, Joplin, Jay, Fort Smith…here's one clear up in Springfield! Several smaller towns in the bunch, few of um from Clifton but not a sangle one from Whisper Ridge."*

"He'z done all kinds of work…farm hand, field hand, crop pickin, dirt work…a little paintin or some roofin and what not…just whatever come along at the time…but mostly auto mechanic…occasionally he dreamed of opening his own shop…being his own boss."

"I'm sure he's out there workin somewhere…could be just about anywhere…I'm surprised though he aint come in for a spell…It's not like him to stay gone this long without checking on his family. He claimed he was savin up to

buy a trailer house and have it put out there in the holler as soon as he could stake claim that he homesteaded that land. Could be that he's off workin on that situation…Still…he should be back by now." Denby said scratching his head before reaching into his sack again.

As he did, Doc found opportunity to ask him, *"Did they ever talk about their families…where they were from…who they were?"*

"Not much." he answered. *"…seemed like a sore subject so I didn't bring it up. On occasion, one of the other might mention a family member but they didn't talk much about their past beyond their courtin days. Earl had an aunt and uncle he lived with down near Winslow…his Mama's brother, I believe… don't know if they still livin…I remember him telling me one of um took sick and died…that's been a while back."*

He pulled from the sack a piece of deer skin and unfolded it on his lap. *"Lookie here…They give me this here vest. Earl cleaned the hide and little Mama stitched it together fer me. Ain't it nice? It was one of many homemade gifts they give me…never had enough money for a store bought presents…these kind was much better anyhow."*

He passed the vest around for all to examine. When it got to me I rubbed my open hand over the fur, brushing the short hairs back and forth. I opened it up to the inside and found myself running my fingers over each stitch in the seam. I remembered watching Mama force the big needle through the tough hide. She had to stop and sharpen it several times before she finished. It made me sad to think she was through making things.

"I didn't realize you kids had made so many new friends." Denby said as he looked around the room. *"I brung this jar of fig preserves from my sisters last batch for the good doctor and his wife…for lookin after my little buddies here…reccon there's enough to share a spoonfull with the rest these folks here?"* Denby asked reaching to hand the jar across to Estelle.

"Sure! How thoughtful of you Mr. Denby…Thank you!" she responded with surprise in her voice.

I was not at all surprised that he did that as it was just like him to do such a thing.

"Got anythang in there fer me?" Ed Earl asked; now up on his knees trying to peer into the sack.

Alma scooted to the front of her chair, leaned toward the boy and politely said, *"Now…Ed Earl…that's not a nice thang to ask…let's scoot back…give Denby a little space, alright?"*

"You know I wouldn't forgit cha sonnyl" he chuckled then reached in and pulled out two small carved pieces of wood. One was whittled into a turtle, the other a frog, both hand carved by Denby himself no doubt. I recognized his workmanship. I was a bit jealous when he gave one to Ed Earl and the other to Learline, though I had my own collection back home in the bus. Yes, years of gifts from Denby.

Scratching around in the sack he said, *"Sassy, I have something for you."* then pulled out a long string of camphor bean seeds that had been made into a necklace. *"Now you be careful with these…don't leave um round for the baby to put in her mouth…the're poisonous to eat."*

"For me?…The're nice." I commented.

"Your mama was wearin this the first time I ever laid eyes on her…said she strung um up herself. She had no idee at the time what kind of seeds they wuz till I told her…but we both agreed they made a purdy necklace. She seen fit ta send it with me the day I left…said she knowed I wuttin gonna wear um but it was something to remember her by…you might have better use fer um…I could never forget her nohow!"

Taking them gently from his hands, I immediately draped them over my head where they rested over my chest. I examined the smooth texture that had a faded worn coat of polish and wondered how something so pretty could be of any danger. Thanking him I jumped to my feet to hug him.

He grinned saying, *"My pleasure to get um back where they belong…I don't think she ever intended for me to wear them…it's really a girly thing…I used to tease her for wearing necklaces around out there in the woods where there wuttin nobody round ta admire um…Sometimes, for no reason, she would try to dress up like she was going somewhere…ya know…pin up her hair and put on a frilly dress she might have picked up from the salvation army…Sometimes she would say she was havin church and she would have you kids slicked up too…She didn't really have no place to go but she liked the idee of getting all gussied up every once in a while…said it made her feel purdy…She had no idea how striking she was all the time…real good natured woman, ya mama wuz…she…."*

His sentence drifted off with wholesome passion as his eyes started to mist over again.

"I'z all time after ya daddy to git her out of them woods and into a nice house where she belonged. She needed to be in town, round other women so's she could make friends. I told him he ought ta least take her to a movie or someplace special ever once in a while. I'd even offer him a little money fer it time and again,

offer to stay and look after you youngins so's she didn't have to worry bout ya'll none whilst she wus away. Earl wouldn't take money fer nuttin. He'd tel me theyz doin just fine,'sayin she never makes out like she needs that kind stuff and that she had babies to keep her company'. Truth is, I thank he's scared she might leave him fer one em city slickers if she had a way. She wouldn't a done that,she was crazy bout him. She made out over him so, like she done you kids!"

Learline, who had been having a hard time sitting still, worked her way up to Denby's lap and wedged herself between him and the sack. She took her wooden frog he had made for her and was hopping it up and down his arm, then up his neck and onto his face while he tried to talk.

Trudy got up to get the baby from him saying, *"Looks like a little spoiled somebody is fightin for her spot as center of attention!"*

"Oh she's just a wantin to play…Here I am just rattlin on…nobody wants to hear an old man yackin when they got a cute little ole tike to play with!" he said, tickling Learline, causing her to squirm and giggle.

He played a bit more with her as they both entertained everybody and had us all laughing. It felt good for everyone to laugh and play; a far cry from the mournful atmosphere that had lain heavy in the air for days before. They played a bit longer before she reached her little arms up for Trudy to rescue her from her torturing tickler. She had done so only to have the baby begging to get down and go back for more.

"Got anythang fer me?" Earldean asked, standing beside the chair with her hand on Denby's shoulder.

"Sure do!" he answered reaching into the bottom of the sack for the last item. He pulled out a rectangular shaped package wrapped in newspaper and tied up with jute string. Everyone eagerly watched as she jerked at the string to untie it then loosen the paper to reveal a framed photo under glass.

"Who's all these folks?" she asked pointing to the image of five people including a baby. Denby squinted at the picture pointing to each face as he identified himself and his sister standing next to Daddy, and Mama. *"Who's this little baby?"* she asked looking closely at the smaller face.

"Why that little tadpole wuz you when ya wuttin no bigger 'na minute." he said with a grin, watching her face for a response of her surprise, while the rest of us gathered around for a better view.

"ME?" she shrieked. *"I wuz'at little? I don't ever remember that! Where did you git such a thang?"*

"My brother-in-law got him a new camera long about that time. He made that stillness of us standin there in my yard, long time ago, when thez come fer a visit." he answered. *"It wuttin too long after ya'll moved to Chinkapin Holler. I forgot all about him a even taken that thang, till I run across it in a box of pictures we wuz lookin through after I moved up younder ta Sikeston. The original one's been taped to the front of my dressin mirror, back at my sisters, for about two years or more now. When she heard about me coming back to see ya'll, she took it down to a place there in Sikeston and had um make a bigger likeness of it and put it in 'at nice frame. She seen fit fer me ta brang it to ya…git it and take care of it fer her."*

Pushing her hair away from her face, Earldean said, *"I cain't believe I wuz a baby one time, zat really me? That don't even look like my Mama and Daddy! Mama looks here bout as big as me now, don't she? And this is Daddy? He looks like a skinny ole boy! You still look the same though Denby…you ain't changed hardly none a'tall."*

We had never owned a camera, neither had Denby to my knowledge so we had never seen pictures of ourselves before except for the one that was taken during the search for Mama. The only pictures we had were some old faded ones Mama had for so long that they were about to fall apart. We didn't know any of the people in them.

"Look at cha Earldean!...you'z a little ole thang wuttin ya?" I said staring over her shoulder. Ed Earl and Learline were pulling at her trying to get a turn to see what all the fuss was about. She held on tightly to it as she bent down to show them.

"Baby Doll!" Learline squealed, pressing her finger against the glass.

"That's you? You wuz a funny lookin baby, Earldean!" Ed Earl cried out in laughter making a funny face of his own.

"*No I wutten, Ed Earl!*" she said in her defense. *"I wuz a cute lit'lo baby see!"*

"Yea you wuz." Alma said, as she took her turn to look at the picture a little closer. *"…cute as a button."*

"Let me git a good look at that." said Trudy who was next in line. "*Aaaawee! Aint that just precious? You were a livin doll, Sweetie!*"

"Yea, a funny lookin doll!" Ed Earl teased.

"ED EARL!" the ladies sang out in unison.

"Come ere boy…" Denby said teasing back, *"…I'll show you funny!"* He reached over and goosed him till Ed Earl balled up in Denby's lap

where he tickled him until he cried for mercy through roars of laughter. *"Who's funny now? Huh?"*

Learline ran to join in the fun, yelling, *"DO ME…DO ME! My turn Bubba…tic-me like Cody do…Do me now!"*

They played around a bit while the framed photo was passed around for all to see. Earldean and I followed it around the room listening to the different comments that were made.

"So these are your parents…they are so young!" one said.

"Well that was about ten years ago…or more." said another.

Then another and so on saying, *"He doesn't look anything like the sketch on the missing person posters!"*

"It was no wonder nobody could find um."

"They were so young…and thin…Look at um!"

"Just babies themselves."

Earldean carefully guarded her treasure wiping the fingerprints from the glass with her shirt tail between each hand off. I too, was mesmerized by the image, holding on to it with one hand as I looked on with each person in the room. With my other hand I twisted the string of beads around my finger, taking in as much tangible evidence of my parents existence than I had in a long time.

When Denby started to get up from the chair, the buzz of conversations fizzled out and every turned to see what he was trying to do.

"Can I get you some more coffee, Mr. Denby?" Estelle asked stepping toward him and reaching for his cup.

"No thank ya, Mrs. Murphy…I've had plenty."

"Ya ain't leavin yet, are ya Denby?" I asked, darting back across the room.

"Naw Sassy" he said. *"This boy is after me ta go see these horses the doctor has out yonder…I've been sittin fer sa long on that car ride here…I need to git up and stretch a bit anyhow."*

Doc got up and reached for the cane then offered Denby assistance in getting out of his chair. *"Need some help?"*

"I got it…my legs tend ta go ta sleep when I sit too long is all…bad hip. Thank ya tho." Denby said. After he made it to his feet, he took hold of the cane saying, *"Now, let's go see them horses."*

"Good Idea." Doc said, thinking the kids were getting a bit rowdy and noticed it might be wearing on Estelle's nerves. *"It's a little ways out there to the pasture…think you can make it alright?"* he asked.

"If we take it kinda slow...ought be alright." he said following Doc and Ed Earl to the back door.

"Put your shoes on Ed Earl...if your goin to the pasture." Alma reminded him.

"Shoes? Ya wearin shoes these days, sonny?" Denby teased.

Half the people there partook in the trip to the pasture while the other half stayed behind to stew in any new information Denby had given them. Doc used the time to ask more questions about our parents and their lifestyle; fishing for clues to piece together the puzzle. He asked about the different places Daddy had worked and if the letters included the names of the people who employed him. He dug deeper for anything Denby might have left out about their past.

I didn't pay much attention to his answers as I was too excited about showing Denby how I had learned to ride a horse.

When we reached the barn, Doc thought it best that we used the time to visit with Denby and not to wear him out on his first day after such a long trip. Instead of saddling up the horses and riding them, we just petted them and gave them some food and water.

He was impressed about how much we had learned about everything around us. He complimented Doc on how well his place looked and figured him to be wealthy. Doc informed him that he had invested his earnings wisely and had been blessed but he was far from being rich. At any rate, Denby told Doc that he appreciated all he had done for us kids and that our Mama would have been grateful and so will our Daddy...whenever we find him.

On our way back to the house, they talked a little about getting us started in school and what it would take to do so.

Denby said that he thought it would have been a little easier on our Mama if she had sent us to school during the day but she insisted on teaching us herself.

They talked about the need for trying to find our birth certificates so that we would be able to enroll before we got any further behind.

In the course of the conversation Doc asked about my middle name and if I had one. Denby told him that I did have one but that he couldn't remember what it was.

He said that Sassy wasn't even my real name but a nickname given to me when Earldean couldn't say sister.

"She was cute and sassy so the nickname stuck…I don't think I've ever heard her real name said again past that first week of her life…not that I recall…so I reccon it's just Sassy!"

I was a little disappointed; I wanted a real name like everybody else…a bona fide name.

"Do you know where their parents…uhh…Earl and Marline might be keeping important papers such as these birth certificates." Doc asked.

"I never thought about it." Denby said pausing to think as well as catch his breath from the stroll. *"Could be anywhere out there. Might not have ever had one; you know all but one of them youngins was born right out there in the holler. They might not have ever thought about it. And, as far as they were concerned if they didn't need it they didn't bother gettin one."*

Doc slowed down his pace to wait on him, turning to say, *"That never occurred to me either. I just took it for granted everybody knows about needing a birth certificate…at least in this country…this day and age."*

In their defense I said, *"Well, I didn't know what one wuz till just the other day when Alma told me bout it! I don't see why come we don't just git some paper and make one. Why don't we just do that? That a way, we can go to school…aint that what we need it fer anyways?"*

"Ya know Doc…Those kids wuz so young when they started out but they appeared to be doin a good job survivin…barely makin ends meet… money wise, but didn't starve ta death. They seemed like good folk…friendly when they needed to be…like they come from good families…somebody taught um right from wrong along the way…but for some reason they wanted ta keep ta themselves and didn't want to be bothered by nobody. Almost like they'z afraid or mad,I never could make out which one, maybe a little of both! Heck, after I got to know um a little…I figured for some reason they trusted me…cause they didn't like nobody else messin around their place. I think I was one of the few people that wuz ever let come around younder."

"Do you think they were hiding something?" Doc asked.

"I don't know what it could be iffin they wuz,they were a little peculiar in some ways bout some thangs,that's what made um special…but naw…they wuttin criminals iffin that's what ya askin…they wuttin hidin nuttin." Denby assured him.

"Yea they wuz…Mama told me what they'z hidin! So did Daddy!" I informed them.

"O Yea…What wuz they a hidein?"

"Well now…I aint spose ta tell nobody…They said it wuz a secret…didn't want nobody ta know bout it."

28
FROM THE LOST & FOUND

I would later find out that while the women waited inside for us to give Denby the outside tour of the Murphy's place, they offered cordial hospitality to his cousin, Harold, who waited with them.

He had their undivided attention as he offered all the secondhand information he could about what Denby told him of life in Chinquapin Hollow with the Johnson family.

He went on to fill in the blanks as best as he could about Denby's predicament as well as his ridiculous idea of moving back to his old house on the lake in spite of his bad health.

Apparently Denby had spoken at length about us to his relatives there in Bugtussle and was concerned about what would happen to us kids without our mother. He knew that Daddy wasn't going to be able to leave us unattended while he worked and was convinced the responsibility would fall to him, since he was the closest thing to next of kin.

His thoughts included the whole family moving out of the bus and into his house that would be better suited for children.

Just before leaving for Sikeston, he had suggested we stay at his house and make use of it while he was away. However, our parents had declined his offer saying they didn't foresee him staying with his sister that long. Denby wasn't sure if it was *their* pride or if it was their support of *his* pride that kept them from taking advantage of his generosity.

Had he known things would have turned out like they did he would have been a little more persistent.

Now, not only was he ready to take on maintaining a household again but was willing to attempt childcare as well.

Denby had no clue as to what kind of shape his old home place was in by this time. At best, it was a fixer upper according to most standards, when he left it. Sitting vacant and unattended over the years had taken its toll on the aged structure and it was pretty close to being dilapidated.

Harold was certain Denby was not physically up to this but was being headstrong in getting back home. His sister thought that maybe if he came back for a visit the trip would tire him out enough for him to see he wasn't up to such nonsense.

They had discussed several other possibilities of what would become of us, depending on whether or not we ever found our father. One thing for sure, Daddy would have to make some drastic changes in order for child welfare to be satisfied with the unusual circumstances.

No matter what happened at this point, life, as we knew it, would definitely be different. They pondered who or what might have killed our mother, with none wanting to believe that her husband had anything to do with it. But what if he did?

One of the other guests there suggested that we were too naive to know what he might be capable of. After all, he appeared to be irresponsible when it came to his family and that he kept us so secluded that we had no other father figures to compare him to.

Harold, in Daddy's defense, spoke up and said that he had never met the man but that he felt like his cousin Denby was a pretty good judge of character. He guessed that with Denby being a good natured man himself, he wouldn't have associated with somebody who was capable of murder. Instead, he came here to help him through the death of his wife, and his children through the loss of their mother.

After being enlightened a little by what Denby had told them, they all had conjured up some new theories of where one might locate our daddy. Surely, somebody in one of these towns would know his whereabouts.

Estelle, with her Perry Mason familiarity, thought that Clifton, being the closest town to Chinquapin Hollow, would be the first logical place to start.

Trudy reminded her that the police there already knew of the situation but, according to Noland, they had not come up with anything yet except a few ill speculations.

Alma recalled the sour attitude that some of the officers there had toward us kids and didn't see the likelihood of help from any of those fellows. Especially the one named Virgil who seemed to take pleasure in intimidating everybody he came across.

Estelle, still in her investigative frame of mind, suspected that this particular character might have had something to do with the disappearance of our father and possibly the death of our mother.

Trudy agreed and said she had her suspicions about him as well and felt he was up to no good from the very beginning.

The whole situation had become the buzz of the town again but not wanting the reputation of being a gossiper Estelle confessed that based on what she heard about him, she had the same notion toward him all along.

They were all puzzled as to how we ended up in Whisper Ridge with the town of Clifton being eighteen miles closer.

Harold suggested we probably didn't know which direction to follow and took the wrong route. Getting turned around on those winding, dirt roads would be easy enough for even a grown person to do in a good frame of mind.

And, for that matter, had we known what we were doing we could have crossed the lake by boat to Denby's old place then gone only six miles to Bugtussel in a whole lot less time.

Alma felt that it was by the Grace of God we didn't know any better, for there was no telling what might have happened to us if we had gone instead to Clifton.

Through the course of the conversation Trudy, having relatives in Bugtussle, discovered that she was related to Harold on his wife's, mother's side. Knowing this gave her a feeling of distant kinship to him; which in turn made her somehow related to Denby…well, once or twice removed.

This unearthing information was found just in time to change the dismal subject as we were returning from our venture out back at the Murphy's.

Trudy's voice broke through the hum of discussions that was going on in the room announcing our presence. She proudly addressed Denby saying, *"Well hey there Cuz!"*

Stepping over and putting her arm around him as he wiped his feet on the rug, she said, *"Looks like you and I are kinfolk!"*

He looked at her with curiosity in his eyes, yet, he was not going to deny this pretty woman the opportunity to back out of her claim. Whatever it was that gave her the inkling to draw near to him was a welcomed occasion as far as he was concerned.

After explaining her reaction, Denby agreed it was a small world and that even though there might not be any common blood flowing through their veins, their common love for us made them family enough.

"These youngins told me how you'z one the ones who took um in…and fed um …and been helpin ta look after um. Well, sounds ta me like ya done a good job a makin um feel right at home, 'long wit Miss Alma there…I want ta thank you gals!" he said.

"After the State Police called me 'bout that old truck I gave Earl, sayin they'z some kinda trouble down here, I called around here and talked to the police. That there Sheriff, he's the one who told me bout all this mess they'z in and where I'z ta find these youngins."

Then turning to Estelle, he continued, *"And I need to thank you too. Hear tell you and the Doctor done a great deal of sufferin right along with the rest of um…Sheriff told me all about how all ya'll seen fit to take um in till they found their folks. He told me how Alma here never left the boy's side when he took sick and had to go to the hospital…said he pert near died from it!"*

He hung his head shaking it saying, *"That little feller might not be here today if it weren't for you folks a doin what cha done! I just wish…his mama could'a been as lucky is all."*

As I watched the color of our old friend's face turn red in his efforts to restrain his grief, I recalled the depth of love he had for his neighbors. He stood, leaning into his cane with his head still hung, when tears began to fall and hit the floor.

It was not my own self pity that brought forth my tears this time, but my pity for Denby and the loss he was feeling right then. I felt a sharp pain in my chest that I now know was my heart breaking for him.

The next few moments were of silent respect while another wave of sorrow swept across the room bringing that familiar lump of pain back to my throat.

When he had heard a few of us sniffling, Ed Earl ran for the box of tissue and made his rounds. I remember feeling proud that my little brother was learning to be considerate of other people's feelings.

At her inquisitive age, Learline followed behind him watching every move that was made as each person pulled a tissue from the box. She made note of the silence and took the liberty to speak, saying *"They got buggers bubba?"*

The sound of her squeaky little voice asking such a question at that particular moment brought forth an unexpected roar of uncontrollable laughter.

About the time we started to get a hold of ourselves, we lost it again when she pulled a tissue from the box, released her crippled doll from the headlock she carried her in and said, *"Now be still baby…let me get dem buggers out choo nose so you won't cry no more!"*

Looking up only for a moment to see what everyone was laughing about, she continued her task before she crawled on Alma's lap pushing a tissue toward her nose, saying, *"Here I help ya…now blow it...blow it!"*

It appeared she was mimicking what Alma had done to her many times in teaching her to do the same.

Still laughing Doc said, *"Well, come on Alma…be a good girl and blow!"*

"Before these kids came along, I had never cried so much…nor have I laughed so much!" Alma said…catching her breath from the latest occurrence of each.

"Me too…" Estelle said with a chuckle. *"…I just thought it was my mood swings!"*

Another outbreak of laughter followed her joke. It was funny to those who understood it but even more so from those who knew Estelle.

"Good one Estelle!" Trudy said. *"These kids have got you pickin on yourself now."*

"Yea…Well with them around, I realize I'm not the only one going through a change of life." she responded light heartedly.

"Well, looks to me like you've softened up that hardened heart of yours." Trudy said with a smile, putting her arm over her friend's shoulder. *"…and I can see you have wiggled your way into their hearts too!"*

"Yea I denied myself the experience at first but they have helped to fill this empty nest."

Alma got up and stood on the other side of Estelle slipping her arm around her waist as she added, *"Ya know…They've brought so much joy into my life too. It's been worth every single worry and every little tear!"*

The three of them stood in embrace and support of one another watching us kids play along with Doc. He was holding the doll up by the arms and pretending like she was learning to walk. *"Good girl! Now...walk to Learline."* We giggled and laughed as she held out her arms and coached her Baby Doll to come.

Denby had sat down to rest on the sofa next to his cousin. He took in all that was going on in the room and could see the care and concern that these strangers had unselfishly taken on for our sake.

I turned to see his face as I heard him breathe a sigh of relief. I believe it was the sound of pressure leaving his chest caused by the burden he thought he had to carry alone.

I made my way to him and sat on his lap with my arms around his neck like I used to do.

He responded with a hug and a kiss on my cheek saying how much he had missed me. Though he didn't complain, I felt the need to shift my weight off his boney leg when he commented that I had really grown.

He caught me staring at the deep lines in his face, wondering what makes that sort of thing happen to old people. As my eyes rested on his, we both grinned at each other over the familiarity of our union. After a lengthy silent gaze that brought back a flood of memories, I grew more homesick than ever before. I suddenly began to cry again.

"Now…Now…It's gonna be alright Sassy…Denby's here for ya!" he softly said as he drew me closer, wiping my tears with his fingers.

I whispered back to him not wanting to let the others know that I was crying again. *"I just missed ya is all Denby…you wuz gone so long…I miss my Daddy…and I aint ever gonna see my Mama again …am I?"*

"Yea…One day we will…" he promised me as he patted my back. *"…She's a waitin up there in Heven with her Jesus, don't ya know? She's a savin us a place fer when it's our turn to go…so's all the people ya love can be together again when we done with this old world! Oh…we'll miss her alright but the achin…well, it'a ease up fore too long and life will be tolerable again…you'll see."*

We were soon joined by Ed Earl and Earline talking about good ole times we had together. Learline made her way onto Denby's other knee as if she had always known him.

Giving him some room to breathe and relief from his sleeping leg I slid to the floor with my brother and sister to listen to his tales.

The adults were entertained as well with some of them waiting for anything that might represent a clue.

Just as some of the others were leaving and saying their goodbyes, the Fletchers showed up with a couple of bags from the Filla-Sack.

"Hey, Sis!" Alma said as Estelle led them into the house. *"…What brings ya'll out this way?"* she asked.

"Well, we just thought we'd bring some things out for the children…ya know... new socks and underwear…a few little toys…extra laundry detergent…shampoo…stuff like that…to help out Doc and Estelle." Mrs.

Fletcher answered taking the bags from her husband and placing them on the counter.

"Oh that's just an excuse...we really came out to meet this famous Denby fellow!" her husband commented secretly to his sister-in law.

Estelle overheard his remark as she passed behind him and said, *"Now, you know good friends like ya'll don't have to have an excuse to come over!"*

"Estelle, it's been like Grand Central Station here with all these people around. How are you holding up, Hun?" her dear friend asked.

"Fine...fine, doin just fine. Everybody has been good to help...seems like the whole town has come to pay their respects." she answered.

Even though his cousin promised to bring him back on Sunday, it was real hard to say goodbye to Denby when he left Doc and Estelle's late that afternoon.

About the only way we would let him go was for Trudy to conjure up a plan for everybody to meet at the Eat-A-Bite after church. That way Denby could check out those crinkled fries and ketchup that Ed Earl had been telling him so much about. She insisted on Harold bringing his wife back with him so they could catch up on the family gossip saying the whole thing would be like a big family reunion.

Though I hardly recognized him out of uniform, Deputy Reed showed up just before they drove off having only enough time to be introduced to Denby and his cousin as they were eager to get back to Bugtussle before dark.

He said that he was sure he'd be seeing him again soon and that he was bound to be of some help in finding our daddy. He told Denby that the investigators were eager to meet with him even though he had already discussed the matter with the Sheriff and State Police over the phone.

We all waved goodbye as they drove off with Trudy turning to the Deputy, saying, *"Well...with all my best Friday night customers over here at the Murphy's I'll be out of business in no time!"*

"I went by The Eat-A-Bite but they said you were out here!" Deputy Reed replied.

"So Noland...Did you drive all the way out here to place your order? You know...I'm not the only one who can wait on you." she said to him in a flirtatious voice.

I was standing just the other side of Trudy and noticed a timid grin come across the deputy's face. Like a bashful school boy, he folded his arms and gently kicked at the dirt in the driveway. Then, to flirt back, he tilted his head toward her and responded under his breath, *"Well...you are the prettiest one there!"*

Trudy gently shoved at his arm saying, *"Oh, Noland...you're just sayin that!"*

"Really you are...Can I help it if I want that special attention that you give me...you know what I'm talking about...like I'm your favorite customer?"

"I thought I was your favorite customer!" Alma said interrupting the two of them.

"Well you two can fight it out here or discuss it over supper back at the diner." Trudy said as she hugged us goodbye. *"I've got to get back to work and let Yvonne go home."*

"We'd better get going and let these people rest up from all the company that's been here pert near all day!" Alma suggested.

Deputy Reed told Trudy and Alma that he would follow them back over there but first he had a little something for us kids.

He went to his car and came back with a tattered, brown paper sack. He turned it around in a way so we could see that on its side was an animated picture of a pig's face.

He held it up and asked, *"Have ya'll been lookin for this?"*

"Our pig bag! Lookie Ya'll!" Ed Earl exclaimed.

"Hey! That's the one we toted our stuff in!" Earldean rejoiced.

"Yea!...Where'd ya find it?" I asked.

29
GET A CLUE
(*BIBLE, BLOOD, & BLUEBERRIES*)

Estelle found that she needed an afternoon to rest up from all the activity that had been going on around her house. So around noontime on Saturday we headed to town with Doc, who had some business to tend to at the Clinic. We would be meeting up with Alma, who normally didn't work weekends, but had been there all morning catching up on paperwork that had been piling up due to her being distracted by our dilemma.

She was still hard at work when we arrived and asked that we play quietly in the waiting area while she finished up.

We entertained ourselves with the drinking fountain and the magazines found on the coffee table.

Earldean, who had been unusually quiet for the biggest part of four days, was stretched out across the folding chairs moaning with a belly ache. She hadn't much of an appetite and had not eaten well for several days.

The adults had diagnosed this as part of her grieving Mama's death as they had tried to get her to eat something light to ease the pain. However, she didn't force herself and I noticed that she would only stir at her food.

It bothered her when Denby had to go back with his cousin to Bugtussle and she was disappointed when she didn't get to go with him. I thought at first she was just pouting because she didn't get her way until I realized that she really hadn't been herself since we were told in fact that our mother had been found dead.

She claimed that she had felt all along that Mama was already dead that first morning she went into the bus to take her breakfast but didn't want to believe it.

When Doc first quizzed her about Mama's symptoms prior to our leaving her, she answered his questions trying not to leave anything out. She told him that she didn't know to listen for a heartbeat, but as far as she could tell it didn't look like Mama was breathing.

Doc, still unsure of what he might find when he got out there that day, had prepared Earldean for the worst.

With her being the oldest, he had asked her to remain hopeful for our sake until we knew for sure but that he was almost certain he'd find her dead.

She didn't want to go back out there with him the next day to find out. That's why she volunteered to stay behind with the two younger ones.

After I fainted and Doc gave a brief explanation of what happened to me, Earldean found it easier to hide behind a slim chance that maybe Mama had fallen into a coma of some kind and was just unconscious.

When she heard that Mama wasn't in her bed that day, dead or alive, Earldean changed her mind and chose to hold on to a string of hope that Mama woke up feeling better and had gone out looking for us. She wanted to believe that, when they found us, we'd all go home, then everything would go back to normal.

Her guilt had consumed her for not staying behind to take care of Mama when we found out that she was found dead. She had told me that she was afraid that Daddy would be mad at her for not taking the responsibility of staying there with Mama in the first place.

She felt somehow she had been disobedient for leaving without permission. He was adamant about that. In fact the last thing he said to her was, *"Stay close by and help ya Mama take care of these here youngins."*

We still weren't quite sure just what really happened but in Earldean's mind, it was all her fault now.

Lying there, she tried to make herself more comfortable by rolling onto her side. To prop up her head she used Mama's bible that she had been protecting since it was found.

In spite of her depression, she was elated the bible had been recovered and returned to us. She announced her gratefulness from the moment Officer Reed handed it over, still in the paper sack we had carried it in.

The crumpled and worn out bag had been found by an employee from the Clifton County highway department while mowing a ditch out on Old Dozier Road.

When the man discovered it several weeks before, he peeked at the contents and assumed at first it belonged to somebody in one of the houses close by. After closer examination, he found underneath the bible some wadded up wax paper with cracker crumbs, a flashlight, loose batteries, and a knife along with some bloody children's clothing.

He had noticed what looked like might be dried blood on the outside of the sack and became suspicious of this evidence. Wanting to be heroes, he and a couple of his co-workers decided to turn it in to the local police where they probed for information on possible crimes that might have been committed in the area.

It happened to be that the closest local law enforcement was in the town of Clifton…and wouldn't you know it…Virgil and his partner just so happened to be the deputies on duty that day.

They kept the sack and its contents locked up as evidence claiming they were onto something really big and sent the men on their way with the idea that they were on the verge of solving a major crime.

Of course they were exaggerating; nothing major ever happened around there.

Our missing parents had been the biggest ongoing story until the election debates and neither of those accounts were crimes…depending of course, on who you voted for.

Truth was, the biggest crime reported in the area around that time was that of an alleged burglary.

Supposedly, someone had come up on Lola Mae Whitley's back porch and stole all of her blueberries out of her deep freeze that she'd put up that summer. Most folks in them parts had their doubts that there were ever any blueberries in the first place because of the heat and drought. Those who knew Lola Mae and her bouts of forgetfulness claimed it could have been that she actually put up the berries the previous summer. More than likely it was she who took the berries out of the freezer over a period of time and was unaware of her dwindling supply.

She had a reputation for reporting to the police on a regular basis claiming she had been robbed when in fact she merely had a bad habit of misplacing things or forgetting that she had given them away.

She kept enough accusations flowing in order to keep Virgil and his partner employed as assistants to the Sheriff there in the town of Clifton.

Other than following up on her fictitious claims, these fellows didn't have much else to do but patrol around in the squad cars and stir up their own trouble.

Most of the people there ignored them saying the only reason they had a job in the first place was because Virgil was the mayors nephew.

They, in their ignorance, tried to link this sack of paraphernalia up to any and everything that came along to make them look like they were big city police. Just like on Perry Mason.

The Clifton Sheriff confiscated this so called evidence that seemed to be the basis for some pretty vicious rumors in his town.

Recognizing it as being a bag from the Piggly Wiggly over in Whisper Ridge, he turned it over to Detective Glenn thinking it might belong to us.

After it made its way across several desks throughout the investigation, it was decided that the said blood came from the little boy when he cut his leg on the barbwire fence.

It was Deputy Reed who remembered we had been looking for the sack with the Bible in it from the first day he met us.

After they recognized several of our names written in its registry they assumed that this Bible must have belonged to our mother.

Notation was made of the whole find as well as the other names written there that may be of further use in the investigation. After seeing that it was not necessary to keep it from us any longer it was released to be forwarded.

Deputy Reed apologized for it taking so long to get it back to us but that it took a while for everything to line up in order to find its rightful owner.

Now, in light of her death, "The Good Book" was our inheritance. It was the only tangible thing to our past we kept with us. Even our wardrobe had been replaced by then.

We must have set the sack down there in that ditch on the side of the road while we were waiting for Huey. That was about the time Ed Earl checked the cut on his leg. Huey had gone to go talk to his Maw about giving us a ride on that first day we met him. Somehow, in and amongst all the distractions, it was left behind in the tall grass, going unnoticed for the longest time.

I remember seeing blood rubbing off of Ed Earl's leg onto the sack as it banged into the side of his steps. We did in fact have to use some of Learline's clothes to help stop the bleeding. The knife was the one we used to spread the peanut butter onto the crackers but I hardly think a butter knife would do much harm in the way of a weapon, but who knows? I guess if somebody wanted to hurt another with something like that they could.

So, looking back, I can now see how Virgil could possibly make such an assumption not knowing what really happened.

I'm just glad somebody had listened to us and had heard the truth of the event. Otherwise, Virgil might have tried to put us in jail based on his suspicions. When our mother's body was found, he accused us of being guilty of killing her and that the contents of this bag, along with the blood, was proof enough for him.

When Alma finished up at the Clinic, we walked over to the Eat-A-Bite for lunch. Though they were in the middle of the lunch rush, all of the employees took a moment to acknowledge us by nodding or waving.

Some other people were already sitting in our favorite booth so we sat up at the counter on the tall stools. With only four of those unoccupied, Alma stood behind little Learline on the end stool not wanting her to fall and decided we would wait for an available booth.

Charlie Wayne and another milk man were still waiting for their order and didn't mind moving down one stool so that we could sit together. Mayor Scott, who had finished eating but was still having coffee and visiting with Fred McMillen, got up and offered his stool to Alma. She thanked him for his kindness but said that she had better stick closer to the wiggly youngsters who she thought would do better in a booth.

He was chit chatting with her a bit about our current state of affairs when Learline started whining about being hungry. She asked the mayor to pardon her while she tended to the little one's interruption.

"Hey Ya'll. How bout some Coke-a-Cola while ya'll waitin?" Yvonne asked. *"Do ya'll want ta look at a menu?"*

"I do!" Ed Earl called out; though he really couldn't read, he liked looking at the pictures of the food that were pasted next to the list.

Looking through the big window, I could see Cody in his paper hat cooking and filling orders. Each time he would lean towards the opening to put a plate on the shelf, he would look at us and smile a tight grin, not showing his teeth, as if it was forced. He had a pitiful look in his eyes that said he felt sorry for us.

I could tell he wanted to say something but was too busy cooking for all the hungry people and didn't have time to talk.

I had heard Trudy say before that folks can be mean when they are hungry and say things they wouldn't say otherwise. So in the restaurant business you have to move fast sometimes.

Several people there came up to Alma and asked her questions about our mother and if there was going to be a funeral service for her.

I had heard someone make mention of such a thing back at Estelle and Doc's house but didn't ask then what that was. I figured while we waited, I'd ask her so she could explain to me what they were talking about.

Learline didn't pay much attention to her response as she was being entertained by Ed Earl who was busy spinning around on the stool and sliding the menu back and forth on the counter.

Earldean and I listened closely as she began to explain what happens at a funeral and a graveside service.

Her explanation was vague and left me with even more questions to follow up with but a booth became available before I could ask them.

It wasn't our usual booth but Alma was eager to get the baby in a booster seat and Ed Earl off of the spinning stool.

For the most part we waited patiently and took in all the norms of a Saturday lunch rush at the Eat-A Bite.

I could hear Cody whistling an Elvis tune in the kitchen over the hiss of steam from the grill and the clinking sound of the dishes rattling as Willy Jay cleaned the table across the way.

Trudy came rushing by with a cup of coffee for Alma in one hand and a pot for refills for the guys at the next booth.

The men joked with the tall redhead as she topped off their cups, smiling, chewing her juicy fruit gum and nodding her head as if she were paying attention to their nonsense.

She walked off laughing and went on to the next table and then the next making sure everyone was satisfied.

Yvonne came to take our order. *"Hey Kido's! Alma, how ya doin today? Ya'll be havin ya usual?"* she asked confidently, not feeling the need to write it down.

"Yea...I believe so." Alma responded. *"...and an extra bottle of ketchup please."*

"Sure sorry to hear about ya'lls Mama." Yvonne whispered, bending down, speaking mostly to me and Earldean. *"...If there is anything I can do to help ya'll...well just let me know...ok?"* She smiled softly as she patted my shoulder then turned to go place our order with Cody.

Brother Jessie and his wife Sharon were just leaving and stopped to say hello on their way out. Mrs. Sharon was the Sunday school teacher for the kids my age and had invited us again to come an hour early for the children's lessons before regular services.

Those classes consisted mostly of kid's whose parents came early too unless they rode the church van there. Brother Jessie reminded us that the van could pick us up if we ever needed a ride to and from church while we were staying in Whisper Ridge. He told us that all we had to do was to just give him a call by the night before.

He pulled a napkin from the bin and his pen from his pocket then began to write. He then handed it to Earldean saying, *"I believe this about your mother...may she rest in peace."*

On the napkin he had written his name and phone number along with a Bible verse that read John 11:25-26. Jesus said to her, "I am the resurrection and life. He who believes in me, though he may die, he shall live. And, whoever lives and believes in Me shall never die. Do you believe this?"

After they left, Alma helped us to find that same verse in the bible and read it aloud. Then Earldean placed the napkin between the pages using it for a bookmark. Carefully closing the book she said, *"I don't understand about all this...what it says here...Ifin my mama believed in Jesus she ought lived...Why come her to die?"*

Alma tried her best to explain over Learline and Ed Earl's playing at the table. *"Well...Ya Mama's body died but her spirit lives!"*

"So, how come me not to see her then?"

"Because she's in heaven, honey...her spirit that is... it's her body that's gone!

"Well, 'while ago you'z said folks wuz a commin to the funeral to morn the body, right?...and now...ya sayin it's gone?"

About that time Yvonne came to the table with our food. Alma settled the little ones down for grace and asked me to say the blessing.

"Lord," I prayed, *"...bless this food...and help us figger out bout what we spose ta do...till we find Daddy...Help us find him purdy quick...Amen!*

By the time we got our food it was close to the end of the rush and the café started to quiet down a little.

We didn't talk much at the first part of the meal for by that time we were hungry and even Earldean seemed to have found her appetite again.

I pondered what Alma had said about the people coming to mourn the body. *"What body?"* I asked.

"What? Err..Oh…Ya talking bout the funeral…Well, ya Mama's body Sassy, that's who the funeral is for." Alma answered.

"Really Alma Fey?" Cody said, coming up beside the booth and sliding in tight next to her, barely on the edge of the bench. *"Now the way I see it the funeral is more fer the living than it is fer the dead…don't you thank? I mean...dead folks ain't got no idea what's goin on but now the ones who's left behind…well, they need family and friends to see um through the sad part…pay their respects to the love they carried for the one that's passed away…right?"*

"Hey Cody!" Ed Earl said with a mouth full of fries. *"Ya want some ezz here taters?"*

"Don't recon I will boy, them's for you!"

"But they'z real good! Ya ought ta try um!" Ed Earl insisted, sliding his plate toward that end of the table. *"Here…dip um in this here ketchup…you'll like it!"*

Obliging his generosity, Cody reached across Alma and took a fry from his plate.

"Now dip it!" Ed Earl demanded

"Dip it…dip it…dip it…like dis!" Learline said, bouncing on the seat as she demonstrated the maneuver for him as if he had never seen it done before.

"Oh…aww ite den." he said, then raked his chosen fry across the blob of ketchup on Alma's plate. *"Mmmmm…mmmm! That's good eatin! Huh, Alma Fey?"*

Alma shyly grinned at him and tried to nudge him off the seat but he held firm to his invasive grounds there beside her.

She asked, "*Shouldn't you be in the kitchen cookin or somthin?"*

"I'm on a ten minute break."

"Well…don't you usually go out back and smoke you a cigarette bout this time?"

"Give um up!" he said nudging her back.

"Really now…I guess you gonna take up pesterin the customers for ya new bad habbit, huh?"

"Naw…not all of um…just regulars like you." he said making a goofy smile at her.

She laughed until she turned red then nudged him again. He overreacted pretending as though she had pushed him hard enough to make him fly from the seat to the floor.

When we saw that he wasn't hurt, we laughed at his silliness. All except for Learline who scolded Alma saying, *"DON'T HURT CODY...ALMA, be nice!"*

"He's ok baby…we's just playin is all!" she said trying to calm her down.

Learline took on a roll reversal saying, *"Don't be playin while ya eat ya dinner!"*

"Oh…Yes mam'm!" Alma said, then turned her attention and full blame to Cody saying, *"Hear that? We not suppose to be playin while we eatin so'z ya best quit messin with me!"*

"Yea Alma Fey…" he teased, *"…better eat bafore your dinner gets cold…if ya know what's good for ya!"*

"Why come you ta call her her Alma Fey?" I asked Cody.

"That's her name, 'Alma Fey Nettles'! That's what her family calls her, 'Alma Fey'."

"We just call her Alma…are you her family?"

"Pert near but not plum! We aint blood kin but we purdy close to her here at the diner…aint that right…Alma Fey?" he said with a big grin, winking at her.

"Yea…that's my name…so, don't wear it out." she said, blushing before she took her next bite of food.

"I think it's cute…Aaaalma Fa-a-a-ey!" he said under his breath, leaning in to her.

She turned red and nudged him once again. Jumping up, pretending to be hurt, he grabbed his arm saying, *"Did ya'll see that!...She playin again Learline you better git on to her!"*

We were tickled as we watched Learline's response, knowing all the while he was teasing but the tot took a bit longer to size up the situation to see if it was necessary to call Alma on it again.

Her frowned face let us know that she was still not sure. Taking no chances, she defended him by yelling in her shrill little voice, *"DON'T HURT CODY…ALMA FAY!"*

It was funny and we laughed about the whole thing…calling Alma by her whole name.

Trudy had just rung up the last of a long line at the register and was about to go check on her few remaining customers when she noticed the uproar over at our booth.

"Alma! What did you do to Cody?" she yelled jokingly across the diner as she made her way toward us.

"Toodie…Alma make Cody cry!" the baby tattled.

"She did? Poor Cody!" she said, putting her arm around him pretending to have pity.

Cody played up the act by hanging on to Trudy's neck with his long arms and limp body. And, in a whiny voice he whimpered,
"Yea…make her stop Toodie!"

We giggled at the adults acting like big, silly kids and saw that it was entertaining the other staff and the customers…including the three who had just walked in.

Earldean excused herself to go to the restroom still laughing as she walked away. Trudy took her place next to me so that she could sit and rest her feet for a minute.

I finished my meal while listening to the three adults carry on with Ed Earl and Learline.

"Oh by the way…I almost forgot to tell you…" Trudy said, interrupting their giddiness. *"Nolan and that other deputy came by not too long before you got here saying they had been out to Chinquapin Holler again this morning!"*

"Really? Reckon what they'z up to?" Alma quizzed.

"Wuz Daddy home yet?" Ed Earl asked.

"Naw son…He ain't made it back there yet." Trudy sadly reported.

"They finally checked out that deep freeze you'z talking bout Sassy." Cody said.

"They did? Did they find our birth papers in there?" I asked.

"You mean birth certificates?" he corrected me. *"...Naw said they didn't find nuttin!"*

"Whatcha mean? Didn't they find the keys round Mama's neck that would open it?"

"Yea they got it open alright…said wuttin nuttin in there!"

"Nuttin? It wuz empty?" I asked wondering what happened to the contents.

"Nuttin septin a few old blankets and an empty pickle jar." he said as he stood up to stretch, then put his hands on his hips. *"Didn't you tell me ya daddy kept his money in that old thang…along wit his guns and ammo?"*

"Yea." I answered. *"Least ways far'z I know, that's were they kept um…they gone too?"*

"I guess so…I tole Nolan what cha said about how that there deep freeze chest wuz where ya folks kept their stuff fer safe keeping and all…but he said ifin it wuz…it's all gone now! Told me that detective wuz gonna be askin ya'll about it."

"Yea from what Nolan says wuttin no guns to speak of." Trudy added. *"Said they met Denby down there with his cousin so's he might could help um look for where else ya Daddy might be a keepin um."*

"What?" Alma asked, *"… the guns or the birth certificates?"*

"Both, I guess." Trudy said. *"I don't think Nolan was suppose to be talkin much about it ya know…on account of that other deputy that was with him… made out like it was some kind of top secret business…You seen him…huh Cody…the way he was carryin on and all…when Nolan commence tellin us about it!"*

"Aww…I didn't pay him much mind" he responded. *"I'm sure he was just tryin to keep anybody else form hearin what they'z talking about. Ya know how folks can gossip when they ease drop on private conversations."*

He turned to see a customer who had come up behind him. Stumbling around, he asked her, *"Oh! Hey Mamm...err..uh uh…you ready to check out? Okee dokee…uh…well uh…Trudy, I believe this here lady is ready to go…ya wanna ring her up please?"*

After Trudy got up and led the customer to the checkout counter, Cody turned and said that he had better get back to work before he got in to trouble with his red headed boss.

"Thanks for the tatter Ed Earl! Oh…and for the ketchup Alma Fey! " he said loudly as he walked away waving with one hand and the other in his pocket.

Alma shook her head and grinned at him until he disappeared behind the swinging doors.

"Wanna go see what's keepin your sister, Sassy?" she said after a few more minutes. *"I don't know what could be takin her so long…she still hasn't finished eating and we'll need to go soon."*

I needed to go to the restroom anyway so I didn't mind. When I opened the door I could hear Earldean crying in the stall.

"Who's there?" she snapped in a whiney voice.

"It's me, Sassy! I need ta pee…what's takin ya so long in here?" I asked. *"Are ya cryin bout Mama again?"*

"NO! Well…yea sortta…Oh Sasseeeee!" she cried with her voice trailing off into a fading high pitch. She caught her breath and sniffed a few times saying, *"I don't wanna die…not like Mama done! I don't wanna to be buried under the ground!"*

"Whacha talkin bout, Earldean?"

"I'm fixin ta die Sassy…Right here! Right now!" she wailed, then broke into sobs.

I pushed the stall door open to see her standing there butt naked with nothing on but her shirt. A thin stream of blood trickled down her leg.

"Where's ya britches Earldean? And, how in the world did ya cut yourself?" I asked reaching for some tissue.

She stood there shaking and crying while I wiped the blood off, only to find no apparent cut or scrape from which she could have bled.

"What happened?" I asked, still examining her leg. *"What did you do?"*

"NUTTIN!…I ain't done nuttin!…I just came in here to pee and found blood all over my drawers and it had run onto my shorts! It's just terrible I tell ya! I had to throw away my clothes in the trash can there!"

"Oh Earldean! I don't know. That's what Mama done and she wuttin cut nowhere…she just died and all her blood come out! Oh Sasseeeeeee!" she wailed again with her voice intensified by the acoustics of the ceramic tile in the room. She grabbed on to me as if to hold her up.

"Turn me loose…Let me go get some help!" I insisted, trying to free myself from her grip.

"NO!" she yelled. *"No don't tell nobody…Ya caint!"*

"Why come?"

"Cause Sassy!…that blood is commin from my private place! Please don't tell nobody!"

"Ya private place? Uhhh…Where's that at?"

"Ya know…down younder!" she said bobbing her head downward toward her crotch.

My eyes followed to the place where she was indicating and when I realized that things didn't look the same as they use to, I screamed, *"OH LORDY EARLDEAN…YOU GONNA DIE!!!"*

30
A NEW KIND OF VISIT
(*FAMILY REUNION*)

It makes sense now, but back then I just could not comprehend why our mother would keep secret such an important thing as human reproduction and all it entails.

Perhaps she was holding back the information on that particular subject until we were better able to understand. It would have only caused a great deal of confusion or maybe prompted more questions that she didn't know how to answer properly.

She probably felt there was no need to bring it up until necessary and until such time, I wouldn't doubt she had rehearsed that speech over and over in her head, getting it just right.

Though I had not paid that much attention, you'd think that her mother would have noticed that Earldean was maturing that summer and her "visitor" would be coming soon.

Had she lived just a few months longer, I'm sure she would have taken pride in revealing the information about the onset of womanhood to her first born daughter.

Alma and Trudy had rushed into the café's restroom when they heard me screaming that unforgettable day. After they assured us both that Earldean wasn't going to die they figured that one of them had some explaining to do.

Before we walked back out into the café, Alma assured me that my sister would be just fine. She asked that I not say anything about it to anyone, as this sort of thing was a lady's personal matter and that Trudy would look after her. She said, *"For now…we'll just say ya sister's monthly visitor come to call…and leave it at that. I'll explain more about it when we are alone…ok?"*

Trudy had the honors of tending to the immediate explanation while she helped Earldean rinse out her panties and shorts in the sink so that she could wear them out of there.

After Alma whispered something in Yvonne's ear, she took off to the back room and returned to with a small package and handed it off to Alma who in turned handed it through the door to Trudy.

A short time later Trudy summoned Alma to the restroom door for a minute where they mumbled under their breath so that I couldn't make out what they were saying.

Anybody that might have noticed anything unusual, which was everybody thanks to my big mouth, had resolved that everything was ok by this time. It appeared that our two heroic women had once again gotten everything under control.

When Ed Earl heard that Earldean had a visitor in the bathroom, he wanted to know who it was. I told him it wasn't a "who" but a "what" and it was something that scared us. After several unconfirmed guesses, he stood firm on his suggestion that it was probably a spider.

He knew that I had never been afraid of spiders but that Earldean had grown to become skittish of the little creatures.

He had convinced himself, Learline and Willy Jay that *"that's"* what all the fuss was about and that our sister was a big 'scaredy-cat' who probably peed on herself over the little ole critter.

His theory seemed inevitable when Earldean stepped out of the restroom in her obviously damp shorts.

Trudy led her to the door in a hasty exit to prevent her any further embarrassment. She held her hands over her face not wanting to chance seeing Cody, Willy Jay or any of the customers gawking back at her.

Of course this only drew more attention to her and her poor efforts were magnified when Ed Earl pointed toward her yelling out, *"SEE! SHE PEED HER PANTS…I told ya Willy Jay! …didn't I tell ya!"*

"ED EARL!" all the women yelled.

She was so humiliated by the time we made it back to Alma's car she swore she'd never go back to the Eat-A-Bite again. It was understood that she would get the front seat unimpeded.

Ed Earl, sitting in the back seat behind her, took advantage of his riding position and immediately found use of a discarded sucker stick. Gliding it ever so slightly down the base of Earldean's neck followed by an urgent warning that he'd seen a spider there.

This sent her shivering, swatting and searching to find the creepy little creature. The only thing she found was that she'd been fooled by her bratty brother, holding his gut as he roared with laughter on the back seat.

Learline was just giggling along for the sport of it, with not a clue as to what for. Alma tried hard to suppress her laughter but when a chuckle forced its way out of her mouth, her hand flew up to catch it, so she had to disguise the sound with a fake cough.

I wasn't really laughing at her but the amusing trick Ed Earl played. I couldn't help it if she was chosen to fall prey to his prank! However, I couldn't convince Earldean of that.

Ignoring the warnings that she had issued repeatedly, backed by both me and Alma, he was persistent in his pursuit. In his adolescent judgment, he reckoned that if it was funny once it should be just as hilarious on his fourth attempt.

Her recent state of humiliation had made her exceedingly vulnerable. Now she was trapped in the cab of a moving car, with no place to run and hide.

When the pesky little scoundrel made his attack, Earldean, in her opinion, had been once again cruelly victimized.

Her reaction was just short of a dramatization of a prisoner who was being severally beaten and tortured. Her shrill screeching pierced the air as we tried to block the noise by plugging our ears with our fingers.

Alma tried to dodge the sound with her right shoulder which caused her to pull at the steering wheel making us swerve a little. She pulled off the road to get things under control.

Though she didn't agree with what Ed Earl was doing, she had a hard time scolding her little friend, so he didn't take her seriously.

I had to practically sit on Ed Earl to keep him from tormenting our big sister who cried all the way back to Alma's trailer.

Once there, I was asked to sit on the steps with the two younger ones for a bit while Alma took Earldean inside and tried to settle her down a bit. It was only a minute or two before we heard through the thin walls of the trailer, the sound of running water filling the tub. It was followed shortly by footsteps then muffled music all canned within the confines of the tiny silver habitat.

After Alma had Earldean calmed down and soaking in a bubble bath, the rest of us were allowed inside.

She found some paper and pencils then asked us to just sit quietly for a few minutes drawing or something while we listened to some music.

She walked over to her hi-fi stereo and put on her newly purchased forty five. I guess she thought it was the most appropriate for the occasion as it turned out to be one of Neil Diamond singing "Girl You'll Be a Woman Now".

Often as a child I wondered if that town didn't get its name from all the whispering that was done around there. It seemed like every time you turned around somebody was talking secretively about something they apparently didn't want others to hear. It didn't do much good though because nobody could keep the secret. They couldn't stand it, they just had to give it away to somebody; even if it was just to their best friend or next of kin.

Since just about everybody in town qualified to be one or the other of those, word could travel pretty fast and didn't have very far to go before it reached the edge then came back for another round.

That's why by then it didn't surprise me when in no time at all, after we got to Alma's and while Earldean was still soaking in the tub, the phone was ringing off the wall with concerned inquiries. Of course Alma was hush–hush about it all, but that little silver trailer was only so big and our "little ears" couldn't help but be so big.

We hadn't been there twenty minutes and already Alma was on the phone with the third caller. About that time Ed Earl jumped to his feet and raced to answer the knock at the door, causing the new record to scratch and skip. Alma scrunched her face then abruptly ended her phone conversation saying she didn't have time to talk right then and that she'd have to call them back later.

At the door was her sister, the one we called Mrs. Fletcher, who had arrived with a wrapped gift and a brown paper bag from the Fill-A-Sack.

It would seem that what Trudy had whispered to Alma through the restroom door was for her to send an urgent request for a delivery of fresh dry clothes and beginners size feminine protection. A.S.A.P!

Apparently, the women secretly formed some sort of an emergency task team choosing to take what had started out as a pretty scary situation and turn it into some sort of secret celebration.

Trudy stopped by after work and brought with her a box of chocolates for Earldean saying, "*There ain't nuttin better to take the bitter out of bad day than the rich sweet taste of chocolate*!"

It worked too. Just after eating her first tasty morsel, a big smile came across her face and she was more than willing to share the experience with the rest of us. She even shared one with Ed Earl whom she had forgiven after he was forced to apologize.

When Trudy left she took Earldean back to her house with her while we stayed the night with Alma.

We spent the biggest part of the evening helping her make up pies for the "Family Reunion" that was to be the next day.

During the course of the evening I found myself asking Alma questions about what happened to my sister.

The most I could get out of her was that it was a normal thing that happens to all girls. So my little brother would be spared but what about me and Learline, we were girls, and so was Alma. Had this tragic thing happened to her? Does it hurt?

She kept putting me off saying she'd explain later when the little ones were asleep but by that time she was passed out on her bed with them.

I made my bed on the sofa in hopes that she would wake up and come in there before I fell asleep myself, but she never did.

Trudy and Earldean didn't show up for Sunday school the next morning. Alma said that we'd see them at the reunion later; I was concerned that Earldean might not be there after she'd threatened to never go back to the Eat-A-Bite again.

On that particular morning at church service, I found that the atmosphere was a bit sobering as the announcement was made once again about the death of our mother.

Having been in such a state of grief we had missed the services the week before, so I think this was done as much for our sake as well as for any who might have been hearing it for the first time. For whatever reason, announcing it from the pulpit seemed to have made our mother's death much more bona-fide.

Brother Hemphill announced that pending the length of time it takes for an autopsy; the funeral arrangements were still incomplete at that time. It was followed by a request to continue praying for the safe return of our father who was still missing.

He asked Sister Turner to come up and sing a special, in memory of our mother. I guess the song was mainly for our memory since nobody else really knew her. I couldn't see how in the world they could remember a woman they'd never met.

Sister Clarice Hully accompanied Sister Turner on the electric organ while she sang her own rendition of an old fashion classic. She created a style all her own as she brought forth the lyrics that revealed a little twang as they were carried out in perfect notes pushing forth a vibrato that seem to shake the rafters.

"Safe in the arms of Jesus,
Safe on His gentle breast
There by His love o'ershaded,
Sweetly my Soul shall rest,
Hark! Is the voice of angels,
Borne in a song to me,
Over the fields of glory,
Over the Jasper sea.

At the time I thought her voice was angelic as she was able to hit those extremely high notes like that. It reminded me of Mama trying to sing the same way and made me miss her terribly. So, I just closed my eyes and pretended that was her up there instead of Sister Turner. I could imagine her all dressed up in white, looking like an angel and just singing her heart out to Jesus in heaven.

After church service the kids didn't come ask us to play as usual. I think they weren't sure just what to say. It was just as well; I was anxious to get over to the café for the reunion.

Doc and Estelle said they'd meet us there as we headed back to Alma's to change clothes and pick up the pies.

Upon arriving at the café, we'd found Trudy had put a note on the door, just under the closed sign, that read, *Family reunion today /private party.*

With not having to worry about bothering with customers, we had the whole place to ourselves to move about freely while we were visiting.

I felt honored to be in a place where only special guests were invited. We had never been to a family reunion before and found it to be an exciting event for all involved.

When I had asked about it the night before, Alma had explained how we were all somehow tied together and that it was our relationships that made us related like family.

Trudy offering to let us gather at the Eat-A-Bite was the perfect idea since there was plenty of room to feed a large crowd. She had cleared the counter and set it up like a buffet fit for a king where everybody had put the side dishes they brought with them.

The main course was bar-be-que chicken that she had hooked Cody into cooking using Denby's special secret sauce he had given her.

She had promised him that if he did, she wouldn't ask anything else of him once he pulled the birds off the pit. When he asked what was in it for him she told him that his reward for doing her the favor would be that he'd have the honor of getting to spend his day off relaxing with her and some other really fine folks.

Trudy had a way of making it sound like he was the lucky one for getting to come. I was glad to see she had talked Earldean in to coming anyway in spite of her oath she had made twenty four hours earlier. I could hardly wait to talk with my sister about her big secret, but I could tell it was still a sore subject with her and thought it best to let sleeping dogs lie until later.

Most of the Diner's staff was there and out of uniform, but were still minding the task of preparing to feed people.

Cody and Willy Jay were pushing the tables together creating one long one while Yvonne and one of the others set out napkins and silverware in front of each chair.

Willy Jay's parents were there as his daddy was the butcher over at the Piggly Wiggly and had given Trudy such a good deal on the chickens, she felt obliged to invite them to join us.

She figured that since Willy Jay's mama was Noland's sister, and that she had invited Nolan to come, it was perfectly all right for them to attend being that they too were just all part of the connection.

That led to the notion that she had better invite the Sheriff and his wife since his chief deputy was coming. She didn't want anyone to notice that she was showing any favoritism.

Trouble with Trudy was she didn't know where to cut off the invitations. Everybody she ran into during the brief planning of this reunion she felt was somehow related and had a right to be there.

Of course Doc and Estelle were there and had come straight from church, as well as the Fletchers; who, not only because they were best friends and went practically everywhere together, but also because the Fletcher's were Alma's kinfolk and had done their fair share of providing things from their store for us kids.

We were excited when Denby arrived, along with his niece who had driven him from Sikeston to Bugtussel.

Also with them were Denby's cousin, Harold and his wife Shirley Jean and their kids, who were also related to Trudy.

Everyone spent the biggest part of the day trying to figure out this hodgepodge of people that had gathered to celebrate "a family".

Sheriff McCoy and Deputy Reed spoke very little of the investigation, claiming it was their day off. At least that's what they would say whenever we came around listening in on conversations. I couldn't help but feel that they was just trying to protect us from something as I'd catch one or the other of them talking in a low voice to Denby or Doc as if they were making some sort of plans to find Daddy.

Trudy tapped against the side of a glass with a spoon to get everyone's attention, letting us know it was time to eat. We circled up and held hands at Alma's request where she asked Denby, being he was the eldest, to say grace before we lined up to fix our plates.

He was reluctant at first but when he was told why he was chosen to do so, he then took the honors and began to pray as the crowd quieted down to a silent reverence.

"Oh Lord…you might not remember me seeins how I aint took time ta talk to ya much lately but I knowed ya gotta remember some these other good folks gathered here. I knowed you are up ere in heaven with a few of the sweetest little ole gals you ever made in all the creatin ya done …."

There was a long pause.

"…Virginia, my own sweet wife of twenty eight years who ya seen fit ta take home with ya and now at litt'lo Marline, these here yungin's mama. I knowed they'z restin good up there and You a takin good care of um…azz both good women that woulda liked to been here today but I reckon you got your reasonin behind it all…and well…bless this food we are about to eat and all these fine folks who came here today to be like family.

Tell my Verginny I miss her still and ain't never, ever yet loved another…Amen."

We all responded together with another big, *"Amen"*.

I was astounded at the number of people that could share a meal together as I looked down the long banqueting table at all the faces. I listened during the course of the meal to bits and pieces of the different conversations.

There was talk of the good ole days when who was who and what ever happened to them. Some told short tales and some told tall ones as each tale led to another.

My favorite part was when Denby, who was sitting at the head of the table, maintained most everyone's attention as he told some of the stories of my parents.

He would forget sometimes and catch himself when he talked of Mama in the present tense. He would apologize for it but I didn't mind because I didn't want to think of her as gone anyway.

All the talk for days prior to this was with questions and guesses as to how Mama really died. Though they didn't say much in front of us kids, I'd still caught people saying things when they didn't know that I was listening.

I had found myself second guessing my own theories when I'd overhear one or the other of them talking about different diseases that we would have to be immunized from.

Maybe I was still in denial but I wasn't convinced that it was her illness that killed her. I was pretty sure, as sick as she had been though, that she must have still been awfully weak when she had gone out looking for us. I could only wonder how worried she must have felt when she realized we didn't stay close like we were supposed to have done.

She had to have looked in all of the usual places first before she ventured out further. In doing so she must have stumbled and slipped down into a crevice, knocking rocks loose and was killed in the pile up of debris. We had all come close to doing that a time or two ourselves and she was the very one who would warn us to be careful about that. I'd cringe at the thought of such a painful death. I could only hope that she didn't lie there hurting for a long time but according to what the adults told me, this autopsy thing could tell me just about how long she might have been out there and if she even suffered.

Alma said she still wasn't sure how they could figure out all that sort of stuff after someone dies but that it takes a special kind of doctor called a scientist to do it.

Throughout the conversations, I overheard several of them suggesting ideas for funeral plans and wondering would they be able to wait until we had found Daddy first. With the time that had passed, some wondered if we ever would find him.

It was difficult for some to imagine any man of integrity leaving his wife and small children in the woods for that length of time without checking on their welfare and safety; especially in the extreme heat of the summer we were having that year.

Denby seemed very concerned about the reputation our daddy was getting with these people who didn't really know him. With some claiming that maybe his broke down somewhere and couldn't get back; Doc, trying not to be judgmental, said he felt that car trouble was unlikely if what he had heard about his mechanic skills were true.

Sheriff McCoy reminded them that there was an all points bulletin out to help find him and the biggest hold up was the autopsy at that time. He said the best thing we could do now was for everyone to take this opportunity to rest their worries and try to regain their strength while our hands were tied.

It was difficult to keep the conversation from heading that way but everyone did their part to make the most of the reunion with stories of the olden days and good comments about the food. It all was delicious; every bit, but my favorite was the chicken. It tasted much like the bar-be-que I remembered eating on all special occasions with Denby. Many of them were begging for the secret of Denby's award winning recipe.

When most everyone was through eating, Trudy and Cody disappeared for a moment to the kitchen then returned through the swinging doors with Cody carrying something in his arms that appeared to be on fire.

With a great big smile Trudy sang out… *"We have a surprise for somebody!"*

As they got closer, I could see that the burning thing was very colorful and was crowned with three of the tiniest little candles I'd ever seen; all the ones we had used back home were much bigger.

Other loved ones who waited near the counter joined in their procession from the kitchen to the big table where Cody sat it down in front of Learline and shouted, *"Happy birthday!"* then began singing the birthday song as everyone joined in and sang along.

It was so pretty that I didn't recognize it as cake at first. It was long and flat with pink, bluc and yellow candied flowers stuck all over it.

Learline was handed several packages wrapped in pretty paper. Cody introduced her to the idea of ripping off the paper to find a toy inside. Ed Earl caught on quicker and assisted her in opening the rest. She wasn't quite sure of what to do with that much attention and just sat there looking around at everyone's enthusiasm.

Though her birthday was the day before, it had been overlooked with all that had been going on. Somewhere between Mama's death, Denby's arrival and Earldean's visitor, we kids had lost track of the days.

When Estelle checked her calendar that day she realized it had slipped up on her too and she wanted to do something special so she called Trudy and Alma.

Trudy thought it would be a good idea to wait and celebrate while we had already had a crowd together. They all agreed it would make a better party…especially if they could keep it a secret from us so we'd be surprised too.

So now in addition to all that I had eaten, I just had to make room for some of that pretty cake that was made especially for my baby sister.

We all ate until we were miserable then sat around complaining about it as if no one knew any better than to do so. Someone offered an explanation for it all saying they didn't want to hurt anyone's feelings by not sampling each and every dish that was prepared. Another responded saying it was all just too good to pass up and that when the pain subsided they were going back for more.

There was enough food left over for everyone to take a sampler plate home with them as they said their goodbyes.

I only wished that our own parents could have been there to celebrate our new found relationships. The irony of this all, was that it was the *absence* of these two people who brought this particular group together in the first place.

31
FAMILY BLOOD

Ed Earl was content now that Learline could hold up three of her fingers indicating her true age. He accepted full credit for teaching her how to do that. I, on the other hand, believe it was the three candles that Trudy put on the birthday cake that finally convinced her it was official.

"It's my birthday…I'm three now!" she'd say often over the next several days, or at least until the cake was all gone. Before the novelty of it all wore off she was pretending that it was Baby Doll's birthday too.

Earldean finally let me in on her secret and informed me that her recent "visitor" would be making monthly calls. I accused her of lying to me at first when she went into details about the biological reasoning behind it all. Why would Trudy have told her such a stupid story that didn't make sense? To me it was just downright gross! However, the more she explained about the baby part the more believable she sounded, especially after she compared the complexity of birth to the vague memories we both recalled of one particular day about three years earlier.

This set the wheels in motion as we brainstormed some ideas about Mama and the condition she was in before she took sick and died. Though Alma and Trudy had promised us that, though you may feel like it sometimes, your monthly "visitor" really won't kill you. But we wondered could it kill a baby after it got up inside you?

Mrs. Patterson, from Child Welfare Services, had been keeping up with the search progress through the State Police and Detective Glenn, as well as keeping in touch by phone with Estelle. After the report of our mother's death she told her she would be dropping by periodically to check on us until they found our father. She let her know that a full scale investigation was being done to find any relatives that would claim us.

Now that they had a few names to go by and a little history on where our parents may have been born they were hoping to make some connections in the efforts of finding a permanent placement for us.

She let Estelle know that things didn't appear to be in Daddy's favor at this point unless he had a solid alibi for his lengthy absence. She agreed with most, that it was wrong for him not to have tried to contact the police on the whereabouts of his children. That is, if he in fact, was supposedly out looking for us as we would have liked to have believed.

Trudy acted a little put out with the woman for some reason but Alma and Estelle agreed that they thought she was nice enough about it and just seemed to be doing her job.

Though they weren't in favor of us leaving Whisper Ridge they wanted what was best for us. Trudy said that it may sound selfish but that she felt placing us with relatives that we had never met before, would be emotionally disturbing to us kids. Estelle had to remind her that she and everyone in Whisper Ridge were strangers to us a little over seven weeks before then.

She hadn't thought about that and honestly, neither had I but I could only hope that if it came to that, we'd find our kinfolks would be just as wonderful as the fine people we had found in this town. It was sad to think that we would have to leave and be far away from them.

If we went back home to live in Chinquapin Hollow with Daddy, we would have to stay by ourselves while he worked.

Had anyone asked me, I'd have told them that without my Mama, the hollow would never be the same again, so I'd rather stay right where we were at with Doc, Estelle, Trudy, Alma and Denby; our best friends in the whole world.

Denby was a great help to assist the police with leads to find Daddy and get him home to bury his wife and take care of his children.

Though each led them to dead ends with no sign of Earl Johnson's whereabouts, they did find they were getting tidbits of information leading to his true identity.

Detective Glenn had already made calls and checked out the address that was on the long expired drivers license our daddy was reported to have carried. He found out that address no longer existed and the town's old school records showed no forwarding.

The phone company had provided a list of customers with the last name Johnson who might live in the area but after calling them all, they found none claimed to be related.

Denby insisted on riding with Detective Glenn to Winslow to try to locate this Uncle Leonard whose last name they were uncertain of. And, if it happened that Daddy was found there, he thought that the news about his wife would be better coming from a friend.

Still awaiting the results of the autopsy, Mama's death was not yet determined and the uncertainty of Daddy's disappearance was beginning to look very suspicious.

The investigators weren't so sure that this woman's husband didn't already know she was dead.

Other than the aged picture his old friend had and the description we had given, the detective wasn't sure what he looked like. He agreed that it would be helpful to have Denby ride along to identify him if they had any luck there. He wasn't quite sure what they might find but he felt that with them being friends, the trust factor might come in handy in the event negotiations were necessary.

Once there, they checked out the bus barn to see if anyone knew of or might have remembered any Earl Johnson having worked there.

The young secretary had not been there long enough to be of any help but she suggested they check employee records.

They did find that an Earl Johnson had worked there part time back in 1954 and part of 1955 but had left his job without notifying his boss, who happened to be a man by the name of Leonard Gibson.

Through the same records, they sought out other employees who had worked there around that same time frame and interviewed them.

They were able to find out that Mr. Gibson was supposed to be Daddy's Uncle Leonard whom he had claimed to have lived with there in Winslow.

A few of them couldn't recall all the details but thought they remembered when the boy had come up missing with some girl. With only the gossip of a small town to go by, some guessed he had gotten this young girl pregnant.

It was an affair that apparently had been long forgotten by the locals who said that neither of the kids lived around there long enough to get to know very well. Authorities too, had assumed they just ran away from home.

The current foreman had worked with Uncle Leonard and took his place when he finally retired from that position. He referred to him as Mr. Gibson, saying he had not kept up with him much since he'd left but he happened to remember that just short of his retirement that his wife took sick and was bedfast.

He estimated that it was about two years later that a tragedy took the life of the woman when their house caught on fire and Mr. Gibson couldn't get her out in time.

He told them that the old man had lived in a mobile home out there next to the burned out ruins for a few years until he sold his land and that the whole place was bulldozed to make way for the new highway.

He had heard that Uncle Leonard took the money and had traveled for a few years but had recently moved back to Winslow with a new wife and had built a decent place out on the outskirts of town. He wasn't sure exactly which house it was but said if they headed east in that direction they were sure to find somebody out there who would be able to tell them.

The detective had the records checked for an address to see where a pension check might be going. With this they were finally able to track down Leonard Gibson, a man who appeared to be in his late seventies and living well for a retiree of the bus barn.

His new wife was an attractive and much younger woman who, according to Denby, appeared to be a little more sophisticated than her husband.

Introducing themselves to the couple, they were invited in to their elaborate home where the old man looked out of place in his overalls.

His spouse, on the contrary, who appeared a bit overdressed for house work, served them lemonade then pretended to be tiding up as they began to converse about the nature of their call.

After talking with him at length, they found that he had no idea where Earl Johnson was and had only talked to him once in almost twelve years.

Uncle Leonard told them he had last seen his nephew a month after his eighteenth birthday when they were out at the county auction.

"All Earl talked about…" his uncle said, *"…was gittin his own place and a set of wheels. The boy had a notion to kill two birds with one stone by getting an old bus to drive and live in at the same time. I didn't think it was a bad idea."* Uncle Leonard added. *"It was about time for him to be gittin out on*

his own but Verdi May wanted him to stay in school. I think she liked keeping him around. She told him that if his mind was made up about a bus, that he could park it next to the house out there to sleep in. That way she could still feed him and get him up for school. He'd been savin all his money so he paid cash for the thing but never got any paperwork done on it. He drove off with his fifteen year old girlfriend before the auction was over!"

Denby interrupted with a question, *"He never told ya he was leavin?"*

"Naw, but he did seem to be preoccupied with something all that mornin. I just figured he was studding the idea of makin his first big purchase. The last time I laid eyes on him, he was standin up on the front bumper of that bus he'd just bought with his head stuck up under the hood. I looked over a little later and seen him drivin off in it. I figured he was just gonnna take that little ole gal of his out for a spin but…they never did come back!"

He told them after a brief pause. *"Had Verdi and me all worried for the longest time!"*

The new Mrs. Gibson didn't seem to be sympathetic to her husband's last comment as she poured refills of the lemonade, saying, *"Sounds to me like he was just ungrateful. I wouldn't have worried…I hope he don't come back looking for a handout from us!"*

"Oh…Did you know Earl too?" Denby, being a little defensive, asked in a way that wouldn't sound disrespectful to the man's new wife.

"No…that was before my time…I'm not from this hick town."

"Well I'll tell ya…" Denby said, *"…It don't surprise me none that he didn't say nuttin before he left, he never was good at sayin goodbyes as long as I knowed him…but he didn't ever ask for anything either and he wuttin one for charity…he never took anything unless he could give somethin back in return…now that's the way I seen him."*

Trying to keep to the task at hand Detective Glenn asked Uncle Leonard how well he knew his nephew's girlfriend.

When asked about it, he couldn't recall her last name and had to be reminded that the girl's first name was Marline.

He said that she had supposedly lived in an orphanage in Little Rock until she was taken in by her foster parents who had moved to Winslow around 1953. He recalled hearing his late wife Verdi Mae talked about some troubles the girl was having just before she ran away.

He and Verdi Mae didn't think too highly of her foster family saying they were accusing their nephew of taking advantage of this girl. She wasn't but sixteen at the time and these people thought that he was too old for her. They were against them seeing one another all along so the young couple had to sneak around to date.

He told them how after they took off, the police had come around asking questions of these kids whereabouts. Apparently, her people were under the impression that when neither of these kids could be found, that perhaps the Gibson's might be hiding them out somewhere. Of course they had no idea of where they might have run off to and were offended by the accusations.

When their foster daughter was not found after several years, her family moved on without her.

Uncle Leonard went on to say that about six months after they disappeared, his wife had received a post card with a California postmark letting her know that he was alive and well but there was no mention of the girl.

Even though they were seen leaving together, his aunt thought only one signature indicated they had probably gone their separate ways by then, however, she had no way to find out any different.

They didn't hear from him again until they received a phone call in November, of '56. He said that Earl had told them that he and this Marline had just had a baby together.

It was easy for him to remember the date because it was just a week after Daddy's Aunt Verdi May was diagnosed with cancer.

The reason for the call, he told them, was that these kids were looking to legalize their relationship through marriage so their baby could have Earl's last name. It appeared they had tried to go about it but were told they needed birth certificates to do so. Neither of them had a copy and needed some help getting it done. They were also told that the girl was too young and would need a parent or guardian's signature. They wanted to know if his aunt or uncle would sign saying they were her foster parents now.

He and Aunt Verdi Mae tried to talk him into coming back to Winslow and do the proper thing but his nephew was hardheaded and stubborn and didn't want to do it that way.

The best he could do was promise a visit and check on his aunt when he came to pick up the birth certificates they would be sending off to the state capital for.

They had apparently used his old address there to have the records sent because a few months after that phone call, some mail arrived from the state capital, addressed to Earl Johnson in care of Leonard Gibson.

He said he assumed that's what it was but that it was never opened because they never showed up to pick it up. They had held it there because they didn't have an address to forward any mail to and they had hoped that one day he would show back up.

When Detective Glenn asked if he still had the piece of mail, he was told it had burned in the fire with everything else, including the boy's Aunt Verdi Mae.

Denby told Daddy's uncle how the youngsters ended up living out in Chinquapin Hollow where he had become close friends with his neighbors over the years.

Updating him on his additional family members with names and ages of each of us kids and what had recently happened to our mother, he could surely see the urgency to find this man's nephew.

Denby said that when he first met them, he just assumed they were married with a baby until one day they asked him how to go about getting legal.

He told them how a Justice of the Peace could take care of it for them but my Mama insisted on a preacher.

Denby wondered should they have had a post office box there in town since the mail carrier didn't come out that far in the hollow.

The Detective informed him that he had already checked out the post offices in several counties to see if he they had a box with that name. There were four Earl Johnson's but out of all of them, none turned out to be him. Denby wasn't aware that they didn't have a way of getting mail. He never gave it any thought or he would have offered the use of his mailbox.

Neither Uncle Leonard nor Denby were really sure if the two of them ever got married.

When the detective told him that Mrs. Patterson from the child welfare department would be contacting him about getting the children to him, he asked them not to bother.

He said that he took in Earl only because he belonged to his late wife's sister and was doing his sister-in-law a favor when the boy's daddy died, claiming she was too crazy to look after and provide for him.

He had been put out with the teen when he acted irresponsible and showed little respect to his dying aunt after what all she had done for him.

Denby told him how Daddy didn't say much about his family but when he did, he had talked only good about his Uncle Leonard and never appeared to be disrespectful toward either Verdi May or him.

Uncle Leonard told him that with the boy coming from such a pitiful situation he and his wife did all they could to help him.

He went on to tell how our daddy's only brother and one of his sisters were killed in a car wreck when Ed, his drunken daddy, was driving them home one night.

Such recklessness left his oldest sister crippled for life. She was still alive, as far as he knew, and living in a home for the handicapped unable to care for herself. He said that Ed and eight year old Earl escaped with only a few scratches.

His mama, Liz, never forgave the man and was eaten up with anger and depression to the point that she couldn't function in her right mind.

Denby listened intently to the story of his dear friend's past seeing now why he never wanted to talk about it.

Though he didn't know if any of this would be of useful in finding our daddy, Detective Glenn jotted down more notes in his pad as the old man talked on.

'Earl was pretty much on his on except the few times his daddy tried to sober up. Ed was never able to pull it off completely and he eventually drank himself to death. Verdi May tried to do what she could for her sister from here, we'd send what money we could for a light bill or groceries to help her out. We got really concerned over some of the letters Verdi got from her…Here it was some eight years later and Liz was still grevin the loss of her dead children…as though it just happened the night before…And…though he was six feet under, her anger toward Ed grew stronger by the day. After all this time she was still mad at him for the misery he'd caused her before he went and killed her kids. Next thang ya know… she's claimin he deliberately left her sick with all the bills.

When she quit writtin all together, Verdi May couldn't sleep at night for wonderin if she was alright. We kept thinkin she'd come around but… she was so wrapped up in her sorrow that she couldn't take care of the two kids she still had left. She just laid up in the bed and cried all day.

That oldest girl was crippled up to the point she couldn't even talk. All she could do was just wail out for help and Earl had been the only one who would do anything for her.

It got to where he couldn't go to school for stayin home lookin after his sister and his mama. Turns out…he'd been doing most everything around there long before…before thangs got worst than they already wuz… Even took care of his daddy when he was dying. A youngin that age ought not to have to do all that! He needed to be out of doors, playin ball and bein a kid!

It got to be more than they could handle so his sister was put up in that home I told ya'll about. His mama had taken a turn for the worse and had to be put in a mental hospital so that Earl had no place to go.

After eight long years of lookin after others, we figured it was time somebody looked after him…That's when he came to live with us here in Winslow...We was all the family he had to speak of that wuttin crazy or crippled.

Verdi May cleaned him up and took him to church where they both prayed for his mama. It was a little over a year later before Liz died too and the boy acted like he was more relieved than anything...He had been burdened with prayin for a woman that didn't seem to want to ever get better....Misery had become a way of life for her and she died in likes of such company there in the nut house."

Uncle Leonard said he didn't know if they ever figured out what killed her. Her sister Verdi May thought it was a broken heart but others claimed she might have taken her own life.

"Me?" he said. *"I think all that anger ate her guts up and she rotted from the inside out!"*

Denby shook his head and said, *"What a shame…Poor feller lost his whole family."*

"Well he seemed to be a happy kid after that…Claimed we were his family now!" Uncle Leonard protested before he caught himself getting riled up. *"…At least we thought he's happy till he run away from home…guess he had a right, after all, he'd been tied down long enough, ya think?"*

"Where did you say he moved here from?" the detective asked.

"Murphysboro." Uncle Leonard answered.

"Is that where his family is buried?"

"Yep, they all buried in the same graveyard. There was no money left to bury his mama when she died so Verdi and I had to pay to have her put under. Set us back a bit but somebody had to do it…we the only family she had left...well except Earl…he'z just a kid…he didn't have no money to speak of."

"What was his parents names again?" Detective Glenn asked as he waited with his pen over the paper.

"Ed…er…well full names, Edward and Elizabeth Johnson."

"Are there any more relatives around there that you know of…any more Johnson's that might be related?"

The old man scratched his head and tried to recall any living family members he might have forgotten. Ed had some older half brothers and sisters somewhere but they had a different last name.

He couldn't remember what it was nor was he sure if any of them were still living. He said his own three sons were grown and gone by the time our daddy came to live with him. They were scattered around the country with their own families and he doubted they'd want anything to do with any more kids. Now that he was remarried, he didn't think his new wife would want to fool with any kids either, especially when they were not her own.

She had indicated this with a few grunts as she buzzed around the room, eavesdropping during the conversation. It was confirmed however by her snapping out, *"Now, don't you get any crazy ideas about me taking care of a bunch of your dead wife's family…We shouldn't have to be the ones to take in that girl's bastard children…we don't even know if they are his anyway!"*

When Detective Glenn could see that this didn't sit well with either of the two older men he interrupted her by thanking her for the lemonade and the time, then hurried Denby out.

Uncle Leonard walked them out to the car apologizing for his wife's behavior. *"Thanks James."* he said shaking his hand. *"For being such a good friend and neighbor to Earl. Glad you was there for him… and I'm sure his aunt would be grateful too."*

Denby responded, *"My Pleasure…He's been there for me…good times and bad."*

"I guess I was hard on the boy when I talked with him last." Uncle Leonard said with remorse. *"He's not a bad kid, he just disappointed me by makin us worry about him all them years. I really did enjoy haven him around…he did earn his keep. I hope ya'll able to locate him for them kids' sake."*

"Me too." said Denby. *"He's got some sweet lit'lo youngins, they'z his too…look just like him and Marline…you aught ta least see um!"*

"It's gonna be hard on him when he finds out about that girl of his… he was crazy about her… If ya find him…have him get in touch with me, will ya?" he asked the detective.

"I will" Detective Glenn said, shaking hands and leaving a card before they drove away.

32
ABOVE GROUND

The weather was fairing off as the morning clouds parted to reveal a brilliant blue sky making way for a pleasant sunny day. The worst of the heat wave had passed, leaving a gentle breeze to freshen the atmosphere, so Trudy had propped open the front doors of the Eat-A-Bite to air out the café.

In doing so the invigorating aroma of spaghetti sauce cooking in the kitchen found its way out the doors and down the sidewalks. It had traveled nearly two blocks away, luring in hungry customers who couldn't resist the temptation to come early for the daily special.

I had noticed the shadows on the floor had shifted ever so slightly, bending and stretching in ways I hadn't seen before. Cody told me it was because the sun was falling more toward the southern sky now and it won't be long until fall.

"Fall?" I pondered the word.

I thought by his description, that he meant the sun was going to fall out of the sky and come crashing down on us and burn up everything. It would be the end of the world and now, according to Cody, that time was getting near!

I remember hearing somewhere before that in the end of times the sun was supposed to fall from the sky. I was scared and wanted to hide. When I had explained my fear to Trudy, she suggested that I not pay attention to Cody's nonsense. She assured me the sun would not fall to the earth and that he was just teasing.

When she finished she marched straight to the kitchen and popped Cody on his shoulder with the back of her hand and yelled, *"Which one of them demons that possess you ever made you tell that child such a thang!"*

"OUCH! ...WHAT?...Whatcha claimin' I done this time?"

"Don't play dumb with me...You know what I'm talking about! You'd better quit tormentin them youngins!"

"Woman! Why come you all time pickin on me?"

She must have told him what had happened and he found it to be funny. As a matter of fact, he saw enough humor in it to play with all day. After he finished laughing about it the first time she smacked him, he leaned his head through the order window and yelled, *"The sky is fallin…the sky is fallin!"* Like in the story Alma had told us once of Chicken Little. I ducked under the closest table until I realized it was a joke.

Trudy popped him again saying, *"What'd I tell you?"*

Though she didn't hit him hard enough for it to really hurt, she left him in the kitchen squawking and acting as though he'd been mistreated in front of his audience of coffee drinkers who were sitting at the counter watching through the big opening.

Although these fellows weren't exactly sure as to what was going on, they found it entertaining enough just to watch these two go at it knowing Cody's reputation for teasing her and fishing for a fight. They also knew Trudy's reputation for taking the bait and her inability to resist being reeled into it.

They were all hiding their grins behind their cups when she returned with an explanation of the seasons which I had already known all too well. I misunderstood what he said when we were talking about the shadows and thought he meant it wouldn't be long until the sun falls!

At first I felt stupid, like I really was a dumb hillbilly and then I felt bad that Cody got in trouble for my silly misunderstanding. It was not his fault that I couldn't comprehend his explanation. He was only being nice and making conversation with me, not meaning any harm.

It was kind of funny after I thought about it, so to make up for it I didn't act like a cry baby when he made wisecracks throughout the day.

I just played along with him and laughed when he said, *"Don't worry Sassy…If the sun does fall…it will spring back in six months...Then itta just hang 'round up in the sky summer* (instead of somewhere)…*till it falls again!"*

After he stirred up a few laughs from whoever might have been listening, he'd asked Yvonne and the others at the counter, *"Hey, do ya'll know where the sun went when it got so cold last year?"*

Playing along, pretending not to know answer to his riddle, she retorted, *"No Cody, where did it go?"*

"It went terr." he said pointing out the front window up towards the sky. "*… that's right…It went terr behind them clouds…that's why it to be so cold…that's why come um ta call it winter…git it?!"*

"Cody…that was so corney." one of the waitresses said.

"Yea...Well it's true...It wuz sa cold last went terr...I'z kinda wishin it fall down and set a fire...ya know...warm us up some."

"Can the whole world catch on fire?" Ed Earl asked Cody.

"Well now the way I see it..." he started to answer before he was stopped.

Tending to business, with her back turned to him, Trudy called his name out slowly but sternly, *"COOOODEEEY!"* A simple warning she used to serve as a reminder of the consequences of his teasing.

"Yes um!" he said timidly before returning to his work.

"He givin ya trouble again Trudy?" Deputy Reed asked after stepping in through the open doors and removing his hat.

Recognizing his deep baritone voice, she was delighted at the thought of his presence and tried to contain her revealing beam before looking up to find him standing tall and handsome in his uniform.

"Hey Nolan...Yea, trouble is Cody's middle name...do ya think you can arrest him for somthin...anything...I don't care!"

"Well, reckon who's gonna do all the cookin round here if I'm locked up?" Cody yelled from the kitchen.

Trudy slowly shook her head and waved Cody off saying, "*Guess he thinks he's the only one who cooks around here...*" Then with a flirty smile she asked, "*...Come in for our special today Nolan?*"

"Thought you were the only thing special round here Miss Trudy." he said flirting back with her.

Denby sent word that he'd catch up with us sometime early that day after he took care of some business he had there in town.

We had all been anxiously waiting to hear of what they found in Winslow. More than anything I hoped it was our Daddy.

I had felt myself growing frustrated and angry because he had not come back on his own yet. He had never been gone this long before. Something was not right for him to stay away and if he was out looking for us, he would have found us by now.

Surely Denby would be bringing us good news.

Estelle had gone to spend most of the morning at the beauty shop getting Melba to wash and pile her hair all up high again. She had dropped the rest of us off at the café but took Earldean with her thinking a new hairdo was in order to celebrate the end of her first cycle.

Estelle wanted to cheer her up, as this experience had been coupled with the loss of her mother, both of which were traumatic for an unsuspecting young lady.

She told Trudy that when they finished there, she needed to go by the cleaners and then to Albert's to see if he could repair a broken heel from one of her favorite pair of shoes.

Alma was working at the Clinic with Doc who had an office full of sick people that morning. Since they all had decided that sending us to school would not be a good idea until after the funeral, we had no place to go that morning except to the Café.

Trudy didn't have the heart to say she was too busy to fool with us when Estelle asked for help. She just couldn't say no, especially when she saw how excited we were, knowing this was one of our favorite places to be.

I had been doing my best to keep Learline and Ed Earl away from the opened doors and busy street so Trudy could do what she had to do.

After chasing those two around for the better part of an hour, Trudy suggested we sit in the back booth farther away from the doors and out from under the customers' feet.

She asked us to play quietly until she found something to entertain us while we waited. We each put our finger over our lips and tried to see who could be the quietest as we made a game of it like Mama had taught us before.

She returned with the box of crayons and color books she had starting keeping on hand for times such as these.

She gave me a pair of safety scissors and had me cutting the models out of a Sears and Roebucks Catalog so that I could have some paper dolls.

This worked for a while until Ed Earl and Learline kept fighting over the same colors. To settle their arguments I offered Ed Earl a turn with the scissors which kept him occupied. He found enough pleasure in cutting the scraps into the tiniest pieces he possibly could, that nobody fussed about the mess he was making.

We were so involved in our play that we hadn't noticed our old friend had arrived. He stood at a distance watching us play for a moment before Trudy came through the kitchen door greeting him.

"Hey Denby…how are you doin? Are ya havin a good day today?"

When she said that, I glanced up in time to catch him poised in this pleasant observation of our innocent play.

He hesitated for a moment, then breaking his gaze he turned to answer her. *"Any day above ground is a good day Miss Trudy…and how bout you purdy lady, are you havin a goodun?"*

Though I had not yet given away my knowledge of his arrival, his familiar voice drew the attention of the little ones who leapt with joy and wiggled their way out of the booth so that they could run ahead of me.

"I believe it's bout good as it gonna git!" she responded with a welcoming hug around his neck. *"…And it cain't get no better now that you're here! These kids have been antsy all mornin awaitin on seein you!"*

"DENBY!" we all yelled as we rushed him at the door with hugs. We clung to his side as he made his way to the closest table. *"Did you find our Daddy?"* we wanted to know.

"Not yet but we're still lookin…we gonna find him…he'll show up you'll see!" he assured us, hoping he was right.

Once positioned on a chair, the old man stretched out his arms and received all three of us; returning the affection we bestowed on him.

Ed Earl took hold of his cane and hooked it on the back of the next chair as he'd seen Denby do before.

"You're a good little ole feller…just like ya Daddy. I bet he'z right proud of ya." Denby said sentimentally while gently patting the top of the boy's head.

"Are ya hungry?" Trudy asked him. *"We got a good batch of spaghetti today or would ya like to look at a menu?"*

"Just water for now, thank ye…my appetite aint what it should be today."

Before Trudy left to get the water she noticed the sorrow in Denby's eyes and could tell by the tone in his voice that he was suppressing his melancholy emotions for the sake of us kids.

"Why come ya didn't find my daddy fer me Denby, like ya told me?" Ed Earl asked.

"We tried son…looked all over…but we seen another feller that knowed him… His Uncle Leonard ya daddy told us about. Said he aint seen hide nor hair of him but he told us about him a livin over yonder when he was a boy."

"Is he my kinfolk too…or just my Daddy's?"

"Believe he'z ya great uncle."

It was a nice feeling to know that there were in fact relatives out there who had ties to me through my parents. I curiously asked, *"What does he look like…does he look like Daddy or Mama?"*

"Neither…he's an old man like me…only he'z got some fat stored up on him…He aint blood kin…he'z married once to ya Daddy'z, mama'z, sister…his aunt Verdi May."

"Did you meet her…does she look like Daddy?"

"I cain't rightly say what she looked like…She'z passed on like ya Mama done."

"Daddy's aunt died too? Oh no…Daddy is gonna be so sad when he finds out two of his favorite people's done died now!" I said sitting on the chair next to Denby as my knees grew weak.

"Yea…it's very sad." he said, patting me on the back. *"Ya daddy's had a heavy load ta tote, looks ta be he'z got a bit more when he finds out bout ya Maw. I figured he likely already knows bout his Antee a passin…but hun…he'z still got you youngins…that's a heap more than some folks got. He'z a strong man, ya daddy…he'z seen some tougher trials than most in his life time…reckon that's why he to be so hardened against the world like he gits from time to time…but he'z gonna pull through this un too on account he'z got the likes of you…a sweet lit'lo gal…You kids the best thang ever happen to him…ya know it? "*

Trudy, returning with the water, asked, *"So, how was ya trip to Winslow? Were you able to find out anything?"*

Ed Earl answered for him showing his disappointment, *"He didn't git ta find my Daddy yet Trudy…we aint never gonna find him, huh?"*

"Oh Hun…" Trudy said as she reached to console the lad. *"We'll find him…you'll see!"*

Learline, sensing his frustration, chimed in with an empathetic cry for her mother. Squatting down to draw her in too, Trudy was at a loss for words and could only express her sympathy with a kiss on the top of each of their heads.

"I want my mama!" she cried out loud again as if nobody heard her the first time.

"It's ok baby…come here let Trudy hold ya…there, there." she said to Learline as she also communicated a cry for help to Denby with her eyes.

Denby looked away with a blank stare for a minute to compose some sort of response. *"Hey! Lookie here what I brung ya!"* Denby said, coaching them out of their depression. The distraction worked as he reached into his shirt pocket and pulled out a treat.

"Lollypops!" we all sang out, except Trudy who stifled the rapid change of heart with a command of discipline. *"Not before you eat! They haven't had their lunch yet. I've been so busy I haven't had time to…"*

"Oh now Miss Trudy…they can eat regular ole food anytime…but it aint ever day a kid can git one these here kinda suckers. These come all way from Ozark Sugar Shack…this here place up in the hills there where they make all kinds of taffies, candies…little ole cakes of sorts…had a sign out there on the road said 'Sweeten up your Sour Day.'

We stopped out there on our way back and I figgered ya'll to be a needin somethin ta pleasure ya sweet tooth."

"But itta spoil their appetites, Denby!" Trudy said. *"…and I was just about to…"*

"Aww come on Trudy…We like suckers…we'll still eat…later…Please let us have our lollypops now!" we pleaded.

"I don't know…if Estelle comes in and finds ya'll eatin candy before lunch she'll skin my hide!

"Please…We won't tell her!" I insisted.

"Pweeze Toodie! Me like candies!" baby sister begged with irresistible sweetness in her puppy dog like eyes.

All were grinning about her desperate request as we turned back to Trudy awaiting the verdict.

In a last ditch effort to help us win the battle, Cody, having heard our cries, came walking up behind her and said, *"Toodie, don't be an ole stick in the mud…let them youngins have their treat…it aint like its gonna be the end of the world! Don't you know the sun has to come fallin out the sky fer that to happen?"*

She turned and gave him a look that stopped him in his tracks and sent him running back to the kitchen yelling, *"Look out! I believe the sun is fallin…the sun is fallin! It's the end of the world!"*

Trudy jumped up as if she was going to run after him yelling back, *"Just you wait till I git a hold of ya…you gonna wish it's the end of the world!"*

Then turning her attention back to us, she could see we had not lost focus on a positive victory as we all stared at her with great anticipation. Even our old friend had an expression on his face she couldn't resist saying no to. After a long evaluating moment she threw up her hands and said, *"I guess I'm out numbered…I give up! Go ahead…eat your lollypops. I guess it won't hurt this one time."*

The whole place then broke out in applause and cheers from the customers, who couldn't help but overhear what was going on.

Apparently they had taken a sympathetic view of the escapade, siding with us and were about as tickled with the outcome as we were.

Trudy was taken by surprise at the response of her guests who cheered her on as a hero.

Facing her audience, she stood with her hands on her hips shaking her head in disbelief yet was pleased that they found the whole thing entertaining.

She caught Cody grinning from the kitchen and wondered had he put them up to it. Playing it up, she took a bow which brought on more cheers. As she walked off, she pointed to a few of her regulars and said, *"Now the rest of you…eat your lunch!"*

How funny I remember that being, when the customers laughed as she pretended to fuss at them. It was so out of character for her who was always so sweet and flirty with them.

I don't know if it was the warm sun coming through the windows or the smiles on all the faces but the whole place seemed to be lit up.

We had hardly gotten the paper off and a few licks in before Doc and Alma came in on their lunch break.

"Oh…no,no,no..don't spoil your lunch!" Alma said rushing to take the candy from the baby.

"We came to eat with you…wait till after we eat!" she attempted to explain as the tot went into a fit.

"NO! NO! TOODIE SAID OK! Gimmie back Alma!" Learline screamed.

"Trudy Pearl! What were you thinking?" Alma said turning to see the customers were finding the whole thing funny.

"Toodie's in trouble now!" one of them said, causing the others to laugh.

"It's ok Alma...this one time…just give the baby back her lollypop!" Trudy argued.

"But…Estelle will git us!" she insisted over Learline's crying.

"Just do it…we'll deal with her later!"

"But…You know this'll jest give her sumthin to fuss at us about…and…"

Doc intervened saying, *"Alma, she was quite content…it won't be the first meal they missed…I'll handle Estelle. Give the baby back her candy…please."*

Doc was the heroic one that time and the customers let him know it with another round of applause and cheers.

"Way ta go Doc!" one yelled then whistled.

The place was buzzing with the humor of it all when two tables were pulled together to accommodate our group.

Some of Alma's friends who had just finished eating, filled her and Doc in on what had just happened before they came in.

Fred McMillen and his wife stopped by to say hello to Doc on their way out. When Doc introduced them to Denby, Fred said he was glad to meet him and that he'd heard a lot of good things about him.

"Ya know Doc…sounds like you gonna have to hog tie that wife of yours to keep her off of Trudy's back over her letting um have that candy like she done." he said, picking around so that Trudy could hear him as she set down a tray of drinks.

She just grinned and said, *"What she don't know won't hurt…so ya'll just hush about it!"* Acting as if she was nervous, she turned to us and said, *"Now ya'll hurry up and finish them lollies…go on…bite um…eat um up!"*

"Now Miss Trudy…A Lollypop's to be enjoyed…sposta last a long long time…you know that!" Denby said.

"That's right…That's right." Fred replied. Then turning to his wife he softly said, *"Come on Hun, we better git incase Estelle shows up…a food fight could break out in this place ya know…Bye Yall!"*

"Bye!" several responded.

Another man who had been sitting at the counter stepped over to the table saying, *"I sho hate to miss the rest of the show but I have to get back to work…I wish you the best Miss Trudy."* He finished with a wink and handed her a tip.

She had just set Doc and Alma's plates on the table with a small plate of spaghetti in front of Denby to try even though he said he wasn't hungry.

All was calming down when low and behold, Estelle and Earldean who were returning from the beauty shop, stepped through the opened doors.

For those who knew who they were in relation to us held their breath awaiting Estelle's reaction to the lollipops. Others figured out who she was when Cody yelled through the serving window of the kitchen, *"Hey Ms. Murphy…Earldean…Like ya'llz hairdo's!"*

The whole place got quiet as heads turned toward the doorway. Even the tinkling sound of the dishes seemed to come to a stop, making their entrance more pronounced.

All dolled up in a new dress, Earldean stood motionless with all eyes on her. Her hair had been piled high in a beehive style just like Estelle's.

Oblivious to what had happened before they got there; Estelle assumed all were admiring their breathtaking beauty.

My sister stood at the entrance of the Eat-A-Bite, in much the same way Cinderella stood at the top of the stairs at the ball. Estelle, acting as the fairy godmother, stood proudly next to her. With a gesture of her hand, she encouraged Earldean to be confident and step forward so that she could exhibit her new look.

Reluctantly but obediently, she took a few cautious steps toward us as a smile started to make its way across her face.

Breaking the silence, Ed Earl blurted out, *"What ta heck cha do to ya hair Earldean?"*

Earldean turned red and ran off to the restroom with her hands pressing down over her fresh new hairstyle.

"Oh…Darn it! Ed Earl! Why'd ya have to go and say that? I like to have never got her come in here! She's embarrassed and thinks her new do makes her look funny…Me and Mable think it's pretty…makes her look all grown up…don't ya'll like it?" Estelle said as she made her way to our table. Once there she stopped and noticed how quiet everybody still was. *"What?"* she asked looking around wondering what was going on.

Other than a little snickering, the only sound she heard was Learline lapping on her lollipop.

With only a nub left on the end of a soggy bent stick, the baby stretched out her sticky little fist which tightly held the remains of her treat. She smacked her lips then primed her tiny voice to ask Estelle *"Wanna lick?"*

Well that's all it took to cause everyone to start laughing again. This was followed by Estelle saying, *"That's awful generous of you but…no thanks."*

Then somehow figuring out what might be going on, she asked to be sure, *"Did these kids eat their lunch yet?"*

"Here we go again!" the man at the next table said as others laughed.

"Yea…They eatin now…" Cody says. *"That's all Trudy would let um have was them suckers there…you see how she is? It's awfull ain't it? I tried to tell*

her it wuttin right but you think she'd listen to me? Naw...Wouldn't let nun the rest of us feed um a fittin meal...Alma wuz in on it too! That just aint right if ya ask me, Mrs. Murphy!"

"CODY!" Trudy snapped. *"Estelle, you had to know I was against it... but...Estelle, Denby brought them lollipops all the way from the Sugar Shack and..."*

"Oh well, I guess it won't hurt this one time." she said shocking everyone with her response, then went on like it was nothing. *"I believe I'll have some of that spaghetti. Maybe that's what Earldean wants too...I'd better go see."* But, before she got too far Earldean emerged from the restroom with her hairdo pulled down and going everywhere.

"There! This is how I'm sposta look!" she said as she stomped over to the table, plopped into a chair next to me then folded her arms with a huff.

She really looked funny with her hair crimped and going every which way from being pinned up. The stiffness from the sticky hairspray kept trying to recoil the curls and she fought to straighten them back out. This had only made matters worse causing it to look like a rats nest in the back but nobody dared laugh, though the urge was hard to resist.

Ed Earl, on the other hand, lacked such control and had just busted into laughter when Alma reached and put her hand over his mouth before Earldean could hear him.

Struggling to break free she whispered something in his ear forcing him to concentrate on breathing and listening to her instructions as she slowly released him.

Ed Earl resisted the urge by hiding his grin with his own hand.

For a moment it was quiet again while nobody knew what to say; that was until across the diner someone started slowly applauding leading others to follow.

We all broke out into laughter including Estelle and Earldean when Denby leaned forward and handed her a lollipop too.

I think it got to be where folks just looked for some reason to come into Trudy's place. Mealtime or not, they'd just come to see what Cody might have to say or what was going to happen next. There was hardly a dull moment.

What a wonderful place that café was. Its' charm warmed the hearts of many people who would make eating there part of their weekly routine for many years to come because of times just like that one.

Its homey atmosphere with good food, family-like friends and memorable times, made the Eat-A-Bite one of Whisper Ridge's favorite spots.

For me, it came to be a place to go when I felt good and a place to be if I felt bad. It was a safe, secure place when I was afraid and lonely…a place filled with people from all walks of life who could set aside their differences while they come together for a common cause.

Brother Hemphill had preached one time about how church should be like this. It was at the Eat-A-Bite where I realized what unconditional love was. I believe it's because they carry church inside them and brought it to the café.

At this little greasy spoon, joy would multiply and the burden of sorrow would be shared. Folks were just regular people just trying to do what God made them to do, love one another in spite of their differences.

It was there we first met some of the most important people in our lives; the very same people who made these life changing events bearable for us. They took their turns picking us up when we were down.

Strangers who had nothing to gain by reaching out to help four little lost hillbillies. Overlooking our ignorance, they were patient in teaching us to live in a world so different from the only one we'd ever known.

These people who gathered at this place, bonded with each passing day as they reported information on the efforts to reunite our family. They gave of their time and from their pockets but most of all from their hearts.

They gave us hope when all was unpromising and in turn it was our strengthened faith that kept them hanging on and not giving up on us.

They had no idea that by doing this, it would change their lives as well…forever.

33
TIME OF THE SEASON

Trudy kept a calendar on the back wall in the kitchen that was marked with X's to count off the passing days we had been there in Whisper Ridge looking for our Daddy.

Flipping the pages back and forth to make sure I had not missed any, I counted and recounted each one. Some had notes by them indicating the information on the search.

It was now Friday, the twentieth of September, and had been fifty one days since we had set out for town. Still, we were no closer in our purpose of coming there than we were the first day. Finding our Daddy was a matter of life or death, of course in the beginning we weren't certain which. Never the less, in time we had discovered that it was the latter.

The preceding days were not in vain however, we had learned many important things and why we needed to know them to co-exist with others in the real world.

A few of those things being our daddy's last name, our mothers first and the possibility that they were never really married.

If that be the case then what was our last name? From what I understood by eavesdropping on the adults, they would have had to be married for us to legally have the last name Johnson.

Now I must tell you that living together and/or having children out of wedlock was just unheard of in those days, especially in this part of the country.

The fad of "shacking up together" had only just started in and among the "Hippy" communes out west. Such immoral ideas would not become popular among a more rebellious generation until the next decade; which was a little over a year away.

Based on that information I could see how some of the town folk might have come up with various rumors that had circulated about this couple I call my parents…my family.

By no means were they the first to come up with the scheme of living sinfully in a shack, or a shabby bus in this in this scenario, but in light of this new information that somehow leaked out to the public one might draw the conclusion that my parents were irresponsible and reckless.

Obviously I had never seen that side of them but there were those who thought that that it could possibly exist and felt that it was important for others to weigh their opinions as being more valuable than mine.

On my behalf, there were those who fought against such accusations and thought that the ones allowing these judgmental comments to get back to the innocent children of such said people are themselves the ones who were being irresponsible and reckless.

The fact that children are born out of wedlock has been going on since the beginning of time but it does not make it the child's fault and therefore he or she should not suffer the price of such an abomination.

If it had not been ordered by God Himself for Joseph to marry the young virgin when he discovered his fiancée pregnant, then Jesus himself might have been called a bastard child.

That couple didn't plan it that way…Mary didn't plan to have a baby at such a young age. When her parents first found out about it, to save her reputation, they sent her off to hide out at her cousin Elizabeth's place in another town. They knew way back then just how cruel folks can be when it comes down to acting on their opinions. She could have easily been stoned to death because of how it might have looked. They would have never known until it was too late that this was the mother of God!

I know, I really shouldn't compare myself to Jesus Christ, nor my parents to that particular saintly couple but I'm just saying that God must have picked my parents out for me because I didn't have any say in the matter.

I could only wish He had sent an angel to tell them to give me a whole name that people could remember. Like he did when He told Mary to name her baby Emanuel…but everybody ended up calling Him Jesus anyway. Well at least it was recorded somewhere and he was counted as a bona-fide person with the rest of the people in Bethlehem when they took that census.

Mrs. Patterson told us that children born to unwed mothers take the mother's last name. In order to be able to give our "proper" name when asked, we needed truth of this vital information to be able to answer correctly and possibly find some record of our birth.

This woman was adamant in getting the correct statistics in order for her complete legal reports to be accurate and precise.

This lead to a burning desire for me to find out just "who" I really was; not this nickname I had gone by all of my life, but one like everybody else. I needed a name with all its parts…a first, middle and last…a "proper name" she called it.

It had not mattered to me when it was just our family living down in the hollow but once we walked out of there, it would be the first question always asked; *"What's your name?"*

I had been asked that same question so many times over those first fifty days in the "real" world that it was obviously important information and I needed to know the real answer.

I needed more than just some half-wit hillbilly name I'd been given by my sister who didn't know how to talk at the time. I stewed at the thought of lying to people for ten years and telling them that my name was Sassy. Of course I didn't know that I was lying and that just made me feel even more ignorant when I discovered it.

I was stuck with this frustration too many times when officials, who were trying to help us, could not go any further with their reports because all I could give them was an unofficial name.

They had told us that because of our emotional status they were waiting until after Mama's funeral to send us to school. However, I had overheard Alma tell Trudy that this name issue was one of the things keeping us from registering for any sort of education.

I had been informed by a couple of the kids in Trudy's neighborhood that only babies don't go to school and that a ten year old should at least know their full name by that age.

I was so humiliated to say the least and even more so when yet another one living over in Shady Grove trailer park had the nerve to tell me that his mother told him I could never be a bona-fide person unless I had a bona-fide name to prove it.

I didn't like the feeling of not fitting in the human race anywhere just because I didn't know my name. It wasn't like I didn't have one…surely my parents gave me one.

Now, more than ever, I needed to know for sure and I wasn't aware of how much it bothered me until that particular day.

Denby and the Murphy's were meeting with Mrs. Patterson that morning and had dropped us off at the Clinic so that Alma could keep us there with her. We knew the routine of how we were to behave in the office when sick people would come in to see the Doctor.

Alma had told us before, that sometimes kids make people nervous and I wasn't about to do anything to cause anyone to react like old Mrs. Riley.

I had already looked at every magazine in the place and knew the pages by heart from going in there so much.

Alma was preoccupied with paperwork and had Learline and Baby Doll on the floor next to her stacking blocks. Ed Earl was on the other side of her hooking together paperclips making a long chain.

Earldean was busy practicing her penmanship so that she could write a letter of girl talk to Debbie. She'd found out through Trudy that her niece had been having a monthly visitor for quite some time so she wanted to let Debbie know about how much they had in common now.

Me, I was bored with my confinement of the small area and longed to be outside in the wide open space.

Alma assured me that the parking lot was not a safe place to play off of such a busy street and the younger ones would want to follow me out there.

She finally consented to let me cross the street and walk down to the café where I had promised to help, not hinder, Trudy in getting ready for the lunch rush.

Trudy had a full staff that morning so most everything was done except refilling the saltshakers. I had gathered them all on a tray and had taken them back to the kitchen so as not to make a mess in the dining area.

I glanced up at the calendar again which had already been marked with the fifty first X and wondered how many more would be scratched before this was all over.

Cody was serenading Trudy and a couple of the waitresses with a new song while they all stirred around preparing vegetables and pressing out hamburger patties.

I was so distracted by this name thing that Cody noticed I was not paying him all my attention he usually got when he showed off. He had accepted it when everybody else could work around him without paying him any mind but he didn't want to believe I had already hardened like the rest of the staff had.

As if he were pursuing a career in nonsense, he made several attempts to get my attention by dancing over and singing just to me.

After shooing him away several times he hadn't noticed that something was bothering me.

"Hey ya'll heard that new song on the radio by the Zombies?" he asked.

"Zombies?" Willie Jay said. *"I thought you were strictly an Elvis fan."*

"Naw…I like um all…if'n thez any count…this one is a catchy tune."

"You talkin bout that one called 'Time of the Season'?" one of the girls asked.

"Yea…I believe that's it." Cody responded.

"How'z it go? another asked.

When Cody began to sing it to them with his usual exaggerated antics, they remembered hearing it then joined in like his backup singers.

"What's ya name…What's your name…Who's ya daddy…Who's your daddy…Does he look like me? Has he takin…Has he taken…Any time…Any time…To show…To show you what you need to live…Ya Daddy should have told you…"

As their singing droned on I grew agitated. I don't know what come over me but I felt like I was going crazy!

Maybe it was the words to the song or the melody, though I didn't think I was paying enough attention. It could have been that I didn't understand how people could be so happy when I felt so bad. Just like that, it set me off and I exploded into a fit of rage.

In the middle of their singing I slammed the salt box down on the counter top, knocking over a few of the full, topless shakers, spilling salt all over the place. I ran screaming out the back door of the kitchen that led to the ally, letting the screen door bang behind me.

Several of them rushed to the door to see what happened when Trudy came running past them yelling, *"Are you ok? Sweetie…did you hurt yourself?"*

Cody was right behind her and followed her out the door where they found me on my knees crying.

"Oh…Honey, let me see!" she sympathized as she squatted next to me examining my hands and arms for possible cuts. *"Tell Trudy what happened baby!"*

"IT'S NUTTIN! JUST LEAVE ME ALONE! …And I'm not a baby!" I protested.

"Well, I know you're not a baby, sugar…I just…"

"I'm not sugar either…or honey or sweetie or nun them names people keep callin me! My name aint even Sassy! I don't even know what my name is!" I cried.

"OH Sweetheart!" she said as she put her arms around me and drew me to her. *"…what are you talking about?"*

"MY NAME AINT SWEETHEART!" I wailed out.

Cody tried to arbitrate, *"She don't want ya ta baby her Trudy…cain't cha see that?"*

"Well somthin's wrong Cody…I caint just let her cry like this…What happened?"

"Well her name is Sassy…call her Sassy…think that's what she wants!"

"Well I know that Cody!" she snapped back at him. Then turning my shoulders to face her, she took my face in her hands and asked again, *"What's wrong hun…I…uh..Sassy?"*

I remember looking into her eyes as she aimed my face toward hers and seeing her genuine concern for me. I grabbed hold of her and held tight for fear I might lose her too.

I had yelled at her and was afraid she might not like me anymore.

"I'm sorry Trudy…Please don't be mad at me…Don't leave me… Please!" I begged through the sobs.

"Mad? Why would I be mad? And I ain't goin nowhere!"

"I…I…y…y…yelled at…sniff…you." I timidly said, earnestly attempting to control my bawling. *"Im, sniff…sorry."*

"Oh I'm not mad at you! You was upset was all…I know you're not a baby…I was just lovin on ya is all…Just a pet name…ya know, like we talked about before?"

"But that's just it Trudy… sniff…all I got's pet names…aint nun of um a real one!"

Cody squatted next to us and said, *"Ya know Miss Trudy here likes to call people all sorts of names…least she calls you some good uns…ya oughta hear some the ones she calls me!"*

I grinned briefly before I resumed my crying. *"I know you just playin Trudy…I really don't mind you sayin all them names…I just wish we knowed my real one…all of um…ya know like Alma Fey Nettles, or Trudy Pearl Teffitiller…then there's Melba Jean Hogan and all them people …"* then looking over at Cody as serious as could be I asked, *"…What's your last name? I know you got one…Trudy here says your middle name is Trouble…least you know that!"*

The two of them fell out laughing at what I'd said with me sitting there looking at them wondering what was so funny.

When they told me that trouble was another one of Trudy's pet names for Cody I felt stupid again but laughed along to hide my ignorance. But as soon as that subsided the tears began to flow again.

Trudy dried my wet face with the tail of her apron then Cody helped me up while brushing the dirt off my knees with his other hand.

He began to apologize about his song selection thinking that was in poor taste under the circumstances. I could tell that his inconsideration was not deliberate.

"I'm so sorry Sassy…I just wuttin thankin. I wuttin sangin it ta hurt ya feelins…that wuz jest how the song goes. I guess I ought not done that one huh?"

"Naw…Ya oughtna!" Trudy scolded him. *"That's what happens when ya don't stop and think Cody…Ya all time teasin an…"*

"Naw…It wuttin just that…" I interrupted not wanting those two to bicker. *"…It's not your falt Cody…Its…Its…"*

"Well what happened…Who done it?" they asked.

"Well its…Well I just wanna be boney fried like everbody else!"

"BONEY FRIED?" Cody repeated loudly in a mocking tone that slid off into a high pitch chuckle. Trudy, working hard to keep a straight face herself, signaled to him that this was not a time to play around.

"Yea…I wanna proper name soz I can be boney fried…"

"What do ya mean…like…bona-fide?"

"Oooooh, that'z what ca tryin ta say? Cody asked with a big grin. *"Now I see…what makes ya thank ya aint already? I mean…What do ya want ta be bona-fide to do?*

I went on to tell them about what that kid had told me and they insisted I pay him no mind. They assured me that I was a bona-fide person and they were pretty sure that I had a real name.

If I had one, what was it? And, if I didn't, why not and how can I get one.

I told them that I was mad at my Mama for not teaching me my name before she died. I let them know how mad I was at her for not staying alive and taking care of me.

"She could a waited til we found Daddy…but…we still ain't found him yet and…and...I'M MAD AT HIM TOO! Why come um to do this to us?

...WHY!" I screamed out before folding with painful sobs that seemed to emerge from the pit of my guts.

Cody picked me up and held me as if I was a toddler but as grown as I was, my long legs dangled beneath me. It had been a long time since anyone had picked me up. I forgot how it felt. Trudy patted my back while Cody held tight to me and rocked back and forth with my legs swinging side to side.

"Shhhhhhhh...I got cha sweet girl...now...now don't cry...shhhhh." he said, doing his best to console me. I held on tight to him until I felt my neck get wet with his tears as he pinned with me.

I heard Trudy sniff as she patted my back. I turned to see she was crying too.

"I AM still a baby aint I?" I said through my tears. *"...Just a big ole baby that don't know her name fer nuttin!"*

"It's always good to be somebody's baby!" Trudy said. *"Aint that right Cody?"*

Cody didn't say anything at first as he just gently set me back down.

"I'm so sorry Sassy...or whoever you are...I wish I could fix it for ya....I'd do anythang I could to help ya...if I just knew what to do." he said softly, showing a tender side I'd not yet seen in Cody.

"There aint nuttin ya'll can do about it...it just makes me mad is all." I told them. *"...sorry about getting ya'll sad too."*

They both assured me it was normal and that I had a right to feel that way as long as I didn't get stuck in it.

Cody said I shouldn't blame my mama because it wasn't like she died on purpose. He said he thought she had done a good job teaching us what she had without any school books and that I knew about a lot of things that most grownups didn't know.

He told me that if he was ever lost in the woods somewhere he would hope he'd run across somebody just like me who knew a thing or two about surviving.

Trudy agreed and added that I knew more about fishing and hunting than her ex-husband, who claimed to be an expert.

Cody, though he wasn't much of a "church goer", said he'd learned more about what the Bible said from me than he had any preacher and had no idea there were so many interesting stories in there.

"I don't know about ya daddy's situation or what could be a keepin him...But, ifin I was ya daddy..." he said, clearing his throat, *"...I would be rightly sick and a goin nuts wonderin were ya was and I wouldn't stop a*

lookin till I found ya!" He patted my back saying, *"Ya folks couldn't be bad people to have raised a good youngin like ya self...just hold on to all them good thangs...and if ya knowed he was ya daddy...well...just take his name and play like theyz married...Heck...you might be worrin fer nuttin on that last name. Let's jest say its Johnson iffin anybody wuz ta ask ya."*

They had to get back to work right then but promised to help me if and when they could. We went back inside and didn't say anything about it to the others.

The Eat-A-Bite was full that day and buzzing with chatter when the static came across the radio that hung from Deputy Reed's hip. All quieted down to hear the broken noise in anticipation of any news of finding the missing man.

Sheriff had radioed his deputy to let him know the results back from the autopsy.

He and Detective Glenn were trying to locate the Murphy's and/or James Denby to meet with them and go over the report. He knew Alma and Trudy would want to be there too and wanted him to take care of getting them all together A.S.A.P.

Deputy Reed told him he was over at the café and that we were all there having lunch. Even though it was a little after one o'clock the customers seemed to linger that day pretending to mind their own business long after they had finished eating.

Some folks ordered desert while others requested refills on their coffee or sweet tea. I guess they really had a right to want to know what the sheriff had to say, after all, most of them had spent a great deal of time in the search efforts.

The Deputy and Doc pulled another table over next to the two that we had already pushed together to make extra room to accommodate the men who were on their way over.

Trudy had just poured them the last two cups then put on another pot of coffee shortly after they arrived. After pulling off her apron, she tossed it across the counter then asked Yvonne to take over for her. She poured herself a glass of ice tea then went and sat next to the deputy at the big table.

Everyone was anxious to hear the results of this report which indicated it was something of importance that would make some kind of difference.

According to what Doc said, they were just going to see what kind of sickness she had. I didn't see what difference it would make, she was dead and nothing they had to say could bring her back.

34
STICKS & STONES

As far as a hundred miles away, newspaper readers were drawn in by captivating headlines of their feature story of that Saturday morning, September 21st , 1968. "Mystery Woman Found Dead, Her Children Search for Their Father" read one.

"Missing Mommy Discovered Dead…Disappearing Daddy yet to be found" read another.

"Children Grieve their Mothers Death...Has their Father Abandoned Them?" read yet another.

Closer to home, The Daily Recorder, chose the front page to print their version of the story along with a big picture of our abandoned bus.

Its headlines read:

"Motherless Children Search for Missing Father" and the article stated:

The body of a dead woman was discovered in the woods of Chinquapin Hollow and police believe it to be that of the missing woman they have been searching for.

Police said that they feel sure this is the mother of the four children who were found wandering out on Old Dozier Road, on Aug. 2nd .

Identifying the body has been a challenge because it appears her only possible survivors were her missing husband and these 4 children, whose ages range from 3 to 11 years old.

The body was sent to Little Rock for an autopsy before a neighbor could volunteer to confirm her identity. Without any dental records to go by a positive identification has not yet been made.

When it was reported that the children couldn't find their parents, State and local police formed a search team that included area volunteers. After combing the area they had all but given up when the body was found Wednesday, September 4th, after a thirty five day search in Clifton County and surrounding areas.

Autopsy findings reveal that the woman was about 26 or 27 years old and had been dead for approximately 35-37 days when her badly decomposing body was found.

It was also discovered that she had recently miscarried and consequently died from infection. Examiners estimated that the pregnancy had terminated in or around the third trimester but the cause of complication was undetermined.

Tracing bruises suggested that she might have struggled with an attacker or had a fall but a precise conclusion was inhibited by the amount of decomposition.

However, they were able to detect that the body had possibly been repositioned several times after she died.

Ongoing investigations have officials puzzled as to the exact time and location of the woman's expiration. Because of conflicting testimonies and recent test results, it may take weeks before anyone knows for sure.

Officials said that if this is in fact the woman they have been searching for, then her alleged husband, Earl Johnson, 29, of Chinquapin Hollow, is still missing after 46 days of trying to locate him.

Research on the couple in nine states reveals no official records have been found of their marriage or the births of their children. However, these matters are still under investigation.

According to Clifton authorities, the couple kept their children secluded in a remote area of the woods near Chinquapin Hollow approximately nine miles southwest of Clifton. Isolated from outsiders, they were never told their last name and said they had never attended school.

A Clifton volunteer, Bubba Franks who was part of the search team, claimed to have seen the rusted out old school bus in which this family had been living and determined that it was an unfitting environment to raise children. He said that the children appeared to be undernourished and neglected. He was unsure as to how long they had been left unattended before they were discovered by police in Clifton.

Clifton County officer, Virgil Green, said they are searching for Johnson who was last seen on July 24th in Jay Oklahoma, driving a brown, '57 model, Dodge pickup truck. It is unknown at this time if Johnson has filed for a license for this vehicle.

"*We're not sure who we're dealing with here,*" says Green, "*... because nobody seems to know the man. As far as we know, this might not even be his real name. He's got to know by now we're looking for him but he has not come forward yet to claim his children or the body of his dead wife which leads us to believe that he may be guilty of something...but we're not sure what yet...He* *could even be responsible for the woman's death for all we know. We do believe that he may be armed so it's possible that he could be dangerous."*

If anyone knows the whereabouts of Earl Johnson, please contact the authorities immediately.

A memorial service will be held in honor of the deceased at 10:30 am on Monday morning at The Elm Street Church of Whisper Ridge. The public is invited to attend.

At Trudy's request, Cody had read the article out loud at the café that Saturday morning after one of her customers pointed it out to her. By the time he'd finished, they said she was fit to be tied and was ready to scratch that Virgil fellows eyes out.

Deputy Reed said he thought that Virgil was a disgrace to the uniform and that a lawman had no business running with the likes of Bubba Franks.

It was suggested they drive to Clifton and meet firsthand with the Chief of Police over there about Virgil's self promoted press conference.

As regulars gathered for breakfast or coffee, the topic was all the buzz of the place. With every comment that was made about it, Trudy found it necessary to set the record straight. She would get so steamed up at times about what she thought were lies and allegations that it would have the whole place stewing and sharing in her frustration.

"Why come him to want to make everybody think this woman was murdered or somthin? And for all we know he mighta been the one who took them guns from that place out there…or his hillbilly friend here…Bubba…why come him to have that shotgun he'z toatin?

"Yea…" Cody added, *"…he need a shotgun to find somebody?"*

"Just look at this…" Trudy insisted, tossing the paper down on the counter in front of a customer. *"Who is this Bubba Franks…and what would he know about a decent living environment for youngins?"*

"Never heard of um…have you?" Cody asked another.

Deputy Reed, looking over the customer's shoulder for another look at the paper said, *"I don't remember Bubba Franks volunteerin for the search out yonder."*

"Me neither…" replied a coffee drinker who had. *"He's probably one of Virgil's friends…ya think?"*

"He'z sa hateful" Trudy hissed. *"How can anybody be Virgil's friend? …That ole good fer nuttin…"*

"Now Trudy…" Yvonne interrupted, *"… making remarks against a feller based on how you see him…After all we don't really know this fellow…he might be a disturbed man."*

"Oh, he's disturbed alright…" Deputy Reed agreed. *"A lawman should have a better head on his shoulder."*

Cody laughed, then said, *"Maybe somebody tried knock it off before…jarred a couple of screws loose…ya recon?"*

"Yea…he'z a nut…" Trudy muttered as she wiped the counter off. She turned to walk away when she suddenly spun back around with her arm in full swing. Still holding tightly to one end, she slung the opened wet rag causing it to slap against the edge of the counter. The sudden loud noise jolted the unsuspecting coffee drinkers.

"…And where does he come off claiming that it was the Clifton police who found these kids…If any one deserves the credit it was Mrs. Pane's grandson…or Alma…she was the one who had them left at her doorstep over at the Clinic! Man…this just burns me up! I have a good mind to call her up and let her know how Virgil has stolen the recognition from her!"

"Wow…didn't see that commin…did we?" Cody said as he passed dry napkins across the counter to everyone so that they could blot their spills.

No sooner than she got the words out of her mouth, Trudy was on the phone with Alma who had not yet read that particular paper. Alma only took "The Weekly Town Talk" circular that consisted of mostly local civic activities, sales ads with cents off coupons and things such as that. The last page held a section reserved for birth announcements and the obituary column where the names and information that showed up in these two sections ran for at least a week just to keep them filled. A good bit of the time, the names that showed up in either section belonged to somebody's out of town relatives.

Now this particular day, the information about my Mama's death took up the whole obituary column. However, it was nothing compared to the one in "The Daily Recorder".

Most of the people in Whisper Ridge had already heard the news through word of mouth long before the ink was dry on the paper.

"The Weekly Town Talk" was simply a formality where folks could confirm the "hear say".

Some folks, like Alma, didn't take the big city newspaper daily. They simply waited to read the shared copy when they came in at the café. However, after this story was printed, Trudy threatened to cancel her subscription with them until they replaced that particular reporter with one who could report the truth from a more reliable source.

So after that phone call, Alma rushed down to the Eat-A-Bite before Trudy took a notion to rip the newspaper into shreds.

Back at the Murphy's, Doc and Estelle had read the same story and were a bit put out with it themselves. Though my reading skills were not fully developed at the time, just watching the reaction of the adults was enough to spark the interest needed for me to see what all the fuss was about.

Estelle had left the front page spread out on the coffee table when she went to answer the phone. Mrs. Fletcher's was one of several calls that she had received that morning and she was on the phone with her discussing her opinion of the matter.

My sisters were sleeping in and I had been in the bathroom when Doc and Ed Earl headed out the door and off to the pasture.

While Estelle was preoccupied with the latest phone conversation, I took the opportunity to check out the picture that took up almost a third of the front page.

A closer look revealed Bubba and Virgil standing proudly beside the old bus as if it were a trophy from a big hunt. Virgil was in full uniform standing at an angle so that his gun and holster could clearly be seen and Bubba, shirtless under his overalls, stood proudly with a shotgun propped on his shoulder.

I thought it was a good picture of the bus and wondered if Detective Glenn had taken it with his camera. I scanned the page for familiar words and tried to sound out the others but none of it made much sense to me.

Estelle, in order to "protect the innocent", often kept such things from us knowing that it would only make matters more complicated. She had seen enough Perry Mason to be able to skirt around questions, explain away comments and speak in a code language when necessary to protect little ears from misconceptions. It was not like her to slip up and leave that article open for us to see.

However this morning, when nobody was looking, I pulled the whole page loose from the others and folded it up for closer inspection later. Doc and Estelle had already gone through their morning ritual of passing the sections back and forth for each to read so it probably wouldn't be missed.

Even if I couldn't read, I wanted to save the picture of my first home to look at from time to time, thinking maybe it would help with the homesickness. I'd later learn that it wouldn't.

In fact it would only make matters worse when I'd see Virgil and Bubba standing in the photo. It would make me ill…as if this whole thing was their fault. I guess I needed somebody to blame it on and they were an easy target. I'd later cut them out of the picture. It worked…I felt more at ease looking at it then.

I'd thought to save the words for a time when I would learn to be a better reader at which point I could make sense of the mayhem.

Except for the hole, where those men once stood, I kept the whole page, folded neatly and tucked away in the shoe box I had saved from my first pair of store bought shoes.

There it was kept along with my other little treasures I had collected throughout this adventure; in a tiny space I called my own.

I would hide my box in a safe place wherever I stayed so that nobody would take it from me. And, whenever I'd get homesick, I'd just pull it out and look these things over.

Nobody ever said anything to me about the missing page I had taken. I guess Estelle thought Doc had thrown it away and Doc assumed Estelle had hidden it from us kids.

The following day, Trudy showed up Sunday for services not only to secure her salvation but to preserve our reputation. She would be there to set the record straight about what the papers said for anyone who might have missed that opportunity over at the diner the day before.

Alma and Estelle were prepared too for any questions or comments they thought folks might ask or say that would upset us.

Before church they stood in the parking lot and went over all possible scenarios we might come up against with the other children.

Apparently, a lot of people are funny when it comes to their children's playmates. They might not want them playing with kids like us who come from a shady background and based on the picture those words painted in the paper, who could blame them?

The women were afraid that our new friends may have been warned to stay away from the likes of us and were afraid that would hurt our tender feelings.

They drilled us on what to say if anyone said this, that or the other.

"Well…you know how cruel kids can be to one another." Alma said. *"Sometimes they just spout off at the mouth when they don't have a clue what's really goin on…I know…I was teased as a kid and words can really hurt!"*

"Yea..but most of it they learn from hearin grownups say things that aint right…some of them can be mouthy and their kids are just like um because nobody ever set um straight…ya know what I mean…well, I'll tell ya…I don't mind helping um out."

Estelle stepped in closer and discreetly placed her hand on Trudy's arm as some of the congregation made their way past us to get inside. Waiting for them to pass, she exchanged smiles and nods as they went by with sympathetic stares. *"Now Trudy…kids will be kids and some adults never grow up…but that don't give us a right to go around correcting their children."*

"That's right Trudy…" Alma told her. *"Folks wouldn't take kindly to us fussin at their youngins."*

"That's why it's important these kids know what ta say…" she replied, brushing Ed Earl's hair with her fingers. *"…so they'll be able to handle it themselves!"*

Then turning the boy around to face her she bent down face to face with Ed Earl and said, *"…So, if they say anything mean…or call you names you just tell um…Sticks and stones may break my bones but words will never hurt me…but… if they throw any rocks…or hit'cha wit a stick you come tell me about it…I will step in... if ya need me to."*

"I can wup em bad boys wit a big stick…if theyz ta try-n-git me!" Ed Earl claimed.

Alma reached and pulled him close to her as if she were protecting him from something. Pressing him in close to her side and covering his exposed ear with the palm of her hand.

"Now Trudy…don't put any ideas in this boy's head…it's hard enough as it is now that he can hardly pass a rock that he don't pick it up and hurl it as far as he can…not to mention… grabbin up any stick he comes across and swingin it around in the air…I'm afraid he might put one of his sister's eyes out one of these days if he don't get a hold of his impulses!"

"That's right Trudy." Estelle added. *"We don't need to breed any more violence…besides…we don't know that anyone will say anything to them at*

all…these are our friends and neighbors …lets give um a little credit for tactfulness."

"That's why I told him to come git me!" Trudy said defensively. *"I don't want these kids ta git in any fights…but you never know what it might lead to…I'm just sayin… if it comes to that…but if we teach um to put a smart-aleck in his place when he says sumptin tacky…well…then they might be able to nip it in the bud…know what I mean?"*

Alma shook her head in disagreement as she released Ed Earl who was struggling from her shielding grip.

"Oh…Trudy that don't work…that just makes um meaner than ever. Naw…it's best if ya just ignore um and don't say nuttin at all…exchangin mean words can hurt both ways and just builds up anger that eats away atcha fer a long, long time.

We watched as the women debated what was best for us and I worried that their disagreement would hurt their relationship with one another. I couldn't stand the thought of being responsible for that and felt compelled to take the chance of interrupting their adult conversation.

"Mama always told us to be careful what we say…She said that bad words could hurt a fella pert near as bad as a knife a goin deep in um!"

Ed Earl hopped around indicating he had just remembered something important he needed to share in relation to the conversation.

"Oooow…and Mama told me that if ya say bad words…your tongue u'll turn into a big ole long knife that can cut both sides of your mouth open when ya try ta talk…and then you'll be a big mouth." He then stretched his mouth out with fingers in either side to demonstrate how it might look before he continued with his theory. *"It'ta hurt real bad…and ya can't eat and stuff like 'at."*

"Oh…Ed Earl…that aint what she said…" Earldean corrected him then went on to explained to the amused women. *"…He'z got it all mixed up…He'z a talkin bout one em ere double edged swords…but she didn't say ya tongue would turn into one…she said it could be like one iffin ya let it make ya say bad words…All'z she wuzza meanin wuz ta watch what'cha say so'z ya don't hurt nobody."*

The women forgot all about their disagreement as they turned their attention to what we had to say about it. I knew then, my plan was working and that my interrupting them had been worth the risk, when I saw their frowns slowly melt off of their face. I watched as their worry wrinkles unfolded from the brows and rearranged themselves into pleasant grins. The noise of their secretive squabbling had been restored to agreeable chuckles.

They were amused by Learline's take on the matter when she mimicked her brother's funny face he'd made. And, before they could go any further with their conversation about verbal abuse, I wanted to tell them the truth according to Mama and her Bible.

"Daddy told us bout them sticks and stones…but Mama said that ole sayin wuz a outright lie cause she knowed first hand it didn't work atta way…So, she seen fit to change them words around and teach um usin a different way. She told us we aught ta remember um like this…" I stood up straight and tall then cleared my throat before reciting Mama's revision of the misguiding, old cliché.

"Sticks and stones can break your bones…and in time they'll heal
But, bad or good…the words we choose…do somethin very real.
They hurt or heal…sting or soothe…give or take away
But, once been said…can't get um back…forever will they stay.
While mending bones…from sticks and stones…may cause a little strife
One bad word…can break a heart…and cripple it for life.

"Awwee…You say ya Mama made that up Sassy?" Trudy asked.

Alma reached and took my hands into hers. Holding them she said, *"Sassy! That was real good you remembered it atta way…you did a good job!"*

"Sounds to me like your mother was a real smart lady." Estelle said as she patted my shoulder.

"Yea, she was…" Earldean added. *"She showed us places all up in her Bible where it said how we's suppose ta talk ta one another in a right way…"*

The memory of Mama's voice began to play in my head as if it had been recorded. I recalled how, on a daily basis, she would teach us things about living a good life. It seemed as though she could find a lesson in every little thing that we did.

"Mama always wuz a sayin we'z to live each and ever' day like we'z plantin seeds…the good we say and do…will always give us sumpin better back…just as the bad…will come back on us like wild weeds out of control…it takes a little while…but there will always be a season fer harvest…She's all time telling us…Ya reap whatcha sow."

The tone of my own voice sounded so much like Mama's that it sent chills down my spine. Ed Earl and Earldean must have thought so too.

"Hey…That's just like the way Mama sayz it!"

"That's right...and she'd tell us how we'z ta one day meet Our Maker face ta face and have ta answer fer ever sangle thang we ever said er done...good or bad!

The women all just stood for a moment looking at one another before Alma said, *"I wish we could have met this lady...I bet we would have all been good friends."*

"Me too." said Trudy, as she leaned down and gave Learline a kiss on her forehead. A perfect impression of her lips had been left from lipstick she was wearing, which in turn got a laugh out of Ed Earl.

While Trudy dug through her purse and found a tissue, Learline enjoyed the attention until she was picked up and perched on Trudy's hip so that she could wipe it off.

"She must have been a purdy good teacher..." she continued, while she gently rubbed the spot away. *"...As it seems...I...myself...mighta learned a lesson here today...a lesson passed on from her star students!"*

"We might be making more of it than necessary so let's just get in there and have church...come on kids." Estelle said as she herded us up the steps and into the door.

It just so happened that Brother Hemphill's sermon was about the very conversation we were having outside before service. When he had asked everyone to turn in their Bibles to Ecclesiastes, chapter twelve, verses thirteen and fourteen, Earldean and I shared Mama's Bible across our laps and rustled through the pages to find it. And, though we were close, Estelle had to point it out on the page.

When the preacher read it out loud, we pretended to follow along with our fingers and moved them across the page with the sound of his words.

"Fear God...and keep His commandments...for this is mans all. For God... will bring every work into judgment...including every secret thing...whether good or bad."

Though we couldn't read well enough to make them all out, the message was clear that Mama's teachings had lined up with the Word of God in this chapter as well as several other examples he gave us that morning throughout The Good Book.

At the end church service an announcement was made about the funeral that was to be held the following day.

There was hardly time for anyone to say a word to us about anything as the women gathered their purses and rushed us out of there during the closing hymn. Estelle said it was because we were on a tight schedule but I couldn't help but feel it was mostly to spare us any insensitive remarks or comments from well meaning people.

She told us that it was because we had to meet up with Granny Pane at Trudy's house. The Fletchers had donated five yards of black fabric after Granny offered to make us some new dresses to wear for the funeral. She said that if we could be fitted in time, she could have us each a simple shift sewn up by Monday morning.

She kept her promise as she and Alma drove out to deliver them by eight o'clock the next morning.

There had been enough fabric left for Granny to stitch up a pair of slacks for Ed Earl so that he wouldn't feel left out.

I don't know how she had the time to do it all unless she stayed up all night; but with the small scraps, she even went to the trouble to make a tiny dress for Learline's baby doll.

When it came time to put on our newly sewn clothes, everything turned out to be a close to perfect fit.

Too young to understand the law of fashion, Learline pitched a fit because she wasn't allowed to wear her new white patent leather shoes to the funeral. Even if it hadn't been after Labor Day, the rule of black was not to be broken at a time of mourning.

Doc argued her in her defense as he fussed with Ed Earl's miniature clip-on tie.

"Estelle…what would it hurt to let that baby wear what she wants…who cares which ones match her dress!"

"I care, Hank!" she explained. *"Those white shoes will stick out like a sore thumb and just draw more attention to the poor child!"*

"Well…what's wrong with that?…She likes to get attention."

"It's a bad reflection on me…that's why…I don't want it to get back to Mrs. Patterson that I'm not taking good care of these kids while they are in our care…What if she's there…what will she think?"

"First of all…I doubt that she'll be there…and second, what does the color of shoes have anything to do with how well we take care of the kids?"

"Oh Hank…you just don't understand…do you?"

"Honestly? I don't…but I do understand that you're making a fuss over nothing…It seems to me…"

"Nothing!…Nothing you say?" Estelle stood stiff with frustration, her arms pressed straight beside her and her fists clenched tightly. *"Oooow…Hank Murphy!…You make me so mad sometimes… I am with these kids night and day and I know the whole town is watching every little move*

we make…just to see if we mess up…so they can run back and tell that woman how I can't even do the simple task of dressing these kids right!"

It was clear to Doc by then that the shoes had nothing to do with the mood swing Estelle was going through at the moment. At any rate, we kids still couldn't figure out yet what the argument was about but we'd do our part to stay out of the way.

Ed Earl took off running up the stairs while Earldean and I fussed with putting on the shoes Estelle had bought special for Learline to wear that day with her black dress.

Her makeup ran as she began to cry so she reached for a tissue to blot her face.

"Oh Darlin…Now don't cry…" Doc said as he tried to console his wife, *"…You are doin a fine job of handlin these kids…they know it…and that's what's really important…I mean…What does it matter what anybody else thinks?"*

He reached out and pulled her close to him. *"I understand you want things to be perfect…you want them to have all the things they've missed out on…right? …but sweetheart, shoes aren't as important as the love and care you give um. That's far more than most folks would take the time to do…It takes more than a handful of people to make up for the loss these kids are going through right now…they can't even began to comprehend what this is all about right now…but later they will be grateful and thank you for trying to fill that void…the best way you know how."*

He hugged her tight and patted her back saying, *"Why don't you just try to relax…you must be exhausted…I'll finish getting them ready to go."*

"No Hank…I'll do it."

"But…"

"No…I want to…really…I'll be alright."

Reflecting back, I can see how frustrating it must have been for Estelle and Doc to have dealt with all the problems we must have caused for them.

Before we came along, they were at a point in their life when all should have been calm and easygoing for them. Their kids were grown and out of the house, finances were stable and they finally had time to spend together. They could come and go as they pleased without having to worry much about having to take care of anybody but each other.

Though they never made us feel unwelcome, the added stress of worrying about us didn't come easy for a woman who was at her peak of menopause. Estelle was not only going through changes in her life but she was dealing with the changes in ours as well.

We stopped at the Clinic along the way to pick up Alma. She had just finished hanging a black wreath on the door there with a note saying they were closed for the day.

Trudy had done the same over at the Eat-A–Bite, except her note said they would be open by three o'clock coffee time, with grill orders only for supper. At the bottom of the page it gave the time and location for the funeral services for Mama. The whole town of Whisper Ridge seemed to have shut down for a few hours that morning when most of them gathered at the church.

It's true that some might have been curiosity seekers but most seemed to be sincere in paying their respects. It's hard to imagine that many people taking time out of their busy lives to care enough to mourn the death of a woman they never knew.

Needles to say, Brother Hemphill was thrilled to have a packed house as people from both of the churches in town came together, along with some who hadn't been in years.

Brother Jessie was there early as he didn't have to run the church van for this service. He and Mrs. Sharon were standing at the back of an opened van receiving several big sprays of beautiful flowers that had just been delivered to the church. It was not the church van but another from a town down the road. This van had flowers painted on the side with the name of a big flower shop over there.

When they saw us coming across the parking lot, Brother Jessie waved down a woman who summoned two men in black suits who then took the flowers and carried them into the church.

Mrs. Sharon made her way toward us and led us in to a small room off the foyer where we waited for Trudy to join us.

While we waited, Alma put Learline's hair up in pig tails then tied tiny black ribbons around the rubber bands.

Estelle fussed quietly the whole time she spent brushing the lent and dog hairs off of my little brother's clothes saying, *'Ed Earl…why did you have to play with Festus, today of all days?…when you're wearin your new black britches that Granny made ya?…Just look at ya…can't you just leave the house one time without huggin all over that dog?"*

"But I don't mind…I love him…he'z my best friend!" Ed Earl explained as he slowly turned to allow her to finish.

"Just look at this! Why can't you just stay clean long enough to get where we're goin?"

"Oh, he looks fine, Hun." Doc said, smiling and patting the youngster on the head in an attempt to press down his cow lick. *"Time flys don't it?"*

"What do ya mean Hank?"

"Well…seems like only yesterday you were here fussin at our little boy about the same thing…remember…at your sisters wedding?"

"Yea…he was the ring bearer…and I had him all ready to go when he slipped out the door and went to the pasture out back. They held the wedding up until we found im…he was a mess!"

"It was in this same room where we had to bring him in and clean him up…you were so mad at him!"

"Can ya blame me? I had fought so hard to get him ready on time then to keep him clean all the way here…He looked so adorable too…before that happened."

"Well…boys will be boys huh?…'Bout how old was he then?" Alma asked.

"He was only four…about yea tall…just a little fellow." Doc answered, measuring the approximate height his son might have been at the time. Then he shook his head and laughed saying, *"But I tell ya…he put up a fight to come in and act prim and proper in the middle of his playin. He was like restllin one of them bulls out there! It took both of us to get him in here…by that time we were all dirty…including the bride! He had tried to hide under her big white dress in order to keep from getting in trouble with his mother. Estelle was about fit to be tied herself!"*

"Yea…I was…I fussed till we both cried…he went down the aisle all muddy and red faced…it's funny now but it wasn't back then. Hank Jr. kept me so busy trying to keep him out of mischief…yea…you're right Alma…boys will be boys."

Then Ed Earl asked if they were talking about that same little boy in the pictures back at their house. Doc told him it was and reminded him that his only son was all grown up now and off fighting in the war in Vietnam.

"He always likes to be in the middle of the action…he's probably filthy dirty in some foxhole over there….I pray he's alright" Estelle said as she brushed some lent off the front of Doc's jacket.

"I'm sure he's doin just fine, Hun….Boys will be boys…right?" he said wiping a tear from her eye with his thumb.

"Right…more than likely he's covered in mud right now and lovin every minute of it…at least I hope it's only mud."

She kept silent as she adjusted Doc's tie then gave him a little kiss on the lips. He repaid her with another then a lengthy embrace that was interrupted only by Trudy coming through the door looking for all of us.

"Here ya'll are! I think they're about ready to start…they told me to wait in here with ya'll and they'll come get us...they're taking care of a few last minute details."

"Toodie!" Learline screeched as we kids all rushed her for hugs.

"Just look how precious you are all dolled up in your purdy new black dresses…and look at you, Ed Earl…some kinna handsome…I tell you!

"Lookie at Baby Doll, Toodie…she gotta dress like me too."

"How 'bout that!…and look at cha sweet little hair do!" Trudy said picking her up to hold her. *"Where did ya git them darlin pig tales and ribbins?"*

"Alma made um fer her…she wanted us to make some fer her doll but the hair wuz too short ta fool with." Earldean answered for her then went on to say, *"Ya look right nice ya-self Trudy…I like em there high heel shoes ya wearin there…Won't be long fore my feet be big nuff fer a pair my own…ya thank?"*

"Maybe so…you keep on a growin like ya a doin…you'll be a young lady before ya know it."

"I already am, Trudy!" she said softly but still loud enough for us all to hear in the small room. *"…don't cha remember…I got my visitor already."*

"Oh…That's right...no…I ain't forgot."

"How could anybody forget bout that, Earldean?" I asked, a little put out with her by then. *"That's all you ever talk about anymore…between you and Ed Earl…the whole world oughtta know by now…I'm surprised you ain't done gone clear to Clifton and told Vergil so'z he can have um tell some more lies…He can lie and say how you'z a grown up woman by now!"*

"Now Sassy…Calm down." Alma said. *"Whatsa matter with ya anyhow…don't cha know ya ain't spose ta talk bout that sort of stuff in mixed company? Ya got Doc…and ya brother in here…they's boys…girls don't say them kinna thangs around the fellers!"*

"Well. He'z a doctor aint he?" I smarted off. *"He oughta know about that sortta stuff…don't cha thank?…And she ain't keeping her secret hid very well from Ed Earl…Everybody knows by now!"* I huffed loudly then pointed

my finger in a gesture of declaration in order to finish spouting off these resentful accusations, *"You seen the way she acts about it! It ain't no secret…They might as well put it on the television news, ' bout how Earldean done got her visitor!"*

Earldean turned beet red then covered her shameful body with her arms as if to protect herself from such an attack.

"Oh ya'll!…PLEASE…Don't let um do somthin like that!" sister yelled out loud, after which, Doc grabbed Ed Earl by the hand and led him quickly out of the room.

"Quiet, Earldean…shhh…not so loud! Estelle hushed her simultaneously with the other two women so that we couldn't be heard through the door.

"Shhhhhh…it's alright sweetheart."

"Ok…ok…let's talk soft, now!"

Alma put her arm around me and walked me to the other side of the tiny room. I could hear Estelle and Trudy explaining to Earldean how she'd never have to worry about anything like that ever happening. They told her newspapers only prints things the general public wants to read about and that something of that nature would be extremely personal.

Estelle was saying, *"There is no way on earth that you will ever hear about such things as a delicate as that on the television…why…I believe that's against the law…huh?…don't you think so, Trudy?"*

"Oh, I'm sure of it…the T.V. is the last place you'd hear something about a female's minstrel cycle! Whoever would want to see such a private matter bein out there for the whole world ta look at that…that would be downright nasty! Naw…that ain't gonna happen, Hun…you ain't never gotta worry about bein embarrassed 'bout somthin like that!"

About that time, there was a knock at the door. It was Doc telling us it was time to get started, though I still wasn't sure what we were about to start doing. Alma kept her arm around me and hesitated while the others walked out first. She then turned to me and said, *"Sassy, I know what it's like havin sisters…sometimes ya have thangs in common and sometimes ya don't…there's times ya love um and other times….well ya just wanna choke um! …But, she's still ya sister…Good Lord willin…you'll grow up to be best of friends."*

"That aint gonna ever happen, Alma…I'll never be the same age as her…she'll always be bigger than me."

"Naw, one day…you'll see…age won't matter…Right now ain't the time to be worrin bout all that…today…well…it's about ya Mama…Now whatcha thank she'd have ta say 'bout you two actin like that toward one 'nother?…Whatcha recon she'd say 'bout them mean words you used on ya sister there?…she wouldn't like it none…now would she?"

I held my head in shame and answered, *"No ma'am."*

"Naw…I didn't thank so…I know ya all out a sorts 'boutcha Mama today…and that's whatcha really upset about now ain't it?…Well that's ta be expected…Earldean is a goin throug the same thang you are…so don't take it out on ya sister…alright?"

I didn't necessarily agree with her but I didn't have time to go into it right then with Mama's funeral about to start.

Once outside the room and into the small area at the entrance, I kept my head down in shame, as much as in embarrassment that somebody might have heard Alma scolding me.

Without looking up I could see only the legs of a small crowd of mostly men, gathered there. I worried that they might have heard through the door what I said to Earldean.

The heavy aroma of Aqua Velva, Old Spice and Brute mixed with a back note of stale cigarette smoke had begun to clash with Trudy's Taboo and Alma's Evening In Paris.

I felt smothered in the crowed area and wanted to go outside for a breath of fresh air but I wasn't sure if I could squeeze through the crowd before I threw up on somebody. I swallowed hard past the lump in my throat, to suppress the thought as best as I could.

The low drone of voices softened to a quiet murmur as the faint sound of organ music began playing a poignant slow tune.

Several late comers shook hands with Doc and whispered things to Estelle, Trudy and Alma as they made their way past us to find a seat.

A weird feeling came over me as I tried to prepare myself for the unfamiliar event about to take place. Somehow it didn't seem like other adventures of my recent past. I had not gotten enough information on what was to take place and what might be expected of me. Nobody really seemed to want to talk about this funeral thing like they did the Labor Day Celebration.

I felt a tap on my left shoulder and turned around but couldn't figure out who was trying to get my attention. Everyone around me seemed to be preoccupied with someone else.

When I was tapped again I spun all the way around but still didn't see who had done that. I was certain someone had tapped me by the third time but it made no sense until I looked over my right shoulder and saw Cody standing there with his arms folded, looking off and pretending he didn't do it. But I knew better; it was just like him to tease me like that.

I hardly recognized him at first without his food stained apron and paper hat. He wore instead, some baggy pants with an oversized jacket and that was very much like one that I had seen Doc wear before. He topped it all off with a purple clip on bow tie. Trudy would later that day inform him didn't really match but I on the other hand thought he looked handsome.

His hair was parted on one side and slicked over with one little curl that appeared to have been purposely left dangling over the center of his forehead.

"Cody?" I said quietly, *"...is that you?"*

He turned, then jumped back and acted surprised to see me.

"Well...Hey there, Sassy!...how ya doin?" he answered in a hushed voice. *"...didn't see ya standin right here by me all this time."*

Alma gently elbowed him, *"Shhhh...Cody, Quit that lyin...you in the house of the Lord ya know!"*

"Lyin?...I ain't lyin Alma Fey!...Sassy...you hear her call me a liar?"

"Shhh...keep it down!" Trudy whispered. When she turned back around, he made a funny face at the back of her head which sent Ed Earl off giggling.

"Whatch do to ya hair?" I asked him in a soft voice.

He smiled, looked around as if to be inconspicuous then bent down so that I could hear him whisper. *"Like it...Look just like Elvis...don't cha thank?"*

"How ge git it ta stay that'a way?"

He leaned back down and softly sang the jingle we'd learned from a radio commercial. *"Brill-Cream...a-little-dab-a-do-ya!"*

I began to chuckle at his little song and dance as he snapped his fingers and tapped his shoe on the floor. This got Trudy's attention; just as he had really planned all along.

"Shhhh...Cody...Quit that sangin...folks can hear ya all the way out yonder!"

"What?...I cain't sang in a church?...Who ever heard a such?"

Pretending to be serious, Trudy squinted her eyes at him and quietly scolded him through her gritted teeth. *"Now…you know that ain't no church song…nobody want's ta hear you sangin 'bout hair oil…now cut it out!"*

"Hey…now listen here woman…" he mumbled, *"…you might be my boss ov'r the Café…but ya ain't the boss of this here place…Naw…God's the boss here!"*

"Yea, that's right…You'll have to answer to him…and He's gonna gicha fret' tere lyin ta little youngin's like ya do!"

"That ain't lyin…It don't count iffin ya just playin!"

"We'll see…now hush…we about ta go in."

"You hush!"

"Well Shhhh then…"

"You shhh…"

Half the folks back there were snickering at them and the other half responded in unison to their banter. *"Shhhhhhhhhhhhhhhhhh!"*

The quiet shuffling of bodies in the small space made way for him to get by as he mumbled under his breath, *"Excuse me…can I git by, please…I'm gettin away from these gals…'fore they git me in trouble."*

Smiling as he squeezed passed them, I heard somebody softly say, *"Leave it to Cody to have folks laughin at a funeral."*

Estelle was handed a red carnation with the stem broke off. I watched as she then turned and fastened it to the chest of Doc's jacket. He stood very still though he seemed confident that his wife would not stick him with the long sharp pins.

Among a small crowd we heard the pastor instruct Brother Jessie to allow him get up to the pulpit before we were to be ushered up the isle to the front pew that had been reserved just for us and all of our caretakers. He seemed to be personally honored to escort us along with Alma, Trudy, and the Murphy's to our places.

As we stepped into the back of the packed out Sanctuary, I noticed the lighting seemed different than it had been before. It might have been all those beautiful flowers in contrast to all the dark clothing everyone was wearing. Everyone that is, except Charlie Wayne the milk man, who had just finished his route and hadn't had time to change out of his white uniform.

He stood at the back against the wall as not to be noticed…but who could help it? Estelle was right; she said that Learline's white shoes would stick out like a sore thumb…and they really did. She and Charlie Wayne were the only ones wearing any white.

Detective Glenn who was leaning against the wall next to Charlie Wayne, unfolded his arms then stood at attention when he noticed us come in.

Some folks turned to see us coming and the hush of voices followed each slow step we made. Working our way toward the front of the church we passed a few faces that we recognized from the Sunday congregation and places around town.

Willy Jay and his parents, as well as Yvonne and the rest of the crew from the café, were there and had all taken up the whole back row. The regular coffee drinkers from over there were sitting in the pew just in front of them.

Granny Pane, who was sitting a few rows up from that group sat next to her daughter Jane. I looked over past them for Huey but didn't see him in the crowd and wondered if he was at school.

Jane leaned over and whispered how nice we looked in our new dresses. She grinned when she saw Baby Doll hanging by one arm from Learline's hand wearing the miniature black jumper like ours. She might have helped her mother with getting our dresses ready by the deadline but if she did, she never took credit for it.

Granny reached out for my hand as we passed and I leaned in for a hug. When she smiled at me, I didn't notice her toothless grin as much as I did the color of her caring eyes. They were the same shade as Denby's.

Melba and the girls from over at the beauty shop were there, dressed in black and all wearing the same big hairdos that they had managed to perfectly duplicate from one another. At a glance, with me being an amateur at distinguishing the different shades of shampoo in color rinse, it was hard for me to tell which one was Melba at first.

The Fletchers were there, seated in the same pew that they normally sat in every Sunday and Wednesday. Next to them were some other folks who were regulars there too.

Doc reached over and patted Fred McMillen on the shoulder and shook his hand as we passed him by. He was seated next to his wife and Collis who had managed to be all cleaned up except for his oil stained, callused hands; one of which he used to reach across and greet Doc's with.

I hesitated to take another step when I turned to see Lester and Myrtle Riley sitting there a few rows up and across the aisle.

With the use of a cane and a stretched out pair of slippers, they managed to come and pay their respects in spite of Myrtle Riley's handicap.

Old man Riley nodded his head as usual, to acknowledge me when he caught me staring at them.

However, the large old woman sat leaning forward, on the edge of the pew, just staring at her folded hands that were propped on the handle of the cane in front of her.

She looked as though she was trying to ignore us then Earldean nudged me a little to move along. At the moment, my feet seemed to be stuck to the floor as I stumbled a little in the procession almost causing Trudy to fall off her high heels.

In the brief commotion, Myrtle Riley cut her bloodshot eyes toward me then quickly back down to her hands again. She slowly shook her head in a way that somebody might think she was in sad disbelief.

My first instincts read her body language to be saying, "No, you stinky little girl…I ain't gonna look at you and don't want you lookin at me either!"

I managed to get a second glimpse of her before I moved along, and saw a teardrop fall from her cheek.

I may have misunderstood her at first. On a second thought, I wondered if she might have felt just a little bit of compassion for the children of the only friend she probably ever had on the face of this earth.

I had no idea that she could possibly care that much; I mean, enough to make her cry. Mean people like Myrtle Riley don't keep friends long and Mama just might have been one of the few who didn't shun her because of her negative attitude.

Myrtle Riley could rearrange blame and spout off mistrusting accusations about every single thing from the war that was going on to who might have broke into her house and stole her big ole dirty underwear. It didn't matter what it was; for every breath of fresh air she took in came out "stinkin words."

Who knows why people like her choose to be so full of hate instead of love…maybe she didn't know she had a choice.

I don't know all of the excuses she may have used for being the way she was but in her own mind she figured she earned the right to be that way. At all costs, she paid the price for her decisions and actions because she reaped what she sowed.

It must have hurt her terribly to lose a friend like my Mama; for she turned out to be one of the few people in Myrtle Riley's life who didn't just walk away from her of their own accord.

Now, all she had left was Lester, who sat next to her patting her knee saying, *"You're gonna be alright…I'm still here."*

Sheriff McCoy and another deputy sat with their wives on one side and across the aisle from them. Sam Hully sat next to his wife Clarice, who was proud to have her husband inside a church house no matter what the circumstances.

Martha Barnett stood up and snapped a picture for the Town Talk circular then sat back down next to her husband the banker. They were sitting with some more old timers who they normally hung out with at the diner.

I remember seeing the Fletchers and two of Alma's other sisters there too. Next to them was the Avon Lady. Her red earrings and neck beads seem to pop out against the dark navy jacket she wore and her hair looked whiter than ever. She was there with one of the checkers from over at the Piggly Wiggly grocery store.

Mayor Scott and some of the town's officials took time out of their busy schedules to attend. Though, back then, I wasn't aware what it was they really did with their time.

Learline broke loose from Trudy and ran up to show Mr. Albert that she still was wearing her favorite shoes that Estelle had gotten from over at his shoe store. It was enough that Estelle gave in and let her wear them, hoping no one would notice but she was sure this would bring it to everyone's attention. He leaned forward with raised brows then smiled and patted her on the head. She grabbed her head and warned him, *"Don't pull my piggy tails!"* causing him and a few other people around him to stifle a laugh.

Old Woody and his son Jimbo was there along with some of the folks from down at the marina.

The twins, Robert and Rebecca, who by this time were college graduates, sat on either of their proud Paw. We had come to know them in passing as regulars over at the Eat-A-Bite now that they both had jobs in town. They both claimed they had outgrown the younger crowd who hung out down at the Burger Doodle.

I didn't think anything of it but Trudy and Alma seemed a bit nervous about the fact that Mrs. Paterson showed up and was there with another lady from the welfare office. They were sitting close to the front and acknowledge us with a nod as we passed them by.

I had been so distracted by all the people on the way in that I had hardly noticed all the beautiful bouquets of flowers at the front of the church. Never before had I seen such a magnificent array of color in one small place.

There were so many different kinds that I'd never seen before all of which had been sent in honor of my Mother.

Brother Jessie guided us to the very front row on the left where we found Denby sitting solemnly by himself. His demeanor altered from gloom to glad at the sight of us rounding the corner of the pew. Of course we greeted him with our familiar excitement where some might have thought we'd not seen him in a real long time.

Trudy turned and winked at her cousin from Bugtussel, who sat directly behind him. Smiling and shaking her head she then leaned back and whispered over her shoulder, *"They're just crazy about him…they do this every time they see him"*.

After he'd seen that we were all seated, Brother Jessie walked over and sat next to his wife Sharon who was sitting by Sister Hemphill and Sister Turner.

I was just getting comfortable in my spot between Denby and Earldean when I turned to see Nolan Reed coming up the aisle. He was not in his police uniform but he still looked handsome in his dark suit.

Following close behind him were Denby's cousin Harold, Huey's Paw Inky, Cody and a Mr. Gibson; who I would later find out was Daddy's Uncle Leonard.

As they all filed in to sit on the pew across the aisle from us, I noticed that each of them, like Doc, was wearing a red flower fastened to their jackets.

When Ed Earl started waving vigorously at Cody, Doc settled him back on the seat between him and Estelle while Alma pulled Learline who was trying to follow suit, onto her lap. Holding on tightly she whispered something in her ear that was interesting enough to keep her attention so that the tot wouldn't be a distraction.

Everyone sat quietly as the organist finished playing her soft, sad music.

Brother Turner stood in the pulpit and tapped on the microphone before he spoke into it.

"Today…Brothers and Sisters…we gather together to bid our farewells to this earthly vessel that The Lord God has now called home to be with Him…Though it is a sad day for us…I believe it is a glorious day for Him as he welcomes to His mighty Kingdom…one godly woman…a Mrs. Marline Johnson…She was survived by her husband Earl Johnson…three daughters, Earldean…Shirline and Learline…one son…Edward Earl. She was preceded in death by her late baby boy…James Leonard.

I was trying to get a perception of what he was talking about when I recognized the names of my siblings. However, two I did not recognize, nor did I hear my name called among them. My mind wandered for a moment to trace what he had said about a baby boy.

"…And, though only a few of us here ever had the opportunity to meet and know her personally…we are here to bear the burden of her passin…for those lives that she has left behind…Yes…brothers and sisters…we must stand behind those lives that must go on without her…We have among us today…a man who was a good neighbor and friend to the young woman…and I've asked him to give us a few good words about her…if ya will…Mr. James Denby.

Denby came off the seat with the help of his cane and was assisted by an usher up the few steps to the Altar. The man adjusted the microphone so that Denby could be heard when he gave the eulogy. The old man appeared to be nervous and uncomfortable in doing so as he cleared his throat and began to speak into it. We could hear his heavy breathing as though he had exerted himself in getting up there. So, at first he talked slowly until he got his bearing.

"I um…I…excuse me." he cleared his throat again. *"I just…um…Well, I just wanna say…its right nice…how you folks seen fit to be here taday…This is a mighty fine thang you a doin ta put this here funeral on fer that gal younder."* he was saying as he pointed and brought my attention to a wooden crate that looked somewhat like a large storage trunk.

There was a spray of flowers that had been laid across the top so that I had not noticed it before.

"…Now I'm glad that they seen fit not to open up that there casket…cause a body that ever knowed her…wouldn't even recognize who they'd seen iffin theyz ta take a look at what was left of the shell she lived in…"

I stared at the box and figured out that that's where they put Mama after they found her. My heart pounded as my mind wandered back and forth between the thought of her suffocating and what Denby was saying about her being in there.

Trudy reached and put her arm around Earldean who had turned toward her to bury her face. She must have had the same thoughts as I did at that moment.

"...Then ya mighta got the notion...of Marline bein just a dead and gone...then soon she'd be forgoton...But I'm here ta tell ya...iffin ya knowed her like I done...that little Mama is unforgettable...Her memory will live on in the hearts of those of us who loved her and ever thang she stood fer."

I tried to imagine that she was just sleeping inside that thing and that any moment she would wake up, push open the lid and say, *"Alright...I feel better now...You youngins come on...lets git back home 'fore dark...ya Daddy ought ta be back any minute now!"*

I resisted the thought of never hearing her voice again though already I had forgotten the sound of it. I just knew I would recognize it if I could just hear it one more time. So I just kept watching and waiting, hoping somehow she would find a way to let us know that she wasn't really dead. I had the urge to go open that thing up and get her out.

Reality was beginning to set in as sat I staring and waiting. I felt a distant coldness as though I was in a bad dream that I couldn't wake up from. And, though I had already cried so many tears over this already, that aching grief grew in my gut and was pushing its way up causing that painful lump to return in my throat.

I turned my eyes back to Denby's talk but when they shifted the grief became unbearable. I was just too weak and couldn't seem to hold it back any more. The tears suddenly broke loose and came pouring down my face. This time I didn't try to stop it...I didn't care...It was just too sad for me to know that I was never going to see Mama ever again...for as long as I lived.

At that moment I wanted to die too. That was until I felt the warmth of Trudy's tender loving hand reaching to include me into the embrace she already had with Earldean.

She too had begun to sob which seem to start a chain reaction across the whole front row except for the two little ones who couldn't tell if folks were laughing or crying. They just had questioned looks on their faces.

Someone had passed some tissues to Trudy who then reached to wipe my tears from my face. In doing so, I realized I had missed some of what Denby had said. It must have been important or the preacher wouldn't have had him come up to talk to everybody. I decided I would focus on his words instead of what was inside the coffin.

"…and first time I laid eyes on her…she couldn't have weighed more than a hundred pounds soakin wet!"

I noticed that Denby wasn't talking about my mother being dead but instead, he was telling everyone about her life. I managed to pull myself together so that I could hear his story about Mama.

Apparently, mine and Earldean's crying must have interrupted him as he kept checking back at us to make sure we were alright before he could continue with his next sentence.

Once he'd seen we were calmed down, he became more comfortable with his position in relating the point.

"…Don't know much bout where she come from or where she'd been…didn't matter…she's where she wanted ta be…right there in Chinquapin Holler…with Earl and them lit'lo babies of hers. They wuz her whole life as far as she wuz concerned…all she had…all she ever wanted."

Denby propped himself on the pulpit by leaning in and taking hold of the top of it. His face, that had started out tight and nervous, seemed to relax along with his voice. He looked at me and Earldean and smiled a big smile. He was nothing at all like a preacher man in the way he talked to everybody in the church. He probably would have been more comfortable if they would have put an old folding lawn chair up there to sit in.

"…I called her Little Mama from the first day I met her…she looked like a youngin herself…a toten 'round a baby doll. I seen how she took good care of that first baby they had…she's the same way wit all the rest of um…Spent all her time a fixin and doin fer them.

Whil'st they'z daddy showed um what he knowed bout makin do with what they had right there in the woods…how ta keep from starving ta death…She's a one who leart em how to read an write…You folks from the church here, might appreciate the fact that the only schoolin they had come from them Bibles they had out younder…I figured they'z too afraid ta send um off to a school house fer fear them teachers might not let um come home if they knowed they'z out there livin in an ole school bus…They'z might a tried ta tak um away from um er somthin.

I don't know…but I thought they'z best be left alone bout that…wuttin no need fer it…them youngin seemed to be happy right where's they'z at. They'z real good ta me… so it seemed right to turn favor on um.

Cain't say fer sure…but…best I figure…they'd done seen 'nuf hard times in their upbrangin and was a hidin out there cause they just couldn't take no more.

I reccon that there'z what caused um ta take a shine to one 'nother in the first place…they stayed to themselves out yonder in the woods...wuttin hurtin no body…no harm done.
…Now I caint see why…well…it ain't like Earl not ta be here today…I…I don't know…"

Denby shook his head as he repositioned himself, tightly gripping the stand with arms stretched out. He held his head down for a moment while he gathered his thoughts.

"She…Marline here…was crazy bout that boy…she worked like a mule round there ta keep thangs goin…so thangs would be good fer him…She could take any old thang he'd drag home and make sumpin useful out of it. She could see somthin in her head that nobody else woulda ever thought of…beats all I ever did see!…And cook!…Why she could fill a piece of dough and make sum the best pies you ever eat…now…how she done it…sho beats me…all she had ta cook in wuz a pit a old bricks Earl stacked up out there fer her…but she made it werk…best she could…she'z right smart a little woman she wuz.
…But the best part of her we can all see…is the love and kindness she put in these here youngins a sittin right younder…Jest look at um…aint they'z the nicesest lit'lo thangs…ain't got a bad bone in um… Yep…I hear tell a Apple don't fall fer frum its tree…and in this case…them'z good ones…sweet I tell ya!
…I see their Mama in each one of um…Take at there baby younder…them purdy eyes and that smile…looks jest like her…And Ed Earl…why he's a prankster like his diddy…but them lovin arms he gits from his maw…and how ya can see them little wheels just turn in his brain like that…That's her…all time tryin ta figure how ta goin bout gittin what ya want without askin fer help from anybody else…independent…that's Marline.
…and Earldean...with her motherin ways…always lookin out after the others and takin care of um…like little Learline is with that there baby-doll of hers…how she carrys it with her everwhere she goes…that's cause their maw had them youngins with her all the time…or she'd know right where ta find um.

He took a deep breath and blew it out slow as he caught me sitting on the edge of my seat waiting to hear if he could see any of Mama in me. Our eyes locked on one another and I could feel his affection he had for her as he spoke.

"…And Sassy…my sweet girl Sassy…You are just like her…not who she had to be…but who she wanted to be…She…like you, would find the beauty in every single thang…She would take a bad situation and find a good lesson in it…She'd find darn good reason for bad weather and wait for nature to prove it so that she could point it out…and she had a love for all the life around

her…even the fresh air she breathed…she was greatful for it. For me…this young lady was like that breath of fresh air…a joy to be around…we're gonna keep on livin without her…she will be missed that's fer sure…but…I can tell you folks…she will not be forgotten."

When Denby stepped down, he took a few steps over past the cluster of flowers and placed his hand gently on top of the closed casket. He stood staring for a moment before rubbing a tear from his face with the back of his hand. Then, making his way back to his seat next to me, he nodded his head to the pastor who stood and proceeded with the service.

He took this opportunity to preach a short sermon on living each day as if it's your last. He said that it was the untimely death of this unknown young woman that made him aware of just how short life can be, how valuable our time here on earth is and that none of it should be wasted.

He said that each new day was a gift from God, a chance to make a difference in our life which in turn will affect the lives of others. He told us that each and every morning when we wake up, we should ask ourselves what we can do today to make a difference.

"What can I do?" he asked. *"What little thing can I do to make a big difference in the long run? Let's not waste any more time…let us take this next minute for example to think about what will be said about us at our eulogy? What will we do with this next precious moment? …How shall we spend it? …will we invest it…or will we waste it?"*

Nobody answered him. Nobody said a word…not even an "Amen!" or "Halleluiah!"

With the exception of an occasional sniff there was total silence and stillness for a long full minute until he continued.

"Now…that moment is gone…You can't recapture it…but hopefully…another will come along for you today…Yesterday is gone…we can't change it…but today is new.

With each passing moment there is a chance to start over…begin again and make the most of what's left of our time here on earth. For it's not where we were yesterday…but where we're going from here that will make a difference…if tomorrow comes for you.

35
YANKED OUT BY THE ROOTS
(*PURSUIT TO ROTTEN TEETH*)

It was in the small town of Whisper Ridge, where folks there had taken on the burden of seeing to it that our mother had a proper entombment, they managed to find enough dirt to bury her properly in the church graveyard. Though Denby thought she should have been laid to rest in the hollow, he was out voted by authorities who made the call when Daddy had not yet shown up in time.

They wouldn't let us watch her being put in the ground; it was just as well, the idea of it was more than my ten year old thoughts could bear.

We did however, go back late that afternoon to the cemetery and place the flowers she had been given on her grave. She didn't have a tombstone like the other graves around there but somebody had made a cross out of wooden stakes and stuck it in the ground.

Attached to it was a note that read:

"Here lies a young mother
Whom God has called home,
He's left us her children
To raise as our own."

Nobody to this day ever admitted putting it there; it could have been just about anyone around at the time...who knows?

I was convinced at the time that it was Mrs. Patterson who was the guilty party when she showed up a week or so later and packed us off to Little Rock to the orphanage there.

It was just one day shy of Earldean's twelfth birthday and our cause for sudden departure blew Trudy and Alma's plans for a surprise party right out the window.

Their secret was out about it when the two of them were pleading with the woman to let us stay a little longer.

"No! Ya cain't take um yet!" Alma declared. *"We weren't expectin ya this soon...We need more time!"*

"That's right...Don't ya know that tomorrow is October first...do you even realize what day that is? Well...just let me tell ya..." Trudy informed Mrs. Patterson as she pulled Earldean into her arms. *"...It's this child's birthday and we have already made big plans to celebrate it with her...You just can't run off with um like that..."* she insisted as she pulled me into her

embrace too. *"…This aint the right time…everybody ain't got ta tell um bye or nuthin!"*

Mrs. Patterson told them that she was sorry but that the time allotted for our father to claim us had run out and that she had her orders to pick us up. She was trying to be nice about it all but her schedule didn't allow her to return another day. She said she had done all she could do and unless something short of our own father driving up right then and there, that we had to go with her to the orphanage.

Time stood still, for that very moment we heard a vehicle pull into the driveway. What were the odds of that? My heart was racing as I pulled myself from Trudy's arms in hopes of finding my knight in shining armor coming to rescue me from this transgression that seemed to be taking place.

We turned to see that it wasn't Daddy but instead it was Doc and Estelle who had come with my two younger siblings along with what few belongings we had accumulated during our stay in town.

They must have known something about it because Estelle looked as though she had been crying for a while when she got out of the car with Learline. Doc too, looked a bit sad about having to see us go as he walked slowly with Ed Earl at his side. They carried our things over and set them down by Mrs. Patterson's car.

In a last ditch effort Estelle quietly tried to reason with the woman, attempting to persuade her to reschedule her task.

Doc put his arm around his wife and said that as much as he would miss us too, that they had to let us go. He told her that Mrs. Patterson had a job to do and it was hard enough without confrontation. I heard him say to her, *"Sweetheart…be strong for the kid's sake…alright?"*

"I'm sorry to have to do this…" the woman compassionately replied. *"I can tell you all have bonded somewhat as their caretakers…I see this sort of thing often enough to know it usually doesn't last long enough to make a difference though…in fact, it could make things worse."*

"How could it hurt anything to let um stay a little longer?" Alma asked.

"It's never easy to say goodbye Miss Nettles, the longer they stay…the harder it will be for them to have to make new adjustments elsewhere. As it is now, they are going to need a whole lot of special help making social adjustments…not only because of their previous living conditions but especially after all they have been through with their parents. We have counselors on staff at the orphanage who are

trained professionals that can work through this with them…help them fit in better in society."

Trudy, feeling a bit intimidated asked, *"They fit in just fine here…What are you tryin ta say?"*

"Before these children came along, you all were living your own busy lives according to your own plans in pursuit of hopes and dreams. As much as you want to help right now, in time you will realize that these children weren't part of that plan. Later…down the road, they may cause infringement on your freedom to come and go as you please…as children can cause certain limitations… the added expense of clothing and extra mouths to feed can all add up with four children…not to mention all the other frustrations that accompany rearing children…You grow tired of the responsibility…next thing you know we get a phone call to come get them…It's really best I take them now…Before they start to take root here."

Trudy, shaking her head no, refusing to accept such allegations put her hands on her hips and said, *"What? Are we talking about plants here? You act like these are some kinda flowers we're gonna neglect to take care of… git tired of waterin and let whilt…Naw!*
…These are children…real live people with feelins…They already ARE part of our lives…we understand um…love um…You're the one'z uprootin um!"

"Please Ms. Teffertiller…I'm not saying you all aren't capable of tending to the children here…We have studied this case closely and feel that we need to start moving toward a more permanent situation for them. These sorts of things have to be handled delicately.

"Trudy…Please…" Doc said in attempt to calm her down. *"…Let me talk to you a minute."* He then took her and Alma gently by their arms and led them off to the side to talk peacefully and reasonably; in that empathetic way that Doc just had a way of doing.

"Mrs. Murphy…you understand don't you?"

Estelle just stood there and sadly nodded her head in defeat.

"…I wish this were easy…but it's simply out of my hands now." Mrs. Patterson explained to her before she turned to us and told us it was time to say our good byes.

Estelle rushed back to her car and reached in to get something off of the front seat. She came back then handed me my shoe box of treasures that I kept hidden under the bed.

"I found this Sassy…I thought it might be yours…I knew you'd want it if it was."

Mrs. Patterson had me place it in the trunk of her car along with the rest of our belongings.

Doc then returned with Trudy and Alma who seemed to be a little calmer and less argumentative, at least Alma was anyway. Trudy didn't cut her much slack and accused the woman of being down right heartless.

Oh, it was not without resistance as we were torn away from Alma and Trudy alongside of the Murphys. It all happened so fast that it is just a blur in my memory today.

Those first days at the orphanage were totally miserable for us as our patched up life was once again torn apart. We couldn't understand how they figured we'd be better off in a strange place not knowing a single soul.

Through the tears, Mrs. Pat, as we'd come to called her, and several of her co-workers did what they could to console us and explain that under the circumstances we would have to wait there for the courts to decide what to do with us until our father returned for us. They said that the environment back in the hollow was not fitting for children and that the town's people couldn't just keep passing us around like that. They told us that we needed a more stable and regimented place to stay.

I couldn't see what difference it should have made to them…it was working for us and our new friends in town seemed to be happy enough with it as they tried helping us out.

How dare these people, who we didn't know, decide what was good for us? Chinquapin Hollow was our home and we loved it there. We didn't mind living in a bus or sleeping on the ground; before Mama took sick we had never known the difference…we were just fine. We didn't need T.V. or electricity, running water or a man delivering milk to the door. We didn't have to dress up in fancy clothes that matched or wear shoes all the time. It didn't matter if we had a tub full of bubbles; we had a wash pan, a bar of soap and a rag; that was all we needed. We just couldn't understand what all the fuss was about…I would take my old life back any day over being forced to live someplace where I had to start all over with unfamiliar surroundings. At that point newness was just too overwhelming.

I didn't care where I lived as long as it was a place where I could be with people that I loved and they loved me back.

Why didn't Alma and Trudy fight harder? Why did Doc and Estelle just stand there and let them take us away? Why didn't Denby move back to his house like he said he would do and let us live with him?

I felt like I had been betrayed and abandoned when first my own mother wouldn't fight hard enough to live and take care of me and then Daddy runs off and leaves us and never came back. Now this! I felt so unloved as if I wasn't worth the time of day.

It didn't matter anymore if I was bona-fide or not…who cares? I didn't need a proper name now because being there made me feel like I was a "nobody".

I sullied up and withdrew into myself and didn't want to ever get attached to another person again. To me it was just not worth it to give your heart away and nobody care enough to keep it.

The days turned into weeks and then into months and my depression blocked my memory of the place but not the pain of my breaking heart.

The only things I remember about the Children's Home was all the rules; which weren't too hard to keep if you just fell in line and followed the crowd of other children.

We went to school and set in classrooms with books and pencils. I remember getting in trouble for daydreaming and staring out the window. I could hardly pay attention to anything the teacher said as I watched the green leaves change to bright yellow, orange and red.

I longed so, to be outside with the brisk cool wind blowing in my face in hopes that a strong gust would pick up my skinny little body and blow it back to the hollow where it belonged.

I'd often craved a vanilla wafer from that old cookie jar that belonged to Alma's great Grand-maw.

I'd yearn for the sound of tinkling dishes, Cody's singing over the sizzling grill and laughter of Trudy's Eat-A-Bite. I missed the security of Deputy Reed being close by and insuring us protection.

By then I would have given anything to hear Estelle explain to me how to do things "the right way". She and Doc could probably teach me how to do arithmetic better than any ole teacher. Doc was a good teacher about horses and if he could do that then he should be able to teach me just about anything I wanted to know.

Denby taught me a whole lot about fishing and other things. Why couldn't he be my teacher? He was old and had been around for a long time; he was always saying how he had learned his lesson about first one thing then another. Surely as long as he'd been around he had plenty of lessons life taught him. He could teach them to me, I thought.

Earldean and I were behind in our education but they put us in classes with kids our age and called it social promotion because we were too big for first grade. We were smarter in some areas than most of those kids who had been going to school for six or seven years. At least that's what Earldean claimed; I don't really know for sure because I mostly just stayed to myself. I didn't care to get to know anybody else anymore.

We had been there only a month when she and I had gotten wind of a rumor that somebody was trying to adopt Learline. I was torn about it at first; I wanted her to have a home with a real Mama and Daddy but I would never get to see her again.

We were told by some of the other orphans that most folks don't want to adopt older kids. They said that most couples just like babies and toddlers because they are cute and sweet and don't have as many problems. It was sad to think that nobody would want me or Earldean. Or, for that matter Ed Earl's chances of ever going home with anybody were slim with him already being well into his sixth year.

We would see him around at school and at meal time but that's about it. He slept in another building with the boys and Earldean and I stayed at another place with the girls our age. We had chores like back home but there wasn't much time for play with all the studys we had to make up for.

Earldean told me to quit telling Ed Earl that Daddy was going to come for us one day. She said that I was just giving him false hope and that it was the same as lying.

She had been convinced by the older kids there that they all came in believing somebody was going to come for them one day but they were all still there. They told her that some get sent to other homes but seldom does anybody have a relative claim them.

They told her that the sooner she accepted that fact, the easier it would be for her to live there. I began to believe them too. After hearing some of their stories Earldean relayed to me, I began to wonder if Daddy left us on purpose. I would find myself comparing incidents of control and him keeping us from other people and wonder why he would do such a thing.

One boy told us about how his daddy would get drunk and not come home for days at a time. I don't really remember seeing my daddy drink any alcohol but I really didn't know back then what it looked like to know the difference. But my daddy did go away for days at a time, he might have been drinking…I wasn't sure.

This one girl told us about how her mama and daddy kept her locked in her room and wouldn't let her out to play with other kids. She told us of some really mean things they had done to her…I didn't believe her. My daddy didn't like us talking to strangers but he never did anything like that to me.

Another girl told us that she knew that neither of her parents were never coming for her because they were both dead and she didn't have any other living relatives.

But one thing for sure…Daddy never came to take us home from that place and we did have that in common with the other children there. But, I didn't want to be one of them…I didn't want to belong to that place. I didn't even want to try to like it there as my mind was made up before I ever went.

By the last day of October I had come to the conclusion that I had better make the most of my new home such as it was.

I had thought about what Denby said at Mama's funeral about how I was supposed to be like her. Like her, I should find the good in any situation but my heart wasn't in finding anything positive about living in an orphanage.

Some new costumes had been donated by a local organization and all week long the other kids had been trying them on for size so they could dress up for some kind of event they had been calling Halloween.

I had not paid it much mind as I was in no mood to celebrate anything but leaving there. However an announcement was made that morning that if we all finished our chores and studies that we'd be treated to a night of some sort of tricks and treating in one of the local neighborhoods.

The kids laughed at me when I asked what that meant. They couldn't believe I'd never gone trick or treating before.

Finally, one of the girls explained what it was and I thought it was a weird idea. Well, at least part of it was but other parts of it sounded intriguing.

"Every year, on October thirty first, kids all over the world get dressed up and disguise themselves as spooky things...most of the time they paint or cover their face so that they won't be recognized. It's fun to guess who might be under a mask cause all you see is their eyes.

Then, when it starts to get dark, they take a sack and go knock on doors yelling trick or treat, scaring people into giving them some sort of snack to put in their bag."

The thought of that made me feel uncomfortable as I had regressed somewhat from addressing strangers. I also didn't care to be any more afraid than I already was, much less attempt to pass that eerie feeling off on anyone else.

I wondered why anyone would reward to such cruel treatment, so I asked her, *"If they'z ta git skerid...why come um not to slam the door...run and hide under the bed or sumptin?"*

"Oh, they won't do that...cause then they'll get tricked...everybody knows that!" she responded with a wrinkled brow. *"...they have to put something in your sack...besides these are grownups we're talking about here...most all of them know we're not real spooks."*

"But what if they'z aint got no treat fer ya...How do ya git um turn a loose of sumpin they'z aint got?"

"Well...It's Halloween! They sort of expect us kids are goinna be commin around on Halloween night looking for a treat, so, they bake cookies or brownies...popcorn balls or candied apples...some sort of taffey...good stuff like that...lots of um just buy store bought candy and have it waiting by the door for you to come by."

"...But what if they forgit...or don't know about Halloween and they ain't got nuttin fer ya?" I inquired.

"They'll get tricks played on um!"

"What's the trick? How do ya play?"

"Well there are all sorts of tricks...I've heard tell of some kids who used four whole rolls of toilet paper and wrapped it around the trees and bushes at this one house for not passin out any goodies..."

My goodness, I thought to myself, how could they waste such a luxurious thing? I bet they wouldn't try that again if they had to use leaves like we did back in the hollow.

"…I've heard of tippin over their garbage or squeezing stinky salve or grease on their door knobs…throwin eggs at their door…mean stuff like that."

"All on account they'z would'n share a treat wit um?"

"Yep."

"I bet they got in a whole heap a trouble fer the likes of such meanness…ya reckon?"

"Not if ya don't get caught…that's why ya wear the disguise…so they don't see who it was who done it." she explained.

It all seemed like a strange way of going about getting people to be nice to you. Mama had always said that we should treat each other like we want to be treated and set a good example for others. She had always told us that what goes around comes around.

I listened on as she chatted away about her experiences of Halloweens past.

"One time, I saw some boys scoop up some dog poop, put it in a paper sack and place it on the doorstep of this one old man's house…then they set it afire…rang the door bell then took off runnin…" the girl chuckled before she finished the tale.

"Some of us girls almost got the blame for it though…we were just standing in the street watchin it all while them boys hid in the bushes and laughed their socks off the whole time. It was sort of scary at first…it could have burnt down the place…when the old man answered the door and saw the blaze…he panicked and stomped out the fire. Needless to say he had made a mess of his shoes and his front steps too…He was fit to be tied…I was worried at first when he thought us girls had done it…that was until he found the boys' hiding in the bushes…it's funny now…looking back at it all."

The girl shook her head and laughed, *"Ya should have see that old man bangin an polkin his cane in them bushes tryin ta run them boys out of there!"*

"That was a nasty trick…don't cha thank? I aint a hankerin fer no treats that bad…Are you?" I thought of Denby and began to picture such a thing happening to him.

"Yea it was…Of course…we're not gonna to be allowed to play any tricks… but most people will be prepared to pass out treats of some kind anyway…most of um are nice and seem happy to play along with us…so you don't have to worry about none of that stuff…just relax…it's gonna be fun!"

Every one scrambled for the newer costumes of the latest Super Hero while those of us who were more timid settled for something from the old trunk of prior years characters.

Some wanted to paint their faces to look creepy hoping to scare the treat-givers into giving them more treats. Two of the otherwise pretty girls dressed as wicked witches with green faces and black lips, but this made them look really ugly.

When I heard everyone speak of ghosts and goblins it made me sort of nervous to hear what they had to say. Some told compelling stories of graveyards and spooks as they would gather in spellbound circles and tell one after another.

It was all confusing to me and I had trouble sorting truth from fiction. Most of what they were saying didn't make sense at all but according to some, they were true stories with eyewitnesses. I would shiver at the thought of such things and felt chills run down my spine.

Earldean, tying to fit in, attempted to relay a story taken from of an episode of Casper. However, she was cut off before she had a chance to finish when one kid decided that a cartoon for babies wasn't spooky enough. Not wanting to break the evil enchantment that was holding the group captive, the kid hatefully laughed at her saying that there was no such thing as a friendly ghost.

Before leaving the hollow, the only ghost I had ever heard of was the Holy Ghost and I didn't see any cause to be scared of that. But the stories and rumors of dead people coming out of their graves got me to thinking about Mama. If she was coming up out of the ground I wanted to be there to see her; I had no call to be scared of her for she was my own mother. But, I wasn't sure about all these other dead people with distorted bodies they talked about. The curiosity in me stirred to want to sneak just a peek at such a thing but staring at those kinds of people I thought, may prove to be difficult.

Earldean had to explain to me that since Mama went to Heaven she wasn't coming back so I shouldn't look for her to come up out of her grave. She reassured me that all that talk was just to scare people.

"I'm afraid about all this..." I told her. *"I don't want one em goblins ta git me!"*

"Sassy...ya ain't got no call to be scared...Ya know the Bible tells us that God didn't give us a spirit of fear...but one of power...love ...and sound mind...all that scary business belongs to the devil...he's a one who want us to be

afraid and confused…that kind of stuff will make ya a crazy person. Naw…That ole devil wants us to lose our sound mind so that he can git control and drive us insane…and a confused mind…well…it's on its way out! …He aint fer us a doin lovin kinna thangs…he's all about us doin hateful stuff."

"But I'm scared of the devil…what if he tries ta git a holt a me?"

"Well, ya see there…he'z a workin on ya already…you ain't got ta give in to him, ya know…Jesus claims allz we got ta do is call out his name and he'll be there…Bible says there's power in His name and aint nuttin that can come against ya can prosper!"

"Yea…I heard that said a time or two…What is a 'prosper' anyhow? …zat like Casper…the friendly ghost?"

"Naw…now Sassy…listen up…prosper…you know…like…do better…ain't nobody better than God…That's what Mama said…and Mama wouldn't lie now, would she?"

"Naw…not no more…she dead…she ain't never gonna tell us nuttin no more."

"That's why we got to hold on to all she did tell us when she wuz alive…we never got scared before then."

"We didn't know bout all this stuff 'fore Mama took sick and died."

"Well I don't know what else to tell ya ta make ya understand that you've got to learn how to sort out the good from the bad…us sane folks…we just cain't pay no mind to their spooky nonsense…itta drive ya crazy iffin ya let it…all that's just crazy talk, I tell ya."

By the time I had gotten up the nerve to pick out a costume all that was left was a dirty sheet with eye holes cut in it, a wrinkled up Dracula cape along with a chewed up set of sharp, plastic teeth and a squished up Charlie brown mask. I chose the latter, though it was the most uncomfortable.

Mrs. Greer, the house mother, tried her best to press out the face of the character, then dug around through the pile of rejected costumes and found the felt pull over sweater that went with the mask. It was too big but she said that if I wore it over my regular clothes it would fit better. I did like the zigzag design it had around the bottom of it.

Just before dark we all gathered in the dining hall and were all handed brown paper bags with handles. We then were divided into groups of ten and assigned to two adults who were responsible for keeping up with us.

I was disappointed when Mrs. Greer wouldn't let me stay in Earldean's group. Instead she thought it best if I wasn't so dependent on my sister and thought I should try socializing with some of the other children.

Ed Earl had paired off with a group of boys he had taken up with and they already had too many in their group. I was forced to be with some I didn't particularly care for because of their bad habit of fighting or teasing beyond the point of fun. I had decided not to let them get to me no matter what.

While we waited for instructions, I caught a glimpse of Learline playing with some other children her age.

There weren't as many in her group and with these being the youngest they were staying in for a little party because they were too young to wander around in the dark. Most of them were afraid of all the scary costumes anyway and screamed at the sight of us.

I waived at my baby sister but she didn't recognize me all dressed up as Charlie Brown. I didn't get to see her as much since we stayed across the way. I didn't realize how much I had missed her until I saw her that night but I had already made up my mind to detach from her so that it wouldn't hurt so much when she was adopted.

I didn't pursue the greeting as she went about playing. She seemed to be adjusting alright which was more than I could say for myself.

The night air was cool and crisp as we made our way out and across a big field to the houses over in the neighborhood. Some were given flashlights to lead the way for their group and we were instructed by our leaders to take turns holding it.

The Director and one of the counselors would be meeting us over on the streets to follow along in station wagons to pick up any of us who would get too tired of walking.

It wasn't far at all and I was looking forward to filling my sack with treats and planned to stop at every house so that I would have enough candy to last a lifetime.

It was decided by our chaperones that the groups would break off and start down different streets so that we could be done in a few hours. We were to go up one side of the street and then the other before moving on to the next.

Though we were told not to run, there were those few who just couldn't resist the urge to do so in all the excitement.

From house to house we rang the doorbells and yelled, *"Trick or Treat!"* Then the home owner would open the door and pretend to be surprised or scared…it had become expected by our group. They had proclaimed that anyone who didn't play along was an "Old Fuddy Duddy" or a "Mean Old Grouch". I heard some of the bigger kids threaten to sneak out and throw eggs at their houses later when everyone was asleep.

We were on the last street and already some had gotten tired and were ready to go back. A few had already climbed into the station wagon that was carrying loads of kids back over to the Children's Home.

When two of the boys started fighting over the flashlight I took the opportunity to duck behind a bush.

The chaperones were too distracted with trying to break them up that they didn't miss me. In fact, it wasn't until bed check when they noticed my empty bed that anyone came looking for me but by that time I was long gone and had walked quite a few miles away.

36
THE EVIL SPELL

If it worked for Mama and Daddy, it could work for me; I thought, as I wondered away as far as my tired body could possibly take me that night.

Now it would be me who would become the missing person. They never found my Daddy and I didn't want them to find me either. I was sure to get by with it as I had the impression that I'd never be recognized because of my disguise.

Thinking I could survive on the treats I had collected, I planed to make my way to that far away place my parents called California and see some of those sights they told us about.

But deep down inside, my heart ached for home; the only real home that I ever knew. Someway I'd find my way back to Chinquapin Hollow and there I'd wait on my daddy.

As I meandered through the streets, passing other trick-or-treaters along the way, I would occasionally walk close enough to a group of them as not to be noticed by any suspecting grownups. This way I didn't have to ring any door bells nor do any begging on my own. I simply fell in line with the rest who held their sacks up to the generous treat givers and no one seemed to notice I had tagged along.

I took this opportunity to fill my bag with enough of what I considered would be my means of survival.

Through the previous three months, I had dealt with the discomfort of my displacement enough for it to become a familiar part of my being. So, this odd and peculiar holiday should have been just another day in my new and abnormal life. Yet, in some bizarre way, this particular type of celebrating made me feel really uncomfortable. I felt a sort of grinding in the pit of my stomach and tightness in my chest. The whole thing was confusing as the good parts mixed with the bad and I couldn't really decide If I liked it or not. Some of these kids were either a glutton for punishment or somehow enjoyed getting scared out of their wits.

I guess I had enough on my mind to magnify the intensity of that evening of fear. When the bigger kids tried to spook the little ones with their monster costumes and loud growls, I too would be startled and shaken by it even though I was old enough to know better.

It was the high pitched screeching caused by an occasional scare that would worry me the most when I'd remember the spooky tales some of those children told me about earlier that day.

My concern would lighten when shrills of laughter soon followed for it was then I'd remember about some of the mean scary tricks big people liked to play on each other as well as unsuspecting little kids.

"*Remember…these er just tricks bein played…don't be sceerd.*" I whispered to myself as I checked back over my shoulder from time to time. I didn't care too much for that part of this holiday; it was just too creepy and hateful.

I shivered at the thought of some of those gruesome stories and realized for the first time I could ever remember of being a little afraid of the dark. Well, it wasn't actually the darkness that spooked me but whatever it was that might be hiding in it.

The only thing that would get me through it was the encouraging Bible verse I'd recall my sister reciting to me.

"God didn't give you the spirit of fear but that of power, love and a sound mind."

I had never before experienced such a strange and uncomfortable night so I believe these words were the only thing that kept me from going crazy. I didn't want to be scared out of my wits because I needed my mind to be sound so that I could clearly think about what I was going to do all on my own out in this big ole world.

As I walked on for the longest time, I could hear dogs barking off in the distance mixed with sporadic howling sounds made by either an animal or a facetious prankster. Thrown in the mix was the occasional call for tricks or treats that continued to echo in the night.

The glow from the nearly full moon was bright enough to light the way down the back road that led me through several other neighborhoods with gigantic trees and lofty massive homes. Many of them were brightly lit up within and from the sidewalk I could see into the ones with opened window dressings.

Abundant life appeared to be abiding within each of them as they sparkled with clean colors of curious objects that occupied their spaciousness.

There were a little less people out in the streets by the time I reached the place with the giant oaks in the middle of the boulevard. There, most of the children had already gone back into their houses.

I stopped and rested on the curbside at the corner of one street trying to decide which way I should go next. When I set my sack down beside me my arm ached a little; I hadn't realized how heavy it had gotten. Under the streetlight I could see enough to know I had gathered some rather desirable goodies but couldn't bring myself to eat anything at that moment. Though I was a bundle of nerves I was proud of my loot and figured it to be more than enough to last for a while.

Several vehicles crossed the different streets at this intersection making their way cautiously as to avoid hitting any children that may dart out in front of them.

Being this was Halloween, I did not appear to be out of place there resting on the curb. In fact, when I first arrived, it appeared to be the meeting point for several children to reunite with their parents.

Some kids had already shed their costumes and were carrying them over their arms when one of them stopped under the streetlight to stuff her outfit into her sack.

"Wait for me!" she said as she worked to make it fit. When she bent down to tie her shoe she looked at me and asked, *"Did you make it down to the Rothschild's house yet?"*

She spoke as if she knew me though I'd never seen her before. She must have thought I was somebody else behind the mask.

"…if not… you'd better hurry because she's almost out of candied apples. Mrs. Marie makes the best treats every year…don't you think?"

"Come on!" one of the girls yelled back to her from a half a block away.

"I'm commin… just wait" she answered.

"Hurry up!"

"See ya…gotta go…it's getting late."

When she caught up with the rest of them, they skipped off a little ways giggling and laughing before disappearing behind a gate.

I wasn't sure about her suggestion of me going down to this child's house. "Roth" to me sounded too much like it might have been a fancy word for "lost". In my mind I pictured it being another orphanage or a place where they kept lost children. I wasn't lost and didn't want anyone to try and make me stay there. This Mrs. Marie person could be the house mother down there or something; who knows?

I just wasn't sure what might happen; candied apples or not, I was not about to take any chances. Besides, I was sure I had already bagged several candy coated apples in one of the other neighborhoods.

Several ghosts and goblins raced past me making their way back home after their mother called them in from their front door.

A few minutes later a man rounded the corner holding the hand of a whiney little fairy that was dragging a plastic pumpkin. The two of them were being closely followed by a small framed Tony the Tiger with a long tail that swung from side to side as they made their way down the walk and faded into the darkness.

After I felt a little rested I snatched up my sack and made my way across the street then down the long sidewalk passing these lovely big homes.

Through the big glass windows I could see inside and longed for a safe place to sleep. I could see well into this one place, so I stopped to observe as the family stood gathered together around a big table. The parents smiled while watching their children as they spilled their candy and treats out onto the table and examined their edible treasures.

When I was startled by a cat that shrieked and ran into the bushes, I turned around to find a man walking his dog and heading my way. Though the streets were nearly empty and it had been a while since I had seen anyone else I didn't think much of it until his dog spotted me then started barking. Thank goodness the man had him on a leash or he might have tried to bite me. When the large animal yanked and pulled his owner in my direction it frightened me until the man gave a short shrill whistle gaining control again.

"Its ok boy. It's just another one of those kids…it will be over soon, shhhhh… that's a good boy…yea." he said, calming his pet down a bit before he spoke to me.

"Trick-or-Treat is about over…its best you run on home."

I wasn't sure what to do at that moment so I just stood scared. I knew I should have obeyed him but I couldn't very well do that as I had no home to go to.

"It's getting late…you go on now…before your folks get worried…go on…scoot!"

With that, I just turned and took off running but when I did, the dog attempted to chase me. The man yanked at the leash pulling him back close to him then told him to hush all that barking.

The sound of my breathing was amplified and I could feel humidity building behind the plastic mask I was wearing. Though it was partially obstructing my view, I continued trotting at a steady pace; occasionally looking back over my shoulder to see if he was following me.

To avoid being suspicious, I pretended to make my way up the driveway of a house close by so that he would think that I lived there. Though he was almost a block away, I turned to see that he was still standing there with his dog, watching and waiting to see that I made it inside.

Slowly I stepped up on the first of three steps leading to the entrance and kept myself close to the manicured shrubs that were growing just next to them. Just as I was about to run out of ideas, to my advantage, the home owner opened the door and stepped out onto the stoop. When he bent down to blow out his jack-o lantern, he saw me standing there.

"Oh my…It's a Charlie Brown!" he said with a big grin. *"You still trick-or-treating this late?"*

"This is my last one." I mumbled through the sweaty mask. *"I'm on my way back home."*

There was no intention of a lie here as this was truly my plan by that time. I had already made up my mind to find my way back to my real home; back at my birthplace in the hollow.

"I just love that little guy...Did you see the Charlie Brown Halloween Special on T.V.?"

I hadn't watched much television and wasn't sure as to what he was talking about so to answer him was easy. I just stood there shaking my head no.

" …all he got was rocks when he went out Trick-or-Treating with the Peanuts Gang…Poor little guy…Well let's see if we have something better than that for this little Charlie Brown."

He turned and stepped just inside the door and reached for a big bowl that was setting on a small table close by. Pulling out a large handfull of wrapped candies, he then extended his arm and held them out toward me.

"Come on...open your bag son…so I can drop them in."

I was so nervous that I had already forgotten the routine. I unclenched the sack handles from the tight grip that I had been holding them together with. Warily, I held it opened to receive the generous offering and as if that wasn't enough he then took and poured the rest of the contents of the bowl into my sack.

"Here ya go…just take the rest if this…don't think anybody else is commin tonight…the misses and I really don't need it!" he said patting his belly with his free hand.

In disbelief, my eyes widened and even though the facial expression on the mask never changed, he could clearly see my delight through the holes provided for my vision. The added weight of the candy proved the measure was more than I expected as the sack lowered almost to my feet.

I stood dumbfounded as I peered over into my treat bag. I was so amazed at how this had really built up my stockpile that I forgot to thank him. I was speechless when I looked back up to see him grinning at me from ear to ear.

"…Now, you run on home now little fellow…a boy your age aught to be in bed by now…good-night and err…Happy Halloween!"

Wow, I thought, my disguise was working; he thinks I'm a boy.

The man backed in and slowly closed the door, watching and waiting for me to leave. *"Good night now…ok?…bye."* he said just before he shut the door.

I realized he was encouraging me to move along but I was afraid that the man with the dog might still be watching too. I had hoped I had tricked him into thinking that was my house.

Cautiously, I turned and made my way back down the drive toward the street hoping the dog and his master wouldn't notice that I hadn't gone in.

I stooped and slowed between bushes and trees until I almost reached the street. I could see that they were still there watching and waiting. When the home owner turned off his porch light, it made it easier to hide from them until they turned and headed back.

It worked! I had tricked them. When they were clearly out of sight I came out from behind the bushes to continue my journey.

The night grew colder and darker as patchy fog settled in closer to the ground. I kept a steady pace down the sidewalk for a while until it ended and I had to take another road.

All of the houses seemed to fade into the shadows of bedtime along with the rest of the world. I too was weary and longed for a safe place to hide so that I could sleep.

Quietness fell with the heavier fog making it harder to see which way to go. Though I was probably less noticeable should anyone else be out that late, I grew nervous about being seen.

The few people that had spoken to me earlier seemed to think that I needed to go home. What if an adult came along and wanted to enforce the idea? How would I be able to stop them, I worried.

Not wanting to be taken back to the orphanage, should anyone find out I'd been staying there; I decided I'd better try to keep out of sight.

It didn't occur to me that anyone might come looking for me. I had figured there were so many children there that surely they wouldn't notice just one missing. That was unless Earldean decided to tell them I didn't come back with the rest when she couldn't find me.

I felt sad and started crying because I didn't get to tell her bye. I had thought of running away before and had even told her about it but I had not really planned to do that this particular night. I simply took advantage of the opportunity to make a move that must have been kept in my subconscious. I didn't want to take a chance of my siblings getting adopted out and me having to stay there for the rest of my life. Though I would miss Earldean a whole lot, I was sure she would do fine without me because she could make friends easily. I was getting used to not seeing Ed Earl and Learline much anymore.

Still, it all made me sad to think about so I had to try to focus on my own survival now.

I put my hand to my face to wipe the tears from my eyes but the mask I was hiding behind got in the way. I ended up caving in the cheeks to that thing after Mrs. Greer worked so hard to smooth the wrinkles out of it. I lifted it long enough to wipe my face on the sleeve of the oversized orange sweater.

I was glad the costume was too big for me so that I had to wear extra clothes under it to make it fit. The temperature had been steadily dropping and the added layers were all I had to keep me warm. As I walked on, I plotted to use all that I was wearing for my future wardrobe until I could get back home to my own raggedy clothes.

My scheme included finding Daddy and the two of us going back for the rest of the family; well, at least whatever might be left of them by that time.

My feet were aching and I began to stagger with exhaustion when I happened upon a city park that included a playground.

Through the low floating mist, the ornate park lamps gave off a dim light through the haze, but I could still make out the different obstacles that indicated this was a safe place designed especially for children.

I made my way across to a big slide and crawled in underneath it as far as I could go without hitting my head. The grass beneath it was taller here so it would make a nice soft bed, though it was a little moist from the dew. The slide would provide shelter in the event of rain so hopefully I wouldn't get soaked.

I settled in, drawing my legs up under the big sweater and placing my bag of treats in front of me to better shield myself from the elements. Relieved to finally be sitting, I kept as still as I could at first until I was sure I had not been seen or followed. After a minute or two I sighed with relief and felt content enough to rest there until morning.

I tried to eat a piece of candy but couldn't fit it through the small slit that had been left open on the mouth of the facemask. Since nobody was there to see who I really was, it felt safe to remove my disguise so that I could enjoy my midnight snack.

The night air felt cool to my face which had been shielded by the plastic I'd been wearing for hours. I hadn't realized how much colder it had gotten and how that thing had been keeping me warm, but without it my breathing was much easier.

When I finished the candy I curled down onto my side resting my head on my sack of treats. It didn't bother me at all lying there on the cold ground, in fact I felt right at home and soon fell sound asleep.

According to the sun, it must have been about mid-morning when I woke up to the sound of children playing. Still unnoticed, I grabbed up my mask and sack and crawled to my feet, dusting debris off my clothes.

A crisp cool breeze was stirring the colorful fallen leaves that whirled in circles close to the ground. The vibrantly blue sky that morning created the perfect shade to contrast the brilliantly colored trees of autumn.

I hid in the shadow of the slide watching some kids playing on swings and seesaws. Though most of them were not dressed in their costumes anymore, there was still this one kid dressed up like Super Man. He was stretched out across the top of the bars on the Merry-Go-Round pretending to be flying in circles.

A few bigger boys were trying to see how fast they could make it spin before they grabbed hold of the bars and jumped on board.

When a small group of kids started congregating around the thing waiting for a chance to hop on too, I took this opportunity to attempt to get lost in the crowd so as not to be noticed by any grown-ups.

Not really awake good enough yet to be interested in playing, I was satisfied standing by and watching the others.

I had my mask tucked down in my sack so that when some of the kids started teasing the one dressed like Super Man for still being in costume, they didn't realize that I was too.

When he cried out for his mother, she came to his defense announcing that it was ok to do that even if Halloween was over. She asked the culprits to please stop teasing her son and threatened to speak to their parents if they didn't do so.

I thought about my own mother and how she use to have to get after me and my siblings for bickering amongst one another. She wouldn't be able to come to my defense any more…I was on my own.

I thought it best if I moved on along at that time as not to chance bringing any attention to myself.

Not far from the playground, nestled in the midst of the most brilliantly colored Maples, was a rectangular shaped, stone building with doors on both ends of it. I was wondering if anybody lived there. If so, I thought, how wonderful it must be to have a yard with a playground so close. This place had flowerbeds that were adorned with purple and orange mums which were in full bloom that day.

As I was admiring its quaint beauty I saw a woman with three kids walking up to it.

With the exception of the boy, who was about my age, the rest of them went in through one of the doorways leaving him to wait just outside. Then shortly after they entered an old man with a cane came through the other door at the opposite end.

At first I thought it was Denby so I ran up closer only to see that it wasn't. The old man nodded and even smiled a little when he hobbled past me but he didn't tell me to get out of his yard.

If the boy on the other end was related somehow to the old man, he didn't let on as though he was. He was too busy making a game of trying to catch falling leaves before they hit the ground.

I saw two other ladies and a little girl come out of the same door that the others went into and wondered if this was a place where anybody could go. It didn't really look like any of the other houses I'd seen before; this one didn't have windows.

When curiosity got the best of me I went to investigate this place for myself. The boy paid me no mind as he went about inspecting the leaves he had caught. In fact, I don't think he even saw me at all. It could be because I was trying to be real quiet so that I wouldn't get caught snooping around.

Stepping in a little closer, I could see a small nook that had been hidden by the landscape and discovered on the back wall of it was a water fountain.

It was a little different from the ones that I had seen before but I had no problem figuring out how this one worked. The cold water tasted very good and I couldn't seem to get my fill. I hadn't realized just how thirsty I was. I was truly grateful for not having to ask anybody for something to drink and that I could get it on my own.

Beyond the walls, I heard a toilet flush and the muffled sound of children asking questions. I heard the woman say to the girls when they exited through the same door they went into, "*...That's because this is a public bathroom...he has to use the men's room...this one's for ladies only.*"

Well, that was easy enough for me. Without any questions on my part, I could figure out the rest and was interested in taking advantage of the added convenience.

Once inside I thought that it would have made a better shelter to sleep in than the one I had chosen, had I known it was so close. The fog was so thick the night before I guess I just didn't see it.

I don't think the smell would have bothered me that much and it would have definitely been warmer than it was under that metal slide.

When I finished my business I washed up and left, letting the spring hinged door slam behind me. I was pleased that nobody fussed at me for that but the lack there-of made me aware, once again, that I was really on my own.

I stopped for a few seconds at the water fountain, unsure as to when I might run across another before I got that thirsty again.

As I walked through the park I noticed two little girls in their princess costumes playing close to their mothers who were visiting on a park bench. So, the super hero's mother must have been right in saying that it was ok to wear a costume even if it wasn't Halloween any more.

Since the disguise worked the night before; I believed it would serve me well to keep it on in the event someone from the orphanage did come looking for a missing girl.

After all, I was wearing my hair much shorter then, so with the mask on, I could fool people into thinking I was a boy.

It felt good to be out in the wide open space with a crisp cool breeze bringing in the first day of November that year.

Still hanging on for dear life, some of the more colorful leaves danced on branches of the trees, while others were forced to let go and join the rest that tumbled around on the ground. It was entertaining to watch and see how far one particular one might be carried off before it would get lost in a pile of others just like it. An occasional gust of wind would swiftly sweep them all in one direction before another came along and swept them all back again.

With winter coming soon, all the trees would be naked and exposed to the harsh elements, as would I if I didn't hurry and get back out to the hollow before then. Trees were used to withstanding icy coldness but little girls have less of a tolerance for such extremes. Feeling grateful that I did have on *some* clothes to protect me, I still could have used a light jacket that day.

They had given me one at the orphanage and had I known I'd be leaving I'd have taken it along with me. My experience of hiking out of the hollow enlightened me a little about distance by those days so I knew that I was in for a long cold walk home.

At least back there we had those old coats that Daddy brought home from the Salvation Army stored with the winter blankets in the deep freeze. They were smelly but they kept me warm and dry. Hopefully Daddy would already be there and could unlock it for me with his key.

It got me to thinking again about how Deputy Reed and the other policeman got that thing open without Mama's key she had kept around her neck.

With the guns gone and money missing from the pickle jar, I'd already resigned to the fact that we had been robbed. Daddy said that sort of thing could happen and that's precisely why he kept them locked up in there, hidden under the other stuff.

I struggled with the thoughts of how he might react when he finds out because I knew he would be aggravated about it. He'll probably say that we shouldn't have left our place unguarded, I worried. I should have never left.

I couldn't imagine who would have taken that stuff but with nobody around to look after things it was bound to happen. For a second, a glimpse of that picture from the newspaper flashed through my thoughts. Though I had cut holes to remove Virgil Green and Bubba Frank's faces from the copy I had saved; in my head I could clearly see them and worked quickly to dislodge that vision from my mind. I shook my head vigorously and tried to think about something better.

On my way out of the park I stopped to select a sweet treat from my stash to eat for my breakfast. When I got the last bite in, I slipped the false face back over my own and set out for another day of conquering those miles back to Chinquapin Hollow.

It didn't take too long before I was able to get out of the neighborhoods and over to a highway that was full of fast moving cars. Their drivers were all so busy and in a hurry to get to wherever they were going that none of them slowed down to let me cross over.

They would only honk their horns as they whizzed past me, with some yelling for me to get back; I thought I'd never make it to the other side.

When I did, I had walked only a short distance before hopping a fence and cutting across a big field. I would meet and cross several more roads looking for possible landmarks that would let me know that I was heading in the right direction.

The environment here was much different than any place I had ever been before. The more I walked the stranger things got for me. There were enough unfamiliar things to keep my mind occupied from my loneliness.

I would stop at times and stare at the amazingly tall buildings all around. They were built in all sorts of shapes and sizes, some with lots of windows, and then there were some that didn't have any at all.

I had seen some tall buildings before but it was from a distance. It was when we first came into the city but this was the first time I got to see any of this up close.

I could hear all sorts of indistinctive noises that indicated movement of life but I didn't really see a lot of people up close.

After walking all day, everything started to look the same and I wondered if I might just be going in circles like one might do if they got lost in the forest. Surely, I thought, there had to be an end to this place.

Though I was anxious to get home, I didn't have to be there at a certain time so when I got tired, I'd stop and rest and eat a treat. It was sort of nice to be able to do what I wanted to do or eat sweets whenever I liked without somebody bossing me around.

I missed my siblings and longed to share this adventure with them; at least the good parts, but if Earldean had been along with me, she might have tried to make me mind her like she used to do all the time. It's weird though, sometimes it might have been worth it to have her around just so I wouldn't have to be all alone and scared.

Because of the tall buildings, I had a hard time making out which direction the sun was; that was at least until days end.

It was then that the whole city seemed to tilt a little toward the northeast as long tall shadows stretched from building to building, blocking the warmth of the southwestward setting sun.

As the golden hue tinted the various textures that was exposed to it, things appeared to take on a whole new look.

Chills ran down my spine as dusk fell, not only because of the lack of heat from the light of day but also because of what took its place simultaneously. Suddenly, a countless number of lights began to now blink on, lighting up the entire metropolis.

Gigantic pictures of advertisements were spotlighted atop of tall structures. Bright twinkling colors of every sort moved about through tubes that outlined assorted silhouettes. Words were spelled out in huge, bold letters that were lit up with pride and could be seen for at least a half a mile away. They were fastened up somehow for everyone to read, those who possibly knew how to do so anyway.

I slid my mask to the top of my head so that I could take in as much of the sights as possible, yet it would be readily available should I have to hide my identity quickly.

The many street lamps and blinking traffic lights were bright enough for any driver to see where they were going, though they all drove around with their headlights on.

Streams of these headlights flowed up and down the streets as far as I could see both ways, making it hard to cross over anywhere. I rounded this one particular block at least four times before I found a safe opportunity to reach the other side.

Amplified sounds of heavy traffic still flowed as it did during the day, echoing off the tall buildings in much the same way other sounds, like those of night bugs and frogs might bounce off of canyon walls.

With it being a Friday night, people were still out walking along the sidewalks stopping in one place or another. I tried to be as inconspicuous as I possibly could but still every once in a while a passer-by would say something in regards to my costume.

Without the glare of the sun on the glass, it was easier to see inside some of these shop windows at night. Many of them had big, lit-up displays of their goods and wares arranged nicely so that folks would stop and look.

Like back at the Eat-A-Bite, some of the places were for dining. The smells of food cooking made me think about Trudy and Cody and all the other friends we had to leave behind down at that diner. I wondered what they might be doing and if any of them had ever been to a big city like this.

I remember Trudy saying something about Alma thinking of moving off to the big city in order to go to nursing school. Trudy said she was afraid that if she did, then she wouldn't want to come back to a small town like Whisper Ridge.

Well, as for me, I'd take that small town over the big city any day. As pretty as the city might be, it was proving to me to be a lonely place, full of lonely people like myself; they weren't as friendly as the folks of Whisper Ridge.

Unlike that small sleepy town, this place seemed to stay up almost all night. It seemed like they never turned the lights out and went to bed. Though I was really tired I couldn't think of going to sleep with all the brightness and noise around me. So I just kept going until I ended up in an area that was a little different from the rest.

This section still had lots of lights but not as colorful. It still had lots of noise but there was less traffic around. It was a while before I saw any more people and even then, it was far off in the distance.

As I wandered out into this foreign region, I took cautious steps, only guessing as to which way to go; stopping to rest when I got tired and ate as many goodies as I wanted to from my sack of treats.

By early the next day I managed to overdose on popcorn balls, caramel apples and candy.

It was a city police officer who took me back to the orphanage after he'd been call to the scene of a little Charlie Brown person throwing up over in the industrial part of the city.

On the ride back, he asked me what I was doing way off over there. I informed him that I was running away and going back to Chinquapin Hollow. He acted like he didn't know where that was so I told him it wasn't too awful far from Whisper Ridge. He let me know that was too far for a little girl to be running away to and that I was headed in the wrong direction anyway.

Later, after I was returned to the orphanage, I was told the same thing...that I was headed in the wrong direction...direction in life that is. And, I would have to live with that on my record they kept there. *"Nobody wants to adopt a run-a-way!"* I was told. And now, just because of me, none of the children would be allowed to go trick or treating the next year or ever again.

Even more so than before, the kids really didn't like me and for days even Earldean wouldn't speak to me. Not only had I upset her and made her ashamed of me, she was afraid that after what the other kids said about me that they would be mean to her because everybody had to suffer the consequences of what her sister had gone and done. I had only made matters worse for myself.

I withdrew even more after my candy was taken away as punishment but that wasn't as bad as being sent to the counselor, Mr. Haskell.

He glanced at a chart about me then pretended to listen to my reasons for running away. Though I could tell he didn't really care, as he said that he had heard it all before. It didn't matter what I told him it was apparently not what he wanted to hear.

He finally let me leave his office after I told him that I just felt like being bad that night. I didn't want to lie to him but I didn't know any other way to tell him what was wrong.

How could I…I didn't know myself.

After that, I continued to be a loner under the wicked spell of that evil Halloween night that caused me to go missing. I had become a curse to my sister and the other kids when every little thing I did was scrutinized and made note of by Mrs. Greer who had to report her findings to Mr. Haskell.

He and Mrs. Pat had a talk with Earldean about the possibility of any other behavior problems I might have had before I came to live there. I'm not sure what all she might have told them about me but I know she let them know about how we used to fuss at each other because I wouldn't mind her. And, there's no doubt she told them I was a crybaby.

She was upset with me about having to go talk with them and said it was my entire fault that she had to be drug into this just because she was my sister.

Eventually, she came around and forgave me a few days later…after her visitor left her. She said she couldn't stay mad at me forever and that she really understood why I might do something like that. However, she begged me not to ever try it again.

The other kids backed off too after a week or so. After all, most of them knew about how I felt and why I might have tried to run away. Come to find out, even a few of them had tried it before.

It made things a little more tolerable to be forgiven though I dared not ask for it. It was not my intention to make all the other kids pay for me breaking the rules, but I was sorry and I believe they just finally figured that out.

37
A CHANGE OF PLANS
(*GLUTTON FOR PUNISHMENT*)

We made it through Thanksgiving and even though it wasn't like the ones we had back home it wasn't all that bad. The cooks there had prepared a big turkey and dressing dinner with all the fixings on the side.

The maintenance man we called "Mr. Cotton" and some of the bigger boys helped to push all the tables together so that the older girls could dress them up so that it appeared to be one long table for the feast.

The staff had invited their families and friends to join us all in the dining hall for a reenactment of the very first Thanksgiving just before we ate. The play was put on by the kids in Ed Earl's group and he got to play the part of one of the pilgrims.

With the help of their teachers they had made their own costumes so they spent most of the time adjusting their hats and such. Their outfits may have stayed on better had they been able to keep from fidgeting so much during the whole show.

Earldean and I sat on the edge of our seats as we were so proud of his courage to be able to do that just as he had rehearsed. He had two lines; the opening, *"Welcome-friends an neighbors."* and the closing words, *"Won't-you-join-us-one-and-all-as-we-give-thanks-for-this boun-ti-ful feast?"*

After that Mr. Haskell asked a visiting priest to say the blessing before we lined up to get our plates.

They let me and Earldean sit with Ed Earl and Learline. It was the first time we'd all been together for any length of time since we had arrived there.

The first light snowfall came with indication of winter being here to stay by mid December. My sister and I were still struggling with our studies and had to spend extra time with a tutor.

All the advertisements on the T.V. and radio were promoting Christmas toys that would make a kid drool just at the thought of having any one of them. Mrs. Greer would turn off the set and find something for us to do in our spare time, so all of us orphans wouldn't get our hopes up for the likes of anything those toy stores had to offer.

She found some green and red construction paper, some scissors and glue and showed us how to make a long chain that we ended up hanging from the ceiling then across the room. We made another to go around the front door.

Mr. Cotton had the older boys up on ladders stringing lights around the eves of all the buildings. They were finished by dark so everyone bundled up and went out into the snow to see how it looked. It was such a beautiful sight to see, with light bulbs of all different colors glowing in the night…like a little city.

Off in the distance we could see that the people in the neighborhoods had the same idea we did. There were little colored lights everywhere! It was amazing to me what all they could do with electricity those days as this put off enough glow to see all around us.

The adults led us in singing some Christmas Carols then allowed enough time for a playful snowball fight. I actually laughed a little and was starting to enjoy myself when they said that it was time for us all to go back inside our houses.

Mrs. Greer made mention of how, at Christmastime, people are nicer and more generous than they are at other times of the year. She said that sometimes the good boys and girls get surprises from Santa Claus. Some are even invited to spend the day with a family and are treated real special. Most people who are adopting want to do so by Christmas because that's thought to be a time for a family to bond together.

I didn't care about the toys and all that but I would sure miss being with my family. We never had much but Mama would find a way to make the time special. She'd get Daddy to cut down a small pine and put in the bus for us to decorate with berries and pine cones tied on with string. Mama would save the tin foil from different packages and would cut out stars from cardboard boxes. She'd then wrap them with the foil and let us hang them on the tree.

She would cook up whatever wild bird Daddy would bring home and dress it up real nice with Denby's homemade sauce.

From different hiding places she would bring out something she had made special for each of us, including something for Denby when he came by.

Daddy would always have some little something wrapped up for her too. It was never much but she was so grateful. You might have thought he had given her the moon.

Yes, this year would be so very different for us; there was no denying it.

Saturday morning, the 21st of December, Earldean and I were summoned to the main office. When we asked Mrs. Greer what it was about she said something about a visit.

We were out the door and across the grounds as fast as our legs could run. Everyone knew that having a visitor was like a badge of honor and you didn't waste a single second messing around.

On the way up the steps we saw a woman walking our way with Ed Earl and Learline alongside her. They broke loose and ran toward us with open arms.

"EARLDEAN…SASSY!" they shrieked in unison.

"Are we gonna git ta visit with them?" Earldean asked the woman who just smiled as we all embraced then said, *"Why don't we do this inside…let's get out of this cold wind before we all catch a cold."*

She held the door while we all tried to squeeze through the opening at the same time. We were tickled to get to be together but nothing could have made us happier than what we saw once we got inside.

It took a brief second to sink in as we stood staring at the happy smiles of some of our loved ones that we had all but given up on ever seeing again.

"I can't believe it…ya came to see us!" Earldean said as she stretched out her arms and ran to hug them all at the same time.

"Alma?…Cody?" Ed Earl shrieked.

We all fell in behind sister, hugging and kissing each one of them several times. The sound of overwhelming joy echoed in the chambers as we said each other's names over and over again. We didn't want to let go so they could sit back down.

"Oh, Toodie…I missed you!" Learline said as Alma passed her over.

"Boy o boy…she's gotten a lot heaver…just look how you've all grown!"

"Hey Deputy Reed…Where's ya police clothes?" Ed Earl asked.

"I'm off duty today…didn't have to wear em." he replied as he shook his hand and embraced him.

"When I grow up…I'm gonna be a cop jest like you…and I ain't never gonna take off my police clothes…I'm jest gonna sleep in um…and stay in my squad

car at night…case I gotta wake up n go catch me some robbers…Attaway…ya see…I aint gotta take so long gettin dressed…I can jest wake up and go fetch um right quick…'for theyz git away!"

"Oh…I see." he said with an agreeing smile. *"I'm sure everybody in Whisper Ridge will feel much safer knowin you'll be out there ready to catch any bad guys that come along."*

"Naw…theyz told me I ain't a gonna git ta go back yunder…I gotta stay right here at this here place…on account I ain't got no Mama no more…so she can't git me a house ta live in up yunder." He sobered a little from the excitement when he gave his explanation but seemed to have accepted the reasons for his being there. *"My Daddy still aint come ta git me yet…don't look much like he'za comein does it?"*

"Naw son…shure don't look that way…but how about if you'z ta have a house there in our town? With a purdy lady to play like she's ya Mama and her husband to be a daddy to ya…since your's aint come back and all. Your sisters could live there too!"

"You mean like if they'z ta adopt us from outta here?" I stepped over to ask him.

"Yea…yall be ok with that?"

"Sure…but where we gonna find another Mama that wants old kids like me and Sassy?" Earldean asked.

"How about…let's say…Trudy here?" he said bobbing his head toward her.

Trudy sat up straight and smiled saying, *"Yea…how bout me?"*

"Trudy, you would make a right good mama…but…you aint got no husband to be a daddy!"

"She does now!" the deputy said putting his arm around her. *"Me and Trudy got married two weeks ago."*

"Married?...how come yall'z ta do that?"

"I love her, Ed Earl…that's why!"

"Oh, really?" he responded. *"Trudy…I thought ya didn't like em husbands?"*

"Well…I like this one…He's perfect for me." she said as she looked at him and winked.

"But…Trudy, you said you wuz a gonna marry me when I growed up!"

"Oh Hun…I wuz just playin with you about that…"

"Shame on you…Toodie!" Cody said. *"You ought not play around witta man's heart like that…ya might break it..specially one that young and tender."*

"Hey now…" Alma spoke up, *"…I thought you were gonna marry me Ed Earl!"*

"I am Alma… I'm gonna marry you AND Trudy."

"BOTH OF UM?" Cody teased. *"…Are you a glutton for punishment or sumpum boy?"*

38
UNPACKED

We were pleased with our new living arrangements, though in those first few months we were still emotionally a mess. In the beginning the adults had regular meetings with the counselors from the Children's Services as well as with Ms. Pat.

After all we'd been through; we were so totally lost as to where we might really end up when it was all over that we were reluctant to settle in and unpack.

Our insecurities led us to think that we would be split up again if Trudy or Nolan changed their minds about us. Though we did our best to behave ourselves, we all were still having nightmares about Mama and Daddy that would often be followed the next day with bouts of depression.

Learline was alright as long she didn't hear any of the rest of us talking about it. Being exposed to a variety of conversations her vocabulary increased somewhat for a three year old. She would dramatically rattle on about whatever she thought we were crying for even though she really didn't understand at all. We finally realized that she was just imitating us according to the way she saw us acting; sometimes quoting the same phrases.

Even so, everyone agreed she was the one adjusting best to the conditions, mainly because back at the orphanage, she had to share the attention as well as everything else with the other little kids her age. They didn't baby her like we all had done before; it was just as well, she was at the age where she wanted to be treated like a "big girl".

Ed Earl seemed to take to the deputy real fast in efforts to secure his male identity. He had often felt outnumbered before, being around mostly females, so having another guy around more often was good for a boy's tough male ego.

At first he kept comparing the way Nolan did things to the way Daddy might have done it better if he were there. The counselors said that the boy was still in denial about the "absence" of his real father and that this was his way of handling it. Because of his age, it was normal for him to test his replacement for accountability and durability. They said that Ed Earl would come around in his own time and accept the new terms. And, he did.

Nolan would come home every night after work unless he was on call for special duty. He was always sure to find a little time to spend with Ed Earl, showing him the ropes of being a great little man.

Sometimes it might be as simple as pitching a ball and teaching him to play catch or letting him help with fixing something around the house. Their invested interest in one another proved that Ed Earl was a quick learner and Nolan was a good teacher. Each task ended with a "Good job, buddy!" then a strong handshake.

Even though Melba Jean offered to cut Ed Earl's hair for free, Nolan started taking the boy to the barber shop with him instead. He was firm in believing that the little man had no business in a beauty shop with a bunch of women, saying that the smell of all those chemicals alone could be enough to cause his reproductive organ to malfunction later on down the road.

The Sheriff said it wasn't safe for Ed Earl to go on patrol with his deputy but they often went places in the squad car on his off duty time when it was allowed.

Before too much longer they were almost in each other's pocket and the entire police department called him their little mascot.

Earldean's "visitor" would come every month like clockwork and every month she played it up for what it was worth.

Estelle managed to convince her that these mood swings she would go through were much like what she herself had experienced with menopause and that there was nothing that could be done about it.

Though the chemistry might have been difficult to comprehend, she should have explained it a little different to my sister about the mild to moderate discomfort that she might experience during her cycle.

Personally, I think that Earldean took the explanation to mean that she could behave anyway she wanted as long as it worked in her favor.

For what it was worth to her, she was guaranteed at least one week a month of what she thought was "much deserved attention" and she took full advantage of the opportunity.

From that, she managed to get special privileges without earning them. She was able to get out of her fair share of work, and she could use her "visitor" as an excuse to blame any of her misconduct on.

Well, needless to say I was jealous and was looking forward to the day I would be paid a "visit" and given such honors. Surely there would be a big celebration with bubble baths and boxes of chocolate in store for me too.

I'd get to stay up past bed time and look at the television or a magazine until I got sleepy. I could shave my legs smooth like all the other young ladies do and paint red polish on my toes and fingernails. Maybe the Avon lady would start handing out samples to me too.

Then, Earldean might see me to be as grown-up as she was and quit treating me like a baby. She did, but by that time I *had* grown up enough to get a better grip on my emotions so I didn't give her enough ammunition to shoot me down anymore.

"Visitations" weren't all they were cracked up to be either. It wasn't as big of a deal with me I guess because I was better prepared than she was and knew more about what to expect when it came my turn.

I would later learn that the special treatment was to help her emotionally adjust to something that was totally natural.

With her having been caught off guard and uneducated about it, Earldean reacted at first as if it were a disease that would kill her or maybe cripple her for life. They said that under the circumstances of our mother having just hemorrhaged to death they could see why she was having such a hard time with it.

The women were simply trying to help by turning the negative into a positive. It took a while but she's much better about it now.

In time, Earldean and I were both more psychologically balanced having been relieved of full responsibility of our younger siblings. It felt good just to be a kid again even though I was getting too old to play the same as I did back in the hollow.

My interest over time would change to fit that of a girl my own age and soon I began to find friends beyond the limitations of that small group.

People eventually quit calling me a little hillbilly and started calling me by my own name…my bona-fide name; Shirline Reed.

We had been living with Trudy and Nolan as our foster parents for about eight months before the adoptions were final. Though we'd refer to them as our parents now, they never insisted we call them Mama and Daddy. They said that nobody else could ever take that place in our hearts and they weren't about to try. However, they did insist we call the deputy by his first name, Nolan; especially after he was promoted to sheriff a year or so later.

They had a great support team of friends and family there in town who all pitched in however they could to help the couple adjust to an "instant family".

Doc and Estelle played the role of our grandparents, spoiling us with gifts, quality time and attention that every child should be blessed with. They included us in all their family affairs right along with their other six grandchildren that eventually came along.

Hank Jr. returned from the war with the tiniest little wife that he got while he was over there. She wasn't much bigger than me at the time but by my 16th birthday, I wore two sizes bigger than her. By then they had two babies and Hank's sister, Amy Sue, was married and had four of her own.

She stayed and made her home out in California with her little family but they would bring the kids to see their grandparents at least once a year. And, every time they came home, Estelle would gather us all up for a group photo of all her "grand-babies" to send along with her Christmas cards each year.

Her own grown children never seemed to mind her doing that even though we weren't blood related. I'm glad it didn't bother them because it was good for us to have "cousins". Through the years we've all kept in touch and have grown closer than the average extended family.

Trudy and Nolan would tell us all the time how much they loved us and they never ran out of hugs. As a couple they were really good for each other. Trudy claimed credit for their happiness on her ability to keep the man fed with *"good home cookin"*; although most of it came from the café. Nolan said it was because he took good care of his wife and paid her plenty of attention and showered her with *"good lovin"*.

They both kept up the Bible reading for us and saw to it that we said our prayers every night just like our own parents had. Eventually, with the extra help from our teachers at school and church, we all learned to read better and we would take turns reading out loud. They said it was good practice for us so that we'd be able to do this for our own children some day.

Once I learned how to read real well I just couldn't get enough of it. I read everything I could get my hands on, including the book that Daddy often said was one of his favorites, "Ole Yeller". It *was* a good story…even made me cry, but I was a little disappointed when I discovered it wasn't about an old school bus.

However, we did start riding the school bus every day. It was more modern and could seat more bus riders than the one we lived in. Often times, on the long ride home I'd reminisce about those stories Mama and Daddy told of their courtship.

Different volunteers helped to teach us the various subjects so that we could catch up in school faster. It got to the point that we were some of the smartest kids in our classes and were making honor roll…most of the time.

Our new parents said they couldn't have done it without all the help of these people who so generously gave of their time and wisdom.

The best help came from our new neighbors, the Gilberts, another newlywed couple who had conveniently moved into the house just across the street from us. We knew them best by their first names…Alma and Cody.

For a wedding present, people from all over town and down at the church house put some money together and came up with a down payment on the fixer-upper. Then, many of them worked on the project of renovating the place. We also got to help with a little bit of the painting; it was like a big party.

And, after a few weeks of honeymooning, they flew right back into helping with…I'd say, about fifty percent of the rearing responsibility.

They opened up their spare bedrooms to accommodate me and Ed Earl when it became too crowded at Trudy and Nolan's Place. They said that this way we could all have our own room.

A couple of folks went into together and bought us beds and some others donated odd pieces of furniture so that we could keep our things put away neatly.

Just like back home, we kids had our chores in helping with the cooking and cleaning. We enjoyed working outdoors, maintaining our lawns while the adults helped each other maintain our education…as in helping us with our homework.

There was always somebody available that could get us where we needed to go if it was farther than *normal* walking distance.

They all joked about these accommodations saying that it was like a six bedroom house with a street running through it.

It was true…we could be found at either place depending on what was going on around there, be it a meal or a movie…coffee time or bath time…planning a grocery list or a party list…the dust could hardly settle in either place.

Oh, there were always those few folks who didn't know the whole story and thought this whole set up was abnormal or a bit over the top, but both couples agreed that those people were never going to be happy anyway.

They said that there's always going to be some miserable "busybodies" who want to pass judgment on everybody they meet, but until they walk in our shoes they'll never change, and even then there's no promise.

Cody supposed they didn't like themselves, therefore, they didn't want to like anybody else any better. *"That's cause misery loves company…Least ways 'ats what Trudy's all time telling me… ain't it?"* he'd say when Alma would be frustrated with them.

Cody could always get Alma to laughing again with something silly he'd have to say about whatever was troubling her.

"You aint got a serious bone in your body…do ya?" she'd enlighten him with a grin.

"I seriously got some bones…now I'll tell ya…" he'd respond, then would run off on some bunny trail about whatever…anything…it didn't matter as long as he could get her to come around to her jolly self again. I still enjoy being around them whenever I can.

Thank God that there were more who agreed with them and supported our efforts to make our lives more livable.

In spite of any few who might have disagreed with our arrangements there were always those who wished to attach themselves to the group…the family…the congregation…the township...the relationships. I guess everybody needs to find some sort of kinship or they will end up a lonely person… *"And God said it wasn't good for man to be alone."*

So, no matter what we were gathering for, there was always one or two of us who would invite a friend along to join in to share in the fellowship and fun.

Often times for family entertainment, we'd gather together for home movies that Doc made with his 8 millimeter motion camera. My favorite one was the reel with Alma and Cody's wedding day on it. Positively speaking, it's still the most memorable event of my childhood because of the influence it had on my thoughts at that point.

It was more to it than the beautiful bride Alma turned out to be or the rented white tuxedo that Cody wore that made him look like a skinny Elvis Presley. It was more to it than the Easter egg colored brides maid dresses that Granny Pane made for me, Earldean and Trudy or the one she made for the precious little flower girl Learline.

Nor was it the adorable part of ring bearer played by Ed Earl. Of all the pretty flowers and fancy dressed people that came to celebrate with us that day, nothing influenced me more toward feeling secure than the vows they made to one another.

They promised to love one another and forsake all others, keeping only to themselves, for better or worse, richer or poorer, in sickness and in health until death do they part or…as long as they both shall live.

I thought of that pair of dreamers whose bus broke down in Chinquapin Hollow that day long ago, and though it was never proven that they were ever "lawfully" married, they held these same vows unto each other.

They *kept only to themselves* and didn't let anyone else come around… except Denby. For over ten years, when things went bad they somehow made it *better* by agreeing things could have been *worse.*

They were *rich* in the eyes of God but *poor* according to the standards of the world. When they were *sick* they'd lie down until they felt better and took care of one another until they got *healthy* again.

The only time Daddy left her out there was when he had to go to work and while they were apart that last time…she died. So, *till death* did they part.

I'll never know for sure if they got married and bona-fide their union but I want to believe in my heart that they at least tried to…God only knows and that's all that matters.

I'll never know for sure if Mama died before or after we left or if she was buried by the earth…or by somebody.

God only knows what happened to all that money they'd been saving in the pickle jar or the guns Daddy kept locked up in that old deep freeze. They did however, recover that one shotgun…the kind that was just like that one Daddy had always left with Mama; it had a shell in it. It was out there along with what they thought might be some of the money rolled and bound with a rubber band.

39
THE LEGEND OF CHINQUAPIN HOLLOW

It was mid December of 1968, when the trees were naked and the wind bitter cold, that some deer hunters who were tracking fresh prints in the bed of a cavernous, wooded canyon, stumbled across something unusual.

Partially buried in the snow, they found a perfectly good hub cap and wondered how it got way out there in the middle of nowhere. They didn't think much of it at first until they came across a whole tire that was still in good condition, only it was still attached to part of an axle.

When their curiosity got the best of them, their eyes followed the path of least resistance to find a large object that seemed out of place. About halfway up a tall, steep incline, that was sparsely covered with bare trees and a few snow capped evergreens, something was shimmering in the morning light.

It was hard to tell exactly what it was at first because it was partially obscured by snow covered limbs and twigs. It was large, whatever it was, and in its determination to get there, it must have made quite a disturbance from looks of the debris it took down with it.

On closer inspection they discovered what appeared to be a mangled up truck, nose down and wedged in a large crevice between two gigantic sections of bedrock.

One of the hunters bravely volunteered to climb up even closer and take a quick look; just to make sure. It was so distorted from the process of getting lodged that one would hardly recognize what it was unless they were almost standing right next to it. In fact, when they came back with the police it took them a little over a half hour to find it again.

With the new fallen snow it was hard to tell just how long it had been stuck there but judging from the condition of the tire and hubcap, it couldn't have been too long. Yet, the evidence of dried leaves still stuck to the broken branches told a different story. This had to have happened when the tree sap was high and still flowing through the veins of its leaves…sometime before autumn.

The gray colored wreckage blended well with the limestone and its surroundings so if anyone had been searching for it, it was easy to see why they might have overlooked it all that time.

Just in case they were wrong about the time frame of the accident, or in the unlikely event that anyone could possibly survive such horrible tragedy; they spent the better part of two days just trying to get close enough to find a body to rescue.

It being so far down the cliff from the dirt road above made it difficult and chancy for large equipment to attempt to dislodge it. Nothing they had available to them would be able to reach it because of the rocky terrain. Getting up high enough or, lowered down low enough to the site proved to be quite a challenge without special gear, so they sent in expert climbers to help with the operation.

Their intent was to go in and retrieve any possible survivors or more likely, a victim of fatality, so stretchers were ready to be lowered in the event there of. After several treacherous maneuvers they finally were able to master their quest of getting there, however the grimy cracked glass made it difficult to see inside the cab.

The crushed doors were jammed shut and impossible to open because of the way the truck was pinned in past their hinges.

One of the climbers yelled over toward the cab to see if he could get a response. When they didn't get one right away they both yelled again. This time, one thought he heard someone comeback with a moan but it was at the same time the others foot slipped and knocked down more debris, so he wasn't sure.

The top of the cab was partially caved in making it even more difficult to see though to the other side but one thing was for sure, whoever was in there found no way out. Though they were all cracked, the windows were still intact except a small section missing from the broken windshield but it was exposed to the outside of the bluff, there was no place for a survivor to go…except down.

The demolished vehicle hinged dangerously above a gap that seemed to drop down into an abyss of darkness. With every little movement the whole thing would sway, producing eerie sounds as if it were crying out in severe pain. Long screeching sounds of metal grating against the jagged rock echoed throughout the wintered canyons and were amplified by the void beneath the ruin.

Crumbling gravel along with loose oddments from the truck readily broke away, dropping far below then disappearing into the bottomless pit, making the rescue team a bit nervous.

The cracked, blood stained glass took only a modest amount of force to completely knock out, in order to see through the back window. Still they couldn't see well enough past the rubble to tell if anyone was in there or not. Unless they were pinned beneath the dashboard…they just couldn't tell.

As much as they would have liked to have been able to just reach in and pull somebody out, the task was looking pretty forbidding. They both leaned in towards the opening and yelled again, *"Anybody in there? Can you hear me?"*

"Knock or something…anything…we're here to help!"

This time they both heard a thud followed by a low short moan.

"Hear that? Somebody's in there!" one exclaimed.

"THEY'RE ALIVE!" the other shouted back to the rescue crew above them, who then cheered as they hustled to get the stretcher down to them as fast as they could.

The first fellow quickly began to pull himself up so that he could climb through the back window. As he struggled for the just right position, he could hear the moaning again which gave him a sense of urgency. He pulled harder then swung his legs over into the bed of the truck for leverage. When he did, the moaning sounds grew stronger and over into more of a high pitched squeal. It was then joined by a grinding drone that sounded like it was coming from the sides of the truck. Next there came a heavy rumbling sound as the whole thing began to vibrate.

"Get off…It's about to fall!" the other yelled out the warning as he was jumping back to save himself.

The dark crevice below grew narrower the further down it went, so, this large piece of scrap iron would never fit much tighter than it already was. However, it might have fallen forward and over the bluff if it turned just right and it had enough forceful weight on it.

More rocks, glass, leaves and snow descended from the commotion as the young man hung on for dear life. Though it swayed and squealed to get loose, the truck was still held captive by the massive rocks either side of it.

The one fellow hanging over the back of the cab was able to reach in and grab the shotgun just before he was pulled off by the other guy. They both slipped from their snowy footing and came close to getting pinned in with the wreck as it rocked back and forth.

The other crew below the site warned them to get back and to abort any further plans to get in any closer. The team above couldn't see as well to tell what was happening but having heard the commotion and not wanting to put anyone else's life in danger, they all agreed to call in the climbers.

While they waited on them to scale back up the mountainside, the rest studied the situation from a safer position. Several suggested possible ways to salvage out the truck but without finding the just right angle it presented a challenge. With the risk involved, they decided it was best to just leave the truck hanging there until they could come up with a better plan.

The only one who got close enough to see inside the cab was the climber who pulled the shotgun out; he said that he was barely able to reach and get that much less a body.

Most everything in there had fallen down under the dash due to the nose dive the truck had taken on impact. The driver's side of the seat had unbolted and was bent almost in half with the broken steering wheel stuck through the back of it.

"There was no way anyone could have survived that crash…" he said *"…but I didn't see any bodies in there…I don't know though…there was plenty of dried blood."*

"I don't know how anyone would have gotten out…" the other reported. *"The hole in the windshield wasn't big enough to crawl through…unless he jumped somehow before it lodged there…but with that steep slope…he'd have to be down there somewhere."* he said pointing to the canyon floor.

"Somebody had to have been banged up pretty bad before they jumped to explain all that blood though…don't you think?" one responded.

"…I don't see how…but…if by chance they did…they've gotta be dead around here somewhere…there's no way they could have gotten up and walked away."

"…or crawled for that matter."

"No…not from a tumble like that!" another agreed.

They spent the rest of the next day in search of a body that could have been buried in snow. So with another storm moving in and Christmas just around the corner, it would be a month or more before they'd make it back out there.

Despite the fact that they combed the whole area as best they could in those conditions, they never found a body for positive identification.

Most thought it would have been too mangled to recognize anyway and some even thought maybe the remains could have been eaten by wild animals but they never found any bones or rags that might resemble clothing to prove that theory.

This truck might have fit the description of the one that was sold to an Earl Johnson in Jay, Oklahoma on Aug. 2nd 1968. But, without being able to compare the vindication number or license plate, it couldn't be proven…so one's guess was as good as the next.

Even the seller of the truck couldn't positively identify it from the photos they took because the thing was so scraped up and bent out of shape…but the make and color was a match.

Earldean and I identified the shotgun as being one just like the one Daddy would leave for Mama to protect us with. However, it was pretty banged up so I couldn't be certain.

The authorities said that our response, coupled with the description of the truck was affirmative enough for them to agree that the driver was more than likely our father. They checked and found that there weren't any other "missing persons" reported in or around the area in that time frame…who else could it have been?

They felt that the estimated time frame of the accident proved to be an explanation of his location and why he couldn't be found during those late summer months when the undergrowth of the forest was much thicker. Though they had searched all the roadsides before, even in the dead of winter it was impossible to see this spot where the wreck was from the road above because of its position.

Based on the report of the person with the only pair of eyes who got to get a good look inside the cab, there was no need to risk going any further with trying to get it down so, they left the truck hanging out there, wedged in the side of the cliff.

With the exception of the broken out back window…its still there today…just the way they found it…still no body…that we know of.

A couple of hunters said that they had looked around when they went back out but…nothing.

In the spring a group of young enthusiasts formed a team to see what else they could find after a couple of sightseers found the cash.

There was over eight hundred dollars in small bills rolled up and bound up with a rubber band. It had apparently been hidden there under some underbrush and exposed to the elements but was still spendable. When the authorities got wind of it, they checked it out but they couldn't prove that it belonged to Daddy, as the finders insisted they should be the keepers. They didn't keep it long though…they blew through it like crazy in no time at all.

Nolan, Denby, and Cody really put up a fuss along with a bunch of the others about that money business. They were a bit put out because they thought the people should have at least had the decency to forgo the money to us kids since our Daddy was the one who worked hard and saved it up for his family.

This too, made the papers that had misguiding reports to beef them up a little as if the truth wasn't enough. Of course everyone had their opinions.

For months later we'd hear of folks driving out there to try to get a look at what all the fuss was about. Rumors spread across several counties and it was *"all the rave"* to plan a day of treasure hunting after having the whole story blown out of proportion.

Some said they had heard that the man killed in the truck was really an old miser who intentionally lived poor because he didn't want folks to know how rich he really was. They said it was because he was afraid somebody would try to steal it all. So he carried his life's savings around with him everywhere he went. As legend would have it…the old miser had it all with him the day he drove himself off the cliff. Some say that only a fraction of the loot was found but there was plenty more where that came from.

Gossip eventually turned into child's play of scary storytelling and is now referred to as the *"Legend of Chinquapin Hollow."*

Some say he fell from his hanging truck into the bottomless pit that led straight to hell for killing his wife.

As if to find reward in it, teens would load up on a Saturday afternoon to go out and look for the missing man and his money. They'd stay till after dark where, in fun and games, they'd scare one another half to death with spooky sounds just for the thrill of it.

On windy nights boys would take their dates parking out there on the roadside in hopes of spotting him walking down the dusty path or just to listen and hear him wailing from the deep dark hole beneath the truck.

Others say that there's a bloody wild man gone crazy who walks about the canyon still looking for his lost children and his money. Yet, others claim that they've heard footsteps and have been followed.

There are also claims to actual sightings of somebody out there walking around looking for something…some say they have even heard him calling out our names.

40
HAPPY EVER AFTER

Trudy and Nolan said that with all those people coming and going out there in the hollow, that there's no doubt they didn't see or hear something…each other!

Alma claimed it was all just the foolish nonsense of devil's play, while Cody thought it would be a good way to get the money back if he bought all that land around there, just so that he could charge admission to get in. This way he could make enough money to make payments on it and enough left over to replace the eight hundred dollars he felt was stolen from us.

Nolan said he thought Cody could make enough to put all of us kids through college. Doc and Estelle claimed they always felt that Daddy must have been going to do something special with all that money to have had it with him that day…or night…whichever it was…but they were all sure he had to be on his way home or out looking for us when the accident happened.

I've often wondered if it was even him at all…It might have been somebody else's truck stuck out there…It could have been some lost stranger just passing through.

Daddy could still be out there looking for us today…who knows?

To me, it was a blessing in disguise…no matter if it was really him or not. Not that I don't care about him, but it's the "*not knowing*" that can drive a person stark raving mad if you let it.

Earldean has come close to madness at times because she has had trouble over the years with all the explanations that end with *"Who knows?"* She just has to know everything…she's often called *"A Know It All"*.

For me, it was the inability to *do anything about it* that I couldn't stand.

It must have been on that exact same December morning when I was still back in the orphanage, begging God for mercy on my very soul, that those hunters found the truck out there.

My sadness was festering into anger from all that I had been through up to that point.

Since I was stuck in the orphanage and wasn't allowed to continue to look for Daddy myself, I had prayed so hard that very same morning for God to help *someone else* to find him for me, so that we could get on with our lives. Without knowing his whereabouts, there was no telling how long we would have had to stay there and wait.

I didn't want to live like that anymore…"waiting"…I thought I'd rather die that morning!

Years later, I had the opportunity to meet and talk at length with one of the hunters that was out there the day they found that truck hanging from the side of the cliff.

He gave me the detailed account of how it all came about. They'd almost canceled their plans to even go hunting that morning because they heard another snowstorm was headed their way and would lower their chances of visibility. They chanced it anyway, in hopes they could get back before it set in.

Though it was unusual, they had not seen any sign of deer until they met up and started to head back. It was then that they came upon the fresh tracks and decided to follow them. He said it was those tracks that led them to the place where they found the wreck.

He told me that they still might have missed it had not the sun come peeping through the thick clouds for that brief second to reflect off of what he thought was probably the rearview mirror.

Now, what are the odds of that happening?

Personally, I don't lend it to a "chance of luck", for I fully believe it was an act of mercy on God's part to answer a child's prayer.

He heard my cry, and then saw me through with a plan better than my own in that without the finding of my Daddy, dead or alive, we would have never been awarded new legal guardians.

In doing so, God also answered many other people's prayers too… in ways of His own.

As for mine, I was given back my life with a family; not exactly the way it was before, but possibly better…I don't know…but God knows.

In the process, I've been given a "Bona-fide" name. My adopted family name, "Reed", follows the discovery of what is believed to be my real given name that was found in my mother's own handwriting.

In the front of the binding pages of the Bible we inherited from Mama, were found seven names that were numbered and listed in various shades of writing.
The ink is faded now, but is still legible as follows:
1. Earl Edward Johnson,
2. Marline
3. Earldean
4. Shirline
5. Edward Earl
6. Learline
7. James Leonard.
Through process of elimination, it was declared that the fourth name was mine. The seventh and final name is believed to be that of the child she had already named, but lost, just prior to her own death as it was written in the freshest ink.
I don't think it was just a "coincidence" that with the number seven being the number of completion, biblically speaking, that little James Leonard came last in the line of birth order.
His two namesakes alone tells me that this was indeed a real little *person* who had a purpose for his short existence here on earth… whether he ever took in his first breath or not…he *was* here and is now buried in it.
Because you see, before this child was ever conceived in his mother's womb, there were at least two people who came before him with strong positive influence on the lives of his parents, Marline and Earl.
The first of them being a man who went the extra mile and who had the compassion of a good father, including the qualities of patience and teachability… *"Everthang I ever learnt 'bout fixin thangs…I learn't frum my Unka Leonard."* my Daddy used to say.
And, the other, the man who lived to be the perfect example of the spirit of love to them. His actions spoke volumes in the meaning of the last of the Ten Commandments…you know the one about your neighbor?
James Denby was also an example of that commission Jesus gave us while He was on earth…that red letter phrase "…Love thy neighbor as I have loved you, that ye also love one another…" That's how our good neighbor was.

Denby died just three short years later after his little namesake, baby James Leonard, passed through this life.

For love suffers long, it is kind, love does not parade itself, it is not puffed up, it does not behave rudely, does not seek its own, is not provoked, thinks no evil; Love does not rejoice in iniquity, but rejoices in the truth; Love bears all things, endures all things. Love never fails. James Edward Denby was all of these…he was Love come to life.

I will always love my neighbor, Denby, and the spirit of his love will be passed on for generations to come. Just as the spirit of Leonard Gibson, my great uncle, was passed on to me, my brother and sisters.

I'm sure when my parents came up with that name together, they were planning to give this child names to live up to…James and Leonard.

To honor them both, their names were passed on for the sake of goodness and were given to another so that all those blessings would continue on. That's what that baby's purpose was…to honor those two men with a namesake. Had they both lived past that delivery, Mama probably would have called our little brother by both of these names…so shall we.

In her honor, Alma and Cody saw fit to name their only child James Leonard Gilbert and we've always referred to him as our baby brother.

In a few years, if I live that long, I will have lived twice as long as my mother did. Then, in another two, God willing, twice as long as my father lived.

I don't know if that's good or bad…but it might have something to do with another one of those Ten Commandments, the only one that comes with a promise. That would be the fifth one: Honor your father and mother and you will live a life of longevity.

I don't believe that you, or I, or any of us, are here on this earth without purpose. Yet, there are many souls who muddle through their lives hopelessly thinking that this is as good as it gets… *"Here today and gone tomorrow."*

I choose to believe that I'll see my Mama and her little baby, my Daddy, Denby and all of my loved ones again one day in a wonderful glorious life here after this one…in the "Ever After." I really believe I'm right about this…if not, what have I lost? Nothing! I'd rather have faith and trust in God while I'm here than to *not* have faith…*not* live accordingly, then die only to find out that I was wrong. Then it would be too late.

They say "Ever After" is a mighty long time.

I don't think God created us because he was bored and had nothing else to do. I believe that He put us here on earth and allows us to suffer trials and tribulations so that when he sends His grace to see us through it all, we will more readily appreciate Him when we meet him face to face.

Compared to eternity, our time here is short and is to be used wisely. Each of us will experience a certain degree of pain and joy in this life. Which one you pick to stay in, is up to you. As for me, I share them both with my Jesus so I don't have to go it alone. He can ease you through your pain and he delights in your joy, if you pray and talk to him. And, I don't know about you, but I don't want to spend eternity with somebody I don't know. That's why I'm doing everything I can to get to know Him now, so I can enjoy His company later.

There are some people who take full credit themselves for all the blessings they've received, but in the end of this time and the beginning of forever, they will see the truth.

It's then, we will *know* that He was…is…and shall always be…truly worthy of *all* our praise and glory.

I might not accomplish all I'd like to while I'm here, but if my purpose is to serve Him well, so be it; I'll give it all I've got, as I will try to glorify Him in all I do.

Mama's life might not have been very long but she definitely served a purpose…so did Daddy. So far, I've seen it in most folks I know. But sometimes, a body has to take *time* out to get it done before they run out of *time*.

Earldean is still working on finding her purpose. She's spent too much time blaming her misfortunes on her past. When she couldn't get a hold of things, she took up drinking to ease her worries. Only problem was, she worried a lot. The more she worried, the more she drank and it got to the point to where she couldn't stop. It was a vicious cycle and after a while she spiraled so far down, that at one point, she almost couldn't get back up.

Well I guess it took hitting the bottom before she could spring back. The bottom is a very low place to be and once you are down, it makes you that much further from the top. Some folks might think that's just too far to reach and they give up trying.

It has taken Earldean several tries, but each time, she gets a little better. I believe she's almost out of the woods…so to speak.

She went out to California a few times with Doc and Estelle, back when they were still traveling. Amy Sue talked her into coming out there to visit after graduation. Well, that visit lasted twelve years. (No, not the kind of "visit" she was famous for!) She lived there, in and around the same area as the rest of our cousins. She got married, divorced, married and divorced again, before she moved back home with two daughters from two husbands.

"Fey" and "Katie" bounced back and forth between their Mama and their daddies before they were finally old enough to be on their own. They both are married and living in West Oklahoma, about half the distance between either parent.

Earldean is a grandmother now, of four grand-children. Fay and Katie bring them to visit two or three times a year. The kids are all excited about the family reunion and visiting with their grandmother they call…"Gramadean."

I'm proud of my sister and how she has managed to pull herself through …by the help and grace of God. Earldean had been caught up in going the wrong direction and somehow, she spun around in such a way that she wasn't sure which way to go. For the longest time, she was going against the grain and things never seemed to run smooth for her.

She seems much happier these days, as things are going more her *new* way. She's been sober now for over three years and our whole family is proud of her. We're glad to have her back again.

She's been seeing Willie Jay, who turned out to be a handsome fellow… and real smart too. He's been widowed for two and a half years now, and is in the insurance business. I really hope it works out for them…he's good for her.

Ed Earl is doing great. He took a different path to handling his past. Though most of the memory he has retained is due to mine and Earldean's recollection of accounts back in the hollow. As far as the transition period goes, he didn't have to see the counselors as long as his older sisters did.

Having strong, positive male influences around really helped him to build a firm foundation for integrity. He took his childhood trauma and weaved it into the fabric of his purpose in life. It was those experiences that have led him in the direction of justice, coupled with his association with the law and order of a community.

Learning the value of a dollar at an early age paid off for Ed Earl, who was always doing odd jobs to earn extra money. On his seventh birthday, Doc handed him five one dollar bills then taught him about the concept of *"Give a little…save a little…spend a little and live off of the rest."*…and how it works best in that order.

We all knew that he had caught on when he asked Cody to bring home four empty, economy size, pickle jars from the Eat-A-Bite. He took and labeled each one accordingly with the words **GIVE**, **SAVE**, **SPEND**, and **LIVING**, then placed them on his dresser so that he could see them every day. They were made of clear glass so he could see exactly what he had to effectively work with. He took the five bills he had been holding on to until he got the jars so that he could implement his plan for his money. Then, he put one dollar in each of the first three and two in the last. Then, for at least three months, he divided every dime he earned in the same manner, not spending even a penny of it until he was certain he had enough to work with.

We all watched along with him to see his money grow and wondered what he was going to do with it all. His self-discipline was amazing for a boy his age so it was easy for the rest of us to be enthusiastic about it. The adults seemed to just look for ways to pay him for something…anything for a nickel…simply so they could all watch him put money in his jars. Always having to make change for him, Trudy got to where she kept pennies around just for that purpose.

Finally, one Sunday morning, I guess when he thought he had enough, Ed Earl came out of his room dressed in his "Sunday Go to Meeting" clothes, and carrying one of his jars; the one that had the word ***GIVE*** on it. He insisted on taking that whole big glass jar with him to church, where at offering time, the congregation waited for him to get the lid off so that he could pour the entire contents over into the collection basket.

Needles to say, the "Spirit of Giving" made a move on Brother Hemphill in a way that he took the opportunity to preach a sermon on tithing.

The next day, Estelle came by to pick us up to go shop for school clothes. This time, Ed Earl came out of his room with the ***SAVE*** jar and a pocket full of change from the ***LIVING*** jar.

When we stopped off at the bank, so that Estelle could make the deposit, Ed Earl took his **SAVE** jar and went in with her. Before too long, they came out with Mr. Barnett, the banker, walking them to the car. Ed Earl was carrying four suckers to share with us and his new savings account card with his own name and number on it.

After we were finished with the shopping, we made one more stop. Ed Earl treated us all with an ice-cream cone, from his "living money" he had been carrying in his pocket all day. He claimed that money was for necessities and felt it necessary to make us happy.

The first money he ever spent from his **SPEND** jar was some time later, when he knew for sure how he wanted to use that money. After everybody in both houses kept fussing at him for using up all the ketchup, he decided to buy his own bottles so that he could have all he wanted without any guilt. He was going through a bottle every other week, so he supplied both houses with plenty to use. In simpler words he told us this was an investment in non-confrontational relationships. It turned out to be more than just a minor investment.

Years later, he had eventually made enough money to fill the **SPEND** jar several times over, so he had to open another account at the bank to keep it all. On his twenty first birthday he took all the money from that account to "spend"…on ketchup! He invested every penny of that money in the stock market with "H.J.Heinz Company". He figured they had been around since 1869 and they probably wouldn't fold any time soon; especially with so many folks around with ketchup addictions. He still has one of the very first bottles of ketchup he ever purchased with his own money. None of us know how he has resisted opening and using it all this time, but somehow, he never broke the seal. It is a special edition bottle of Heinz's 100th year anniversary that he purchased in November of 1969.

He paid his own way through college and earned a degree in criminal justice and started with some pre-law. Estelle thought he'd make a good Perry Mason and encouraged him to go back for more schooling. Instead, he ended up as a private investigator, not for the money; he just loves solving mysteries.

He recently turned down the position as a detective for the city of Wheaton and decided to stay where he was at so that he could spend more time with his wife Becky, and twin boys; "Easy" and "Early", who will be fourteen next week.

Their real names are Ezekiel Ray and Earl Cody, named after their "Grand-paws", Nolan, who's middle name is Ray and of course Daddy, then Cody, who gave them their nick names when they were babies, too little to argue with him. The idea of such stuck.

They're living just north of Kansas City where Ed Earl coaches his boy's softball team. He has been active in The Boys and Girls Club for years now and just loves it.

He still gives, saves, spends and is making more than a just living. He has been wise with all the money he handles and is now the treasurer at his church and financial advisor for its members.

He is a really great Dad for his boys and a wonderful husband to Becky, who is still just crazy about him...*and* his ketchup! She takes good care of all her boys and is there to cheer them on in all they do. As a family, they love to go camping, hiking or boating but most of the time, they're happy enough just to go fishing in the lake behind their house.

It's a charming country home that Ed Earl built for Becky after the twins were born. It's on a nice little stretch of land big enough for his three horses..."Whitey, Blackie, and Wild Flower."

Learline finally put 'Baby Doll' up on the shelf long enough to finish school and court the fellow of her dreams. She went ahead and married young, just as she had planned, because she knew her purpose in life was to be a good wife to a preacher man and to be a wonderful mother to six children...she is.

Her husband, "Preach", is the pastor over at that new non-denominational, Bible church in town called, "Word of Faith". Together, they are actively involved in their church activities, their children's school functions and a variety of sports. She still has her beautiful voice and sings on the worship team there at church and she has headed up a Mom's support group in town.

Thanks to all of her coaches, Trudy, Alma and Cody, in the process of learning to cook, she turned out to be a better cook than all of them. Because she's been around the restaurant business most of her life, she has learned how to cook enough to feed her small army and she heads up all of those big church dinners.

Many years of loving and taking care of "Baby Doll", as well as all her other dollies that were given to her after she moved to Whisper Ridge, was just practice for all the nurturing she has had to do for her real live babies. For just as planned, she did give birth to those six kids she and Preach claimed they wanted and they gave them all names with good virtues to live up to; Grace, Faith, Hope, Charity, Joy, and Love. Learline had used all these names for her other baby dolls when she was little so she held on to the idea in hopes that one day she could name her real babies those same names.

They have one boy stuck in the middle of all those girls. "Charity", was supposed to the baby's name if it was a girl. She never had any *boy* dolls…just girls. So, they had to come up with a boy's name at the last minute that would mean the same.

Preach had already said he didn't want to name his son after him because he was afraid he'd be nicked named "Junior". He thought there were enough of those running around that neck of the woods and didn't want his son to get lost in the crowd on account of something like that. Learline was relieved because, even though she loved the man dearly, she didn't think it was necessary to let another child suffer with a name like "Wellford Harlow Givin".

She was grateful that he found his calling at an early age and was given an appropriate nickname before she ever met him or otherwise she might not have ever given him a chance. It was the name, "Preach", that hooked her in the first place.

They wrestled with several ideas and suggestions to name their new born if it turned out to be a boy. Finally, they came up with one that they both thought was absolutely perfect. Preach explained to Ed Earl about how Learline came up with that one while she was still in labor.

Between contractions, she was talking to her husband about the "act of charity" and what it meant. That lead to her discussing how she had always noticed that particular quality in her brother, saying that Ed Earl had been giving of himself and his money for as long as she could remember. With him being such a charitable person, it would only be fitting to name their son after him out of respect of his generosity. After a few close contractions and her repeating herself several times… in her country slang, *"Yep, he's been given…been givin"*, her eyes lit up. They named the boy Benjamin and nick-named him "Ben". It worked out ok, especially since their last name is "Givin".

Her youngest, Lovie, just turned thirteen and her oldest, Gracie is now twenty-two and married. Learline just became a real "bona-fide" grand-maw nine weeks ago. Oh, and they also have an old collie dog named "Justice". She says life is good!

As for me, well I'm blessed and it would take me an eternity to tell you all about it. Oh, I'm exaggerating, eternity is a long time and there's only one of um! So, if we end up in the same place, I'll be happy to fill you in.

But I will tell you this much…Huey and I will be celebrating our Silver Anniversary this year…That's 25 years, for those of you who are color-blind like my husband.

We still live here in Whisper Ridge and have over the years done our part to help keep it populated. We have five grown children…well almost grown. Our youngest graduates this year…YEA! Huey and I are going to celebrate till the cows come home. We'll be tired by then as we don't fare as well these days with staying up late like we used to do when they were all just babies. We have ten grand-children already and the kids tell us there's two more on the way. All of us are real excited about the new additions as that will make a "dozen cousins" for this generation. Can I tell you all of their names? Well, that's another story…another whole book…we'll see. Hmmm…a book about all the Pane's Family. Now, I can tell you some stories about them, that's for sure, but Cheese-n-crackers!…It took me the longest time just to learn spell enough words to try and tell you *this* story. I had to learn how to pronounce them first! And then, I still want to spell them like they sound…datburnit! Well, maybe later.

I have to go now and get started on cooking some supper, then make some phone calls about the big "family reunion" coming up soon. They'll all be here in town for it. If I get a chance, I'll tell you all about it later, but for now, Huey is trying to get my attention messin round wit me a sayin... '*Woman, why come ya ta spend sa much time writtin them stories these days? Reccon ya aught ta ba a good wife and git back in younder in the kitchen and bake me a pie er sumppin? Im'a gittin houngry and gotta hankerin fer some good eatin…na come on!"*

Oh don't mind Huey, he's such a fun lovin tease! He likes to mimic grand-paw Pane.

God rest his bitter old soul!

41
BE BACK IN TIME

Last week, we all got together for a big family reunion on the Fourth of July weekend. Somebody suggested we all drive out to Chinquapin Hollow and take a look around…just for old times' sake. We got up early Saturday morning, before it got too hot, to take the long ride out there.

Due to the extra warm weather and the anticipation of the perilous exploration, the Great Grandma's Trudy and Alma quickly volunteered to stay behind to help watch the toddlers.

Of course, Great Grampaw's Cody and Nolan, being the feisty old fellows they are, enjoyed teasing their wives about it as they went around boastfully claiming to be sure footed enough to take on such an adventure, even at their age.

Never the less, when it came time to go, they felt obliged to stay and assist our younger brother James Leonard, who has taken over his daddy's roll as chief cook of the family. When it comes to feeding large crowds he is the pro; especially after he, being the only namesake, personally inherited the secret recipe for Denby's Bar-B-Q sauce. He had already made up a batch big enough for everybody to take a jar home with them as a souvenir from the family reunion. James proudly pressed on each jar neat labels that read:

Uncle Denby's BBQ
Secret Family Recipe
In Loving Memory of James Denby

Though they are getting on in years, Estelle and Doc were honored to be asked by our grandchildren to come go with us. They had already rehearsed their excuse as to why they could not go either. They were already scheduled to pick up the gigantic birthday cake that had been ordered for the twins who were celebrating their fourteenth birthday that day. However, Estelle did send her digital camera so that we could take pictures for her. She often can't remember how to use it but there's always somebody around to help her figure it out. She still loves her pictures and certainly didn't want to miss out on any of these!

It took a caravan of several SUV's and a minivan to get the all of rest of us out there. Each vehicle had at least one story teller riding in it, reliving the tales of how this all came to be. Most of us, now spoiled to the comfort of such luxuries as air-conditioned automobiles, found it amazing how four little waifs survived walking so far in such miserable heat.

With several new homes in the area and the roadways being much better than before, things looked quite different from the last time we had been out that way. Because it had been over-grown for so long we had a hard time locating the old home place. That last part of the stretch, though it had been graded and made much wider, was still a dirt road. Once we got to that part, I had Huey stop several times so that we could get out and scout for the entrance. By the fourth stop we still weren't sure at first because underbrush was covering what had once been the beginnings of a driveway. Just beyond that however, on the slope down into the holler, we could see the place where Daddy had spent so much time cleaning off that hillside for that shortcut.

Years of erosion had taken over and had finished the job, washing away the surface so that it was now down to bare rock. Though it was too rugged to drive over, it would make the climb down much easier than we anticipated. Once we were sure we were at the right place, the kids were all warned to watch out for snakes and other critters as they scrambled out of the vehicles to began the exploration.

Though they had all heard about our strange past, I guess it took seeing it with their own eyes to believe those accounts must hold some truth to them. It was fascinating for them to learn that we really lived there. Though by now, the bus could barely be seen as it sat camouflaged, with decades of decaying, fallen leaves and limbs all around it. The unmistaken form was smothered by clinging vines that seemed to be holding it permanently in place.

In its day, our old home place was already considered to be secluded, but today, if somebody happened to stumble across it, they would be truly puzzled as to how anybody could have possibly gotten a bus out there. All paths and lower trails were completely grown over except for that which had been kept down by the deer and other wild animals who had taken to going this way, now that it all was just abandoned backwoods.

The old A frame was nothing more than a pile of crumbled rust on the ground. Had we not been looking for it, we would have never found its remains. We discovered that the old supply trunks were in about the same sort of condition; just heaps of oxidized memories.

Full grown trees were growing where the garden use to be. One had even made its way up through the fire-pit. Nature had certainly taken claim to what had once belonged to her in the first place. After all, it had been a lifetime ago.

It was so very different, yet familiar, as we looked all around and tried to remember how it used to be, when the traffic from our bare feet kept the grass and weeds down in the clearing…there was no clearing now.

Remnants of our life back then looked primitive, as we stumbled across objects that were obviously out of place on the forest floor.

The younger children brought us their findings to be identified then compared to the modern things of today. As we examined them together, we were taken back in an instant to the last time we had used and touched these things. It made me feel old when I scanned the area and realized how much time had passed. Where did it all go?

Wiping the perspiration from my brow, I tried to imagine how my life would have turned out, had that sad day never come when I had to leave my mother just lying there, dead or alive. Though not as much in recent years, Earldean and I had discussed it many times; would we have ever survived that sweltering summer so long ago?

Would it have made a difference, had we gone left toward Clifton instead of right toward Whisper Ridge? I know it would have. As it turns out, that even as innocent little girls, our instincts about that cop named Virgil were right. That creep ended up on the wrong side of the law when it was discovered that he was a no good, wife beating, child molester! I shook my head at the thought of that; no telling how things would have turned out in the hands of that monster.

Huey, Ed Earl and our brother-in-law "Preach", Learline's husband, cleared a path to the old bus by rolling a huge log to trample down the tall weeds. Easy and Early found some big sticks, then went about hacking at the thorny vines and thistle that were in the way.

When they reached their destination, they could see that the hooded stoop was dangerously unstable, due the shifting of one of the decomposing posts. Together, they firmed it up by lifting and resetting it and sliding some flat stones beneath it to hold it up higher.

Earldean and I, who had been watching from a safe distance, slowly made our way to the bus by way of the newly trodden trail. Watching our steps, we were looking out for not only snakes but for any old relics of our past.

I looked up in time to catch my husband Huey take off his ball cap and swat at the curtain of cobwebs that laced the entrance. We got tickled when Ed Earl teased him about disturbing nature that way saying it could easily come back to bite him in the butt if he wasn't careful.

While Huey was momentarily occupied with picking the clinging debris off of his cap, Ed Earl snuck up behind him with a fresh, sharp pine needle and poked it through the back of Huey's pants causing him to jump about a foot off the ground. To intensify the shock factor of the moment, Ed Earl had hollered out, *"Look at the size of that thang on you Huey!"*

All who saw it got a good laugh watching Huey go spinning around in circles, slapping at the seat of his britches until he realized it was just another one of Ed Earl's pranks.

Seeing what he was up to, we all got tickled watching them as Ed Earl started to slowly back up. He gravely asked, *"What's a matter? One done gotcha, huh? I told ya! Best leave them bugs alone!"*

Once Huey was sure he had not taken on any spiders to fight in the process, he engaged in recreation by trying to smear some of the sticky strings across Ed Earl who was squealing and dodging out of the way. He did however manage to wipe his cap off on Early's shirt while he was bent over laughing so hard, from such amusement. When the boy tried to run, Huey jokingly grabbed a hold of him around the waist in order to finish what he started. As they scrambled around Huey taunted him, saying, *"What's so funny, huh? Hey, Easy…better get over here and help your brother check himself for little ole spiders!"*

When he stepped over to rescue his brother, Huey let go of Early and pretended to wipe some of the spider web on Easy too before walking away satisfied he had gotten his payback to his brother-in-law by way of his sons.

As they brushed off their shirts, the twins were still grinning from the childish fun they had just made with their Uncle Huey.

After one final inspection of his cap, Huey felt safe enough to put it back on. He then grinned at me, winked and said, *"That brother of yours…I tell you what…!"*

Long after the foolishness subsided, several wished that we would have recorded that part of the trip. Had we known it was going to happen, we could have entered it in the America's Funniest Home Videos. It could have won the ten thousand dollar prize to say the least. Guess you'd have had to be there to really appreciate it. I still chuckle at the thought of it even now.

That was just like Ed Earl to find a way to put the fun back in the adventure. No harm done, everybody needed a good laugh.

I know him and the other fellows were just trying to make things light hearted as the mood had gotten weighty for me and Earldean. I don't think either of us was really prepared to be so overwhelmed with the sights we had taken in, thinking for some silly reason, we would find things as we had remembered as children; having kept them preserved in our minds all this time.

It was just kind of heartrending to see it all this way.

Mama and Daddy would have been sad too. The old yellow bus that had sheltered us back in those days was hardly yellow at all anymore. It's buried under layers of pollen and corroding sap having settled under that canopy of trees for decades of seasons.

The words that Mama had hand painted along the sides could hardly be read through the vines. Most of the letters had faded completely or simply cracked and flaked off through the years.

We could see that some of the dust crusted windows had been broken out either by vandalism or more likely, years of flying debris from the many storms the old place had weathered. Draped through one of the gaping holes was some old, faded, dry rotted fabric, torn in flight, no doubt from the shards of glass it has passed time after time.

It was identified as what once was one of Mama's pretty curtains, still hanging from a rod she had secured there herself, a very long time ago. A few of the others still barely hung in place but were in about the same condition. The rest were torn down by nesting birds or other animals that might have intruded while seeking shelter of their own.

Having come this far, there was no doubt that the plan was to pry open the doors so that we could look around inside.

Ed Earl attempted to do the honors before Preach decided to assist him, after he saw that it wasn't going to be an easy task.

For a few moments, I felt like I was in a dream state of mind. My chest had grown tight before I realized that I had been unconsciously holding my breath with anticipation; for what, I'm not sure. That lost lump in my throat returned once more, causing me to hear myself I swallow hard. I felt for some strange reason it was necessary to suppress my tears.

Somewhere deep in my imagination it was as if when the doors were opened, they'd find Mama still laying there where I'd left her.

Eerie squeaks from the corroded old metal signified the resistance of the taut hinges that seemed to be struggling to keep the ghostly past held hostage. This unnatural screeching was amplified by the terrain and echoed a sadness that caused critters in the area to scramble to safety. At the same time, it got the attention of some of the other family members, as if to call them closer to watch the historical unveiling.

I choose not to go in. I was doing good to control my emotions as it was. Instead, I turned away and stood, trying to absorb the same beauty of my surroundings that I had often found in my early childhood. Those treasured views were interrupted every few seconds by flashbacks that served as bitter-sweet reminders of those last few weeks there with Mama, and the last time we said goodbye to Daddy.

My mind raced back and forth, bouncing from the thoughts of playful innocence to wondering how things might have played out had she not miscarried.

As naive children, we had not noticed that she was pregnant; we just presumed she was putting a little meat on her bones. My guess is that she thought we weren't old enough to understand what was going on, or it was just too hard for her to explain it in a way we'd be able to comprehend.

I looked around again, at the woods surrounding this secluded habitat, and wondered where she might have hidden herself from us, while all that took place. It crossed my mind again, as it had many times over the years, when I'd tried to recall the details of those last days, when that supposedly happened, but nothing ever came to me. Had we somehow missed her crying out in pain? How could she have kept such anguish hidden?

But then again, Mama seldom complained about much of anything. My heart grieved at the thought of her going through that horrible experience all alone, with nobody around to help her through the physical, emotional and spiritual pain of it all.

My only consolation was that she had Jesus, who she had come to know as her best friend and savior. She had told us many times that we were never alone…He was always with us.

I slowly spun myself around and stepped closer to face the old sweet-gum that was still standing among the other aged but familiar trees. Judging from the ground beneath, it was now past its fruit bearing years. Yet, the crooked, crippled limbs, still held tightly to its' leaves it had put forth this season and was able to provide shade from the scorching summer sun.

Though it seemed much lower than I remember, the trunk of the tree had truly claimed the faded Orange haired lady as part of its own, for now even more of the old Coca-Cola thermometer was engulfed with bark. Though one could barely make out what she might have looked like at one time, the image was permanent in my mind. On closer inspection, I could see that the needle seemed to be stuck on the one-hundred degree mark, just as it was that day I'd last seen it.

I was abruptly brought out of my trance by the ruckus behind me. Though they had not been inside the bus long, the fellows came flying back out, yelping and swatting wasps. Thank goodness nobody was stung in the escape of their brief expedition.

Once we were sure everyone was alright, Earldean immediately started in asking questions about what it looked like inside. She too had not made it in and was working up the courage to do so just before this happened. Everyone else rushed over to see what all the commotion was about.

Still a bit shaken about the assault, the fellows were all talking at once when it tapered off to just Ed Earl comparing the past to what was left.

Apparently, nature had invaded this territory as well, leaving little preservation.

He briefly told us about finding most of it, the bench seats, the table, the crates and all that we had left behind, was now nothing but musty old rubbish.

Even the old mattress was found in the same place but it appeared to have shrunken with age and corroded with dried up, old bugs and bird droppings. Apparently quite a few different creatures had made their way in through the broken windows.

Early, fanning his nose, interrupted to proclaim how bad the smell was comparing it to the cages at the zoo. Easy backed him up but said he thought it was far worse than that.

In his hand, Ed Earl gripped some bits and pieces of aged, shredded paper that he managed to salvage from the bus floor before he ran out of there.

His examination in better light proved them to be torn pages from a bible. Preach stood looking disturbed and holding the leather binding with the gold lettering.

We just all stood quietly in the moment as nobody knew quite what to say right then. Vandalism, I thought. I don't know why anybody would want to tear up a Holy Bible but somebody did.

Huey held in his hand a small stack of old pictures that were stuck together, no doubt because of the long exposure to the elements. They tore when anyone tried to pull them apart. Mama would be upset if she knew that they had been neglected. We didn't know anything about the people that could once be seen in the images but they must have been important to her at one time for her to have ever held on to them in the first place.

Easy managed to salvage what appeared to be the head of a little ceramic donkey, among the few what-nots that had been broken and shattered into pieces. It had once been a gift from someone in her past and was one of the few things she had brought along when she and Daddy had run away together. For the most part, it had just sat on a high shelf in the bus, along with a few other tiny curiosities.

Ed Earl, Earldean and I recalled several times, when she took it down to let us see it up close. Often, the occasion would linger as we watched her admire it before putting it back in place.

Trying to recall any stories about what this little figurine might have meant to her, I strolled around rolling the broken off head around in my hand for a while. Rubbing off some of the dust, I could see the color had faded under the glaze that was now dulled and crackling.

Figuring I possibly could glue it back on if I could only find the rest of this beheaded treasure. It was really worthless to try but the sentimental urge to do so was overwhelming at the moment. It was as if I needed some tangible evidence to prove that my mother, Marline, had really once existed; as if her four grown children and all of their descendants weren't enough.

As the others strolled about in small groups close by, cautiously kicking under leaves and such for more buried relics, Earldean and I found ourselves still lingering in along closer near the bus. We made our way behind it we could see where the old deep freeze that had been left open was rusted and caved in on its sides. It too was partially buried under fallen limbs and leaves.

She was sifting through some of the rubble and came across a find. Stepping over closer to show me, we shared the emotion of discovering Mama's button collection. Miraculously, that little glass jar had managed to remain unbroken after all it had been through. The fact that the lid was rusted on made it air tight and was how they were able to be preserved so well.

When we made teary eye contact, we laughed as we shared the same idea out loud. *"Mama! So that's where we get it from!"*

We dotingly elbowed one another because we had said it simultaneously, knowing we had developed a reputation for being pack rats because we saved and stored things in jars. We didn't realize it until then that we'd learned this habit from our own mother.

No doubt, Earldean was keeping this as a memento.

After the wasps seemed to have settled back on their nest I was drawn over closer to the bus thinking maybe I'd just take a peep in. Although there was hardly a breeze blowing, the stifling atmosphere inside had been stirred enough to cause the overpowering, musty smell to seep out into the open air. I had to hold my nose at first as I peered in through the doorway.

On the floor beneath the steering wheel I could see that one of the boys must have found the old box of shoes. The pasteboard had shriveled to almost nothing and must have disintegrate when they tried to pull it out, leaving two whole sides exposed so that I could see that all the shoes were curled up and dry rotted.

I gazed through the opening and could see the old potbelly stove that looked much smaller than I remembered it being. I reminisced back to the day Daddy installed it and about how clever I thought he was for doing so. Even back then it would have been considered primitive to Whisper Ridge's standard, but I was grateful for all the times it most likely saved our lives from the frigid cold.

I strained to recall how Daddy's voice sounded as he told his stories or read from the Bible between stoking the fires he had burned inside of that antique contraption.

I began to get a little queasy from the smell, the heat and the dust and decided I'd seen enough to move on. The only thing that had ever really been worth saving from the inside of that old bus in the first place was Mama. God knows I tried! I had done all a ten year old could ever have done back then to save her.

I followed the others who were all making their way down toward the creek. Earldean wanted to show them where we used to bathe and get our drinking water. On the way, she stopped and waited for me to catch up with her. When I did, she proceeded to reminded me about how somebody found Learline's doll down by the water that day, during the search they had long ago.

We knew we had lost it along the way into town. However, we never really knew for sure who found it and brought it back. We could only guess it must have been our own father who had come across it while maybe out searching for us. He probably recognized it as being Learline's and might have been in the process of bringing it home for her. But still in all, it didn't make since as to why he would have left it down by the creek.

We considered the possibility that Mama might have come out of her unconscious state and she went out looking for us. Perhaps she had taken the doll down to the creek to wash it and was distracted by something…maybe Daddy…Who knows?

There was so much of that still remained a mystery to us as our minds raced back to those days…What really happened to Mama and how she was found buried under all those rocks.

And we can't help but wonder what really happened to Daddy. They never found his body to prove him dead. But if he was alive, surely he would have found us by now.

A big part of me wishes he was still out there looking as I *still* ache for him to find us.

Up ahead, Ed Earl stooped down and picked up a few objects that were setting on a stump alongside the path. His eyes lit up and a big grin came across his face as he held out his clutched hands to me and said, *"Here, I believe these are yours."*

Amazingly, he had found a few of my wood-carved animals that Denby made me a long time ago; a bird and a little deer. The deer he had given me after my heart broke over the little yearling. I don't know how they managed to stay there on that stump all these years without falling off; even through the wind and rains, snows and storms.

Somebody had to have been out there in the past thirty-nine years…there's just no telling.

Later that evening, we were back at my house and everyone was gathering in lawn chairs in the front yard, awaiting the firework display that was to be put on by this festive little town of Whisper Ridge. The hillside provided a perfect view of the Water Front Park and Marina, where the large crowd gathered for a closer look, although the show was sure to be seen from miles away.

From the platform of an extra large pontoon, provided by Woody's, the middle of the lake was not only the safest place to discharge such an exhibit, but with the reflection of the colorful explosions that would be decorating the night sky, it was guaranteed to be doubly effective.

Right at dusk, Huey stuck his head in the front door just as the first big boom drew out the responses of OHOOO's and AHAAA's from my excited kinfolk outside.

"Commin Shirline?" he called out to me. *"It's startin ya know!"*

"I know hun…be there in a minute…save me a seat!"

I took the two miniature carvings, blew the dust off of them then placed them in that fragile, old, worn out shoebox I had been keeping my treasures in for so long.

For my sixteenth birthday, Alma had bought me a nice silk covered hat box that was decorated with pretty bows and gave it to me so that I'd have a "pretty" place to keep my little "treasures" in instead, but I still held on to this one for sentimental reasons. Oh, I still have that one Alma gave me…and use it also, because of her thoughtfulness.

However, *this* particular box came from Albert's with my *very first* pair of store bought shoes in it. My most sentimental valuables are kept in this one...like the belt Debbie gave me for my thirteenth birthday. She had made it herself out of aluminum pull tabs that came on the new soda pop cans. Also, a chain she made from all those Juicy Fruit gum wrappers I got from Trudy....Then, there are the caster bean beads that Denby gave me; strung by my own mother's own hands, before I was ever born...The newspaper picture of my very first home...the one where Virgil and Bubba Franks were standing beside the bus...only, I had cut out their faces and replaced them with mine and Earldean's from the Polaroid snap shot that Detective Glenn took of us that day...the very first picture to have ever been taken of me in my life. The scotch tape that held our faces in place had yellowed but I never changed it out because that particular tape was the first strips I'd ever used on my own. Amazingly it still worked.

I would have put Mama's Bible in there too, if it would fit; instead, I just tore out the page that had Psalms seventy-seven: the one I had read to her that last night I was with her. She had pulled herself together long enough to quote these verses, and as far as I know, they were the last words she'd ever spoken.

And, the most prized possession that I keep in this box is a copy of my birth-certificate.

After the adoption was final and legal, the very first records of our births were put on file down at the State Capital where all other vital and important records are kept. When our copies came in the mail, just in time to register for school, Trudy asked Cody to go to a place that he knew of, that made carbon copies, and have a duplicate made.

In keeping with the promise they had made me, of them helping me to find my own identity, they thought I should have one of my very own to keep with me at all times.

This way, I could carry it around and prove to the other kids... and anybody else that ever questioned it... that I had a *real* name and that I was indeed, a ***"bona-fide"*** person.

In Retrospect

What a privilege to be part of something so much bigger than just myself, more than just what others might see when they look at me, or where I live…or how I live.

When someone really gets to know me well, they learn that I've been redeemed. They learn about all of these relationships that I've been blessed with and how they help make up the person I've become over the last…almost half a century. For there, in my life, no matter how I might have felt at one time or another, I was never alone.

We've lived together, played together…cried, laughed and prayed together.

We've gotten mad…and gotten sober…gotten together…gotten over it.

We've learned new habits, unlearned others…learned the value of sisters and brothers.

We're side by side through ups and downs, for births and deaths, 'till the lost is found.

We've fought, forgave, forgot, felt loved again…stuck it out through thick and thin.

We did it because we're family…nothing can take its place. No matter how big or small, everybody needs to be a part of one…to fit in a place where they belong.

No matter how self-sufficient we think we are, at some point we'll need or want them.

God said it is not good for man to be alone. With other "people", you can say **"We"**.

ABOUT THE AUTHOR

B.J. Tassin, a Louisiana native, moved to Northwest Arkansas with her husband Scott on the first day of 2002 after the last of her three children were married and were off to start lives of their own. They now reside in Bella Vista, and are business owners of Cloud 9 Mattress in Bentonville.

She enjoys spending time with her growing family that now includes 8 grandchildren.

Though BJ has had a passon for writing since a teen, other than a few poems, articles and art work published in her home town of Monroe, Louisiana, this is her first "Bona-fide" novel to be published.

COVER ILLUSTRATIONS

by

BJ Tassin

64554298R00303

Made in the USA
Lexington, KY
13 June 2017